'A sweet and flirty short story, I really enjoyed it. I can't wait
to see what Nikki comes up with for the next book in the
series.'
Sky's Book Corner

D0766774

NIKKI MOORE

I've adored writing and reading since forever and have always been a sucker for love stories so I'm delighted to be part of the fabulous HarperImpulse team! I write short stories and fun, touching, sexy contemporary romance and really enjoy creating intriguing characters and telling their stories.

A finalist in writing competitions since 2010, including Novelicious Undiscovered 2012, I'm a member of the fantastic Romantic Novelists' Association. I blog about three of my favourite things – Writing, Work and Wine – at www.nikkimooreauthor.wordpress.com and am passionate about supporting other writers as part of a friendly, talented and diverse community, so you'll often see other authors pop in!

You can find me at www.facebook.com/NikkiMooreAuthor or www.facebook.com/NikkiMooreWrites or on Twitter @NikkiMoore_Auth to chat about love, life, reading or writing…I'd love to hear from you!

Picnics in Hyde Park

A #LoveLondon Novel

NIKKI MOORE

Harper*Impulse* an imprint of
HarperCollins*Publishers* Ltd
1 London Bridge Street
London SE1 9GF

www.harpercollins.co.uk

A Paperback Original 2015

First published in Great Britain in ebook format by Harper*Impulse* 2015

ISBN: 9780008127244

This novel is entirely a work of fiction.
The names, characters and incidents portrayed in it are
the work of the author's imagination. Any resemblance to
actual persons, living or dead, events or localities is

To my sister Natasha, who may be younger than me, but who is infinitely wiser some (but not all) of the time! Thanks for everything, love you Sis x

To my big little brother Ryan, we may not have a lot in common but when it matters, we're there for each other. Lots of love, x

To Mark, my family and friends; thank you so much for the support during the last nine months of #LoveLondon madness! x

To Charlotte Ledger, for being so fantastic. Look what we did! x

#LoveLondon Series

1

Matt Reilly is a complete, unbelievable bastard and I'm going to make him pay, Zoe Harper vowed as she pounded the gold lion-head knocker against the door of his exclusive Knightsbridge residence.

When there was no response, she switched to thumping the glossy black wood with the side of her fist.

Thud. Thud. Thud.

Answer. The. Door.

Utter fury was squeezing her chest so tight it felt like her ribs were suffocating her lungs and a horrible pressure was building behind her eyeballs, the sure sign of a tension headache.

Where the hell was he? She stepped back to gaze up at the impressive facade of the town house, which had to be at least four storeys tall including the basement area below her. The top two floors were exposed brickwork but the ground and lower floors were painted white, decorated with manicured window boxes. The property screamed refined wealth, as did the beautiful leafy communal garden area in the middle of the square. He must have paid extra for the property, which sat back from the road slightly. It was one of the only houses with off-road parking.

She turned to look at the gravel driveway. Someone had to be in, there were three cars parked up; a garish, canary-yellow convertible sports model, a sexy low-slung black supercar and a more modest silver Prius hybrid.

Thudding the door again, there was still no answer.

If she was some kick-ass action movie heroine she could bust the door down, flatten whichever of the selfish idiots was inside (although both at the same time would be preferable) and just be done with it. But at five foot seven, as well as pounds lighter than she'd been in years, she hardly looked or felt the part. Still, if there was anything guaranteed to bring out her fighting side it was protecting her younger sister Melody. She was her only proper family left apart from their Great Aunt Ruth, who'd always been distant and had all the affection of a watermelon.

What it came down to was that anyone who hurt Melody deserved justice. But she didn't really believe in violence, and ruining her beautiful nails with their miniature stars and stripes design on every tip didn't appeal either. The manicure was a present from her ex-boss Liberty, named after the statue of. It was something to remember New York by, a city she'd come to love. But better not to think about that, or what else she'd loved and lost.

Where the heck was Mr. High and Mighty Reilly, or for that matter, his younger brother Stephen? Surely they had enough staff to answer the bloody door for them. A girl could die of heatstroke out here. The midday sun was ferocious and prickling heat along the back of her neck. It was sure to be scarlet by dinner time.

Thud. Thud. Thud.

Her hand was never going to be the same again. Then she'd be suing the sods for personal injury as well as emotional trauma for Melody. Her sibling had been crying so hard at Jemima's flat in multicultural, packed Holloway that Zoe hadn't been able to get the full story on arrival from Heathrow. There'd just been a lot of mumbling and sobbing around swollen red eyes and handfuls of soggy tissues. Still, what she'd figured out had been enough to instantly trigger her big sister reflexes. The stale, stuffy black cab had made for a nightmare journey across London but the sunlight glinting off the windows had matched her heated, murderous thoughts perfectly. She'd avoided direct eye contact with the chatty driver, jaw clenched as she replayed the fragments of her sister's story in her head.

Fell in love with Stephen... Matt ended it, fired me... kicked me out without notice... never see the kids again... looked after them for three years!

How dare he? It was bloody outrageous and unbelievably unfair. How could anyone be so uncaring that they'd do someone who trusted them out of a relationship, job, home and salary all on the same day? So here she was outside of his posh, rich-guy's, *I'm so fabulous* home, fully intending to grab her sister's belongings as well as telling Matt Reilly exactly what she thought of a guy who'd treat a naïve twenty-two year old like dirt. If she could grab his brother by the scruff of the neck at the same time and give him a good shake for helping break her sister's heart, she'd do that too. He had a lot of explaining to do as to why he wasn't answering Mel's calls.

Bloody men. They were a faithless lot at the best of times, the reason she'd left the States after five long years. But her sister's boss had reached new levels of bastardom, if that was even a word.

Part of her wished that when confronted, Matt might admit he'd made a terrible mistake, beg forgiveness, tell Melody that of course she was good enough for his brother, and ask her to come back to them. But the text that had just pinged on her mobile meant the idea was a non-starter.

> **Appreciate the support Sis, but**
> **please don't cause a scene and**
> **DON'T try and get my job back.**
> **I'm never going back there.**
> **M x**

Zoe didn't really want her sister anywhere near them anyway. Still, an apology from Matt, an opportunity for Melody to say goodbye to the kids properly, pick up her belongings and be offered some kind of compensation for the notice pay she was surely entitled to would be something. Along with some explanation as to why Stephen had gone AWOL and seemed to be letting Matt make all the decisions. Perhaps he didn't feel able to stand up to him? Or maybe he was intimidated by his older brother's success.

According to the tabloids, Stephen was abroad a lot of the time, a playboy who basically partied and shopped his way around Europe with the family money. Why her sister had fallen for him she couldn't understand. At thirty, Matt was older by seven years, a famous music producer who was hardly ever out of the press, despite his attempts to evade the spotlight. Snapping pictures of his children was a rabid hobby for British journos and there were rumours of a new girlfriend every week, although you couldn't believe everything you read in the papers. She and Melody were close, despite the vast miles that'd been between them, and Melody had told her a lot about Matt's children via Skype and text messages but nothing about any of his personal relationships, respecting her boss's right to privacy. Not that she'd got any thanks for that loyalty and professionalism.

Zoe banged her fist on the wood one last time and to her satisfaction finally heard footsteps. The door was yanked open by a dark-haired guy in his twenties.

'Yes?' he drawled, stepping out into the sunlight, forcing her to move backwards down the three concrete stairs and onto the pavement.

Cocky green eyes ran over her flat black shoes, tight black jeans and the fashionable short-sleeved print top that hung off one shoulder. Having had no chance to change out of the clothes she'd travelled in, she felt rumpled, sticky and at a distinct disadvantage.

She couldn't afford to jump to any conclusions, but this guy had to be Stephen.

'Are you planning to say something today, or not?' he demanded, looking her up and down again, a bit too slowly for her liking.

Sucking in a deep breath, shudders of rage and adrenalin swirled with the giddy exhaustion of jet lag and noon heat, making her feel light-headed and dangerously out of control. Face scalding, she started shaking, hands bunching into fists around her over-sized bag. Ignoring the feeling, along with the urge to ask if he was done checking her out and start demanding what the hell he was playing at with her sister, she expelled the breath. If she lost it too soon it was game over; he'd likely slam the door in her face. Getting over the threshold was the important bit. *Then* she could tear strips off them both.

'Yes, sorry. Hello. Matthew Reilly?' It was Matt's house and it might seem weird if she asked for Stephen.

'God, no! Definitely not,' smirking, he turned his head to yell over his shoulder. 'Matt, there's some Katy Perry lookalike-wannabe here for an interview.' A pause. 'I'm off.' Shrugging when there was no reply, a strange expression flashed across his face. 'All right,' he hollered, 'see you when I'm back.' Reaching back inside the hallway, he grabbed a travel bag and hustled past her, leaving the front door yawning open behind him.

See you when I'm back?

'Wait—' she yelped, spinning around as his comment registered.

But the arrogant jerk ignored her, running down the steps and leaping into the yellow open-top car like some Dukes of Hazzard extra. Screeching away with a spin of tyres, gravel flew everywhere in an unholy rain of stones and he barely paused before roaring off towards the main Knightsbridge road. God knew how many people he was going to take out driving like that. Complete maniac.

Then his other words sunk into her sluggish, travel-addled brain. *Katy Perry lookalike-wannabe?* He was a cheeky bugger! She might have black hair and blue eyes but was no wannabe, wasn't here to audition for some tacky talent show, didn't care that Matthew Reilly was in the music business— Hang on, interview?

'That was my brother Stephen. I'm Matt.' A deep, terse voice said behind her.

She swung around to face the door, stumbling slightly. She needed to get out of this relentless sunshine, she was starting to feel pretty sick.

'Ready?'

'Ready?' she repeated, thinking. She'd missed her chance to have it out with Stephen for now, but it was this man stood in the shadows who was ultimately responsible for her sister's confused distress.

Keep calm, just breathe. She squinted, hardly able to make him out. The inside of the house was too dim and it was so bright outside, red dots blurring her vision.

'Look, I'm very busy. Are you here to interview for the nanny position or not? I haven't got any time to waste.'

He'd got rid of her sister only yesterday and was already trying to replace her.

At her dumbfounded silence, he began shutting the door. 'Okay then, goodbye.'

'I, uh— hang on! Sorry, of course I'm here for an interview,' she thought fast. 'There's just a slight problem.'

The breath hissed loudly from between his teeth. 'Which is?'

'I flew in from New York this morning and came straight from the airport, as you can see from my lack of a suitable outfit,' she gestured to her jeans, 'so I don't have my CV with me.'

'How did you hear about the job then?'

It was hardly surprising he was suspicious. 'A contact at the agency called me, knowing I was due back in the UK today,' she fibbed, hoping she was right. 'Zoe Harper, pleased to meet you.' She nodded briskly in greeting to avoid shaking his hand. 'I was added to the list at the last minute,' she finished the lie, 'haven't the agency emailed the updated schedule?' She prayed it was the same agency that'd placed Melody here originally, the one Zoe had also got the placement in America through.

A ringtone filled the hallway. Blowing out an exasperated breath, he prised a sleek mobile from his pocket and after checking the screen, cut the call off.

As he tucked the phone away, she chattered on. 'When this job was mentioned,' ironically one she was more than qualified for, 'I asked to be put forward, especially when it's working for you and this is such a lovely area to live in.' Sucking up to him felt wrong but if it gave her an in, it'd be worth it.

'My assistant is off sick, I haven't had time to mess around checking emails and my kids are due back in two hours,' he said in an irritated tone, 'so I'm sorry but—'

'But I've come all this way—'

His phone started ringing again and he swore, wrestling it back out of his pocket. 'Sorry.' After a quick glance at the screen, he answered. 'Matt Reilly,' he barked. 'Yes?'

She forced her lips into a polite smile while she waited. It wobbled when she realised he was talking to the recruitment agency.

'No, it's not good enough. I'm completely dissatisfied with the level of service I've received. You know I need a new nanny urgently. You sent someone else along, but— What? Oh, never mind, forget it.' He hung up, clenching the phone in his fist.

Jeez, was he this grumpy all the time? He must have been a joy for her sister to live with. Or maybe he was just having a bad day. If that was the case, it wasn't going to get any better with her arrival.

'That was about another no-show. Incredibly, the third today.' He paused, then shook his head, as if already regretting what he was about to say. 'I've only got this afternoon set aside for interviews, I suppose as you're here you may as well come in.' Gesturing her over the threshold. 'You can talk me through your experience and the agency can get me your details later if things go well,' he bit, slamming the front door behind them.

Gee thanks, don't do me any favours. She stuck her tongue out crossly at his back as her eyes adjusted to the light inside the house, then blanked her expression as he moved past her.

But he didn't stop, striding off down the wooden parquet

8

hallway so that she had to hurry after him. 'This way.'

She caught a flash of a staircase to her left and a dazzling though unlit chandelier overhead, but her focus was on following Matt. The scents of vanilla polish, flowers and some unnameable but appealing fresh male aftershave drifted over her as she caught up with him.

'I'm presuming the agency will have up-to-date references for you, along with an enhanced DBS clearance,' Matt threw open a door and lead her into a massive lounge filled with windows and light.

Zoe made a non-committal *mmmm* sound, taking in her surroundings. The parquet flooring continued straight through from the hallway, but apart from that everything was white; the ceiling, the walls, the fireplace that looked like it had never been used. On the far side of the room two French doors opened onto some kind of outdoor space, with matching conifers in square black pots sat outside them. There was very little furniture and no paintings on the walls. She walked over and sat on one of the shiny black sofas that faced each other across a blocky glass coffee table. Hiding a grimace, she slung her handbag down on the floor. It was so impersonal, more like a show-home than a real one. She hated it. It was way too pristine. How on earth did kids live here? Where was the personality, the clutter, the colour? Perhaps the children were kept in a cupboard under the stairs like Harry Potter, she thought unkindly, tongue in cheek.

She knew from her sister that Matt's daughter Aimee was seven years old, didn't talk much and was exceptionally bright, and that his son Jasper was nearly five and about to start school. Melody had described the little boy fondly but seeing her sister's sometimes strained face on the laptop screen and listening to funny stories about what he'd got up to, Zoe had concluded he was a bit of a handful.

'Anyone in there?' a gravelly voice broke into her thoughts.

Straightening, she lifted her chin and met Matt Reilly's gaze properly for the first time. 'I—' Oh.

Oh, man. The Americanism resounded in her head. Freezing, heart thudding, her mouth dropped open. Realising she must look like the village idiot, she shut it immediately, teeth clicking together. 'Yes. Sorry.'

'Good.' Leaning forward, he grabbed a notepad and silver embossed pen, and made a few notes on the paper.

She sucked her bottom lip into her mouth. She'd seen blurred photos of Matt in the press, but he was always ducking his head away or wearing sunglasses, so there'd never been an opportunity to see what he really looked like.

The reality was that he was outrageously, jaw-droppingly gorgeous.

He shared his brother's colouring, the green eyes and thick dark hair, but the similarity ended there. Stephen was tall and wiry, but with the long spread of his ridiculously muscular legs and the breadth of his shoulders Matt was far bigger and better built. In fact, he looked more like an international rugby player than some arty creative type who spent most days holed up in a dark studio.

And though she could understand why Melody found Stephen attractive, Matt was far more appealing. His face was leaner, rugged with stubble and with a fierce intelligence shining in his gaze under thick dark eyebrows. James Marsden chiselled cheekbones and a stern mouth might have given him a rugged male beauty were it not for the two tiny imperfections she'd always been a sucker for. A sinking feeling tugged at her tummy as she stared at a bump on the ridge of his nose, perhaps from a break, and a small, inch long scar that ran down into his top lip.

She'd had a thing about bad boys since a teenage crush on Harrison Ford in the *Indiana Jones* films, sparked by watching Christmas re-runs with Ruth. Their great aunt, who'd raised them since Mel was seven and Zoe was thirteen, loved adventure movies despite her appearance and stilted manner. Since then, the rebel characters in TV series and films had prolonged Zoe's obsession with bad boys. It was unfortunate for her, because Matt definitely looked like the kind of guy who'd ride up on a motorbike wearing leathers and whisk a girl away for a dirty, dangerous weekend. The sinfully tight blue jeans and black t-shirt clinging to his broad shoulders reinforced the image.

'Shall we get started?' he asked, frowning.

'Of course,' she straightened in her seat, trying to reassert her professionalism.

His phone pinged. 'For the love of—' putting the pad aside, he checked his mobile, reading something and scowling like it was telling him the end of the world was nigh. 'The sooner my assistant is better, the sooner my sanity will return,' he muttered absent-mindedly, touching the screen and typing a reply.

The deadpan delivery was unwittingly amusing and made him seem less grumpy. Zoe couldn't help chuckling under her breath as she stared at him. A tingling awareness ran through her, a purely sexual heat beating between her legs and tightening her skin, raising bumps along it.

No. You detest him. He hurt Melody.

A pretty face and a toned body mean nothing.

Men aren't to be trusted.

Get over it.

It was easy to clamp a lid on her unruly hormones as she reminded herself of those facts. Plus the intense physical reaction was ridiculous and just too much. It had to be down to the jet lag and fury, as well as her spinning, conflicted emotions about coming home.

Then she sighed, studying him as he tapped away on the phone. Damn. One thing she didn't usually do was lie to herself and the truth was she'd never had such an overwhelming and immediate attraction to someone before. Fancied them, sure. Had flings, a few. Longer term boyfriends, yes... which unhappily lead her thoughts to Greg. What an awful waste of five years he'd turned out to be.

Why didn't I see it coming? Why didn't I know?

Rage swamped her, despair pulling her down. She was obviously no judge of character where men were concerned. She'd virtually abandoned Melody to follow Greg across the ocean, and in return he'd betrayed her.

She straightened her shoulders, setting her jaw.

No. No man was ever going to come before her family again. She owed her sister more than that... and she owed the Reilly brothers revenge.

2

'I'm sorry,' Matt silenced his phone and placed it face down on the glass table. 'Today's been nightmarish,' he ran a hand distractedly through his hair, 'to say I'm short-staffed is an understatement.'

If part of the reason for his stress hadn't been down to him throwing her sister out on her arse, Zoe might have felt sorry for him. He looked genuinely pained. But it was his own stupid fault.

'That's okay,' she said politely, wondering how much of the interview to go through with before sharing the real reason for turning up on his doorstep. She felt like she needed to know more about him first. What if she started accusing him of what he'd done to Melody and he denied it all, or threw her out too? No, that wasn't good enough. She had to think about this strategically. It was just a shame that dragging tiredness and anger were befuddling her brain.

'Right, the phone is being ignored and I'm not going to answer the door if the bell goes,' he declared. 'Let's get on with this.' Leaning forward to grab the notepad again, the movement showed off strong chest muscles shifting under the cotton of his top.

Her eyes flew up, noticing the petal pattern in his forest green irises, and how focused his gaze was.

'So, tell me more about why you wanted the agency to send you over for this job in particular?' he asked, pen poised over the paper.

'Er... um,' she stuttered. It was an easy warm-up question, but her brain couldn't seem to come up with an answer. What the heck had she said earlier? She couldn't remember clearly, she'd been so intent on getting through the door.

'Well?' he raised both eyebrows.

Glancing out of one of the French doors, Zoe caught sight of a flowering indigo plant and a section of deck railing. It looked pretty out there, idyllic. Which nudged her memory. 'Like I said, it's a lovely place to live,' she mumbled.

'That's it?'

'Yeah,' she said lamely. God, this was awful. She was acting like a space cadet. *Get it together.*

Matt twisted his wrist and checked his battered but expensive looking watch. 'Are you sure you're actually here for an interview? To be frank, I'm really busy, so...' he started unfolding his tall body from the sofa.

It was enough to shake her from the fog. What was she doing? She was here for a reason, couldn't blow it. 'N-no,' she squeaked, and then cleared her throat before speaking with more confidence. 'I mean, no.'

Shooting up and stalking around the coffee table, he jerked her from the sofa by one elbow. 'Why the hell are you here then?'

She stumbled against him, letting out an *oof* as their bodies clashed awkwardly. Typically, his muscles were as solid and defined as they looked and her face bloomed pink as scorching sexual awareness ran through her, hardening her nipples. She glanced down quickly to check he couldn't see them through her top. Luckily he was more focused on other things, like drilling her for information. He didn't seem to notice how close they were or how tight his grip was.

'Are you with the press?' he demanded softly, the tone somehow scarier than if he'd shouted.

'No! Absolutely not! I'm not part of *that* lot.' She hoped her tone was suitably scathing and convincing, given that one of her best friends was a journalist. 'And can you let go of me please? That's way too tight.' The determined shake of her arm must have convinced him of something, even if it was only that she wouldn't put up with any high-handed crap.

He let go immediately. 'Sorry. I hope I didn't hurt you?'

To his credit he looked sincere. It was the perfect opportunity to make him feel bad, but he hadn't actually hurt her. Plus, if she went on the attack, it might make him defensive, which would get her nowhere. 'You didn't,' she shrugged, 'don't worry.'

'Good. So now you can explain yourself.' He crossed his arms across his chest, shoulders tense.

'Sure. Okay. When I said no, I only meant that no, I didn't want to leave. You were getting up and I thought you were going to say it was over before it had even begun. I don't usually perform this badly at interviews, I swear. I wasn't talking much because I'm jetlagged and feeling a bit funny from the sun.' She fanned herself to illustrate the point. Did she look as stupid and fake as she felt? But hey, she was committed now, and might as well go for it. 'I only landed a couple of hours ago, it's really hot outside and I burn easily. I mean look at this rubbish pale skin.' She pointed to her face. 'I may have a bit of heatstroke, but I feel better now I'm inside.' She mustered her best acting skills and smiled brightly. 'So perhaps you could offer me a glass of water and a minute to compose myself then we can start again? I'm not from the press, honestly.' It was easy to hold his gaze, given it was the truth.

There was a long pause as he stared at her. 'Fine,' he said, expression guarded. 'I suppose.'

'Really?'

'Yes. I know journalists. If you were one you would either come clean and bombard me with questions or maybe try to tempt me with something,' his eyes flickered over her body, 'in exchange for an exclusive story.'

Her spine stiffened and she smiled coldly. He was either deadly serious and an absolute pig, or was testing her.

'Luckily neither of those applies. Anyway, what would someone from the press want with you at the moment?'

'You really don't know?'

'Nope.'

Now she was fibbing, having read about a supposed broken engagement in a trashy celeb magazine on the seven hour flight home. The break-up was allegedly because his pop star fiancée had set up a cosy photo shoot with his kids without permission, prompting him to storm into a conference room to collect them, followed by hustling them out of the private entrance at the back of the hotel. As well as leaving with his children, he'd also apparently left with the massive diamond rock he'd proposed with six weeks before.

He shook his head. 'Never mind then. It doesn't matter.'

Was he embarrassed? Ashamed? Hurt? None of the above, surely. He didn't look particularly heartbroken.

'Hang on. I think it matters. If you gave me the job would I have to live with the papers breathing down my neck all the time? For instance, do your children get followed?'

'Getting a bit ahead of yourself based on your input so far, aren't you?' he asked dryly. 'Talking yourself into the job. A bit over confident, maybe?'

Arrogant was the unspoken word hanging in the air. From the glint in his eye, he wanted to see how she would react when provoked. But he wasn't going to see that side of her. At least, not yet.

'Over confident? No.' She shrugged. 'Over qualified? Maybe. I got a CACHE level three Diploma in Home-based Child Care when I left school before it was replaced with the QCF framework, and worked in a nursery for a few years. I progressed to a degree in Psychology with a view to specialising with children, but hated the job itself when I did my placement year at an independent school. So I left uni early, got a Paediatric First Aid award, did basic health and safety training, undertook a food hygiene certificate and became a nanny. My plan tomorrow is to apply to get onto the OFSTED Childcare Register so I can care for under eight year olds...' She continued talking, reeling off her experience and skills, taking great pleasure in shutting him up. By the time she was done, his eyebrows were so high they'd almost disappeared into his dark hair.

'Now we're getting somewhere,' nodding his head, 'we'll get on with the set questions after I've got you that glass of water.' He loped away, long legs carrying him quickly to the door.

Her eyes dropped to his deliciously muscular butt and she twisted away, swearing. She was almost twenty-eight, not a teen-ager. She should not be susceptible to crushes on the latest bit of man-candy in the media.

Think of Melody. What do I do about the indefensible way he treated her?

Matt was so self-assured that Zoe doubted simply taking her sister's stuff and having a go at him would have the slightest affect, never mind making him feel bad enough to offer to make amends. Her hands curled into fists, picturing her sister's pale face and bloodshot eyes. According to Jemima, Melody had hardly spoken or eaten since rolling up on her friend's doorstep unexpectedly the previous day.

Matt walked back into the room and placed two blue glasses filled with sparkling water, ice and neat slices of lemon on the table. Zoe dropped onto the sofa and thanked him politely, hiding her churned up feelings behind a bland expression. As she sipped her drink, her hand was steady, a new determination burning a hole in her stomach. She wasn't sure how she was going to get even with him yet, but would ignore his physical appeal if it killed her.

'So,' she put her water down and clasped her hand together in her lap, 'what's the next question?'

For the following half hour, Zoe answered his competency-based questions calmly, talking about educational standards, setting up

17

routines, and how she handled behaviour management issues through shared partnership and agreed strategies with parents. She was candid with her professional opinion of what Matt's children needed based on their ages, following up with questions about their likes, hobbies and extra-curricular activities to show her interest. At times she accidentally slipped into enjoying the challenge of the interview and as much as she hated the idea of thinking anything positive about Matt, it was obvious from his probing questions that he was bright, sharp and knew what he wanted for his kids. She was shocked to feel genuinely interested in the job when Matt gave an approving smile to her last answer and asked if she had any questions of her own.

'I assume it's a live-in position?' she said after quizzing him about the hours, salary and next stages of the interview process.

'Yes, you'd have your own bedroom, bathroom and a small lounge area on the top floor.'

'Great. Could I see them please?'

'Not today,' he said brusquely.

No wonder. Melody's things were probably still in her bedroom and he'd be unable to explain why. Because, after all, not many people would voluntarily leave their stuff behind, and he'd hardly want to admit to slinging a previous employee out so quickly he'd not let them pack up their belongings.

'Okay, maybe next time, if I'm invited back.' Sliding forward on the sofa, she leaned toward him with her head tilted to indicate interest and encourage honesty. It was basic psychology. 'So, am I allowed to ask what happened to your last nanny?'

His lips tightened, a pulse beating in his stubbly jaw. 'I'd rather not discuss it,' he replied, shuffling his paperwork together on the table.

'It's important for me to know, given I'm applying to replace her,' she said, peering at him so he had to meet her gaze or appear rude. 'Did she leave for professional or personal reasons? Was she not happy here? What have you told the children? If I get the job I need to know what happened so I can be prepared for any questions your son or daughter might have about her going. They may be upset, or miss her. They could feel like she abandoned them. Particularly after what happened to your wife...' she trailed off as his expression turned grim and his knuckles turned white around the notepad. 'I'm sorry,' she said, meaning it. 'I didn't mean to upset you.' She might not like the guy but she wasn't a robot. There was genuine grief and regret on his face. One thing they had in common.

'Its fine,' he said in a taut voice, 'it's common knowledge. It's not as if my family has any right to privacy or anything.'

She sidestepped the bitterness in the remark, choosing not to get into the debate. It was his choice to have a career that put him in the spotlight, so it was for him to deal with the consequences. It was just a shame if it affected the kids. 'I appreciate it must have been difficult and I don't want to pry. I'm thinking purely of your children's welfare.'

'I understand that. And I suppose you might be right about needing to know what happened. But how do you know my last nanny was a woman?'

She nearly lost her nerve but wouldn't give in that easily, holding his gaze. 'Statistically, the number of women in the field compared to the number of men makes it more likely your nanny was female.' Pushing a strand of black hair behind her ear, she watched his deep green eyes flicker along her collarbone before returning to her face. That was interesting. 'Seriously, I know I'd have to meet Aimee and Jasper and pass all the clearances and checks, but if you offer me the job I'd quite like to know what happened to the last employee in it.' Forcing a nervous laugh. 'She's not buried under the patio or anything is she? Or chained up in the basement? What's the big mystery?'

His smile was fleeting. 'No mystery, just simply not pleasant. She, ah,' he picked over his words, 'did something I didn't agree with that meant she was no longer suitable to be my children's nanny. It turned out she wasn't the person I thought she was. It was disappointing,' he shrugged one shoulder casually as if he didn't care, but there was something in the set of his chin that suggested otherwise, 'but these things happen, and I need to replace her urgently. Does that tell you enough?'

'I guess so,' she replied through stiff lips, longing to jump up and yell at him. 'Thanks for sharing.' He really was an absolute bastard. It felt like every muscle in her face was clenching, but she breathed in and out deeply, striving to keep calm. Since when was falling in love such a crime that it meant you were unfit to look after children? And he could have said anything, taken the diplomatic line and said his nanny had left for personal reasons. Instead he was suggesting Melody had let him down, when the truth was that it was the other way around. Especially after all the time, energy and passion her sister had devoted to his children, who she'd grown to genuinely care about.

Zoe could hardly believe it. He clearly had zero conscience. Was it the industry he worked in that made him think he could treat people this way, or did the nature of the industry happen to support an arrogance that had already existed before he'd made it big? She resisted the urge to bounce out of her seat, grab his precious bloody paperwork and whack him around the head with it repeatedly, very hard and with great satisfaction. Fury didn't even begin to cover it. Bloody, bloody men.

'So, what about you?' he asked, looking at her expectantly.

'Sorry?'

'Why have you just left your job after five years and come back to the UK? You must have liked it over there to stay that long? You still sound very British but I noticed you use American slang quite a bit.'

'I guess it's normal to pick things up when you're living and breathing it every day,' she said shortly. 'And in answer to your question, personal reasons, including to be with my family again.'

'Fair enough,' he stood up. 'Right, I think we're done here.

Thank you for your time.'

'Can I have another glass of water before I go please?' She needed a minute to think, as well as rein her anger in.

'Sure,' he checked his watch, 'but it'll have to be quick. The next candidate will be here any minute.'

'That's fine. Thanks.'

He nodded and picked up the glasses, leaving her alone. Springing off the sofa she strode across the room and flung open the nearest French door, propping herself up against the frame. Her heart beat a rapid *ga-doom, ga-doom, ga-doom* in her chest, pumping adrenalin around her body. What a bastard Matt was.

The scent of freshly cut grass filled her nose and normally the heady smell of British summer would be a lovely distraction, a balm to the last few years of homesickness. Not today. Her fingers clenched around each other, knuckles tight.

Then as if her system had used the last of its energy up with the hot blast of anger, belated jet lag hit hard again. A drowning wave of languor washed over her, making her eyes go gritty and heavy. Just like that, she couldn't wait to get out of this house and away from the whole sorry mess. God, she was weary. Curling up in a ball and sinking into a deep slumber suddenly held massive appeal. She hadn't slept properly for almost two weeks before leaving New York. There'd been too much to do, wrapping up her life and returning to her old one. The nights staring dry-eyed at the ceiling hadn't helped either. Somewhere inside her there was a healthy need to grieve and cry, but she hadn't been able to manage it before leaving the States.

It had been a mistake coming here, a knee-jerk reaction. Would it be better if she simply left? Went back to Melody and helped her put her life back together, while doing the same for herself? But then she heard Matt moving around the kitchen, whistling along to a pop song currently in the UK download chart, perhaps one that he'd produced. He sounded so happy, so unconcerned. It was completely unfair. Why should he be acting as if life was peachy

21

when he'd practically ruined her sister's?

She went to shut the door and her head jerked as she spotted a wooden bench tucked away in a corner of the manicured lawn, not far from a sturdy apple tree and rose-beds resplendent with pearl-white blooms. Her gaze zoomed in on a scrap of fabric draped over the seat. It was a rich mulberry colour. Melody's cardigan, one Zoe had bought in Bloomingdale's and paid to have shipped back to the UK for her last birthday. Next to it was a book, left open face down to keep the page. The spine would be permanently creased by now. They'd always argued about Melody's inability to treat books with respect. Then it dawned that her baby sister had been ejected so quickly she'd not even been able to grab her things from the garden and she shook with regenerated rage, adrenalin boiling up and smothering her exhaustion.

It was time to give Matt, a guy too similar to Greg for comfort, what he deserved. He needed to feel humiliation and hurt on every level. She was sick of men who thought they could treat women like that, tossing them aside when they were done. It wasn't right and it stung. It ripped apart your self-esteem so you were left wondering, *what's wrong with me? Why aren't I good enough?* It ripped apart your heart so you thought, *I never want to go through this again.*

Matt Reilly would pay, and not only for making her sister jobless, homeless and breaking her heart with the help of his brother, but for all the other women he'd hurt in the past. She'd read the articles. Sure, you couldn't take everything you read in the tabloids as a given, but there had to be a grain of truth in them. If only a fraction of the hearts he'd reportedly broken since becoming a widower three years ago were true, the line of devastated women would stretch from London to Brighton and back again.

But how was she going to do it?

Then there was that sweet, magical moment when inspiration hit. As Matt swept back in and she turned to him, smoothing her hands down over her top, she saw an appreciative glint in his eyes, quickly hidden. Put that together with his near paranoia about

22

the press and his desperation for privacy and she knew exactly what to do.

This was going to be so goddamn satisfying... if she could pull it off.

3

'I don't know about this, Sis,' Melody twisted a piece of long, dark blonde hair around her nail-bitten finger, frowning. Lowering her voice so customers nearby couldn't overhear, she leaned forward. 'Aren't you worried it might backfire?'

Zoe stared at her sister's pale, hollow-eyed face. 'I don't see how it can,' she replied, putting her mug of latte down on the sticky table. They'd met at a cafe near Jemima's flat in Holloway, given that part of the plan relied on Matt and Stephen not finding out they were related. 'The risk is all his,' she added, sliding the coffee aside so she could grasp her sister's chilly hands. 'And don't you think he deserves it? Don't you think it will do him good to be humiliated and confused, the way you've been? I mean, you still don't even know why, do you? Not properly. All Matt said to you that day was that you weren't suitable for his brother or to look after his kids and had to leave immediately. There was no conversation, no chance for you to ask why. He just threw you out.' Melody had told Zoe more about it a few days earlier. About the way that one day she'd been a girl in love, part of Matt and Stephen's family unit, and the next she'd been out in the cold with barely any explanation. 'But you said that Matt seemed okay about you and Stephen seeing each other before then? You'd been together a few months?'

'Yes.' Melody gnawed her bottom lip, dark brown eyes looking bruised. 'He was. I just don't get it. Why the change of heart? And why wasn't I good enough? Because we're not rich? He never seemed like a snob to me.' She gulped. 'I thought he liked me.'

'I don't know. It doesn't make sense.' Zoe paused. 'Unless he thought you and Stephen were just casual, and then when it started getting serious he wasn't happy? You said that you and Matt always got on well though. Why wouldn't he just talk to you about any concerns he had?'

Melody's eyes brimmed. 'No idea. Yes, we did get on well, he was more like a big brother than an employer sometimes.'

Zoe sighed, her sister's naivety paining her. 'Oh, Mel. You should never confuse professional and personal relationships. That way can only lead to hurt.'

'Pardon?' Melody stared at her, dazed eyes clearing.

'You should always keep a personal distance from the people you work for. You know that.'

'Don't start lecturing me. You don't know what it was like.' Melody flashed, yanking her slim hands away. 'I was with the family for three years. It's a bit late to wade in and start pulling your big sister act just because it's suddenly convenient!'

'Right,' Zoe murmured through dry lips, throat aching. Ouch. Direct hit.

'I'm sorry,' Melody gasped immediately, 'I didn't mean it. You know I didn't. I'm just such a mess...' she dropped her head into her hands, shoulders heaving, 'and I'm so angry.'

'I know. Don't worry.' Melody was normally the gentlest person in the world. Zoe scooted her chair around the table to get closer, the legs scraping on the tiled floor. Placing a hand on her little sister's back, she waited quietly, giving her time.

If she'd been there for Melody, maybe none of this would have happened. Mel wouldn't have gone looking for the guidance and friendship from her boss that she should have been getting from her big sister. Even though they'd texted and Skyped a lot, it hadn't been the same, living on opposite sides of the ocean. Zoe might blame Matt and Stephen for her sister's heartbreak, but part of the responsibility rested on her shoulders too.

The look on Matt's face when he talked about Melody letting him down flashed across her mind and as much as she wanted to dismiss it, or think he'd been lying, there'd been something there. Something he was unsure of or puzzled about. It would do no good to tell Melody what Matt had said because it might upset her. But perhaps her plan could serve two purposes; not just revenge, but finding out just what the heck had happened.

She stroked her sister's back soothingly. 'I know you're worried about my plan, and don't really agree with it but maybe if I can find out *why*, it will give you closure?' She nodded at Melody's raw, tear-filled eyes. 'I take it that Stephen still isn't taking your calls or answering your messages?' Thinking of his travel bag and *see you when I get back* holler to his brother. 'I suppose he could be abroad. Perhaps he's having problems with his phone.'

Melody shook her head, a lone tear running down her cheek. 'I don't think so, and he can more than afford the roaming charges. I just don't get it. Everything was fine. We were happy. And I just can't understand the way Matt acted— Oh, Zoe, I don't know what to do-oo...'

The last word ended on a wail and reignited the hot, rolling rage and fiercely protective instincts in Zoe. She sucked her bottom lip into her mouth, rubbing her sister's back more firmly, wanting to scrub away the hurt. 'I'm sorry. I didn't mean to upset you. But Matt hasn't been in touch to check how you are either. I mean, you could be living on a park bench somewhere for all he knows. It's disgusting. I really think he needs to be taught a lesson.' She looked into her sister's face, jaw set, thinking of the added insult of a few days before, when she'd gone to Matt's house. 'Let me do this for you, Mel,' she said fiercely. 'Let me get answers and teach them they can't behave this way. That you can't ignore people and pretend you've done nothing wrong. It'll be fine, I promise.'

26

Melody sighed heavily, running a finger over some spilt grains of sugar. 'Okay,' she whispered.

'Good. It's the only thing that makes sense.' Zoe paused. 'Also, I know that Jemima is happy to have you,' she broached, 'but sleeping on her couch is less than ideal. What do you think about me calling Ruth and seeing if you could stay with her for a while? You always got on well together, right? I'm sure she still has the guest room set up ready. It might give you some distance. Fifty miles might not be very far, but it's not on Matt's doorstep either. One of the worst things about a break up is running into the person, or the possibility you're going to. If Stephen gets back soon, you'll have two people who upset you to avoid. I don't want you to think I want shot of you,' she added, 'because I can't wait for us to spend some quality time together after I've been away so long. I'm just thinking of what's best for you right now.'

Melody sniffed. 'It would be good to have some space, and be somewhere familiar. I know it never seemed like home to you, and Ruth isn't the huggy sort, but I feel safe there.' She nodded. 'Can you call her please? If you can do it without arguing that is. I'm going to splash some cold water on my face.' Pushing her chair back, she grabbed her bag and hitched her chin up, trying to be brave.

Zoe watched her go. Poor thing. Sucking in a deep breath she dialled her aunt's number, dreading the conversation. 'It's me,' she said when Ruth answered with a curt hello.

'Oh. You are still in the land of the living then.'

'I did text you from the airport the other day.'

'Messaging relatives is no substitute for a good old fashioned phone call,' Ruth said in a sniffy tone. 'I expected you to follow the text up with a call. I knew you'd be jetlagged but surely you could have—'

'I've had my hands full,' she cut across her aunt's accusation, picturing her grey hair in its no-nonsense bun and the pursed lips, shoulders bolt-straight, her dark eyes cool and unforgiving. When in this mood, the result was stilted accusations Zoe didn't have the time and energy for today. Obviously she still wasn't forgiven for what had happened before her departure for the States, despite the birthday and Christmas cards she'd always sent, accompanied by luxury gifts. However, now was not the time to try and sort it out. That didn't mean she shouldn't be conciliatory. 'I'm sorry, you're right, I should have called. The thing is, Matt's fired Melody and kicked her out, and Stephen's gone AWOL.'

'What? What on earth do you mean? What happened? The absolute brutes.'

'I'm not sure yet.' Zoe didn't know whether to be grateful or sad that her aunt would jump so easily to her sister's defence, when if it had been her the first thing Ruth would have asked was *what did you do*? 'I'm trying to sort it out,' no way was she telling Ruth the details of what she was up to, 'but in the meantime I think it would be good for Melody if she came home for a while. We've talked about it and it's what she wants, if you'll have her.'

'Of course I will. The guest room is made up for when she visits during the holidays. Put her on the first train you can and let me know when she'll be arriving. I'll pick her up from the station. She can stay as long as she likes.'

'Okay, thank you,' Zoe said, relieved. At least that was one less thing to worry about. There might be a lot of muddy ground between her and Ruth, but Melody's well-being was always a given. 'I'll text you. I'm aiming to get her on the train this afternoon if I can manage it.'

'Right. And what are you going to be doing in the meantime?'

'I'll be trying to work out what's gone on, and see if the situation can be retrieved.' She had to talk in the language that Ruth understood.

'You do that. Keep me updated, will you? If you need me to speak with either of the swines let me know. I don't know enough about Stephen to comment, however it's odd about Matthew, I didn't think he was like that. He always seemed so nice. I met him a few times when I came into London for lunch with your sister.'

'That's what Melody thought too,' Zoe replied. 'I'll be in touch. Bye.' She hung up, sitting back in her chair. Formidable was not the word for her aunt. She almost felt like setting her on Matt because it was what he deserved, but that wouldn't get them anywhere. She was convinced that direct confrontation wasn't the route to take. Staring down at the greasy table top, she frowned, anxiety coiling in her stomach. Was it always going to be this way between her and Ruth? Was there ever going to be a time that they could come to some understanding? Or when Ruth would tell her why she'd always been the odd one out in their little patched together family?

When Melody returned a minute later, Zoe forced a smile. 'Good news,' she said. 'You can go to Ruth's as soon as this afternoon if you want. We can grab your things from Jemima's and get you on the train in no time.' She thought longingly of the coarse sandy beaches of Southend-on-Sea. Pictured the world's longest pleasure pier, the row of multi-coloured beach huts, the rides and roller coaster of Adventure Island on the Western Esplanade. Could almost taste the salt that carried on the sea breeze and always tangled her hair. While Ruth's house with its dark shadows, locked rooms and no-nonsense air had never felt like home, she loved the seaside town she'd spent most of her teens in.

'That would be good,' Melody murmured. 'I do think I need to get away and the sooner the better.' She closed her eyes then opened them again, looking horrified. 'I haven't even asked about you, Sis. Are you doing okay? Funny that we're both going through break-ups at the same time.'

'I'll be fine.' Zoe grabbed her bag from under the table and started rooting through her purse. 'At least I know what happened,' she muttered, head down. The memory of that last night with Greg flashed in front of her eyes. 'Besides, I've got other things to concentrate on. I'll be checking out of the bed and breakfast in a couple of days' time and moving in with Matt.'

Melody shook her head. 'That's the part of the plan that makes me nervous.'

'Why?' Zoe frowned at her sister as she threw a ten pound note down on the table. At least that was one thing; she was returning to the UK with money in the bank, courtesy of her ex-fiancé and their cancelled plans. 'You think he might rumble me straight away?'

'No. It's more that while he has a tendency to be closed off from the children, and really distracted, he's a nice guy. Kind of charming actually. I never saw him that way but lots of women—'

'Not such a nice guy that it stopped him from doing what he did to you,' she interrupted, 'and that's all I'm interested in. Don't worry, I won't fall for the act.' Thinking of Greg, something in her chest twisted. 'There's no chance.'

Later on, when they said goodbye as Melody boarded the train, her shoulders slumped like a puppy that had been kicked one too many times, a new determination burned through Zoe. The sooner this was done, the sooner Melody might be able to move on with her life, and come back to London, where the two of them belonged side by side together again. Sisters.

Huffing out a breath, Zoe slung another huge canvas bag on the bed, a trickle of sweat snaking down her back. She bit her lower lip, pulling out her phone to re-read her sister's text from that morning.

> **All settled and Ruth is
> looking after me. I'm still
> not sure about this Sis.
> But if you're going to do
> it, please be careful. M xx**

Melody was obviously worried so Zoe had done her best to reassure her.

I'll be fine.
Can't wait to see the
look on Matt's face when
it all comes together.
Then on to Stephen! xx

It probably was a kind of madness, moving in with a guy she detested. But it was part of the plan. Besides, if she wasn't meant to do this, why would the universe have co-operated quite so nicely? When the agency had called the day following the interview to tell her Matt wanted her to go back and meet the kids, it'd felt like cosmic rebalancing, like it was meant to be. Not that she was superstitious. But the agency—Exclusive London Nannies—had been happy to re-register her, delighted to make money from the placement. Once Liberty had supplied a glowing reference and Zoe had registered with the online DBS service, her enhanced disclosure and barring clearance available within days, with her certificate of good conduct on its way from America, it had been too easy to meet Aimee and Jasper. To convince Matt of her suitability to be his nanny. Of course it had helped that Melody had been able to give her some inside tips about the family.

Surprisingly, the children weren't the spoilt brats she'd expected. Maybe that was down to her sister's influence over the last few years. They did however have a few issues that Melody hadn't articulated.

Number one was that they were crying out for their dad's love, the net result being that Aimee was so incredibly shy she was virtually mute, finding it hard to hold eye contact and hesitant about speaking, while Jasper's behaviour was so demanding and energy levels so high he was on the verge of hyperactivity. Zoe couldn't help feeling Jasper was attention seeking, trying to establish communication with his only parent.

Number two was they were bored out of their skulls and weren't engaging with the activities Matt had chosen for them.

She'd seen it all within an hour; interacting with the three of them, noticing Matt's distracted and distant manner, the way the light went out of his kids' eyes whenever he glanced at his phone, or gazed off into space with a faraway look, or scribbled something on a notepad he kept in his back pocket. They weren't a happy, cohesive family unit. Not at all.

She could do a lot of good for these kids. It was a shame she was only here for a few weeks to get revenge, which she'd started referring to as *Plan Nannygate* in her head. Nothing over the past week had made her feel like Matt didn't deserve it. What she hadn't mentioned to her sister in the cafe was what had happened during her brief third visit, just after accepting the job.

Finally allowed to see her living quarters, she had been horrified to find Melody's things shoved into black bin liners and left carelessly in a pile in one of the upstairs hallways, the contents overflowing and getting trodden on every time Jasper ran past. Which he invariably did, as his default speed setting appeared to be supersonic. The lack of respect for her sister's stuff had her fuming, never mind the health and safety hazard to the kids if they tripped over the bags.

'This is really dangerous,' she'd raised an eyebrow at Matt. 'You must have storage space. It needs to be put away.'

'Dangerous?' he'd answered her without lifting his head, typing something into his iPad.

'For your children. They could fall over the bags and down the stairs?' She pointed out exasperated, before realising she had to watch her tone. She couldn't be bolshy. He was about to become her boss and she wanted to earn his trust, so she had to play nice. 'I'm just concerned. I have a duty of care towards them, remember?' Like he did as their parent.

He swiped the tablet screen to lock it and looked up, shaking his head as if bringing himself back to planet earth. 'You're right. Sorry. I hadn't even noticed. I'll get our cleaner Roberta to move them tomorrow.'

'Or we could do it now?' she suggested, not giving him much

chance to disagree, scooping up two bags and running downstairs. 'Where shall we put them?' her voice echoed up the spiral white staircase.

A loud, resigned sigh sounded on the landing above her. She bit the inside of her cheeks to stop from smiling as she heard the rustle of plastic bags, followed a moment later by the beat of approaching footsteps. It was satisfying knowing she'd annoyed him, just a little bit.

'There's a double garage, and I only use one of them when Stephen's away because I always have one car on the drive. We can put these in the empty side.'

'Is it clean and dry?' she prompted. 'We wouldn't want it all getting ruined. I'm guessing your old nanny might come back for them at some point?' The last was uttered through gritted teeth. *Sweetness and light Zoe*, she reminded herself.

He looked troubled by the thought. 'It's possible,' he turned around, 'garage is this way.' After twenty minutes of traipsing up and down, everything was safely stowed away and Zoe felt like she'd scored a victory. The garage was easily accessible from both the front and side of the house, so at some point she'd make plans with Melody to collect her stuff with Ruth. Or perhaps she'd smuggle it out a bit at a time, she mused, like illegal contraband.

The fact that, as well as failing to check on her sister's welfare, Matt also had no respect for her belongings reinforced Zoe's feeling that he didn't give a crap. Well, she thought grimly, he needed to be taught to care.

So here she was, in the enemy's house surrounded by her clothes, shoes and other belongings. The original idea had been to sling a few suitcases in the car and live out of them, but she'd realised it would look suspicious if she brought hardly anything with her after accepting a permanent position. So she'd called the storage company and asked them to deliver some of the boxes shipped over from New York and phoned Rayne, who'd been letting Zoe use the loft in her attic flat for some of her old stuff, pre-America.

'It's so great to see you,' Rayne had hugged her earlier, before stepping back to study her appraisingly. 'I know coming back to Blighty now isn't what you'd planned,' she paused as they looked bleakly at each other, knowing what *had* been planned, 'but I'm still glad you're here. I'm not that pleased to see how skinny you are though, Zo.' Squeezing her friend's narrow waist. 'Tell me the truth, how are you doing?' She swept her black fringe out of her eyes, Cleopatra sharp bob falling back around her face, multiple cocktail rings glinting in the early morning sun.

'It's good to see you too.' Zoe smiled tightly. 'And, yeah, okay,' her throat closed up, and she realised she'd barely thought about her own heartbreak because of dealing with the fallout of her sister's. Maybe that made it easier. 'You know what it's like after a break up. The weight falls off, doesn't it? Best diet around,' she joked weakly.

'Hmm. Well, just don't lose too much will you? I don't want to let that bastard make you ill. I still can't believe he—'

'Can we not talk about it?' Zoe touched Rayne's arm. 'Another time, all right?' She wasn't ready to deal with the implosion of her life yet.

'Sure,' her friend looked worried but nodded, turning to gaze up at Matt's house. 'Wow, it's really something. You've landed on your feet haven't you? I know you're here for less than savoury reasons, but still.'

'Thanks.' Zoe replied dryly. If there was one thing you could count on, it was Rayne being honest to the point of bluntness. *Less than savoury.* Her plan wasn't going to cover her in glory, but it was justifiable in the circumstances. 'You're going to help me, right?'

Rayne hesitated. 'If you're sure this is what he deserves, and you're not going to get hurt.'

'I'm one hundred per cent sure,' Zoe said firmly. 'This is what I need to do. I mean,' she said hastily, 'what Melody needs me to do.'

'All right then, I'm in,' Rayne nodded, 'you know you've always got my support. If he's as much of a bastard as you say he is, let's go for it. When the time is right, I'll put you in touch with some of the celebrity reporters I know.'

'Thanks.' Zoe moved the conversation on. 'And what about you and Adam? How's it going?' The question choked her a bit. It was hard being newly single when the rest of the world seemed to be coupled up, but she couldn't begrudge her friend's happiness. Rayne had run into her uni ex-boyfriend at Wimbledon a few weeks before and after nearly five years apart they'd ended up giving it another go.

'Amazing so far,' Rayne grinned, practically glowing, 'the way it was back then, but even better. He's still lovely, and *so* much hotter too. You remember he had that preppy handsome look going on at uni? Well he's got a few rough edges now, cut his hair, got a tattoo and he's much more relaxed. You'd love him. But not too much,' she teased.

'I do like bad boys,' Zoe mused, wondering how the heck she'd ever ended up with Greg, who was polished Kennedy-American uptight, 'but I draw the line at body art.'

'Fair enough, each to their own,' Rayne smiled easily. 'Adam would like to see you again. We've been going on double dates with Lily and his intern Flynn, but it would be nice to get more of the old gang back together.'

'Sounds great, how about we do something in a few weeks' time, once this is over,' Zoe gestured at the property behind them, 'and I'm settled somewhere else?'

'Cool, but if you end up needing to escape the madness with a girlie night out sooner, let me know. We can try and get your sister involved; Adam has plenty of spare rooms in his place in Islington she could stop in. We might be able to convince Frankie to put Zack down for a minute and join us too. It would be good to get the dark trinity together again.'

Zoe laughed at Rayne's description of how madly in love their other best friend was with her boyfriend, and the name Adam had given the three of them at uni because they all had black hair. 'Yeah, thanks. I will. I don't really feel like going out at the moment though.'

'Fine, but don't lock yourself away for too long,' Rayne ordered. 'You need to keep busy, not mope over that deaf, blind and dumb idiot, which he totally is to do what he did as well as letting you go so easily. Besides, I don't want you turning into some sad old spinster who's going to get chewed on by her cats. Especially as you're such an oldie.' Referring to the fact Zoe was two years older than her.

'Gee, thanks for the sympathy.' Zoe stuck out her tongue, playing along, knowing Rayne was trying to cheer her up. 'I'll let you know when I'm ready to leave the fortress of solitude,' she smiled, 'but nothing too wild, for gawd's sakes.'

'Nooo,' Rayne said, backing away, holding her fingers out in front of her in a cross sign, 'she's turned American on us! Quick, call the Queen!'

'Ha ha. I probably have picked up some bad habits. I was over there for long enough. You can be in charge of my conversion back to British citizen if you want.'

'It's a plan.' Rayne saluted, clicking her heels together. 'I'd better run. I've got a story to finish and a meeting with my editor. Sorry I can't help you move your crap upstairs,' she finished cheekily, her turquoise blouse bringing out her navy blue eyes, which flashed with humour.

'Sod off, it's not crap!' Zoe replied automatically, reverting back to their uni days. 'And it's fine. You're a star for getting it down from your loft and dropping it over. Thanks so much.' Zoe leaned in for a quick hug before shooing Rayne away. 'Go. Speak soon.' She shook her head as her friend roared away in her sporty black Mini, a Union Jack design on its roof. The girl certainly had personality.

God, she'd missed her. Had missed all her friends. She'd given so much up when she'd moved to the States. Pretty much everything in fact. And all she had to show for it was a bare left hand, a few extra laughter lines and a dress she'd never wear hanging in her closet.

By the time she'd heaved all the boxes and bags up to her top floor living quarters, she was hot, sweaty and swearing. She was also grateful her new boss and his kids weren't around to see what a complete mess she was; damp dark hair coming loose from its high ponytail and sticking to her slippery face, denim shorts creased and the straps of her dust-smudged white vest top falling off her shoulders. It was a scorchingly hot day and although the lower floors of the house were cool and spacious, the upper floor was carpeted, more compact and suffered from heat rising upwards. Throwing open the skylight windows hadn't helped much, there was no breeze outside to offer any relief.

Thankfully Matt wasn't due back for hours as he was holed up in his studio with some new talent he'd discovered and both kids were visiting with their grandma, his late wife's mum. It was his way of giving her time to settle in, which she should be grateful for, but instead of abandoning her maybe he could have stuck around to see if she could do with a hand?

She shook her head. It wasn't his job to help her move in. Why on earth should he? Looking at all the stuff spread out over the length and breadth of the bedroom, a mixture of old and new, cases and boxes of clothes, shoes and her beloved books, knowing there were more in the lounge area, she blew out another long breath. It was strange to think that this set of rooms had been her sister's home for three years. She felt uncomfortable, like an impostor. It was going to take hours to unpack too. Mind you, there was no bookcase so her books could stay packed away for now, which would save some time.

As she opened the first crate from America and a long black and white Marc Jacobs gown slithered to the floor, her addiction to clothes caught hold and she forgot how uncomfortable she was. Leaping up, she unpacked everything else in delight, rediscovering old friends from before she'd left, including the ancient Alaia chain-link leather sandals she'd saved up a month for when living at Ruth's. Haphazardly laying clothes, shoes, belts and handbags across the bed and every available surface, she stroked them lovingly, holding the soft, luxurious fabrics against her face. God, she adored all this, and given enough money would shop every single day. New York had been a revelation. She'd fallen in love with the stores as much as the loud, straight-talking people. She'd also been lucky that even though Liberty had been bossy and occasionally unreasonable about her children, she was generous and had fallen into the habit of gifting her collections to Zoe after every season. She was going to sorely miss that perk of the job, along with her charges Ava and Grace, and a hundred other tiny little things she'd come to love about NY.

As well as the life she'd had planned. One that Greg had robbed her of with his stupid, selfish behaviour.

All of a sudden it flowed over her.

Bastard! How could he *do* that to her? After everything they'd been to each other... Friends, lovers, partners. But clearly she'd been fooling herself, because if that was really the case, he could never have done what he'd done. For god's sakes, it was the oldest story in the book, sleeping with someone else. Couldn't he have at least been a bit original? Or ducked out of their relationship if he wasn't happy? She wanted to punch him, yell at him, tell him all the ways she'd like to make him suffer, how much she hated what he'd done, how three and a half thousand miles between them would never ever be enough.

She ground her teeth. Watching him hurt would give her satisfaction, definitely. But she wasn't sure it would make her feel any better, and there was no way she was going to give up her dignity by losing control. Sometimes all a girl had left was her pride, along with her instinct for survival. The best thing was to cut him off completely, forget he even existed, until she could speak to him without having a total meltdown.

Picking up a hot pink, strapless dress she'd worn to a party not long before leaving for New York, she shook her head. What *had* she been thinking? She couldn't imagine wearing it again. Her mum, if still alive, would have probably told her to put it in the bin or give it away, that once things became useless, you should just get rid of them. But Zoe was feeling sentimental, so she tucked the dress into the back of the massive built-in wardrobe in her new bedroom and hung up a beautiful sequinned blue top. Spying her favourite black Manolo Blahniks she slipped them on, mood instantly lifting. She'd saved up her bonuses to buy them and they were totally impractical, but boy, did they make her feel great.

Grabbing a cropped jacket she'd once worn to a rock concert, she stroked it before hanging it up, smiling at the memories of the blaring music and sweaty, jumping crowd. Unpacking her old things, marvelling over them and remembering the girl she used to be, along with the good times in New York, might be the closest she'd been to happiness in a while.

That, and the thought of Matt's face when he was plastered all over the weekend papers, his precious privacy blown sky high. There might be a confidentiality clause in her contract, but she had absolutely no fear of breaching it. He'd hardly want the publicity of a big court case, and she would do whatever it took to do right by her sister.

4

Matt crashed his car keys into a bowl on the expensive white sideboard, kicking the heavy black front door shut behind him.

He hissed out a swear word. The studio had been a nightmare. For some unknown reason the singer with the incredibly rich, adaptable voice who'd seemed so passionate, enthusiastic and energetic when he'd offered her a contract after weeks of sound tests and negotiations with her agent had today been listless and disinterested. It was like working with a different person. He could only hope the chance he'd taken on her wasn't going to backfire. The fact it might frustrated him, made irritation burn inside. She had it in her to be amazing, world-class. So what the hell had happened to change her so radically? To make her avoid his gaze and mutter that she was fine, when she quite clearly wasn't? He would never get women. Why did they always *do* that? Not that he'd been thinking of her as a woman, despite her fragile blonde beauty. He only saw her as a gifted artist. The talent was always off limits, at least in his code of practice.

He pulled a hand through his dark hair, itching for a cool, calming shower and a strong black coffee before going to his office and dealing with the tedious mass of emails he was behind with because his assistant Sadie was still recovering from her procedure. He supposed he should do the polite thing and find his new nanny first though. Say hello, ask if she needed anything.

Taking the two sets of spiral staircases in large leaps, up from the ground floor and past his and the kids' rooms on the first floor, he strode down the top floor corridor and swung into the doorway of Zoe's living space. Not in the white and beige lounge area. She must be in the bedroom. If the door was closed he'd knock, but it was open, so he walked straight in, impatient to get it over with.

The greeting he'd planned died on his lips, breath unexpectedly clogging in his throat. There was a knee-jerk response in his lower body, his jeans going uncomfortably tight.

Bloody hell.

Of all the beautiful women he'd worked with over the years—the singers and divas with their glamorous designer outfits and fashionable haircuts, manicures and pedicures, their gym-perfect toned bodies and fake tans—she was by far the sexiest he'd ever seen.

Sitting on the plush blue bedroom carpet, she was leaning against the ivory wall-paper, head tipped back as she gulped thirstily from a can of coke. Her creamy skin was flushed and her shapely but slightly too slim bare legs were on display, stunningly shown off by a pair of ultra-high black heels and some nearly non-existent cut-offs. A white vest-top outlined generous breasts and a tiny waist, the plain top a contrast against her black hair, dark brows and lashes.

Tamara Drewe eat your heart out, he thought, recalling the scene in the film where the intrepid journalist had made an all too memorable picture striding through a Dorset country field in tiny denim shorts.

When interviewing Zoe, of course he'd noticed she was attractive. Okay, striking, with a lovely face and athletic body. But he was surrounded by good-looking women most of the time. For a start, his recording artists were almost always easy on the eye. Not fair maybe that looks should be as important as talent, but the paying public invariably preferred something appealing to look at with the music. It was part of why Taylor, Rihanna and

41

Rita had done so well.

He'd never had a problem keeping his hands off his artists, never had an issue keeping the relationships strictly professional. When Helen had been alive, he'd believed in being faithful and sticking to his marriage vows, even if, as it turned out, she hadn't felt the same. Since she'd been gone, he'd had two small children to worry about, a successful business to keep afloat and an income to bring in if he wasn't going to rely on the family inheritance the way his brother did. Was it any wonder he'd avoided getting close to women over the last few years? The complete opposite to what the press thought, the flames of publicity fanned by his PR Officer to give him and his clients maximum exposure.

Whatever, Zoe had been the best candidate for the job by far and it had been an easy and pragmatic decision to offer her the post. He'd had no expectation that moving her in would be an issue, but now wasn't so sure. She was absolutely gorgeous, though a little on the thin side; her upper arms were a bit too defined and the slight ridges of her ribs were visible through the top. Nonetheless in this outfit she had an earthy sexiness that was going to make it hard for him to be around her without being in physical discomfort.

The thought brought back his earlier irritation. The last thing he needed was a complication, especially after everything that had happened with his last nanny. Getting involved with Zoe would be inappropriate. She was an employee. Look what had happened with Melody and Stephen, how that had turned out. Thinking about it brought on new waves of anger and disappointment. He'd thought Melody was such a sweet girl. So caring, so selfless. *Wrong.*

Frustration edged his voice as he stepped further into Zoe's bedroom. 'What's going on? I didn't realise you were moving your worldly possessions in. It's like a jumble sale in here!'

Zoe looked up at him, then at the devastation around the room, flushing. 'Oh. Well, I'm not finished yet, and wasn't expecting you back so soon.'

'Obviously.'

Jumping to her feet, rocking on the high heels, her black hair trailing down her back in its loose ponytail, her eyes flashed. *Great, the view's even better up close. Focus on talking Matt, look her in the eyes, not anywhere else. Definitely do not drop your gaze to those eye-popping breasts.*

'I didn't realise there was a limit on the number of items I was allowed when I took the job,' she said defensively, tucking her hands in her shorts pockets. 'Sorry, did I miss something in the contract?'

'No, of course not. Don't be silly—' he clicked his teeth together, seeing from her scowling face how well the comment had gone down. *Deep breath, try again.* Maybe if he didn't look into those massive baby blues he'd be okay, so he stared at her collarbone instead. 'I'm sorry, what I meant to say is, no. There's no limit. I was just, er, it's just that—' his gaze dropped a few inches, and he frowned, fighting an overwhelming urge to grab her and bury his face in her cleavage. *You're acting like a schoolboy, sad and needy. Get a grip.*

'Just that what?' she crossed her arms.

Shit, it just made the cleavage thing worse. *Eyes up.*

'I was just a bit surprised by the mess,' he muttered. 'I'm not in that great a mood either. My version of a bad day at the office. I shouldn't have taken it out on you though, so I apologise. I'm sure you'll have it all put away soon.'

'Yeah,' she hitched her chin up a few centimetres but didn't look very confident. 'I hope so.' Giving him an uncertain smile. 'What time are the kids back again?'

'Just under two hours. Let me help,' he said instinctively. Why had he done that? He'd never offered to help Melody in that way. He also had loads to do. The cold shower, the emails, phone calls to return. This was a bad idea, a stupid one. He should leave her to it. Instead, to his surprise, he stepped further into the bedroom.

A funny feeling swirled in Zoe's stomach as Matt came closer. He lifted a hand, rubbing a long finger over the scar that ran into his top lip. If it were anyone else she might have thought he was nervous, but he was so confident she knew that couldn't be it.

'Thanks for the offer, but I'll be fine.' She edged away, aware of his body heat and how big he was, towering over her. 'You don't want to help unpack a load of clothes and shoes, surely? I hardly think that it's part of your job description as my boss.'

He shrugged muscular shoulders in the clinging grey t-shirt he wore so ridiculously well.

'I want you to feel at home here,' he wandered around the room with an easy grace for such a tall, well-built guy. 'If you do, the kids will feel it. So whatever it takes. Where do you want me to start?' Frowning, and looking at the tottering piles of shoes in three different parts of the room. 'I take it you've seen there's shelving for shoes? Although,' he glanced at her, 'I'm not sure you'll fit them all in.' He bent over and plucked up a patent red stiletto, letting it dangle from one finger, raising one eyebrow.

She blushed and bit her bottom lip. The shoe looked tiny in his hands. It was a strangely personal feeling as he ran assessing fingers over the curve of the arch and turned the heel over. He might as well be delving into her lingerie drawer. Something about the confident way he handled the shoe sent a ping of lust zipping through her pelvis. Plus he smelled incredible and looked sexily rumpled with his hair in tufts, presumably from where he'd raked through it with stress, and she couldn't help noticing again the way his t-shirt stretched over his well-defined chest.

She was mortified to realise as he looked over that she was staring.

What? No, no, no! Stop salivating over him. He's a pig, remember? Remember why you're here.

'So, is this it or is there still more to come?'

His question threw her, given the battle she was fighting against rebellious hormones and the need to hang onto some brain power.

44

'No, that's it. Anyway, does it matter?' she asked, clearing her throat when realising how breathy she sounded. 'Because you've said I've no limit on the amount of stuff I can have, I mean.'

'It'll matter if this only scratches the surface and we end up with a house so full we can't move,' he grinned disarmingly. Then he looked down at the shoe. 'You've got expensive tastes, haven't you? Got a rich guy secreted in the States somewhere who keeps you in the good stuff?'

'Sorry, but that's not really any of your business, Matt,' she said stiffly. He was only joking but the comments hurt. Yes, she'd had a guy in the States, but contrary to what he might think she couldn't be bought by pretty things, wouldn't be blinded by them.

Temper flared in his eyes at her tone, but he didn't respond straight away, instead gathering up the matching red shoe and disappearing into the cupboard, presumably to put the pair in the rack. 'Fair enough,' he said casually as he came back out, picking up a silk top from a pile on the side, 'as long you're not going to have some guy turning up out of the blue.' He glanced at the king-sized bed behind her, and something in his expression tumbled her stomach, along with the way he was running his fingers absent-mindedly over the lace of the top's neckline. 'I don't allow sleepovers in this house. That *is* in your contract.'

She turned to stare at the bed. Her eyes closed on a rush of heat, her skin prickling with awareness and she suddenly felt tongue-tied. *Get it together. Anyone would think you were a teenage girl alone in your room with a boy for the first time.* As much as she was aware of his astonishing hotness in her weaker moments, she wouldn't act on it, mainly because of the whole Plan Nannygate and not liking him thing, but also because she wasn't ready for anything after Greg's betrayal. But back to the issue at hand, his comment on overnight guests. 'That won't be a problem.' She met his gaze. 'I'm single, and happy to stay that way.' But she mustn't be too adamant about it. At some point she needed to try and build a relationship between them, or at least the appearance of one. Which meant humour, trust, affection. Yuck.

'Great! Good.' He looked completely wrong-footed by the words flying out of his mouth. 'I mean, that's easier for everyone. I just don't like the thought of strange men wandering around my house with the children here—'

'No. One strange man is more than enough,' she joked, crossing the room and easing the silky top from his hand, raising her eyebrows. 'Could you please kindly stop feeling up my pyjamas?'

His eyes shot to hers, then down at the fabric. 'Oh. I, ah... sorry, I thought that it was a top. That you wear out, I mean. I-I'd better go, I have a lot of work to do.'

'You're not going to stay and help after all?' She couldn't resist teasing him, seeing his discomfort.

'I think its best you sort it out,' he started backing toward the door. 'If you can get the room straight and then get changed into something more suitable before Jasper and Aimee get home, that would be appreciated.'

She frowned. 'Something more suitable?'

He took a few more steps back. 'You're the other responsible adult in this house at the moment and need to set a good example. I'd rather not be confronted by my seven year-old daughter trying to wear shorts that go up to—' he paused before nodding at her bare legs, 'well, you know what I mean.'

Turning, he headed off downstairs before she could respond, leaving her standing in the messy room, face turning a slow bright red. Lovely. He'd just practically accused her of looking like a prostitute. What an ass. So much for Melody saying he could be kind of charming. Although he hadn't been doing too badly at first. Maybe Melody was right. Maybe this was a mistake.

She had to get out of here, get some fresh air, figure out what she was doing. She wasn't officially on duty until the morning, but had planned on spending some time with the children before their bedtime. So she'd unpack, shower and change into something Mr

Clothing Police might approve of, see Aimee and Jasper for half an hour, and then she was escaping for the evening.

Matt was sitting at the breakfast counter in tight blue Levi's and a navy t-shirt watching the news when Zoe sloped into the kitchen early the next morning.

She murmured a quick greeting and looked around the room, admiring again the luxurious black and silver flecked marble counter tops, chrome equipment and spotlights set against the white walls and cabinets. Moving behind Matt to fiddle with the coffee machine, she placed a porcelain cup under the spout, frowning at the variety of buttons and levers. It looked more like a dashboard from a spaceship than something for making hot drinks. If she got desperate enough she'd ask him for help, but she'd give it a darned good try on her own first.

She poked at a black button, waiting for the chrome machine to do something. The orange *ON* light was lit up, and there was steam coming from somewhere, but nothing happened. Come on, she needed coffee.

They'd not spoken since Matt's comment about her shorts the previous day. He'd been in his office and she'd been with Aimee and Jasper in their playroom after they'd come back from his mother-in-law's and once they'd gone to bed she'd headed out, mooching around a few still open shops before trekking down towards Sloane Square and along Chelsea Bridge Road to take a walk beside the sluggish River Thames. The evening was balmy and bright, cars rushing past with beeps of horns, stressed commuters and cheerful locals streaming past her on the way to their next destination. She'd always loved London at this time of year. The sounds and smells of summer and the sense of endless possibilities. After her stroll she'd gone to see a late night comedy at the cinema.

She'd felt better and calmer on returning to Matt's. As much as he'd embarrassed her, reflecting on his behaviour she'd realised it was unintentional rather than trying to piss her off. Also, for the plan to work she had to get Matt on side. Which meant not sending waves of palpable dislike his way every time he moved or spoke. So the only sensible thing was to temporarily put aside what he'd done to Melody and concentrate on being nice and becoming part of the household. She also didn't want to live in a house filled with tension. It wouldn't be good for any of them, least of all the kids. They mustn't be hurt by all this. It wouldn't be fair.

Muttering under her breath, she stabbed at a different button on the machine.

'Here, let me.' The deep voice sounded behind her and she jumped, the top of her head thunking his chin. His teeth clicked and a long, muscular arm grabbed the counter beside her waist, clutching it for support.

'Shit!' She span around, dismayed to see Matt's eyes clenched shut, face white, a trickle of blood running down his chin. 'I mean— argh! God, I'm so sorry. You took me completely by surprise.' She took hold of his arm, scared he was about to topple over. Breathing in his aftershave and noticing how hot his body was really shouldn't have been possible at that moment but somehow she managed both. Damn it.

'Uh-huh,' he groaned.

'Here. Sit down,' she ordered, guiding him back to his stool and pushing his head between his knees with a firm hand on the back of his warm neck. 'Stay there a minute.'

He didn't reply, staying put, so she edged away to get him a glass of iced water from the dispenser on the front of the big American style fridge and grab a piece of padded kitchen roll from the side, which she dampened. 'Here you go,' she held them out under his nose and after hesitating, he lifted his head slightly, grabbed the tissue and dabbed his mouth with it, followed by taking a few careful sips of water.

'I'm so sorry,' she repeated again, wincing. 'It was a complete accident.'

Making a deep *hmmming* sound of acknowledgement, he stared

at the floor in silence for a minute, taking slow deep breaths.

As Zoe hovered next to him, she tried to take some satisfaction in his pain—after all, she'd regularly fantasised about punching him since her return to the UK—but totally failed. She hadn't meant to hurt him and the guy was so pale he looked bloodless. It wasn't funny what a sorry sight he was. 'Are you okay?'

Straightening up, he rubbed his jaw, poked a gentle finger in his mouth to check his tongue, and ran assessing fingers under his stubbly chin. 'I think so.'

Zoe sucked in her cheeks, expecting to be bawled out for being clumsy. Greg would have been furious with her for the lack of care. He'd also never been good at dealing with pain. In contrast, Matt had sucked it up and been a man about it.

Shaking his head and dabbing his mouth with the kitchen roll again, he smiled gingerly. 'I think I saw stars. And I definitely bit my tongue.' A pause. 'That is the last time I'm offering to help a woman make coffee.'

She was so surprised she burst out laughing. 'Sorry, again. I was zoned out thinking about something. You made me jump.'

'Clearly. Who would have thought you could jump so high though?'

'I know, like I was on springs.' She chuckled before turning serious. 'But are you sure you're okay? You might bruise under your chin. Your tongue will be sore for a few days too.'

'It's just a little cut. I'm sure I can cope. If there's a visible mark under my chin I'll make something up. I wouldn't want the world thinking my nanny could take me...' he trailed off, an odd look in his green eyes. 'In a fight I mean.'

'No,' she cleared her throat, stepping away as a tingling flush ran up and down her body. 'Obviously.' Spinning around, she went back to the fridge, opening it and sticking her head inside to cool down. 'Maybe I'll just have an orange juice. Safer for both of us that way.'

'No, I'll do you a coffee,' he replied, slowly getting up. 'You just stay over there where you can't injure me, and make toast or cereal or something.'

'Seems fair.' Emerging from the fridge she took two pieces of bread from the bread bin on the counter and put them in the toaster, pushing the button down and watching the elements glow red. The only reason her face was still warm was from the heat of the toaster. It was not about the thought of 'taking' Matt.

'So,' he looked over his coffee cup once she was settled across from him with her breakfast. 'Any injuries at your end?' Nodding at her head.

'A bit of a sore spot, but I think I came off better than you.'

'You might be right.' He grinned, but not too widely, wiggling his jaw. 'Look, I wanted to talk to you before the kids get up.' He slid a quick look at the digital clock on the front of the high-tech oven. 'They usually are now. It's past seven.'

'I'll establish a routine with them, but they both seemed tired and a bit out of sorts last night so I thought I'd let them sleep in this morning.'

'That's fine. It's the start of the summer holidays after all. As long as they're back in their routine for September—'

'They will be, no problem.'

'Good.' He pulled a face. 'Thinking about it, they do come back from my mother-in-law's a bit ratty sometimes.'

'Why do you think that is?'

'I... I've never really thought about it.' He stared into space for a moment. 'I suppose... it might be that she's not the warmest person in the world.'

'Yeah, I know someone like that,' she mused, thinking of Ruth. 'Or maybe their gran reminds them of their mum?' she suggested softly, off the back of a comment Jasper had made the previous evening. He'd said Gran had the same curly hair as Mummy, he knew it from photos at her house. There were no pictures of Mummy at home, Daddy didn't like them.

Watching Matt struggle with her suggestion, she was worried.

A parent who knew their kids would instinctively know what was going on. Why was he so out of touch with them?

'I don't think so,' he said at last.

Feeling he was wrong, she also knew now was not the time to push. It was too soon. She'd barely been here five minutes and he was unlikely to trust her opinion yet about something so sensitive and personal. 'Okay.' Watching the news on the flat screen TV built into one of the walls, she chewed some toast and drank some of the delicious coffee. Gulping, she studied him. 'So, you wanted to talk to me about something?'

'Oh, yes. I wanted to say sorry for the comment about your shorts yesterday.' He looked down into his coffee cup. 'It was clumsy.'

'Thank you. I understand they might have been a bit skimpy, but—'

'But I could have been a bit more diplomatic,' he interrupted, flicking his gaze to her face. 'I sounded like a pompous git.'

Her mouth swung open, and she laughed. He wasn't at all what she'd been expecting. 'Well, I wouldn't have said that.'

'Well I can. I apologise. I just don't know how to talk to women anymore.' It was the last thing she'd have predicted him sharing and he looked embarrassed. 'I didn't mean to say that.'

'Obviously. After all, what about your reputation as a serial dater in the papers? And your last nanny was a woman, you must have talked to her?'

He scowled. 'You shouldn't believe everything you read. Besides, Melody was different. I wasn't—' he clenched his teeth. 'Never mind.'

'What were you going to say?' Was he about to open up, give her an inkling of what the hell had caused him to fire Melody and kick her out?

'Nothing. It doesn't matter. Next subject.' He drained his cup.

'If it's something I need to know, something that could affect the children—'

'It's not,' he said tightly, before making a visible effort to breathe in and out to calm himself. 'There was something else too, Zoe.'

'Oh?' Obviously she needed to let the subject of Melody drop, but it was weird how stressed he looked about the whole thing. 'Go on.'

'I'm um— not sure what time you got in last night but I really need you to be dedicated to the job, not coming in and out at all hours, dragging yourself around exhausted. Especially not smelling of alcohol.' His mouth tightened, the scar cutting into his upper lip turning white. 'Aimee and Jasper need stability and a responsible adult. I'm not unreasonable, you have a right to a life outside of work, it just has to be appropriate and come further down the list of priorities. My kids come first. Do you understand?'

She nodded, feeling a bit like a child who'd been told off for staying out to play too long, but she could see his point; she'd got in pretty late and was here to do a job. Plus how could she argue when he was looking out for his children? All she'd ever want from any parent was that they be child-centred and put their children's best interests first.

'Yes, absolutely,' she nodded, 'I want the best for them too.' Hopping down from her stool she stacked her plate and cup in the dishwasher, before straightening up to look at him. 'Just so you know, I wasn't out drinking. I went for a walk and saw a film. I like going out and having fun occasionally but that's it. I'm not a party girl.' Hangovers and looking after children were not a good combination. She'd learnt that the hard way when she'd worked at the nursery in her late teens. Coming into work hung-over, dealing with the noise and demands of young children had been like slow-roasted torture and she'd ended up in tears before lunchtime. 'Is there anything else?'

His eyes raked over her beige safari shorts, a respectable mid-thigh length today, the floaty white vest top, chunky necklace and lace-up sandals.

'Yes,' he met her gaze. 'I can't let you leave the house like that.'

'Pardon?' Her eyes widened. He couldn't think this outfit was too revealing?

'The other nannies dress a certain way.' He ran a hand around the back of his neck, seeming awkward with the direction of the conversation. 'I'm afraid that's not it.'

'I was planning on taking the kids out somewhere, spending some quality time with them. I'm not going to a fashion show.' No one loved clothes more than her but you had to dress for the activity.

'I appreciate that,' he rose from the stool and strolled over to her, 'but the thing is that I need you to fit in with my lifestyle, not the other way around. That outfit,' he looked down at her shorts, 'is too casual if you're going out. You're bound to bump into some of the kids' friends and their nannies or parents. I wouldn't want either of my children feeling...'

'What?' she questioned lightly, trying not to take it personally. 'Embarrassed to be seen with me?

'Not embarrassed! But you won't fit in. I'm saying this for your benefit as well as theirs. Think of it like wearing a uniform. There's a certain way you're expected to look for this job. You must have come across that before.'

The truth was, she had. Liberty had expected Zoe to be immaculately groomed in well-cut clothes to fit into the society she lived in and she'd done it happily. But she hadn't really thought it through when she'd put her clothes on this morning, because her professional head wasn't on in the way it usually was, given she was here to get even, not make a living. She had to take more care. 'So what kind of thing do I need to wear?' she asked lightly, gazing past him out the window at the bright sunlight filling the manicured garden. 'Given it's not even half seven and already twenty degrees out? It's supposed to be another hot one today.'

'I don't know really. I think Melody wore a lot of dresses, but I never took proper notice. Just something smarter I guess.' To his credit he looked genuinely flummoxed.

She let out an exasperated sigh. 'Right, that's helpful.' Not. 'I'll go and change.' Marching out, she made for the top floor. At least he'd been more tactful than he'd been yesterday. They were making progress.

It was confirmed as she ran up the stairs, when he had the grace to yell, 'Thank you, Zoe!'

It made her smile, despite the fact everything inside her said it was wrong to.

5

She was downstairs again half an hour later, this time accompanied by Jasper and Aimee. After putting up with five minutes of moaning and groaning when she'd tried to get them up—aware of what they were like in the morning from Melody—she'd resorted to motivating them with a little competition. *Zoe's Ten Minute Challenge* had worked like a dream with Ava and Grace and it had worked a treat with Matt's children too. The added opportunity of picking a place of their choice to go had acted as a wonderful incentive for them to get washed and dressed with teeth brushed within the allocated time.

Aimee had narrowly won the contest which had triggered a tantrum from Jasper. Zoe had felt distinctively unimpressed and worried about a child of school age reacting like a toddler, and after telling him she'd be in the other room, had waited him out, pulling his door halfway closed while she helped Aimee pack a rucksack. The girl had looked at her a few times, mouth opening to say something but had shut it again each time.

'I give him two minutes,' Zoe had whispered out the side of her mouth.

Aimee smiled, as if to say, *in your dreams.*

He was done in just under. It wasn't long, yet he hollered pretty loudly and she was half expecting Matt to come thundering up the stairs to demand what was going on, but he didn't appear.

Seeing Jasper's feet approach from the corner of her eye, she'd stood up, passing the rucksack to Aimee. 'Ready to go downstairs?'

The girl nodded, her auburn ponytail bobbing, blue eyes wide and looking impressed, possibly by Zoe's prediction about the length of Jasper's tantrum being right.

Jasper inched forward. 'Can I come too?' he hiccuped, rubbing at his green eyes, so much like Matt's.

Zoe wasn't fooled for a second; if they were real tears she'd put on trousers and call herself Bob.

'I suppose so,' she replied briskly, 'if you're ready?'

He pursed his lips like he was considering his options, then tucked his hands in his pockets, small dark head bobbing. 'Yes.'

'It was sort of silly behaviour, wasn't it?' she remarked conversationally as they wandered down the stairs, Aimee trailing behind them. 'After all, you can't always win. You'll just have to try really hard next time to be even faster. And I heard that you're a big boy. Your dad told me you're starting school soon and your birthday is not long after.'

'Yes!' his eyes brightened. 'In forty sleeps time on the second of September I go to school. It was forty, Melody helped me count before she went,' his little face clouded over, 'and I've been counting by myself but I'm not sure I'm right...and my birthday is on the third day of September. I'll be five,' he finished proudly.

Zoe gulped hard, upset for him and her sister that Mel wasn't going to be here to see him start school, or for his birthday. But she said nothing. It would do no good to upset him further and it wouldn't be fair to quiz a four year-old about adult decisions. 'Well then, you need to have a big think about what you might do at school if you lose a game, because if you get cross like that the teacher will probably make you sit on your own and the other kids might not want to play with you. I bet you want to make friends, don't you?' she affirmed by nodding.

'Yes,' he agreed seriously.

'So you have to find ways to not be cross. It's okay not to win everything, all right? As long as you try your best that's all that matters. If you feel angry about something, tell me and we can work out how to make you feel better. I know some really cool counting games. Can you do that for me? Will you let me know?'

'Uh-huh. That would be super cool. Holly might like to play those games with us.'

'Holly?' Her face froze, and she stopped on the spiral staircase. Who the heck was Holly? Had Matt moved on to someone new already? He'd only supposedly split with the pop star ex-fiancée just over a week ago. No wonder the kids were confused and insecure if he paraded an endless stream of women through their lives. Why wouldn't he have told her about a girlfriend? As their nanny, she needed to know these things. Every person in his life was part of his children's world, a role model or an influence.

'She's 'Ncle Noel's girlfwiend.' Jasper lisped as he stared up at her.

Zoe had noticed that one of his two front teeth was not quite fully grown and occasionally affected his speech, but knew it would improve as the tooth grew. 'I thought the only uncle you have is Stephen?' she said. 'Did your mummy have a brother?'

'No, don't think so,' Jasper looked puzzled, glancing over his shoulder at his sister, who shook her head.

'So who's Noel then?' she asked gently, switching her gaze between both children.

'Daddy's friend,' Jasper replied, 'and my g- g...' He screwed his face up, rounded cheeks puffing out. 'My g- something. Can't remember. But Holly is really, really, really good at ice skating,' he said excitedly, 'just like me, we can both skate backwards but she can do spins but I can't yet and she has long yellow hair and blue eyes and white skin and her teeth sparkle and she makes 'Ncle Noel smile even though he hates Chwistmas and can be really gwumpy,' he finished on a gasp of breath.

'Wow!' Zoe grinned, 'Holly sounds amazing! Noel is a lucky guy.'

As Jasper nodded eagerly at her summation, Aimee leaned into

Zoe's side and whispered softly in her ear. 'Godfather.'

'Ah. Thank you Aimee,' she turned her head and murmured back in a low key tone, trying not to look too triumphant that the girl had actually spoken to her. Neither should she get a big head. Aimee had probably only supplied the information through frustration at her brother's inability to remember Noel's role in their lives.

When she looked at Aimee and saw her downturned face and pink cheeks, she knew it'd been right not to make a fuss. Starting down the stairs again, she watched to make sure Jasper didn't trip over his own feet.

'So, I bet you'll be extra quick tonight when you get ready for bed, Jasper. Do you think you might be able to beat your sister then?'

'I'll try my best!'

'Good boy.' Another victory, he'd taken something on board. 'Same goes for you,' she said casually at Aimee over one shoulder, 'anything you need, just ask.'

Aimee didn't reply, but her expression when Zoe flicked a look at her was quietly grateful.

Zoe felt strangely nervous on reaching the ground floor. Matt had given the impression the other nannies dressed smartly, but she had no idea what they wore in Knightsbridge, so had gone ultra-smart. Was she over-egging it in her grey knee length skirt and matching nipped-in jacket? She probably looked like she was off to the city for an interview. Plus she was going to fry in it. Her body temperature was already climbing.

She gestured the children to go in front of her. 'Come on, time to say good morning to your dad.'

Aimee turned around, pale red brows drawing together.

'But we can't go in and see Daddy in the morning,' Jasper piped up, 'we're not allowed into his office. He finds us to say hello and goodbye when he leaves for work if he can.'

'Sometimes,' Aimee supplied in a barely audible voice, staring

58

at her feet.

What? Melody had said he could be closed off from the children, but she hadn't expected that they weren't allowed to see him in the morning. 'I'm sure he'll want to see you now that you're up,' she said blandly. 'Don't worry, come on.'

Jasper took a step forward then stopped again and Zoe's feet tangled with his. 'Whoa!' She grabbed him and steadied them both.

'Melody never let us into Daddy's office,' he insisted.

Unluckily for your dad, I'm not Melody. She thought inwardly. *I'm far more stubborn for a start.*

'I understand that,' she said, holding his anxious gaze, 'but I do things differently and I think your dad will want to say hello to you.' She squeezed his shoulder. 'Come on.'

Aimee raised an eyebrow and Zoe could read in her clear blue eyes that she thought their new nanny was making a mistake, but given Jasper had changed his mind and was now racing ahead, she shrugged and followed her little brother to the office door.

Zoe reached above their heads and knocked on it twice firmly, feeling sweat forming in the small of her back. It was so darned hot already. This suit was going to kill her. When there was no answer, she knocked again. After a minute, she lost patience and reached around Jasper's head, grabbing the door handle and nudging the kids into the room.

Matt spun around in the ergonomic office chair, a scowl on his incredibly good looking face, the desk behind him a chaos of paper, pens, Post-It notes and gadgets.

'Yep, what is it?' he turned back to the Mac screen.

'Aimee and Jasper wanted to say good morning.'

'Sorry. I'm busy.' He tapped a few buttons and rubbed the back of his neck.

'I'm sure you can spare a minute.' She kept her tone light.

'Not really.' He replied vaguely, moving the wireless mouse around. 'I'm in the middle of something.'

She gritted her teeth. What the heck was the matter with him?

Where was the kind, light-hearted guy from earlier in the kitchen?

'They're not sure you'll find them to say goodbye before you leave,' she explained in a gentle voice for the children's sakes, 'which I understand happens sometimes?'

As she said it, Aimee dropped her gaze to study the floor and Jasper started jiggling up and down on the spot.

'Hmmm?' Matt tapped some keys again.

'Matt? Matt!'

'Yes?' He looked at her over his shoulder, eyes distant.

Maybe he wasn't being rude, he was just caught up in what he was doing. She chose to give him the benefit of the doubt. 'I know you're not saying you don't have time to say good morning to Aimee and Jasper,' she stared at him meaningfully, 'and I'm sure that if you need uninterrupted work time you'll go to the office.' She let that giant hint sit there. 'It's fine if you don't want to speak to me about that other thing now,' she said softly, giving him a way to make this quick, 'so this will only take a moment. Kids, go and say morning to your dad. Give him a big squeezy hug.'

Jasper stared uncertainly from his big sister to his dad and back to Zoe, who immediately saw the tension in both children's shoulders. Looking across the room she saw an equal tension in the set of Matt's arms, and the way his jaw was clenched.

What was going on here? They never hugged? Zoe was utterly shocked, looking at her boss's closed expression. What kind of family was this, so shut off from one another? And why hadn't Melody told her how bad things were? They were young children for God's sakes. They needed warmth, love and affection to build their self-worth, to feel secure and happy. Self-esteem was crucial to their development and the people they would become.

'No. I mean, we don't usually...' Matt started saying, trailing off as Zoe shook her head slightly then nodded at Aimee to show him how his daughter's chin was tucked tight against her chest, fingers twisting nervously in the hem of her top. She gestured with a small wave at Jasper, bopping up and down, green eyes wide.

Don't push your children away, can't you see what you're doing to them? Zoe tried to communicate what she was thinking to Matt, looking at him with begging but determined eyes. Her tone was firm. 'We'll be out of your hair as soon as it's done. Just a minute, I promise.'

Staring from one child to another, he tapped his fingers on his knee, shoulders hunched over. Zoe could see the pained indecision on his face, but after a brief hesitation while he studied Aimee's pose, he conceded with a curt nod, face twisting with something she couldn't peg.

Full of relief, Zoe smiled brightly at Matt and his mouth swung open, looking surprised. Bending over she peered up into Aimee's face. 'Go on,' she encouraged. 'Your dad's ready for his hug now.'

Aimee frowned.

'He is. Come on, look at him. Get to it!'

The girl gave Zoe a look of pure disbelief but cocked her head around her to look at her dad. He crooked his fingers at her, jaw flexing again.

Aimee bit her lip and threw her a look. *If this goes wrong, it's on you.*

Zoe smiled bravely. *Fair enough.*

Shrugging her thin shoulders, Aimee wandered towards her dad, throwing a quick glance at her little brother, who was watching the action with interest, still jiggling away. Matt flushed as his daughter approached him, face still rigid, but moved forward in his chair, normally graceful movements strangely uncoordinated.

They wrapped their arms around each other hesitantly, and it was one of the most awkward hugs Zoe had ever seen, but then something in Matt seemed to unravel and he relaxed, muscular arms tightening around Aimee, eyes closing. He rested his head against her auburn hair, swallowing hard, and then opened his eyes and arms, inviting his son into their little circle.

Jasper sprang across the room like he'd been waiting for years, hurling himself at his dad and sister, his small face full of innocent joy as he snuggled into them. Matt scooped them tighter against his broad chest, closing his eyes again and Zoe melted a little as she saw his love for his kids. Why he wasn't usually affectionate with them she didn't know. He was a natural once he loosened up. And why she found him so extraordinarily sexy holding his children, her knickers melting along with her heart, she couldn't work out. She fanned herself. It was getting hotter inside and outside.

Maybe it was a biological thing programmed in by evolution, the sight of a big, capable tough man protecting his children triggering a need to make more. It might explain why the famous Athena poster of a bare-chested man holding a tiny baby had sold so many millions of copies. God only knew, but whatever it was, she didn't like the tender feelings racing through her. It was totally and utterly wrong. She started backing toward the door, intent on escape and happy to leave them to their private family moment. Maybe she'd splash her face with cold water to cool down.

'Kids,' Matt said huskily as he opened his eyes and saw her exit attempt, 'can you go into the kitchen and sit at the table? Zoe will be there in a minute.' He released them, standing up. 'Close the door on your way out please.'

Oh, crap.

Both children smiled widely at her as they left the room, and Zoe smiled back with pleasure for them but a sinking feeling in her stomach. As soon as the door shut she stepped forward, needing to take control of the situation. Waiting to be bawled out was awful. 'I'm sorry if I ambushed you, but I had no idea that's the way things were,' she was aware her voice was both apologetic and defiant, 'and really you can't expect me to let you reject your children by not hugging them and they're bound to want to see you in the mornings, they're kids, they need to know you love them. Also how would you feel if you didn't see them and then something happened to one of them, you'd regret it and—'

'Whoa! Slow down, Zoe! Wait a minute.' Matt held up his

hands, walking toward her, forest green eyes searching her face. He shook his head and blew out a long, slow breath, gathering his thoughts. 'Look, I wasn't pleased at the interruption when you first came in, I'll admit. When I'm disturbed I find it really hard to get back into whatever I'm working on and sometimes I have to start again, which seems to take twice as long. I guess it comes with being creative. I get so immersed I lose track of myself and what's going on around me, and then when I'm yanked out of that place I find it jarring. I know that can be difficult for other people to understand,' he stated. 'I'll also admit that I don't like feeling slightly bullied by you and your steely, *don't mess with me* eyes... I mean, at one point I was scared you were going to kill me if I didn't hug the kids,' he chuckled, 'but I can see that you were in a tough position. You weren't to know that we're not really the hugging types,' he trailed off, looking uncertain. 'When you forced me to look at Aimee and I saw... what I saw, well, you were right to insist. But you don't get to tell me how to raise my children, and there will be some things I won't give in to,' he emphasised.

'It was the right thing to do, and I don't regret it,' she defended, 'but if you feel bullied, I'm sorry. I also accept that you're their dad and should know what's best for them.' Except that for years he'd given them little physical affection and appeared to have kept them at the periphery of his attention. She also knew from Jasper's chatter at bedtime the night before, that Matt had signed them up for hobbies they detested, like horse-riding, draughts and fencing. So at the moment, she needed convincing that he had their best interests at heart.

'Why do I feel like there's an unspoken criticism in there some-where?' he asked dryly, rubbing a hand through his messy dark hair.

She shrugged, letting him fill the silence. Sometimes you had to let other people do the talking, to realise things for themselves.

'Look. I love my kids, and I spend a lot of time protecting them,' he stated. 'Not everyone shows their love in the same overt way. Everyone's different. But believe me, I work hard to provide for them and be a positive role model,' he sucked in his cheeks, 'I just hadn't realised how much the lack of affection has affected them. Melody, my last nanny, never said anything about it and she was with us for three years,' he frowned.

No way was she going to criticise her sister, even if she was wondering the same as Matt. 'Perhaps she shouldn't have had to. In any case, as you said, everyone's different. Maybe she didn't feel able to bring it up with you. You can be a bit… erm, never mind,' she raced on when he raised both eyebrows, 'I'm just more confident than some people. So, when and why did you stop hugging them?' She gazed at him, wanting to know the story despite the fact that she shouldn't care.

'I'm really intrigued as to what I'm a bit of, but won't hold you to it,' Matt's stern mouth quirked up on one side, before his face turned grim. 'I don't want to talk about it though Zoe, if you don't mind. However, I'll make more of an effort going forward.' His expression was written with guilt. 'They both looked so happy.'

'Well, that's good, and as long as I'm not in trouble—'

'Don't speak too soon,' he replied. 'What exactly are you trying to prove with that?' Pointing at her jacket.

'Nothing,' she hitched her chin up, doing her best to pretend she wasn't incredibly hot and wanted nothing more than to rip the stupid suit off. 'You said I wouldn't fit in, that I needed to dress the part so as not to embarrass the children. So I got changed into something smarter, like you said.'

He shook his head, looking impatient. 'Not a suit! And I told you it wasn't about embarrassing us. Now go and change.'

She shook her head, even as sweat broke out on her face. He hadn't even said please.

His mobile started ringing on the desk. Stalking across the office he grabbed it and pressed the end-call button. 'Shit! I've got that meeting soon. Sadie, please come back, all is forgiven.' He cast both eyes up at the ceiling and joined his hands together in mock prayer. 'I'm not sure how much more of this I can cope with,' he said to Zoe. 'I'm so used to Sadie organising me. I don't know whether I'm coming and going, and all I want to do is get back into the studio. I just hope she recovers soon and that the hamper I sent helps... But anyway,' walking back over to Zoe, he threw her a hard look, 'I'm sorry, but I haven't got time for this. We both know you're being a little ridiculous. Please go and change.'

'I'm fine.' He was right, but she'd look silly backing down just like that and she didn't like being bossed around. It made her wonder if this is what he'd been like with Melody the day he threw her out. Her fingers curled into her palms. She couldn't forget what a bastard he'd been to her sister, even if he did seem to have some redeeming qualities, like wanting to be a good person for his children, and being nice to sick staff and having a sense of humour. *Stop it.* 'Really,' she insisted, 'I'm fine.'

'But you won't be, with the predicted temperature today. I can't believe you're serious. You'll bake if you leave the house.' He glanced down at his watch, swore and moved away from her to start grabbing things off his desk, throwing his iPad, notepad and a sheaf of paperwork into a messenger bag before looping it across his chest.

'It's not that hot,' she answered.

'It will be,' he shot back, stalking back over to her. 'Come on,' he stepped closer, eyes narrowing. 'Look how overheated you got at our interview; ready to fall over from standing on the doorstep too long. You'll make yourself ill, and then where will my kids be? Take it off.' Reaching out, he curled a big hand around the jacket collar and tugged her closer.

She froze, smelling his aftershave, far too close to his broad, muscular chest, her body flashing with heat, but not because of the weather this time. She mustn't sway towards him. Couldn't ask him to put his fingers down inside her collar, to run them over the tops of her boobs, to—

'Is this wool?' he asked in disbelief, testing the material between two fingers.

'Er—' she pulled a face. 'It might be.'

'It's the middle of summer. You're completely insane,' he joked. 'Right, that's it. Take it off. I don't want to get done at tribunal for not ensuring the health and well-being of my employees.'

'No!' She might have given in at that point but quite apart from sticking to her guns, there was a really good reason she didn't want to remove the jacket in front of him.

'Yes!' he insisted. To her shock, he started unbuttoning it, and she wrestled with him, trying to bat him away.

'Matt, don't!' *Oh shit,* she thought fleetingly. 'I said don—'

Unfortunately the jacket only had four buttons, his fingers made mega-quick work of them and she stepped back at the same time as he undid the last one.

The jacket flew open, revealing her pale, round breasts encased in a red lacy bra.

'Bloody hell!' His breath whooshed out, eyes all but popping out of his head as he took in her cleavage. 'You're not wearing a top!'

'Thank you Captain Obvious, I didn't know that,' she muttered, yanking the jacket back together, doing it up with fumbling fingers, face burning as he spun around to give her some privacy. This was so embarrassing, and would probably forever be known as either jacket-gate or bra-gate. Why it had to happen in front of Matt of all people, she didn't know. It was just her luck. 'Sorry,' she thought of how her sarcastic Captain Obvious comment must have sounded, 'I didn't mean to be rude.'

'That's fine. I'm sorry too. I-I just meant... Bloody hell,' he repeated. 'Why?'

'It is too hot,' she grimaced. Now the outfit choice looked really stupid. 'And I didn't think it would matter that I had nothing on underneath. You can turn around now,' she said. When he obeyed, it was like he couldn't quite bring himself to look at her, fixing his eyes on a spot on the wall over her left shoulder. She gazed up at him, seeing the nonplussed expression on his face. For some reason her mouth quirked up on one side. They must have looked like complete idiots during their little struggle, her trying to keep the jacket on, him trying to get her out of it. 'I wasn't planning on taking the jacket off,' she explained, 'and I didn't foresee a madman coming along and trying to wrestle me out of it,' she finished drily.

'No,' he conceded, dropping his eyes to her face, 'I don't suppose you did.' For a moment he looked solemn, but then his mouth curved, a spark of warmth in his eyes.

Their gazes connected. There was a silence.

'It was like a comedy sketch or something,' he choked out. 'Your face! I've never seen anyone look so panicked!'

She couldn't help it, grinning back. 'Well, you can understand why now.' She gave into laughter, holding her side. 'We must have looked pretty ridiculous. I mean, imagine if the kids had seen us,' she snorted.

'They'd think that we've lost it,' he agreed, laughing. 'Not a great example to set for them.'

Oh, bugger. The kids. She'd forgotten all about them. It'd never happened to her before. In her other jobs she hadn't ever neglected her professional responsibilities. 'Oh, God, they're alone in the kitchen. I should go.'

'Yes,' Matt crossed back to his desk, looking puzzled, 'me too. That's right, I have work to do, a meeting to go to.' He rammed his phone into his jeans pocket, hunting around in the mess of music sheets and other random items. 'Keys… keys. Argh… bloody things.'

Zoe stood by the door, watching as he cast various papers and a spare tablet around. 'Um, Matt.'

'Hmmm?' He picked up an expandable file, shook it, put it back down. Picked up a mug of all things, as if the keys would be hiding in it or under it somehow.

'Don't you put your car keys in the bowl by the door?' she asked, raising an eyebrow.

'The bowl,' his head came up and he glanced over at her, face clearing. 'Yeah, you're right, I always do. I can't think why I forgot—' his green eyes flickered over her chest. 'I've got to go,' he blurted, racing past her out of the office. 'See you this evening. Bye kids.' She heard him yell, followed by the slam of the door and the quiet purr of the Prius rapidly fading into the distance.

Shaking her head at his odd departure, Zoe walked into the kitchen to find Jasper standing by the fridge, face covered in strawberry jam, slices of bread, utensils and bowls littering the floor and work surfaces.

'I got hungry,' Jasper explained woefully, staring up at her with an expression on his face that said *please don't tell me off*.

Aimee was completely oblivious, head stuck in a thick book of fairytales with line drawings on the cover.

'That's okay,' ruffling Jasper's hair, Zoe lead him over to the sink and started wiping his hands and face with a damp cloth, 'it was my fault. I took too long with your dad.' She blushed as she thought of all the things they could have done if they'd had more time. If when he'd opened her jacket he'd sunk to his knees and buried his face in her cleavage and—

No. Remember why you're here.

There was no doubt about it, Matt was hot, but her sister came first, she wasn't letting her down again. Plus, no good came of getting involved on the rebound. 'Next time come and get me, okay?' she asked the little boy, shaking her head as she found a clump of red jam in the hair behind his ear. 'When you want jam, remember it's supposed to go on something, Jasper. Like toast. Not the floor, or yourself,' she smiled.

'Yes, Zoe,' he nodded.

'Great. Now how about giving me a hand clearing up this mess?' Stooping over, she picked up a bowl and two spoons.

'Do I have to?' he whined. 'Melody wouldn't have made me.'

She loved her sister, but had she been half asleep on the job or something? At seven and nearly five, these children were old enough to know the difference between right and wrong, and to be clearing up after themselves. Just because their dad was super-rich and super-successful, it didn't mean they couldn't learn some traditional values and personal responsibility. She must ask Matt about it, and talk to Mel too.

'It would be great if you could,' she said to Jasper casually. 'But if you're worried I can pick up more things faster than you...'

'No, you can't!'

'Can!' Wiggling her eyebrows.

'Can't.' He giggled, racing over to grab a couple of forks off the side and bring them to her.

'Good boy,' she nodded approvingly scooping up slices of bread, and randomly, a bottle opener. They were definitely not being left alone in the kitchen again, until they were better trained. 'Everything that's been on the floor will need to go in a pile in the sink so I can wash them up.'

'Ok-ay,' Jasper sang cheerfully, clattering a mixing bowl and wooden spoon into the sink, along with a broken egg.

God only knew what he'd been trying to make.

'So, what would you like for breakfast kids? And where do you want to go today? Aimee's choice remember, because she got ready the quickest. Aimee?'

At the sound of her name, the girl's head jerked up, wearing the same look of fierce concentration as her dad when he was immersed in something. It was sweet.

'What do you want for breakfast? And where would you like me to take the two of you?'

Aimee bit her lip, squinting. 'Pancakes please. And...' she paused, started to say something then seemed to change her mind, 'um, the library?' she finished instead.

Jasper let out a little groan behind her. 'The library? Bo-ring.'

'It's Aimee's decision, Jasper,' she said firmly, while wondering how the heck she was going to keep him occupied in such a quiet, contained environment. 'Come on, books are fun. We'll find some good ones for you too, okay? I'm sure there's a nice children's corner,' praying wholeheartedly it was true. 'Aimee,' she asked hesitantly, 'how would you feel about going to the park on the way home? Just for ten minutes or so? The nearest one is Hyde Park, right?'

Aimee nodded, then shook her head. 'I don't want to. Maybe another day.'

'Are you sure? I thought it was a nice one, though I've never been. It's not far at all, and it's lovely and sunny today.'

But the girl shook her head resolutely with her lower lip sticking out and returned her attention to her book.

Ordinarily Zoe would go over to her, ask what was going on, but Jasper was tugging at her jacket insistently and it was obvious Aimee wasn't ready to open up. There was no point in pressing too hard; it had taken two visits and as many days to get Aimee to even speak to her in half sentences.

'No problem,' she said matter-of-factly, 'we can always find some games to play in the back garden.' She turned to Jasper, seeing Aimee pull a relieved face from the corner of her eye. 'So Mister, pancakes?'

'Yay! Pancakes! Pancakes!' Jasper started jumping up and down.

'Okay. If you calm down you can help me make them.' He really was a bundle of energy.

'Yay!' He bounded over to her, grabbing hold of her hand. 'Super cool! I want you to stay, Zoe.'

Aww, bless. 'That's lovely Jasper. Because I'm letting you help me make pancakes?'

'Because you're nice,' he decided solemnly.

'Oh. Thank you.' She gulped, his remark both warming and worrying her. They were good kids at heart, they just needed boundaries and the right kind of attention-slash-authority. But what she hadn't thought through properly when embarking on *Plan Nannygate* was that the kids might get attached to her.

'What about you, Aimee?' she asked gently. 'Are you happy with me being here?'

The girl looked up with a distracted air, and nodded once.

'Do you think I'm nice too?'

'Uh-huh.' She focused back on her book, turning the page. Zoe thought she was done, but just as she went to turn away Aimee spoke again. 'You got Daddy to hug us. It's been forever.'

Zoe bit the inside of her cheek, insanely sad for the kids. The plan was for revenge, but while she was here, there was no harm in trying to make things better for them as a family, for the good of the children. Was there?

6

It was a harried trip to graceful Mayfair library, during which Jasper caused near mayhem. Running around the ends of stacks, he pulled books off shelves and talked in the loudest voice possible despite stern glances from a staff member. Zoe used every behaviour management tool she could think of, along with repeated shushing, but eventually had to take him for a time-out, letting Aimee know she'd be out front for a few minutes.

They sat on the stone steps of the entrance while Jasper calmed down, his Ben 10 baseball cap pulled down low over his eyes, feet tapping on the pavement. She relaxed in the balmy sunlight, reading a leaflet picked up from the foyer about the weddings they performed in one of the two ceremony rooms. From the pictures, the venue looked romantic and intimate. Zoe could think of few nicer places to get married; surrounded by books in a nineteenth century building with the beautiful Mount Street Gardens next door, perfect for taking photos.

It was a far cry from the wedding she and Greg had planned at the *St. Regis* on Manhattan Island, which was as glamorously luxurious as it was hideously expensive. Greg had made his money on the stock markets and was more than happy showing his wealth off. She had insisted on contributing to the cost of the wedding but wondered now how comfortable she would have been on her own wedding day in such rich surroundings, when at heart she was an orphan from the British seaside. She also wondered how comfortable she would have been moving in with him permanently, subject to his world twenty-four-seven. Still, if they'd loved each other enough then it wouldn't have mattered. They'd have made it work.

Shrugging the thought off, she reminded Jasper of the need to behave and lead him inside by the hand with a firm grip. In sharp contrast to her brother, Aimee was in heaven in the library. Walking purposefully between shelves, she ran her fingers along scripted spines and stroked glossy covers. When she stuffed her rucksack full with the maximum amount of books she could borrow, checked in by a librarian who knew her by name, Zoe was surprised to see a copy of *To Kill a Mockingbird* go in. It was advanced reading for a girl her age.

As they walked home along wide Park Lane which guarded the eastern boundary of lovely Hyde Park—Zoe looking longingly at the green spaces and trees she could see across the road—down to Hyde Park Corner and along Knightsbridge, Aimee walked with her nose stuck in the Harper Lee classic. Zoe was tempted to tell her not to, especially with how busy the streets were with teeming crowds of tourists snapping away with cameras, shoppers swinging branded bags filled with new summer wardrobes and countless black cabs zipping past. It would be hypocritical though. She'd read books in the street right into her teens, skilfully learning to step around lamp posts and avoid people, and still recalled the guilty pleasure of every possible stolen reading moment. Heck, if she could get away with it now, she would. So she held Jasper's hand and settled for placing a guiding hand on Aimee's shoulder as the girl traipsed along.

When they got home, Aimee shut herself away in her room without a word and Zoe decided to leave her to it. She could hardly complain that one of her two new charges loved reading and was happiest when expanding her mind and vocabulary. In that way, she was a dream. On the other hand, she could do with learning a few more social skills. It wouldn't do her good being too insular.

For a few hours Zoe and Jasper painted and coloured-in while sitting up on stools at the kitchen units, newspapers spread out to protect the expensive marble, aprons on to protect their clothes. Zoe opened the window to let in some fresh air, and turned the radio on so that pop music created a white noise in the background. Occasionally the buzz of a lawn mower drifted in, punctuated by a child's laugh or call. There must be other kids in the neighbourhood, and Zoe wondered if Jasper or Aimee were friends with any of them.

Just before noon the beeping of horns and high-pitched two-note tone of a siren sounded, getting ever closer. Jasper jumped at the noise, arm freezing in place, paintbrush clutched in his sturdy fingers. Somewhere above their heads, a thud sounded.

'Everything all right?' Zoe frowned at the ceiling, and put a hand on Jasper's back.

Turning his head, he stared at her with solemn green eyes. 'Don't like sirens,' he answered in a tight voice, trembles rippling through him. 'Mummy went when sirens came.'

'Oh.' There were some residual memories of the accident then, even though he'd been so young. 'Well, there's nothing to be worried about now, okay? We're here, your sister is upstairs with her book, and your dad is safely at work. Besides, ambulances go to help people, right? They nee-naw like that to move cars out the way so they can get to people in trouble as quickly as possible. Everything is okay,' she soothed, stroking his back until the sirens faded away. 'See? They've gone.'

With a nod, he dipped his brush in the blue paint and started outlining swirling clouds. Zoe gazed down at his ruffled hair, marvelling at how freely he'd shared his fears with her, so soon after she'd arrived in his life. Still, that was kids for you, especially younger ones. They were open books. They barely had filters at this age and blurted out pretty much everything they thought.

'Stay there for a minute, all right? Just keep painting. I need to check on your sister.' Thinking of the thudding noise. Racing upstairs, she knocked on Aimee's door, pushing it open gently when there was no reply. 'Everything good up here?' she asked, hoping Jasper didn't get into too much mischief while she was gone. She stared at Aimee's downturned head, nose only a few inches from the page. 'I thought I heard something hit the deck,' Zoe said, 'was it in here?' There was no answer, just a slight tightening of the little girl's pink lips. 'Oh well, I must have imagined it then,' she added lightly, 'never mind. I'll leave you to it. Lunch is in a bit, by the way.' Aimee's gaze flickered upwards and she nodded once, but Zoe could see that her eyes were suspiciously bright. Maybe Jasper wasn't the only one affected by sirens. 'If you need anything, we're in the kitchen.' She backed out of the room, leaving the girl alone with her thoughts. When she was ready to talk about it, she would.

Zoe wandered down the spiral stairs, hand clutching the curved white rail. She could still remember the horror she'd felt when Mel had told her over Skype, brown eyes tear-filled, that both children had been in the car crash that killed their mum. Mel had only arrived with the family a few days before, and Matt had been battling along without help for three months before hiring a nanny. It had been a difficult time for all of them and Zoe knew that her sister, who could be emotionally fragile at times, had found it hard to deal with their grief. Slowly however, she knew things had gotten better. Or thought they had.

When she sloped back into the kitchen, heart weighed down with the sad thoughts, Zoe halted, mouth opening. 'Jasper,' she breathed, fighting not to laugh, 'what did you do?'

Grinning proudly, he pointed to his face, which was painted a bright shade of blue, save for a crooked, naked stripe down the middle over his nose. 'I'm Braveheart. It's one of daddy's favourite films. He won't let me watch it but 'Ncle Stephen lets me sneak peeks sometimes. This is what they do when they fight.'

'It is.' Shaking her head, she tried to be serious but sniggered instead. He looked so earnest, and more like a haphazard smurf than a warrior. The fact he'd managed to miss his hair was a minor miracle. 'But that kind of paint is for paper, not for faces,' she pointed out. 'If you want to do this again, please let me know and we'll buy some proper face paints.' Reaching for her phone from one of the shelves, she held it out in front of her. 'Can I take a picture?'

'Yep! To show Daddy!'

'That's a great idea,' she said, deftly pressing two buttons and taking a selection of photos. 'We won't tell him you didn't ask permission, but I'll send him a picture if you promise that next time you will.'

He nodded decisively, blue dripping off his chin and plunking onto his plastic red apron. 'Deal.'

Grinning, she sent Matt a picture via WhatsApp, with the caption *Your son has the same movie tastes as you.* 'Right, done.' A reply wasn't necessarily something she expected, but a minute later a smiley face icon and *Lol, that's my boy* comment pinged her mobile. Smiling, she tucked her phone away and dampened some kitchen roll, standing Jasper at the sink to wash his face off.

After cleaning him up, they made fresh bread for lunch. At the end of the bread-making session, Jasper had managed to get little white-flour finger marks over himself, Zoe and most surfaces in the kitchen. With a chuckle Zoe wiped the sides down and they got the kitchen roll back out, turning the radio up and bopping around while they got clean again, before setting up a picnic in the garden. This time Jasper helped her without complaint.

When Zoe called Aimee for lunch, it took a full ten minutes to coax her from her bedroom at the same time as trying to keep an eye on Jasper, who was banging something about in his jam-packed room across the hall.

'Aimee,' she resorted to quiet authority after nice requests and cajoling had failed, 'you can't starve, and I'll be more than happy to discuss your favourite books with you or let you carry on reading after lunch, but if you don't come downstairs and eat with us before all the food gets swarmed by ants, I'm going to have to withdraw a privilege.' The girl looked at her with wide eyes, waiting to see what she'd do. Zoe knew it was a test. So she let out a big sigh, shaking her head sorrowfully. 'I would really, really hate to have to take one of your books away, because I understand how much you love them. I'm a big reader too,' she confessed. 'There's nothing better than getting lost in another world and making new friends. But you have to live in the real world sometimes, okay?' Throwing the door open wider, gesturing to the staircase. 'Come on. You can have a quick bite then sit in the shade and read some more, or you can have a longer lunch and we can talk books while your brother plays on his swing set. The choice is yours.'

Giving kids options seemed to help. It worked with adults too. But sometimes when you gave someone enough room to make a choice, they ran away from you instead of staying close, as you'd hoped. If you love someone set them free. That was the saying, wasn't it? If they loved you, they'd fly back of their own accord. But what happened when they didn't? In her experience it was heartbreak that could send you hurtling into the wrong man's arms. Heartbreak that could divide a family already poles apart. Because would she have fallen for Greg and moved to the States if she hadn't been so heavily on the rebound from her first love, Henry? And surely Greg was the wrong man for her after what he'd done? She gulped down the lump in her throat and breathed through the ache in her chest. It didn't matter. The break up with Henry was distant, hellish history. The only reason she was thinking of it now was because she was in that precarious state again, everything she'd known and planned wrenched away from her without warning. But she would get over that, and Greg too, in time. As soon as the anger was no longer a living, breathing thing inside her.

Smiling approvingly as Aimee trudged past into the hallway clutching her book, Zoe called for Jasper and they made their way down to the tartan blanket in the garden, her heartache fading away. After a lunch of bread, ham, cheese and fruit that dried out and quickly turned brown in the baking sun, and a few minutes to loll around and digest their food, she and Jasper set about playing a game of *tag*. It was almost unbearably hot. Running around the garden and dodging each other's footsteps, Zoe was glad she'd changed out of her suit after breakfast, exchanging it for a lemon sorbet coloured sundress with a cut-out hole at the back.

Aimee refused to join in with their game, resting against the bottom of the apple tree with her book instead. Every so often though, Zoe caught her watching them play, flicking her eyes back to the page whenever Zoe lifted her head. She wasn't sure why the girl was so reluctant to take part. Was it that she didn't like playing or that she didn't know how to? Melody must have played with the kids. She would have to call her sister on the quiet in the next few days and have a chat. She was starting to wonder if Melody leaving was having more of an impact on the kids than she'd first thought. Maybe Aimee was hanging back because she didn't trust that Zoe would be around for long? She wasn't wrong, Zoe thought, flushing with a pang of guilt. She didn't want to hurt anyone. It was only Matt's pride and self-important ego that she wanted to damage. He had to learn that actions had consequences.

She gradually slowed to let Jasper catch her, 'Okay, okay.' She held her hands up in mock surrender. 'You win!'

Jasper laughed delightedly. 'Got you!' he yelled, ploughing into her.

'Well done, you're very fast… for someone with such short legs,' she quipped, laughing as he stuck his tongue out at her.

He went quiet and looked up into her face, green eyes wide. 'Thank you for playing with me, Zoe,' he said, and then his mood flipped. 'Daddy doesn't weally play with us anymore,' he lisped, bottom lip trembling, a quaver in his little voice. He wrapped his arms around her waist and buried his head against her stomach.

As she looked down and stroked his dark head, glad not to

have to abide by the more rigid child protection rules of a nursery that restricted physical contact, she felt an unexpected and overwhelming pang of emotion. Jasper was hard work, but adorable too. The realisation wasn't good for her peace of mind, given she'd only just arrived here and it might take weeks to set her plan in motion.

Surely she was just feeling vulnerable after her break up with Greg? He'd hurt her, badly. She was bound to be a soppy mess.

'It's okay,' she said, hugging him briefly before easing away. 'You can always talk to me about things like this. Thank you for telling me. Your daddy is really busy but he loves you, always remember that.'

She crouched down in front of him so that she could look him in the eye. Casting a quick glance at Aimee, she saw the girl had finally put her book down but was peeling bark intently from the apple tree whilst pretending not to listen.

Zoe brought her gaze back to Jasper's and straightened his black and green Ben 10 t-shirt. She knew that Matt probably preferred them in designer stuff but it was what Jasper had chosen that morning so she would side with him if it came to it.

'I'll see if I can get your daddy to start playing with you a bit more. How about I ask him to slot some Jasper time into his diary?' A reassuring smile at Aimee. 'I'll also do the same for your big sister. Perhaps the three of you can get some time together every week, maybe have dinner out somewhere too. Would you like that?'

'Yes!' Jasper punched the air in reply to her proposal.

She didn't normally like setting expectations without first having discussed these things with parents, but she would find some way to convince Matt that his children needed some quality time with him. After all, he wasn't unreasonable; when he'd understood what was going on this morning, he'd done the right thing. She only hoped he would this time too.

Realising that Aimee had left the tree and was edging closer, casually picking flowers to disguise her interest in their conversation,

Zoe suppressed a grin.

'Zoe?' Jasper said brightly.

'Yes?'

He looked up at her thoughtfully, sucking his lower lip into his mouth, which she knew all too well was a habit he was already learning from her. Kids were like sponges at this age. They picked things up so easily. 'Can you come out with us to dinner too, Zoe? Please? Please, please, please?'

Her eyebrows pleated as she contemplated how to answer. It was important the three of them have time together as the family unit they should be. She wasn't a part of that, she was just doing a job and not even properly. They needed to learn to function as a family without her so that if, she mentally adjusted that to *when,* she left it wouldn't all fall apart. Added to which, it would be mortifying if Matt thought she was trying to wangle some kind of date-night via the kids. Plus, for her plan to work and be convincing, it all had to come from him.

'I don't think so, Jasper,' she answered in a soft voice, careful not to reject him, 'but thank you for the thought, it's very sweet. You'll spend lots of time with me without your dad around, so your time with him should be your special time, just the three of you. Anyway,' time for a change of mood she decided, 'you've got me now, and I think I know two children who might need to run round the garden some more, or be tickled!'

Swinging round, she lunged at Jasper with a pretend growl and on the rest of the spin lurched toward Aimee, who skipped out of arms' reach with a squeak.

Within minutes they had her pinned down on the perfectly manicured but somewhat prickly lawn, the smell of flowers and freshly cut grass filling her nose. She sneezed, the bright sun beating down on her head and shoulders. A bee buzzed somewhere and a breeze blew the leaves of the tree above their heads, pretty shadows dappling the lawn around them. Jasper laughingly pulled up short bunches of grass and threw them on her as she sat up, the blades tangling in her hair and going down the top of her dress. Aimee let out a series of uncharacteristic giggles as she saw what a mess her nanny was in. Somewhere in the distance a car beeped.

Throwing her head back and laughing like one of the evil geniuses in the programmes that according to Mel, Jasper was occasionally allowed to watch—*mwah-ha-ha*—Zoe jumped up to go after him, and was rewarded with a cackle of glee from Aimee, who stuck more grass down the back of Zoe's dress through the cut-out hole. 'You little troublemakers!' She ran after Jasper, grabbing him and lobster-pinching his waist to tickle him.

'Stop! Stop,' Jasper howled, giggling as he squirmed away, 'I'm going to wee myself!'

Aimee and Zoe shared a look and burst into fresh laughter. Zoe released Jasper and sank down onto the grass and Aimee copied, clutching her stomach. When Zoe rolled over onto her back, Jasper bundled on top of her, his sweaty, compact little weight half-crushing her. A wave of nausea hit her square in the tummy. Ignoring the sick feeling because they were all having such good fun and it was the most that Aimee had come out of her shell so far, Zoe wrestled the little boy onto the lawn, tickling him this time by squeezing his chubby knees.

Another wave of nausea swept over her as she sat up, touching a quick hand to her hot cheeks and moist upper lip. She didn't feel so good. She'd done a thorough job of protecting the kids from the sun, slapping sun cream on them, keeping them well watered and in the shade, but had obviously not done such a great job on herself. The kids giggled as she sat on the ground recovering, the sound making her smile despite the way her stomach rolled over in a sick flip. Yuck.

A shadow appeared over her and she arched her back to peer upwards, hand shielding her eyes from the sun. 'Matt.'

'What's going on out here?' he asked, hands on hips. 'I could hear the noise from out on the driveway!'

He'd returned early to work from home and catch up on some emails in Sadie's absence, but had been drawn outside by the sound of the kids' screeches of hilarity. They both quietened as he looked from them to his new nanny. She was certainly making herself at home, he thought. Walking through the house he'd noticed the paintings hung up to dry with pegs and string, paint pots and brushes drying on the draining board, the fragrant loaf of fresh bread resting on the kitchen unit and the sweet smell of pancakes, presumably from breakfast.

He couldn't remember the last time he'd heard his children being so noisy. Melody had spent most of her time trying to tame them into nice, quiet, obedient kids. Not that it had always been successful with Jasper, he mused. But he'd appreciated her efforts. He couldn't think properly when there was clamour going on around him, it made it almost impossible to work. Yet Zoe seemed almost determined to undo whatever Mel had done and make his kids as loud and distracting as possible.

Still, as he gazed down into their beaming little faces, he noticed that they also appeared happier than they had in a long time. The photo that Zoe had sent him of Jasper covered in blue paint had been hilarious. His mouth quirked, shoulders relaxing. As much as what had happened with Melody pained him, perhaps the change would be good for all of them. Even him, set in his ways. Zoe didn't seem afraid to challenge him, and although it was a bit irritating to have to explain himself, she also appeared to know what she was talking about, her bold confidence about children that she hardly knew somehow comforting. Hopefully she would stick around for a while. He'd just have to make sure he didn't let Stephen anywhere near her. It was probably just as well his younger brother was yachting on the Med to get over what Melody had done. Stephen had his own brand of arrogant charm (he'd once referred to himself as similar to Spencer out of *Made in Chelsea*) and it drove a lot of women crazy. Matt didn't want to lose another nanny because of his brother's love life. He grimaced at the thought of Stephen with Zoe, a pang of annoyance shooting through him. She'd said she was single, and bagging a young, rich playboy might appeal. That had certainly been the case with his last nanny.

His gaze dropped to his new one, where she still sat at his feet. 'Are you all right?' he asked abruptly, taking in her pale yellow sun dress, the top half filled with mouth wateringly generous curves that made his palms itch to touch them. Even in the studio, a place that was sacrosanct, he hadn't been able to get the sight of her stood in her red, lacy bra out of his head. He jerked his eyes upwards, away from her creamy cleavage. Her tangled blue-black hair was peppered with bits of grass and her cheeks were flushed with heat. She looked like she'd been for a tumble in a country field. His groin immediately tightened at the image that filled his mind. Her beneath him naked on a bed of grass, her breasts rosy and round in the sunlight—

'Y-yes,' she said, dazedly pushing her hair back from her face, cutting across his frustratingly inappropriate thoughts.

He frowned, taking in the slightly unfocused look in her eyes and the dewy hint of sweat on her face.

'You don't look it. You look as if you're suffering from the heat. If you're in this state, what on earth have you done to the kids?'

She pushed herself up hastily. 'Now wait just a minute! I—' too hastily as it turned out, because she swayed and stumbled forward into his unprepared arms.

He caught her against him with a surprised grunt, his muscular arms tightening around her as he looked down into her flustered face and then lower to her rounded cleavage, spying blades of grass tucked down there that he suddenly, desperately wanted to get rid of with his teeth, with his tongue—

He cursed as his body hardened even more and she must have noticed because she thrust herself away from him.

'Can you watch the kids please?' she said huskily as she turned to jog toward the house, 'I'm sorry, I—' she planted a hand across her mouth, 'I think I'm going to be sick!'

She ran off and left him, looking from her departing back to Aimee and Jasper in astonishment. He wasn't every woman's cup of tea—he could be distracted, tetchy and knew he kept people out of reach, plus he was her boss—but it wasn't often that he made grown women throw up.

Almost two hours later, after a long cooling bath and a power nap to ease away the worst of her mild heatstroke, Zoe came downstairs to tidy the kitchen and start prepping dinner. She met Matt coming out of his office.

'Hi.' He gestured at her loose pastel pink t-shirt and baggy white shorts. 'Feeling better?'

'Yes, thanks.' She peered around him, concerned. 'Where are the kids?'

'They're fine,' he replied. 'Sadie popped round to see me as she's feeling a little more human, so they're in there with her,' he hitched his thumb over his shoulder, 'playing hangman and chase the monkey.' He raised an eyebrow as she opened her mouth. 'It's okay, they've known her for years, and she was happy to help. Besides, what she's got isn't catching. It's a gynaecological... thing.'

'Oh, right,' she murmured, moving on quickly. 'Well, I'm sorry she had to look after them. I'm not usually unreliable but I felt pretty ill. This is the hottest summer I can remember for a while and I keep forgetting to apply sun cream and stay in the shade. New York was stifling in the summer, so we always retreated into the nearest air-conned building. I'll be more careful in future.'

'Don't worry,' Matt said, shifting nearer and touching her elbow, 'as long as you're better now, and don't make a habit of it.' He frowned as she jerked her arm away. 'Sorry. I was going to come and knock on your door to see how you were doing, but I thought it was better to leave you to it.'

'It was. Thank you.'

'I hope I didn't make you uncomfortable,' he said gruffly, 'out in the garden.'

'Uncomfortable?' she frowned. No. Not uncomfortable, just supremely conscious of his hard, muscular body despite battling rolling nausea.

'When I caught you, you backed away pretty quickly. I wasn't coming on to you, I promise. Jesus, that sounded so cheesy and sort of insulting.' He puffed out a breath and tried again. 'What I mean is, you work for me and I'm not really dating at the moment, haven't since Helen died and—'

'Wait. What? You said this morning I shouldn't believe everything I read in the papers, but you're seriously telling me that you haven't dated any of the women you've been seen with? What about your fiancée, the pop star?'

'We were never engaged. She just liked costume jewellery, and wearing the ring was good PR, according to my publicist,' he explained, a frustrated expression crossing his face. 'But me storming out of the hotel with the kids was true enough. Though how the press got tipped off for that one, I don't know. As for the dating,' he shifted from one foot to another, rubbing the small dark bruise under his chin from earlier in the morning, 'it's a fluid term, isn't it?'

She stared at him. 'Oh?'

'Well, what I mean is, I date occasionally,' his face started to burn a slow, deep pink, 'I just don't have significant relationships. So you don't have to worry about Aimee and Jasper, I don't bring women home with me, I just—'

'Stop, please,' she interrupted in a pained voice, holding a hand up, palm out. 'Wow, you really don't know how to talk to women anymore,' she sighed. 'Look, its fine Matt, don't worry about it, I get that you were just trying to help in the garden. I didn't read anything into it.' Talk about awkward. Though it would have been the perfect opportunity to learn more about his love life if she was going to get close enough for her plan to work, there was a strange reluctance inside her to pursue the conversation. She bit her lip, staring at the frayed collar of his t-shirt. 'So, um, how long has Sadie been here? Did she arrive right after I went up?' It was oddly disappointing that he could have played with his children but had instead got his assistant on the job.

'Don't leap to conclusions,' he shook his head. 'And definitely don't scowl at me like that. I've been playing with them for the last half hour too. I didn't have much of a choice, given your second-hand directive.'

'Huh? Sorry, what do you mean?' She squinted at him.

Matt tapped his chin with a long finger, as if he was pondering one of life's great mysteries. 'Let me see. How did Jasper so delicately put it? *Zoe says you have to spend more time with us.* Tell me, do you normally use children to try and manipulate men?'

Her mouth dropped open and her face flushed at the accusation. 'No!' Still, although she hadn't used the exact words Jasper had, the message was close enough. Bugger, she'd wanted to talk to Matt first. He had a cheek though. He of all people was in no position to judge someone else's behaviour after what he'd done to her sister, tearing her life apart without a backward glance. 'No,' she repeated defensively. 'Absolutely not, I only—'

The office door opened behind him.

'S-sorry.' Aimee stopped, picking up on the tension.

'That's okay,' Zoe replied in a soothing voice, talking to the girl and studiously avoiding Matt's gaze. 'Were you after something, Aimee?'

'Jasper asked about dinner.'

'I'm just on my way to sort it out. Can you tell him it'll be about half an hour please?' She turned to Matt as his daughter nodded and went back into his office. 'We can talk about this later. I don't want the children to overhear. Will Sadie be staying for dinner?' she asked in a neutral tone, studying the skirting board to keep her cool.

'Why would she?' Matt asked, confused.

'Um, because it's the polite thing to do, especially as she's just been playing with your kids?'

'Oh, right,' it was like the thought was alien, had never occurred to him. 'I don't think so. She never has before. I should think she wants to get home to rest anyway.'

'Are you going to ask?'

He raised both eyebrows. 'I guess I am now.' Stepping around Zoe, 'Sadie,' he called, 'can you come out a minute please?'

The door opened and an attractive fox-faced brunette stuck her head into the hallway, 'Yes, Matt?'

'This is my new nanny Zoe,' he gestured. 'Zoe, this is Sadie.' He gave the women a moment to exchange polite nods. 'Sadie, Zoe wants to know if you're staying for dinner?'

'Matt!' Zoe muttered, shaking her head.

'Matt, you're a sod!' Sadie scolded, a dimple flashing in her left cheek, dark eyebrows arching. 'I need a break from the rabble for a while, but thank you for asking, Zoe. Matt never would have. He finds it hard to observe social niceties and talk to normal people, especially when he's working with a new artist.'

'Hey, I'm stood right here,' Matt protested, folding his arms.

'I know,' Sadie said impishly, ducking back into the room, 'that's the best time to talk about someone.' Her voice floated out into the hallway, full of mirth. 'You've got me for twenty more minutes. Then I'm escaping.' The door swung shut and she said something else, causing the children to chortle.

'I like her,' Zoe said as Matt turned to face her.

'Huh, I wonder why,' he remarked drily. 'Now you'll both gang up on me,' he said with a mournful expression.

'Oh, you poor baby,' she rebutted in mock sympathy, still so used to the banter of her relationship with Greg that she forgot who she was talking to. God, she'd better not be flirting with Matt, it didn't bear thinking about. 'Right, I need to get on.' Twisting away she started toward the kitchen. He trailed along behind her.

'Aren't you going to go back into your office?' Zoe said in a hopeful voice, his footsteps echoing hers.

'Nope,' he replied, 'we need to talk.'

The weight of his gaze on her back tingled a warning along her spine. She thought of the comment he'd levelled at her about manipulating men through children.

This should be fun.

7

'You're cross with me,' she pre-empted Matt as he rested against one of the marble countertops with a scowl. Reaching up to take Jasper's paintings down from their pegs, she tested them with careful fingers to check they were dry. 'However, if Jasper had given me time to talk to you first,' she continued, 'I would have explained that what I'd said to the kids was that I would *ask* you if you could spend some quality time with each of them, with some time as a whole family too.' Setting the paintings aside she put her hands on her hips. 'I don't do things through the children Matt, that's not my style. I approach things with parents directly, and prefer to work in partnership with them so we have common goals.' She nodded. 'Jasper was right though, I do feel that way. Living in the same house is one thing, but actually talking to each other and sharing your lives is another.'

'I appreciate your professional opinion,' he answered tersely, 'but we sit together in the lounge some evenings.'

'You sitting playing on your iPad, with Jasper on another and Aimee scrunched up on the other side of the room reading with her back to you both isn't what I'm talking about. You need to do some activities together, have a chance to connect, find some shared passions. You don't put them to bed, you barely see them in the morning, and you don't talk much,' recalling what Jasper had told her as they'd strolled along Park Lane. 'Look, I'm not having a go,' she held her hands out in front of her, 'I'm just trying to do my best for them, based on what I see,' she chose her words carefully, 'and what I see already is that they're great kids but could be happier. They also have some things to work through—'

He straightened away from the worktop, shoulders taut. 'What do you mean?'

'An ambulance went past today and Jasper got a bit upset. He mentioned something about his mum?'

'They saw the accident,' stumbling over the word, 'happen.' He tightened his lips and the scar running into the top one turned white.

'I know,' she said quickly, stepping closer. Trying to ignore how sexy the scar made him look. Bad boys, eat your heart out.

'How?' he frowned, black eyebrows pulling down. 'How do you know?'

Shit. She thought fast. 'It was in the kids' development folders that your last nanny left,' she blurted, 'and from what Jasper said it wasn't hard to put it together.'

'I see.' His mouth relaxed a little. 'I didn't realise it still bothered him.'

'I'm not sure,' she said hesitantly, 'but I think Aimee may be struggling with it too.'

'It is? I didn't realise. It was three years ago. They were so young.' He closed his eyes. 'She never said. Neither did Melody.'

'It might be that she found it difficult,' she answered, thinking of her sister's gentle nature, how she probably wouldn't have wanted to upset him. 'And your daughter's not exactly the world's greatest talker, is she? I mean, she'd rather escape into a book than talk to people. She's a bit like you in that way.'

Matt opened his eyelids, blinked, green gaze settling on her intently. 'In what way?'

'Like you said this morning, when you're working on something you get lost in it. She has the same focus.'

'I suppose. It's funny,' he mused, gazing out the window at the apple tree, 'Aimee always reminds me so much of Helen.'

'Maybe in looks, but she has a lot of you in her, personality wise. It's the nature versus nurture debate, isn't it? Genetics versus environment. Jasper is the spitting image of you though, lucky thing. He's going to be a heartbreaker,' she said unthinkingly.

'I'll take that as my first compliment,' his mouth edged up on one side.

'Pardon?' Realising what she'd said. Bugger. 'Oh. Sorry, I didn't—'

'It's fine,' Matt chuckled, 'relax. It's a relief to hear something nice from you.'

'Am I horrible to you then?' she said, alarmed.

'No. Just insistent about some things.' He nodded, 'As long as you're doing your best for my children though, I'll find a way to cope.' There was the smallest hint of seriousness in his ironic drawl.

'Good. So, anyway,' she hurried on, 'Aimee's social skills need to develop but otherwise her concentration is a good thing. I'm sure she's reading well above her age group. Have the school ever been in touch?'

'I don't know, Melody always handled that side of things.'

She pulled a face. Hadn't he even been interested? Why did this guy have so little buy-in to his children's lives? He did seem to love them in his own way, but the lack of engagement was puzzling.

'Before you say it, I work long hours and Melody was the expert, not me.'

'Whatever you say,' she shrugged, struggling to keep the disbelief from her voice. These were his kids. His to love, his responsibility. 'I'll take another look at the development folders and phone the school at the start of the term. I'd like to know what milestones they're setting for Aimee. She needs to be appropriately challenged or she'll get bored.'

'Fine by me. I was impressed by her hangman skills,' he added, 'in fact, she almost thrashed me.' He looked surprised. 'She's got a great vocabulary.'

'It's all the reading.' Zoe blew a breath out, sensing the conversation was calming down. 'So, what do you think about spending more time with the children? I understand your work commitments and it's great you have a hard work ethic, but can you spare one evening a week with each of them, with a morning or afternoon at weekends together? Proper time to talk and touch base would be really valuable for you as a family.' She smiled, 'Before you know it, they'll be teenagers and all you'll get will be grunts from Jasper and flouncing about from Aimee after she's applied a ton of foundation and taken endless selfies.'

'Don't scare me! I'm barely coping with them at this age,' he joked. 'I'll see what I can do, I'll talk to Sadie about my schedule once she's back at work.'

For a moment she thought he was still joking, but when it became apparent he wasn't her fingers curled into fists. He was an adult, so he should make time for his kids in his own goddamn schedule. They should be his top priority. She held her tongue though. It was a start and if she went at him too hard he would only retreat. 'Okay, sounds good.'

'So, um, should I be worried that an alarming amount of my son's paintings feature aliens having gun-fights, complete with spatters of blood?' he asked, picking up the pile of pictures and resting back against the counter as he flicked through them.

'No. I don't think it's anything to be concerned about. It's not unusual to be into gory stuff at his age. Besides, he's a big Ben 10 fan so it's hardly surprising.' Going over to the fridge she started pulling courgettes, onions and tomatoes out of the bottom drawer.

'Oh yeah,' he looked vague, 'Ben 10, that's right.'

'The boy with the watch? He's a hero and turns into different aliens?' Really, did this guy occupy another planet? She slammed the fridge door shut, rinsing the courgettes and tomatoes under running water over the sink. Yanking an expensive copper frying pan and a matching saucepan from a low cupboard, she filled the saucepan with water and set it on the hob to start heating, throwing in a pinch of salt.

'Yeah, that's right. Jasper's got a duvet cover and clock in his room,' Matt supplied. 'Melody bought them for him. For a birthday I think.'

Zoe kept her face straight as she set the food down on the chopping board, hiding her frustration. 'Do you ever take him out to buy stuff yourself?' She made sure her tone was curious rather than accusatory. 'Have you ever sat and watched an episode with him?'

'Not really.' Matt put the paintings aside. 'Shopping isn't really my thing. Neither are cartoons.'

She drew a knife from the knife block and held it up to the light to check it was sharp. 'When you have kids,' she said wryly, 'sometimes you have to do things you don't like. You should watch the programme with him sometime, it's quite good fun, and it would give you something to start talking about.' She started slicing the courgettes into small chunks.

'I don't need a cartoon to help me talk to my kids,' he crossed his arms over his broad chest.

'Oh?' she raised an eyebrow. 'What do you talk about then?'

He sucked in his cheeks, looking unsure. After a moment, 'Fencing. Horse-riding. Dra—'

'Draughts?' She finished for him. 'Thrilling stuff. I wasn't sure draughts were still played this century. You do know they don't enjoy those activities, don't you? Aimee doesn't mind the horse riding but Jasper finds it scary, they're both bored to tears by draughts and they could take or leave fencing.'

'Really? Melody picked them out. I asked what the kids should be doing and she spoke to some of the other nannies and suggested those.'

Maybe they were activities the children should be doing with their lifestyle. Yet Jasper had told her how he and Aimee felt about them, and if he'd told her then why not Melody? If Melody knew, why wouldn't she have spoken to Matt? He wasn't that unapproachable. 'You do live in Knightsbridge, I suppose,' she excused. 'It's a pretty affluent area and some of the kids go on to attend Independent schools. I'm guessing the nannies are very competitive about their charges, and those activities aren't necessarily wrong. I just feel they're wrong for your children.'

Matt watched as she slid the cut up courgette aside and started chopping the tomatoes. 'What do you think they should be doing instead?' he quizzed.

'Ask them.'

'Pardon?'

'Ask them. They'll tell you. Then it's up to you as their dad to make a decision as to what's practical and appropriate.'

A pulse beat in his jaw. 'Okay, I will.'

'Good.' Concentrating on not squirting tomato juice everywhere, she cut the tomatoes up with single-minded purpose, aware her shoulders were so tense they were near her earlobes. She must talk to her sister ASAP about what had been going on in this house and she had to wake Matt up before he missed the whole of Jasper's and Aimee's childhoods. Not that she owed it to him, it was the kids she was thinking of.

There was a dragged out, tense silence. Matt released a heavy sigh.

She flicked a glance at him as he pulled up a stool at the breakfast bar and sat down, the jeans tightening around his muscular thighs.

Rubbing his scar. 'I know what it must look like,' he muttered, looking troubled.

'What's that?' Moving the tomatoes aside with the flat of her knife, she started peeling the onion, hoping it wasn't too strong.

'I was much more of a hands-on dad once. When they were little. It's been complicated since Helen died.'

'Uh-huh.'

He tried again, 'I work really long hours.'

'Uh-huh.'

'I had to earn a living—'

'Uh-huh,' her voice climbed higher.

'Melody was here to look after them.'

'Uh-huh.' Picking the knife up and chopping the onion in half in one smooth motion.

He scowled. 'What does uh-huh mean?'

'Nothing,' she shrugged, turning half the onion on its side, glancing over her shoulder to see if the water was boiling yet.

'Argh, I hate it when women do that. Say one thing but mean another. Just like when you use the word fine, but are plainly not. The new singer I signed has been like that recently, all withdrawn and non-committal but still insisting she's okay.'

'Well, men are from Mars, women are from Venus,' she shrugged again, cutting the onion into neat lines.

'Just tell me, Zoe please. Say what you're thinking.'

'You won't like it.'

His expression was determined. 'Even so, I want to know. Although you're being pretty presumptuous for someone who hardly knows me, I promise not to take offence or fire you.'

She laughed bitterly, thinking of Melody, chopping the onion harder, the knife hitting the heavy wooden chopping board beneath with unnecessary force. 'You'd be lucky,' she breathed. 'Fine. What I think is that all those things you listed are excuses, not reasons.'

'What?' he shot off the stool, the legs scraping along the floor.

'You asked,' she reminded him, 'so here's what I think. You work for yourself so you could set your own hours and it's common knowledge that you have family money, so you could use that rather than driving yourself into the ground making a living. Melody was your nanny, employed to help care for your children, not to raise them for you.' She held his eyes, gaze direct. 'Those aren't the real reasons you're not involved in your children's lives.'

'What is the real reason then?'

'You need to figure that out for yourself.'

'Oh, for God's sake don't talk in riddles,' he glowered.

She stopped, surprised, and set down the knife. 'I'm not. I'm just not certain myself. As you said, I don't know you that well. I'm sure if you take some time to think about it and are honest with yourself though, it'll come to you. It's important for your family.'

Her concession appeared to deflate the worst of his anger and he sat back down, looking a mixture of thoughtful and annoyed. Hesitantly, she picked up the knife and resumed cutting up the onion, eyes starting to water with the fumes.

Matt pulled one of Jasper's paintings towards him, tracing a long finger over a self-portrait stick-figure that his son had topped with a shock of black hair, one hand holding a giant grey laser gun. 'This is Jasper,' he muttered, 'this is Aimee,' pointing to a red-haired figure in a barred cell, a taller one with long black hair next to it, 'and this must be you. And he's either locked you up or is trying to save you, but where am I?'

Zoe shifted from one foot to another uncomfortably. That's exactly what she'd asked Jasper earlier. 'He said you were at work. And he's trying to save us because you're too busy making cool music.'

'I see,' he cleared his throat, putting the painting aside and staring into space for a moment. 'Well,' he shook his head, 'I can't say it wasn't painful to hear what you think of my parenting skills and you're treading a fine line with some of your comments, but I said I wouldn't take offence, so thanks for the honesty. I'll give it some thought. That doesn't mean you're right though.' She didn't reply, letting him have that one. After a moment he sprang up, appearing restless. 'I need a cup of coffee. You?'

'Please, if you don't mind.'

'White, one sugar, right?'

She tilted her head as tears blurred her vision. 'Yes, as long as you don't poison it.'

'It's tempting but I'll hold back this time,' he teased. 'So, the little girls you looked after in the States,' switching the subject as he clanked cups and turned knobs on the chrome coffee machine, 'what were their names?'

'Ava and Grace.'

'Seriously? Were their parents into classic movies or something?'

'You've got it.' She put the knife aside, arranging the pieces of onion into a pile.

'If they'd had a third, do you think they would have called her Marilyn, as in Monroe?'

Zoe chuckled, thinking of Liberty's extrovert ways. 'Probably.'

'Do you miss them?' The machine made a few hissing noises and started producing steaming black coffee. Matt moved the mugs along the spouts, topping them up with hot milk as he looked at her questioningly.

Zoe thought about the day she'd had playing with Jasper and coaxing Aimee out of her shell. There was something about children's innocent joy that lifted the spirits. She was exhausted, couldn't sleep and had no appetite and the anger, humiliation, hurt and disappointment over her ex-fiancé was raw, running a constant circle of questions in her mind as to why she hadn't been good enough. Somehow though, Matt's kids were getting her through, keeping her too busy to brood or mope. Rather than longing for Greg, New York and the girls, she was coping. It was like this job had been waiting for her just at the perfect time. She shrugged the thought off. It hadn't been, she was here by default. This was her sister's life really, she mustn't forget it, or the plan. 'Do I miss them? A bit.' She'd been fond of Ava and Grace, but had never bonded with them in the way she was already bonding with Aimee and Jasper. Perhaps it was because Liberty had always been there in the background making demands, whereas these kids were motherless. 'Not as much as I thought I would,' she mused. 'Still, its early days.'

Matt spooned sugar into both coffees and set hers down in front of her, resuming his position on the bar stool.

'What about New York? Do you miss the city? You must have had friends there? You said you were single but there must have been someone at some point?'

'Thanks for the coffee,' she gestured to the mug. 'Honestly? I'm not sure it's been long enough to miss anything properly. Yes, I had friends. Yes, there was someone. That's over though.' Tears blurred her eyes again. 'Definitely over.'

A hand reached over and curled around her wrist. 'I'm sorry, I didn't mean to upset you.'

Freezing, she took a breath. 'You didn't,' easing her arm away, she sniffed, 'it's the onions.'

'Oh,' he murmured. 'Well, now I feel like an idiot.'

She laughed, 'You said it.'

'Oi!' Sipping his coffee, he watched as she spun around, poured some olive oil into the frying pan and put it on the hob. Studying the now boiling water, she rooted through one of the units and pulled out a bag of pasta, emptying three quarters of its contents into the saucepan. 'Do you like cooking?' he asked.

'It's all right. I prefer it when there aren't kids running around under my feet. Makes it more relaxing. I love my job and being a nanny though,' she tacked on quickly.

'Don't worry, I know what you meant.' He paused as he heard his name called. 'Excuse me, I think that's Sadie on her way out. Back in a minute.'

As soon as he was gone, Zoe dropped her head and sucked in great gulps of oxygen. What the hell was she doing? She wasn't supposed to be bonding with the guy, or helping him out, she was supposed to be getting revenge. Her phone beeped and she raised her head, grabbing it off the side and checking the screen.

**Hi, Sis. How's
it going? Found out
anything yet?
M x**

Yes, as it happened. A fractured family. Things that didn't make sense, given how nice Matt could be some of the time. But replying to her sister by text wasn't going to do it. After the kids were in bed, they'd talk.

**I'll call you
this evening.
Around 8? Z x**

'Sadie was flagging,' Matt said as he walked back into the kitchen, 'she said to say bye.'

Flustered by Matt almost catching her texting Mel, Zoe threw her mobile into the corner, where it span in a lazy circle. 'Okay.'

Matt raised an eyebrow at the action. 'Everything all right?'

'Yes,' moving over to the chopping board, she heaved it over to the cooker, clumsily tossing the veg into the frying pan and seasoning it. 'What are the kids doing?'

'I've put them in their playroom with the TV on. I didn't think dinner would be long.'

'It won't,' she grimaced at him as he sat down to finish his coffee, 'but is there anything in there that Jasper can cause mischief with? Felt-tip pens, crayons, paints?'

'No, plus I put Ben 10 on for him, as Aimee's sat in the corner chair reading.'

'Again,' Zoe smiled. '*To Kill a Mockingbird* is holding her riveted today.'

'It's a great book. Prejudice, justice, love, hate. The nature of the human heart.'

She stared at him, 'Yes. I like it too.'

'Don't look at me like that. Music is my passion, but I enjoy reading books. I read *To Kill a Mockingbird* as a teenager for school and I still read occasionally.'

'Have you ever talked to Aimee about it? The books you enjoy?'

He paused, 'No, I don't think I have.'

'You should,' she suggested, planting the seed. 'I read as much as possible,' she stirred the vegetables, 'anything I can lay my hands on. Have you read anything good lately?'

'Harlan Coben is pretty good. Noel and I swap his books sometimes.'

'Ah, yes the famous Uncle Noel.'

'Have the kids been talking about him?' Matt drained his mug.

'Yes,' wandering across the room, she picked her coffee up and wrapped her hands around it, 'and about Holly.'

'Noel's my best friend. They're a nice couple.'

'I gathered that from Jasper's chatter.'

'He does talk a lot.' He leaned in, whispering conspiratorially, 'It makes my head hurt sometimes.'

Leaning closer to him across the breakfast bar, she whispered back, 'I get why.' Seeing the sudden spark of something in his deep green eyes, she straightened. Clearing her throat, she wiped the sides down, placed the chopping board next to the sink and prodded the pasta with a wooden spoon. 'So, uh, Sadie.' She pictured the brunette and didn't like the squiggle of discomfort in her belly. 'She's very attractive. Is she married?' She could have kicked herself for asking such an irrelevant and possibly sexist question. Why did she care?

'No.' He wandered across the room and leaned around her to put his mug in the sink, making her ultra-aware of his height and the breadth of his shoulders. She inhaled sharply as she saw muscles shifting under his navy t-shirt.

The room seemed to be getting smaller. She tugged at her top. Was it getting hot in here? It must be cooking over a hot stove that was responsible.

'She has a boyfriend,' he said. 'They're trying for a baby. The procedure she had was to remove some cysts. I'd appreciate you not saying anything about it though, especially to her. She's quite sensitive about it and it's very personal.'

'Poor her. Of course. Thanks for telling me.'

'You're both my employees, and I can trust you right?'

Holding his gaze was incredibly hard because the last thing he should do was trust her, but she managed it, and nodded. Silence stretched between them. He looked tired, slight bags under his eyes. Most men would look awful but for Matt it just added to his bad boy air. The hush between them continued and she felt as if they were in a bubble, well away from the real world. It was just the two of them.

She wrenched her eyes away from his and saw his chest expand, heard the soft whoosh of his breath as he exhaled. She could hear the murmur of the TV in the room above them and through the open kitchen window she could make out someone's radio, tuned to an old Blues station. A stupor crept over her, his body heat wrapping around her. Swaying, she leaned closer, closer...

'Zoe,' his low voice made her jump.

Stepping back, she shook her head, pulling herself from the daze with an effort. 'Yes?' She should be with her sister in Southend-On-Sea, she thought. Not stuck in the lifeless high-tech kitchen of a big house in Knightsbridge with a man who both annoyed and excited her.

'Is something burning?'

'Oh, crap,' whirling around, she stirred the veg, which had started breaking down into a saucy tomatoey mess and turned the heat down on the pasta, 'I mean, oops. So, um,' her voice sounded unfamiliar and croaky, 'I know it's possibly very un-PC of me to ask but how old is Sadie?' She stirred the sauce, the fragrance of onions and herbs wafting from the pan.

'It's probably indiscreet of me to tell you, but I don't think she'd mind,' he offered, 'forty-two.'

'Really?' she whipped around, spoon in hand, spattering sauce across his t-shirt.

He jumped back, swearing. 'Argh, that's hot!'

'Oops, sorry,' she choked, biting her lip.

His eyes narrowed under his black eyebrows, the break in his nose highlighted by the angle his head was tilted at.

'Yeah, you look it,' he answered drily. He gave her such a look of

101

reproach she couldn't help but burst out laughing before flinging a wet cloth at him from beside the sink. He caught it in mid-air, 'Thanks.'

'I am sorry,' she repeated as he wiped the front of his top down, her mouth going dry as the damp spots made the cotton cling to his chest. What would he look like shirtless? She wondered, feeling uncomfortably hot. 'I was just surprised,' she explained as he threw the cloth into the sink. 'I would have put Sadie in her early thirties at the most.'

'Yeah, so surprised you pelted food at me,' his mouth quirking in amusement, he pulled the top away from his body, unknowingly exposing a patch of hair roughened chest. 'I'll have to tell her. She'll be pleased, no, thrilled.'

'She definitely looks a lot younger than she is.' She gulped down the huge lump in her throat and turned back to the sauce, stirring it round in lazy circles, perhaps trying to hypnotise herself into not staring at him. Turning away, she got another pan and went over to the sink, filling it with cold water. She liked to plunge the pasta in fresh water once it was done.

'That's good,' Matt said, 'because her boyfriend is a lot younger than her. Yeah, good old Sadie went and got herself a toy boy.'

She was so astonished at his laughing admiration that she twirled around holding the pan against her stomach and a huge wave of water crested over and spilt down her top.

'Urgh,' she squeaked, ramming the pan onto the kitchen unit and jumping back.

Matt clutched his side and chortled as she stretched the cotton away from her body so it couldn't cling to her bra. The wet t-shirt look was not a good one to sport in polite society. She pulled a face at him.

'Sorry,' he said around a wide grin, 'sorry. Sadie and I have known each other so many years I'm used to joking around like that. But it might have sounded odd the way I put it. You have to admit though, it was quite funny. I've never seen anyone move so fast. You also thought it was amusing when you got me,' he said as she grabbed a kitchen roll and ripped off pieces, ineffectually dabbing at her soaked top.

'It's not quite the same, is it?' she grumbled as water dripped onto her bare toes.

'Okay,' he held his hands up, 'I'll give you that. You go dry off and change and I'll mop up and serve dinner.'

'Are you sure?'

'Yes, I'm sure I can manage to drain some pasta and put food on plates.' His eyes dropped to her chest before resolutely forcing them upwards. 'Shall we eat together at the table in the dining room?'

'Actually, I prefer the kitchen,' she said, starting to blush at the way he was looking at her, 'it's cosier.' She studied the marble and chrome equipment surrounding them. 'Well, by contrast to the dining room it is anyway.'

'What's wrong with the dining room?'

'It's the same as the lounge,' she blurted.

'What's wrong with the lounge?' he demanded.

'It's so,' she shuddered, 'bleurgh.'

Putting his hands on his lean hips, smiling slightly. 'What's bleurgh?'

'White, pristine, cold. It reminds me a bit of my aunt's house. Homes should be warm, cosy and comfortable.'

'I see.' Matt looked bemused. 'I didn't appreciate that you were an interior designer as well as a nanny.'

'I'm not— oh. Ha-ha.' She flushed, 'Sorry, I shouldn't be criticising your home. I'll go and change. I'll send the kids down to help set the table while I'm up there.'

'They're going to do what now?'

'They're more than old enough, Matt, don't look so astounded,' backing away, she hustled towards the door. 'Oh, by the way, there's parmesan on the side too.'

Dashing up the stairs, she called for Aimee to please put her book down and Jasper to turn the TV off so they could go and help their dad because he was going to join them for dinner. Her tone brooked no argument. Fleeing to the top floor, she slammed into her room and sank down onto the edge of the bed, curling her toes into the blue carpet. What had she gotten herself into?

It didn't get any better later that night after she'd tucked the kids up in bed and called Melody. After the niceties were done and she'd consoled her sister that of course only crying three or four times a day was better than crying every hour, she got straight to the point.

'What's going on, Mel?'

'Pardon?' her sister asked warily.

'The kids, Matt. It's all wrong.'

'Wrong? What do you mean, wrong?'

'The way they are together.' Zoe rolled onto her side, hugging a cushion. 'There's no quality time, they're doing activities they don't like, Aimee's so introverted she's nearly a hermit, Jasper's bouncing off the walls trying to get his dad's attention. When I sent the kids into him this morning and told them to hug him goodbye—'

'You did what?' Melody exclaimed, sounding horrified.

'I didn't know, did I? It's normal for kids to say hello to their parents and have some affection from them. I didn't think I was doing anything outrageous.' Chewing her lip. 'Did you uh, ever challenge him with it?'

'Challenge him?' Melody said. 'You don't challenge your boss. You do what they tell you to do.'

Zoe sighed, remembering this had been Melody's first real job since leaving college. 'It's okay to raise things with them though, to make recommendations and provide advice. It's part of what we're paid for. Ultimately what the parents say goes, unless we've got safeguarding concerns in which case we refer it on to social services, but that doesn't mean you shouldn't try.'

'I did say something once or twice when I first started but

Matt wasn't interested. So I left it alone. Besides, I didn't think it was that wrong. Some families just aren't that demonstrative, are they? I mean, Aunt Ruth isn't a big one for hugs, but our childhood was okay.'

'Maybe you were happy, but I wasn't. Is that what you want for Matt's kids?' Zoe said sharply, sitting up on the bed and throwing the cushion aside. 'Nights lying awake wondering if they're loved or not? Waiting for praise and attention but never getting it? Feeling lonely and alone?'

'Wait a minute, I care about those children!' Her sister spoke fiercely in a voice that Zoe hardly recognised. 'And it probably doesn't help that you and Ruth have never agreed on much, does it? Also you have to remember that not everyone is like you, Zo. We don't all have your confidence, like Dad's.'

It was true enough, and perhaps Melody and Ruth got on better because Melody was content to follow orders, happy not to ask questions or want to share her opinions. Unlike her. Zoe knew she was lucky to have inherited or learnt the confidence Mel was talking about from their father, a trait that ran through her like the words imprinted down the middle of the sticky seaside rock they'd eaten as children. 'Still, you could have—'

'You've been there a couple of days.' Melody's voice was low and tight. 'I was there for three years. When I agreed to this plan I didn't think you were going to wade in and start judging me. I did my best given how inexperienced I was when I got there.' Dropping to a whisper. 'I thought what I was doing was right.'

Zoe gulped at the defeat in her sister's voice, feeling awful. 'I'm sorry, sis. I didn't mean to upset you. The last thing you need at the moment is me having a go. I'm just a bit shocked at the set up here, that's all. Listen, it's not beyond repair and it's really not that bad. You've done a good job with them and I genuinely think they're missing you.'

'They are?' Melody's voice was thick with tears.

'Yes,' Zoe said firmly. 'No matter what else happens, if there's any way at all I can arrange for you to see them, or say goodbye, I will. But sis, why didn't you tell me? I know it was difficult with me in New York, but I would have talked it through with you. I'd always be happy to give you advice. We Skyped regularly, but you never once said anything about the way things are here.'

'Like I said, I thought it was normal. Besides, it's hard enough to live in your big sister's shadow without having to run to her for help. The only reason I became...' she trailed off.

'Became what?'

'Nothing,' she murmured, and Zoe could picture her little sister twisting a lock of dark blonde hair around her finger, dark eyes huge in her pale face, 'it doesn't matter.' Melody cleared her throat. 'Sorry, I have to go. Ruth's calling me for dinner. Speak soon.'

She rang off abruptly, leaving Zoe staring at the phone open mouthed. It wasn't like Melody to end a call like that. Not with her anyway. She hadn't even asked how the plan was going or whether she'd found out anything from Matt, or about Stephen's whereabouts. Also, Ruth always served dinner at seven o'clock on the dot, one of her regimental rules, so Mel should have eaten over an hour ago. Zoe picked the cushion up again, hugging it to her, thinking about her sister's comment about living in her shadow. What had she been about to say? The only reason she'd become what?

Her phone beeped and she picked it up eagerly, thinking it would be a message from Mel to say sorry or send her love, but to her shock it was a text from Greg.

I miss you Zoe.
We need to talk.
Call me.
All my love, Greg x

She stared at it, black rage climbing up inside her throat. He had a damn nerve. He missed her? He loved her? He could go f—

She hurled the phone onto the bed before leaping up and marching into the bathroom. Twisting the taps on violently, she started running a bath, accidentally throwing nearly a whole tub of bath salt in with shaking hands.

If you loved someone you didn't cheat on them and humiliate them in front of the whole of New York society. If you loved someone you treated them with honesty, trust and respect. If you loved someone you didn't ask them to marry you and plan a wedding with them, only to wreck it all two weeks before you tied the knot. And if you were going to miss someone, you'd better make bloody sure you were okay with letting them go in the first place.

Zoe sighed as she stared down at the whirling, swirling bubbles in the water. What the heck was going on with everyone around her?

8

As the dog days of July melted into August, Zoe and the children built a routine together. Breakfast and showers when they got up, greeting Matt before he went to work, an activity or outing in the morning, some quiet time at home over lunch followed by another outing or activities in the afternoon. Most nights she got them involved in making dinner, mashing potatoes up in a bowl with butter or folding pastry for a pie. They got used to setting and clearing the table with her every night in exchange for a scoop of ice-cream and a topping of their choice which they ate enthusiastically while she loaded the dishwasher.

Jasper wasn't that keen on her rule about there being no TV for an hour before bedtime, or when she insisted he have a warm bath filled with lavender oil to help him get sleepy every evening, and neither was he a big fan of reading together in his room before lights-out. However, after four nights of complaining and Zoe compromising by reading his favourite Ben 10 annual, he gave in with a faintly resigned air, accepting that she wasn't going to change her mind. By the end of the week he was looking more rested in the mornings, and was a little more settled in the day.

Aimee was interacting more often and loved that Zoe put half an hour aside every day for them to talk about books and pore over the small library in the girl's room while Jasper played a fun but educational game on his iPad. They had great fun talking about their favourite stories, and discussing why characters did things and felt the way they did. Zoe made sure to give Aimee lots of praise when she said something particularly insightful, impressed with her almost adult-like perceptions.

She didn't get much of a chance to push *Plan Nannygate* forward because she hardly saw Matt apart from for a few short minutes in the morning. It was probably just as well for her piece of mind, because every time she was near him the breath hitched in her lungs and warmth tingled over her skin. The broken nose, lip scar, broad shoulders and deep green eyes made her a goner every time. It was unfair for one man to be so scandalously sexy.

Thank God that although he was spending more time at home than she'd originally anticipated, leaving by eight every day and returning just before lunch time, he immediately hid himself away in what she discovered was a soundproof recording studio in the basement. He would often stay there until the early hours of the morning and never joined them for meals. However, a few times she caught him in the kitchen making a coffee and a sandwich. Watching the kids play in the garden, there'd be an expression on his face she couldn't place. It was somewhere between longing and fear, she thought, but wasn't sure.

They did make some progress because on two occasions he popped up from the studio to say goodnight to the children, giving them quick hugs before loping off, while she stood in the hallway to give them some privacy. Each time, he disappeared before she could speak to him. If she'd had something urgent to talk to him about she would have followed him down to the basement and insisted they catch up, but there was little to say at the moment so she left him to it. She didn't want to do anything to make him suspicious, and appearing for idle chats when she knew he was so busy would surely make him wonder if she was after something.

One balmy day Zoe and the children joined some other nannies and their charges in Green Park, with its tall trees, rolling lawns

109

and deckchairs.

'You lucky thing. Matt Reilly!' Beth, a blonde haired girl who worked for a family in Belgravia, sighed dreamily. 'He's so gorgeous. Are you getting on with him okay? His last nanny Melody never said much about him.' Her blue eyes widened. 'Well?'

She reminded Zoe of a golden retriever, all high-energy and bouncing enthusiasm. 'Fine,' Zoe said in a non-committal tone. 'Nice.' She raised her hand and shielded her eyes from the sunshine to check on Jasper, pleased to see him racing over the grass playing a good natured game of football with the little tow-headed boy Beth cared for.

'Seriously?' Monica exclaimed. 'That's all you have to say?' A brunette with yellowish eyes who worked for a single mum entrepreneur in Chelsea, she was definitely the leader of the group with her expansive arm gestures and strident voice.

'I didn't even see the job advertised,' Phoebe remarked softly. A tiny Asian nanny who looked after a six month baby girl for a family in Knightsbridge, she was dressed neatly in a lilac dress with a high collar, her feet tucked under her while she rocked the shiny, expensive pushchair beside her back and forth.

Zoe liked her immediately. There was something calming about her gentle manner. 'I got it through an agency,' she explained to Phoebe, smiling politely.

'Has he got another girlfriend yet?' Beth quizzed.

Zoe glanced over at Aimee to avoid their expectant stares, seeing the girl lying on her belly in the shade of a tree, nose stuck in a book, beribboned straw hat protecting her fair skin. She'd finished *To Kill a Mockingbird* the previous week with a sad but satisfied expression, and had moved onto *Great Expectations*.

'So?' Monica prompted.

One of the core parts of being a nanny was discretion and confidentiality and while that might not be the case once her plan was achieved, for now she couldn't afford to say anything indiscreet that would give Matt a justifiable reason to fire her.

'Come on, spill,' Beth said, 'we won't tell anyone, it'll just be between us. The nanny code and all that.'

'Nanny code?' Zoe angled her face to the sun's belting rays, glad she'd remembered to apply sun cream.

'We gossip amongst ourselves, but never to anyone outside the group.'

'I see.' Zoe felt uneasy about the use of the word gossip, but didn't want to spend the whole afternoon getting hounded, or face being excluded by them for being snotty. Maybe she could tell them something that wouldn't be an issue if it got back to Matt. Sitting up, she checked on Jasper again, watching with a smile as he tipped his Ben 10 cap further back to see the football better, face stripy with neon-pink sun block. 'Well, in that case, Matt seems nice. He loves his kids, and works a lot. I don't think he's that interested in a relationship at the moment though. He's working on a big project.' The last thing Matt or the kids needed was all the nannies in the area bowling up on the doorstep on some kind of manhunt. She was shocked at the protective instinct that ran through her at the thought.

'Oh,' Beth looked disappointed. 'I've heard he's nice, though a bit work mad, which is why what I heard about what he did to Melody doesn't make sense. She always said good things about him.'

'In what way doesn't it make sense?' Zoe asked, struggling to keep her voice level instead of achingly curious.

'You know about it?'

'I know that she left in a bit of a rush, Matt told me that, but not much else.'

'I don't want to worry you, especially if you're getting on well, but supposedly he fired her without notice and threw her out the same day,' Monica said bluntly, 'apparently she did something really awful. But that doesn't seem like her. She was so sweet and kind. Great with the kids too,' glancing at Aimee, who was still reading, 'it's so strange.'

'Do you know what she's supposed to have done?'

111

'No, just something bad.'

'Where did you hear that from? Matt?' Zoe asked.

'No, he keeps himself to himself, and I've never heard that he's said a bad word about anyone.' Monica frowned, 'I can't remember, a friend of someone who knows his brother, I think. Everyone was talking about it a few weeks ago.'

'Please,' Beth shuddered, blue eyes glinting, 'let's not ruin the afternoon by talking about Stephen.'

Phoebe glanced over at her, pushing a black wing of hair behind one ear. 'Are you okay?' she asked her friend quietly.

'Yep,' Beth sighed.

Zoe raised both eyebrows, 'What's this about Stephen?'

Monica looked to Beth, who sighed and rolled her eyes. 'Go on then.'

'Melody was lovely, but she had lousy taste in men,' Monica stated.

'You didn't like Stephen?' Zoe asked, keeping her voice steady. It would be interesting to hear what they thought of her sister's ex.

'He's immature, spoilt, and a serial dater. He's been with half of London, including three quarters of the local nannies. Beth was one of them,' she nodded at the blonde, who pulled a face to indicate her own stupidity, 'unfortunately he's not that great at finishing one thing before starting the next.'

'He really sucked me in,' Beth muttered, staring down at the tartan red blanket they were all sharing, 'I thought he liked me. I should have known better when I was never allowed around the house to meet Matt, and when he only came to mine late at night.'

'Of course he liked you,' Monica squeezed her knee, 'why wouldn't he? Remember, you're too good for him.'

'I was a booty call and you know it. I just didn't realise it at the time.'

Monica put an arm around her shoulders. 'You're not the first girl to fall for it. Come on, you'll be okay.' She hesitated, and grimaced, 'I've got to admit though, Stephen's different with

Melody. Kind of softer, and from the way he looks at her he seems to really care. They do look quite loved up. Sorry,' she told Beth.

'Don't worry about me. I'm over it.' The opposite was quite clearly the case, but no-one said so.

Zoe wondered if the sense she'd got that Beth may be interested in Matt was anything to do with making Stephen jealous. Making a play for your ex booty-call's brother was sure to get the booty-call's attention.

'Anyway, she's welcome to him,' Beth added, 'I hope he's being useful and comforting her somewhere.'

'He's not,' Zoe said absently as she watched Phoebe get up and lift a beautiful little girl dressed in pink lace from the pushchair. 'He's gone abroad and she's gone home.'

'Really?' Monica's eyes widened. 'She's got an aunt over on the coast hasn't she? And how did you know they're not together?'

'A sister too,' Phoebe chipped in, looking at Zoe over the baby's head, 'although I think she's in America somewhere?'

Zoe's drew her focus back to the group, realising what she'd said. Bugger, she hadn't meant to blurt that out about her sister. And now they were asking questions about Mel's family. This was getting too close for comfort. A warning claxon sounded in her head. *Divert, divert.* Fighting a mad urge to scoop up the kids and run, she forced herself to stay seated and appear relaxed. 'Matt must have mentioned it,' she answered, waving a hand at a fly that dive-bombed her face.

'So they've broken up?' Beth asked, leaning forward. Monica flashed her a look. 'Not that I care,' the blonde added lamely.

'Not sure,' Zoe answered, 'it doesn't really affect me so I haven't asked.' She was such a big fat liar. 'Anyway,' time to change the subject before she landed herself in trouble, 'enough of that. Let's talk about something more interesting.' Something that would get them talking. 'So, how does a girl go about finding eligible men around here?'

Phoebe blinked at her as she placed the teat of a bottle into the baby's searching pink mouth and Monica stopped in the act of lifting a drink from a cooler by her side.

Beth looked at her like she was crazy. 'Um, I can't imagine why you need to ask. You're living with one of the most eligible men in London!'

Zoe stopped at the entrance of Hyde Park next to the cute, white pillared Alexandra Lodge. The traffic along Kensington Road flowed behind them, red double-deckers roaring past at regular intervals, motorbikes darting between slowed cars with high-pitched purrs. Clutching Jasper's hand and a picnic hamper, she looked at Aimee's down bent head anxiously. The little girl had told her the previous night that if Zoe really, really wanted to visit Hyde Park, they could go the next day. However, she'd been staring at her bookshelves and her tone had been hesitant as they'd sat side by side on the small pink sofa in her bedroom.

'Is that what you want Aimee?' Zoe had asked, surprised the girl had raised it when she herself hadn't mentioned going for a while.

'I think I want to try.' Aimee nodded. 'I want to do it for you too, because you've never been.' Gazing into space, 'I think you'll like it there. It's pretty.'

'Well, that's nice of you. I appreciate you doing that for me. But what do you mean, you want to try?'

Aimee tilted her head so she could meet Zoe's quizzical expression. 'It's been a long time. Daddy only took us once and Melody never took us because I told her it upset me.'

'Won't it upset you now?'

'Maybe,' she looked serious, eyebrows lowering over her blue eyes. Her voice dropped to a whisper, 'But I miss her.'

Zoe was confused. 'You miss Melody?'

'No. Yes. I miss Melody but I was talking about Mummy.'

Zoe edged away a bit so she could turn to face the girl, tucking one leg under the other on the sofa. 'You want to go to Hyde Park because you miss Mummy?'

'Yes. We used to go there. All four of us. Me, Mummy, Daddy and Jasper. We used to have picnics, Jasper was really little and we used to laugh.' A shadow crossed her face. 'There's a piece of her there.'

'A piece of her?' Now she was completely flummoxed.

'I'll show you when we get there.'

Zoe smiled. 'All right. Would you like me to pack a picnic?'

Aimee looked torn. A bit happy, a bit sad. 'Can I tell you in the morning?'

'Of course you can,' she laid a hand on the girl's arm, 'that's fine. Right, shall we read something?'

Her face cleared, 'Yes, please.'

Now Zoe wasn't sure if going into the royal park was such a good idea. Aimee had been unusually quiet this morning, playing Connect-4 with minimal enthusiasm and staring off into space at odd moments.

Jasper tugged on her hand. 'Come on, I want to splash in the water.'

Whatever was troubling his sister he didn't seem bothered by it. All morning it had been, water this and water that and did Zoe have his swim shorts and was there a towel and could he take a ball with him?

'Ready?' Zoe asked Aimee.

The girl sucked in a breath and rolled her shoulders back, like she was bracing herself. 'Yes.'

'Good,' Zoe led them over to the big tourist information sign and the map setting out the park and immediate surroundings with red circular tube signs dotting the edges. A large light green rectangle marked out the boundaries of the park, darker green indicating trees and bushes, beige lines carving out paths, buildings in browns and greys neatly labelled, the Serpentine a long blue curving body of water that cut diagonally from top left near the fountains, to bottom right near the Queen Caroline Memorial. Immediately next to the entrance they were standing at were the

115

pavilion, a bowling green and junior tennis courts.

'What are you doing, Zoe?' Jasper asked, pulling on her hand again. 'Come on, I want to play.'

'Looking at the map.'

'I know the way,' Aimee dipped her head, watching with big eyes as a smiling couple walked past them holding hands.

'Even after three years?' Zoe asked, moving the picnic hamper from her hand to further up her arm, crooking it against her body.

'We came every Sunday, even in the winter,' Aimee explained. 'We just wrapped up, that's all.'

'Great, come on then. Aimee, you lead the way.'

Zoe followed the girl in through the open black wrought-iron gates, scores of trees lining both sides of the drive.

'We have to go and see the Princess.' Aimee pointed forward and off to the right.

'The Princess?'

'Mummy said she was beautiful and kind,' Aimee replied solemnly, 'and liked to help children and people who were sick.'

'I see.' She wasn't sure what the girl was on about but it was bound to become clear soon. Strolling along the pavement while Jasper bopped up and down at the end of her arm, which made it feel like her shoulder was about to pop out of its socket, she dodged the numerous other visitors to the park, handbag swinging against her hip. The crowds were made up of both locals and international visitors; groups of teenagers in black garb, chattering families from exotic places driving pushchairs with other children racing along beside them, teenage girls in barely-there outfits, mature couples with walking sticks but purposeful strides, a fair Norwegian-looking pair with the woman almost as tall as the man, an expensive camera hanging around her neck from a Nikon strap. Most people were in shorts and t-shirts, with a lot of the women in colourful summer dresses, due to the weather. It was another bright, sweltering day and the heat of the sun on the back of Zoe's neck was like a presence pushing her to the ground. She felt like she wanted to take a nap and it was only just gone noon.

She adjusted the hamper on her left arm, already regretting the amount of food she'd packed because the straw basket seemed to get heavier by the minute, the twisted handle leaving marks on the inside of her arm. It also made it difficult because she didn't have a free hand for Aimee. At seven, the girl was a little old to hold hands but Zoe still preferred to have one spare in case anything went wrong. Still, there were no cars to look out for; it was more about keeping track of both kids in the steady procession of people.

'We go down there,' Aimee pointed to a path that branched right, the tennis courts on one side before being hidden behind a row of leafy trees, and a thick thatch of bushes on the other. They walked along the path for a few moments before skirting left around the bushes.

Zoe smiled. 'Wow, this is nice.'

In front of them was a space encircled by a dark green metal-railed fence with loops and arches along the top. Inside the fence was bright emerald grass, graceful trees and children playing and splashing happily in a stone fountain set into the ground in a large circle, with a raised lip. The water sparkled and glinted in the sunlight creating diamond reflections on the surface and the sky above it was an endless, deep blue. 'This is where the princess is?' she looked down at Aimee.

'It's a fountain for the princess, because she liked children.'

'Ah, I see.' Now it was starting to make sense. It must be the memorial fountain created and built to honour Princess Di. Zoe gestured to the nearest gate. 'Shall we go in?'

Jasper gave her a gappy grin and Aimee smiled slightly, moving ahead to hold it open for her.

'Thanks, Aimee.' Zoe hoisted the picnic hamper higher, releasing Jasper's hand and following them both in. 'Pick somewhere to sit,' she encouraged.

Aimee gestured to a spot over on the far side closest to the Serpentine and some kind of statute, but not so far from the fountain that Zoe wouldn't be able to keep a safe eye on them from a sitting position. 'Okay, off you go.'

Cheering, Jasper tore across the space, looping around the side of the fountain and coming to a halt on the spot his sister had picked. Jumping up and down, he grasped the bottom of his t-shirt and wrenched it over his head. Zoe was laughing by the time she and Aimee joined him, shaking her head wryly. 'Hang on, hang on. Don't you want to eat first? Aren't you hungry?'

'Nope,' Jasper jerked his head from side to side. 'I want to play.'

'What about you, Aimee? What do you want to do?' Zoe asked, setting the hamper down with a sigh of relief and flexing her arm. Letting her handbag slide to the floor, she gazed expectantly at the girl.

'I'll sit down for a minute,' Aimee decided, sinking to the grass and arranging the skirt of her cotton dress neatly across her knees, 'I'm not hungry yet.'

'All right. Are you okay to stay here and keep an eye on our things while I take Jasper to the water?' Not having been before, she needed to know how deep it was.

Jasper hopped from one foot to another. 'Come on, Zoe. Pleeeeeease.'

Aimee nodded, biting her lip.

Zoe held a hand up. 'Hang on a minute, Jasper.' Hunkering down, Zoe looked into Aimee's eyes. 'Are you sure you're okay with this?'

'Yes,' she whispered, eyes confused. 'I just want to sit down for a while. It's nice to be here again though.'

'I'm glad. We'll only be a few minutes.' Standing up, Zoe kicked her flip flops off and grabbed Jasper's hand. 'Right then, you. We don't need to put any sun cream on because we did it before leaving the house, but if you get your upper half really wet, we'll have to put some more on, okay?' The coconut scent still clung to her hands.

'Uh-huh,' he agreed, tugging her along.

118

Zoe laughed at his eagerness and they broke into a jog. Stepping over the raised lip of the fountain and jumping into the water, Zoe sucked in a breath. It was clean and fresh but frigging freezing, her toes immediately numbing and a line of ice lapping against her calves.

'Jeez,' she breathed. 'It's a bit cold isn't it?'

Jasper scrunched his face up and broke away. 'Don't care,' bending down he scooped up a handful of water and threw it in the air.

'Nooo,' Zoe squeaked, stepping back as the droplets rained down on her. 'Urgh.' She stopped, turning her face to the sun and feeling the slight breeze drying the water on her skin. 'Actually, that's quite refreshing,' she smiled at Jasper. Peering back over her shoulder to check Aimee was all right, the girl waved at her reassuringly, looking less troubled than before. That was good. She faced Jasper again, who was now running back and forth through the water, churning up waves on either side of his legs. 'Guess what?' she asked, squatting to plunge both hands into the water as the boy paused to look at her.

'What?'

'Water fight!' Flipping both hands up, she sent a shower of water over him, soaking one side of his shorts.

'Hey!' Chortling, he danced out of the way. 'I'm not in my swimmers!'

'Doesn't matter,' she grinned, pleased to see him have fun, 'you can change into them later and we can put those to dry on the fence like other people have, while we have lunch.'

'Cool.' Jasper grinned in return, and sent a cascade of water over her with a light kick, plastering her short, white summer dress to one thigh.

He backed away as she growled and pounced towards him with dripping hands.

They played for a few minutes, chasing each other, careful not to slip and fall in the fountain, hooting and splashing around. Zoe glanced at Aimee a few times to make sure she was okay, and on each occasion the girl was either watching them with a tiny smile or gazing out along the Serpentine.

Three screaming children ran past Zoe and Jasper, two boys and a girl yelling at each other to stop but continually spraying each other with water, before turning and scampering back past. 'Play with us,' one of the boys slowed, arching an eyebrow at Jasper and curling his hand into a *come here* gesture. He looked about seven or eight but had the confidence of an older child.

Jasper swivelled his head to look at Zoe. 'Sure,' she agreed, sitting down on the granite lip of the fountain and stretching her legs out in front of her. 'Go.' Her lips curved as she watched Jasper join in with the group, instantly flicking water at the girl, who also looked a few years older. The other boys gave a cheer and joined in and Zoe wondered if the girl was going to hightail it or start crying but instead she charged at them, guffawing and lifting her legs in ever higher kicks that sent water spraying in all directions.

Zoe rested back on her arms and studied the circle of the fountain as Jasper played happily. Wider at some points and narrower at others, one section of water was tranquil and on the opposite side the walls curved and tiny waterfalls cascaded over small steps or jets of water bubbled up in the stream. The space in the middle of the fountain was grassy, though some paths ran along the inner edge and one intersected the middle, and a few trees dotted around provided some shade from the relentless sunshine. *Princess Diana* was engraved into one of the fountain walls just above the surface of the water. Scores of kids were mucking around, leaping in and out of the fountain, scampering down the mini-waterfall, sitting in the water and swirling their hands through it, some in swimming costumes and others in vest and knickers. Children's laughter and shrieks floated on the air and somewhere a mother called out that lunch was ready. Soft grass cushioned Zoe's hands, and the meaty smell of sausages drifted past from a nearby family who were unwrapping onion-filled hot dogs from crinkled foil. It was noisy but lovely and Zoe exhaled, relaxing a notch at a time. She was suddenly glad she'd returned to the UK.

Her stomach growled as the tangy scent of mustard from the hot dogs filled her nostrils. Five more minutes and she'd tell Jasper it was time for lunch. Tilting her head to the left, she cast an eye at the spot where Aimee was sitting and was shocked to see the hamper and her bag abandoned on the grass, the girl nowhere in sight.

Shooting up, Zoe gulped, scanning the grassy area. Fear lurched in her stomach. Where the heck was Aimee? She should be there, sat down. Oh my god, what if she'd lost her? What if she'd wandered off and couldn't find her way back or someone had taken her? She'd only looked away for thirty seconds. This couldn't be happening. Tendrils of anxiety wrapped themselves around her ribs, squeezing tight. Eyes focusing on the area inside the grass, she examined each group of people in turn, trying to see if a little red-haired girl with narrow shoulders was among them. Nothing. Shifting her attention to the fountain, she looked all the way around it frantically, searching among the cavorting children for Aimee, while making sure she knew exactly where Jasper was. Nothing, again.

Lifting her hands, she cupped them around her mouth and shouted Aimee's name, projecting her voice across the grass. She would never forgive herself if something happened to the girl, and neither would Matt or Jasper. 'Aimee!' she repeated in a bellow, mentally starting to plan her next steps. Grab Jasper, get her bag, alert a member of staff, call the police, call Matt—

A flash of red just outside the metal fence caught her eye. She squinted, breath stuttering in her throat. Was it...? 'Aimee!' The person moved in response, and then a small hand lifted and waved. Oh, thank god. She was so relieved she almost cried, but held back. She didn't want to scare the girl. Jogging over to Jasper, she motioned for him to come out of the water. 'Sorry, Jasper. It's time for lunch and we need to go and get your sister.' She checked to make sure the girl was still in the same spot. 'Come on. Now, please.'

'But I want to play some more.' The boy waded through the water, legs stiff, expression pleading.

'You'll have a chance to play some more after lunch, okay? Right now I need you to come with me.' She smiled gratefully when he heaved a sigh and gave his newfound friends a double-shouldered shrug, as if to say *what can you do*?

'See you later,' he waved to them.

'Thank you,' she said, as she helped him out of the fountain. Hurrying past their belongings with Jasper traipsing along behind her, she opened the gate nearest the banks of the Serpentine and urged Jasper to follow her over to his sister. The girl was standing next to a statue of a stork or some kind of bird with its neck arched over, beak resting against its wing. Made out of a greeney-blue marble, the statute was graceful and communicated a sense of peace. Set into the plinth at its base was a silver coin slot, encouraging people to donate to the park and education centre. Radiating from that were loops of end to end metal plaques encircling the statue in long looping lines set into the ground. They were filled with inscriptions. Some had a simple name, others a longer message with dates.

'You worried me, Aimee,' Zoe clasped the girl's shoulder in a light grip, keeping her tone non-confrontational. 'I didn't know where you were. We agreed you would stay by our stuff, remember?'

'Sorry. I didn't mean to scare you.' The girl didn't lift her head, staring intently at something on the ground.

'That's all right. Just don't do it again please.' Letting go of Aimee's shoulder, Zoe put a hand on her own chest, echoes of the piercing fear bouncing back on her. 'It's important that I always know where you and your brother are. I have to make sure that nothing bad happens to you.'

'Because you're our nanny and you'd get in trouble?' Jasper questioned, cuddling into her side and looking up at her with big green eyes, so much like his dad's. 'Or 'cause you like us?'

Returning his trusting gaze, something in the region of Zoe's heart squeezed and then flipped over. She didn't give a toss if she got in trouble, she realised. It was about keeping them safe, wanting to protect them from all the bad things in the world. She never wanted to see them hurt, or sad.

Oh no, she was falling utterly in love with Matt's kids. This was not supposed to happen. It never had before.

'A bit of both,' she choked out, hugging him close. 'But anyway,' breathing in deeply for composure, 'that's not the point. You both need to stay near me. Got it?'

'Yes,' Jasper replied in a piping voice as his sister mumbled her own agreement.

'Good. What are you looking at, Aimee?' Zoe narrowed her eyes at the floor.

'Mummy,' Aimee pointed to a tiny metal plate in a ribbon of them. *Helen Reilly. Gone Too Soon. 04-06-12.*

Zoe could make out the sheen of tears in Aimee's eyes.

A piece of mummy, the girl had said. She supposed that to a child who'd lost a parent at four years old that must be what the engraved memorial plate seemed like.

'Ahhh,' Zoe nodded. 'That's nice.' Yet the idea that Matt had been sweet and sensitive enough to remember his wife in this way, in a place they'd been happy as a family, a place that was close enough to home that his children could visit it if they wanted to, jarred with the image of him firing and throwing Mel out. It didn't fit. She had to make it a priority to try and find out more about what'd happened between Stephen, Melody and Matt.

'What's nice?' Jasper tugged on her dress. 'And where's Mummy?'

Seeing the panicked expression on Aimee's face, Zoe motioned to the plaque. 'There's a little rectangle of metal there with your Mum's name on it. It's a way of remembering her.'

'Oh.' Jasper glanced at it quickly, but it obviously meant nothing to him as he turned to watch the other children playing in the Princess Di fountain. He was possibly too young to understand the significance of it. Neither did he ask what the numbers were. Zoe assumed they were the day Helen had passed away, yet didn't memorials usually have the dates of someone's lifespan on them, to celebrate the life they'd lead, rather than focusing on the day they'd lost it? Also, where was the usual wording about being a wonderful wife and loving mother?

The plaque raised all sorts of questions Zoe shouldn't want the answers to.

'Are you ready for lunch now, Aimee?' she queried. 'We can come back afterwards if you want.'

The girl lifted her head and scrubbed both hands over her damp cheeks. Something tugged in Zoe's chest again.

'It's all right,' Aimee met Zoe's gaze directly, 'I feel better. It was nice to see her. I told her things in my head. I'll eat lunch and then I'll play in the water with Jasper, while you sit down and rest,' she finished solemnly. 'But can we come here again? Maybe we can come back on Sundays, like we used to before?'

'Maybe.' Zoe gritted her teeth to stop from bursting into tears, the bittersweet comments taking her back to a time when she'd been caught in that awkward age between child and adult and had lost both parents at once. She'd been the bigger sister too, like Aimee. Memories flashed past. Melody's smaller hand slipping into hers as they stood in Ruth's shadowed porch, waiting to start their new lives. The lemony smell of her mum's hair and then the absence of it. The deep timbre of her dad's voice as he told them all a lame joke. The sticky, tangy multi-coloured Opal Fruits (she'd never get used to calling them Starbursts) her parents used to pass to them in the back of the Fiat on long car journeys. She swallowed down the aching lump in her throat. Her life seemed to be a catastrophe of losses of some sort or another. Her parents, Henry, and now Greg. No. She was getting maudlin. That wasn't who she was. 'Right then,' she said brightly, 'lunch.'

Swinging around, she put her back to the Serpentine Bridge curving over the water and the people enjoying the sun, pedalling

124

lazily in blue pedalo boats.

Grasping both children's hands she took them back into the memorial fountain grounds, unfurled the blanket from the hamper, and brusquely set up their picnic. The question of what to do about the attachment she was forming to the children would have to wait.

Half an hour later, Zoe lounged on her front on the blanket, chin propped her hand as she watched the kids play in the water. Replete after a generous lunch of sandwiches, chicken, crusty sausage rolls, fresh fruit, cheese, mini scotch eggs, coleslaw, potato salad, crisps and juice, she felt a drowsy contentment stealing over her. She'd have to be careful not to fall asleep with the sun's warm rays pulsing down on her head. It was so lovely to lie here and watch Aimee playing with her brother. It was even better when she went one step further by talking to the girl who Jasper had been splashing earlier on, the two other boys rushing over to join in with the conversation.

When her eyelids drifted shut and her chin slid off her palm, she forced herself to sit up to stay awake. Grabbing her mini laptop from her handbag, she opened the lid and created a new Word file, glancing up to check the kids were playing nicely. Pausing, she sucked her bottom lip into her mouth before starting to type.

The Truth About Matt Reilly

It's well known that infamous London-based music producer Matt Reilly is fiercely private and camera shy. He never gives interviews to the press, and seems uncomfortable at public events, preferring the focus to be on his artists. In an exclusive story, the girl who was his nanny for X months shares a kiss and tell story about his love life, his relationship with his two children and his ruthless work ethic.

Stopping, Zoe went back and deleted the part about the kids.

It didn't feel right to talk about them. What could she say about his love life from what she knew so far?

Claiming not to have dated anyone seriously since the tragic death of his wife three years ago, Matt told his nanny that most of the women who accompanied him to social functions were friends or fellow celebrities seeking publicity, agreed via his PR Officer. However, we can exclusively reveal that he did in fact have arrangements for sexual-

Zoe paused again, a sick feeling swirling in her stomach. This felt wrong. Hearing her phone ping with a message, she hit the *Save As* button and named the file *Nannygate* before shutting down the laptop and shoving it in her bag. Retrieving her mobile at the same time, she cast a quick look at the kids before opening the text. Surprised it was from Matt, who hardly every contacted her during the day, she stood up and moved closer to where the kids were frolicking in the fountain.

Hi, just wondered
when you'll be
back? May join
you for dinner. M.

She was insanely pleased. He hadn't joined them for a meal since the day Sadie had dropped round. The flutter of excitement she felt at the thought of them all sitting down together was for the children, and only them. She wasn't bothered personally, of course not. Wasn't looking forward to the prospect of hearing about his day, seeing his face light up when he talked about his latest project or turned to listen to Jasper's chatter, like he had when he'd tucked them up the other evening.

That would be lovely.
The kids will be happy.

**We're having a picnic
in Hyde Park atm. Back
around 4 p.m. Dinner
about 6 p.m. That ok? Z.**

She could see the message had been delivered and he'd read it, so was puzzled when there was no immediate reply. Going over to sit down on the lip of the fountain but out of reach from getting sprayed, she watched Aimee and Jasper play with their friends and tried to relax in the sunshine over the next half hour. It proved to be impossible because worry nagged at her stomach. Checking her phone repeatedly for a return text, she chewed her lip. It could be that he was just busy, but he'd read the message so why not take a moment to send one back? What was going on? She didn't like the feeling she'd done something to upset him. Worse was feeling that way when it shouldn't matter. She should want to upset him after treating Melody so horribly. Increasingly though she couldn't square the person Matt seemed to be with the person she'd thought he was from his actions towards Mel. Mind you, she acknowledged bitterly, she was hardly the best judge of character. For five years Greg had fooled her into believing he was one thing, when he'd turned out to be another.

Finally she sent another message, unable to push away the squiggle of discomfort at Matt's lack of response.

**Everything ok?
Will those timings
work for you? Z.**

A message pinged back a few minutes later.

**Yes, fine.
See you later.**

There wasn't even a sign off. The message was either brief or cold, depending on which way you looked at it. Checking the messages she'd written it dawned on her. How could she have been so dense? *We haven't been in three years.* Aimee had told her. *We used to go – me, Mummy, Daddy and Jasper.*

She'd casually dropped into a text that they were having a picnic in Hyde Park as if it had no significance. But of course it might upset him that she was with the kids in a place he'd come with Helen as a family and that the mention of it could cause him pain. God, maybe she should have checked that he was all right with her bringing the kids here. It hadn't occurred to her, she was just so pleased that Aimee was continuing to open up and had thought it was a good step forward for her. Bugger, she'd have to try and speak to Matt before dinner. To apologise for her lack of sensitivity.

When her phone received another text, she hoped it might be her boss adding a polite sign off. But it was Greg again, with a message very much like the other three she'd received over the last few weeks.

Zoe, this is silly.
Call me please.
Lots of Love, G x

She stabbed at the phone to close the message. He was having a laugh. She was silly? No, he was crazy to think for one minute that she would want anything to do with him. Besides, if he was that bothered about talking to her, he'd call directly, not hide behind a text. Not that she wanted to talk to him. But when it came to serious issues, texts were for cowards. She'd been unable to believe it when one of her American friends, a nanny who looked after the four boys a few doors down, had been dumped by text. What kind of person did that? When had it become acceptable to ditch someone you'd been intimate with, in love with even, in truncated written form? If you had something important to discuss with someone, you picked up the phone, or spoke to them face to face.

Zoe sighed, shaking her head again. Hypocritical or what? She'd been avoiding it, but there were a few things she and her Aunt had to say to one another. It couldn't go on like this, especially now they were living in the same country. Even if what she'd done before leaving for the States had been for the right reasons, she'd hurt her aunt and needed to make amends. Especially if she was ever going to have the relationship she wanted to with her sister again. The three of them—Mel, Ruth and herself—might not be perfect but together they formed a lop-sided triangle. At the moment, she was the weak link.

Hitting the contacts list and call button before she could think too much about it, she held her breath as the phone rang, standing and wading through the chilly water while watching the kids. Jasper was giggling joyously as he zigzagged back and forth across the fountain in a game of chase with his sister and their new friends and Aimee had a rare, wide smile on her face.

'Yes, hello?'

'Hi, Aunt Ruth. It's me.'

'Oh, hello.'

'I thought I'd call and see how you are, and if you and Melody are getting on okay?'

'We're fine,' her aunt's voice was as frigid as the water Zoe was standing in.

She took a deep breath, pressing on. 'Good. How's Melody doing? I spoke with her the week before last and have sent her some messages but she's not really been in touch, so—'

'I'm not sure what you said to her, but she was ever so upset,' Ruth cut across her.

'Oh. Was she? We had a bit of a disagreement, it's true, but I hadn't realised I'd upset her this much.' That explained her sister's minimal contact. 'I apologised at the time. Can I talk to her?'

There was a pause. 'She's not here at the moment. She's gone down to the pier to meet an old school friend.'

'Anyone I'd know?'

'I don't think so, with you two being so many years apart in age.'

Zoe stared at the azure sky, praying for patience. No matter what she did, in her aunt's eyes it was wrong. Why did it have to be so difficult? 'Fine. I'll try her mobile then.'

'I wouldn't bother. She's left it here on the sideboard.'

Zoe wondered if that was a fabrication and was half tempted to ring her sister to prove her aunt wrong, but the point-scoring games between them had to stop. 'Okay,' she said reasonably. 'I'll try her later. In the meantime, I thought it might be good for us to talk. The next day off I have, I'd like to come and see you.'

'You would?' Her aunt sounded taken aback. 'Why?'

'We have things to discuss. I'd like to clear the air. I know you don't agree with what I did, but you shouldn't take it personally. It wasn't a criticism of your care, I just wanted—'

'You're right,' Ruth interrupted, 'you need to come visit. This conversation is hardly one to be done by phone. I have things to say too.'

Zoe winced. Of course she did. What a lovely discussion that was sure to be. 'I'll let you know when I can come.'

'I'll wait to hear from you. In the meantime, are you getting any further on with finding out what on earth happened? Your sister still hasn't heard from Stephen.'

'Not really,' Zoe admitted, feeling like a failure. Thinking back to the afternoon in Green Park with her fellow nannies. 'Other than Melody is supposed to have done something pretty unforgivable, though I don't know what.'

'Tosh!' Ruth exclaimed. 'I don't believe it. You need to keep digging.'

'I know. I will,' Zoe promised. Staring at Aimee and Jasper having such a great time together, she gulped. Siblings should always be there for each other, no matter what. 'Take care, Aunt Ruth. Bye.' Ending the call, her shoulders slumped. How did she do right by her sister, while also doing right by Matt's children? If she hurt him, she hurt them.

9

'Matt, I'm sorry,' Zoe said as soon as he loped up the stairs from the studio and into the kitchen later on that evening. 'I didn't even think to ask if it was okay to take them to Hyde Park.'

Not answering, he acknowledged her apology with a curt nod. Striding over to the sink he turned the tap on with a jerk, grabbing a posh blue glass from one of the cupboards. She stared at his broad shoulders outlined in a thin white t-shirt, the shifting muscles of his back visible through the light fabric. Gulping, she leaned over and checked the homemade lasagne through the orange-lit glass on the front of the oven, peering in at the cheese bubbling nicely on the surface of the pasta.

Thank goodness he'd come up before she'd served dinner. It gave them the chance to talk alone while the children listened to what Jasper referred to as *Daddy's Music* in the enormous white lounge. The last time she'd put her head in, they'd been bopping around the room to the latest pop track by one of the cutting-edge girl groups signed to Matt's label. Throwing their arms in the air and shaking their heads, they'd danced with no inhibitions and no self-consciousness. Zoe had grinned with amazement at seeing Aimee express herself so freely, remembering the little girl of a few weeks before who was only interested in reading. Jasper had catapulted himself onto one of the white sofas and was bouncing up and down on it with sweet abandon. Wondering if she should tell him to stop, she decided the furniture must be mega-expensive and should therefore be strong enough to cope.

Straightening now, she spun around to find Matt right in front of her, only a few inches between them. 'Oh, hi.' She fumbled with the tea towel in her hands. 'Wow, you moved quietly. Look—'

'Melody never took them,' he butted in, 'so I've never had to deal with how it might feel.'

'I completely understand. Next time anything like that happens, and I think it could be a sensitive issue for you because of Helen, I'll check with you. Melody probably didn't take them because she didn't want to upset them. Aimee wanted to go though, so I thought we should try.'

He expelled a breath. 'I'm not angry, Zoe. I was just upset earlier. I find it hard.'

'Yes,' she said in a soft voice, understanding his grief, 'I get that. I lost both my parents when I was in my early teens and when I went back to our old house a couple of years later it was one of the most challenging moments of my life. Thinking of the happy times and memories of my parents only highlighted that I'd never have new memories to make with them. Seeing another family living where we used to, a bike I didn't recognise propped against the porch, the eaves painted beige whereas Mum had painted them an ice-lolly orange, a strange tabby cat licking its paws in the garden... ' Pausing, she swallowed past the enormous lump in her throat. 'I think that was the first time I truly started to accept that they really weren't coming back.'

'I'm sorry,' he said in a deep voice, eyes compassionate. 'That must have been tough, losing both of them at once.' Touching her arm, he shifted closer, and she had nowhere to go, crowded against the oven.

'Thank you,' she replied, gazing into his forest green eyes, noting again the pretty petal pattern within the irises. 'The reason I mention it is so you know I appreciate what you're going through and how you must feel about the thought of going back there.' She raced on, determined to stick to the subject and not get distracted by the tingles of warmth spreading through her body. 'But the kids enjoyed it, Matt. Jasper didn't seem to remember it much, but Aimee talked about a lot of happy times when you went as a family.' He stepped back and put his hands on his lean hips, dropping his head. Zoe sped on, needing to get it all out before he closed down again. 'She showed me the plaque you commissioned. It was a lovely thought. I think having it in a beautiful park rather than visiting a gravestone might help Aimee deal with missing her mum. It did her the world of good. They want to go back again. Maybe you can take them once a week or something? Even if you don't have time for them to play in the fountain each time, I still think it would be a nice idea to—'

'Zoe, don't. Stop, please.' Matt lifted his head and she was so stunned by the depth of pain in his face that she sucked in a sharp breath. He shuddered. 'I can't.'

'I understand you must miss her and it would make you sad. But it might be good for you as well as the kids.'

'Yes, that's it, I miss her and it would be very sad.' Matt repeated almost robotically.

She frowned. It wasn't the response she'd expected, or at least, not the delivery of it. 'Can you just give it some thought?' she murmured. 'I think it would mean a lot to them. If you want, I can take them until you're ready to?'

He stared at her so long that she raised a hand to her face to make sure there was nothing on it, wiping her cheeks. Nope, no crumbs, no food.

'You would do that?' he asked at last.

'Yes. I care about them.'

His mouth curved, eyes crinkling. 'Yeah, I can see that.' Nodding, 'I'd appreciate it. Thanks. I'll go and get the kids to set the table.' He swung back around to face her, 'Oh, remind me at dinner I've got something to give you.'

'You have? What is it?' she asked, clutching the tea towel. 'I love surprises. Well,' she crinkled her nose, 'good ones anyway.'

'It was going to be a surprise, but I'm rubbish at keeping them. My face can't lie. Hopefully it's a good one. I thought you might like your own car.'

Her eyes widened. 'Really? I mean, I'm happy to walk and Jasper loves going on the bus, but that would be great. It'd be nice to take the kids somewhere a bit further afield.'

'It's no problem. Just be warned, it's not very flash.'

'Hey, I'll take anything I'm given.' She grinned at the thought of taking the kids on an adventure. About to turn away to see to dinner, she was totally shocked when Matt suddenly scooped her up in a quick hug. Her toes barely scraped the floor and she clung onto his shoulders with a squeak, scorching awareness shimmering down her spine as the heat of his toned chest warmed her boobs. 'Matt?'

'God, you're great. Thank you so much,' he said into her neck.

'That's fine,' she choked, staring up at him as he released her and stepped back.

'Sorry, that wasn't very appropriate, was it?' He looked sheepish. 'Bosses don't usually go around hugging employees. It's just that you've made such a difference to the kids already. I'm really grateful. Melody was nice to the children and they got on well,' a flicker of uncertainty crossed his dark features, 'but you've arrived and straight away seen everything so clearly, everything that the kids needed that I couldn't recognise. Even though we've had some difficult conversations that must've been as uncomfortable for you as they were for me, it's all been to make my kids happier. And they are.'

Zoe gulped, feeling both flattered and guilty. 'I'm just doing my job.'

He waved a hand. 'It's more than that,' he dismissed. 'But anyway, I won't embarrass either of us any longer. You get dinner sorted and I'll get Aimee and Jasper.'

She nodded, mouth hanging open as he loped from the room. She could still feel his body imprinted on hers.

'I don't believe it!' Zoe hissed her annoyance through gritted teeth. She'd walked out of the house, Jasper and Aimee ahead of her, ready to drive them down to Longleat Safari Park and Matt's Prius was blocking her in on the gravel drive.

Again.

For the fourth time in a week. Arghh. What was wrong with the guy?

She'd been so touched when he handed her a set of car keys at dinner the day she'd gone to Hyde Park, guiding her and the children out the front of the house to reveal a smart white BMW 1 Series Sports Hatch. 'Nothing flashy?' she'd said, raising an eyebrow and stroking a hand along the bonnet.

Shrugging both shoulders, 'Not in the same league as my McLaren,' he pointed at the sexy black supercar on the driveway.

She laughed. 'No, but I expected a cheap little run-around or another Prius.'

'I don't do cheap, not anymore.'

'What do you mean?'

He ran a hand over Aimee's red hair absently as she stood in front of him. The little girl rested back against her dad, a tiny smile on her lips, like an adorable kitten basking in the sun. 'When I was younger the first car I bought myself was a second-hand Ford Escort,' he pulled a face, 'it was snot green. You could see me coming for miles. Mum hated it, said it brought the whole neighbourhood down. She's terribly upper class,' he mocked.

Her laughter pealed out as she propped both elbows on top of the car, watching Jasper as he started running round the Prius and BMW in loop-the-loops, arms out like an aeroplane with accompanying sound effects. 'Really? Why didn't your parents buy you a car?'

'They offered, I refused. I wanted to earn my own money and

buy my own things. I'd seen too many spoilt rich boys at school and didn't want to turn into one.'

'I see. What about your brother? Did he feel the same?' She was pretty sure she knew the answer.

His mouth turned down. 'I hoped I'd been a good role model, but no, he doesn't work. He has a trust fund. He bought that yellow monstrosity with part of it.'

'You don't seem that keen about his choice of cars, or lifestyle,' she blurted, before adding, 'sorry.'

Jasper scuttled past, increasing the volume of the roaring engine sound.

Matt dropped his hand to his daughter's shoulder, eyes narrowing as he nodded his head. 'No, it's okay. The truth is, I wish he wasn't so heavily reliant on the family money and that he'd find something worth doing with his time. He always seems so restless, although he travels, socialises and shops a lot.'

'Is that where he is now?' she asked in a careful voice. 'Travelling?'

'Yes, on our yacht in the Med. The poor guy's been through a rough time,' he explained, 'a girl broke his heart.'

'She did?' her voice came out high pitched and weird. What the hell was he talking about? It was Stephen who'd broken Melody's heart, not the other way around.

His eyes narrowed further and he focused on her flushed face. 'Yes. It's the first and only time I've ever seen it happen. Usually he's commitment-free, but Melody seemed to change him. I thought he was settling down.'

'Melody?' She bent at the waist and caught Jasper automatically as he stumbled and almost went over on the gravel. 'There you go.' She righted him and sent him on his way with a pat on the back.

Spinning around, Jasper glared at both adults. 'I like 'Ncle Stephen,' he piped, 'he's fun.'

'I like Uncle Stephen too,' Matt replied, 'and yes, he's fun but we both know he can be a bit of a handful too. Like you, right?' he teased.

Jasper stuck his tongue out with a grin.

As he resumed his flying game, Zoe gazed at Matt. 'Melody, as in your last nanny?' Her heart was pump-pump-pumping in her chest, knowing she was getting closer to the truth.

'Yes,' he looked grim.

'That must have been complicated, your nanny slee—' flickering her eyes at Aimee, 'I mean dating your brother.'

'It wasn't ideal, I'll admit. I thought it might get messy, but when they came and talked to me about it, I felt reassured. I was fine with it as long as it didn't affect the kids. My parents might not have felt the same because they're self-confessed snobs, but I just want my brother to be happy. Besides, I liked Melody until...' He looked down at Aimee at the same time as she looked up. Seeing her features creased in a question seemed to jolt him.

'Until?' Zoe prompted. If he was telling the truth, he'd had no objection to his brother having a relationship with Melody. So what had changed?

He stepped back and stuck his hands in his pockets. 'It doesn't matter,' he muttered, looking panicky. 'It's all over and done with now. It's also probably not something we should be discussing in front of the kids.'

Bugger, he'd been about to spill. She mustn't spook him. 'Maybe not,' she agreed. 'Anyway,' she clapped her hands, 'thank you for my Bimmer. It looks great.'

He relaxed, 'I considered a Prius, but wanted to get you something with a little more energy and power. I thought this would suit you. It's yours for as long as you're with us.'

'Thank you,' she twisted away to open up the boot so that he wouldn't see her wince. How long she might be there for was an increasingly troubling issue in her mind. 'This isn't a bad space,' she talked to the carpet lining the boot rather than Matt. Needing a minute to steady herself.

'It's insured and ready to go. I hope you enjoy it.' Crossing to the back of the car, he came and stopped beside her, touching her arm gently. He waited until she lifted her head. 'Please be careful with my children, Zoe. I'm putting a lot of trust in you. To be honest, I'm very nervous about it. I asked Melody once if she wanted a car, but she didn't have a license. You can imagine how I feel, given the accident, which as you know...' Halting, his eyes rested on Aimee, who was observing them both with pained eyes. 'You know what I'm saying,' he finished gruffly.

'I know.' Zoe nodded reassuringly. 'I'll drive sensibly, I promise. I had to get used to driving in America and it's pretty hectic on the roads over there, so I have plenty of experience. I always got Grace and Ava safely from A to B.'

'Thank you, that's a relief to hear. Now why don't you take it for a spin? I'll stay here with the kids.'

'Are you sure?' How sweet, giving her a chance to enjoy her new car.

'I'd rather you get used to it without Jasper chatting away at you from the back seat.'

'Oh. Thanks.' Not so sweet then, merely practical.

Since then she'd used the BMW, or tried to, almost every day despite the London traffic and everything being basically within walking distance. She loved how smooth and responsive it was, the high gloss interior effortlessly modern and cool.

However, Matt constantly blocking her in was driving her insane. How he managed it she didn't know, but the total disregard it showed and the level of inconvenience wound her up. He was here all the time too, he never seemed to go into the City any more.

The first time he'd blocked her in, she'd gone to his office and very politely asked him to move his car.

'Sorry, haven't got time,' he'd grunted over his shoulder, not even turning from his Mac screen to look at her.

'Please, Matt?'

'I said, I haven't got time,' he ground out, yanking a hand through his hair. His desk was even more chaotic than usual, balled up pieces of paper littering the floor and discordant music playing on the Mac. 'Do you mind leaving me to it? I'm in the middle of something. I'm sure you can walk if you want to go out.'

Just as quickly she was dismissed from his thoughts. It was a replay of his behaviour on the day he'd interviewed her and she wondered if Sadie's continued absence for an extra two weeks was taking its toll on him. It wasn't often he was snappy, but when he was, he was a pro.

In the interest of keeping the peace and because both Jasper and Aimee had been standing in the hallway behind her, she'd backed out. 'No probs, sorry to disturb you.' Smiling easily as if it wasn't a problem, she'd motioned to the children to follow her. 'Come on, your dad can't move the car at the moment, we'll walk down to the park instead, or do you want to take the bus somewhere?'

When it came to the parking situation, he just wasn't thinking, she decided, and he was incredibly stressed and busy. But now that it'd happened two other times with similar results and she'd geared the children's expectations up for a day trip, she'd had enough. No matter what he tried to say or do today, he was moving his damned car.

Leaving the children waiting patiently in the front hallway with promises of seeing monkeys if they didn't behave like ones while she was gone, she hurried down the basement stairs and rapped on the studio door.

Nothing. No answer.

She swore under her breath and knocked again.

Silence.

Curling her hand into a fist, she used the side of it to bang, bang, bang on the door.

Still nothing.

A flash of memory shook her, the action reminding her of knocking on the door of Matt's home nearly a month ago. If she'd known then what she would end up doing in the name of revenge, how much it was costing her when she was falling a little more in love with Matt's kids every day, would she have carried on knocking or walked away?

She wasn't sure any more.

Sick of waiting for an answer that might never come, she grabbed the door handle and thrust the door open, almost falling into the room.

Matt swung around in a chair set in front of a darkened large plate window, his hands on a massive soundboard filled with buttons and sliding switches. 'When people don't answer the door,' he hit a switch to cut the music, a nerve ticking in his jaw, eyes flashing, 'it's usually because they don't want to be disturbed.'

'When people don't answer the door,' she shot back 'and when they speak to people the way you just spoke to me, it's because they're rude and ignorant.'

'Pardon?' He jerked out of his seat, the chair shooting back and hitting the desk with a heavy bang that made her jump.

Replaying what she'd said to him, she crossed her arms over her chest. The air con set into the low ceiling sent goose bumps over her skin and she fleetingly regretted the belly-grazing white vest top she wore with an Indian patterned ankle-length summer skirt. 'Crap. I'm sorry, Matt,' she shivered, 'I didn't mean that the way it came out, but if we're too noisy for you or you don't want to be disturbed, then maybe you should go and work in your off-site premises? I also understand that you're under pressure at the moment but the only reason I keep disturbing you during the day is because you keep parking the Prius across the driveway and blocking me in. All I'm asking for is a little consideration...' she trailed off at the expression in his green eyes, noticing the dark stubble edging his jaw, much thicker than usual. 'What's the matter?' she asked.

'Why do you care?' he demanded irritably.

Taking a step back, her spine hit the doorframe and she winced. Had he found out who she was related to, and why she was here? Was that why he seemed so cross? But if that was the case surely he would just come out with it.

'I care about anything that affects the children,' she replied, 'which includes you. Unfortunately.'

'Unfortunately?' he glowered. 'Oh, that's charming.'

'Well, I'm sorry but you're not being very nice at the moment.'

He went to answer, paused, closed his eyes and took a deep breath. 'You're right. I'm not. I'm sorry.' He went quiet again, jaw clenching and unclenching as he inhaled and exhaled.

Zoe regarded his still pose, wondering if he was trying out some new-age Zen exercise. He looked pale, with crescent shadows under his eyes like he wasn't getting much sleep. With his broken nose and the scar above his lip, he was more bad boy and dangerous than ever. It was a look that worked entirely too well for him, and which caused an entirely unwanted reaction inside her. Knees feeling floaty, a familiar tingle of lust pinged between her thighs, heat sweeping in a slow burn through her body. Her hands curled into fists, nails biting into her palms. She was glad the door was propping her up and pinning her to reality because she desperately wanted to launch across the room and kiss him until it hurt them both. Wanted to have the kind of hot, angry sex that came with making up after an argument. The biting, clawing, sweaty kind that left you breathless, satisfied and purged of frustration. It was wrong to want it with him, but she couldn't control her thoughts, and her body was as traitorous as her imagination.

She moved forward to stand under the air con, hoping the stream of cold air would cool her raging hormones. 'Maybe you need to slow down, take a break?' she suggested into the taut silence. 'Sometimes when you're too close to something it makes it harder to see clearly. Feeling wound up can also make you less productive. I take it work isn't going well?'

Opening his eyes and letting out a harsh laugh, he returned to his seat, stretching out his long muscular legs and staring at the ceiling. 'You could say that. But it's not just that.'

'Do you want to talk about it?'

'Not really.'

There was another drawn out silence, the bristling kind that set her nerves on edge.

'Right, fine,' she said finally, frustration edging her voice as she thought about the eager children upstairs waiting for their fun day out, 'still, having stuff on your mind doesn't stop you parking considerately. If you're not going to talk to me, Matt, can you at least just come and move your bloody car?'

At his continued silence, she shook her head, swung around and thundered up the stairs.

The exasperation in Zoe's tone as she blazed from the room made it clear to Matt that she was mightily pissed off. He couldn't really blame her; she had every reason to be. He knew he'd been rude lately, as well as distracted. He was trying to do as she'd asked by joining them for dinner and tucking the kids up in bed a few times a week but kept slipping back into bad habits. He had a natural tendency to withdraw into himself when he was working, and had to stop himself from resenting every small interruption and biting people's heads off when they needed something.

It didn't help that the new female vocalist he was working with was still completely off-piste both vocally and emotionally. There was no way they were going to meet the deadline he'd set to cut her debut album if things carried on like this. The delay frustrated the hell out of him, made him twitchy and anxious. Something about the girl's fragile manner told him they needed to keep the momentum going or it might never happen. And she was capable of platinum albums and sell-out tours, he knew it.

He'd already started popping antacids like sweets and at times could feel himself shaking with sleep deprivation, catching only a few hours rest a night.

It also didn't help that Stephen had gone AWOL, not answering the satellite phone or radio aboard their yacht, which had last been reported as anchored up in a rocky Corfu port. There was probably nothing to worry about, it was in character for his brother to fall out of touch for days or weeks at a time, but Matt couldn't help feeling uneasy anyway. He'd give it a few more days then start contacting Stephen's international friends and likely places he'd moor up, before approaching the appropriate coastguards if necessary.

There was something else nagging at him too. Talking to Zoe about Melody had made him wonder once again if his old nanny was all right. He'd felt like a bit of a bastard firing and then chucking her out, but after what Stephen had told him, he'd had no choice and tried to comfort himself that he was one hundred per cent justified in his actions. She was just lucky he hadn't done worse. Still, it didn't stop him feeling a sense of responsibility towards her and hoping she wasn't living in a cardboard box somewhere. On the other hand, girls like her always landed on their feet.

As for Zoe, she was one of his biggest problems at the moment, and a definite contributor to his bad mood. She worried at him like a nippy terrier with a bone, insisting he do things differently for the children, challenging him to be a better dad, but what he'd said the other day when he hugged her was true. She was making the children happy and he couldn't fault her for that. The problem was, the living situation was making him ratty. He could think of little else but her. His concentration was shot. The way she smiled with that lovely pink mouth, the shine of her glossy black hair, the warmth of her voice when she spoke to the kids, her big baby blues when she fronted up to him, the compassion in her face when she mentioned Helen, the incredible body underneath clothes that he ached to rip off... It was distracting and unnerving and his physical frustration was spilling over into everything else, amplifying his shitty behaviour. Which included being a royal pain in the arse towards Zoe. Take the car thing. Would it really be so difficult to park at a different angle, or move the cars around when he got home? He sat up, blinking. Was blocking her in a way of keeping her close, or annoying her so she'd confront him? Had he subconsciously been trying to get her attention?

No, that was ridiculous. He wasn't interested in getting involved. His late wife had taught him that emotions tied you down, restricted your choices. Put you at someone else's mercy. Three years after her death Helen still had a hold on him and he didn't know how to break free. There was no chance he was interested in falling under another woman's spell.

One side of him longed for Zoe to quit just so he could have his peace of mind back. The other side wanted her to stay and share her good heart and generous spirit with him and his children. To continue teaching them to be more loving and open than he was capable of nowadays. To show them that independence and individuality should be encouraged, just like he did with his artists, nurturing and helping them to grow as people. He frowned. If he could do it for them, why wasn't he doing the same for his children? That wasn't right. What was holding him back? Fear, or the ever present black guilt? Zoe had said he should think about why he'd distanced himself from Aimee and Jasper, and he wasn't quite there yet, but like a window blind being raised to let in the daylight, Matt suddenly knew what he had to do. Grabbing his phone off the side, he flew up the stairs after Zoe.

As she reached the top of the basement stairs and arrived in the ground floor hallway, Zoe was muttering under her breath at Matt's stubborn behaviour. The children stood up from their spot on the bottom of the spiral staircase.

'Can we go on safari now please, Zoe?' Jasper asked excitedly, skipping up and down on the spot. 'I weally want to see the monkeys.'

An automatic grumble about 'your dad' sprung to her lips but she held it back. It wasn't fair to involve them in her and Matt's bickering. God, they were like an old married couple.

Where had *that* come from?

Nope. No way. Imagine being tied to a bloke who was light-hearted and funny one minute, and distant and infuriating the next. Talk about unsettling. Or exciting, a little voice whispered. She shook her head firmly to dispel the silly thoughts. It was just hormones, with Matt being such fabulous eye candy. Any woman passing him in the street would take in the height, the built body and that roughly hewn face and think the same.

Aimee interrupted her inner ramblings, tucking a stray bit of red hair into her ponytail where it had slipped free. 'Daddy won't move his car, will he?' she asked softly, eyes full of disappointment. 'I bet he's too busy.'

Damn him. Both children had been looking forward to this so much. She played the logistics in her head. A bus or taxi to the station, a train journey to Wiltshire, a taxi on the other end. It might be expensive but Matt was rich enough to bear the cost. That wouldn't make up for the increased travel time though, and it was already gone nine in the morning. Going by train rather than car was going to cost them a couple of hours at least, cutting into the day she'd planned.

She noticed Jasper's eyes welling up and realised she hadn't answered Aimee's question.

Her back went ramrod straight and a wave of irritation swept over her. No. This wasn't happening. She wasn't letting Matt upset his children because he was having problems at work and whatever else it was he'd alluded to.

'Don't worry,' she told them, pawing through the bowl on the side table to locate Matt's Prius keys and stuffing them in her bag, 'we're going to Longleat. If he hasn't got time to move his car we can do it for him, or use it ourselves. He can always drive the P1 if he needs to go out.'

She grabbed her bag and the picnic hamper she'd packed early that morning before the temperature had started climbing. Running a critical eye over the kids, who were both dressed in baggy light t-shirts and shorts, she cocked her head. 'Did you both put sun cream on after you washed, like I asked?'

'Yes,' Aimee said, 'and I helped Jasper with his, and put the bottle in the hamper like you said to. Our hats are in my backpack.' Turning around to indicate the '*I Love Books*' bag perched on her shoulder.

'Thank you, good girl. Right, let's go.'

Throwing open the door she ambled down the front stairs onto the driveway, the gravel crunching under her Greek style sandals. The Prius opened with keyless entry when she touched her hand to door handle, detecting that the fob was in her bag. Cars sure were smart things nowadays. Sometimes smarter than people? she wondered.

'Daddy won't like this,' Aimee told her.

'Oh, well, I'm sure there are lots of things that he—' she broke off. It wasn't fair to badmouth Matt to the children. It wasn't professional of her or helpful to their self-esteem. She was better than this. She smiled brightly, her black hair swinging in her face. Reaching up, she tied it into a knot at her nape. 'Aimee, it will be fine. Come on, get in.' She couldn't be bothered to mess around moving the cars, and would be covered for an accident through the fully comp car insurance Matt had taken out for her on the BMW.

Aimee shrugged her shoulders and clambered into the back whilst Zoe loaded up the boot and took Jasper around to the other side, buckling him into the booster seat while he chattered on about lions and hippos.

He turned to his big sister as Zoe slipped behind the wheel. 'Daddy is going to kill her,' he said in a matter of fact tone tinged with awe.

'Yes, she's very brave,' Aimee agreed.

Zoe looked over her shoulder and rolled her eyes at them playfully, grabbing the door handle. Pulling on it, she met with resistance. 'Huh?' She switched her attention to her arm, and found Matt stood in the space between the car and the door, jamming it open.

'What do you think you're doing?' Matt demanded, a firm hand grabbing her upper arm and pulling her from the car.

'Ouch!' she yelped, unbalanced as he tugged on her arm again, sandals slipping on the gravel. She fell up against his solid chest, gripping his belt to remain upright. His lips brushed her earlobe, the touch making her body do funny, trembly things.

Her mouth opened in shock. 'Matt—' she squeaked as big masculine hands settled around her waist to steady her, their heat burning through the material of her top, a couple of fingers grazing her bare tummy.

He was strangely pale, his cheekbones standing out starkly. 'I said, what do you think you're doing?'

She tried to shake his hands off without success. 'What am *I* doing? I was just going to borrow your car. What are *you* doing? Are you crazy? Let go of me, please.'

He gritted his teeth and started answering but glanced at Aimee and Jasper in the back of the car. Jasper had unclipped himself and thrown himself across his sister's lap, little nose pressed up against the window so that he could watch the action.

'Aimee, can you take your brother into the house please? I need to talk to Zoe.'

His daughter nodded, exiting the car through the opposite door and leading her brother up the steps by the hand. 'But I want to go to Longleat,' Jasper's plaintive voice carried across the drive as he waved his free arm around expressively.

'Shhh,' Aimee murmured, pushing open the front door, 'let's go in and play. Just be patient.'

As soon as they were safely inside, Matt towed Zoe over to the front of the house near the garage doors. 'We don't need to stand in the middle of the driveway in plain sight for this conversation.'

When they stopped, Zoe took a step back at the look on his face. It wasn't just anger, it was fear and something else she couldn't read. Talk about an overreaction. 'Matt, what is it? I don't understand. You wouldn't move the Prius and I promised the kids I'd take them to Longleat so I didn't think there was any harm in using it. If I'd thought you'd mind I would have asked.'

His green eyes fixed like lasers on her confused face. He went whiter still and swayed, dropping to sit on the gravel like his legs could no longer hold him.

'Matt!' Zoe crouched down. What was going on here? 'You're scaring me.' Putting a hand on the back of his neck to check his temperature she saw it was warm to the touch, but not boiling. 'Are you ill? You don't feel that hot.' She sat down next to him, rearranging her skirt so the stones wouldn't cut into her legs.

'No.' Raising his head, he gazed at her. 'Please don't ever get into my car with my children when you're angry, Zoe,' he begged. 'I'm sorry. I didn't mean it. I won't block you in again.'

'Angry? What?' Whatever was going on here she needed to know. For all their sakes. He looked haunted. This was not possessiveness over his car or about proving a point about whose driveway it was. Her eyes were unwavering as they met his. 'I was annoyed, but I wasn't angry. I just wanted to fulfil my promise to the kids, but you're acting as if I'm committing some crime.' He flinched at her words, skin becoming paler if possible, and she felt another twisting pang of unwanted concern. 'Why did you react like that?'

She squeezed his neck, knowing she should let go, stop touching him, but it was like a magnetic force was joining them together.

She thought over the last few minutes. The kids, the car, his comments. 'Is this about what happened to Helen?' she queried calmly. 'Was she upset with you before she got in the car? Before the accident? I am so, so sorry if the situation reminded you of that, but I swear I would never drive in a temper, or hurt the kids. Whatever happened back then—'

'Please don't start telling me you understand how I feel,' Matt interjected, eyes bleak. 'You don't know a thing.'

'What you feel?' She lost her cool a little at that. Forgetting the barriers between them as employee and employer, too cross to care. 'Do you actually feel anything? You're so closed off sometimes. No wonder Aimee is so reserved.'

The statement fell into the silence between them like a dead weight, an albatross hanging around their necks.

'Excuse me?' his voice was hoarse, as if she'd caused him real injury.

'You know what I'm talking about,' she whispered. 'She's closed off Matt, just like you are.'

'Aimee's fine. There's nothing wrong with her,' he uttered, but his eyes were shadowed.

He had his head stuck in the sand if he believed what he was saying. She finally lifted her hand from his neck, craving the warmth of his skin straight away. 'There's being introverted and quiet, Matt, but that's not what this is. She's getting there, but it's still like she's afraid to show emotions sometimes. I'm not saying this to be horrible, I'm just trying to help.' She gazed at the eggshell blue sky, because it was easier than looking at his gorgeous but hurt face. 'Kids learn behaviours from the role models around them. They're sensitive creatures.' Turning back to him. 'Can't you see how much they need you? How much they want to be shown love? You need to show them that it's okay to feel, to have emotions. I'm not just saying this with my nanny hat on, I have personal experience.'

'I love my children, Zoe,' he answered, the passion in his voice clear, 'and I want the best for them. I would do anything for them, including leaving my comfort zone. So if you say I need to try harder then I will, but I have been trying, honestly. It's just not bloody easy, is it?' Frustration came through his husky voice. He cupped a hand around her jaw, his thumb stroking her cheek, and shuffled closer. 'And if I'm unfeeling, then why do I want to do this?'

Before she had time to answer he lowered his head and kissed her. It was tender with a hint of restrained need that drove her wild. Everything she'd imagined it would be and more. His lips shaped hers, tongue slipping into her mouth and sliding sexily against hers. She sighed, sinking into him and kissing him back, murmuring at how good and right it felt. Tingles flowed up and down her spine, boobs swelling and straining towards him, waiting for his touch. Her hands went to his broad shoulders, wanting to push him away, knowing in a dim corner of her mind it was the sensible thing to do and that it should feel weird kissing anyone but Greg. Instead, her fingers clung to his muscular neck and she edged closer to his tall, hot body.

With a rough sound he yanked her onto his lap, pulling his head back enough so that his teeth could nibble her bottom lip. The warm tingles turned into a full on fire, and she wiggled on his thighs, aware of his hardness against her. Lust throbbed between her thighs and if he'd suggested in that moment they go upstairs and get naked, she'd have agreed in a heartbeat.

This was Matt. It was wrong, and God knew she had reason to dislike him, but there was something about him that kept drawing her back, sucking her in, and he was so outrageously sexy her hormones took over. She tipped her head back and his hands curled around her narrow waist, hauling her nearer.

Her hands climbed from his shoulders to the back of his head and into his hair, grasping handfuls of it to hold him tight. She kissed him back with everything she had, completely absorbed in him. She could smell fresh, spicy male scent rising from his stubble coated neck, could feel the thick silkiness of his hair beneath her palms, the rasp of his tongue against hers.

It was incredibly hot, searing and absorbing. The best kiss she'd ever experienced.

And just as abruptly as it had started, it ended.

Matt suddenly tore his mouth from hers. 'Shit!' he said dazedly. 'We're in broad daylight. If we got photographed now, necking like a pair of teenagers... ' he shook his head. Depositing her carefully on the gravel, he scrambled to his feet, hauling her up with one hand. He put his hands on his hips, chest rising and falling rapidly. His eyes flickered over her generous breasts, clearly peaked beneath the thin cotton of her top. She blushed, struggling to come back to reality, praying her knees would hold her up.

Dark colour ran along his cheekbones. 'I'm sorry, Zoe. I shouldn't have done that. Look, take the Prius, and have a great

150

day with the kids.' He smiled but it didn't reach his eyes. 'I need to get back to work.'

'Matt—' she stepped towards him.

'I'll send the kids out to you.' Turning on his heel, he took the concrete stairs two at a time, leaving her standing in the middle of the driveway. Wondering what had just happened between them and what it meant.

10

Zoe cupped her hands around her mouth. 'Aimee! Jasper! You've had your extra ten minutes,' on top of the twenty they'd begged for previously, so reluctant to leave the fun behind and head back to London, 'it's time to go home now! They're closing for the night. If you're not careful you'll get locked in with the spiders and snakes!'

Smiling, she watched Aimee grab her brother's arm and start towing him to the entrance of the kids Adventure Castle area where Zoe waited on a bench, basking in the balmy evening sunshine. Jasper looked longingly over his shoulder then gave in, trudging as slowly as humanly possible back to his nanny.

Getting her phone out, she texted Matt a quick message.

**Hi. Stayed longer
than planned.
Just leaving.
Back around 8
if traffic's good.
Z.**

She didn't necessarily expect an answer. The previous two texts she'd sent had received no reply. The first had been to let him know they'd reached their destination safely, and the second at lunchtime was to ask how he was and say the kids were having a great time. Tempted to put a *P.S. we need to talk* at the end of the last one, she was glad she hadn't bothered when he'd not acknowledged either message. Besides, some conversations definitely needed to be face to face.

'Okay?' she asked Jasper and Aimee as they walked up to her. 'Do either of you need the toilet, or are you ready to rock and roll?'

Jasper looked confused, but Aimee got it. 'I'm fine. Do you need a wee, Jasper, or can we leave?'

'Oh. No, I'm okay. We can go.' Looking over his shoulder again regretfully.

'Come on, then.' She set off for the car through the main courtyard with various closed food stalls, making sure the children followed. 'Maybe we can come again, another time?'

'Yay!' Double yells of glee greeted her question, and she grinned.

They'd had an amazing day at Longleat but it had also been tiring packing so much in, especially with the beating sun so high in the cloudless sky, sweat dripping down their backs and prickly heat making their arms and legs itch. Despite wearing excessive amounts of sun cream and hats, Aimee's nose was looking distinctly pink and Zoe felt a little frazzled. It was gone six and she was looking forward to getting the drive home over and done with, and tucking the kids into bed. As it was they'd stayed longer than planned and were going to have to stop off for a fast food dinner on the M3 motorway services somewhere.

It had been worth it though, Zoe thought once they'd loaded the car up and were on their way up the wide, sedate tree-lined road, heading away from the stately elegance of Longleat House. The kids had loved driving around the Safari Park and seeing the animals in the wide grassy spaces and shadowy forests, winding up their windows to ensure they had no unwelcome visitors for the first and last sections. Their favourite was the monkey enclosure with its '*roof surfing zone*' where the monkeys ran up and leapt onto cars, clambering over them, peering in through the windows and rubbing their rude bits up against the windshields to Jasper's hysterical delight and Aimee's wrinkle-nosed disgust. Pulling off aerials and number plates with a self-satisfied air they passed them to one another to play with and hitched rides on car roofs. Thankfully they'd not managed to pull anything valuable off Matt's car. At the gate a teenage girl with a white stick made sure that park visitors '*took no extra monkeys home other than the ones they'd arrived with*', a sign that amused Aimee no end.

They saw enormous rhinos, dun-coloured camels, graceful giraffes and bright pink flamingos. They fed deer through rolled down windows with cups of dusty food, laughing with glee at their tickling rasping tongues and butting heads. They drove through the leafy forest enclosures that housed the lions, tigers and wolves with locked doors and wide eyes at seeing such magnificent animals up close. No activity or enclosure was left unvisited. The gorilla on his solitary island in the middle of the lake with TV for company, seen on the boat trip in Jungle Kingdom, sea lions coming up to the boat and clapping for the fish thrown in by uniformed staff members. Walking through penguins and standing in the enclosure with them, Jasper chortling when one pooed on Aimee's foot, her face filled with revulsion until Zoe handed her a wipe to clean up. Then there was the winding maze which Zoe solved in a few short minutes, taking the children's hands and giggling as they raced through high hedge walls. The air in the Butterfly House was heavy and humid, multi-coloured tiny wings flapping gently past them and from there they went into the tarantula and snake handling area that Jasper revelled in, but which made the girls shudder. They wandered around the newly opened exhibit of dinosaur statues complete with sounds, before walking through beautiful gardens packed with flowers and heart-shaped shrubbery.

The children even enjoyed the grand luxuriant interiors of Longleat House itself, the three of them dressing up in fur-trimmed cloaks and crowns, pretending to be royalty as they swept through the large rooms with rich tapestries and elegant French furniture.

The flat manicured lawns and fountains outside were just as pretty and provided a good place to rest and enjoy the ice lollies and fizzy drinks Zoe treated them to, though she knew she was probably going to pay for it when it came to bedtime. She'd just craved a day of innocent, childish fun for them. A special day they might remember when they were older, the way she still remembered and treasured a day trip to a theme park with her parents and sister when she was ten.

Sitting down with a glass of wine later on was something she was relishing the thought of, Zoe mused as she joined the M3, leaving plenty of space for a lumbering lorry to roar past. It was Friday today so in theory her day off tomorrow. Whether Matt remembered that or not was another matter. So far on weekends, while she curled up on the sofa in her lounge with a series of thrillers she was reading, he'd tended to drift in and out of the house looking sheepish, or arrange for the kids to have play dates with their grandmother or Noel and Holly. Zoe really hoped that Matt wasn't going to do the same again tomorrow given her conversation with him this morning about the need to show the kids affection.

As for the incredible kiss they'd shared, it had niggled away at her all day, like a label on a piece of clothing that scratches your neck and drives you half mad until you have no choice but to cut it off.

One part of her was mortified it'd happened, that it had been so bloody enjoyable, and—this was the worst bit—that she wanted it to happen again. That part told her to forget the plan, pack her bags and get out. That she was edging into dangerous territory like the lion enclosure earlier and should run now before she got torn apart and devoured.

The other part of her said to stop overreacting, that it had meant nothing, and Matt himself had said it shouldn't have happened. To stop being so damned wet and just get on with things. The truth was, until she had it out with Matt, she wouldn't know what the right thing to do was.

She probably needed some distance and time away from him and the kids after the last few weeks of intensity, so she'd arranged to see Ruth the next day and also sent texts to Rayne and Frankie to ask about a girly night out the following evening. Rayne had texted straight back stating that hell yeah, she was up for it and Adam was a big boy who could amuse himself for the night. Frankie had replied a few hours later, confirming she'd had a cancellation for a party she'd been due to take photos at so she would love to come, her boyfriend Zack offering to drop her off and pick her up. They'd agreed on dinner and drinks, and 'who knew what else' after that. Zoe was looking forward to having a proper catch up with her two best friends, and a bit of advice about her current living situation might not go amiss.

After that, she'd finally got hold of Melody on the phone to see if she would come to London for the night, having a job convincing her that a bit of fun would do her good. When Melody had been reluctant, Zoe had resorted to big sister bossiness and told Mel she was planning to visit Ruth the next day so could bring her back and would eject her sister from Ruth's sofa forcefully if necessary. And, she added, the two of them needed to talk alone and the drive from Southend back into the capital would give them the opportunity. After a lot of sighs, and *I'm not sure*'s, Melody had agreed.

It was gone half eight by the time Zoe pulled up in front of Matt's house, and by then she was seriously dragging and ready to end the day. Looking at the spot on the gravel driveway where she and Matt had sat and kissed, she shivered, flushing all over. Bugger, how was she going to keep it together when she actually faced him? Peering around the front door and listening for her boss as Jasper and Aimee clattered in ahead of her, she was relieved when it was quiet. A few minutes to settle herself would be good. Sloping into the hallway, she slid the Prius keys into the bowl Matt usually kept them in, and set the picnic hamper on the floor.

The door of Matt's office flew open and he stuck his head out. Zoe had to hold back a laugh because it reminded her of the inquisitive meerkats they'd seen earlier at Longleat.

'How was your day?' he asked them all. 'What did you get up to?'

She groaned, shaking her head. That was a mistake; the kids would be talking for hours. As their excited chatter and descriptions filled the high ceilinged passage, Jasper doing his habitual hopping on the spot, Zoe picked up the basket again. 'I'll just go and empty this out in the kitchen.'

'Hang on kids. Everything okay, Zoe?' Matt caught her arm as she passed him.

Fixing her gaze on his left ear and ignoring the tingle where their skin touched, she forced a smile. 'Yes, fine. They've been really well behaved. It's been a long day, that's all.'

'All right. Well, you do that and I'll take them upstairs to start getting ready for bed.'

'Oh, Matt, that would be great, thanks. I'll be up in five.'

'No problem. It's getting late and I don't expect you to be on duty at this time of night,' he joked.

She stared at him. He was so calm and collected, whereas she was a bag of nerves thinking about their kiss. He'd been telling the truth; it really had meant nothing. She should be happy and relieved, but instead she felt flat. Jerking her arm from under his hand, 'I won't be long.'

He looked puzzled. 'Okay. Right kids,' he clapped his hands, 'upstairs.' He motioned them ahead of him. 'So what was your favourite part of the day?' she heard him ask as they disappeared up to the first floor together.

Her shoulders slumped as she emptied the picnic hamper, dividing the contents between the recycling and food waste bins, and the fridge. What on earth was wrong with her, that she should find Matt's carefree attitude upsetting? The best case scenario was that they forget the kiss ever happened, and she finished what she'd started here.

Telling herself to grow up and get over it, once she was done she made her way upstairs, amused to find Matt stood in the hallway between the children's rooms with a lost expression on his face. Trying to convince them to settle down, change into PJ's and brush their teeth, he turned to her with his hands out, *what do I do now?*

'Need some help?' she raised an eyebrow, taking pity on him.

Yes, please, he mouthed.

'Right, you two,' pitching her voice higher to get their attention, she held direct eye contact with each of them for a few seconds. 'We've had a brilliant day, but now it's time for bed. If you want to do something like that again, you need to show us that you'll behave once back home. Let's go. Hurry up. Who can win Zoe's night time challenge?'

Matt tilted his head questioningly.

'It's a task and reward system,' she explained, gesturing at Jasper and pointing at her watch. 'They get to do something of their choice the following day, or pick a treat.'

'Ah, I see. Genius.'

'I'd reserve judgement until we see how well it works, or doesn't work, tonight,' Zoe chuckled, some of her earlier awkwardness fading away. If he could act like nothing had happened between them, so could she.

As predicted, it was a nightmare getting the kids into bed. While she was wiped, they were energised, excited and continued to rattle on about their day. Aimee was quicker to settle with a promise that she could read an extra chapter of her book at bedtime the following night, but Jasper tried every trick under the sun to delay. A toilet trip, needing to tell Daddy something really important that couldn't possible wait until the next morning, another wee, a water to drink, he was too hot then too cold and his bed was too lumpy.

In the end Zoe promised to take him out shopping for a sticker chart the following Monday, explaining that if he could get a gold star at least four days in a week he could pick an item out of her special prize box. Unknown to him, and Matt as yet, she was also going to remove all the gadgets and gizmos from his room and put them in the playroom. He needed fresh air and intellectual challenges, not an overload of consoles and tablets. The promise of reward for good behaviour might help prevent any temper tantrums about the limited technology time.

Matt watched with interest while she talked to both children, and then he hugged them goodnight once she had. Zoe was pleased to see the cuddling was starting to look and feel more natural.

When the two of them finally closed the kid's doors and stood in the hallway, Matt leaned back against the wall, pretending to mop his brow. 'Phew, that was hard work. I don't know how you do it.'

'It's my job,' she quipped, 'and it's usually quicker than that.' She slumped against the opposite wall, exhausted. 'They were over-excited from our mini-adventure. I'd hoped they'd be tired out by the time we got back, but...' she shrugged feelingly.

'Fancy a glass of wine in the garden then?'

She hesitated. 'I'm pretty tired.'

'We need to talk, don't we? Plus, you get a lie-in tomorrow.'

Studying his open expression, she couldn't see how to reasonably refuse without looking petty or like she was upset with him. Besides, a glass of wine outside had already been in her plans. 'Yes. Okay, a wine would be lovely, thanks.' With her eyes on his broad back, she followed him down the spiral staircase.

They were soon settled on matching wooden sun loungers on the decking overlooking the large green lawn and abundant apple tree ripe with fruit. The white rose bed was in full bloom, lending a quaint English beauty to the hidden garden in the heart of London. Vibrant turquoise and mauve flowers in pots surrounded Matt and Zoe, their delicate floral scent filling the air. A dewy glass of white wine sat on a low table between the loungers for her, with a condensation covered beer for him. The air was still warm so there was no need for the cardigan she'd left hanging over the deck railing that morning after her daily dawn coffee. Although they were only a few streets away from the main Knightsbridge Road, there was surprisingly little traffic to be heard, as if a strange hush had fallen over the city.

'Thank you for giving them such a fantastic day.' Matt leaned over to pick up his pint and took a few deep gulps, eyes on her the whole time.

She wiggled on the lounger cushion self-consciously. 'No problem.'

'They seemed really happy. You must have had fun.' He looked wistful.

'I've got some nice photos on my phone if you want to take a look. Yeah, it was a nice treat for them, but it really doesn't take that much to keep kids happy,' she rubbed the bridge of her nose, 'just some time and attention. If there's a fun activity thrown in, even better.'

He rolled his eyes, 'Yeah, yeah,' he teased, 'I get it. I need to spend time with them. Which is why you'll be pleased to hear I've cleared my diary and am spending the day with them tomorrow. I was thinking of taking them to the Harry Potter studio tour.'

'Matt, that's brilliant. I'm so pleased.'

'Actually, I was wondering if you wanted to join us?' he said casually. 'I know it's your day off, but—'

'Sorry, I can't,' she avoided his gaze by leaning forward to pick up her white wine. The curved glass was cool and smooth against her fingertips. She was tempted to say yes to Matt, but spending down-time with them all as a family wasn't going to help her see things any more clearly. Besides, she had a commitment to keep. It was time to finally sort things out with her aunt, if that was possible. Five years was too long a time for the divide between them not to have been bridged. 'I've made arrangements to see my—' she paused, realising it wasn't a good idea to mention Ruth by name in case Melody ever had, 'a friend tomorrow. I'm also going out tomorrow night. But thank you. It sounds like fun. It's probably just as well you get a chance to bond with them alone,'

160

she added, taking a big gulp of wine, 'if I was there I'd probably wade in all the time.'

'A friend, huh?' For a moment he looked like he was going to ask more. Instead he added, 'As for wading in, it wouldn't bother me.'

'But the children need to see you as an authority figure too,' she answered. Deflecting any further conversation. 'Nice wine by the way, what is it?'

'Pinot Noir,' he supplied, looking disappointed. 'Anyway, if you don't want to come tomorrow that's fine. Another time maybe.'

'Maybe,' glugging some more wine back, Zoe exhaled, letting the edgy notes of a Jessie J song spin her away for a moment, tapping her free hand on her thigh. Matt had put the radio on and opened the kitchen window so they had background music and Zoe could already feel relaxation beginning to seep into her muscles. Her eyelids were becoming heavy with wine and a hectic day in the sun with the kids. She rested back in the lounger, tipping her face to the wide, azure sky over the tops of neighbouring houses and trees. It was gone nine o'clock but was still light, with no trace of twilight. However, the blue of the sky was softer and vaguer than it had been that afternoon and the ferocious heat of the sun's rays had abated.

Matt seemed content to listen to the music and stare off into the garden, pint glass balanced on his knee and tense shoulders unwinding an inch at a time.

The silence stretched out, but it was comfortable.

Zoe released a long, low sigh. For the first time since leaving New York, she felt really and truly content. It hadn't been that long since the break-up but the five years with Greg were already hazy, like they'd been part of somebody else's life. It was surprising how quickly you could adjust to change if you had to. She was also surprised to realise it was a life she wasn't necessarily that sad to have left behind. Though thinking she was happy at the time, she was starting to wonder if working in America and marrying Greg would have been settling, rather than truly living. There had been no grand passion between them like in the movies, and she was starting to question if she'd really loved him. The shape and sound of her ex was already dissipating, the idea of him like a mirage rippling in the distance.

The pain and embarrassment of his betrayal was still there, niggling away under her skin like a splinter, but the fury had lessened and relief was starting to creep in. Yes, maybe she'd had a lucky escape. If he'd cheated on her a few weeks before their wedding, then why not once they were married or later, when there were children on the way? When confronted, Greg hadn't been able to articulate why it had happened. And if he didn't know why, what would stop him doing it again?

She glanced across at Matt, his black hair striking against his light grey t-shirt, the fabric pulling taut across his chest and shoulders. This was her life now, her normality. Her boss, his kids, the luxury home, summer in London.

But it was all a daydream, or a nightmare, depending on how you looked at it.

She shook her head. These weren't the kind of thoughts to have in front of him. He might see the truth written on her face. 'You always have music on,' she murmured. 'When you're not producing it, you're listening to it.'

'Music's in my soul, it takes me to another place. I just love closing my eyes and letting the running beat and notes wash over me, or energise me. It can make me laugh, or smile or get me,' he put a fist to his chest, 'right here. It's powerful stuff.'

'I feel that way about reading,' she confided, drinking her wine, the liquid cool and crisp on her tongue with a faint echo of peaches and lemon. 'I can travel to different times or lands and live inside someone else's head rather than my own.' She chuckled, 'No wonder Aimee and I get on so well.'

'Yes, I noticed. I also noticed loads of boxes of books in your room. How come you haven't unpacked them?'

'There's no bookcase to fit them all in, and I've got a bit of a thing about them needing to be arranged in orderly rows, according to genre and then within that alphabetically.'

'Yeah, you're very neat. You tidy up as you go along, your stuff is always folded, you don't leave things lying around the house. In that way you're the complete opposite to Melody, who always left a trail of mess in her wake.'

She nodded and kept her mouth shut to stop from blurting out that Mel had been the same when they'd been kids. It was the only thing she and Ruth had ever disagreed about, their aunt constantly having to remind her youngest niece to pick up after herself. While Ruth thought Melody had got better, in truth it was that Zoe had covered for her, sweeping along behind her putting things away and sorting her laundry.

'My office must horrify you then,' Matt remarked, 'the overflowing bin and all the paperwork. It's not usually that bad, but without Sadie it's got a bit out of control.'

'Yep,' she quipped, 'stepping into your office traumatises me, which is why I don't come in that often. I also don't want to encounter the grumpy troll who lives in there sometimes.'

Throwing back his head he unloosed a husky laugh that made her smile and set a flock of butterflies free in her tummy. 'Sorry about that,' he replied, 'I know I can be a bit of a grump at times. I don't mean to be, I just get caught up in what I'm doing. But I'm getting better, right?'

'A little. But you could spend a bit less time down in your man cave, Matt. It would be nice for us to see you more often.'

'It's not a man cave,' he said with a straight face but a twinkle in his eye, 'it's a studio, and very important work goes on there, I'll have you know.'

Waving a hand, 'It's in the basement, it's dark, you have a mini-fridge in there full of drinks and snacks, and no-one else is allowed in. It's a man cave.' She studied his lean face, the chiselled cheekbones and slash of dark eyebrows. 'Was it always music for you? Did you ever want to do anything else?'

'No, it was always music. That was always the dream,' he spoke with absolute certainty. 'It was the only thing that really made me happy when I was young. I couldn't stand the stilted atmosphere at home during the holidays. My parents are good people—both retired senior government officials and currently travelling the world on Mum's family money—but they're both very reserved. There wasn't much warmth or fun growing up. Stephen and I were sent to boarding school when we were old enough, because our parents travelled a lot for work or sometimes had overseas postings. I used to escape to my room to listen to music when I came home between term times.' One side of his mouth quirked up. 'And when all the other boys at boarding school were playing tennis or learning the violin, I was up in my dorm listening to techno and teaching myself to play the guitar and electric keyboard.'

Her laughter pealed out into the evening air. 'Techno? You don't strike me as that kind of guy. Most of your acts are Pop, or R 'n' B, aren't they?'

'Yes, they are. But I listened, and still do, to all sorts of music. Dance, Pop, Jazz, Blues, Rap, R 'n' B, Opera. Every type of music is inspiring in a different way. Every type of music means something to the person listening.'

'And every piece of music tells a story.'

'Yes,' he grinned so widely she was almost blinded by his straight white teeth, 'exactly.'

'You play instruments, that's so cool. I'd love to be talented in that way. I always wanted to learn something but never got round to it.'

'Actually, I play on some of the tracks I produce but don't put my name to them.'

'Why not?'

'I don't want to be known for being a musician, or have the focus on me. I want to help other people tell their stories. I love working with artists or bands, helping the finished song emerge from the raw ideas and melodies. Mixing the sound until the

164

magic comes out.'

'But what about telling your own story?' she shifted around on her side to face him, propping her right arm along the back of the lounger, glass clutched in her left hand.

'Nah, that would be boring,' he said dismissively. 'No one would be interested.'

'I am,' she blurted before she could think better of it, the wine making her feel mellow and a teensy bit reckless. 'Go on.'

'There's not much to tell.' Taking a contemplative gulp of beer, he wiped some white froth off his top lip. 'There's not that much to add about my childhood and teens.'

'Oh, come on. There has to be. At least about your teens. What about girls, and parties, and hanging out with mates? And if your parents were posted overseas you must have got the opportunity to travel when you visited them?'

'Not really.' He looked uncomfortable, rubbing his lip scar. 'I guess there's no harm in telling you. After all, you are subject to that confidentiality clause.'

'Uh-huh,' she murmured, thinking of the article she'd started about him on her laptop. A squirming sensation wriggled along her spine and she prayed her face wouldn't go red.

'Well, to be honest,' Matt explained, 'they didn't send for us that often. I remember a few airports and an embassy, but really I stayed at boarding school most of the time. To be honest, I was happier alone with my music. Of course I went to parties—I even DJ'd occasionally—and there were girlfriends, but again that was hard because of being at an all-boys school and not going home much. I was part of a crowd of boys, but I preferred to have a few quality friends rather than being Mr Popular. Nowadays I've always got one eye over my shoulder about my privacy, so it's simpler to keep a few people close, which is why there's only really Noel and Stephen. I met Noel when I was eighteen. We were in a house-share together in Wembley.'

'Wembley?'

'Yeah.' He chuckled. 'The roughest part. I was still on my *just because I'm a rich kid it doesn't mean I can't live a normal life* kick. My parents were horrified and would never come visit me there, but it was what I wanted. I had a pretty great time during those three years.'

'Good.' It was fascinating, this peek into the real Matt Reilly. She could understand why he was the insular, passionate, single-minded guy who spent hours alone in his studio, shut away from the real world. After all, he'd spent numerous, lonely years at a boarding school because the people who were supposed to love him the most—his parents—had sent him away for the sake of convenience. Unless that was unfair; maybe they'd wanted to give their sons the stability they couldn't because of their jobs. She realised Matt was looking at her expectantly. 'As for friends, there's nothing wrong with being selective about who you spend your time with,' she added. 'I'm the same.'

'Really?' he looked bemused.

'Yes.' She paused in the act of lifting her glass to her mouth. 'Why are you looking at me like that?'

Putting his pint down, he turned on his seat, mirroring her pose so he could talk to her face on. 'It's just that you're so confident, and warm. I imagined you with a wide circle of friends, the person in the centre of the crowd.'

Her cheeks heated. Although his comment had been delivered in a matter of fact tone, it sounded like a compliment and she felt like a flustered schoolgirl. 'Thanks, but not really. I was friends with a lot of the American nannies in the neighbourhood I lived in for my last job, but it was a loose kind of friendship created by geographic proximity and our jobs more than anything. I have two best friends,' three when you included Melody, who didn't seem to be her biggest fan at the moment, 'who live here in London. Frankie is lovely, just a really nice, considerate person. She works in retail and has her own freelance photography business, and is madly in love with her boyfriend Zack, who apparently is very different to her last boyfriend. Not that I've met Zack yet,' she said with regret. 'Then there's Rayne.'

'Rayne? That's an unusual name.'

'Her parents were new-age. She's a real character. Independent, feisty, outspoken, not afraid to be different.'

'How so?'

'At uni she was the girl with the piercings and the skimpy, colourful clothes who did what she wanted and didn't care what people thought. She still is, to a degree. She has that amazing effortless sense of style that makes me feel boring in comparison, and says what she thinks. I love her individuality.'

'Oh, I don't think you're too shabby,' he mused, before straightening up and clearing his throat. 'I mean she uh, sounds like some of my artists. You said her parents *were* new-age?'

She kept her face blank but smiled inwardly at his awkwardness. There was something kind of endearing about his lack of smoothness when it came to women. 'They died in a motorway smash a year before she joined us at Loughborough University. It was something we had in common, losing both parents. Rayne, Frankie and I got on really well straight away, although I'm a couple of years older than them because I worked for a few years before taking my degree. Rayne's just got back together with her uni boyfriend after they bumped into each other at Wimbledon last month. He, Adam, used to call the three of us the Dark Trinity because we all have dark hair. There's also Lily,' she thought of the petite blonde who looked like the American actress Amanda Seyfried, 'but she's more reserved and was closer to Rayne.'

'They sound great.'

'They are. I've missed them a lot, so I can't wait to see them tomorrow night.'

'Ah, so that's who you're going out with.'

Was that relief on his face? If so, why? she wondered with a nervous jump in her stomach. 'Is there a problem?'

'No, I just thought you might be going on a date or something.

Not that it's any of my business.'

'I told you, there was someone and now there's not. But anyway, it would be too soon.' The fact she'd only split with her fiancé just over six weeks ago should be a factor, but nope, she grasped as she stared down into her empty wine glass, that wasn't it. The truth was that the idea of spending time with another guy seemed plain weird, especially after this morning's kiss. Shit, was she in a mess. Get back on track, fast. 'Back to you,' she said. 'You were talking about boarding school? What happened afterwards?'

He seemed taken aback by the change of topic, but nodded. 'I got some credible exam results but rather than study for A-levels with a view to going to Oxford or Cambridge as my parents expected, I came straight out of school. I took a music technology course, followed by a variety of music business, engineering and performance courses.' He smirked. 'My parents were mortified. It was far too creative and artsy for them.'

'Well it should be about what makes your kids happy, not what you expect for them. Children have to make their own way in life,' she raised her wineless glass in an imaginary toast, and realised she might be a bit tipsy. 'When I have children I'll keep them with me, rather than shipping them off to boarding school. I'm not denying that a better level of education or excelling at sports might be attractive, and it might be the done thing in certain social circles, but it just seems a bit cold. No offence to your parents. But you feel the same way, right?' she paused and he nodded. 'I'm so glad you're letting the kids go to a mainstream school, Matt. Aimee seems happy enough and at least Jasper will be able to see her on the playground if he's feeling a bit lost. It must have been the same for you and Stephen?'

'Not really,' he seemed sad. 'There are seven years between us, so we were in different dorms in school.' Something dark flitted across his face. 'We never really hung out. We got to know each other better when we got older. After Helen died he half moved in here. He stays in one of the spare rooms when he feels like it.

There's a flat in Chelsea but he's never there much. He's one of those people who doesn't like being alone.'

'Right.' Zoe tilted her head to one side. In that way Melody and Stephen were well-matched. Mel had always had a big circle of friends at school, and if she wasn't with them would sit in Zoe's room chatting away for hours, at times bugging the hell out of her older sister, who wanted to be left alone to read. Mel had never been at peace with her own company, so it must have been hard for her living here with Matt and the kids with Ruth a train journey away and only Jemima across town. Zoe knew she'd lost touch with a lot of her old school friends. 'Sorry, you were saying about doing all those music qualifications. What happened next?'

'Well, when I left college I managed to get a job as a glorified tea boy at a tiny music production company and also started putting ads out in local papers, looking for soloists or bands who might be interested in collaborating, or having some free production time from me. I worked my arse off trying to get up the ladder, and went without sleep for about two years while I went to obscure backstreet bars and smoke-filled gigs finding new talent to nurture and record music with, before setting up my own company on the side. There are different types of music producer, but I don't just do the creative bit producing the music and coaching the musicians and artists, I also have a wider role managing the budget, schedules, contracts and negotiations. Of course when my boss found out I'd created what one day might be a rival company they fired me, but by then I'd started to make a name for myself. Professionally speaking, the rest is history. I've worked with some amazing artists and have had some fairly big hits, probably more down to good luck and somehow being ahead of the market than anything else. I have put in a lot of blood, sweat and tears though. Especially tears,' he kidded.

She knew he was being modest by underplaying the platinum albums and worldwide successes as well some of his artists singing at the White House, but didn't want to make him uncomfortable by saying so. 'What about Helen? Where does she come in?'

'Helen.' He rolled the word around in his mouth like it had a bad taste. Looking away, he drank the rest of his pint in one smooth motion and slammed the glass down on the table between them.

She jumped at the sound.

'Sorry.'

'That's all right.'

'I'll get us a top up,' he grabbed their empties and climbed off the lounger, 'back in a minute.'

Watching him push through the doors into the lounge, she rubbed her forehead. The face he'd pulled at the mention of his late wife's name hadn't been one of grief. Her instincts told her it had been more like disappointment, guilt or anger. God, this was getting complicated.

He was back within thirty seconds with two fresh wine glasses and the Pinot Noir in a metal cooler. 'I thought we might as well finish it off. It's been a stressful week, and it's a nice evening.'

'Thanks.' It was probably a dangerous idea but she took the full glass he handed to her, and settled back against the cushion. 'If you don't want to talk about Helen, I'll understand, Matt.' She was such a liar, she was dying to know what the situation was.

'No, it's okay. You've made me realise over the past week that the kids are going to ask questions and want to know more, and I'm going to have to be ready for that. Though obviously what I tell them might be different to what I tell you.'

'Sure.'

'Okay, here goes.' He swallowed some wine, expression pensive. 'I met Helen in a bar when I was twenty-one. She was two years younger; beautiful, smart and outgoing. We wanted the same things, and she was ambitious for us as a couple, pushing me forward, initially handling my marketing and publicity. I'd had the company for two years at that point and was making pretty good money. Exciting things were happening. She loved that I had my own company and brand, and after four months we moved

170

in together. I bought us a house near Primrose Hill and we got married.' He smiled briefly. 'We were happy. She loved shopping and the flash side of being married to a successful music producer; the parties, dressing up, having fun.' Two more gulps of wine went down. 'But then she got pregnant with Aimee and it's like a spark in her died. I feel awful and disloyal saying this, but she just didn't seem happy to be pregnant. After Aimee was born she was more interested in spending money and getting her figure back at the gym than bonding with our daughter.'

'She was quite young for a first child, and possibly overwhelmed. Could she have had post-natal depression?'

'It's possible,' he admitted, 'but she didn't seem low or anxious. It was more like she wasn't that bothered. Don't get me wrong, she was a good mum in some ways. I never worried about Aimee's safety with her, I just felt that she wasn't high up enough on Helen's priority list. After that, Helen lost interest in the business, and started resenting the amount of hours I had to put in at work. When she found out we were having Jasper she seemed uncertain at first but came round to the idea. The first year and a half after he was born were fine. We did things as a family, and I started to think things were getting better.'

'But?'

'She died soon afterwards,' he said, expression set. 'That's it.'

There was plainly more to it given his choice of wording, but he'd already opened up a lot and his face was set in hard lines. No wonder he felt torn about his wife's death if things had been difficult between them in the months leading up to it. She was mulling over whether to prod him about it a bit more when he leaned across the table and touched her arm, distracting her. Shivering at the tingle of heat his fingers produced, she squeezed her thighs together. She would not, absolutely not give into the urge to hurl herself into his lap, to sit across those rock hard thighs and offer her mouth to him.

'What about you?' he asked. 'I know about your education and career path from the interview, you've told me about your parents and an aunt that made you feel unloved, but what about significant relationships? Have you ever been married?'

'Nearly,' she confessed, repositioning her arm so his hand dropped away from her skin. She couldn't think properly when he touched her. Holding her thumb and forefinger up a couple of millimetres apart, she squeezed them together so they almost touched. 'This close.'

'So what happened?' Swivelling around, he sat up on the side of the lounger so the table wasn't between them, leaning forward.

'He cheated. I found out two weeks before the wedding. I found *them*.' It slipped out and hung in the air between them like a mist.

'What? You're kidding,' he sounded shocked.

She puffed a raw breath out, turning her attention to the apple tree. Thinking of the picture Greg had made, twined naked around Shelly like it was the most natural thing in the world, eyes filling with panic when Zoe had burst into the room. What the hell was she thinking, telling Matt about it? It was humiliating, and stung. The wine was definitely getting to her. 'Unfortunately not,' she muttered, wishing the heavens would open and provide a distraction, but of course this was England; it only rained when you didn't want it to.

To her shock, Matt crawled over to sit on her lounger, his hip against her thigh, placing a finger under her chin so he could look into her face. 'Hey, are you okay?' His eyes were sympathetic, his breath warm on her cheek.

'Sure,' she squeaked. 'It's just that... everybody knew but me. And it was with one of the other nannies. Also, I still don't really know why, what it was about me that wasn't enough.' She was horrified when with an odd little pang in her chest tears welled up in her eyes. Oh, jeez. Not now, and not in front of him, not after almost two months of being unable to cry. It must be the wine, sun and tiredness.

'Come here.' Scooping her close, he pressed her face into his neck, a searing hand rubbing her back in gentle circles. 'It's not about you, you're great. It was about him. There was something in him that meant he thought it was okay. But it's not. It's never okay to cheat,' he said fiercely, and she almost lifted her head to ask him if he'd had personal experience, but he carried on talking. 'As far as I'm concerned, he's a complete bloody idiot. Just let it out if you need to, Zoe. You're safe here. You can trust me.'

Everything in her rebelled at the idea of seeking comfort in his arms, for a multitude of reasons—Melody, the kids, he was her boss, it was embarrassing—but he was right, she did feel safe. Tears leaked out unbidden and he held her as she cried. They weren't the racking great sobs she'd expected, they were quieter tears that were more about sadness and regret and release. She snuggled into him, her hands grasping his waist. He moved a hand up to stroke her hair and the two of them stayed there for several minutes while she let the hurt, shame and disappointment go.

It was astonishing how much better she felt for it afterwards and she tightened her grip on Matt, feeling soft and gooey with gratitude towards him for being there, for his understanding. But slowly the gratitude slipped away and was replaced by something much more intense. She became aware of the burning heat of his body. The imprint of his long soothing fingers in her hair and on her back. His uneven breathing against her ear lobe. The tension in his thighs. The smell of his sexy aftershave, spicy and fresh, emanating from his neck.

Pushing her boobs against his chest, she could feel his heart thudding through his thin t-shirt.

He inhaled deeply. 'Zoe,' he said in a warning tone.

'Yes?' Lifting her head, she met his scorching gaze.

Moving his other hand up to her head, he used both thumbs to wipe the tracks of her tears from her cheeks. 'This isn't a good idea. This morning... we shouldn't have kissed.'

'I know,' she agreed, dropping her eyes to watch his mouth as he spoke.

'It's too complicated. You work for me. You're my kids' nanny, and they need you. I don't want to blow it for them.' He didn't mention Helen, but he didn't need to. It was clear that there were some feelings there he hadn't resolved.

Complicated? she thought. You have no idea.

'I understand,' she mumbled, in a corner of her mind knowing she should ease away, let go of him and get to bed. Run away from temptation. But that corner was wrapped in a fog of wine and lust and she couldn't. She didn't want to. Right this moment she wanted to be held by him, wrapped up in him.

Staring into his eyes, she trailed her hands from his waist all the way down his thighs, and then up again, feeling the taut strength under her fingers. He hissed out a breath and yanked her face to his, kissing her frantically, passionately, lips firm, their tongues tangling. He kissed her like he'd been holding back for an eternity, like he was desperate to have her and would fall apart if he didn't. A thrill of excitement buzzed along her veins. It thrummed through her blood and pumped through her heart, making it thud in her chest.

Suddenly his hands dropped to her hips and he grabbed her bum, swivelling on the lounger and scooping her forward so she was straddling him. She gasped, clutching handfuls of his dark hair and holding on as the kiss continued, his even teeth nibbling at her sensitive bottom lip, his fingers digging into her bum. She rocked her hips against him, feeling like she couldn't get close enough, that if they didn't get naked she'd explode. He groaned and dipped his mouth to her neck, blazing a trail of kisses down it, his teeth moving aside the strap of her top and bra together to bare her shoulder. Hoisting her up, he nuzzled his face down between her round, heaving breasts and turned his head to one side. Before she could work out what he was doing, her nipple was in his wet mouth and he was sucking on it in a rhythmic motion.

'Oh my god, Matt,' she choked. Thigh muscles clenching, pelvis scorching with heat, she bucked her hips against him, feeling his straining hardness rubbing against her clit.

Lifting his head slightly, his breath whispered over her naked skin, making her shiver. 'Do you like that?' he mumbled. 'I've been dreaming about doing this ever since I wrenched that stupid jacket off you in my office.'

'Yes! Don't stop. Harder,' she moaned, rocking her hips again as he went back to sucking her nipple. His erection pulsed against her in response, making judders of pleasure race through her. She was on fire, feverish, sweat breaking out over her skin. She twisted against him, pushing her hands down inside his t-shirt, raking her nails over his smooth, muscular shoulders then up to his hair, holding his mouth demandingly against her.

She couldn't believe how breathless and sizzling it was between them. It had never been like this before, she'd never ignited for any other man the way she did for Matt. When he switched his attention to her other nipple, making her moan again, she lowered herself slightly and ran questing fingers down over his toned stomach. When her hand landed on the zip of his jeans, and the bulge jutting up beneath it, he jerked and pulled away.

'Jesus, Zoe.' Grasping her hand, he brought it up and held it against his chest, easing back so there was some space between them. 'We have to stop.' He looked up at her, regret shadowing his eyes.

'Yes,' she whispered.

The evening air hit her bared breast, making the nipple stiffen even more, and with a groan he gently slid her bra and top back into place, before untangling her legs from his hips so they could sit side by side on the lounger.

'Wow,' he said, shifting uncomfortably and picking up her hand. 'That was... wow.'

'Yeah,' she said, dazed, turned on, confused and a little embarrassed. Not to mention guilty as hell. How was this helping her sister, or her peace of mind? She had a tough decision to make and having sex with Matt in his garden was not going to make it any easier. Which was what would've happened if he hadn't pulled away. She closed her eyes, a blush creeping up her face.

'I'm sorry,' he murmured, tracing his thumb over her palm, which made her squirm. 'I really like you, you know I do, but...'

'It's okay.' Opening her eyes, she edged along the cushion and slid her hand from his. 'It was my fault,' she met his stare directly, 'you said not to, but I kissed you anyway. I get what you're saying, and agree. It is too complicated.' Shaking her head, thinking about the two kids upstairs she was totally besotted with. 'It was inappropriate and unprofessional. It won't happen again.'

'Hey,' turning so that his knee touched her thigh, causing tingles to run along her skin again, 'don't be like that. It was both of us, and we're only human. I'm just as bad. I'm your boss! You could sue me for sexual harassment.'

'Oh, hardly,' she blurted, 'more like the other way around.'

He chuckled, 'I think we were both as bad as each other, so shall we call it even?'

'I guess.' God, she was so sexually frustrated she was going to have to take the longest cold shower in the history of the world. A bucket or two of ice might be required as well.

'So, what are we going to do?' he asked, studying her face.

'I don't know.' She chewed her bottom lip, noticing the way his eyes tracked the movement. 'Be adults, and control ourselves?'

He hesitated. 'Okay, deal.' Standing up, he shoved his hands in his pockets and backed away. 'I, uh, should clear up.'

'Do you want some help?'

'No,' he rushed, 'I'll do it.' Clearing his throat, he shuffled sideways on the decking. As he came into her eye line, she realised why he seemed so uncomfortable.

'Oh,' she gulped, her mouthing going dry as she wrenched her eyes away from his bulging groin. 'I'll, uh, leave you to it then. Night.' Bounding up, she snatched up her half-full wine glass and lit out of there like a pack of wolves was nipping at her heels.

Racing through the house on light feet, she didn't stop until she reached the top floor. Banging her glass down on the bedside unit, she hauled her top over her head, stripped her shorts, bra and knickers off, and walked into the massive double shower cubicle. Hitting the switch to start the water, she dropped the temperature to something so freezing it would probably cause frostbite.

Resting her forehead against the wall, she recalled Matt's confident hands on her body, his passionate kisses and the way he'd used his searching, clever mouth on her.

What the fuck was she doing?

11

Zoe's fingers clenched around the steering wheel as she swung the BMW onto her aunt's driveway. Nerves fluttered in her stomach. The whole way here she'd had the windows down and music turned up high, a summer hits dance album filling the car as the breeze fluttered her hair around her face. Usually she'd find the taste of freedom relaxing, but two of the tracks had been by artists of Matt's. There was just no getting away from him.

She'd hidden like a coward on the top floor this morning, making a coffee in her lounge area with the small pod-based drinks machine. Waiting until Matt and the kids had left the house, unable to bear facing him just yet. She had slept like crap and there were dark circles under her eyes when she'd been brushing her teeth in front of the mirror. There was no doubt about it, she looked and felt fragile and should definitely be in a stronger frame of mind for the conversation ahead. However, she kept her commitments, so here she was.

Grabbing her handbag and locking the car she smoothed down the navy dress with the flock of white birds dotting it and squared her shoulders. Gazing up at her aunt's imposing three floor house with the black railings leading up to the open porch, she traced uneasy eyes over the dark, old-fashioned dormer windows in the roof and the twin curved towers at either end of the property.

The place reminded her of the Bates Motel for some reason. There were other similar properties a few roads away that'd been converted into hotels or bed and breakfasts, but Ruth had always been steadfast that this was her home and she wasn't letting people traipse through it and certainly wasn't selling it to developers.

The front door swung open. 'Are you going to stand there all day, or were you planning to knock on the door at some point?' her aunt asked.

Zoe jumped, putting a hand to her chest. 'Jeez, you scared me.' Taking a deep breath and summoning all of her patience and courage, she walked forward and climbed the wooden stairs, stopping in front her. Ruth had aged over the past few years. Her pale skin looked sallow, new lines fanning out from her dark eyes. Zoe was shocked. The woman had always seemed so solid and unchanging. 'Hello, Aunt Ruth. It's good to see you.'

'Zoe.' She inclined her head and stepped back, holding the door open for her niece to pass. 'Come in.'

No response about it being nice to see her too, Zoe mused dryly as she ambled into the hallway and back into the past. Nothing had changed. The corridor was still dim, the skirting boards and high ceilings painted an immaculate but dull white, the carpet the same violent swirl of dark reds, the mahogany banister gleaming with polish. The scent of beeswax filled the air.

'Through to the front room,' Ruth directed behind her, and obediently Zoe swung to her left, pushing the glossed wooden door open and going into the lounge.

'Is Mel here?' she asked, taking a seat on the burgundy sofa and flickering her eyes over the glass fronted cabinet full of expensive china plates and Dresden figurines. Nothing had changed in here either.

'She's gone to London to see a friend,' the older woman said abruptly, 'Jemima, I think. Tea?'

Zoe's mouth dropped open. 'But she knew I was coming. I was supposed to be taking her back with me to London tonight.

We're going out to dinner with Rayne and Frankie. Why would she do that?' What the hell was going on with Mel at the moment? Was she avoiding her? The other day when they'd spoken on the phone her sister had been a little cooler than usual but for the most part Zoe thought Mel had forgiven her for the comments she'd made about Matt and the kids. After all, they'd only been made out of concern.

'I think she said she would text you about where to meet.'

'Right.' Zoe set her lips in a firm line.

'Don't be cross with her.' Ruth's face softened. 'She's going through a difficult time at the moment. The break up has caused her a lot of distress.'

What about my break up, Zoe wanted to scream. I was about to get married. But it wouldn't make any difference to her aunt, who'd always seemed immune to her eldest niece's feelings. Besides, Zoe wasn't as devastated about her break up as Melody seemed to be about hers. But after what the other nannies had said about Stephen and her only glimpse of him that first day on Matt's doorstep, Zoe wondered if Mel had also had a lucky escape.

'Zoe?' Ruth prompted, smoothing her hair back into its low grey bun, 'Tea?'

'Yes, please.' Sitting back as her aunt left the room, Zoe took in the familiar oppressive oil paintings on the walls, the lace doilies on the two round oak coffee tables, the same red carpet running in from the hallway. It was all very old-fashioned and proper. Very unsuited to the grieving but energetic and noisy girls who'd arrived on Ruth's doorstep one winter's day. The wind had blown so fiercely it'd made a whistling sound through the trees, sending rust brown leaves rushing into the hallway with Zoe and Melody as they'd stepped into their new guardian's home. Really, Zoe thought, the house had been as unsuitable for her and her sister as the girls had been for her aunt. Of course Ruth had done her best, but there must have been a reason why she had never gotten married or had children of her own. Still, it didn't explain why she'd always displayed a more tolerant and softer approach towards Melody than she had to Zoe. It was strange, and something Zoe had wondered about a lot of times over the years.

'Here you are.' Ruth had slipped back into the room while Zoe was lost in her thoughts. She placed a silver tray with a teapot, two cups on saucers, a jug of milk, a box of sugar and spoons down on the nearest table. Shortbread biscuits were arranged neatly on a small matching china plate. She sat down across from Zoe.

'Thank you. Why didn't you ever like me, Ruth?' she blurted. Bugger, that wasn't how she'd meant to start the conversation.

'I beg your pardon?' Ruth froze in the act of arranging her beige skirt across her knees.

'You know what I'm talking about,' Zoe said in a soft voice, deciding she may as well go with it now she'd started. 'I'm not referring to what happened in the year before I left, I know that upset you. This is about when Mel and I were growing up, when we were young. I'm not blaming you or looking for an apology or an argument. I just want to understand. Why did you treat us differently?'

'I thought we might do the polite chit-chat thing first, but apparently not,' Ruth tucked her skirt around her legs. 'So after five years, you're finally ready to have a conversation instead of arguing, or running away?'

Zoe felt her cheeks go red. Damn her fair skin. 'That's not fair.'

'Isn't it?' Her aunt's dark eyes were cool. 'All we did was argue.'

'Mostly when I was a teenager,' Zoe flashed, 'and it takes two to argue.'

To her surprise, Ruth let out a low laugh. 'It does. You're right. As for the running away, I'm not referring to when you were a teenager. I'm talking about America.'

'I didn't run away. I made a new life for myself.'

'It didn't have to be halfway across the world.' She raised a hand, palm out. 'Don't respond, just think.' Sighing. 'You haven't changed much, have you?'

'Neither have you.' Zoe shot back, before realising how childish she sounded. They couldn't ride this merry-go-round again. Something had to change. Surely things could be different now that they didn't have an ocean between them. Forcing herself to relax, 'I know I wasn't easy when I was younger,' she conceded. 'I answered back a lot.'

'You were stubborn and obstinate like your father.' There was something in her expression that made Zoe pause. A hint of pain, a tinge of regret. 'But maybe we are both older and wiser now and can talk like adults.'

'I'd like that.' Zoe twisted her fingers in the fabric of her dress. 'That doesn't sound like a good thing, what you said. I thought you liked Dad.'

Ruth sighed, looking troubled. It was the most human expression Zoe had ever seen on her aunt's face. Growing up, she'd been used to either cold disdain or stern anger. 'Do you want the truth?'

Zoe raised her chin, bracing herself for the blow. 'Yes.'

'All right.' Staring across the room at the china cabinet, the older woman set her shoulders. 'Do you know that when your mother and I were girls, we used to play with the figurines over there?'

'Yes, they were your mum's. Gran's.' Who had been a single mum when it was a mark of shame, and who'd died when Zoe was five. The only thing she remembered about her was a dark haired woman with a stony expression. 'They're worth a lot of money.'

'That's right,' Ruth nodded. 'I can still remember the way Susan used to take them out and sit on the floor running her fingers over them, holding them up to the light to study the curves and patterns.'

'Mum liked pretty things,' Zoe agreed, puzzled as to where the conversation was going. But it was the longest she and Ruth had ever talked without arguing so she let her aunt take the lead.

'I loved your mum a lot. She was my little sister.' It was a tiny smile, but it was there. Her eyes were misty. 'I looked after her. I enjoyed it. She was the only one I felt comfortable with. There was only three years between us. We used to stay up late, talking for hours, sheets strung between our beds to make a den. We understood each other.'

'I feel the same way about Mel,' Zoe said, the thought of her sister taking a train to London rather than sharing a car with her piercing a small hole in her heart. As girls, they'd had a pink and yellow plastic Wendy house in the back garden of their parent's house. Inside were quilted blankets and a table complete with tea set. Zoe had always played in it with her little sister, even when Mel was six and Zoe was a teen and too old for such things. But it had been worth it to see Melody's toothy grin stretching her mouth wide, her outstretched hands holding out a brush and hair band for Zoe to plait her fair hair. She missed those girls, so full of happiness and hope.

'I know,' Ruth replied, leaning forward to pour the tea. 'It's the one thing you and I have always had in common. That we feel so strongly about taking care of our younger sisters. I've often thought it was the reason you became a nanny.'

Zoe frowned. 'I've never thought of it that way before. I've always loved kids so it was natural that I make a career of working with them. But I suppose it makes sense; I must have got my love of caring for children from somewhere. I'm not sure about Melody though.'

'Melody loves you and wants you to be proud of her.' She added milk and sugar to both cups while her niece tried to assimilate what she meant by that comment. 'You know,' she went on, 'I never loved anybody as much as I loved your mum. Although I'm talking about two entirely different kinds of love, it's part of the reason I never married. That, and the fact that I was petrified of being abandoned by a man, the way our father left our mother. The bastard.'

Zoe's fingers stilled. 'I've never heard you swear before.'

'Well, it's not a good example to set to children under your care. But I think you and Melody are old enough now that an occasional swear word won't matter. When I was a teenager you should have heard the words I used, until Mother washed my mouth out with soap. Your mum held my hand when I was sick afterwards.' She fixed her eyes back on Zoe. 'I was lost and resentful when Susan met your dad, but once I got to know him and saw how happy they were together, I was happy for her. We were still close, even after they moved in together and got married. I'm not sure you remember but I used to come round when you and Melody were small?' Zoe shook her head. 'Well, your mum and I used to sit in the postage-stamp sized back garden of the house on Sycamore Grove, drinking lemonade and chatting while you and Melody played in the paddling pool.'

'No, I don't remember that. So what happened?'

'Your dad got home one night and heard me make a remark he disliked. It wasn't meant that way but I was struggling to articulate a concern I had and he came in at the wrong time after a stressful day at work. We had a horrid argument,' Ruth shook her head, picking up her tea and staring into the milky brownness, 'it escalated rather badly and he ordered me out of the house. I tried to speak with him a number of times, and your mum tried too, but he wasn't willing to listen. Which is why I made the stubborn and obstinate remark about you. With your father it worked against me, but it can be a strength when you're defending the ones you love.' She drank some of her tea. 'For years your mum and I had to see each other in secret. She was worried it would upset your dad to know she'd seen me, and she loved him so much she didn't want to hurt him. It was very hard. As you and Melody got older she couldn't bring you along in case you told your dad. Which meant as you got older, Susan and I saw each other less and less, just talking on the phone when we could. Which is why you didn't know me that well when you had to come and live here.'

'It sounds awful,' Zoe sympathised, not wanting to contemplate the idea of she and Mel not being able to be part of each other's lives, or having their time together limited. She felt sorry for her aunt, being isolated from the one person she'd cared for more than anyone else. Lifting her tea, she drank a few mouthfuls. 'What was the argument with Dad about? What did you say?'

'They were planning to have another baby. I was worried, and suggested they should wait.'

'They were?' Zoe gaped. 'And why were you worried?'

'She had such an awful, dangerous birth with Melody I was worried it was too much of a risk to have another baby. The doctors told her it wasn't a good idea. Your dad thought I was trying to interfere, to make your mum's decision for her. He was worried she would be swayed by me instead of talking to him about it, who of course was the person she should make that decision with. I wasn't trying to influence or persuade her, I was simply expressing a concern. I thought they should wait a bit longer. Melody was only one at the time.'

'But you were just looking out for her!' Zoe said, trying to reconcile the man her aunt was describing with the laughing, easy going dad she remembered.

Ruth shrugged, tightening her grip on the fine china. 'It doesn't matter now. What matters is that for the last few years of my sister's life I didn't have the relationship with her that I'd had before. And I blamed your father. I also blamed him for your mother's death.'

'What?' Zoe placed her cup on the saucer with trembling hands. 'But it was an accident, right?' She closed her eyes, fearing her aunt was about to rip her world all apart. That she was going to say her dad had been driving recklessly, or worse, drink driving. That it was his fault his daughters had been orphaned. She'd asked for the truth though, and would have to face it.

'Yes,' Ruth said, and Zoe's eyes sprang open. 'Yes, it was an accident. There was no fault found against your father. Except that the day they died he'd turned up here, having found out she'd come to see me because of something you said. He made her leave. I tried to apologise again, explain my comment from all those years before, but he was too angry at your mum for

185

lying about where she was going to listen to me. The last time I saw her, she was looking at me through the window, mouthing that she'd call me later.' Her face creased up with grief. 'If only he hadn't made her leave. If only they had stayed and had a cup of tea and talked it through.'

'Something I said?' Zoe screwed her face up, trying to remember the traumatic day her parents had died. She'd been thirteen, Melody seven. She'd been in year eight at school, and on the school newspaper. Staying behind to work in the library with other pupils on the second issue, she'd returned home just after five to find her mum gone and her dad sitting at the kitchen table with a newspaper.

'Good day at school?' he asked as she shrugged out of her navy school blazer and went over to the fridge for a glass of milk. 'Let me guess,' his blue eyes crinkled and he pushed a hand through his black hair as she looked over her shoulder at him, 'you learnt loads and got another grade A?'

'Ha-ha,' she answered, shutting the fridge and turning around. 'But yeah, pretty much. Where's Mel?'

'At Mrs Briar's until half past.' The lady two doors down who picked her sister up from primary school three times a week so her mum could work at an upmarket clothes shop in town. 'Do you know where your mum is? I called the shop and they said she left at four today.'

'I overheard her talking on the phone last night when you were in the bath,' she replied carelessly, sitting across from him and wiping a hand across her mouth to get rid of any milk moustache. She tightened her high ponytail where it had started slipping out. 'I think she was going to visit a friend.'

'Oh?' he pushed the newspaper aside and there was a tension to his body language Zoe didn't understand.

'What's the matter?' she asked as he stood up, reaching for his car keys off the kitchen counter. 'Are you angry?'

'Of course not,' he reassured, although a vein was standing

out on his forehead, 'your mum's allowed to have friends. I don't suppose you know which one it was?'

Zoe stood up, sensing something was wrong. 'No, I didn't get a name, but there was something about meeting at the beach where they used to go?'

'Right,' he rammed the chair into place at the table. 'Zoe, can you go and get Melody in ten minutes or so? I'm going to go and see if your mum needs a lift home. We won't be long. Just watch TV or something, okay?' he ruffled her hair as he went past.

She squirmed and moved away. 'Dad, I've told you not do that. I'm not a kid anymore.'

'You'll always be my kid,' he dropped a kiss on her head, striding for the door. 'Love you, Zo.'

'That was the last time I saw him,' Zoe told her aunt as they sat together. 'I waited for two hours before I started to get worried, but Melody started getting upset and I didn't know what to do. That's when I went back to Mrs Briar's and she called the police and we were told that...' She brought a hand to her mouth, biting her knuckles as she remembered the two policemen turning up on their neighbour's doorstep, their faces solemn and drawn. Her stomach churned, eyes growing moist. 'If I'd have known that telling him that would lead to... Oh, God.'

'You couldn't have known what would happen, Zoe. You were a child. It wasn't your fault. I knew that, but it didn't stop me resenting you,' she admitted, looking ashamed, 'especially when you look so much like your dad, and have his confidence and stubborn streak. I was so angry with him.' Shaking her head. 'As for Melody—'

'She looks so much like Mum,' Zoe finished, 'it was natural that you'd want to be with her.'

'But it was wrong of me to treat you differently, Zoe. You're both Susan's daughters. She loved you equally, so I should have too.' She came over to sit with her niece. 'I'm sorry. I was wrong.'

'Thank you. I-I really appreciate you saying that, and explaining this all to me even though it must have been so painful.' Heaving out a shuddering breath. 'I'm sorry too. For trying to get Melody to leave you in that last year before I left for the States. Just because I wasn't happy here, it doesn't mean Mel wasn't. I assumed she'd want to live with me. I said some unforgivable things to you.'

She gripped her aunt's hand, trying to communicate how much she regretted her words and actions, 'I never should have asked her to choose between us. You looked after us after our parents died and I'm grateful for that. You were never cruel or hurtful, you put a roof over our heads and fed us. You just weren't warm and loving the way I needed you to be. I guess what it came down to was that you weren't Mum and Dad.' Ruth nodded, eyes looking suspiciously damp.

'I also shouldn't have threatened to try and get custody of her from you.' Zoe shook her head, hardly believing her cheek. 'It was stupid. She was sixteen for God's sake, nearly an adult, and I wasn't even in my mid-twenties. It was just that I was madly in love with Henry and caught up in the fairytale, with the idea of the three of us being a happy family. When Melody said she was staying with you and Henry broke up with me, I could hardly cope. I was lost. I guess that's why when I met Greg a few weeks later, he bowled me over. I was on the rebound.' As she said it, she knew it was the absolute truth. The sense of relief she'd felt about the break up the night before doubled.

'He swept you off your feet,' Ruth agreed, 'the rich American promising you the world.'

'I could be a nanny anywhere,' Zoe said, 'America was as good as any place, especially as he could pull strings for my visa. But maybe you're right, maybe I ran away.' She surprised both of them by clattering her cup down on the table and hugging her aunt.

Ruth stiffened but didn't pull away, her slight frame trembling in Zoe's arms. 'Five years.' Zoe murmured, sitting back. 'It's a long time. But I'm home now. We could try and get to know each other properly if you want to? I know it'll take some time.'

'Yes, that would be nice,' Ruth wiped something from her eye, blinking hard. 'I've never been an affectionate type of person, Zoe. Probably because Mother was so cold. But you girls are the only family I have, so I'll try to unbend a little.' Standing up, she tried for a smile, the expression looking odd on her face. 'Shall we go for a walk down by the beach? There will be a lot of tourists out because the weather's so pleasant, but it would be nice to get some fresh air. We could have an ice-cream, if you like.'

Zoe pushed off the sofa, feeling clean and light, as if a weight she hadn't known she'd been carrying had been lifted. 'Like when we used to go down on Sunday afternoons, and skip stones?' She paused, remembering the day she'd managed five skips in a row. Ruth had let her have a double scoop and dripping chocolate sauce on her Mr Whippy from the ice-cream van as a reward. Of course Melody had wanted the same as her older sister, so Ruth had bought her one, but Zoe hadn't minded. Maybe her teenage years with her aunt hadn't been all bad.

'Yes.' Ruth stood up. 'So, young lady. I know you're living in London and trying to figure out what happened to your sister with those Reilly boys, but apart from that, what's your plan? What's next for you?'

Zoe gulped, her mind drifting to Melody, Matt and the kids. 'I don't know, Aunt Ruth. I really don't.'

Zoe smiled as she heard the children clatter into the hallway, the front door slamming behind them.

'Hang on,' she heard Matt yell as they thundered upstairs, 'Zoe might be busy doing something.'

'Zoe's not doing anything,' she called, making her way carefully downstairs to the first floor in her red stilettos. 'How was your day?' Holding her arms open so that kids could give her a hug.

Aimee and Jasper raced forward and cuddled into her, babbling about Harry Potter and Hagrid, Diagon Alley and Butter Beer, which daddy had hated and Jasper had loved, and Aimee had said tasted like sick.

'You look pretty, Zoe.' Aimee said, leaning back and looking up into Zoe's face.

'Thank you.' Zoe nodded. 'So do you,' tweaking her nose, she pointed at Aimee's fashionable nautical jumpsuit.

'You look like Snow White,' Jasper bounced up and down on the spot.

'I do?' Zoe cast a look down at her short black and red kimono style dress. She'd bought it that afternoon on Oxford Street after returning from Ruth's, feeling like a changed person and wanting the wardrobe to go with it. It was funny how one meaningful, cathartic conversation could make you see things in an entirely different light. 'Well, apparently Japanese styles are trending this summer. But I thought Snow White wore a nice flowing princess dress.' Thinking of the famous Disney animated film.

'Not in the version with Chris Hemsworth as the Huntsman,' Matt said, stepping into the hallway. 'But I think Jasper is referring to the black hair, fair skin and blue eyes.' Dipping his head, 'And, wow by the way.'

'Thanks.' She blushed at the appreciative look on his face, glad she'd decided to keep her make-up simple because the dress was so bold, choosing to line her eyes with black kohl and slick on some red lipstick. 'I'm going to have to get going actually. Come on kids, let's go downstairs and you can see me off.'

'But we've only just said hello,' Jasper protested.

'I'm only going out for the night, and you can see me tomorrow as long as you don't wake me too early. Maybe your dad will let you have a movie night. That way he can relax for a bit before you go to bed. I'm sure you tired him out today.'

Matt looked at her gratefully before switching his attention to the children. 'That's a fantastic idea. You can pick something you both like, and I might call for pizza and even let you have some popcorn. Why don't you go and have a look at the DVD's, so Zoe can get going?'

'Okay,' Aimee nodded at her brother, and they both released

their nanny and ran for the stairs. 'Come on.'

As they disappeared, Matt turned to Zoe and offered her an arm. 'Those heels are pretty high and the carpet's pretty deep. Do you need a hand down the stairs?'

'I should be all right, thanks.' It was thoughtful of him, and she loved a guy who knew how to be a gentleman, but keeping some space between them was necessary at the moment. Otherwise she might be tempted to jump him. He was looking particularly gorgeous in a pair of jeans and a black open necked shirt. His green eyes looked amazing, practically glowing against the darkness of the top. 'Oh.' She looked down at her shoes nestling in the fluffy beige carpet. 'Unless you want me to take them off? Sorry, I should have thought. If it helps, they're new, so they're clean.'

'Don't be silly. I don't care about that.'

'Well, I'm sure I can manage one flight of stairs.' She strode towards him, but as she reached the top step her ankle turned. Stumbling forward, she let out a squeak of alarm, but his arm was already under hers, holding her upright.

'Whoa! I've got you.'

'Thank you.' Her heart was racing at the prospect of a headlong tumble down the stairs. 'Seems like I overestimated myself,' she said with a twist of her lips. Bloody hell, it was typical. Just because she'd insisted she was fine, this had to happen.

'Or underestimated the shoes,' Matt replied, fighting back a smile.

'Oh, shut up,' she grumbled good naturedly. 'You were right, okay?'

'I always am,' he quipped.

They walked down slowly, their shoulders rubbing and their thighs occasionally brushing.

She gulped, heat rising up her chest and into her cheeks. Why did she have to be so ultra-aware of him? It was like every cell in her body was straining towards every cell in his, wanting to mesh and create sparks.

191

'That really is a stunning dress,' he said as they arrived in the hallway. Pointing at the slit, where her bare thigh was peeking out. 'Particularly that bit.'

His eyes rose to stare into hers, and she couldn't look away. He was still holding her arm, his fingers sending tingles down into her hands, which curled into fists. She could feel the scorching heat of his body only a few inches from hers, and forced herself to breathe normally. Panting would be so lame.

'I'm a bit worried about you going out like that actually,' Matt confided.

'What do you mean?'

'Well, it would be easy for some handsome, rich guy to swoop you up, looking like that.'

'And? What's the problem with that?' she raised an eyebrow.

'Well, before you know it he'd be wining and dining you, taking you out for fancy meals and inviting you to his private yacht for a holiday in the Maldives, and then you'd be swanning off to be put up in his penthouse flat by the Thames.' He looked mournful, but she could see a teasing glint in his eye. 'The kids would be devastated.'

'They would?' She daren't ask him how he'd feel, that was far too dangerous. 'You got all that from one dress?'

'I did.' He shook his head, the scent of his sexy aftershave weaving into the tiny space between them. 'It's easy for the imagination to run wild when we're talking about a dress like that.'

'The dress apologises for any offence it causes,' she laughed, 'but it's staying on and I'm going out. Don't worry, I'll be good. I'm not after hooking up with any millionaires any time soon.' *At least, none that live outside this house*, a sneaky shocking voice whispered in her head.

'Fair enough. It's just that I heard Henry Cavill hangs around these parts.' His fingers traced down her arm and she shivered in reaction. 'Please promise you'll look after yourself though?'

'I'll be with friends, don't worry.' Whether Melody was going to be there was still an unknown. Earlier on she'd texted the name of the restaurant they'd be at with the ETA, and all she'd got back in response was an '*okay, thanks*.' She had to sort things out with her sister. With that promise in mind, she managed to step back from Matt. 'I should go.'

'Do you want me to give you a lift, or come and pick you up?'

'That's kind, but not part of the terms and conditions of my contract,' she answered, deliberately reminding him she was his employee. She had to use anything she could to create a barrier between them while she got her head together. 'Besides, you need to feed the children soon and you'd have to get them out of bed later to come and get me, and that's not fair to them. I'm also planning to have a few glasses of wine tonight and I'm not sure I'd want you to see me in that state, or vice versa,' she joked.

'All right, but at least use the black cab company I have on retainer.'

'You don't have limos or a corporate car hire firm taking you places when you don't want to drive?'

'I don't like to attract attention, and I'll definitely do that if I go everywhere in flash cars. I like the anonymity of black cabs.'

'What about the McLaren P1?' she said, 'A high performance supercar is hardly subtle is it?'

'That's different. I love that car. Besides, good sense can't win out all the time, can it? Anyway, I have an account with the cab firm. Put the fare under my name. Call it a perk, but I just want to make sure you get back safely, no matter what time it is. They'll look after you. Here,' he dug his wallet out of his pocket and handed her a business card.

She stroked the glossy, embossed card, 'Thanks. I'm getting the bus there but I'll take advantage on the way back.'

'No problem.' He smirked, 'I don't expect to have to hold your hair back for you when you get in though. If you come home drunk and feeling ill, you're on your own.'

'Have you done that for many women?' she wrinkled her nose.

'Only Helen, she had the worst morning sickness when she was pregnant with both the children. She used to spend at least two hours every morning slumped on the bathroom floor. I used to get her ginger biscuits and provide damp flannels. Sometimes I'd sit in there with her and read *Vogue* to take her mind off things.'

'That's sweet.' When she'd been unwell with Greg he'd swerved away sharply, like a London bike rider around an open car door. He wouldn't see her again until she was better. *I just wanna give you space to get better baby,* he'd say, looking concerned. But maybe the concern had all been for himself. It was the only real reason she could think of why she'd had to rely on the other nannies to bring her soup and other provisions when ill.

'I don't know about sweet,' Matt said. 'It was just right. I was half to blame for her being in that state.' He frowned. 'I hadn't thought about that for a while.'

'I'm sorry. I didn't mean to bring back painful memories for you.'

'No, it's fine. I brought it up. And they weren't all painful.' He added in an odd voice, like it had only just occurred to him.

'Daddy, we've chosen a film now!' Jasper's voice echoed along the hallway. 'We're hungry too.'

Matt jumped. 'I shouldn't keep you, Zoe. You'll be late. Have fun tonight. You deserve it, you've worked hard.'

'Thanks, I plan to.' Grabbing her clutch purse off the side from where she'd left it earlier, she flung open the door.

'Aren't you taking a jacket or anything?' Matt asked, following her out.

'No, Dad,' she rolled her eyes. 'It's August, Matt. It's warm. I'll be fine.'

'If you say so,' he raked one last look over her outfit, 'just make sure the dress behaves itself.'

'I will,' she giggled, shaking her head. Swinging around, she picked her way carefully down the concrete steps and over the gravel driveway. Turning back to wave at him, a thought occurred to her. 'Oh, by the way, Jasper birthday's coming up in less than two weeks, isn't it? What have you got planned?'

A look of horror crossed Matt's face, dark eyebrows drawing together. 'Oh, shit. Nothing. Melody usually plans his parties. Jesus,' he threw a quick glance over his shoulder to check the hallway. Scrubbing his hands through his hair, he muttered. 'Oh, this is bad. Really bad. I am a bad parent.'

He appeared so guilty she didn't have the heart to agree. 'You're not a bad parent, it's just slipped your mind because you've been so busy. Don't worry. We'll sort something out.'

'We?'

'If you want me to help I will, but you have to be involved this time.'

He nodded. 'Sounds fair.'

'We can sit down and discuss it tomorrow, but not until the afternoon. I'll be sleeping in.'

'Deal. Have a nice night. Remember what I said about those millionaires. We've only just found you. My kids aren't ready to lose you.'

Nodding, she made for the pavement, striding as quickly as she could away from the house and its owner. Tears stood out in her eyes. She wasn't ready to lose them either. Any of them. When, she wondered, had it started becoming more about that than about getting justice and the truth for Melody? Was she once again failing her sister?

12

Clattering off the red double-decker bus in her matching stilettos, Zoe made her way through the cobblestoned alleyway into Soho, heading for the trendy bar-restaurant Rayne had chosen. Tonight she was just a twenty-something girl on the town, she'd decided on the way. She needed to have some fun. Life had been far too serious and stressful recently. The air was balmy, the summer night was young, London was pulsing and she was about to spend time with some of her most favourite people in the world.

As she approached the entrance to the bar, an orange neon sign hanging above the doorway, a group of middle-aged men in suits spilled out into the street. A few raucous laughs echoed between them, and a few 'good evenings' were tossed her way, along with a 'Wahey, nice dress love'. The comment made her think of Matt. *Stop it.* 'Thanks, lads,' she grinned.

Most of the group moved past her, but one guy with blonde hair and a shading of stubble stopped and held the door open, leering admiringly as her thigh slipped out of the dress as she stepped forward. Rolling her eyes at how blatant he was, she thanked him and slipped past into the bar, a low hum of conversation and pumping background music filling the space. The man took her eye-roll with good humour, acknowledging it with a nod. She shook her head. Didn't men realise how obvious they were, and that largely speaking, it wasn't a turn on? She smiled wryly. Typical English blokes.

But his cocky demeanour made her realise it was good to be home, good to be back in the UK. As much as she'd enjoyed the experience of living in another country and how great living in sprawling, thrilling New York had been, being in London and visiting Southend had shown her something. While she'd been wholly committed to staying in the States with Greg, this was where her heart was. It's where it would always be. And two of the best reasons for that were somewhere in this room. She hoped that the third would decide to turn up tonight as well. She missed her sister. Returning to the UK, Zoe had hoped they would spend time together, but instead all they'd done was spend it apart.

Her eyes swept over the heavy slab of glass that was the bar, balanced on two black pillars with blue up-lighters beneath it. Plush black sofas were set against designer blue and black printed wallpaper and islands of chest-high round tables and stools filled the room. The restaurant was off to the side and Rayne had texted to say she'd booked a table for half past seven. They'd agreed on drinks first, and she couldn't wait until she had a cocktail in her hand.

First she spotted Rayne waving madly at her from one of the tables with glasses dotted on it, chunky cocktail rings flashing on her long fingers. Then Frankie turned and beamed at her, sweeping her jaw length black hair behind her neat ears. With a massive sigh of relief, Zoe saw Melody occupying a third stool at the table, a small sad smile on her face.

Dashing across the dark wooden floor towards them, Zoe threw her handbag down and grabbed Melody in a fierce hug. 'I didn't think you'd come. Why didn't you stick around for me to bring you back, like we agreed? Are you still cross with me?'

Melody eased away, 'I didn't want to sit around waiting for you. I wanted to see Jemima. No, I'm not cross with you. We're okay.' But her eyes didn't meet Zoe's for long, and she untangled herself to reach for her wine.

'Hey, you,' Rayne exclaimed, brushing her blunt fringe out of her eyes and wrapping her arms around Zoe. 'It's fab to see you. You look incredible. You've managed to put a bit of weight on, I see.'

Zoe laughed, 'Just come right out and say it, Rayne. Are you trying to tell me I look fat?' Putting her hands on her hips.

'Noooo, of course not. It's just that the last time I saw you, you were far too skinny. I could almost see your ribs. You're looking much healthier now. It suits you. You look a lot better than I expected actually, under the circumstances.'

'Gee, thanks. You really don't hold back do you? You look fantastic too by the way.' She admired Rayne's gorgeous sapphire cutaway dress, swatches of fabric cut out on both sides of the waist to reveal silky bronzed skin.

'Aww, thanks. And you know I love you, sweetie,' Rayne pinched Zoe's cheeks playfully. 'We also know each other well enough that I can say what I think.'

'Except you do it with everyone,' Frankie said, giving Rayne a teasing look and standing up. 'Let her go. It's my turn.' Scooping Zoe into a hug, she whispered in her ear, 'It's so nice to see you.'

'You too,' Zoe smiled as they broke apart. 'I'm loving the hair.'

Frankie pulled a face, unusual violet-coloured eyes amused. 'It's taken about eight months for it to get to a length I'm happy with. My friend Davey is a hairdresser and he cut it really short just after Christmas. While I was panicking about the amount of hair on the floor, he was telling me not to worry because it made me look like Frankie from *The Saturdays*.'

'It looked cool,' Rayne said, hopping onto her stool and crossing her legs. 'Stop moaning. Besides, Zack liked it, didn't he?'

Frankie stuck her tongue out at her friend, jumping onto her own stool and pointing to the fourth one for Zoe. 'Zack's a love-sick idiot,' she smirked, 'he'd like me even if Davey had shaved all my hair off.'

'I don't think Zack's the only lovesick idiot,' Zoe noted as she climbed carefully onto her stool, mindful of her short dress, 'you look the prettiest I've ever seen you.' She gestured at her friend's clear glowing skin, taking in the tight black jeans, high heeled boots and this season's neon yellow top. 'I guess ditching the rich guy for the sweetheart has worked out for you, huh?'

'It has. Although there was a year's break in between them. I have to admit, I used to hate being stuck in a cramped, damp flat above a kebab shop, but I don't really care anymore because I've got Zack. Speaking of which...'

'What?' Zoe could see Frankie was desperate to share some news. 'Go on, just spit it out.'

'Ooh, what have you been hiding, you sneaky thing?' Rayne leaned forward eagerly, elbows on the table.

'Zack and I are moving in together!' Frankie grinned, eyes sparkling.

'That's amazing! Congratulations,' Zoe screeched, drawing the attention of the next table over. Oops. She slid down in her seat, lowering her voice. 'I mean, congratulations, I'm really happy for you.'

'That's ace, Franks,' Rayne toasted her friend. 'Spill the details then.'

'Well, we've both given notice on our tenancy agreements and we're getting a new place together in Richmond. We'll be renting to start with but our plan is to save up for a deposit for our own place.' She grinned wider. 'God, I can't wait to wake up next to Zack every day.'

'Bleurgh.' Rayne stuck her finger down her throat, pretending to be sick. 'Come on, I've just been reunited with my first love after almost five years and even I'm not being that soppy.'

'Oh, come on. We all know it's just a matter of time before Adam proposes,' Frankie picked up a cocktail napkin and threw it at Rayne, who laughed and ducked out the way.

'Hey, we've not even been back together two months.'

'You wore his ring through most of uni,' Frankie pointed out, 'don't deny that it's been round your neck for the last few years,' she pointed at the chain dangling between Rayne's boobs, something nestling in between them.

'Damn it, caught out.' Rayne stuck her tongue out at Frankie and tossed the napkin back at her.

'Behave, you two,' Zoe mock scolded, easing back into the warm friendship that had been there since their uni days. She was aware of Melody sitting silently to her right, watching them mess around. Her dark eyes looked too big for her thin face.

'I'm so sorry,' Frankie said suddenly, looking at the sisters. 'Here we are babbling on about our relationships, when you two have just gone through break ups.' She put a hand to her mouth, eyes full of guilt. 'We're such bad friends.'

'Shit,' Rayne said, 'you're right. That was bad. Sorry.'

'Don't be silly,' Zoe reached across the table and touched Frankie's arm, smiling at them both. 'Just because our love lives have imploded, it doesn't mean we begrudge you your happiness. Does it Mel?'

'Of course not,' Melody murmured, but there was a hollowness to her words that was worrying.

'Besides, I had a lucky escape. I'm not into guys that cheat. Do it once and I'm done with them.' Her jaw clenched as she thought of Greg. 'Anyway,' shaking the annoyance away, 'thanks for coming guys.' She slid a hand under the table to squeeze Melody's cold fingers, which were clamped together in her lap. 'I can't wait to catch up and have some fun.'

'Well, we'll definitely be doing that tonight.' Rayne poured Zoe an excessively large glass of wine from the metal cooler in the centre of the table, coloured metal bangles jangling around her wrist. 'We started without you, so you need to catch up,' Rayne ordered when Zoe pulled a *steady on* face. 'You too, Melody,' topping the younger woman's glass up with a generous splash of Pinot Grigio.

'I agree,' Frankie piped up.

'I guess we have no choice,' Zoe replied, trying to involve her sister in the conversation, 'after all, who are we to argue with a big-time city journalist and a talented freelance photographer?' Taking a sip of wine, rolling the sweet, crisp floral taste on her tongue, she looked expectantly at Melody. 'Come on sis, relax.'

With a nod, Melody took a sip of wine. 'I'll try.'

Zoe looked at Rayne and Frankie. 'So apart from both of you being ridiculously loved up, what else is new?'

She listened as Rayne launched into an amusing anecdote about some players she and Lily had interviewed at Wimbledon, and nodded in all the right places, but her head was tilted towards Mel, noticing how the black top and skinny blue jeans she wore hung off her slight frame. She gave her sister's hand another reassuring squeeze. No matter what, she would make sure Melody got the closure she needed.

It was half an hour before the conversation came around to Zoe, by which time they were into their second bottle of wine and had ordered their first round of cocktails. A Pimms for Rayne, who'd got the taste for it at Wimbledon; a Manhattan for Frankie, who'd had one on New Year's Eve at The Ritz, the night she'd been choosing between two men, and a Cosmo for Zoe, her favourite New York tipple. Melody stuck with wine, insistent she was feeling tipsy enough already. It was true her eyes were starting to cross slightly, and Zoe wondered when the last time was that her sister had eaten properly. She circled a hand around Melody's wrist, her middle finger and thumb touching. That wasn't good.

But at least Melody was talking now. It had taken twenty minutes but she was finally mellowing and joining in, laughing with the girls about the time she'd come to Loughborough to visit Zoe. She'd been sixteen, with Zoe twenty-two and fiercely overprotective. Melody had been a big hit with the guys in the dorm, and Zoe had spent the whole weekend scowling at them all and reminding them in firm tones that Mel was barely legal.

'I was so embarrassed,' Melody laughed. 'I wasn't sure I was ever going to forgive you,' shaking her head at Zoe.

'Hey, I was just doing my big sister duties,' she held up both hands.

'I'm not sure they're supposed to extend that far,' Mel answered lightly, but there was something in her tone that suggested she wasn't talking about what had happened almost six years before.

'To be honest,' Frankie picked up on the tension, trying to defuse it, 'I just kept expecting Zoe to walk out of her room wearing a black suit, like a bouncer's outfit.'

'Believe me, I thought about it.'

'Right. Enough of that.' Rayne raised one perfectly arched dark eyebrow. 'My curiosity is killing me. Tell all—how are you getting on living with The Bastard?' Her eyes were aglow with interest.

'What's this?' Frankie asked, straightening on her stool 'I think I've missed something. I know that Melody's boss fired her and kicked her out for no reason, and his younger brother who you were dating,' she nodded sympathetically at Melody, 'has gone AWOL, but what's this about living with a bastard?'

'Zoe's moved in with Melody's boss to find out what really happened, and get revenge for Melody,' Rayne lowered her voice as a waitress sauntered past holding a tray of drinks aloft, 'by selling a kiss and tell story about Matt to the tabloids. He'll hate it, has massive privacy issues. Zoe's going to use my contacts.'

'Really?' Frankie swivelled her head to Zoe, mouth open. 'That seems a bit extreme. Does he deserve it?' She looked at Melody then back to Zoe. 'Is he a bastard, Zo?'

'Um...' Zoe used the pretext of taking a large slug of wine as an opportunity to gather her thoughts. How could she answer that without giving away how uncertain she was feeling about everything? That no, she didn't think Matt was a bastard. 'Well...' But if that was the case, it made her a sister either a liar or there was something seriously screwy going on, which she hadn't got to the bottom of yet.

She gazed at her sister, whose attention was on a napkin she was turning in circles on the table. She couldn't back out of the plan now, could she? Otherwise it would mean that she was choosing a man over Melody again. The way she'd chosen to go with Greg to America rather than facing her sister and aunt to make amends. Leaving her family behind rather than staying and dealing with her heartbreak like other people did, one day at a time. Melody had been so upset when she'd left the UK. It had taken months to get her to contact Zoe with any regularity. She couldn't blame her. After all, she had abandoned her. 'That is... Yes, he's a bit of a bastard.' She stuttered as she said it, blaming the alcohol, which was making her feel fuzzy headed.

Melody lifted her head, looking surprised.

'Wow, that was totally convincing,' Rayne drawled, 'not. Now tell us the truth.'

Zoe opened her mouth, wanting to try again, to say Matt was rude, sarcastic, ignorant, and arrogant. That he really was a bastard. That he had taken pleasure in Melody's downfall. But it wouldn't be true. He could be distant and a little rude with it, and he'd shut himself off from his children for far too long, but he was a good guy. Except for what he'd done to her sister. That still didn't make sense. She felt like she had two puzzle pieces that should match up, that were roughly the right size and shape, but when she laid them down next to each other, they wouldn't fit together.

Anxiety churned in her stomach, her fingers clenching round the stalk of her wine glass. She looked at her sister, who deserved so much better. 'I... I can't.' She gulped. 'I'm sorry Melody. After what he did to you, I know you must hate him—'

'Why are you apologising?' her sister asked, lifting her head to meet her eyes. 'I told you he wasn't a bastard. I've thought about it a lot, I've done nothing else with Stephen shutting me out. I'm not sleeping and I'm never hungry. I can't get over him when I don't know why it's over. But Matt must have thought he had a good reason for doing what he did. It's the only thing that makes sense.'

'He does,' Zoe acknowledged, thinking of the way she'd circled around the subject with him, and what the other nannies have said, 'I just don't know what. But I get the impression it's really bad. Are you sure you don't know what it could be? It's not about you and Stephen seeing each other, you were right about that.'

'No,' Melody said in disbelief, a spark of anger kindling in her eyes, 'I have no idea whatsoever. What's happening here? Do you believe them over me now, is that what this is? I never did anything to hurt Matt, the children or Stephen. You're going to take Matt's side?'

'What? No. No!' Zoe hissed, putting her hand on Mel's arm to stop her as she tried to get up. 'Don't. I'm not saying that. I just wondered if there was anything that could have created confusion, or where wires might have got crossed. There are no sides here. I'm trying Mel, I am. I just can't get any clarity. Every time I try to talk to Matt about it, he shuts down. And I don't know where Stephen is, other than sailing on the yacht...' she trailed off as something Matt had said struck her.

'What is it?' Melody sank back down onto her stool, face draining of colour. 'What? Is it another girl?' she flinched.

'No. It was weird. Matt said you broke Stephen's heart and he'd gone away to get over it. But obviously it was the other way around.' She hesitated, unsure whether this would help or not, 'I also spoke to the other nannies. The way they told it, he was devoted to you. You'd reformed him. He was a bit of a player by all accounts.'

'He was. It took me six months to convince me to date him because I'd heard of his reputation. I was also wary of getting involved, with him being Matt's brother. But eventually he won me over and it was just me. At least, as far as I know.' Melody ran shaking hands through her hair, pressing her fingers against her temples. Frankie and Rayne kept quiet, watching the sisters with concern. 'I don't get it.' Mel said, bewildered. 'It was going so well. We'd arranged to meet by the Statute of Eros in Piccadilly for lunch and he just didn't turn up. I called and called but got no answer, so I went back to Matt's. Stephen wasn't there, and neither was Matt. The kids were at a friend's, so I sat in the garden to read a book, and that's where I was when Matt confronted me. I've never seen him look so furious. He wouldn't talk, wouldn't explain. He just wanted me gone. There was this look on his face, like he was disappointed with me but was holding back. It wasn't like him. I'd never seen that side of him before.' Mel finished, trembling. 'But he definitely wasn't enjoying it. He looked hurt. That's why I say he's not a bastard. You should know that, Zoe, living with him.'

Zoe got up, wrapping an arm around Melody's shoulders. 'Yes. I do know that. He's really kind of,' pausing, her face softened, 'nice.' It was a completely inadequate word to describe the passionate, funny, intense guy that Matt was, but she couldn't let on how she really felt about him and the kids. 'Things are getting better between him and the children too,' she tacked on unthinkingly, trying to give her sister something positive to hold onto.

'Meaning you're doing a good job of cleaning up the mess I made,' Melody muttered, jerking out of Zoe's arms, tears winding their way down her cheeks.

'Mel, don't be like that. I didn't mean it that way, I swear.' Taking her sister's face between her hands. 'I said sorry. I thought we were okay. I'm not saying you got it wrong. We're just different.'

'You mean you're better.'

'No!' Zoe released her and stepped back from the accusation, left ankle twisting in her stiletto.

'Come on, Melody,' Rayne interjected, 'your sister would never think that, let alone say it. She loves you.'

'I know you're angry with Stephen,' Zoe put a hand to her chest, feeling something tearing inside, 'but I don't want to argue with you. I did it for you, going to live with Matt, and—'

'I never wanted you to. I never asked you too,' Melody burst out, the effects of alcohol glazing her eyes and making her cheeks ruddy.

'What?' Zoe murmured, aware of people around them starting to whisper at the commotion. This wasn't the evening she'd planned.

Melody subsided in her seat, as if letting the confession out had deflated her. 'I agreed because you so obviously wanted to do it, whatever I was going to say or not say. You're stubborn, Zoe.' An expression of despair crossed her face. 'You were determined and had this idea in your head that they had to pay. Oh, you were angry at them with good reason and I appreciated you wanting to defend me,' her voice dropped, 'but I think it was Greg you were really angry with.'

'What?' Zoe gawped at her, clambering back onto her stool and draining her wine glass. She winced at the pain in her ankle, eyes welling with tears. 'That's not fair. How can you say that? I was doing it for you.' She felt like grabbing her clutch bag and running away from her sister's words, and was giving it serious thought when Frankie touched her on the shoulder in a comforting gesture. It grounded her, gave her strength. She thought about this morning's conversation with Ruth, one that felt like a million years ago. She'd run away before and would not do the same again, no matter how much it hurt.

'I'll admit I want to know why,' Melody's voice was determined, 'but I never wanted you to splash him across the papers. You're just so used to coming in and making decisions... my big sister taking charge.'

'It's what you needed after Mum and Dad died,' Zoe defended.

'But we had Ruth to be the adult, and I don't need you to make my decisions for me, Zo,' Melody's voice was kinder now, 'not anymore. Believe it or not, I've grown up while you were away.'

'Yes, I can see that,' Zoe blinked, Mel's face a blur. 'I'm sorry I missed it.' Holding back a sob, she grabbed her sister's hand. 'I'm sorry.'

Melody's face softened. 'Don't be, you were just trying to protect me. And don't be sorry for going to America. Whatever Ruth says and you might feel, I wasn't angry with you. I just missed you and I was sixteen so I was more interested in hanging out with my friends than sitting in front of a computer to talk to my older sister.

Teenagers are like that. They're the centre of their own universe.'

'Really? You mean that?' Zoe asked, the knot in her stomach starting to unravel.

'Yes. Please, stop torturing yourself. Don't feel guilty. You're back now.' Taking a deep breath. 'But respect me, Zo. Let me try and sort my own life out. I know I look a mess,' she held a hand up at them all when they opened their mouths, 'please, don't even try for the empty platitudes. I look awful and I feel shocking. But I'll get there. I had a resilient older sister who showed me how to survive.' Curling her other hand tighter around Zoe's. 'This whole thing has given me time to think. I'm done being a nanny. I wasn't passionate about it, and you were right about Matt. I should have tried harder. The children in our care deserve better. I only became a nanny because you did.'

Zoe nodded, thinking of what Ruth had said. 'I'm sorry if you felt pressured.'

'I didn't, I just wanted to be like you.'

'That's a compliment,' Rayne joked as the tension at the table started to unfurl and drift away, 'though why she'd want to be like you is a total mystery.'

'Oi,' Zoe protested, wiping her eyes on a napkin. She felt exhausted after a day of revelations. 'So, what now?' she asked, clenching her jaw as Melody chuckled and Frankie smiled. They didn't understand the enormity of the question. Without a reason to stay with Matt and the kids, she'd have to leave. She would be anchorless, like a severed buoy adrift on the River Thames. The thought of leaving them caused a physical pain to arrow through her.

'Zoe, are you actually asking me what I want?' Melody teased, holding her hand to chest and feigning a heart attack.

In that twinkle of a moment, Zoe could see that Mel was going to be all right. 'Hey, I'm not that bad.' A pause, 'But yes, what do you want?'

'I don't want you to put Matt in the tabloids. It wouldn't be fair to him or the kids.'

'Oh, Mel, I'm really glad you said that,' Zoe huffed out a massive rush of relief, shoulders shaking, 'because I can't do it. I wasn't sure how to tell you, but it wouldn't be right. It's been eating away at me. I've felt so uncomfortable. I couldn't bear the thought of hurting the kids.' *Liar*, a little voice whispered in her head, *it was about Matt too*. 'But I didn't want to let you down.' Dropping her face into her hands, she took a moment to gather herself, thinking back to how she'd felt on arriving at Jemima's from Heathrow to find her sister so devastated. The sun beating down on her head and burning the back of her neck, rage and adrenalin charging around her body. 'You're right,' she whispered, looking up, 'the *Nannygate* plan was fuelled by my fury at Greg for cheating on me and deceiving me, for making me feel shitty and worthless. I got off the plane angry and when I found out what happened to you, it made me a hundred times angrier. I transferred that to Matt and Stephen. I did.'

Pausing as a waiter arrived and served their drinks, she smiled politely without registering how cute he was. She downed the pink citrusy Cosmo in one go, coughing as she slammed her glass down.

Frankie took a sip of Manhattan, pulling a face and looking unsure as to whether she liked it or not. 'Don't be too tough on yourself, Zoe,' she remarked, 'you were heartbroken.'

'I thought I was,' Zoe corrected her, reaching across and robbing a sip of Rayne's tangy Pimms.

'Steady on,' Rayne laughed, 'or you'll be under the table before dinner.'

'Nothing wrong with that,' she quipped.

Frankie waited until the chuckles had subsided, then cocked her head at Zoe. 'You're not heartbroken?'

'I expected to be, I was incredibly hurt and it was a huge shock, but when I look back, it wasn't right. You know, sometimes it's not until you have some distance from a situation that you can see it for what it is. I thought I loved him, but it wasn't the kind of love you should build a marriage on. And when he contacts me now—'

'What?' Rayne slapped her hand down on the table. 'He's had the cheek to get in touch? I hope it's to apologise.'

'He's said he's sorry and loves me, and wants to talk.'

'And?' Frankie asked, as Melody put a clammy hand on Zoe's arm.

'I have no interest in talking to him. I don't miss him, and nothing he says would change things. The thought of being near him makes my skin crawl. I'm still really angry with him, but there's absolutely no temptation to hear him out or go back to him. He would never be the same person to me again, not after what he did. Besides, I don't want to go back to the States. Now that I've been home I know this is where I belong.'

'Good,' Rayne exclaimed. 'I'm glad to hear it.'

The four of them smiled across the table at each other, all with suspiciously moist eyes.

'I'm happy to hear that too.' Melody tightened her hold on Zoe's arm, leaning in. 'You asked me what I want, sis. Well I've got one thing back that I wanted. You. Do you want to know what else I want?' Her voice was slurred, the alcohol sweet on her breath. 'I'd like to know the truth. So with Stephen still gone, do you think you could stand to be in the house for a few more weeks? Could you try one more time to get to the bottom of what I'm supposed to have done?'

'Sure.' Zoe threw an arm around her sister's shoulder, heart pumping. As much as she was relieved to be going home to Matt's tonight, there was also a piece of her that was petrified of getting in any deeper. 'Anything.'

'Thank you,' Melody rested her forehead against Zoe's and they sat there for a moment, making peace.

'Enough of the drama now girls,' Rayne tapped short burgundy nails on the table, 'we've done our Oprah section, established our female solidarity,' she teased to lighten the mood. 'Now to have some fun.' Grinning as the sisters straightened in their chairs, she looked at them expectantly, 'So, is he hot?'

'Who?'

'Marvellous Matt,' she said, tongue-in-cheek. 'He looks pretty fit in the papers, on the rare occasion he gets papped. Is he?'

'Yes,' Melody answered.

'No,' Zoe denied.

They spoke simultaneously and Zoe shot a frown at her sister for the affirmative answer. Melody returned her look with a level gaze and a raised eyebrow, some of the spark returning. *Oh come on,* her expression seemed to say.

Zoe's cheeks went red and she pretended a keen interest in the stocky blond barman who was shaking cocktails for a couple at the bar.

Rayne swept her gaze from one sister to the other, a smile quirking the side of her mouth up. 'Er, what are you two not telling us? You don't think he's attractive, Zo?'

'I guess he's quite good looking,' she said casually.

'Quite?' Melody arched both fair eyebrows. 'Sis, you are either in denial or blind. I never liked him that way, but even I can admit he's gorgeous. I mean he's got that scar above his lip and his nose is a bit crooked where it's been broken. He's also a bit old-' she stopped as Rayne snorted.

'He's only thirty,' Rayne said, amused.

'Well, I'm twenty-two, but as it happens I was going to say he's a bit older than me. He's also too serious. Stephen is twenty-three, so closer to me in age. We had more in common. Or at least, I thought we did.' A shadow passed over her face. 'Anyway, Matt's just a friend—or was—and my ex-boss, but he has these lovely green eyes and great cheekbones. Actually, Zo, I'm surprised you'd say he's only quite good looking. I would have thought he'd be right up your street. You always liked bad boys. Matt fits that description almost perfectly. He's tall and broad shouldered too.'

'Not really,' Zoe mumbled evasively, still pretending a fascination with the barman, desperate for her face not to go any redder.

'What are you on about?' Melody demanded, clutching Zoe's arm.

'Huh? Nothing,' Zoe turned to face her sister and friends.

'Oh my God, you like him,' Rayne said in a slow voice.

'I—ah, no I don't.'

'Zoe?' Melody peered into her face. 'Do you like Matt? Because if you do, maybe it's not such a good idea for you to—'

'I don't.' Zoe stared into her sister's deep brown eyes. 'I don't.' It was an easy fib. What she felt for Matt was far more complicated than like.

'Right. Enough of that,' Rayne summoned the waiter and Melody let go of her sister, 'more cocktails, followed by dinner. Anyone fancy a dance later?'

Zoe rolled her neck, feeling the tension in her shoulders. 'Oh, yes,' she smiled, 'I'm up for that.'

'Oh, God,' Zoe clutched her head. 'Have they gone yet? I think I'm dying. Their voices were going right through me.'

Matt chuckled. 'You're safe. They're playing in the fountain. I can keep an eye on them. You rest up.' He looked down at her with amusement as she readjusted her big black sunglasses and lay back on the grass. 'You know that if this was a working day for you, I'd have to seriously consider firing you?' he mocked, tugging down the peak of the baseball cap he'd worn to conceal his identity.

'It's because it's not a working day for me that I saw fit to get myself into this state.' She groaned as Hyde Park span around her, the cobalt sky sitting at an odd angle, the grass beneath her feeling like it was tilted at forty five degrees, instead of flat. 'And you know that because it's a day off for me, that's why you have to keep an eye on them? Don't try and act like you're doing me a favour, Matthew.'

He laughed at her use of his full name and lay down beside her on his front, chin propped on his hand so he could watch Aimee and Jasper splashing in the water. 'Like the favour I did you when you stumbled out of the black cab at four this morning and needed help making it up the stairs?'

She covered her face with shaking hands. 'Oh, please don't remind me,' she moaned. 'Sorry about that. But I told you, it was because I'd been dancing in heels for five hours and was crippled.'

'It had nothing to do with the massive vats of alcohol you'd consumed?'

'No,' she whimpered. Just the word alcohol gave her flashbacks to the drunken, loud meal that had followed the cathartic conversation with her sister, the hazy, laughing bar crawl and the banging club they'd ended up in. Somehow she'd acquired a penis helium balloon from a hen party and Rayne had given away all her bangles to random strangers. It had been one of those nights that had been planned as fairly low key but that'd ended up as unexpectedly fabulous. Her mouth curled at the memory of tequila shots. They'd seemed like a good idea at the time. 'Urgh.'

'What's wrong?' Matt asked, touching her arm.

'It hurts to smile,' she complained. 'And why is it so bloody sunny? It's making me feel sick.' Pulling her loose ankle-length patterned dress away from her body, she flapped a hand at the scorching sun, 'Go 'way.'

'God, you stink!' Matt fanned a hand over her face.

'Gee, thanks a lot.'

'Of alcohol. It's drifting out of your pores. Do you feel better for it though? Are you glad you had a night out with the girls? What about the dress, did it behave? You weren't in any fit state when you came home to tell me if you ran into any millionaires.'

'No millionaires and the dress behaved impeccably.' She swallowed away a wave of nausea, the sound of a nearby radio playing an R 'n' B tune driving spikes through her head. 'Let's not talk about feeling better at the moment. Ask me again on Wednesday, which is probably when this hangover will last until.'

He shook his head, 'You're really feeling sorry for yourself, aren't you?' He sat up. 'Here,' rooting through the straw picnic hamper

212

he'd brought along, he handed her a bottle of icy water and started unwrapping a sausage sandwich from crisp foil.

'That's really kind, thanks,' pushing herself slowly onto her elbows, she took the water off him and unscrewed the top, tentatively drinking some, 'but I can't stand the thought of that at the moment.' She pointed to the sandwich, which was wafting meaty, tomatoey smells in her direction.

'Okay, but you might just want to try. When I used to have a hangover the only thing that worked for me was eating my way through it.'

'Not right now thanks. Has it been a long time since you had one?' she asked, flopping back down onto the grass and squinting at him. He was the most relaxed she'd ever seen him in a pair of deck shorts and a white t-shirt, his face missing that usual tense, set expression he had when he was working.

'About three years.'

The amount of time his wife had been dead. 'Oh.'

'Anyway,' he glanced over at the fountain, smiling as he saw Jasper chasing Aimee, flinging bucketfuls of water at her, 'we were going to talk about Jasper's birthday. Do you still feel up to it?'

'It's why I came isn't it? Although,' she pressed her fingers against her forehead, trying to massage the pain away, 'I'm not sure whether all of my brain cells are intact today, and those that are left have probably been pickled.'

'So you're saying it might be an improvement then?' Matt kidded.

'Hey!' Zoe rolled onto her side to face him and punched him on the shoulder, immediately regretting it when her stomach lurched. 'Oh, Jeez.'

Matt grabbed hold of her wrist, smiling down into her eyes, 'I'm pretty sure you're not supposed to physically assault your employer.'

'It's a good thing I'm off duty today then.'

'It is. Are you okay? You've gone a shade of white I'm not sure I've ever seen.'

Zoe breathed in and out deliberately, sweat breaking out on her forehead, another current of nausea making her bare her teeth. 'I think so.' Please, do not let me throw up in public, she thought. Still, it didn't stop her being aware that they were lying on the grass facing each other, her boobs only inches from his chest, their legs nearly entwined, his fingers stroking the inside of her wrist. A prickle of heat grew at the bottom of her spine and was echoed in her pelvis, expanding outwards along her nerve endings. She had a desperate urge to snuggle into him, to curl up against his warmth and ask him to stroke her hair. God, she was such a sap when she was hung over.

'Lie down,' he ordered, 'you can rest while we chat about Jasper's birthday and I'll make notes on my phone.' Waiting until she rearranged herself on the grass, an arm thrown over her forehead. 'So, what sort of thing do you think he'll want? Should we try and rent out a hotel or restaurant do you think?'

'He's going to be five, Matt,' she murmured, 'he doesn't need anything fancy. You don't like him and Aimee being exposed to publicity because of your fame, so why do something a typical celebrity would? You could take him and friends out to an activity-based party, or better yet, why don't you have a party at yours and book some entertainment?'

'Really? I suppose it would be nice for us to do normal.'

'It's definitely worth considering. Personally I think Jasper would love having his friends over and would appreciate you being there and just being his dad for the day. Besides, there's less than two week to go now. All the function spaces are going to be booked out, especially as its summer.' She sucked in her cheeks. 'Why not make it a themed party?'

'What theme?'

Lowering her sunglasses, she stared at him over the top of them.

'Oh,' he tutted at himself, 'Ben 10?'

'I'd say so.'

'What about food? Shall I get the caterers in?'

214

'If you're going for normality, we do it ourselves. We could do a finger buffet, this is a bunch of four and five year olds we're talking about after all, or we could—'

'What about a BBQ?' he interrupted eagerly. 'I'm not bad at those.'

'What is it about men, meat and fire?' she rolled her eyes and then groaned as the action sent fresh barbs of pain through her head. Why had she drunk so much? 'Yep,' she exhaled, 'I think that would work. Most kids like burgers and hot dogs, but we'll have to include vegetarian and gluten-free options.'

'It's a bloody minefield,' Matt commented, typing furiously on his mobile phone.

'I just hope enough kids are free to come,' Zoe frowned, 'with it being bank holiday on the Monday, people might be away for the weekend.'

'Do you know what?' Matt paused. 'If we're going to do it, let's go large. We'll invite loads of people, not just Jasper's friends but their nannies and parents too plus my friends and family. You should invite Rayne and Frankie as well, I'd love to meet them.'

'Why?' She tensed. What if one of them let something slip accidentally?

'Why not? If you're going to be with us for a while your friends should feel comfortable visiting. I know it's my son's birthday, but it would be a nice event for them to come to if there are a variety of people there. Right,' Matt went on, oblivious to Zoe's expression behind her sunglasses at his comment about staying for a while, 'let's talk about the guest list and the kind of entertainment Jasper might like...'

They spent the next twenty minutes discussing ideas and arrangements for the party until with a feigned sob of distress, Zoe begged Matt to save what they'd done and leave it alone. 'We'll divvy up the tasks tomorrow at breakfast,' she said, 'but please, let's have a quiet half hour now.'

'Aww, is it time for a nap?'

'Not quite, but my brain is grinding to a halt,' she admitted.

'Fair enough. I do appreciate you doing this on your day off you know, and for helping me. Thanks.'

'Thank you for making the effort to come to Hyde Park with the kids,' she said, 'I know it wasn't easy but they're really enjoying it. I think it'll make a difference to you all.'

'I think so too. You were right, and I'm glad you got me to consider it. I have to admit,' Matt sat up, removing his baseball cap and scrubbing his hand through his thick black hair, 'it's not been as bad as I thought. Walking in was hard, I'm surprised I didn't cut off the circulation to Aimee's hand, but once I got past the first five minutes and faced the memories,' he sucked in a deep breath, 'it got easier. It probably helped that I had you to make fun of,' he said with a straight face, putting the hat back on. 'It's been great entertainment.'

She sat up, sticking her tongue out at him and reaching for the hamper. 'Whatever. Come on, let's get the kids over and get stuck into this picnic.'

'You're okay to eat now?'

'I should probably try, you're right. And if I'm not,' she said tongue in cheek, 'I guess you and kids will just have to carry me home.'

13

It had been a good week, Zoe mused as she sat at the breakfast bar the following Saturday morning. She and Matt had barely had any time alone, but he'd eaten with them most nights and there had been an easy banter around the kitchen table as the kids chatted about what they'd got up to that day. For the most part, she'd been doing her share of secretly organising Jasper's party around looking after them. Sending Ben 10 invites out, following up with whispered phone calls to apologise for the short notice and checking if people could come, sorting out decorations and ringing around children's entertainers had kept her more than busy. The last task had proved to be a fruitless one because as predicted everyone was already booked for the peak summer season. Matt had suggested asking one of his world famous acts to come along and perform a mini-concert in the garden but Zoe vetoed the idea; it would be absolute mayhem with security and sound requirements and hardly up Jasper's street. He'd agreed, so they'd had to come up with some creative alternatives, usually discussed over text during the day so there was no danger of the kids overhearing.

Matt had started writing out a food list, thinking about a birthday present and enlisting friends to help out with the BBQ. On Friday they were going to traipse around a supermarket together to get the food and drinks while Sadie watched the kids. She was back at work part-time phasing her duties and hours up and had offered to watch Aimee and Jasper for a few hours. It wasn't really in her job description, but she was so insistent that Matt agreed. Zoe thought she was probably trying to get some practice in looking after kids, if she and her boyfriend were about to start actively trying for a baby.

Matt had pulled a face at the idea of a food shop, telling Zoe they could just get it delivered from a luxury food supplier he used, but she'd teased him that if he wanted normality for his kids, he should try normal too. Besides, it was part of the fun.

'Look at this!' Marching into the kitchen, Matt flung a newspaper down in front of her.

'What's the matter?' she frowned.

'Check page fifteen, celebrity news.' His lips were compressed, the scar above his lip burning white.

Pushing her coffee away, she flicked through the paper until she came to the article he was on about. *Matt Reilly In Love Again?* screamed the bold headline.

'Oh.'

'They're bloody vultures! Why can't I ever have any privacy? I wore a hat for God's sake.' Spinning away from her, he moved around the kitchen slamming cupboard doors, clattering mugs around and flinging a metal teaspoon down on the side. 'Bloody hell.'

'It can't be that bad.'

'Read it.'

Zoe bent her head over the paper as he made a coffee. Bugger. A picture of her and Matt filled half the page. They were lying on a patch of grass facing each other, his head tilted towards hers, his hand holding her wrist. They looked cosy, as if oblivious to the world around them. It must have been taken the previous Sunday at Hyde Park when she'd punched him for saying she smelt of alcohol. There was a smile on his face as he gazed down at her. Luckily her back was to the camera so they couldn't identify her, or see how awful she'd looked that day. But it was still invasive and disrespectful, not to mention pretty damning. No one studying the picture would think they were looking at a boss-employee relationship. Although from what she could remember the conversation had been an innocent one.

She scanned the article, which alleged that, '*A mere five weeks since his broken engagement with his celebrity pop star ex-fiancée, Matt has been spotted snuggling up in Hyde Park with his children's pretty new nanny.*'

'Oh, shit,' she cringed, face burning. They'd identified her despite the sunglasses. Still, as she read on, she was relieved to see they didn't seem to know much about her other than she'd started working for Matt recently and was thought to have spent a spell of time working abroad. It would have been worse if they'd mentioned all the gory details about Greg, or worse still, revealed her family, meaning Matt would have found out about her relationship to Melody in a horribly public way. If they kept digging into her background and published a follow up, he still could. Oh, double, triple shit. Panic filled her, clammy fingers smudging the black print of the newspaper into the margin. She should come clean as soon as possible. At least if the truth came directly from her, she would have a chance to explain things from her perspective.

She carried on reading, dreading what was coming next. The female celebrity journalist went on to set out Matt's dizzy climb to fame and the death of his wife three years before. It was written in as spectacular fashion as possible, pulling out all the old speculation and rumours about Helen's death. Zoe winced at the details, at the pain it must have caused him to read it. Turning the page to read the last paragraph, she found it bookended by another picture, this one taken later on in the afternoon when they'd had a lazy wander along the banks of the winding Serpentine. Aimee and Jasper were in the middle with Matt and Zoe bracketing them, all of their hands linked together so they formed a chain. They looked like a happy family.

'We have it on good authority that Matt used to visit Hyde Park with his late wife Helen and their children,' the reporter finished, 'and he's never been pictured with another woman there since, so could wife number two be on the horizon for our favourite home-grown music producer?'

'Oh, for the love of—' she hissed. Talk about leaping to conclusions. 'Now they've got us getting married? How totally ridiculous. They've included a photo of the kids too,' she scowled at Matt, protective instincts for Aimee and Jasper kicking in, anger rising in her throat. 'That's not on.'

To her surprise, he said nothing about the marriage rumour.

'No. It's definitely not.' He banged his coffee mug down on the counter, steaming black coffee sloshing over the sides. 'I work so hard to protect them and now they're splashed right across the national papers! Printing any of it in the first place isn't on either. They didn't even ask my PR Officer for a quote. I'm really pissed off,' he gritted. 'Sorry,' he added as an afterthought.

'Don't worry about it. The kids are still in bed and I've already sworn once. I'll make it twice. I'm pissed off too.' It felt like an unbearable violation, making something public that was a private moment. It felt knotty and uncomfortable, the notion of all those people up and down the country reading the paper over breakfast, making judgements and jumping to conclusions about her and Matt.

Her face burned brighter, chest itching. She scrunched her eyes up in horror at what she'd been planning to do to him with *Nannygate*. A kiss and tell story would have been so much worse than this. What the hell had she been thinking? She was unbearably relieved she'd not gone through with it. It would have hurt him and potentially the kids, exposing them to all sorts of scrutiny and unwanted attention. It would have hurt her too. Her reputation would have been shot and she wasn't sure she would have ever been able to look herself in the mirror again. Also, how could anyone have ever trusted her after that? Even if the article had been printed anonymously, it wouldn't have taken much for people around them to put two and two together and disclose who she was.

'They're comparing me to Jude Law.' Matt rubbed the back of his neck as she opened her eyes. 'The whole scandal with his nanny.'

'Well, that's rubbish. It's completely different. Jude Law was engaged when he had an affair with his nanny. You're single.' She stared at him, swallowing hard. 'Unless there's something you haven't told me.'

'What? Of course not.' Putting his hands on his hips, 'Do you really think I would have kissed you if I was involved with someone else?'

She dropped her gaze to the silver flecked black marble. 'Some guys wouldn't have a problem with it. Besides, it shouldn't have happened.'

He strode over to her, tilting her chin up with his finger. 'Hey,' he said fiercely, 'I'm not like that. I'm not your ex-fiancé. I don't start one thing unless I've ended another. I swear.'

The comment echoed through her mind as she tried to ignore the sparkling sensation on her skin that his touch caused. She'd heard something like it before. Where had it been? She strained to remember who'd said it but it eluded her like a cloudy dandelion seed dancing on the wind just out of reach.

'But you're right,' he added, 'it shouldn't have happened. We've got to control ourselves.'

'Yes,' her mouth dried up as her eyes flickered over his tall solid frame, his muscular thighs and broad shoulders lovingly outlined in the habitual jeans and t-shirt he wore. She wished he hadn't said that. Telling her they shouldn't give in just made her want him more. The curse of forbidden fruit was that it tasted even better when you caved to temptation and took what you wanted.

Matt stepped back and walked across the kitchen to grab a damp cloth. 'You uh, don't know anything about it, do you?'

'Know anything about what?'

221

Crossing back to the breakfast bar, he moved the mug and wiped up the coffee he'd spilt. 'The article. You didn't tell anyone where we were going?'

'Are you accusing me of tipping off the press?' Her voice shook with suppressed anger. She knew nothing about it. Still, the fact it was so damned close to what she'd originally intended sent a sharp stab of guilt through her.

'No. I'm just asking if there's a possibility—'

She leapt off the stool, its feet scraping on the tiled floor like the screech of chalk on a blackboard. 'No, Matt. I didn't tell anyone where we were going.' Her conscience was clear on that. 'I had nothing to do with this, nothing,' she emphasised, sweeping around the counter and standing in front of him. 'I wouldn't do that to you or the kids. And it's not just you affected, is it?' She crossed her arms. 'I'm right there in those photos and they've named me. People are going to assume we're sleeping together, which hardly makes me look professional. We look like...' she was going to say *we're in love*, but held back. That wasn't the case and it would just embarrass them both saying it out loud. She ran her hands through her hair, thinking of what Mel and Ruth were going to say. 'God, my family are going to be asking me all sorts of questions. What a mess!'

He studied her face, breathing hard. After a moment he slowly exhaled. 'You're right. I'm sorry. You're caught up in this too; I'm afraid it's one of the risks of working for me.' He touched her arm, 'I didn't mean to suggest you were involved. Sorry. I do trust you.'

Nodding, she squirmed. But he shouldn't have trusted her. This was getting even more complicated. 'That's okay, I understand you're upset. It was probably a natural question to ask,' she edged away from him, returning to her stool and picking up her lukewarm coffee. 'So, why do you think they waited until today to publish the story? They've sat on it for almost a week.'

'I should think it's because there's a higher circulation on a Saturday,' Matt answered with a bitter twist to his lips.

'Right. And what are we going to do about the article? Will you be taking legal advice?'

His mouth quirked at her use of the word *we*, but he didn't comment on it. 'I've already spoken to my solicitor, although I already knew the drill. It's too late for an injunction as they've already run the story. We could consider taking formal action against them for libel, but we'd have to prove defamation and that would be hard to evidence definitively.'

'Sorry, you've lost me. What does that mean, in words of one syllable?'

'Defamation is when a false claim is made. Libel is proving that what's been printed has caused me or my reputation injury or exposed me to public ridicule. It would be almost impossible to prove we're not in a relationship, with you living here and...'

'And what?'

He looked her square on, 'With me not being able to swear openly and truthfully that there's never been anything between us.'

'I see,' she murmured, her tummy dipping like she was back home in Southend on a rollercoaster, the sea breeze flapping her hair around her face at the speed of the ride.

'As for the libel,' he continued when she didn't say anything more, 'it would be hard to prove the story has caused injury to the kids simply by being photographed and as for injury to me that would be even harder. I'm single so it doesn't put an existing relationship at risk or make me look like a cheating bastard. I do look like a bit of a player though, moving on from my supposed ex to you within weeks. I don't want it to look as though I'm a serial dater.'

'What, when the truth is that you don't date at all? Does it really matter what other people think? The two most important people in your life,' she pointed to the ceiling, 'won't know anything of what's going on unless you tell them.'

'I know that, and you have a valid point, but I still don't want people to see me that way when it's not the truth. They had no

223

right to print the story,' he seethed.

'No, they didn't, but I guess it's the price you pay for doing what you do. You love what you do, right?'

'Yes,' he nodded, 'absolutely. So I suppose it's worth it. Not everyone gets to do something they're passionate about for a living, do they?' He paused, calming down. 'I am lucky for that. I'd hate to be stuck in a job I hated. Life is too short.' He looked pensive. 'To answer your earlier question, after speaking with my solicitor and considering the options, unfortunately there's no point in pursuing a case. It'll simply draw more attention to us. As my solicitor pointed out, today's newspaper is tomorrow's chip paper. If I don't respond or retaliate hopefully they'll get bored and move on. As for looking like a serial dater, I'll just have to make sure I'm not seen with anyone else.'

At his words, the memory she'd been reaching for earlier arrived in a flash. She pictured outspoken Monica with the other nannies the day Zoe had joined them in Green Park. The other woman had been criticising Mel's lousy taste in men. '*He's immature and spoilt, and a serial dater.... unfortunately he's not that great at finishing one thing before starting the next.*'

'So that you don't look like a serial dater like your brother?' Zoe blurted in reply to his comment.

'Where did you hear that?'

She shrugged. 'The other nannies talk, Matt.'

'Of course. Well, the rumours are probably true, so I can't really be angry. The truth is,' he rested a hip against the kitchen counter, looking troubled, 'that I love my brother, but he's not got the best track record with women.'

'What about Melody, your last nanny? What was he like with her? You said she broke his heart?' Rising from her seat she crossed the room, emptying the dregs of her coffee in the sink and bending over to load the mug into the dishwasher.

'He was different with her; he seemed to really care. That was probably why he took what happened so hard and was in such a mess when she left. It would explain why he felt the need to get away.'

Breathing in deeply, she clutched the edge of the dishwasher door. *But she didn't just leave. You made her go, and without telling her why.* Straightening up, she opened her mouth to ask him outright what had happened. She would tell him why she wanted to know and confess that she was Melody's sister. It was time to get it out in the open. Even though a piece of her didn't want the answer because it would mean she no longer had a reason to stay, at least she would have closure for Mel. Plus, she couldn't do this anymore. Anxiety was gnawing at her stomach all the time, a grey cloud of apprehension hovering over her shoulder. With the newspaper article added in, it felt a hundred times worse. 'Matt,' she said shakily, 'I—'

'Morning, Zoe,' Aimee skipped into the kitchen fully dressed, hair combed into a neat ponytail. 'Morning, Daddy.' Putting a book down on the breakfast bar, she walked around the counter and put her arms around his waist.

'Morning. Did you sleep okay?' Returning the hug, he looked down into her face as she pulled away.

'Yes, thanks.'

'What are you reading?'

'The first Harry Potter book. I really enjoyed the studio tour but realised I've only seen the films, so I wanted to read the books too.'

'That's a great idea,' Zoe said, slipping past the two of them and heading for the door, ridiculously pleased to see the new ease of affection between father and child. 'Let me know how you get on. I'm off out for the day. Have a good one.'

'Were you saying something, Zoe?' Matt asked as Aimee clambered onto a stool.

'Nothing important. It doesn't matter.' There was no way she was having this conversation in front of Aimee, it would have to wait until another opportunity to speak with him alone came up.

'Doing anything nice today?'

'I'm going to a few galleries and lunch with—' she almost said *my sister*, but held back at the last moment. It would create questions she wasn't prepared to answer in front of his daughter. She paused, wanting to be honest with him about at least one thing. 'With someone I haven't spent quality time with in a while,' she finished, smiling sadly. 'You know there are those people you drift away from sometimes that if you spend a few hours with it'll be like you were never apart? Today I'm seeing one of those people.'

'I've never really experienced that. I've never had enough people in my life to drift away from.'

'That's sad, Daddy,' Aimee said seriously, in the act of picking up her book. 'You need more friends.'

Matt's face relaxed and he laughed. Zoe couldn't help but join in.

'Yep, I probably do,' he agreed, leaning across the breakfast bar to run a hand over her silky auburn hair. 'But as well as Noel and Stephen, I've got Zoe now too, right?'

'Yes,' Aimee beamed.

Zoe bit the inside of her cheeks. What'd happened to the boss-employee relationship? Since when had she become his friend? The problem was, she couldn't deny it. The last thing he felt like was her employer. 'I've gotta go,' she muttered, stepping backwards. 'Tell Jasper I said good morning when he gets out of bed.'

'Will do.' Matt picked up his coffee, the action stretching his top across his toned chest.

God, the man was so hot he was virtually on fire.

'Will you be home for dinner?' he asked as she turned to leave.

'I don't know. I may stay out late. Don't wait for me. In fact,' maybe time away from him would be a good idea and Ruth might be willing to put her up for one night now they were on better terms, 'I might not be back until the morning.'

'Right,' a nerve pulsed in his jaw, eyes narrowing. 'Well, you're an adult. It's your decision.'

Zoe pulled a puzzled face. Why was he being so weird about it? It was her day off tomorrow too.

He cleared his throat as Aimee gave him a look that echoed her nanny's. 'Never mind,' he said. 'Will you uh, be back in time to come to Hyde Park for a picnic with us tomorrow?'

'You want to do that? Even with...?' she gestured to the newspaper by his elbow.

Aimee cast an anxious look between them, 'Yes, Zoe, you've got to come. Pleeeeeease? Jasper will want you too as well.'

'I'm not going to let them stop me living my life,' Matt answered. 'The kids enjoy it, so that's the only thing I need to know. We'll just have to get better at disguises.'

'Disguises?' Aimee wrinkled her nose.

'I'll tell you about it later,' he squeezed his daughter's shoulder.

'Okay, if I stop out, I'll be back in time for the picnic,' Zoe agreed, not sure if it was the best idea. 'See you later.'

As she ran to her room to pack an overnight bag, the newspaper article weighed heavily on her mind. She thought about the softness in Matt's face as he gazed down at her in the main photo, and the other picture of them together with the kids, playing happy families. She thought about her reasons for coming here and the way she'd grown to care about Matt and his children. Then she thought about the fact she wasn't being honest with him and how the concept of leaving them caused her real, visceral pain and a sense of loss so acute it made her want to double over.

Physical disguises weren't the only type, she realised. There were emotional ones too; you could hide the truth from yourself as well as other people.

The next week passed in a flurry of activity which included taking the kids to the uniform shop to get ready for school. They were due to start on the Wednesday following Jasper's party, so she was in danger of running out of time. Matt was busy finishing a project in order to have Saturday off for the party, so Zoe took them alone. Nearly crying with pride when Jasper came out of the changing room looking both incredibly grown up while still just a baby, she sent Matt a photo of him in the grey trousers and red polo top with the emblem of the infant school on the chest. He was so impossibly cute in the outfit with his rounded cheeks and big green eyes.

> **Just look at how adorable
> your son is. Having a
> #proudnanny moment
> right now. Z :-)**

> **Sorry I couldn't be
> there, but having a
> #ProudDad moment
> too. Will ask him
> about it over dinner.
> M :-)**

> **p.s. don't cook tonight,
> will treat us to a take away.**

Aimee walked around the shop solemnly, picking out grey tights and gingham red hair bands to go with the white blouse, red jumper and grey skirt Zoe had already set aside with the help of a knowledgeable staff member. Remarking to her nanny that she was looking forward to going back to school to learn more, Aimee added pencils, a maths set and notebooks to the pile with a pleased expression that was utterly adorable.

How was she ever going to leave them? Zoe agonised.

Now it was the day of Jasper's birthday party and she wasn't any closer to an answer. There had been no chance to speak to Matt alone either. He'd been getting home excruciatingly late from his city studio, or they'd both been with the kids, or organising the party or he'd been down in the basement.

Stepping from the kitchen out onto the decking, Zoe peered up at the clear sky which was so bright it looked leached of colour, unlike the deep blue of the previous few days. The guests had started arriving half an hour before and the party was going well so far, pop music playing in the background from an iPod and speakers set up on the wooden table between the sun loungers, clusters of children and adults dotted around the emerald lawn laughing and chatting. The day had dawned warm and sunny, and it was beautiful BBQ weather. It was all just about perfect. The complete opposite to the crappy excuses she was making to herself about failing to come clean with Matt. The fact was she should have told him but hadn't. She didn't want to, wanted just a little more time. *I'll get them settled at school and then I'll sit down with Matt and tell him everything,* she promised herself.

It was no wonder she wasn't ready to let it all go yet. The latest picnic in Hyde Park the previous Sunday had been hilarious and they'd had the best fun together. Wearing matching baseball caps like an American family, Zoe and Aimee's hair tucked up inside theirs as part of their makeshift disguises, Matt had also bought them all silly eighties-style neon framed sunglasses and suggested they wear their most casual, grotty clothes. For Matt that meant a pair of discoloured grey deck shorts and a black t-shirt from college with a logo so faded it was indecipherable and a rip along the armpit seam. Zoe put on her denim shorts and a bright red baggy top that fell off one shoulder. She'd once worn it to paint a room, meaning there were streaks and splashes of ivory paint all over it. Jasper was in incredibly tight Ben 10 shorts and a t-shirt he'd grown out of the year previously but had insisted on keeping and Aimee had cheated by claiming she had no grotty clothes, wearing a pale pink dress with a belt that tied in a bow at the back.

They looked like the most mismatched group ever and Zoe had been aware of people giving them funny looks the whole afternoon. That hadn't been helped when Jasper jumped into the Serpentine from the pedalo he'd been on with his dad after deciding he was too hot. It had resulted in a damp, uncomfortable walk for him across to the modern kids' playground on the southern boundary of the park, which was Japanese in appearance with a climbing frame that looked like it was made from giant green and beige bamboo shoots. Once Jasper had dried out and the children had played, Matt had treated them all to ice-cream cones as they meandered home. Zoe had presumed Matt would be twitchy at the potential for the press to be camped out looking for them, but if he was it didn't show. On the contrary, he'd seemed to enjoy himself and at one point had slung a companionable arm around her shoulders, until with a sigh of regret and a hot twist in her stomach she'd eased away from the warmth of his body and fresh sexy scent of his aftershave. He'd been so relaxed that day she'd been able to convince him to invite Helen's mum to her grandson's birthday celebration after only a few minutes of persuasion.

Muttering that she was, 'impossibly stubborn,' Matt had rolled his eyes.

'Guilty!' Zoe had laughed, dancing away from him, holding Aimee's hand.

Padding along the decking in her jewel-encrusted sandals and down the stairs onto the grass, Zoe pushed the happy memories away to focus on Jasper's party. She was pleased at what they'd been able to achieve in just two weeks. Hanging from the apple tree was a bespoke Ben 10 Piñata full of goodies, the children taking turns with a solid plastic stick to batter it until sweets tumbled out at their feet. Frankie's boyfriend Zack was supervising the action, making sure that none of the kids got stick-happy or overzealous. He was good-looking in a pleasant way, his fair hair brushing his collar at the back and a dimple in one cheek that was higher than the norm adding a mischievousness to his face. He seemed like a sweet guy from what she'd seen so far. Frankie was laughingly supervising him in turn, clad in shorts and a long white button-down shirt, face tilted back as she giggled at something he said.

Zoe had decided that as much as she was worried about her friends letting something slip by accident, she trusted them and needed their support. Having them here would help her feel less outnumbered by Matt's friends and family, along with the parents and nannies of Jasper's friends. The only people who were missing were Matt's parents. He'd told her they were on a cruise and not due back for another few weeks, but she wondered if they'd have come even if they were back from the Caribbean. Apart from the time they'd spoken about his childhood and their past relationships, Matt barely said a word about them.

Strolling down the garden, she fiddled with the Ben 10 plates, napkins and cups that were set up on a table against the garden fence, accompanied by endless rows of bottled fizzy pop and jugs of iced water and orange squash. A variety of sauces and pickles were lined up in jars near heaving bowls of deli-style coleslaw and potato salad, numerous containers of crisps and dips set out alongside them next to plates of ready-cut seedless burger baps and hot dog rolls. Matt's eyes had nearly popped out of his head at the amount of food they'd bought at the supermarket the previous day. Two trolleys had been needed to get it all back to the Prius, but Zoe had told him it was better to have too much than not enough, offering to go halves with him if he couldn't afford it. Matt had laughingly told her to shut up and get in the car.

She swept her eyes across the lawn. Set against the back fence was a bouncy castle that children were crawling, roly-polying and jumping in and out of at will, and a small ramp next to it with micro-scooters should any of the children be feeling particularly active or brave. Although it was anchored with ropes, Rayne was keeping a tally on how many kids were using the bouncy castle so that there was no danger of it tipping over. Her black bob and cocktail rings flashed in the sunlight as she counted them in and out with a stopwatch on her mobile phone. In her short Indian print dress, she was like an exotic colourful flower in a bed of plain English daisies, and Adam was hardly able to keep his eyes off her. Standing a few feet away to look after the kids using the ramp, his attention continually returned to his girlfriend. Zoe took in the tattoo on one of his brawny arms peeking out from a short-sleeved top, his short brown hair and the soft stubble covering his jaw. Rayne was right; he did look a bit like the actor Tom Hardy nowadays. Though from the giant hug he'd given Zoe on arrival and the soppy expression on his face now, he didn't have the hard-edged mob persona of Tom's most famous roles.

The massive double BBQ was in the far corner, manned by Matt and his best friend Noel, who'd she'd finally met when he'd arrived late morning to help set up. He was around the same height as Matt but with light brown hair, brown eyes and a friendly face. Zoe hadn't been able to see the grumpiness that Jasper had first talked about, but as she saw him concentrating on methodically turning sausages, his features settled into a fierce frown. Ahh, there it was. Equally she could see that Jasper had been right about Noel's girlfriend Holly. As the tall blonde walked gracefully towards the BBQ, her boyfriend glanced up. On seeing her he grinned, eyes lighting up. 'Come here, gorgeous,' he called.

'Whaddya want?' she asked playfully.

Pointing a finger at her, he mouthed *you*.

'Nah, I'm all right thanks,' she stuck her tongue out, 'I have other boys to look after.' Smiling cheekily she turned and made her way towards a group of children bouncing around on space hoppers, herding them away from the sumptuous white rose beds. Shaking his head as he watched her, Noel turned and made a remark to Matt, who smiled and clapped him on the back.

Matt was looking particularly gorgeous and summery in a pair of shorts and short-sleeved white shirt that showed off his black hair and forest green eyes. Zoe had spent the morning trying to avoid him so that she didn't do anything stupid. Every time she got near him her fingers twitched to undo his shirt buttons and her palms itched to smooth over his naked, hairy skin.

She'd spent over an hour hanging red, white and blue bunting along the fences to keep out of his way, followed by twisting tiny white fairy lights around the apple tree's branches and the decking rail in case the party went on into the evening. The overall effect of the garden was lovely, a mixture of British tea-party and sticky, good old fashioned fun for the children. Seeing that everything was under control for the moment and with the burgers, hot dogs and chicken on its way to being served, Zoe grabbed one of the red and white striped deckchairs she'd hired. Sinking down into it with a blissful moan, she smoothed the full skirt of her strapless watermelon coloured sundress over her knees. Getting up at half past five and running around like a mad thing ever since had been a mistake. She was knackered already and there were hours left to go. This might be her only chance to sit down for a while.

Rolling her head to the side, she watched Matt's tall, lean, dark-haired cousin Nathan for a moment. He was standing by a table full of assorted tumblers, glasses, drinks cartons and wide mouthed bottles. Shaking virgin cocktails and flipping plastic shakers over his shoulder and under his arm rapidly to entertain a group of children—mostly girls—he was mesmerising. They were all gawping in awe at his mixology skills. Among the five year olds sitting cross-legged on the lush lawn was a young petite blonde with rippling gold hair flowing down her back. Dressed in hip-hugging jeans and a red belly top, she looked just as impressed as the younger members of the audience but with an appreciative glint to her eye. Zoe assumed she was Nathan's girlfriend, Sofia. It was confirmed when he winked at her and she raised an eyebrow suggestively in response.

'Hi,' a guy with an open face and shaggy brown hair folded himself down into the deckchair next to Zoe.

'Hello,' she turned to him, wondering who he was. 'Sorry, it's been a bit hectic today, have we met?'

'Not yet,' he lifted a hand in easy greeting. 'I'm Leo.'

Zoe screwed up her face, trawling her memory.

'I'm Georgiana's boyfriend.' He pointed to a girl who was talking to Matt. Her brown hair was swept back in an intricate knot and she was wearing a black eye patch decorated with coloured gems.

There was a faint scar down one side of her face from her cheek-bone to her pink mouth. It was a shame her skin was marred by it, but she was beautiful anyway.

'She's pretty,' Zoe observed, remembering something Aimee had said, 'and Matt's cousin, right?'

'That's the one,' Leo answered, his head tilting to track Georgiana's movements toward the bouncy castle. She walked with a slight limp, favouring her left leg, but didn't appear self-conscious about it. 'Matt and the kids seem happier,' he said, glancing back to Zoe. 'Correction, I mean happy. The last time I was here they hardly spent any time in the same room together and were pretty rigid with each other. I'm guessing you're the one to thank for the change.'

Zoe flushed. 'He wasn't doing such a bad job before I arrived. Neither was his last nanny.'

'It's nice of you to say that, as well as loyal, but I work with children with special educational needs,' he explained, 'so I'm very aware of behaviours and emotions. I told George after our last visit that something needed to change, but I didn't feel it was my place to say anything to Matt, not when I've only been part of the family for six months. They're not completely at ease with each other yet but they will be. You're getting them there, right? I've seen how you are with the kids, so positive but firm too. You're the same with Matt.'

'You got all that from the last half an hour?'

'Don't look so surprised. I can see that caring for other people is an instinct in you. It comes naturally. I wouldn't be surprised if you had a younger brother or sister. Am I right?'

'Yeah.' Shifting with discomfort at his probing, she toed her sandals off and curled her feet into the grass, the soft blades tick-ling her soles. 'You're very perceptive. Are you sure you're not a woman?' she said, trying to distract him from further questions, before colouring and wondering if he might be offended. 'Sorry.'

'It's cool. No, I'm definitely a man,' Leo grinned, 'and thank god. Because I've met her,' he pointed at Georgiana, 'and she's the love of my life. Last Valentine's Day on Primrose Hill was the best day ever. I'd given her a reason not to trust me, although it was a misunderstanding really, but she came and found me anyway. We sat drinking champagne and eating a picnic overlooking the London skyline.'

'In February?' she gave a mock shiver.

'I brought blankets, hats and hand warmers too.'

'Oh, that's lovely,' Zoe blinked, 'so romantic and thoughtful. She's lucky to have you. Not a lot of guys these days know how to do old-fashioned romance.'

'No. I'm lucky to have her, and she makes me want to do those things for her, just to see the expression on her face. Plus, everyone's idea of romance is different, isn't it?' Pausing, he stared off into the distance as if recalling another memory, before shaking his hair out of his eyes. 'Anyway.'

'Anyway?'

'Matt's a good guy you know. Despite his issues.'

'Why are you telling me this? And what issues?' No way was she going to be the one to reveal anything first.

'I'm telling you because I think you should know, and as for issues, it's obvious he's still grieving.'

'Hmmm,' she made a non-committal sound as Matt flipped a sizzling burger and let out a shouting laugh when it landed on the grill and the BBQ smoke turned grey, wafting up into his face. He waved his hand over it, dispersing it jokingly towards Noel.

'Why do you think he's such a good guy?' she asked curiously. There was something about Leo that made her feel comfortable, even if some of the conversation was challenging. She got the sense he cared deeply about people. He also didn't seem to have any hidden agendas.

'He's the reason Georgiana and her parents could move to London for a fresh start after her accident. He owns a few properties and lets them stay in one rent-free. They insist on paying the bills of course, but he could still make a killing if he rented it out to someone else because of its location near Primrose Hill.'

'He's doing it because they're family,' she reflected. 'I guess it must be the house he bought when he and Helen got married.'

Leo jerked his head back, surprised. 'He's talked to you about her?'

'A bit. Sometimes. Her mum's here today. I thought it might be nice for all of them.'

'Wow, you're either a hypnotist or a miracle worker. As far as George is concerned, he doesn't talk to anyone about Helen and as far as I know he's never invited Cynthia into this house. The poor woman's not made it across the threshold in the last three years. Maybe he wants to keep it all separate in his head. You know he never lived here with Helen, don't you? He and the kids moved in a couple of months after she died.'

'Really? I hadn't realised. He never said.' She didn't suppose it had been relevant for Melody to mention either. She was oddly relieved. Helen had never been a presence here in this house because of the lack of photos and mementoes, but she'd still wondered a couple of times how Matt felt about going to bed in the room they'd shared. It had made her feel both sad for him but uncomfortable too, because of the tiny sting of jealousy.

'Well, he doesn't open up very often, does he? Most of the stuff I know is either from George or my own observations. What I want to know is how you managed to convince him to invite Cynthia?'

'I have no idea. Maybe he's just turning into a softie,' she murmured.

'Or maybe it's something else,' his gaze drifted over to Matt. 'I saw the newspaper article with the photos of you together.'

She groaned, thinking of Matt's reaction and the concerned, questioning phone calls she'd had to deal with from Ruth and Melody, her sister telling her in no uncertain terms to drop it and get out from under Matt's roof ASAP. It had taken more than twenty minutes to convince Mel that she could handle herself. 'It was awful,' Zoe answered Leo. 'He was so furious. I hate that they printed the photo of the kids and I also feel totally violated. The thought off all those people speculating that we're in a relationship, with me being his nanny,' shaking her head, 'gossiping and assuming that we're...'

'Assuming that you're in love,' he filled in dryly. 'Yeah, what a shocking idea.'

'What do you mean?' she asked in a high-pitched voice. She fanned her face, the sun's rays pounding down on their heads.

He dropped his voice. 'Well, it wouldn't be the worst thing in the world, Matt being loved up after so many years alone. You seem like a good person and you're great with the kids. I get that it's complicated with you working for him, but that shouldn't be a barrier if you really like each other. But please be careful with Aimee and Jasper; they've already lost too many people.' He unfolded himself from the deckchair, standing up and looking down at where she sat with her mouth agape. 'I'm sorry if I've been a bit blunt, Zoe. I hope I haven't upset you, especially when we don't know each other. I'm just looking out for Matt and the children. There are other reasons I'm grateful to him on George's behalf, so anything I can do to return the favour...' His mouth curved into a smile that could probably get anyone to forgive him anything. 'George often tells me I have a habit of saying exactly what I think, even when I shouldn't. It was nice to meet you. Hopefully we'll catch up again later.' He loped off before she had time to recover or reply, crossing the grass and sliding an arm around Georgiana's waist, dropping a kiss on her forehead when she turned to him.

Zoe clicked her mouth shut. Where had all that come from? Who had told him that she and Matt liked each other? She should probably be pissed off with him for being so outspoken when they were strangers, but there had been a complete lack of guile in his eyes that said he was only saying those things because he cared and thought it was the right thing to do. He seemed like a nice guy and there had been no trace of cockiness in his voice.

She sighed, thinking of his words. Shame and regret twisted together in her chest. Leo thought she was a good person, that she was great for Matt and the kids. On one level he might be right, somehow how they were making it work, the four of them. But on another level he was absolutely wrong. How was someone who had arrived in their lives with the sole intention of hurting Matt and then leaving, a good person?

It wasn't something she had time to fret over because as she started pushing herself from her seat, Cynthia sank down gracefully in the chair Leo had just vacated, a silk lilac high-collared dress making her look very Lady of the Manor.

'Good afternoon, Zoe. How are you?' She kept her eyes on her grandson, who was currently bouncing on a yellow space hopper, burbling in glee as he and his friends bumped each other playfully.

'Fine, thanks.' They'd met in passing a few times when the woman had come to drop the kids off and Zoe had thought her very polite, though a little reserved. 'And you?'

'I'm exceptionally well today. Thanks to you. It's so lovely to see Jasper enjoying himself, and Aimee too.' She pointed an elegant finger at the girl, who was launching herself into the bouncy castle under Rayne's watchful eye.

Zoe smiled. 'Matt and I organised the party together, I can't take all the credit.'

'The party is delightful, but I was talking about the fact that I'm here to see it in the first place. I suspect I owe that to you, and I'm very grateful.'

Zoe scrunched her fingers into the skirt of her green dress. Cynthia's comment was an echo of the last bit of her conversation with Leo, and it made her feel like a fraud. 'It's nothing. He was happy for you to be here,' she answered diplomatically, 'and it's nice for the kids.'

'Nonetheless,' Cynthia studied Zoe's averted face, 'in three years I have never been invited to any of the children's parties and neither have I been asked to come into the house. The only factor that is

238

different about the equation is you. I'm not criticising Matthew, you understand. He's been wonderful in letting me maintain my relationship with Jasper and Aimee and he's happy for them to come and visit me, even if they find it a little raw.'

'Because you remind them of their mum?' Zoe guessed.

Cynthia dipped her head, 'I wasn't sure at first why they always seemed so unsettled with me. I thought I was too strict for them, or they didn't know me well enough. However, over time it's become apparent that the photographs of Helen in my home are the only ones they have access to, and that I'm the only one who talks to them about her.'

'I don't think it's deliberate on his behalf,' Zoe defended, relaxing her hands and looking at Cynthia, 'but I understand it's important for them and you to keep her memory alive. It's just very painful for him, I think.'

'There is no doubt he finds it hard, however—'

'Do you know that they've started visiting the memorial plaque in Hyde Park for her again?' She held a hand up, 'I'm sorry to interrupt, but I really think he's trying and you need to know that. The children talk to me about your daughter too sometimes, and when they do I encourage them to remember the happy times.'

'Yes, I was aware of the picnics in Hyde Park, I've seen the paper, the pictures of you all.' Her lips tightened.

'It's not his fault. We didn't know the press were there, and he definitely didn't want the kids splashed across the tabloids.' She paused, wondering whether to say the next bit or not, but feeling like Cynthia might need the reassurance. 'I'm not trying to replace Helen. I wanted him to start going to Hyde Park again because I feel the three of them need it. I'm just the nanny.' Even as the words poured from her lips, her face was tingling with a blush. Technically she *was* the nanny, but she'd never had a post that felt less like a job. She'd never had a post where she'd kissed her boss, or had come to care so much for her charges.

'I'm annoyed that the press are interfering,' Cynthia said crisply, 'but I don't blame him for the newspaper article. I suppose I could because by being his children they're automatically subject to that kind of interest, but I've seen how much he loves music, and how he's always tried to protect them from public scrutiny. At heart he is a good father.'

'He is.' Zoe watched as Matt starting serving burgers onto a large ceramic plate, movements fluid and face cheerful. When first arriving she'd been horrified at the disconnect between him and the kids, how much he distanced himself from them, but he had taken on board all the things she'd said, and what she'd seen recently was someone doing his best for his children, no matter what the personal cost to him. He genuinely loved them, she had no doubt about that, and Leo was right, they would get there. To a place they should be, where they were secure and comfortable in each other's company. The question was, would she be around when it happened?

'As for the other, no-one could ever replace my daughter, however Matthew does need to move on. Everybody does.' She paused. 'He blames himself, you know.'

'Sorry?' Zoe frowned.

'For Helen's death.' The pale blue eyes that lifted to Zoe's were haunted, grief etching lines into her face. 'It wasn't his fault though. My daughter was headstrong and made the decision to get into that car all by herself.' She put a hand to her chest, rubbing the spot over her heart. 'I've tried to talk to him about it, but he doesn't want to. He simply shuts me out.' She paused again, nodding to herself. 'I can't bring my daughter back, but I can make sure her children are happy, and they won't be unless he is. He deserves to be happy in his own right.'

'Of course,' Zoe agreed automatically. Why did people keep telling her these things today? It was like they were trying to give her their approval, or sell Matt to her as a catch. But he didn't want to be caught. He'd been very clear he wasn't looking for a relationship with anyone—let alone his kid's nanny. Her right hand rose to her chest, unconsciously mirroring Cynthia's pose, covering the same spot over her heart, trying to rub away the ache.

14

Lying back on the sun lounger with her legs curled under her, Zoe let out an exhausted but happy sigh. The food had been devoured under the baking sun, the children had played riotously for hours, the birthday cake's candles had been blown out by a puff-cheeked Jasper and most people had gone home around seven o'clock contentedly clutching party bags and extra chicken. Cynthia had offered at the last minute to have the children overnight and as it was Jasper's actual birthday a few days later rather than today, after a moment's hesitation Matt had agreed. Jasper and Aimee had seemed happy to go, the little boy's eyes starting to go heavy-lidded from the afternoon's excitement. He'd still been insistent on taking all his presents with him to unwrap however, so after some wrangling and Cynthia promising to make a list of the gifts and who had given them for Jasper to write thank you notes that had been agreed too. Zoe had chucked their things into bags while Matt had said goodbye to the last of the parents and nannies, and then they'd loaded Cynthia's car up together with the kids and their belongings, waving them off with matching expressions of relief. It had been a long day.

A few select friends and family members had stayed for some adult chill out time, and after picking at the buffet again and having more than a few alcoholic drinks, it had seemed like an exceptionally good idea to take turns on the bouncy castle, space hoppers and even the micro-scooters. Several people had fallen off various pieces of equipment, and general hilarity had ensued. It was hard to imagine they were all tax-paying adults, Matt had remarked, just before he'd slid sideways off the space hopper and onto the grass, causing hysterics. Now they were all sitting on the decking, the light fading as it ticked towards midnight, the evening winding down. Zoe had turned the fairy lights on and lit some citronella candles to keep the mosquitoes away. It was pretty and relaxing, and she stifled a yawn behind one hand, feeling mellow and trying not to think about how great it'd been to see Matt shrug off his responsibilities and take joy in some innocent though drunken fun.

'Here you go,' he handed her a glass of sparkling water and sat on the other lounger clutching a bottle of Mexican beer.

'Thanks.' She'd had more than enough alcohol, and had a sinking feeling a hangover was in her near future.

Across from Matt, Leo lounged in a deckchair, Georgiana sitting on a cushion at his feet so he could idly stroke her dark hair, which he'd unwound from its knot. Next to them, Nathan and Sofia were cosying up on the wooden bench they'd carried from the bottom of the garden, Nathan's arm resting around Sofia's shoulders and idly stroking her slim forearm. Holly and Noel had said they were leaving an hour before but were still reclining in deckchairs a few inches apart, their joined hands dangling in the space between them. Frankie and Zack were cuddling in a cushioned wicker two-person love seat that had been delivered that morning at Matt's request, and Rayne was sitting on Adam's lap on a wooden lawn chair, her arm curled around his neck, resting up against him as she sipped a tall glass of Pimms.

The couples all looked happy and in love and Zoe was pleased for them, but creeping jealousy coiled in her stomach anyway. She stole a look at Matt, wishing she had the right to sit on his lap like that, knowing at the same time that the thought was utterly crazy. Eyes stinging, she gazed at the fairy lights twisted around the decking rail until their bulbs had burnt dancing dots into her retinas.

'I swear to god I'm going to bruise,' Sofia muttered, rubbing her hip. 'We are such children.'

'Stop moaning woman,' Nathan said good-naturedly, 'a tumble off a micro-scooter is nothing. You do far worse to yourself when you come off your skateboard.'

'Or when you miscalculate with one of your cocktail shakers and it flies across the room at me,' she quipped back immediately, causing howls of laughter among the group.

'I'm surprised at you, Matt,' Georgiana tilted her head to look at her cousin when everyone had calmed down, uncovered blue eye twinkling, 'given you're the oldest by far and one of the hosts of this party, I thought you'd have been ordering us off the stuff, not taking the lead.'

'Hey, less of the old,' he exclaimed, 'I'm only thirty. And I know how to have fun, just like anyone else. Besides, my kids weren't around to see it, so I wasn't setting a bad example for them, was I?'

Zoe lifted her head, 'I think they'd have enjoyed seeing you like that actually. Although, probably not drunk.'

'You can be quiet,' Matt teased, 'you should have been keeping me on the straight and narrow as the other responsible adult in the house. But no,' he said mournfully, 'a few glasses of wine and the strict nanny persona goes completely out the window.'

'It probably went to the same place as your grumpy, serious *I'm a very important and dedicated music producer* guise,' she answered, raising one eyebrow.

'God, you are so cheeky sometimes,' he shot back, grinning and raising his glass, 'cheers to that.'

Rayne mumbled something into Adam's ear and then stumbled off his lap. 'Right, we're off, guys,' she said, 'it's been fab, but I'm whacked. It was lovely to meet you, Matt,' she gave him a brief hug and turned to Zoe, holding her arms out.

Zoe jumped off the lounger and swayed. 'Oops,' she giggled. 'Great to see you, speak soon.'

'Call me if you need anything,' Rayne whispered in her ear as they hugged, breath sweet with alcohol, 'and be careful.'

'Huh?' Zoe pulled back.

Rayne fluttered her eyelashes and patted Zoe's cheek. 'You know what I mean.' Her eyes flickered to Matt, who was shaking Adam's hand.

'Whatever,' Zoe tutted. 'Night, Rayne. Adam,' she wrapped her arms around him and squeezed, 'it's been lovely seeing you again.'

'Not quite like the uni days,' he grinned, 'but pretty close, huh? I remember the night with the trolleys...'

Zoe chuckled, before yawning again. 'Let's have that conversation another night.'

'Fair enough,' he released her and stepped back. 'Come on, you,' he turned to Rayne, 'let's get some fresh air and walk down to Hyde Park Corner to get a cab.'

She grabbed his arm, snuggling into his side, 'Good idea, lover.'

Their departure caused a flurry of activity and Zoe and Matt were soon waving everyone off, agreeing they'd do it again sometime.

Leo leaned back against the front door waiting while Georgiana and Matt said their goodbyes on the gravel driveway. He looked at Zoe, who was standing next to him on the top step. 'Was I out of line earlier?'

'Probably,' she said in a light tone, studying his face, 'but don't worry about it. It's done now and I bear no grudges.'

He smiled, 'You're cool. I like you, Zoe.'

'Why thank you, kind sir,' she did a mock curtsy but the effect was ruined when she tripped over her own feet and ended up clutching his arm for balance. 'I did *not* mean to do that.'

Shaking his head, he laughed. 'Not very elegant.'

'Everything okay?' Matt appeared next to them, a mild frown on his face as he took in Zoe's hand on Leo's arm.

'Fine. I nearly fell over,' she hiccupped, transferring her hand to Matt's forearm, 'I'm happy for you to prop me up instead.'

Matt's expression eased, 'No problem. Night, Leo.'

'Night, Matt. See you soon. Zoe,' he nodded, walking backwards down the stairs to join his girlfriend. Putting his arm around her waist, they wandered off, heads together as they talked, Georgiana limping slightly.

Matt escorted Zoe inside, locking the front door behind them. 'Have fun?'

'Yes,' she nodded solemnly, 'but I have a horrible feeling I'm going to pay for it in the morning.'

'Well, at least the kids aren't here first thing,' he said, 'we have the house to ourselves.'

'Yes.' Her mouth dried up as they stood in the shadows at the bottom of the stairs.

'What did you think of Leo?' Matt asked suddenly.

'He's a nice guy. A bit blunt, but nice.'

'It looked like he was flirting with you.' Shoving his hands in his pockets.

'What? Don't be silly!' She let out a disbelieving laugh. 'He absolutely adores your cousin. I can't imagine him doing that to her. We were just being friendly, there's nothing between us. If anything, he was encouraging me—'

'What?'

'Nothing,' she licked her lips.

'What was he encouraging, Zoe?' His voice was low.

'It doesn't matter.'

Matt took a step forward, hands sliding from his pockets. 'It does. Tell me.'

'No, it doesn't, because it's something you've already decided can't happen.' The remark slipped out, the wine fogging her common sense.

'Something—? Oh. Us?' Stepping nearer, he caged her in against the wall with his arms, body aligned to hers, green eyes starting to simmer.

'There is no us,' she breathed, gulping as she felt the heat of his skin. He was so big and strong and gorgeous, it was torture being this close to him and knowing she shouldn't get any closer.

'Maybe I was wrong. Maybe there is.' His eyes gleamed and he shifted nearer, dipping his head towards hers.

She groaned. 'You're drunk, Matt.'

'So?' Leaning in, he kissed her gently, sliding his tongue across her bottom lip and then nibbling it with his white, even teeth.

Sighing, she tilted her head back and opened her mouth, inviting him in. With a sound at the back of his throat, his kiss deepened, their tongues tangling. Their hands grabbed at each other and her fingers dug into his bum to haul his hips in against hers.

He jerked away, panting. 'Jesus, Zoe.'

'You'll regret it in the morning,' she whispered, staring at his mouth, watching it getting ready to form more words that were totally irrelevant because all she was listening to was what her body was telling her, which was to rip his clothes off and sink into him. Let him fill her, hold her and take her. Now. Hotly and desperately. Nothing else mattered. Her reasons for being here, her dishonesty, her need to tell him who she was and what she'd come to do, all faded. She was sick and tired of fighting the sexual spark between them. Tired of fighting her feelings for him. Tired of fighting herself. It was exhausting.

'I want you, Zoe. More than you can know,' he said hoarsely. 'And I'm pleasantly drunk, not hammered. So what if I regret it in the morning? All I care about is now.'

His comment was like a vat of iced water being tipped over her. If he'd have said he wouldn't regret it, that they could find a way to make things work, then she'd have launched herself at him again, kissed him until he begged her to stop. But he was agreeing he would regret it, and things were bad enough without adding extra dollops of guilt and shame to the mix.

'Then, goodnight.' With curled fists she slid out sideways from beneath his arms, and sprinted up the stairs as if the Ripper was on her heels along a cobbled London street.

'Zoe, wait,' Matt called after her.

But she ignored his words and flew up the two spiral staircases, not stopping until she'd slammed into her bedroom and was resting up against the door. Don't think about his kisses, *don't* think about his kisses, she commanded herself tipsily. So of course she thought about his kisses. Her hands fisted again and her heart pounded in her chest, lust scorching her face as she recalled how devastating and sexy those stolen moments had been.

Kicking off her sandals she flung them into a corner and wrenched the green dress over her head. Maybe a cold shower would help. It was what guys did when they were frustrated. God, was she frustrated. They had been so close, so close to... Yes, a cold shower. It might be the only alternative to going downstairs, pinning her boss down on the floor, peeling his clothes off and riding him until—

'Shit!' She was losing her mind. The sooner she could get into the shower the better. The sooner she could get out of this house the better.

Turning as a knock sounded on the door, her mouth opened, 'Wai—' but the handle turned and Matt strode in before she could finish. Her hands flew up to cover her cleavage and she took a step backwards, the back of her knees hitting the bed. 'Matt, you're supposed to wait after knocking before coming in.'

'You're in your underwear,' he said stupidly, blinking as he took in her pale, creamy curves in the black strapless bra and shortie knickers.

'That's what happens when you take your clothes off,' she said breathlessly, rational thought fleeing at the way he was gazing at her so blatantly, so appreciatively, so hungrily. It had made her feel amazing and indescribably sexy, as if she was the most beautiful woman in the world. It was a heady feeling, but it was less about her ego and more about it feeling like he wanted her as much as she wanted him. It also put a serious dent in her willpower, making it that much harder to resist the overpowering urge to give into the magnetizing chemistry between them. Their gazes clashed. Hot sexual awareness flashed between them, his eyes darkening, reading the message in hers. Her mouth went dry, her lips parted slightly and the oxygen in her lungs hitched.

He kicked the door shut deliberately, and with intent.

'What are you doing?' her voice shook.

'I won't regret it in the morning,' he grated. 'How the hell could I? Look at you.' Striding across the room, he grabbed her upper arms and hauled her against him. Her rounded breasts squashed against his muscular chest, her skin went hot all over in one massive wave and she felt the burn of his touch all the way down to her toes.

'Are you sure?' she stared up at him.

'Yes.' He started running searching, open mouthed kisses down her throat, and she gasped.

She should be scared. Emotionally this was the last thing she needed, it would make things so much more complicated than they already were. But physically, she'd never wanted a guy more. She'd never experienced a sexual curiosity like it, a hunger so strong. It wasn't fear that had made her voice shake. It was overwhelming excitement and the thought, *oh thank God, finally.*

His large hot hands swept down her back to her waist, his fingers settling and stroking the silken skin on her spine just above the line of her knickers. Her breath huffed out and her knees went to jelly, her heart pound, pound, pounding in her chest. 'Oh, Matt,' she moaned.

He gathered her closer, the muscles in his upper arms flexing and she made a weird squeaking sound as she felt the hard insistent nudge of his erection against her bare stomach. The muscles and nerve endings between her thighs quivered, her knickers damp- ening with lust. Her mouth dropped open as she tried to inhale, but it didn't work. She couldn't breathe properly. She was lost and taking him with her. All the way.

Throwing her arms around his neck she lifted her face to his, seeking his mouth, stealing tiny biting kisses as she rubbed up against him, twisting her hips. The next thing she knew he'd grabbed her around the waist and was throwing her back onto the bed as if she weighed nothing, following her down to lie on top of her. That action was like a spark lighting a firework and suddenly it was fast and frantic, his long muscular legs tangling restlessly with hers, the material of his shorts rubbing deliciously against the bare skin of her legs and feeling deliciously naughty. His hands held her face steady so that he could kiss her hungrily, insistently, his fingers in her hair.

He was so gorgeous, *this* was so gorgeous and so unbelievably hot, she thought dizzyingly. Arching her back, she tried to get even closer to him. He let go of her jaw to run blistering hands down her waist and over her flat tummy, then grabbed both thighs and wrapped her legs up around his hips so their pelvises aligned.

She rubbed against him as she felt his pulsing erection pressing against the material of her damp knickers, rocking her hips in greedy rhythm so that her clit rubbed along the rigid length of him. Grabbing the hem of his top she pulled it over his head so fast she was surprised that it didn't give him scorch marks. He drew back, panting slightly, his dark hair ruffled and sticking up in spikes. His dilated pupils were so large she could see only a rim of his green irises.

'You are so unbelievably sexy. I can't believe how hot it is between us,' he said huskily, before wriggling down to peel her bra away and feast on a swollen, hard nipple.

'Mmm,' she moaned, squirming and clutching his head to her breasts, encouraging him to suck harder and keep going. It felt like she'd waited forever, a lifetime to get naked with him, be with him. It felt right. Dangerously so. He unhooked her bra and tossed it away, taking her knickers off easily as she wriggled her hips to help him. The sweltering warmth between her thighs grew, her pelvic muscles twitching in eager little jumps, her nipples rubbing deliciously against his hairy chest as he kissed her passionately.

He drew away for a moment to strip off the rest of his clothes and after a rustle of foil while he sorted out protection, his naked body met hers from top to toe. She moaned as his dark head dipped and licked around her nipple before sucking on it in a bold steady beat again, one that had her twisting back and forth and opening her thighs so he could settle between them.

'Now, Matt. Please. Now.'

He let out a muffled groan but carried on sucking her nipple while he inched his hips away and dropped a hand down between them to press a long finger against her, rubbing back and forth in a steady, relentless rhythm. Staggering heat gathered tighter in her pelvis, tingles shooting through her as he quickened the pace and moved his head from her breasts to her mouth. They were half kissing as she moved her hips demandingly against his hand, erect sensitive nipples pushing against his chest as she urged him on, biting his shoulder and then biting his bottom lip. 'Faster,' she breathed, 'yes, right there, oh God. Don't stop, Matt.'

'Like that?' he asked, tilting his face to look down into hers before gazing down at her body. 'You are so beautiful, Zoe.'

'You are too. Kiss me,' she ordered, tunnelling her hands into his hair and yanking his mouth to hers, 'kiss me.'

He did as she asked, tongue flicking against hers, hand moving faster and building the heat inside her to fever pitch. Her fingers clenched on his broad shoulders and his thighs trembled against hers in response.

'Tell me what you want,' he whispered, nuzzling her ear lobe. 'Tell me, Zoe. Harder? Faster?'

Nodding in agreement, she rolled her head on the pillow, skin going dewy. 'Yes. Yes, I'm going to co...' her voice got strangled in her throat as pulses starting racing outwards from her pelvis to the rest of her body. But it still wasn't enough. 'No. I want you inside me,' she whimpered, 'quickly, now.'

Pulling his hand away, she locked her legs around his back and

251

jerked her hips up. She felt him prodding at her wet heat and then he was sliding all the way in and they were both groaning with pleasure.

'Zoe,' he groaned, sinking his face into her neck and pumping his hips.

Wrapping her arms around his shoulders, she hung on tight as he surged in and out, hard and fast, pounding into her almost roughly. She rocked with him, matching his movements, pleasure making her skin prickle and waves of shimmering warmth shooting through her and she was urging him on, moaning in his ear, telling him how unbelievably good it felt to have him inside her, racing to the finish line with him. Then he was kissing her desperately and the feeling was escalating and she was gasping, shaking and melting with an almost unbearable orgasm, calling his name over and over. Her inner muscles were pulsating and holding him tight and he said her name through gritted teeth and then fell over the edge into hot oblivion with her.

As they lay tangled together afterwards panting, Zoe took a deep, slow breath, waiting for Matt to do a runner. She was sure it was going to happen when he gently disengaged and shuffled to the end of the bed. But after disappearing into the bathroom for a moment, he slid back under the covers and gathered her close, tucking her into his manly, slightly sweaty body. With a satisfied murmur, he kissed her forehead and mumbled goodnight in a low, deep alcohol addled voice.

Her damp face creased in confusion. She wasn't sure how she felt about what'd happened. It had been mind-blowing and spine-tingling and that was based only on a quick, frantic tumble so who knew what would happen if they did it again taking their time—an explosion probably—but what did it mean? Where did they go from here? Was it just amazing sex or something more? Could they get past her deceit, the unanswered questions about Melody, and his grief for his late wife? Did they even want to?

Screwing her face up, she struggled to think clearly but failed.

A day of food, sunshine, endless glasses of wine and incredible, earth-shattering sex swept her towards sleep and even though she fought to stay awake to make sense of it all, with a murmur that echoed Matt's she snuggled into him and drifted away.

When she woke up in the morning with a pounding head, he was gone. Sitting up and clutching the covers around her, she swept her eyes around the room. Not a trace of him. So he hadn't done a runner last night, had probably been too drunk, but he had done one as the day had dawned.

'Fuck.' She dropped her face into her hands, shoulders slumping. He'd said he wouldn't regret it in the morning, had promised he was sure. Now she was here alone in her room and wished she could crawl back under the covers and never come out.

She'd had sex with him. It had been unbelievable, like nothing she'd ever experienced before, but with his absence a bolt of pain sliced through her. She felt tainted, uneasy. How was she going to face him after what had happened between them and he'd walked away without any explanation? She was living with him. Looking after his kids. Was he going to pretend it had never happened? She cringed. It would be excruciating.

Seeing her phone on the bedside cabinet, she scrambled towards it, forgetting about the hangover. As she saw a message icon on the screen hope soared in her chest, but when she opened the text it was from Frankie sent at half past midnight and thanking her for a nice night. *We liked Matt*, her friend had added on the end followed by two kisses.

Zoe winced, chucking her phone on the floor. Not a word from Matt. How could he? A note left on the bed saying 'speak later' or some other casual dismissal would have been better than him sneaking out of her bed without a word. Anything would have been better. She'd thought he respected her, that they'd built a friendship of sorts, even though they were supposed to be boss and employee. He'd told Aimee that they were friends. But this wasn't how you treated a friend. With friendship there was warmth, trust, respect, loyalty. Running away after having sex was none of those things.

'What the hell were you thinking?' she muttered out loud, pushing her shaking hands through her long knotted hair. Knotted from when she'd rolled her head back and forth on the pillow when he'd been sucking her nipples and—

'Stop it.' Lurching from the bed, not sure how much of the shaking was down to the alcohol from last night and how much was from anger and disappointment at Matt, she traipsed into the bathroom. Stepping into the shower, she turned it to the highest setting to scald away her shame and disillusionment. She'd thought Matt was better than this. She really had. More fool her. Stupid, stupid girl. She berated herself while shampooing her hair and scrubbing his smell from her body. How did she always get it so wrong when it came to men? First Henry, making her fall for him and then casting her aside after deciding he wasn't ready for a serious relationship. Then Greg cheating on her and sounding the death knell of their relationship, a cancelled wedding left in its wake. And now Matt, who she'd had no business getting involved with in the first place and had sorely misjudged.

What was wrong with her? Images of them in bed together the night before flittered through her mind. It had been so amazing, so intense. Surely he couldn't have looked at her that way, touched her like that if he didn't feel anything for her?

No. It had just been fantastic sex. That's all it was. That's all it could be.

Shaking her head vehemently as she turned the shower off made her groan. She had such a headache. What had she been thinking of drinking so much last night? If anything she should have been trying to keep a clear head given Rayne and Frankie's attendance at the party. It was because they'd been having so much fun she realised. Her and Matt, and the five couples who were all such lovely, good people. Wrapping a large bath towel around her and knotting it over her breasts, she brushed her teeth roughly while trying not to be sick and promised herself a couple of paracetamol ASAP. Striding into her bedroom, she dried off briskly even though it magnified the pain in her head by about a hundred and pulled on underwear, jeans and a loose, thin grey top. Sitting down on the edge of the bed, she tilted her head forward and used a hand towel to dry the ends of her hair.

'Oh,' a deep, surprised voice said above her head. 'Morning.'

Freezing, Zoe fought back a crashing wave of mixed emotions and took a deep breath. Some demons were best faced straight away. Flipping her head upright, she met Matt's eyes, desperate for the next few minutes to be over already. 'Hi.'

'I didn't think you'd be awake yet. It's only just gone nine and we had a late night.' He extended a tray full of mugs and plates towards her, his face pale. 'I went out to get us some pastries for breakfast. I needed some fresh air. I made us coffee too.'

'Oh,' now it was her turn to sound surprised. 'I woke up half an hour ago. Eight thirty is a lie-in for me compared to when I get up in the week.'

'Right.' Setting the tray down on the bedside cabinet, he joined her on the edge of the bed. 'But you got up straight away.' His eyes went to the pillow he'd slept on, the indent of his head still there. Dull colour seeped into his face. 'So you must have thought I'd left without saying anything. That I'd just left you.'

'I um…yeah, I guess I did,' she muttered, staring at the towel and twisting it between her hands. This was so awkward. Had she gotten it totally wrong?

'I'm sorry if that's what you thought, but that's not my style,' he pushed her thick damp hair behind her ear to see her face, then frowned and yanked his hand away as if the contact had burnt him. 'I thought you knew me well enough by now to know that, Zoe.'

'Sorry,' she said, gathering her courage and turning to look at him. His eyes fluttered away from hers, avoiding eye contact. 'But this wasn't supposed to happen, was it?' she pointed out. 'So you can hardly blame me for thinking the worst when I woke up and

255

you'd gone.'

He sighed. 'I don't. I get it.' His shoulders slumped and he shifted away, a divide of wrinkled duvet appearing between them. 'Look, we need to talk.'

'Oh, Matt. Can't you come up with anything more original than that?' A huge lump lodged in her throat and she had to swallow twice to carry on. She wasn't sure she could bear this but at the same time knew that what he was about to say was probably the best for both of them under the circumstances. 'What are you going to say? It's not me, it's you? Or—'

'Hang on! Don't start making assumptions—'

'Of course I'm going to assume. You can't even look me in the eye. It's obvious you regret—'

'Don't tell me what's obvious!' Jumping up, he walked to the window, movements uncharacteristically jerky. Staring fixedly out of the window, he lowered his voice, 'You don't know how I feel or what I think. I walked to the bakery so I could get my head together before talking to you. I needed to get it all straight, needed to understand how I was feeling before I spoke to you. It's only fair.'

'Okay, so you've done that. Now tell me how you feel. Make it fair. You're saying you don't regret us sleeping together, but your body language is screaming with tension.' She breathed in, deep and slow, praying the answer to her next question would be no. 'Do you want me to leave, Matt? Is that it? Do you think it would be better but you're worried you'll come across as a bastard if you ask me to go now?'

'No. It's not regret, okay?' He span around to look at her, face flushed. 'It's guilt.'

She frowned. 'Guilt? Why on earth would you feel guilty? Okay, I was drunk but I knew what I was doing. It's been there between us for a while, hasn't it? So don't feel guilty on my account.'

He waved his hand to dismiss her words. 'No. It's not that.'

'What then?' she shot off the bed and marched over to him, grabbing his forearms, feeling the heat of his skin and the strength

256

of his tense muscles beneath her fingers. 'Tell me. What is it?'

'Helen!' he ground out, a nerve pulsing in his jaw. 'It's Helen.'

'Oh, shit. I didn't think. I'm sorry.' Softening her voice, 'I know it's hard, but you shouldn't feel bad. She died three years ago. At some point you need to move on. I'm not saying you're doing that with me. I'm not asking you for anything, but its normal that… What I mean is that when you love someone, are married and lose them—'

'Zoe.' He met her eyes. 'It's not that. She was my wife, yes. But this isn't me being afraid to move on because I'm still in mourning. I've tried to fight what's between us for so long, but I couldn't. Which is why I feel so bloody awful.'

'What is it then? Matt, what are you not telling me?'

'I don't deserve to be happy!' It burst out of him in a rush, his voice strangled.

'What?' She let out an astounded laugh. 'Don't be so stupid. Why on earth would you say that?'

'Because it's true,' he shouted, his breath hot on her cheek. 'It's true.'

'What?' She stepped back and released his arms, mouth dropping open at the fury in his voice.

'It's true, Zoe,' he repeated in an undertone. 'I'm sorry for yelling at you, but that's the way it is. I'm just being honest.'

She studied the pain on his face, the milky complexion under the ruddy cheekbones, the eyes filled with remorse, the tight lips. 'I'm sorry I didn't take you seriously,' she answered. 'I shouldn't have laughed. I didn't mean it in a ha-ha way, it was genuine disbelief. You're a good person,' pausing, she thought of what he'd done to Melody and how distant he'd been from the kids when she'd arrived, 'even though you may have made mistakes. But everybody does. It's what makes us human. We don't live in a vacuum. We live among other people and we're all messy, complex creatures.' Thinking of herself and of the plan she'd once had. 'So please tell me what you mean.'

He hesitated, expression torn between confusion and despair.

'Please, Matt,' she begged, sliding her hands around his wrists again to anchor him. She stroked them soothingly, reassuring him without words that no matter what, she was there.

Closing his eyes, he started talking. At first it was stilted and slow. 'I don't want to speak ill of the dead.'

'So don't. Just tell me the truth in your own words. I know it's hard, but focus on the facts. Besides, I'm not here to judge you.'

'All right,' he sighed. 'I... I told you that things were difficult between me and Helen towards the end. That she seemed to resent being a mum, and lost her way a bit. I explained to you that things were bad and then getting better. Or so I thought. The truth is, we'd simply found a way to rub along for the kids' sakes.'

Zoe winced. She'd seen on more than one occasion what staying together for the kids did. It caused two unhappy parents and equally miserable children. It was laudable to want to keep the family unit intact, but not at the expense of everyone in it.

'I thought I still loved her,' he continued, opening his eyes. 'I wanted things to work between us. I thought we were going through a rough patch. Sometimes we had spats, sometimes we virtually ignored each other, and sometimes there were these shitty, hideous silences. It went on for months. And then one night I tried to talk to her about what was going on between us and the way it was affecting us all. The way she only really seemed excited about shopping or seeing friends. How she'd been drinking more and more. It was no way to live.' Now that he'd started, it was like he couldn't stop, the words flowing out of him. 'She reacted badly. We had a massive argument and she was so unreasonable, almost hysterical. When I lost my temper and said maybe we should have a temporary separation, that I wanted her to take some time to go and figure out what she wanted, she freaked out. She was ranting and raving that I couldn't take it all away from her. Then she,' he gulped, eyes filling with horror, colour leeching from his skin so that it looked ash white, 'she grabbed the kids from their beds and

258

ran out while I was in the kitchen at the back of the house. She put them in the Land Rover I'd bought for her and roared away. It scared the hell out of me. She'd come home after a few wines over lunch with friends, or at the time that's who I thought she was with, and had another few glasses over dinner.' He stared at Zoe sightlessly and she could tell he was lost in another time and place, re-living that harrowing night. She tightened her grip on his arms, stepping closer to him. Contrary to his usual heat, he felt cold, tremors wracking his body. 'When I realised what had happened I grabbed some shoes and looked for my car keys to follow her, but I couldn't find them.' His face paled further, lost in his own private agony. 'I couldn't find them and I didn't know what to think. I was frantic, couldn't breathe properly and didn't know whether to call the police or keep searching for the keys. I didn't think I'd ever see the kids again. I thought she was going to be one of those women who absconded with the children, or used them as weapons in some ugly war. But most of all I just kept thinking to myself, she's drinking and driving and my babies are in that car with her.'

'God, Matt.' She drew in a sharp breath, aching for him. So that was why he'd reacted so badly the day she'd got into the Prius to go to Longleat with the kids and he'd thought she was angry. She'd guessed there was something at the time, had asked outright about Helen and the accident, but he hadn't felt able to tell her. It must have brought it all back for him. That was also the first time they'd kissed, she realised. When he'd been vulnerable and hurting. So perhaps it wasn't about her, but about the comfort he'd needed that day.

She should let him go, break the physical contact between them but couldn't convince herself to release his arms just yet. So she simply listened as his sentences got shorter and shorter, racing through remembered pain.

'I eventually found the keys—she'd hidden them in one of Jasper's shoes—then ran out of the house. I leapt in the car and drove up the road. I wound the windows down. It was pouring with rain, even though it was June. Bloody British weather, I remember thinking. It was so strange and surreal. I was gasping in the warm air, praying to a God I never really believed in to keep them all safe when I heard the crash. I found out later it was over a quarter of a mile away.'

Her mouth fell open in dismay at the thought of the kids being hurt, and what it must have been like for him to hear the sound of the accident. It was so awful she could barely comprehend it.

'I got to the car and it was crumpled, concertinaed into a tree at the side of a residential road. It was starting to spark and smoke. I thought I'd lost them all,' his voice broke on the last word, 'and I felt as if someone had punched a hole straight through my chest. I ran over to the car, afraid to look, afraid of what I was going to see, afraid not to look. I- I saw Helen. She was badly injured. Her head was crushed against the windscreen and bleeding, her neck was at a weird angle and the airbag hadn't deployed. She'd talked about disabling it at some point but I didn't think she'd actually done it. She was in a bad way, but do you want to know what my first thought was? It wasn't that I should get her out, how I could help her, it was for the kids. I looked in the back seat and they weren't there. The kids weren't there.' His eyes were anguished, hands curling into fists and sending quivering ripples into her hands. 'I could smell petrol and the car was sparking. But still it was the kids that I was worried about. My brain knew they weren't in there, but I still ran around the car wrenching the doors open. Searching for them. Leaving Helen in the front, unconscious and bleeding. And then I heard Aimee calling me.' He ground his teeth, a vein pumping in his forehead. 'I spun around and she was standing further down the road holding Jasper's hand. There was a woman with them. I didn't know who she was or what was happening, so I started running toward them and then there was a clunking sound and a whoosh behind me and I was thrown to the floor by an explosion, straight onto my face. The fall broke my nose.' Freeing his arm from her hold, he rubbed the bridge of his nose with a trembling finger. It must be a constant reminder of the accident, Zoe thought, every time he looked in the mirror.

'When I stood up,' Matt continued, 'blood pouring down my top, the car was a burning wreck and Helen was dead.'

Zoe's eyes filled with tears, a sharp tingling sensation shooting down her nose. It was truly horrific, what this family had gone through. She didn't know what to say, or if she should say anything. All she knew was that she wanted to hold him and soothe him and take away his pain.

'The emergency services arrived only a few minutes later. The woman standing with the kids had called them. She lived nearby. She'd heard the crash and come out to help. When she'd found the kids she moved them away and kept them safe for me. If she hadn't...'

'But she did,' she whispered, picturing Aimee's shiny red hair in a neat ponytail as she bent over a book and Jasper's dark hair and green eyes full of excitement as he bopped up and down about something. Her heart swelled with affection and relief. She couldn't assimilate how close they had come to being hurt, or worse. 'They were fine, weren't they? They weren't injured?'

'They were fine, physically. It turned out that Helen had stopped and let the kids out at the side of the road. What she was thinking of abandoning them like that I don't know, and why she did it is a mystery too. Maybe she realised leaving me and having two children to look after wasn't going to be much fun. Or maybe it was because she was having an affair and thought the kids would be an inconvenience.'

'She had someone else?' she asked, astounded.

'Yes. A friend of a friend as it turned out. They'd run into each other at the gym. He came to see me after the funeral. I never forgave him for telling me. He should have kept quiet, said nothing. It was like a kick in the teeth on top of everything else. I haven't seen him since.'

261

So that's why when she'd confided in him about Greg cheating he'd been so understanding. He knew what it was like from personal experience. It was also possibly why he'd been so adamant after the newspaper article that he would never start something with someone if he was already in a relationship. She couldn't imagine why anyone would want to cheat on Matt. He was so warm, funny and caring. Not to mention gorgeous. Then again, if a person was unhappy, perhaps they could justify anything to themselves. So maybe it said more about the person who was being unfaithful, than the person they were cheating on. Maybe it wasn't about being unworthy, but about no longer being right for each other.

As for the other thing Matt had said... 'He may have thought you deserved to know the truth, Matt. So that you mourned the real person and not a wife you believed was loyal and faithful. Or maybe he was grieving too.'

'I suppose it's possible. I never thought of it like that. I was too angry.'

'But if you can't forgive other people, how can you get closure yourself and be happy? It'll always be hanging over you. And what you said about Helen taking the kids out of the car, have you ever considered that her mother's instinct kicked in? Perhaps she realised she was drunk and that they shouldn't be in the car with her. You told me before that even though she wasn't that emotionally invested you never normally worried about their safety with her.'

'It's possible. I never considered it that way. I just thought she was being irresponsible, but maybe it was the opposite. She did love them in her own way, I never doubted that. But why wouldn't she have simply pulled over and waited for me to catch up?'

'Who knows? We never will, because we can't ever know what was going through her head at the time, can we?'

'Well, what I do know from the Road Traffic Collision investigation is that she pulled straight into oncoming traffic and hit the tree at more than forty miles per hour when she swerved to avoid a car. She was accelerating at the time. They said that she can't have been paying attention. She was nearly double the legal drink driving limit.' He dropped his chin, staring at the floor. 'I saw tears on her face when I found her in the wreck, Zoe.'

'And it's your fault,' she filled in softly, slowly putting it all together. The way he hardly ever talked about Helen to the kids, how uncomfortable he was around Helen's mum, the way he'd distanced himself from Aimee and Jasper. It was the guilt he'd referred to.

At her words, his head snapped up and back as if she'd slapped him. She could see the misery in his dark green eyes.

'It's your fault, that's what you think,' she expanded. 'You feel guilty and responsible and that's why you think you don't deserve to be happy.'

'I don't. I was responsible,' he gritted out. 'If I hadn't argued with her, she wouldn't have taken the kids and got in the car. I shouldn't have lost my temper!'

'Did you hit her, or threaten to?'

'No. Of course not.'

'Did you get in her face and make her feel afraid? Did she look scared?'

'No. I raised my voice but I didn't get in her space. She looked pissed off that I was suggesting we take a break, but that's all.'

'So you didn't drive her out of the house, did you? She wasn't fleeing for her life and I doubt she believed her or the kids were in imminent danger. She could have chosen one of any number of other options; gone to bed, gone to another part of the house, called someone to come and get her, or called a taxi. You need to think logically, remove yourself from the situation. She was drinking and she was angry. We make our own fate in life, Matt. The argument would have happened one way or another at some point. It was bound to if you were both unhappy. But there was no way you could have predicted it would end like that. Helen was the one who decided to drive under the influence. It was her who pulled out into traffic.'

'But I could have gotten her out of the car. I told you, I knew the kids weren't in there. I wasted time looking,' his voice, raw and twisted, broke again. 'I could have pulled her out. Should have.'

'And you could have caused her further injury, paralysed her if she'd hurt her neck or back,' she pointed out sharply, 'and you didn't know the car would go up so quickly, did you?'

'But I still can't help feeling I could have done something. If I hadn't been so focused on...' he drifted off.

'What?' she inched nearer to him so that their chests were touching and she could stare up into his face. 'Looking for your children, who were God knows where and needed you? Who were what, two and four years old? Don't ever apologise for putting your children first! That's what parents are supposed to do. No,' she amended, 'that's what good parents do automatically.'

'But I wasn't a good parent. Because of me the kids lost their mum, because of me she died!' Screwing his face up, his shoulders shuddered on quick indrawn breaths, his eyes glazed with a sheen of tears.

'Yes, they did,' she nodded solemnly, pleading with her eyes for him to listen to her, and to take in what she was saying. 'But only because you care about them and love them so much. You were frantic, you said so yourself. What you've described, from arriving on scene, probably only happened in thirty seconds or so. You didn't have time to think, to weigh up the choices. You followed your instincts, which was to find and protect your children. It was unfortunate and sad that it ended as it did. It's a regret for you, obviously. But it's not one that should rule the rest of your life.' She freed one of his arms and lifted a hand to his face, stroking his jaw. 'Oh, Matt. Stop torturing yourself. You do know that Cynthia doesn't blame you, don't you?'

His expression turned shocked, pupils dilating. 'What do you mean? What do you know about what Cynthia thinks?'

'We spoke at the BBQ. She told me how good you've been,

letting her see the children. She also said that you blame yourself for Helen's death but shouldn't. She misses her daughter, Matt, and she'll always mourn her, but she doesn't hold you responsible and you shouldn't either. The only thing she's cross about is that you don't talk to the kids about their mum. That there are no photos of her here.'

'I thought it was for the best. They were so young when she died. I thought it was better not to remind them of what they were missing. What they'd lost.'

'Which would have also made you feel even guiltier,' she pointed out gently. 'They need to know they had a mum who loved them, and what she was like. It might make them sad that she's not around, but they need to know where they came from so they can understand themselves and their place in the world. It's absolutely vital for their self-esteem. I told Cynthia we've been going to Hyde Park, that you've been visiting the memorial plaque for Helen. I think that helped her feel a bit better. I do think it's been good for the three of you too. Remembering the good times, making some new ones together.'

'You're right, it has. We've done that with you. Because of you. Thank you.' He covered her hand with his, where it rested on his face, holding her fingers against his warm, stubbly cheek. Staring down at her, he nodded. 'Maybe you're right. Maybe I got it wrong. They should know their mother. It will be painful for me, but if it's what they need, of course I'll try.' Pausing. 'As for Cynthia, I haven't been able to look her in the eye for three years. I didn't dare. I guess I was afraid of what I would see.'

'I think you should talk to her. It would probably be cathartic for both of you. And I think that if you look in her eyes you might be surprised by what you see. Compassion. Understanding.' She smiled, a tiny hopeful hitch of her lips, 'You need to try and start moving on from this, Matt. Talk to someone professional maybe, see a counsellor or something. But please find a way to live with it. I mean really live, not this horrible half-life where you haven't been properly involved with the kids. It's getting better, don't get me wrong—you're more affectionate and more engaged—but there's still some way to go. I understand you've been feeling guilty for thinking you lost them their mum, but then in some respects you've taken their dad away as well. Give him back to them,' she pleaded, 'you all deserve more. You also deserve to move forward in your personal life. Don't let what happened hold you back. Three years is a long time, Matt.'

'Just like that?' he asked sadly, 'You think three years of feeling like shit about it is going to disintegrate overnight? That I'm suddenly going to feel fine?'

'No, I don't. But perhaps if you acknowledge it, if you make a conscious effort to start working through it, it'll get easier, until one day you'll realise the pain and guilt that used to tear you apart has faded to a dull ache. It'll be like a niggling little stone in your shoe. It's there and you can feel it but it doesn't stop you functioning. Do whatever you need to do, go to the basement and turn the music up loud and scream until you're hoarse, go and sit on Primrose Hill and watch the sun rise, or take a break from work and do something fun with the kids. Do anything you need to do that will help you deal with it and move on.'

'How do you know about dealing with grief? Oh, your parents,' he acknowledged. 'I guess you know what you're talking about.'

'I was a lot younger when I lost them. I didn't know what to think or feel. All I knew was that one day they were there and the next they were gone. It was like a chasm opened up under me and I was free-falling. I was powerless and needed control, so I got up every day, went to school and did everything I could to make them proud. To be honest, their deaths only really hit me in my mid-teens. I started acting out, coming home late, drinking, smoking and lying, but luckily before I could went too badly off course my teacher realised what was going on and referred me to a counsellor. It didn't bring them back, but talking about it and sorting through my feelings helped me cope when I had a bad day or felt overwhelmed by everything. It was the talking therapy that got me interested in doing a psychology degree, even though I ultimately ended up not using it. Counselling isn't the be all and end all, and it's not for everyone, but it's worth considering.'

'Okay, I'll think about it,' he said, eyes serious. 'But what about the guilt, what makes you the expert? You can't have blamed yourself for your parents' death, you weren't with them, were you?'

'No, it was just them in the car. But I live with guilt every day,' she admitted softly, knowing that after Matt had exposed himself so openly, had shared something so deeply personal, she had to tell him the truth now. No matter what the consequences might be. 'I left my younger sister to go to America, to make a new life for myself, to follow a man who ended up being worthless. I was heartbroken after my first serious boyfriend had dumped me. I shouldn't have gone. I shouldn't have left,' she reiterated. 'And no matter what she might say to me, I know I was selfish and hurt her and because I wasn't around, because she lived with my aunt who's not the type to talk about feelings, I feel like she didn't learn how to protect herself. She's naive. Trusts the wrong people and gets hurt. I've been trying to make up for it since.'

'It sounds like you're being a bit hard on yourself, Zoe, although I can appreciate that's going to sound a bit hypocritical given you feel I've been doing the same thing about Helen.' He narrowed his eyes. 'And I didn't know you had a sister. Why didn't I know that?'

She bit her lip. 'There's a lot that you don't know about me.' Sliding her hand from under his and letting go of his wrist, she backed away. She needed distance between them to do this. 'We all have our secrets, Matt.'

'Meaning?'

Taking a deep, shaky breath. 'Meaning I need to tell you something.'

'I knew it. I knew there was something. You've been seeing your ex, right?' He raked his hands through his hair, leaving it sticking up in uneven ruffles.

'My ex?' Shuddering at the thought of it. 'No, he lives in America. Why would you say that?'

'There have been times you've been twitchy about your phone and you've gone off to spend time with someone, but haven't said who. Obviously you don't have to tell me as your boss, but on a personal level I thought you might, and with what happened last night, I figured you'd come clean now...' he trailed off, shaking his head. 'You stayed out last Saturday night, Zoe. All night. So I was sure you were with him. I've half been expecting you to hand your notice in. But then you don't seem the type to sleep with me if you're starting up with him again. Look, just level with me. Are you with him or not? Are you going back to America?'

'No! Urgh, I'd never go back to someone who cheated on me. Never,' she reiterated, edging backwards. 'The trust is gone and I don't feel I could ever get it back. He contacted me a few times by phone, but it was half hearted. He gave up after a couple of weeks when I ignored him. Maybe if this was a romance novel he'd turn up, beg my forgiveness and try to whisk me away but it's not. This is real life. This is *my* life. I haven't answered any of his messages. It's not him I've been talking to and seeing, I swear.'

'Come on, do you think I'm stupid? Your face says it all, you're literally a picture of guilt,' he stuffed his hands in his pockets, 'so don't bother denying it.'

'I'm not lying, Matt. I want to tell you the truth. I have done for some time, but at first I didn't trust you and then—'

'Didn't trust me? Why?' he demanded, but she just shrugged helplessly. 'And then, what?'

'I got in too deep,' she confessed, hoping he might find some way to understand what she'd done. 'The truth is,' she moved even further from him, putting her back against the window sill, bracing herself, 'the truth is that the younger sister I told you about? The one I abandoned? It's Melody.'

15

'Melody? As in my last nanny?'

'Yes,' she lifted her chin, dreading his reaction but ready for the blow, uneasiness curdling her stomach and making her hands curl into fists.

'Melody is your sister?' he said in disbelief. 'The sister who looked after my kids? The sister I fired and told to leave? When you came to the interview you didn't say anything. Why?' he demanded. 'Jesus, right from the beginning, it was always about that,' realisation dawned as he blurted out the words. Horror washed the colour out of his face and put a hardness in his beautiful green eyes that she hated. It was like looking at a stranger and Zoe gritted her teeth to stop from crying out at the loss. 'These last few months, living in my house, caring for my children and all along you were her sister. We talked about her, you asked about her and Stephen but still you said nothing. There was this ulterior motive the whole time. You betrayed us.' His face was screwed up in bewildered anger, trying to make sense of it. 'So, what is it you were after? What was it you wanted? Revenge? Or was it spite? Tell me. For fuck's sake, just say it.'

'I wanted answers,' she cried. 'I wanted to know why you would treat Melody so badly. I came here to confront you both, but Stephen was so cocky and left so quickly I didn't get a chance to say anything. He mentioned the interviews before he went and it was a way in so I used it. I held you largely responsible, so I wanted to have it out with you. Once I was inside the house you were so impatient, dismissive and—you might not like this—arrogant as well, that I didn't think you'd tell me what had happened, let alone be willing to explain yourself. You seemed so unaffected and oblivious to the consequences of what you'd done. I was furious with you and your brother, cut up on Mel's behalf because she was so devastated and clueless as to why you'd fire and chuck her out without explanation. I had to do something, she's my sister. I needed to get the answers for her, Matt.'

He didn't need to know what she'd intended, about the kiss and tell expose, *Plan Nannygate*. It didn't matter now and would only hurt him more. She took a breath, forcing calmness into her quivering, high pitched voice. 'I thought that if I worked for you, was here, you would open up and tell me. But instead I got sucked in. I didn't want to like you but somehow you grew on me.' She winced when he shook his head and muttered a swear word. 'It's true,' she insisted. 'You weren't what I was expecting. Not at all. I've grown to care about Jasper and Aimee so much, Matt. You have to believe that. I've never felt this way about children I've nannied before. There's a genuine bond there and I would never do anything to hurt them, I swear. I almost left a few times, nearly told you a few more, but after a while I didn't want to leave, and the timing was always off.' She spread her hands, desperate for him to listen, to understand. 'After getting to know you I realise you're not dismissive or arrogant. You were just stressed the day of the interviews and you disappear totally into your own world when you're concentrating or working on something. As for the answers I was looking for, obviously you think Mel did something wrong, something unforgivable which gave you grounds for your actions, but I never found out what because you always shied away from the details.' Shaking her head. 'You don't talk about things Matt, not how you should. You need to face things in life, confront them head on and deal with them. Not bury your head in the sand.'

'You're wrong. I wasn't shying away from it; I just had my reasons for keeping the details to myself. I have confronted things. You've made me. I trusted you!' He looked agonised, pacing the room back and forth, out of reach and then within reach but a thousand miles away. 'Jesus, Zoe, I confided in you and listened to you. And all the time you were here because of Melody.'

'I was protecting her! I'm her big sister and I wasn't there for her. I left her to go to America because things were too painful here. I ran away and have felt guilty every single minute since, whatever she might say to try and make me feel better. That's why I said you have to face things, because I didn't and then it was too late. My sister and I, our relationship, it's not how it's used to be and that's my fault. So yes, I wanted to help her. I wanted to give her closure, help her understand why the boss she got on with so well and admired took everything away from her. I wanted to know why Stephen stopped taking her calls and cut himself off after they'd been so happy together.'

'Happy?' Matt froze, turning towards her. 'I don't think so. I told you, she broke his heart.' He shook his head. 'You may as well know the truth now. I don't see what there is to lose. If you tell anyone it's not as if you'll be a credible source given what you've done. Maybe you also have a right to know what kind of person your sister really is. Perhaps I owe you that much, given what you've done for me and the kids.'

She tried not to flinch at the condemnation in his words. 'So what is the truth?' she whispered, waiting breathlessly for the answer she'd first set out to discover.

'She tried to blackmail him.'

'What?' Her lips went numb with shock. 'No.'

'Yes. He came to me, begging for help. He didn't know what to do. She'd found out he had a criminal record for drug offences—'

'What?' Of all of the things she'd expected, it wasn't that. Drugs always seemed so sordid and dirty, not something an entitled

271

playboy would be involved with.

'It happened during his time at private school. He and a few friends got caught doing some relatively low level dealing—not that I'm saying any dealing is right—when they were eighteen. They got expelled from school. Unfortunately, drugs can be rife among kids that age from privileged backgrounds,' the remark made it obvious he didn't count himself as part of that group, 'they like to party and think nothing of taking Class A drugs for recreational use. It wasn't that big a leap from Stephen and his mates taking them to supplying them to friends. The school wanted to cover it up to avoid damage to its reputation, because to a prestigious institution like that image is everything. However, the Crown Prosecution Service wanted to make an example of them and they could be tried as adults because of their age. I guess the thinking was, why should they get away with it just because their parents were rich? My parents didn't want to go to court, partly for Stephen's benefit and partly to protect the family name and their professional reputations, being senior civil servants. So he admitted the charges, sold out his supplier and got a warning. There was no custodial sentence because of mitigating circumstances and it being a first time offence, and we always managed to keep it quiet.' He stared at Zoe, eyes as unyielding as steel. 'Stephen told me Melody said she had evidence he was dealing again and would testify he'd supplied her drugs if he didn't give her hundreds of thousands of pounds. She threatened to go to the police and the press. He was frantic. Knew what it would look like with his background, and that he might not escape a sentence this time—'

'Bullshit,' she spat, 'Melody would never do anything like that. She's completely incapable of it. She's the most honest person I know. How could you believe it of her? Why the hell would she blackmail someone she was in love with? She's not into money and definitely isn't deceitful—'

'Not like her older sister, you mean? Your bar is hardly high seeing as you've lied to me for coming up to two months about

272

who you are.'

Her jaw clenched, fury started taking over from the hurt she'd caused him with her lies. 'Oh, don't give me that. You didn't know Mel was my sister but you know my name, my background, the way I've behaved with your kids, the hard work I've put in to bring them out of their shell and calm Jasper down. You know what I've done to build you a better relationship with them. It's no good being all self-righteous when you're the one who turfed a defenceless twenty-two year out on her arse without giving her a chance to understand why.'

'I had to,' he came towards her, face twisted. 'What did you expect me to do? He's my brother.'

She gazed at him, fingers clenching. It all made sense now. How out of character Matt's actions had seemed in relation to the person he actually was. 'You really believed him,' she said in amazement. 'So in your eyes, you were protecting him.'

'Of course I was. I couldn't let her do that to him. So I called her bluff and threw her out. I didn't even mention the money, I just told her to go and never come back. I figured that if I played the hard line, like it wasn't even worth discussing, she'd know there was no point in pursuing it. That we wouldn't give in to blackmail.'

A wave of relief crashed over Zoe. It was all a big mistake. Melody hadn't done anything wrong. Stephen was a liar and however misguided his actions had been, the only reason for Matt's actions was protecting his brother from something he perceived as a threat.

All along it had been about an older sibling driven to look out for a younger one. It was exactly what she'd done, so how the hell could she judge him for it? God, what a mess. 'But that also means you never asked her if it was true,' she pointed out, struggling to understand the way events had unfolded. 'You didn't give her a chance.' It didn't stack up. Why would Stephen make up such disgusting lies about Melody, who by all accounts he had genuinely cared for and changed for?

'It had to be done quickly,' Matt ground his back teeth, lip scar burning white. 'I was so furious I just wanted her gone and so did Stephen. We both felt betrayed and he was hurting, big time. I could have called the police you know. Blackmail is a criminal offence.'

She put a hand to her temple, massaging away the dull ache. 'But you didn't, even though you believed him,' she murmured as the fuzzy picture, the pieces that hadn't made sense started to slot together and come into focus. 'Why?'

He sighed, looking troubled. 'She was a nice girl until then and you were right a minute ago, we got on well. She was good to my kids. For some reason I couldn't just put that aside.'

'You didn't want to see her hauled through an investigation or face prison so you cut her loose as quickly as possible?'

'Perhaps. But more importantly if she left and didn't follow through on the threat of blackmail there would be no court case, no media circus and it wouldn't hurt my brother any more than it already had.'

In his own way Matt had tried to be fair, Zoe recognised. He had picked the least damaging option for Melody despite what he thought she'd done. An idea occurred to her. 'Or was it that there was a part of you that believed it might not be true?' she tilted her head, studying him thoughtfully. 'Don't tell me you never questioned whether Stephen might be lying?'

'No, I didn't.' He held his hands up. 'Wait. Just hang on a minute. Stephen's not perfect. He can be cocky, fickle and yeah, doesn't have the work ethic that I do or a history of stable relationships. And God knows he made a mess of it with those drug offences, but he was a screwed up kid at the time. At the end of the day he's my brother and wouldn't have any reason to lie.'

'Neither does Melody,' she put her hands on her hips. 'She has no clue about any of this; would be mortified and shocked at even a hint of it.' Her eyes flashed with heat and she stepped forward, jabbing him in the chest with one finger to emphasise her next point. 'She loves him and is as heartbroken as you claim he is. When I flew into Heathrow and found her at Jemima's she was in absolute bits. I had to take her home to our aunt's to recover. She's lost weight. Looks haunted.'

'Well, Stephen's gone AWOL somewhere in the Med,' Matt threw back, pushing her hand away, 'and I haven't heard from him in weeks. In fact I've put feelers out for him, have contacted a few of his friends and am starting to get seriously worried. But he's done this before when he's been in a bad place, so I'm hoping that he just doesn't want to be found at the moment. I'm afraid your sister hasn't got the monopoly on hiding away and hurting, Zoe.'

'No, I guess she hasn't, after all you've been doing it for three years right here in this house,' she lashed out unthinkingly, stung by the suggestion that her sister was somehow dramatising the situation, or not entitled to her heartache.

'Well at least I didn't run away to the other side of the Atlantic like a selfish child,' he retorted.

'What?' She couldn't believe it, the biggest regret of her life ripped open and used against her. 'You bastard. Well, if I'm so selfish you may as well watch me do it again,' she yelled, hardly knowing what she was saying, face flushed and chest tight with rolling anger. Racing over to her wardrobe she wrenched the doors open, yanked a case out of the bottom, unzipped it and began jerking clothes from hangers and flinging them into a haphazard pile.

'Fine by me. I wouldn't want you here after the way you've lied to me anyway.' Marching across the room, he slammed out of the door like it had personally injured him in some way. Just like she had.

Matt bolted down both spiral staircases and stormed into the garden, rage blazing through him. Sitting down on the wooden deck stairs, he leaned forward, elbows on thighs, head in hands. How could he not have seen it, not known that there was more to Zoe than met the eye? He'd suspected she was keeping something from him, but not this. He'd been convinced she was talking to

275

her ex again but had hoped she wasn't, given how well the two of them had been getting on lately. Given the feelings he had tried to push aside but had failed to contain.

He thought back to the last accusation he'd thrown at her. She'd lied to him. He'd been fooled by another woman. Helen had been sneaking around behind his back for months and he'd been blind to it. Now Zoe had done the same. Well, not the same. But both situations had been betrayals. How could she do that to him, to them? Act like she was just there to do a job, when all the while she was trying to trip him up and catch him out?

Sighing, he rubbed the back of his neck, wishing he hadn't had so much to drink last night. His head was pounding and he felt sick. He supposed that could be as much to do with the emotional turmoil as the alcohol leaving his body.

Maybe he wasn't being fair to Zoe. He could see her side of the argument; it was reasonable to want to find out the truth. If Melody had genuinely acted like she didn't understand what'd happened, then of course Zoe would have been furious and puzzled on her sister's behalf. Also, unless Zoe was a Hollywood actress, the astonishment on her face about the blackmail had been sincere, as was the surprise at hearing about Stephen's criminal record. For the hundredth time, Matt wished Stephen had been a bit more focused and a bit less stupid and selfish as a teenager. Then again, everyone made mistakes and there were few things in life that you could never atone for, or come back from.

Screwing his eyes up, he went back over the last six weeks in his mind, scrutinising Zoe's behaviour, the initial anger subsiding as he picked it over and pulled it apart. He didn't get it. She'd hardly ever asked about Melody and what had happened. They'd only discussed Stephen a couple of times. She'd always seemed so focused on the job and getting to know the children, nurturing them and trying to help the three of them become a family again. Because they hadn't been one before she'd arrived. She was right. They had been going through the motions. At least, he had. He'd kept a roof over his children's head, food on the table, made sure Melody looked after their basic needs, but he hadn't given them proper attention or affection. They hadn't been happy, he could see that now. Aimee had been withdrawn and hesitant, with Jasper bouncing off the walls. Zoe had changed that. He thought about the things she'd said about liking him and caring for the children. Reflected on how hard they'd worked together to make Jasper's party a success. How welcoming she'd been to his friends and family. How everything she'd done since her arrival appeared to have his family's best interests at heart.

From the first time he'd met her she'd challenged him on every level. Emotionally, mentally, even physically, because it had been torture keeping his hands off her and he'd had more cold showers over the summer than hot meals.

It had felt genuine. It had felt real. How long had it been since someone had engaged him, made him feel excited about getting up in the morning and spending time with his children? How long had it been since a woman had made him smile at the thought of coming home every day?

'Hello?'

Matt lifted his head at Cynthia's well-spoken tones.

'We tried the doorbell but no-one answered, so we used the side gate,' she explained, walking forward. 'Is everything all right? I'm sorry we're so early but Jasper kept talking about it being Sunday, the day for Hyde Park.' She looked worried, a frown creasing her forehead into lines.

'Yes,' the word came out croaky so he tried again, 'I mean, yes its fine.'

Jasper sprinted over, wrapping his arms round Matt's neck and squeezing tight.

'You okay, buddy?' Matt asked around the lump in his throat.

Jasper leaned back. 'Yep, we had fun with Nanny last night, but I wanted to come back. We're going for a picnic today, right Daddy? I love our picnics.' He gave his dad a big gappy grin.

It was Matt's favourite smile. One he might have been oblivious to if not for Zoe. He pulled Jasper back into the hug, savouring the warmth and sturdiness of his son's body. It was affection they might not be capable of if it wasn't for Zoe, coaxing them all along in the right direction.

'I love our picnics too,' he agreed.

He and his kids had been happy over the last month and a half. Because of Zoe. No matter that she'd lied to him, betrayed him in her own way, she had done a lot of good for them. She was a good person. No one could fake that so successfully and so intensely when living with a family twenty-four seven.

And while he couldn't forgive her right this minute for lying, he could see how it must have looked to an outsider who didn't know the situation. Her motives for coming here had been the same as his for making Mel leave. Love and loyalty for her family. How could he criticise her for that, or fail to empathise?

The truth was she'd done no harm other than hurting him and that was something he could get over. She'd told him the truth the first opportunity she'd had after they'd slept together. Plus, she could hardly have planned or wanted to get involved with a guy she thought had treated her sister so unjustly, a guy who must have looked like a cold uncaring bastard without knowing the context of Mel's behaviour.

What was less clear was what they could do about the situation when she was so adamant her sister would never do such a thing and he was equally adamant Stephen wouldn't fabricate a blackmail plot. The reality was that they might never know what had really happened between Melody and Stephen.

But maybe that's the way it should or would have to stay. Yeah, it would be difficult and no doubt awkward, but it didn't necessarily have to end what he and Zoe had started, did it? Whatever that was.

He wasn't sure. There was so much to process. All he knew was that there was a weird feeling in his chest at the idea of going to

Hyde Park alone with the kids, of waking up tomorrow and Zoe not being part of their home. It made him feel empty. It made him lose his breath.

Shit.

He couldn't let her go.

'Are you going to play with us?' Jasper wiggled away, eyes cajoling as he unknowingly pulled his father from his inner turmoil. 'I really like it when you do that.'

Matt put his best parent face on, smiling slightly and releasing his son. 'Yes, in a minute. Go and play on the bouncy castle for a few minutes first though, okay? The party equipment isn't being picked up by the hire company until tomorrow morning, so you may as well make the most of it.'

'Yay!' Jasper pelted off to the bottom of the garden, taking a running leap and disappearing into the depths of the yellow and red castle, a smiley face forming the entrance.

'What's the matter, Daddy?' Aimee traipsed over to him, a thick Harry Potter book in one hand and a pink rucksack on her back. 'You look upset.'

'I'm fine.' He stood up and gave her a quick hug. His acting skills must be woeful. 'Go and play with your brother for a minute, okay?'

'Sure,' she agreed, sliding the bag off her shoulder and handing it to him with her book.

Bemused, he looked down at the items as Aimee went to join her little brother, her striped skirt ruffled by the slight breeze that was stirring the leaves on the apple tree.

'Parents have many uses,' Cynthia said as she strolled over to him, having waited patiently while he greeted the kids, 'being a pack mule is one of them.' Taking Aimee's things from him she laid them on the nearest sun lounger and placed a slim, lined hand on his arm. 'What is it, Matthew? What's going on? You look terrible.'

He barked out a laugh, and looked at her. 'Thanks.' He almost dropped his gaze before remembering what Zoe had told him. There might not be the censure and accusation in her face that he was expecting. As he met Cynthia's blue eyes, the irises clear and so much like Helen's, he saw that Zoe was right. There was only curiosity and concern greeting him. No condemnation, no anger. The wave of relief made him feel dizzy. Zoe might be right about the guilt too. Could it be that Helen's death wasn't something he needed to torture himself with every day?

'I don't mean it like that. I just wondered if there's something I can do to help?' she asked hesitantly.

'Thank you, but no. It's very kind of you to offer though. It's more than I deserve. I'm afraid I've probably made a mess of something and I need to figure out how to fix it.' He craned his neck to glance up at Zoe's bedroom window, where she was no doubt busily packing. He'd been reeling, but he shouldn't have made that comment about her running away to America. It had been low and uncalled for. Although she'd been at fault too, with her comment about hiding. The difference was, he acknowledged, she'd been right.

Cynthia followed his gaze. 'She's quite lovely, isn't she? She also has a thing for you.'

Matt laughed again, this time in surprise. 'A thing for me? That doesn't sound like you.'

'You don't know me that well,' she rebuked gently. 'We never really got to know each other while you were married to Helen. As for what you deserve, it's as I told Zoe yesterday; you shouldn't be so hard on yourself. I know it might seem odd for me to be at peace with the prospect of you being with another woman given you were married to my daughter, but she's not coming back. It's taken me almost three years to accept that. At the end of the day, you never know what might be around the corner. You have to get on with it.' Squeezing his arm, 'You have a life to live with my grandchildren, Matthew.' The corners of her eyes drooped with sadness, but her smile was brave. 'So I'm sure you'll sort it out with your nanny, whatever it is you've done.'

He took a deep breath, shame flipping his stomach and making him trip over his own words. 'C-Cynthia, I'm so sorry if I haven't made it easy for you to talk to me since Helen died but I just felt so guilty.'

'Let's not do this today. Another time.' Lifting her chin, moisture gathered in her lower lashes. 'It's kept for the last few years so it will keep for another few days. Just knowing you're ready to start talking about it is enough for me. The only thing I'll say in parting is that she was my daughter and I loved her, but she wasn't always right in the things she did or the way she acted.' She sniffed. 'I'd better go. You have more pressing things to sort out.'

'Are you sure?'

'I am.' She dropped her hand from his arm, and straightened her pink satin blouse.

'Okay.' He started across the lawn with her, tucking his hands in his pockets, hardly able to believe how angry he'd been with Zoe less than ten minutes before and how much lighter he felt from Cynthia's accepting attitude. 'Thank you, Cynthia, for everything. For understanding. For having the kids last night too.'

'It was a pleasure,' she replied, turning to face him as she opened the gate, 'we'll have to do it more often so you can have a little more time for yourself. As for the other, I'm just pleased you've found someone who seems to understand what you're going through and who's so determined to make you all happy. She's marvellous with the children and they seem a lot more settled and confident. It's a gift when you find someone who loves you to the degree that your happiness is more important than their own, you know. So please don't do anything silly and throw it away.'

'Love?' His fingers gripped the black wrought-iron handle as he prepared to shut the gate behind her. 'I don't think so.'

'Don't you?' she answered, before slipping past him into the narrow, rose-lined alley.

He stared after her long after she'd gone, his heart pounding in his chest.

'Don't go.'

'Pardon?' Zoe fumbled in the act of packing another pair of shoes in the case, her hands still shaking with the emotional upheaval of their argument.

'You heard me.' Matt clicked the door shut behind him, walking over and sinking down onto the carpet next to her. 'Don't go.'

'You don't want me to leave? Why?' Afraid to look at him, she rearranged another pair of shoes, turning them so they were top to tail, slotting together perfectly. 'So I can look after the kids? So they're not losing a second nanny in the space of two months?' Shame, longing and dread rumbled through her and she couldn't look at him, too afraid of what she might see in his face or what he might read in hers.

'There is that, yeah. Of course. I love my kids and they need you.'

'Oh.' She gulped, lifting a cardigan up and refolding it.

'But I want you to stay for me as well.'

Her eyes flew to his. Suddenly she could look at him, and needed to know what was there. She clutched the cardigan to her chest, voice squeaking. 'Really? Even though I've lied to you for the last month and a half?'

'Really.' His face was deadly serious, his voice hushed. 'I'm not going to pretend I'm not bloody angry with you, because I am. But I can get past it if you can say there's nothing else I need to know, if you can get past what I did to Melody, and if we can put aside what she did,' he put a finger to her lips when she went to protest, 'or didn't do, to Stephen.'

'Right,' she said, her mouth moving against his finger, lips brushing his skin. She jerked her head away. Touching him made it harder to keep a clear head. This wasn't just about them, or what they wanted. There were children involved too. As well as her sister and his brother.

'What's the matter? Don't you want to stay? From what you said about liking me and caring for Aimee and Jasper, how upset you seemed, I thought you'd want to. I'm sorry for what I said about you running away to America. I didn't mean it. I promise

I'll never throw that in your face again.'

'Thank you. But it's not that. I mean, it hurt a lot but I shouldn't have said what I did either. I'm sorry. Sorry for everything. I never should have moved in here. It was crazy, stupid and ill thought out. I shouldn't have kept who I was a secret for so long.' She shook her head. 'I do want to stay, but it's just so messy, isn't it? What we've both done, what happened between Stephen, Melody and you. I'm going to have to tell her what you think she did, Matt. It's going to hurt her so much. It'll be horrible. Plus it wasn't so long ago I was engaged to be married, and you've got those issues about Helen. We have to think about the kids too, we need to be careful.'

'I know it's complicated, but nothing of value is ever easy, is it? Stop that. Come here.' Prising the cardigan away and throwing it across the open case, he wrapped his arms around her waist, sliding her across the carpet and onto his lap.

She didn't put up much of a fight, the idea of staying here with him and his kids making her feel giddy, even though it shouldn't. This wasn't part of the plan. Now she knew the lies that Matt believed, she should leave. Except she didn't want to. But then again, when had life ever gone according to expectations? It was usually the unexpected things that made it interesting and worth living.

'I don't know, Matt.' She sighed, closing her eyes and inhaling his aftershave, the scent and sexiness she'd come to associate with him. It was all out in the open now. He knew who she was and why she had come here. Well, it was nearly all out in the open, but she definitely wasn't going to tell him her original intentions. There was no point. He'd asked if there was anything else he needed to know, and there wasn't. It was done with.

Maybe they could face the other issues together. Give whatever it was they had a chance. She just hoped Mel wouldn't see it as a betrayal. But the last time they'd spoken about it, her sister had said Matt wasn't a bastard and must have had good reason for chucking her out. At least Zoe would be able to confirm that was the case. That he wasn't a bad guy after all. She just hoped it didn't break her sister's heart again to hear what Stephen had accused her of and what Matt had believed.

'Stop making excuses,' he ordered, and she opened her eyes to look at him. 'I get that you're scared and the situation is hardly an ideal way to start a relationship and we don't even know what it is or where it's going to lead yet,' he continued, 'but come on, Zoe, we've been happy together, the four of us. I like being around you. We laugh together, have fun together, you challenge me and make me think. You make me a better dad.' His arms tightened around her as she fought and lost the war to rest her cheek on his chest. 'You're kind and caring,' stroking her hair, 'and then there's the bonus of the great sex,' he half-joked.

'Hey, easy buddy,' she answered, lifting her head and thumping him on the shoulder.

'Are you going to deny that last night was amazing, as well as bloody hot?' He pointed to the rumpled bed.

'No,' she said, 'I just don't want you to get a big head.'

'No chance of that with you around,' he mocked, 'you're always telling me how it is. And just think,' he added, a wicked glint in his eye, 'that was half drunk, fast and furious. Just imagine what it might be like if we were sober and were taking our time. Imagine me peeling off your clothes and covering your whole body with kisses, before sucking on your—'

Slapping a hand over his dirty mouth, she squirmed on his hard thighs and moaned. 'Stop. I heard Cynthia bring the children back. They're down in the garden, right? So we can't do anything now.'

He pulled a sorrowful expression. 'You're probably right.' He shifted so that she could feel the rigid length of him against her bum. 'It'll have to be a date for tonight,' he suggested, 'if that's what you want?'

She hesitated, thinking hard. 'It is. I do want to be with you, Matt. Even though it flies in the face of everything I should want under the circumstances. But you're right, we have been happy.

So let's just take it a day at a time and see what happens. Right?'

'Right,' he smiled. Then a shadow fluttered across his face. 'Are you going to be offended if I ask something?'

'We need to be discreet for the children's sakes,' she guessed the source of his concern, 'so I'll wait until they're in bed. Then you can come to my room or I can come to yours, but either way we go back to our rooms for morning. We mustn't confuse them, especially as we have so much to work through and figure out for ourselves. We're probably going to have to talk to Stephen and Melody at some point you know.'

'I know,' he said solemnly, before ruining it by grinning. 'You're so brilliant. Thank you for always putting the kids first.'

'I wouldn't have it any other way.' She looped her arms around his neck, kissing him gently, just once. 'I still can't believe you're okay with this.' The prospect of him finding out who she was had been a massive hurdle in her mind. She'd assumed he'd throw her straight out, but that fear hadn't materialised.

A warm feeling started to unfurl in her chest. He wanted her to stay. She made them happy. Though she hadn't wanted to admit her reluctance to leave even to herself, the truth was that they made her happy too. What should have been an awful time in her life with her break up, boxing up her old life and struggling to make a new one, had instead been an adventure.

'I told you,' he tapped her nose, 'I'm angry and hurt but I'll get over it. Of course, you may have to offer me some therapy for a while, just until I'm over the worst. You did suggest it might help.'

'What kind of therapy?' she asked suspiciously, wondering where this was going.

'I've heard that sex therapy is enormously beneficial. What do you think?'

'I think you're misquoting me,' she leaned in and bit his lower lip, before pulling away to watch his green eyes darken and smoulder, 'but I think we can experiment a bit and assess the results.'

'Great. Nine o'clock tonight? My room?'

Grinning, she wiggled around on his lap, making him groan. 'Perfect.'

He wrapped his arms around her and leaned in to kiss her, but with a laugh she jumped up and held out her hand. 'Enough of that. Come on, we have kids to see and a picnic to pack for.'

Groaning, he struggled to his feet, tugging his jeans away from his groin and linking his fingers with hers. 'Fine, you mad woman. Let's go and get ready to go to Hyde Park. But if Jasper jumps into the Serpentine again, you're on lifeguard duty.'

Rising on her tiptoes she planted a quick hard kiss on his mouth. 'Fine by me, as long as you buy us all ice-creams again.'

'Deal.' He swatted her bum as she let go of his hand and danced out ahead of him, the coffees and pastries on the bedside cabinet forgotten as they made their way down to the garden, the sunshine and his kids.

16

The next few days passed in a steamy haze of incredible sex and stolen kisses. Matt was sweet and attentive, helping her cook Jasper a special birthday dinner and spending the last few days of the kid's summer break at home, joining the three of them for lunch every day and even inviting them down into the basement to learn about the soundboard. Surprisingly, Jasper was a natural, with an ear for music and a fascination for the various buttons and functions that delighted his dad.

Zoe crept into Matt's room every night and left early every morning, but still managed to fall asleep in his arms. To her surprise he was a snuggler, enjoying the way her body tucked into the curve of his, complaining when her alarm went off at half past five and she left his bed, trying to tug her back in for just five more minutes, sounding like an older, more petulant version of his son. It made her smile, and melt.

They took the kids to school together on the first morning of term, waving Jasper off proudly as he started in Reception, the pretty brunette teacher talking to her new pupil reassuringly while making eyes at Matt.

Zoe had noticed all the women looking at him, surreptitiously finger combing their hair or dabbing on lipstick.

'What?' he'd asked innocently when she'd given him a dirty look.

She raised an eyebrow.

'Can I help it if they think I'm gorgeous?' he joked in a way she never would have imagined him capable of on the day of her interview.

'I suppose you're okay to look at,' she shrugged, 'but you might want to consider getting the nose fixed and the scar lasered. Some people might see them as flaws.'

'Good thing you don't,' he growled, yanking her into his arms, apparently not bothered by the people around them who were all staring avidly. 'I happen to know you find both sexy and adorable.'

'Bugger, I knew I shouldn't have told you that.'

'Well, we were in bed and I'd just rocked your world,' he whispered in her ear, making her knees fold. 'It's moments like that when women get all soft and gooey, isn't it?'

Pushing him away she's smacked his arm lightly. 'Not as bad as you, Mr Snuggles,' she said loudly. Grinning to herself she'd skipped off to the car, leaving him to trail along behind her muttering retribution.

After that they soon settled into a routine, Matt disappearing to his city office and studio every morning and Zoe doing the school runs each day and redecorating the kids' rooms in between. It was a task she'd begged for in order to occupy herself in the daytime and because it sorely needed doing. Although jam-packed with books and gizmo's respectively, Aimee and Jasper's bedrooms were as white and soulless as the rest of the place and needed some colour and personality. They were already enjoying sharing their ideas with her on themes and motifs and helping her pick things out of high end furniture catalogues.

Matt made a special effort to say goodbye to both children every morning and wish them a good day, and was always back by six to help them with their homework while Zoe made sandwiches for lunch boxes and cooked dinner. They were happy and it was working, although neither Matt nor Zoe had quite built up the nerve to tackle the question of Stephen and Melody yet. They were just enjoying what they had. Or maybe just hiding from reality and hoping for the best.

Until one morning when Zoe came home juggling wallpaper samples to find Matt in her bedroom, kneeling on the floor with an odd expression on his face.

'Hiya. What are you doing in here?' she asked. 'Why aren't you at the office? You didn't say anything about being here today when you left earlier.'

'I came back to let the delivery men in.' He said in a curt tone that she hadn't heard in weeks. 'I was getting a bespoke bookcase built for you.' He waved a hand at the new shiny oak shelves spanning one side of the room. 'It was supposed to be a surprise. I thought you'd be at the shops for longer. I started filling it with the books you'd unpacked. I was sorting them by genre and alphabetising them for you. You told me once that's how you liked them.'

'That's right.' She beamed at his sweet gesture. 'Thanks so much. It's such a lovely thought.' Flinging the samples down, she made to run across the room to him.

He stood up, holding his hands out, face washed of colour. 'Don't come any closer.'

'What? Why?' she frowned.

'Because I finally know what a lying, deceitful bitch you are and I don't want you anywhere near me. Or for that matter, my children.'

'What are you talking about?' She felt the blood seep out of her face and swayed. 'Why are you talking to me like this? You know about Melody. You said we could get past it.'

'I could. But you said there was no more, nothing else to tell me,' he hissed.

'Matt, what are you on about?'

He stalked towards her. 'This!' Thrusting a balled up piece of paper at her chest so hard that it would probably leave a bruise. He backed up rapidly, distaste curling his lip. 'You promised me once you weren't a journalist. And you're not. God, you're worse.

At least some of them are up front about who they are and what they're after.'

'I don't understand.'

'Read it,' he snarled. 'It might help jog your memory. I found it inside a book you were reading a few weeks ago.'

Slowly unfolding the piece of A4 paper, her mouth shaped a succinct, 'Shit,' as her eyes traced the words on the page.

The Truth About Matt Reilly

It's well known that infamous London-based music producer Matt Reilly is fiercely private and camera shy. He never gives interviews to the press, and seems uncomfortable at public events, preferring the focus to be on his artists. In an exclusive story, the girl who was his nanny for X months shares a kiss and tell story about his love life, his relationship with his two children and his ruthless work ethic...

'Oh, fuck. No.' She remembered the night she'd printed the rough draft out, the way she'd read it and how lousy she'd felt, realising what a cow she was being. Tucking it into the back of a beach read she'd picked up in a street market one Saturday morning, she had forgotten all about it. 'Matt, hang on a minute. It's not what you think—'

'It's not?' he exclaimed in mock amazement. 'You mean you didn't write that? You're not the nanny that's quoted?'

Now was the moment for total and utter honesty. No more lies or half-truths. 'I did write it,' she met his gaze squarely, 'I am that nanny. But it was written a while ago, before I really knew you properly,' her voice grew pleading at the closed off expression on his face, one she hadn't seen since first arriving, even the day they'd argued when he found out she was Melody's sister. 'I was frustrated, angry, confused and venting one day, and yes, I'll level with you, it *was* my plan to do this originally,' she waved the crumpled piece of paper in the air, 'to expose the guy I thought had treated my little sister so despicably. A guy I thought was a heartless, immoral shit, but within a couple of weeks of being here I knew I couldn't do it. I didn't want the kids to get hurt, or later on, you.'

'Really? Is that what I'm supposed to believe?' he said, voice heavy with sarcasm.

'Yes,' she rushed across the room despite what he'd said about staying away, and stepped into his space, 'you have to understand that I wasn't in the right frame of mind when I set out to do this. I was heartbroken at Greg's deceit, or thought I was at the time, and how I'd lost five years with my sister for a cheating pig. Then Melody was so broken, so devastated, I lost it. But you have to believe me—'

'Let's get one thing clear.' His jaw was taut, lips as white as the plump roses in his garden. 'I believe fuck all of what you say.' He laughed bitterly, 'Jesus, now you'll be telling me it wasn't you that tipped off the press that day we were in Hyde Park when you were hung over.'

'It wasn't. Honestly, it was nothing to do with me. It's just a coincidence.'

'A coincidence? You must think I'm a complete idiot. It's a coincidence that an article that would have set you up so neatly as a credible source just happened to be published in a national newspaper weeks before you were going to do your sordid little kiss and tell about my sex life, and who knows what else?'

Flinching, she balled the paper back up and tossed it aside. 'I swear on my parent's graves that it was nothing to do with me and that the article I planned was never going to see the light of day. In fact, I wrote another one. That's the one you need to see.'

'Let me be clear. I have no interest in seeing anything you want to show me, or hearing anything either. That day, the one after Jasper's birthday party, when we'd slept together and you told me about Melody, I asked if there was anything else you needed to tell me. If there was anything else I needed to know. You said no, there was nothing. So why the hell should I believe you now when you tell me you were never going to use this? Why?' he shouted, eyes glinting, a vein pulsing in his forehead.

'You didn't need to know. I wasn't going to go through with it, so why hurt you by telling you?' she cried. 'As for why you should believe me, I don't know. I've given you every reason to distrust me, but I never meant any harm. Please, Matt. I love your kids, and I didn't think I'd feel this way about anyone so soon after Greg, but I do. The last few weeks have been amazing. Let's not throw that away.'

'You threw it away the moment you made the decision not to tell me. If you'd come clean, told me what you'd planned, shown the article to me but sworn it was never going to be used and destroyed it in front of me then I might have faith now. I might trust you. But you didn't. It's another betrayal.' He yanked his hands through his dark hair. 'You and your sister really are two peas in a pod, aren't you? You definitely share the same morals. To think what I've been exposing my children to. It makes me feel ill. All that publicity if the article goes out...'

'That's not fair! Don't bring Mel into it. She's done nothing wrong. This is on me. I made a mistake. We all make them, so please don't act as if you're immune. As for the kids, I told you, it's not going out. I swear. I would never do that.'

'Whatever.' He turned his back on her, staring fixedly out the window. 'You need to go. I'll arrange to send your stuff to you in a few days' time. Text me your address.'

'Matt?' she said uncertainly.

'I said, go.'

'You can't mean that.' Her eyes filled with tears.

'Can't I?' he gritted, broad shoulders tense and set. 'Get the hell out of my house, Zoe. Now.'

'You're repeating history. You're doing to me what you did to Mel. You were wrong then, and you're wrong now. Give me a chance to prove myself.'

'How exactly are you going to do that?' he asked without turning around.

She hesitated, thoughts whirring. 'I-I don't know right at this minute, but there must be a way.'

'I don't think so.' He dropped his hands to the window sill, clutching hold of the edge, knuckles pale. 'Leave.'

She could see he wasn't going to change his mind right now. He was too furious. Maybe if she gave him time, he might come around. 'But what about the kids? I dropped them off and they're expecting me to pick them up. I can't just leave without saying anything. They'll feel abandoned again after Helen and Melody—'

He span around, eyes wide, 'Don't you dare talk about Helen. And you don't deserve to say goodbye! You would have exposed them to the worst kind of ridicule at school with that article, would have marked them out for bullies. Did you ever think of that, or were you just too intent on getting revenge?'

'I've already told you I wasn't going to go through with it. Let me just see them, please. We can tell them I'm going away for a while, taking a holiday or something.'

'I'll tell them you had to attend to a sick relative. I'll say that you'll be gone for a while and then after a few weeks I'll tell them you had to leave for good. They'll understand. They'll get over it.'

She gulped, a sob lodged in her throat and a burning pain throbbing in her chest. 'But maybe I won't,' she whispered.

'What was that?'

'Nothing. I'm sorry. About everything. I'm telling you the truth though. One day you'll know that.'

'What I know is that you've got exactly five minutes to pack anything you can into a bag and get out of my house. You can take the BMW because right now I want you as far away from us as quickly as possible. I'll get it collected when your belongings are dropped off to you. But to be honest, at this moment I don't care if you keep it. I want you gone and it would be a small price to pay.' Marching across the room, he grabbed hold of the door

293

handle and gave her a hard look. 'Don't bother coming to find me when you go. I'll be busy calling my solicitor. Goodbye, Zoe.' He slammed the door behind him with a scary finality.

She heard his footsteps recede as she stifled a sob, feeling numb and dazed at the same time. What had she done? How had she messed up so spectacularly and caused both of them so much pain?

Eyes glazed with moisture, she stumbled around the room, drunkenly stumbling from the bathroom to the bedroom and from one piece of furniture to another, hardly aware of what she was stuffing into a small vanity case. Holding it together, just, she lost it when she found a painting Jasper had given her, one of the four of them in Hyde Park sharing a picnic, a giant splodge of yellow sunshine in the upper right corner, lines of dark blue depicting a summer sky. Tears rolled down her cheeks and plopped onto her top as she carefully tucked a bookmark Aimee had made for her into the inside pocket of the case.

A minute later she was ready to go, but there was one last thing she did before leaving the house that had become her home in such a short time. Scrabbling around the lockable drawer of the bedside unit, she slid out the redraft of the kiss and tell article she'd written one night and sealed it in an envelope. Sneaking into Matt's room with guilt scorching her cheeks scarlet, she left it on the pillow she'd slept on for the last few nights, hoping he would understand what she was trying to tell him when she'd barely been able to put it into words herself. When she was only just in this moment realising what it was she was losing.

Zoe and Mel hugged tightly, a bulging backpack at their feet. The sisters had travelled into London from Southend together by train and had lunch before parting ways outside the gracefully arched building that housed Fenchurch Street Station. Zoe clutched Melody against her, desperate not to let go but knowing she had to. 'I'm going to miss you.' She laughed and sniffed at the same time as a few people jostled past them with the arrival of a train. It was mid-September and most of the tourists had returned home. She couldn't believe the summer was almost over. It was especially hard to process when the days were still so balmy and the evenings so light. They'd got the Indian summer that had been predicted after all. 'Are you sure this is the right thing to do?'

'Yes,' Melody drew back.

'Funny that this time it's not me running away, it's you,' Zoe remarked. 'That I'm the one staying put.'

'Living with Ruth will give you both a chance to keep on rebuilding your relationship.' Mel smiled, a sparkle in her dark eyes that Zoe hadn't seen in months. 'And I'm not running away. I'm going to find who I am.'

'You think travelling across Europe will give you that?'

'I think Jemima and I are going to have some wonderful adventures,' Mel said firmly, taking Zoe by surprise with how confident she sounded, 'and seeing the world will give me a chance to think, really think about what I want to do with my life and who I want to be. The last career decision I made was based on wanting to impress and be like you and while I still admire you loads I have to do something I'm passionate about. Plus it'll finally help me get over Stephen. We know he's back in the UK now,' they'd caught a snippet in the celebrity gossip pages the previous weekend which had included a tiny picture of her ex going into his Chelsea apartment, 'but he still hasn't been in touch and after what he told Matt about me, I don't want him anywhere near me anyway.' Pain and bewilderment scrunched up her face but with an effort she forced it away, relaxing her mouth and blinking away tears.

Zoe nodded, squeezing her sister's hands, 'Well, it's your decision. You have to do what's right for you. I'm not going to try and boss you around. I have learnt something from this whole mess.'

'Thanks, Sis. Thank you so much for the money too, I really appreciate it. I'll pay you back, I swear.'

'There's no need to, honestly. You deserve this, and I'm happy to share it with you. I saved up a lot when I was working for Liberty and I got back the share of the money I put into the wedding when I cancelled it. Ruth was pleased to help out too. She told me she's had no-one to spend it on since we've both been gone.' She smiled, thinking of her improved relationship with her aunt, one that meant she had somewhere to stay while she got her head together and tried to assimilate what she was going to do next. What the future may hold for her without Matt, Aimee and Jasper. 'Actually,' she shared, thinking of Ruth's future too, 'I was thinking that travelling and expanding her world might be good for her at some point. Maybe when you come back and tell us all about your adventures, we might persuade her to travel abroad?'

'That's a great idea. I've always thought she was too self-contained and should experience more of life. Not necessarily because she never got married or had kids of her own—after all, she had us—but more because she doesn't have many friends or go out much.'

'Well, I'll see what I can do about that while you're away,' Zoe said decisively.

'Good.' Melody nodded. 'You'll be fine, you know. You always are. I'm sure interviews and job offers will start flooding in soon.'

'Perhaps, if Matt even gives me a reference,' Zoe gulped, mouth twisting. 'I'm not that bothered about getting a job right now though, Mel. I don't need the money immediately and I've been thinking I might do something else for a while. It's just that I miss them so much. I should have handled things better. If only I'd told him the whole story when I told him I was your sister.' She had so many regrets. But on the other hand, she had her family back. She and Mel were more than okay and after two weeks at her aunt's home, coastal Southend was starting to feel comfortable.

She sighed. Actually, the truth was that she longed for London, the size and shape of it, the people and places, the buzz and the hum, the architectural marvels amongst the modern skyscrapers, the wide open green spaces in the middle of the teeming city. She'd left her heart here and she wasn't sure she'd ever get it back.

'I know you miss them,' Mel acknowledged. 'It's the sight of your moping face that's driven me to fly to Paris,' she teased, 'and even Ruth is beginning to feel sorry for you.'

Zoe's face fell.

'Hey, I was joking.' Melody's eyebrows pulled down in concern. 'Look, are you going to be all right? I should be leaving to meet Jemima soon. Our flight is only in a few hours.'

'I'll be fine. Go.' She didn't tell her sister she still hadn't brought herself to text Matt with Ruth's details. That she couldn't face the thought of all her stuff being dropped off to her, a tangible milestone that would signal the end of her relationship with him and the children for good. Clearing her throat, 'Don't forget I'm expecting regular Facebook posts and albums with anything too outrageous to share sent to me by email.'

'I know, I know.' Mel frowned, 'Do you know what the time is?'

'Hold on,' she bent her head to dig her mobile out of her handbag. Squinting at the phone, 'It's just gone two 'o' clock,' she said absently as she opened a text from Rayne.

**You need to pick up a copy
of The Telegraph. It'll be
worth it, I promise.
Let me know how it goes.**

xxx

Wondering what on earth her friend was on about and if she should call her to find out, Zoe jerked her head up as Melody made a startled sound.

'Is that Matt?'

'What? Where?' Zoe asked breathlessly, spinning around.

'No. In the paper.' Her sister pointed at the front page on a pile of newspapers on a stand along the concourse from them, where a grizzled guy in a flat-cap was taking money and giving out folded up papers to passers-by.

'What the hell?' Zoe hurried over to the man, rooting around in her jeans pocket for the right change and practically throwing it at him, almost ripping the paper out of his hands in her haste to see it.

A picture of Matt sat under a bold headline. *The Truth About Matt Reilly; an exclusive interview.* The name of the journalist was one she recognised, a freelancer Rayne worked with sometimes.

Mel was on her heels as Zoe wrenched open the paper looking for the right page.

'An interview?' Mel said. 'I don't get it. Matt never gives interviews. He hates the press.'

'I know,' Zoe murmured as she found the article, hope soaring in her chest, the newspaper jumping up and down as her hands shook. She started reading.

I was lucky enough to interview a handsome, exhausted Matt Reilly yesterday, and he's not at all what I expected. Staring out at the beautiful garden of his multi-million pound property in Knightsbridge, the famous music producer who has a reputation with the ladies looks reflective and answers my questions candidly. Everything I ask him about (save for his children, who he is very protective of)—his career, his ambitions for the future, the death of his late wife, his love life—he responds to with a brutal honesty that takes me by surprise, given how fiercely guarded he's been in the past. The turnaround is surprising, but it soon becomes clear why he has chosen to make an exception. 'I've learnt a lot about myself over the last few months,' he states when I ask him what his biggest regret is, 'that I'm quick to judge; that I trust the wrong people sometimes, which regrettably may include family; that I am human and it's alright to make mistakes; and that I should follow my gut instinct and heart in knowing what's best for me and my kids. Most of all I've learnt that contrary to what I thought, it's okay to forgive myself for the things I can't change, and move on. My biggest regret is that the person I most want to move on with, the girl I love and who loves my children, is out there somewhere and I don't know where. So here I am, laying myself bare in the hope that she will read this and come find us. So that I can tell her how I feel, so that I can say sorry. If it's a Sunday afternoon, she'll know where we'll be.

'Oh my God,' Zoe breathed on a small sob, clutching the paper to her chest and gazing open mouthed at her sister. 'He loves me?' she said in wonder. 'He loves me. I can't believe he's done this. Rayne must have helped set it up, that's what the text was about.'

'It's you. It can't be anyone else.' Mel shook her head.

'It is me,' she whispered, starting to smile before faltering. 'But what about you?'

'Don't worry about me,' Mel grabbed her elbows, 'just because I don't get my happy ever after, it doesn't mean you can't have yours. Go to him. Go to them,' she pleaded. 'You've been so miserable, there's no way you can ignore this. We know why he sacked me and chucked me out now. I don't bear any grudge against him. It wasn't his fault, he just believed his shit of a brother when he shouldn't have done. It's understandable. You would always believe me, wouldn't you?'

'Of course. I love you. But I can't do this again. You're my sister and he's a guy—'

'Uh-nuh. No way,' she started softly. 'You're not doing this. I know you feel guilty about the whole going to America thing after your break up with Henry, but I told you we're cool about that. Plus, this is not the same thing. You're not choosing Matt over me. I'm going travelling and I don't expect you to put your life on hold while I'm gone.' Her voice gained strength. 'As long as you promise that you'll stay in touch and that when I'm back we'll always make time for each other, then that's all we need.'

'I promise. Of course I do.'

'Good.' She pushed Zoe away almost roughly. It was unchar-acteristic and Zoe realised the breakup had changed her sister. But maybe it wasn't a bad thing. Maybe it would make her more resilient and less naive. 'Now get going,' Mel instructed. 'I have a plane to catch today and you have a family to reclaim. Tell them I said hello, by the way. That,' she waved at a red bus that had just pulled into station, 'is probably going to be your best bet at getting to them.'

'Thanks, sis. Love you heaps,' Zoe hugged Melody again, and started backing away, a sense of urgency filling her. 'Safe flight, text me when you take off and land. Don't forget to text Ruth too.'

'I won't,' Melody rolled her eyes at her sibling's bossiness. 'I'll see you in a couple of months. Love you too.'

Zoe turned to go but stopped at the last moment, studying her sister's face, memorising the curve of her cheek, the arch of her fine eyebrows, the dark eyes and blonde hair. 'Have a brilliant time, Mel. I hope you find what you're looking for and you're happy. That's all I wish for you.'

Welling up, Melody ran over and gave her one last hug. 'Thanks. Now you know I hate goodbyes, so please go.'

Zoe chuckled as they separated. 'We'll make it a *see you soon* then.' Blowing her a kiss, she sprinted to the bus and clambered on just as the driver was closing the doors. 'Wait,' she begged, 'there's somewhere I have to be.'

Zoe threw a shadow across Matt as she stood over him in the afternoon sunshine near the Princess Diana Memorial fountain. It reminded her of the first time she'd brought the kids here. It wasn't as roasting hot as it had been that day, but the air was still balmy and the sound of happy children rolled over her along with the tinkle and swish of water. Matt was lying on the familiar picnic blanket, eyes closed but looking far from relaxed with a crinkle between his eyebrows.

The newspaper was rolled up in her hand and she'd read the whole interview three times on the agonising, crawling half an hour journey to Hyde Park.

'Hi,' she said simply.

'Zoe.' His eyes flew open. 'Hi.' He leapt up, an uncertain expression on his gorgeous face. It was just like she'd remembered it. The crooked nose, the sexy scar, the beautiful green eyes. 'You came.'

'I did,' she agreed solemnly. 'Was I right to? Am I the girl?'

'What?' he looked dumbstruck. 'Of course you're the girl!'

'Good.' Now she was here, she wasn't sure what to say, how to act. She had missed them all so much. Why wasn't he grabbing her and kissing her senseless? 'Where are Aimee and Jasper?' she swivelled her head to search for them.

'Over there,' he gestured to a spot ten feet away where the kids were sitting on the stone edge kicking water at each other. 'I only had my eyes closed for a moment.'

She smiled. 'I'm sure you did. Don't worry, I won't call the police on you.'

'Great.'

'So.' Zoe shifted from one foot to another.

'So... shall we sit down?' Matt gestured to the blanket.

Why was he being so formal? 'No. This is bullshit, Matt. What's going on? You give this unbelievably romantic interview saying you love me and to come find you and when I come running, you act all weird.'

'You thought it was romantic?'

'Um, yeah,' she answered, 'any girl would.'

'Aren't you angry with me about making you leave? And that I believed Stephen over Melody?'

'Yes,' she said bluntly, taking a step towards him, desperate to feel his strong arms wrapped around her now she knew how he felt. 'And no. I was hurt and pissed off that you didn't listen, but once I calmed down I could see how it must have looked. Do I think you should have given me more of a chance to explain myself? Yes. Can I blame you for feeling betrayed or mistrusting me? No. I said so at the time and like you said in the interview, people make mistakes. As for Stephen, I understand why as his brother you would want to believe him. Mel and I have talked about it.

She doesn't have an issue with you, only him. She gets it. I do too.'

'Right,' he nodded slowly.

'So what did happen with Stephen? And how did you find out?'

Matt shoved his hands in his pockets. 'He popped up out of nowhere a week or so ago like he'd never been away and never worried me sick. When he saw the state I was in, he felt really guilty, got drunk one night and turned up on my doorstep at three in the morning. He started going on about loving Melody, rambling on about fucking it up and being scared,' he took a deep breath, 'and after a very painful hour, admitted to me he'd made the whole thing up because he was petrified of commitment and panicked. Would you believe it? He didn't want to break up with Melody because he'd fallen for her but he couldn't face the thought of settling down either. So he forced me to do his dirty work. He's a coward. I guess if it was me that made her leave, he could fool himself it wasn't his fault. He was miserable when he was away though and said he'd been a tosser. I didn't disagree. He shocked me by apologising for being stupid, selfish and causing us all a lot of pain. To be honest I think he wants her back but knows he's gone too far.'

'He has. I honestly don't think she could ever forgive him for it. God, what he did is really messed up,' Zoe muttered, wondering if it would be a good idea or a bad one for Mel to know that what had been an awful thing for Stephen to do had been fear borne out of the strongest emotion of all. Love. 'So what did you say to him?'

'I was too furious to say anything. I rang a taxi to take him back to his place in Chelsea and haven't spoken to him since. It's been a week. He's left a few messages but hasn't worked up the courage to come round yet.'

'What will you do when he does?'

'I don't know. All I know is that I'm so, so sorry for what I did to Melody.' He pushed his hands through his dark hair, looking wretched. 'I got it wrong and feel awful. I really want to talk to her, to try and make amends. At the very least she should get some notice and holiday pay, right? I need to see her. Would that be okay, do you think?'

'I think it's too late for that, Matt.'

'Really? Shit. She hates me.'

'No, she doesn't,' she reassured him. 'She's gone travelling for a few months. But I'll happily let her know you'd like to see her when she gets back. Whatever happens after that is between the two of you, okay?'

'Yes. I'd appreciate that, thanks.' He hesitated. 'What do you think I should do about Stephen?'

Shrugging, she edged closer to him. 'I'm not sure. If you're looking for me to tell you never to see him again, never to forgive him, I won't. Firstly, because it's not my place to or my decision to make, and secondly because as much as he broke my sister's heart and I'll have a hard time reconciling that, life is too short to shut people out of it forever. I think it's like we agreed once when we were talking about us. You take it one day at a time, and see how you feel.'

'Sometimes that's not the right thing to do, though,' he answered, striding forward and finally scooping her up in his arms. He kissed her cheeks, her forehead, her neck, her mouth as she laughed. 'Sometimes you don't take it one day at a time,' he continued, 'because when you've found something that might last forever, you want to commit to it, make it yours. You never know what might happen or when it might be taken away.'

From the look on his face, Zoe could tell Matt was thinking about Helen. About how precarious and precious life was. 'Say it then,' she ordered.

'Say what?' he pulled a puzzled face, before burying his head in her neck and whispering, 'you smell so good. I've missed you so much.'

'Me too. Now say you love me.'

Lifting his head, he smiled down at her. 'I love you. I'm sorry I doubted you. When I read that other article you wrote and spoke

303

to Rayne, I knew I was wrong. You never would have done that to us. Do you love me?' he demanded. 'Is that why you came?'

'Yes. As well as the fact that you still owe me an ice-cream.' She yelped when he pinched her bum. 'Okay, I love you too,' her lips curved, knowing it was the improbable, wonderful truth. She thought about the redraft of the kiss and tell story left on his pillow.

The Truth About Matt Reilly

There are many truths about Matt Reilly, infamous music producer. He is rich and doesn't mind spending his money on expensive cars. But he is also generous towards other people and thinks about their needs. He doesn't have many friends because he doesn't trust the people around him, but he is fiercely loyal to those he does have and their happiness is important to him. He is hard working and driven to be a positive role model for his children, and though this can mean he is distant and works long hours, you can't doubt his love for them. He gives himself a hard time when he shouldn't, but doesn't always hold a mirror up to himself when he should. He is funny, caring and an all-round nice guy with firm principles. The truth is, though he might not realise it, he is imminently lovable. The question is, will he let himself be loved?

'So you'll come back to mine? You'll be the kid's nanny again?' Stroking her hair off her face, Matt tucked it tenderly behind her ear.

She turned into his touch, revelling in it, feeling safe and loved. 'No. I won't be their nanny again.'

'What? Why?' he dropped his hand, confusion and distress creasing his face up.

She held a hand up to his stubbly cheek, delighting in the rasp of his whiskers. 'They don't really need me in that way now if they're both settled at school. But we'll tell them I'm their nanny and I'll move back into my old rooms until we're ready and they're ready for it to be more, if you want that?' She smiled at the relief on his face as he nodded emphatically. 'I'll do the school runs and help with homework in the evenings, but I'll be doing it because I want to, not for pay. And we'll redecorate their rooms together. While they're at school I'll be pursuing other career options. How does that sound?'

'That sounds perfect,' he hugged her close, laying his chin on top of her head and breathing in deeply. 'Let's do it.' Leaning back, he stared down at her. 'So what other options are you thinking of?

'I have some money put away, so I was thinking of training to be a counsellor. What do you think?' she held her breath, dreading the idea that he might laugh at her as Greg would have done.

'I think you'd be brilliant at it. I also think that whatever you want to do, I'm a hundred per cent behind you.'

'Thank you. That means a lot,' she grinned, knowing she'd found someone lovely. Someone who would always support her dreams. Someone who would always help her reach for the stars in the summer sky.

'Zoe! Zoe!' Jasper's excited cry greeted her at the same time as two extra pairs of arms did.

'Zoe,' Aimee's more sensible voice piped up. 'You're here.'

Zoe shrieked at the dampness seeping through her top. 'Jasper, you're soaking.'

'Sorry,' the little boy said sheepishly, moving back slightly.

Aimee shook her head at her brother, ponytail swishing. 'You'll make her leave again,' she tutted.

'Its fine,' Zoe reassured, hungrily taking in their adorable faces. 'I have missed you guys so much.' She looked at Matt, who nodded and mouthed *home*. 'I'm sorry I left but I'm not going anywhere. I'm back. How do you feel about that?'

Jasper let out a, 'Yay!' and delivered an air punch, while his sister gave a more sedate but equally enthusiastic nod.

'Great. What about a little rest before we have ice-cream? I don't know about you, but I'm a bit tired.'

'Kay,' Jasper dropped to the blanket, followed by Aimee. They both looked expectantly at their dad.

'I guess I'm the lucky one who gets to go underneath,' he said with a raised eyebrow, appearing far from horrified by the idea, green eyes warm and full of affection.

She winked at him, love swelling her heart and her chest. She was back where she belonged. 'I guess you do. If you're really lucky we can do that tonight too,' she said suggestively under her breath.

Without hesitation he lay down and waited for them to clamber over him and get comfortable.

Zoe grinned widely as she lay down and rested her head on Matt's flat stomach, her arms around his adorable but complicated children as they snuggled into both adults.

For the first time in a long time, she was hopeful that she would get her happily ever after. She was also certain that for many years to come they would enjoy picnics in beautiful, leafy Hyde Park.

Bonus Material

If you enjoyed *Picnics in Hyde Park*, see where the #LoveLondon series began and read Holly and Noel's story in *Skating at Somerset House...*

Skating at Somerset House

Noel Summerford hated Christmas.

The intense, harried craziness drove him half nuts every year. The pressure to buy everyone presents they didn't want and would never use. Shoving, rippling crowds on the streets forgetting their manners, desperate to cross every item off their shopping lists. People parting with their hard earned cash at rip-off prices that would reduce to near zero as soon as it hit Boxing Day. Endless turkey dinners with dry overcooked white meat, lashings of sickly cranberry sauce and stodgy stuffing. Unwanted, twee greetings cards with their cutesy reindeer or Santa cartoons. Cheesy, artificial music piped into every shop for months, seasonal tunes playing on every radio station until he thought his ears would bleed, especially as the girls in the office insisted on turning the music up to near deafening volumes. His female colleagues wearing silver bauble earrings and pressuring the men to dress in novelty ties and festive knitted jumpers made him grind his teeth, but worse was how they clambered up on desks in ridiculously high heels to hang decorations from the beige walls and white-tiled ceiling. It was an annual health and safety nightmare, given that he was the Corporate H&S Officer for a high-street retail giant.

Yes, Christmas was definitely his least favourite time of the year, and his preference would be to hide in his man-cave for the whole of December. He therefore couldn't think of anything worse than ice skating – or in his case falling on his arse countless, humiliating times – at Somerset House. It was London's favourite outdoor ice rink according to The Evening Standard magazine, or so Matt had informed him. He could admit that the main sandstone neoclassical building, set in a square shape around the central courtyard, *was* quite impressive with its graceful columns, Victorian style black lampposts, mini white-encrusted trees in massive gold leaf pots and grand entrances on the Strand and the Embankment. Right now that was contrasted against the modern single-storey, white-framed, temporary buildings that housed Tom's Skate Lounge, the Cloakrooms/Box Office and main skate entrance. Mint green and teal SKATE posters were displayed prominently and matching Fortnum & Mason flags flapped in the winter breeze. You couldn't deny there was a great buzz to the place with all the noisy, excitable visitors chattering and skating, both locals and tourists from the sounds of it. But Noel was a disaster on the ice, and the giant Christmas tree in a huge wicker hamper was overdecorated and overdone… as well as a sharp reminder it was only a few days until the dreaded C-day. There was no escaping it.

Leaning up against the transparent waist-high wall guarding the rink, taking a much needed break from skating, he shivered and shifted from one foot to another. Cold vapour formed in a puffy cloud in front of his face as he exhaled. It was seriously bitter today. He checked the watch that'd belonged to his grandfather; rectangular face, brown leather strap, built to last. It was three in the afternoon, so it was only going to get colder and bleaker. Although, if he froze to death, at least it would be a merciful release from this ice-encrusted hell. This was the last time he was doing a favour for a friend. Not that refusing had really been an option, given the favour was to carry out perfectly reasonable god-fatherly duties for Jasper, whose dad Matt was Noel's best friend.

Teeth chattering, as he watched people – including Jasper – whizz around the ice, he decided he was going abroad for Christmas next year. Somewhere he could sit on a beach, dewy beer bottle in hand and read a crime thriller while soaking up the sun's rays. Because even though he was wrapped up in black jeans, a long sleeved top, thick green jumper, woollen winter coat, scarf, thermal lined gloves and a beanie hat pulled right down to cover his hair, he was still bloody freezing.

As if the weather wasn't bad enough, every time he got on the rink four year old Jasper skated rings around him. It was embarrassing to be a thirty year old guy with no sense of coordination who couldn't push away from the wall, stop, or glide along the blindingly white ice without falling over … but it was mortifying that Jasper, who'd only skated once before (or so he claimed) was showing Noel up with such natural talent. Already having taught himself to do some kind of spinning stop, he was currently attempting to skate backwards, forcing his heels together then apart in curved S shapes. The kid had absolutely no fear, throwing his little body around like it couldn't be bent or broken. But that was kids for you. They were resilient little things, unlike some adults.

No. Not today. There were other things to worry about, like looking after Jasper, which was why he'd fought the temptation to dive into the Skate Lounge with its windows overlooking the rink and rainbow coloured assortment of round paper lanterns hanging from the ceiling, and was staying put. He should probably get Jasper to calm down a bit, stop with the tricks and skate in nice sensible circles holding Noel's hand instead. That was what the H&S part of him would do with a potentially dangerous activity; minimise the risk. Except:-

a) the kid probably wouldn't listen to a word he said,

b) Jasper was always on the verge of hyperactivity so it made sense to tire him out,

and most importantly,

c) it was probably safer for Jasper *not* to hold his hand.

The little tyke came hurtling towards him in an expensive blue ski suit, stopping with a scrape and spraying ice up into Noel's face.

'Jasper!' he snapped, scowling and scrubbing the sharp ice crystals off with his gloves.

The boy's round-cheeked face fell, eyes widening. Noel sighed, feeling like a complete bastard. It wasn't cool to upset Jasper, just because *he* wasn't enjoying himself. Besides, he was genuinely fond of the little whirlwind and loved being his godfather.

'Never mind,' he joked, forcing a grin and stretching over the wall to straighten Jasper's hat, 'it's only a bit of ice. I was getting bored anyway, needed something to wake me up!' Rolling his eyes in an exaggerated cartoon character way, he crossed then uncrossed them, making the boy giggle. 'How's it going? Enjoying yourself? You're doing some good stuff out there, Jay.'

'Uh-huh,' Jasper nodded, dark head bopping up and down like the dog in the insurance ads, 'it's really, really awesome. But it would be better if you were skating with me 'ncle Noel.' He beamed, showing a gap where his two front teeth should be, reminding Noel of the carol, *All I Want For Christmas...*

The hope that Jasper might be ready to go after nearly three hours of skating died, and the boy's expression became pleading as Noel fell silent. The rest of the day would be spent with a storm cloud of guilt hanging over his head if he said no. Jasper had been bugging Matt about skating at Somerset House for months, ever since one of his friends had mentioned going the year before.

Time to do his duty. Careful to keep the dread off his face, Noel nodded. 'Sure, I'll give it another go.' *My seventh one today.* 'Be right there.' He clomped through the skate entrance building and stepped on to the ice. Clutching the wall for support, trying to balance on the metal blades, stupidly risky if you asked him, who would think to put knives on a pair of boots? He pulled himself over to his godson, sure his knuckles were not just white but positively glowing beneath his gloves. Perhaps he could manage a circuit without making an idiot of himself this time.

Nodding at Jasper, 'Come on then,' he smiled bravely and

carefully pushed off from the side. Walking/wobbling more than actually skating, arms extended like a pair of crippled wings, knees shaking, doubt flashed through his head. *There's a snowball's chance in hell of me not landing on my arse again.*

Holly Winterlake loved Christmas.

The chaotic, festive madness of it all thrilled her every year. The delight of spinning and dodging around people in shops to grab the best bargain to cross off her gift list, bought with her Christmas slush fund which she saved up towards monthly. Scrumptious turkey dinners with moist white meat, lashings of fruity cranberry sauce and fragrant, tasty stuffing, not to mention crispy butter-slathered roast potatoes. Exchanging cheery greetings cards featuring cutesy snowmen or North Pole cartoons, watching the assorted envelopes dropping onto her parents' doormat every morning. The jingling, jingly, upbeat tunes playing everywhere to get everybody into the Christmas spirit, which she turned up to maximum volume on the radio while she and her mum bopped around the breakfast table each morning. Having the perfect excuse to wear her favourite tiny silver snowman earrings. Hanging the circular red berry foliage wreath on the front door, set off perfectly by the green ivy twined around a wire topiary frame. The optimistic pining for snow and a white Christmas. Catching the tube with her mum's favourite metal tray if it did snow (more fun than a sleigh because you had to cram your legs onto it, tuck your chin into your knees and hope for the best) to slide down a steep Hampstead Heath hill.

Yes, Christmas was definitely her favourite time of year. In fact, Holly's preference would be to celebrate it every month, and pretend that summer with its muggy, prickly heat and scorching sun that burnt her fair skin and bleached her blonde hair lighter didn't exist. This December she couldn't think of anything better than ice skating for a living. It was a dream come true to be an Ice Marshall at Somerset House, being paid to loop the rink to make sure members of the public were safe, providing them with help where they needed it, issuing skates on request and helping the Ice Technician clean the ice when it became dented and scarred from use. The skating test before the job offer had been as easy as breathing, she'd completed the training at the beginning of the previous month easily and she was lucky enough to have picked up five shifts a week, working up to eight hours a day. Her mum might be worried about her overdoing it on the ice but the money would all definitely add up towards her start up fund. Come the New Year, she was going into business.

She glanced around, grinning. The forty foot Christmas tree near the North Wing, sprinkled with twinkling lights, gorgeous silver, gold, white, bronze and teal baubles and miniature Fortnum and Mason hampers, was an exciting reminder that it was Christmas Eve the next day.

Letting out a small squeak of anticipation, and checking she had enough room, Holly did a quick one foot spin, the first she'd learnt as a child. Starting with arms outstretched and pushing off with her right foot, twirling around she brought her arms in and her foot up against her knee, then span back out, ending with her arms crossed over her chest, both feet planted. Laughing, she did it again, joy and exhilaration zinging through her as the familiar move brought back a thousand happy memories of her professional figure-skating days. Those years had been filled with hard work, endless hours of practice, more bruises, grazes and sprains than she could count, and little time for friends or hobbies, but had also included some of the best moments of her life. When you got it right, it felt like you were flying.

It was a shame she could no longer do a Lutz or Axel as easily as a one foot spin, but she couldn't take the risk.

When she came to a stop, a small boy with big green eyes and a mop of brown hair peeking out from under a winter hat was staring at her. Steady on his feet, he looked more comfortable on the ice than the majority of adults. She'd seen him earlier, confidently gliding along. He hadn't needed her help and she'd been busy helping a family with twin girls, blonde hair in matching plaits, so she hadn't had a chance to tell him how well he skated.

'Wow,' he breathed, showing off a massive gappy grin. 'That was sooo good. You're a really cool ice person.'

'Thanks. I'm Holly, one of the Ice Marshalls.' Rather than someone who sounded like they were actually made of frozen water. She smiled. He was adorable. All massive eyes and cherry red cheeks. 'What's your name?'

'Jasper.'

'Well, I'll let you into a secret Jasper.' She scooted a little closer to him, bending down to his height. 'When I was only a tiny bit older than you, just after I started school, I started skating. I was in competitions, and won things. So I've had a lot of time on the ice.' Before the injury. When her world turned upside down. 'How long have you been skating? A few months?'

'Nope,' shaking his head, 'this is my second time. Daddy works a lot and Melody has gone home for Christmas. But she'll be back as soon as she can and she promised, promised, promised to bring me lots of presents and hugs. She said I'm a busy boy who keeps her running around but I'm on Santa's good boy list.' From the way he said it, he'd heard it a lot in the past few weeks.

'I'm sure you are,' Holly agreed, amused at his babble. 'Melody sounds cool.' Who she was, Holly wasn't quite sure of, obviously not the boy's mum, but would his Dad's girlfriend really disappear off for Christmas? 'But is this really only your second time? You're very good you know.' She paused, 'Do you want me to show you a few tricks a bit later on?' Strictly speaking she was here to help the customers who needed it but she could wait until the end of the afternoon, when it got a bit quieter, to spend some time with him.

'Would you?' he jumped, heels to his bum, and landed perfectly again on both skates, which was harder than it looked. 'That'd be super cool!' he paused, expression dropping. 'I have to ask if it's okay though.'

'Ask who?'

Spinning around in a perfect one eighty, he glanced around the rink. After a moment he extended a podgy finger, glancing at her sheepishly. 'Him ... he's not very good.'

'I'm sure he's not that bad – Oh.'

They watched in silence as a man wrapped up to the max with a face like a British thundercloud under a beanie hat slipped and lurched around the rink, arms flailing, even though every few feet he was using the wall to steady himself.

From the look on his face, Jasper was embarrassed. Heck, Holly felt embarrassed, but it was for Jasper's dad on his behalf, rather than not wanting to be seen with him. 'Well, at least he's trying,' she said from corner of her mouth, 'he might get better.'

'Ummm ...' the boy gave her a doubtful look.

But bless, you had to give the guy points for being here for his son, and making a bit of an idiot of himself in the process. Maybe he just wasn't very fit. He looked a bit bulky and soft around the middle. Or perhaps he didn't have good balance. Shame he wasn't a child; otherwise he could use one of the penguin skating aids available for the younger skaters in the separate area down the South Wing end.

Right. Two birds with one diplomatic, tactful stone then. 'Come on,' she gestured the boy to follow her, 'let's go ask him about you trying something a bit more adventurous.'

'Hi, there!' Her tone was friendly as she skated up behind the man, but unfortunately it unnerved him. Whipping his head round, his feet scissored, arms wind-milling. Trying to find his centre of gravity but failing, his legs started to slide in opposite directions. 'Oops!' Acting on instinct, Holly moved in, threading her arms under his to hoist him up, leaning forward for balance. 'Woah, there you go. I've got you.'

Practically spooning the guy upright wasn't the most professional way to help and she might get a telling off by the Front of House Manager, but it was the best she could do at short notice.

316

He didn't reply, just made a grunting sound and shook his head.

With his back plastered to her front and bum tucked into the curve of her hips, she realised he wasn't as bulky as he first seemed; it was the never ending amount of layers he was wrapped in. No wonder he was having issues, his upper body was totally constricted. No, he wasn't soft around the middle; he was actually quite nicely built.

'Okay?' she asked a little breathlessly. Untangling their arms, she steadied him with a firm hand and glided them over to the side, checking to make sure Jasper was still with them. The little boy gave her a reassuring nod, keeping pace.

'No, I'm not okay,' the guy spat as soon as he was hanging on to the wall, 'you scared the crap out of me!'

Author Q&A with Nikki Moore

1. The #LoveLondon series is an interesting concept. Can you tell us what led you to write it?

The series was born out of me pitching my second full length novel *Picnics in Hyde Park* (a romance set in London) to my lovely editor Charlotte and her commissioning me to write a number of London based short romances linked to the novel and each other. I thought it was a brilliant and very exciting idea and couldn't wait to get started.

My debut *Crazy, Undercover, Love* was partly set in London and I've always loved the city and get a real buzz every time I visit, so I knew I wanted my second novel to be wholly set there. I find our capital endlessly fascinating because there's so much to see and do, and it's very diverse. I love the pace, architecture, nightlife, landmarks... I think I could live in London and still never come closing to experiencing all of it. So when I had to fit in a few research trips for this series, I was very happy! It is totally true that I #LoveLondon.

2. How did you create each story to make it unique while linked and thematic?

The idea for the series evolved a number of times. Charlotte and I eventually settled on a series that would lead up to *Picnics at Hyde Park*, starting at Christmas with *Skating at Somerset House* with a story to follow roughly once a month to capture key dates or events in specific places in London, with one character in each novella either related to or friends with one of the main characters from Picnics. And so *New Year at The Ritz*, *Valentine's on Primrose Hill*, *Cocktails in Chelsea* and *Strawberries at Wimbledon* were created to follow my Christmas baby. :-)

In terms of the plots, these initially grew from the titles, covers, events and places and had to be about two people falling in love, or at least embarking on the possibility of it. What I found when I wrote the series was that each story was about a slightly different kind of, or source for, romantic love. One is about love unfolding from the differences between people and how those can strengthen the individuals; one is about choosing between old love versus new love; one is about love growing out of friendship; one is about love happening despite conflict and misunderstandings (a kind of modern comedy of errors); one is about revisiting first love, and one is about finding love when you least expect it. However, what really gave me the nitty gritty of ideas for the stories were the characters that came to me for each book and what they wanted or needed, what their hopes, dreams, challenges and fears were.

What I also found was that the setting and timing of each story naturally gave it a particular theme or 'feel.' For instance, *Skating at Somerset House* was set at Christmas and was more of a 'sweet' romance, whereas *Valentine's on Primrose Hill* asked questions about what love and romance really is, and was therefore deeper and strangely, darker. *Cocktails in Chelsea* had more of a sexy 'springtime fling' feel to it so was trendier and hotter. I'll leave you to make your mind up about the rest.

I have to admit that I really enjoyed catching up with the five couples from the novellas again in Picnics and seeing what they were up to. It was like visiting old friends, and I hope people who have read the rest of the series, or some of them, also enjoyed the chance to revisit some of those characters.

3. What's your writing schedule like? Where and when do you write?

I work full days in Human Resources over a nine day fortnight, meaning I get two Fridays off a month as dedicated writing time. I'm a single mum with two kids, one of them a teenager. They see their dad regularly but are with me day to day. Sometimes I write between 6.00 – 7.00 a.m. before the school run, but usually it's after my youngest has gone to bed from 9.00 p.m. until I fall asleep over the laptop. I do this at least three times a week but it can be closer to five or six evenings and weekends too if I'm up against a deadline.

Sometimes I fling food at the kids and tell them I'm neglecting them for a few hours, before closeting myself away. Mostly they accept this with good grace, as does my lovely boyfriend, who is more patient than I deserve. :-) My friends and family also accept falling by the wayside if I have a deadline. Equally, housework drops from my usual gold standard to bronze level. It's a delicate act to keep all the plates spinning but if I keep moving, I'm usually okay!

I do most of my writing either in my writing room (dining room at the front of the house) which contains my bookcase, laptops and a filing cabinet and has my book covers stuck up on the wall. I like writing in there because it's very light and airy. However, sometimes I write on the sofa or in bed when I want to be comfy and warm (really bad for the neck, back and shoulders though), in the staff room at work, on trains or even in cars. To be honest

I can write pretty much anywhere as long as I have my laptop and there's a plug handy, or if I have paper and a pen. Over the years I've learnt not to be precious about my writing time, or where I might do it, but to just do it whenever I get the chance.

4. Tell us a bit about your writing journey.

I've wanted to be a writer since I first learnt to read, at about five years old. I got addicted to getting lost in stories, being transported to different times and places, making new friends along the way in the characters. I thought it'd be amazing to be able to make up stories of my own for a living. I read a lot of romance novels in my teens and simply put, love writing about love. I was on the school newspaper at secondary school and my favourite subject was English, because I could write essays and short stories.

I first started writing seriously in my early twenties, when I wrote my first two novels which were romances targeted at Harlequin Mills and Boon. Shockingly (as when I look back at them now I cringe), the first one got as far as an acquisitions meeting with HM&B and the second had interest shown in it by another romance publisher but I didn't pursue that because I was uncomfortable with what they were asking me to do with the story (probably the right decision because they went out of business shortly afterwards). Writing took a back seat for eight or so years in the middle while I pursued a HR qualification and had my son, and I came back to writing in 2010.

I was a member of the Romantic Novelists Association New Writers Scheme for four years. I submitted two books for critiques (completed by an anonymous author/editor/agent), each of them twice. I can still remember the thrill of getting NWS reports that said my work was publishable, and giving me tips on how to improve it. The book I graduated to full RNA membership with in 2014 was my debut *Crazy, Undercover, Love* although it had a different title originally. I rewrote it several times, partially based on the reader's critiques that I received, and this definitely made it a much better book. When I was published I sent my readers' thank you cards.

Other highlights on my writing journey have been:

Getting an Honorable Mention for the RNA Elizabeth Goudge Trophy in 2010 and the phone call from Katie Fforde (one of my favourite authors, and the judge that year) that followed, congratulating me and telling me to keep writing.

Being offered my first publishing contract for my short story *A Night to Remember* published in the bestselling RNA/ Mills and Boon anthology in February 2014 alongside massive women's fiction authors such as Katie Fforde, Carole Matthews and Adele Parks.

Being offered a four book contract with HarperImpulse in October 2013 after meeting my editor Charlotte Ledger at the RNA Conference in July 2013. Thrilled doesn't even begin to cover it!

The day my debut novel *Crazy, Undercover, Love* was published in April 2014.

Being contacted by readers, bloggers and reviewers to say nice things about my stories or ask if I can write an article for them/ what I'm writing next/if I'm going to write a sequel.

Crazy, Undercover, Love being shortlisted for the RNA Joan Hessayon Award 2014 (for new writers) and attending the award ceremony in May 2015, where I was presented with a certificate and cheque alongside the other lovely finalists.

The success of the #LoveLondon series. :-)

There's not a day that goes by that I don't feel incredibly lucky and grateful to be doing something I love so much. Consequently, I always try and do what I can to encourage aspiring authors by offering them advice or sharing my experiences.

5. What's next for you?

Having written around 180,000 words over the past year and a half or so, alongside promoting the #LoveLondon series, the day job and the kids, I'm going to have a very short break from writing to spend some time exploring different marketing options for the #LoveLondon series. For instance, I'd love to try and do some magazine and radio interviews.

However, I also have a women's commercial fiction novel up my sleeve that I've been working on for some time, and I'm planning to get back to working on that in the autumn. And who knows what else I might do for HarperImpulse - I've always fancied writing a New Adult romance...!

Reader Q&A

1. Some people might find the idea of Zoe's plan for revenge uncomfortable. Do you think she was justified in what she originally intended to do? Why / why not?

2. What did you think of Melody, and the relationship between the two sisters?

3. Matt says that it's been 'complicated' since his wife died. What do you think he meant, and did you agree with Zoe that the reasons he gave were just excuses?

4. What impact do you think your childhood has on your adult life? How was this communicated through this story?

5. Before it was revealed, did you guess the reason Matt had for throwing Melody out? Were you surprised by the lie Stephen told and the reasons he did this?

6. What did you think of the end of the story? Did you find it was satisfying? What, if anything, would you change about the ending?

Author Note

Authors need Readers and Reviewers!

I am so grateful that readers and reviewers like you have taken the #LoveLondon series to heart and made it so successful.

I would really appreciate it if you could spend a few minutes leaving a review on Amazon (UK/US) and/or Goodreads.

As an avid reader, I always try to leave reviews and also love connecting with writers whose books I have enjoyed or whose stories have resonated with me. It would be great if you felt able to do the same, so please do write a review and/or drop me a line on Twitter @NikkiMoore_Auth or via FaceBook at https://facebook.com/NikkiMooreWrites.

Remember, authors need reviews!

Thanks so much, Nikki x

WRONG BROTHER, RIGHT KISS

JOSS WOOD

THE ONE FROM THE WEDDING

KATHERINE GARBERA

MILLS & BOON

First Published in Great Britain 2022
by Mills & Boon, an imprint of HarperCollins*Publishers* Ltd
1 London Bridge Street, London, SE1 9GF

www.harpercollins.co.uk

HarperCollins*Publishers*
1st Floor, Watermarque Building,
Ringsend Road, Dublin 4, Ireland

Wrong Brother, Right Kiss © 2022 Joss Wood
The One from the Wedding © 2022 Katherine Garbera

ISBN: 978-0-263-30376-6

0322

WRONG BROTHER, RIGHT KISS

JOSS WOOD

Prologue

Tinsley Ryder-White adored her grandfather's study, the vast collection of books sitting on the floor-to-ceiling shelves. She was seven years old and she loved nothing better than to crawl under his enormous desk, tuck herself into the corner and hide out from the world.

It was the summer holidays, and nobody would look for her here and she'd be left alone for a few hours...*yay*!

Tinsley tucked a cushion behind her back and flipped open the cover of her book, sighing with pleasure. Reading was her favorite thing in the whole wide world.

She hadn't gotten past page three when she heard the heavy door to the study open and her heart leaped into her chest. Her grandfather was back and when he found her, she'd be in a heap of trouble.

Tinsley froze and prayed that Callum—he wouldn't allow them to call him anything but his first name—

didn't sit down and stretch out his legs. If he did that, she'd be discovered.

It was a grown-up game of hide-and-seek. She just had to stay still and keep very, very quiet.

"Good morning, Callum," Daddy said, and Tinsley had to slap her hand across her mouth to smother her squeak. She'd thought Daddy and Callum had left for work already... Man, why hadn't she checked?

"Don't bother sitting down—this won't take long," Callum said, sounding cross. Then again, Callum always sounded cross.

Tinsley held her breath and buried her face in her hands.

If they found her, she was toast.

"I met with my lawyer yesterday and updated my will."

"Let me guess. I'm not in it," Daddy said, sounding tired.

"Au contraire. Since I have no other male heir, I have little choice but to leave everything to you," Callum responded, sounding angrier than she'd ever heard him. "But I placed a provision in the document that if I find another male heir, anyone with a close connection to me—but not to Benjamin—he shall inherit my thirty percent share of Ryder International, all my properties and my financial assets."

"I knew you disliked me, Callum, but I never realized you hated me this much." Daddy sounded like someone was choking him.

"I told you not to take Benjamin's side, that there would be consequences if you defied me. The only silver lining to Benjamin being homosexual is that he wouldn't have sired any children."

"Jesus, Callum, you can't say stuff like that. Your

brother didn't want to marry a woman—he wanted to be with Carlo. I just supported his wish to live his life the way he wanted."

"And your support gave him the courage to tell the world he was gay and to move in with that man! He probably left his share of Ryder International to him, someone with no connection to us!"

"Firstly, as I've told you before, there's no proof he left his shares to Carlo and if he did, why would Carlo hide his identity behind a blind trust? And I was in my early twenties when all this happened and even if I had discussed his will with him, which I didn't, I would've had no influence over him! Like you, Ben made his own decisions. You are punishing me for something Ben did and that's not fair."

"Life's not fair, boyo. Haven't you realized that yet?" Callum demanded.

"What about Kinga and Tinsley?" Daddy asked and Tinsley's eyes widened at the sound of her name.

"What about them?"

"They, like me, carry the Ryder-White name, the only heirs who do. You could leave everything to them—they carry your genes."

"They are silly girls. Ryder-White males carry the name, the genes, the blood." Callum's voice was low and nasty. "Your daughters are beneath my notice. I have no interest in them. But, do not doubt me on this, if they put a foot out of line and tarnish the Ryder-White name, if they are anything less than perfect, *you* will bear the consequences, James.

"You and your family live here, at Ryder's Rest, because I allow it. You are paid an overinflated salary because I choose to give you that money. You certainly are not worth it. Your lifestyle depends on my generosity.

I gave you everything and I can take it all away. Make sure your family understands that you live in my house, under my rules."

Callum was horrible, Tinsley thought. A part of her wanted to scramble out from under the desk and kick his shins and scream at him for being nasty to her dad but another part of her was scared, terrified, actually.

Because, as he said, if she stepped out of line, bad things would happen.

One

Six weeks ago

Well, hello to the New Year.

Tinsley Ryder looked down from the balcony of the newest Ryder International bar and watched a dark-haired man spin his blond partner and dip her over his arm. She laughed with delight and gave him the look that suggested he'd get lucky later. Tinsley wrenched her eyes off them and stroked the skin on the ring finger of her left hand. She'd removed her engagement and wedding rings two years ago—six months after their divorce—but despite so much time passing, she still missed JT.

Correction, she didn't miss her husband; she missed being married, being half of a whole. She missed sex and having someone to talk to at the end of the day.

For nearly half her life, she'd seen in the New Year

with JT and the memories—counting down the clock while standing in San Marco Square, watching the ball fall in Times Square or while holed up in a cabin in Aspen—bombarded her. This was the second New Year she'd seen in solo and, honestly, it sucked.

JT had someone new, but she, well…she was *still* coming to terms with the death of their marriage and the dreams she'd made, the life she'd planned. She could still accurately remember the details of the forever house she'd designed, recalled the names she'd decided on for the three kids she wanted, could recite the itineraries of future holidays.

Planned and perfect.

Yet her flawless life fell apart when JT up and left her and moved to Hong Kong, just as his brother had predicted all those years ago.

Despite knowing that five minutes had passed since the countdown, Tinsley looked at her watch again. She wished she could leave and return to her hotel room just a block away, but this was the opening of their newest bar and it was her job, as cohead of publicity for Ryder International, to be here.

Ryder International opened one or two new bars a year and the preparations took up to two years from conception to implementation. Ryder employed various teams to get the new bar up and running but it was her job to ensure the new venue received the maximum amount of publicity. To achieve that, she contracted Gallant Events to stage an opening night that would wow the celebrities and influencers and make the bar the hottest, coolest spot in the city.

Her publicity team and Cody Gallant's event team had worked together on four other opening nights. They were exceedingly good at their jobs. Tinsley always flew in a week before opening night, and she knew both teams—hers and Cody's—dreaded her arrival as she came with a million questions and another million demands. She saw the eye rolls, heard the frustration in their voices and reminded herself that it was her job to provide perfection.

It was what Ryder International was known for and perfection was what she delivered.

Kinga was equally dedicated to the pursuit of perfection, a good thing since they ran the PR department together. They did, however, have distinctly separate responsibilities and Tinsley was glad that she wasn't running point on organizing Ryder's very exclusive Valentine's Day Ball. Especially since Callum, their unreasonable grandfather and boss, had decreed—on Christmas Day no less!—that he wanted Griff O'Hare, the baddest of Celebrity Land's bad boys to provide the entertainment at the ball.

Kinga was not happy with Callum's suggestion, and Tinsley didn't blame her. She had no idea how her sister was going to resolve that thorny problem but had no doubt she would.

They were both very experienced at pulling last minute rabbits out of top hats.

The DJ cranked up the volume, another bartender joined the attractive staff at the bar and alcohol flowed like water. Tinsley sensed that she wasn't going to get to bed before dawn and the thought made her want to cry. She'd worked eighteen-hour days for three days straight and she was exhausted. She wanted her bed, to cuddle Moose, her enormous Maine Coon cat, to spend New Year's Day with her just-older sister, Kinga, and Jules, her best friend.

Tinsley straightened her shoulders and rolled her head

from side to side, trying to ease the stiffness in her muscles. She needed a double shot of caffeine, or an energy drink, and she would be fine. Okay, maybe not *fine* but she would cope. Coping was what she did.

She refused to let people see her looking anything other than happy and content. She might be paddling like crazy under the surface, but she was damned if she'd let anyone see her sweat. Even when her husband bailed after twelve years together and their divorce rocked the foundations of her world, nobody except for Kinga had seen Tinsley cry.

No, she was a Ryder-White and they did not wear their hearts on their sleeves. She would rather be thought of as cold and unfeeling than pitiful and weak.

Tinsley felt movement behind her and turned, holding back her sigh. She didn't feel like dealing with Cody Gallant right now...

Truthfully, she never felt like dealing with Cody.

Cody held two champagne glasses in one big hand and a bottle of Moët in the other. After pouring the pale gold liquid into the glasses, and handing one to her, he placed the bottle on the high table between them. Echoing her earlier stance, he rested his forearms on the railing, his gaze moving from the action on the dance floor below to the VIP area across from them. She had seen Cody in that area earlier, chatting with the men and charming the women, utterly at ease with Toronto's elite. She wasn't surprised; Cody could talk to princes and peasants, celebrities and custodians. As the owner and operator of a company specializing in staging spectacular events, from music festivals to sports races to high-society weddings, he knew how to work a room. The Gallant and the Ryder families ran in the same Portland, Maine, circles but even with a pedigree, one had to be at the top of their game to secure Ryder International's business. Cody did that in spades.

Tinsley didn't understand why he'd chosen to grace this event with his presence. She knew his company was staging massive New Year's Eve parties in both Los Angeles and New York tonight. He should be there, at either of those events, so his appearance here hours earlier had surprised the hell out of her.

Tinsley refused to ask for an explanation. She tried not to speak to Cody more than was necessary. She sipped champagne, thinking of the differences between her ex-husband and his brother. Cody was four years older than JT and different in looks and personality. Whereas JT was blond and thin, Cody topped out at six-three or -four, and under his tailored designer tuxedo was a hard and muscled body.

With his rugged, masculine looks—square jaw, long nose and quick-to-smile eyes and mouth—Cody looked like he could grace the cover of any men's fitness magazine. JT had been a hipster before hipsters were fashionable—wearing a beard and his blond shoulder-length hair pulled back into a stubby tail. Cody kept his wavy, dark-as-midnight hair short. The brothers shared the same eyes, a deep green shade that reminded Tinsley of freshly cut Christmas trees. She could always read JT's eyes, but Cody kept all his emotions behind a green velvet curtain.

It was commonly accepted that Cody was bigger, hotter, so much sexier than his younger brother. JT was bookish, nerdy, intense…and, when people compared him to Cody, they seemed to imply that JT was a faded version of his brother.

It was a truth she could now admit and yet another bullet point on her list of things that annoyed her about

Cody. Others were that he'd never tried to get to know her and that he kept his distance from her. And when he did talk to her, he was terse, sometimes borderline rude. She'd never been the recipient of his famous charm. Not that she wanted to be but...*whatever*.

Tinsley released a breath, reminding herself that her biggest gripe with Cody was that he'd never approved of her and JT's relationship. He'd even, the night before their wedding—the one she'd planned with exquisite attention paid to every detail—begged her not to go through with the ceremony. It wouldn't last, he told her. He had been proved right and Tinsley hated that he'd predicted their future.

She still desperately wanted to know what he'd realized back then that she hadn't, but her pride refused to allow her to utter the words.

And what did it matter? She and JT were divorced, and he had a new wife and a new life. She had her job at Ryder International.

"Why are you here, overseeing this event?" she demanded.

Cody turned his eyes on her; they were the most amazing color and they always made her feel a little off-balance and jumpy.

"What do you mean?"

"I know you have events happening tonight, one in LA and another in New York."

"And one in New Orleans, too."

That wasn't any type of an answer. Tinsley released an irritated sigh. "Surely those events should be higher on your list of priorities."

Cody stared down at the dance floor, his broad back hunched. "I decide my priorities, no one else. And I employ good people who can handle the events."

"You didn't answer my question,"

He turned his head to look at her and Tinsley felt like a bug under a microscope. She had known him since she was fifteen years old and, although almost another fifteen plus years had passed, she still felt like a gawky teenager. Something about him made her feel edgy.

"Ryder International was my first client and there would be no Gallant Events without the chance your grandfather gave me. I will always look after Ryder International business personally," Cody replied.

Tinsley released an annoyed sigh, reluctantly impressed by his statement. Cody was one of the few people who got along well with her crabby grandfather, and he was someone Callum could tolerate for more than a half hour.

Callum Ryder-White was exceptionally difficult, but he was also the most talented businessman of his generation. When he took control of the family-owned chain of bars, with help from his younger brother, Benjamin, the company was facing insolvency. The brothers turned the business around. After Ben's premature death, Callum flew higher, achieving heights his father and grandfather had only dreamed of. Now, after forty-five years at the helm, Callum was in control of a ten-billion-dollar chain of luxury bars situated in fifty luxury hotels in twenty countries. Callum might be a brilliant businessman, but he lacked people skills, and his family and staff, for the most part, annoyed him. He was a hard-driving, cold leader who pushed his family to be the very best—and then constantly undermined their talent.

The same couldn't be said of Cody Gallant. Tinsley had worked with many of his employees and she had yet to hear a bad word spoken about him. He was, reputedly, fair and supportive. He paid well and treated his staff with respect. He and Callum were very different, but they still got along, possibly because Cody had never been afraid to stand up to the old man.

Callum also respected Cody's ambition and his drive, often saying that few people could match Ryder International's meteoric rise, but Cody came close. Gallant Events had branches all over the country and Cody had satellite offices in London, Tokyo and Sydney. Callum liked taking credit for being the first to recognize Cody's talent.

Callum liked taking credit, period.

Cody stood up straight and gestured to the masses below. "Would you like to?"

"Would I like to what?" Tinsley asked, confused.

"Dance."

"With you?" She and Cody didn't dance—God, they barely *spoke*.

"No one else around so, yes, with me."

"Why would you ask me that?" Tinsley demanded, pushing away the thought of what it would be like to be plastered against that hard chest as they swayed to a slow song.

"I like to dance and it's New Year's Eve," Cody responded, his mouth lifting in his world-famous half smile, half smirk. It was, Tinsley reluctantly admitted, as sexy as hell.

"I saw you in the VIP area earlier, and there were at least five women who passed you their phone numbers. I'm fairly sure any of them would accept your invitation to dance," Tinsley replied. "I'm working."

He didn't respond but he kept his eyes on her, intense but also a little amused.

"Besides, I don't dance," Tinsley reluctantly told him.

"Everybody dances." Cody shrugged. He downed his glass of champagne and poured another.

Everyone but her. She was rhythm and music impaired. A flaw she'd never managed to overcome.

"Not me. It's not in my skill set."

"You can't be that bad," Cody insisted. "Surely even you can shuffle your feet and bob your head."

She probably could, but she'd seen Cody dance at various functions over the years. He was one of those annoying men who had rhythm, someone who was naturally graceful. First on the dance floor, the last to leave it.

No, dancing with Gallant was out of the question. Tinsley sighed, wishing she could move her body with confidence, feel the music deep inside and let go. But that wasn't who she was. She kept a tight lid on her wilder impulses. She was a rational, thoughtful and logical person, and there wasn't much space in her life for the uncontrollable, for coloring outside the lines. She believed in structure, in schedules, and hated surprises or situations where she felt out of control. Or foolish.

Dancing made her feel very foolish indeed.

"No, thank you."

"I will get you to dance," Cody softly told her, his voice just discernible over the pounding music. "Hopefully, sooner than later."

Tinsley handed him a cool smile and deliberately glanced at her watch. "It's nearly time to bring out the midnight buffet. I'm going to check on that." She nodded to the VIP area, where two scantily dressed women wearing very low-cut dresses were hanging over the railing, desperate to get Cody's attention. "You'd better go before they fall off the balcony and into the crowd."

"They aren't nearly as interesting as you," Tinsley

thought she heard Cody say as she walked away. But
that couldn't be right. She and Cody didn't like each
other. They'd been enemies for years and had they not
been business associates and connected through their
families, they'd avoid each other.

They had, as it was said, irreconcilable differences.

When Tinsley disappeared from view, Cody turned
his back to the VIP area and ran his hands over his face.

So, that went well.

He'd decided, a few days ago, that if he was going to
make a New Year's resolution—something he wasn't in
the habit of doing—it would be to improve his relationship with Tinsley Ryder-White.

It might be a fool's errand. But after fifteen years of
snapping and snarling at each other, it was time to get
over themselves. She'd married and divorced his all-but-
estranged brother and it was time they moved the hell
on. They weren't kids anymore, for God's sake.

Cody could remember the first time he saw Tinsley,
later to be known, along with her sister, Kinga, as Portland's Princesses. It was summer and he'd dragged JT
away from his computer to join him and some friends
for a day on the beach. He'd been worried about his
younger brother and thought he needed to get out more.
Cody accepted that JT wasn't a people person like
him, but social interaction was important. As was getting the occasional dose of vitamin D. And breathing
fresh air.

Cody had been walking out of the surf when he saw
Tinsley approaching JT, who sat on a towel, looking
miserable. She wore a conservative black one-piece
bathing suit under a pair of denim shorts and her dark
hair, a couple of shades lighter than his, was pulled off

her heart-shaped face into a high tail that bobbed when she walked. She was young—too young for him—but she was gorgeous. Pale skin, pronounced cheekbones and a mouth made to sin. At twenty-one, he'd liked to sin…

He'd watched as Tinsley stopped in front of JT and spoke to him. It took JT a moment to respond and then, to Cody's amazement, his shy brother patted his towel and invited her to sit down. Cody stared at them, blond and dark, and felt despair swamp him.

She wouldn't be good for JT. He wouldn't be good for her. They'd eventually hurt each other.

It was a snap judgment, and he'd had no evidence to support his feelings, but he'd known it like he knew his name. He'd been proved right.

Cody shook off the memories. That was in the past. She and JT had been divorced for a while now, and his brother lived on the other side of the world. Cody's oldest and classiest client was Ryder International and, while his contracts with them weren't his biggest or the most lucrative, being associated with the famous brand was a shining star on his corporate résumé.

Tinsley co-led the publicity department with her sister, and with this year being Ryder's centennial year, they were planning some kick-ass events that would garner massive attention. He'd conducted a series of meetings with Callum and was expecting contracts to organize various events both in the States and overseas.

The events wouldn't be piddly opening nights, but multimillion-dollar projects that would garner international attention. That his company was well respected and enormously lucrative was in no doubt. But organizing the Ryder centennial events would make Gallant Events the go-to company for rich, exciting clients from every corner of the world, and he'd be right up there with the best of the best.

Exactly where he'd always aimed to be.

But to get there, he would have to personally oversee the initial stages of every project. If he was going to sink or swim—and he very much intended to swim—it would be by his efforts, not by anyone else's.

He'd have to work closely with both of Portland's Princesses. He and Kinga got along, but Tinsley was his brother's ex. JT had left for Hong Kong with no warning and a few days later, Tinsley received a call telling her he wasn't returning and that he'd filed for divorce. Cody still wanted to rearrange JT's face for blindsiding her and for being such a selfish prick.

He thought he'd raised his brother better than that.

But JT hadn't given Tinsley, her feelings or his marriage another thought. Cody even flew to Hong Kong to talk some sense into his brother, but it was obvious that JT had moved on and that he no longer wanted to be with Tinsley.

JT said he wasn't interested in lectures and that he was a grown man and didn't need Cody telling him what to do anymore, or how to do it.

They hadn't spoken since.

Cody sighed, remembering their tense discussion and his inability to reach his brother. To him, marriage meant family and family equaled obligation and responsibility. After his mom's death the year he turned twelve, his father told him it was his duty to look after his younger brother. So Cody listened and did what he was told. It took him a long time to realize his father hadn't wanted to be inconvenienced by his sons so he'd passed the parenting buck to his oldest child.

Cody'd been the one to raise JT. He'd bought him clothes, made sure he did his homework, that he was eating right and wasn't being bullied because of his big brain. Thanks to his father's selfishness and emotional distance, he'd been an adult long before his time.

And, yeah, because he'd spent his teens and early twenties looking after his brother, he'd vowed he'd never again allow himself to feel trapped. A permanent lover—a girlfriend or a wife—was just another person to feel responsible for. Emotions were pointless and only got in the way. So he limited himself to one-night stands and quick flings.

Marriage was completely out of the question and definitively not for him.

Cody allowed his gaze to drift over the room, satisfied that everything was as it should be. Waiters were starting to set up the late-evening buffet in the far corner behind the bar and guests were already lining up to fill their plates. He lifted his eyes to the VIP area and the blonde from earlier who still had her eyes on him. He knew that if he wanted it he'd have company for the rest of the night.

He wasn't even tempted. When he compared her to Tinsley, she came up short. She was too over-the-top and in your face. Unlike Tinsley's classy gown, the hem of her dress was about six inches too short, her top far too low. She was trying too hard...

Tinsley didn't try at all.

Cody shook his head, wondering what the hell was wrong with him. He was a guy and normally never objected to short skirts and low tops. In fact, he appreciated them. And why was he comparing Fun Girl to

Portland's prissiest princess? The one didn't have anything to do with the other.

Despite having known Tinsley for half of her life, she was only a work colleague and he intended to keep it that way.

Princesses were a pain in the ass.

Two

Tinsley left the bar and pulled a scarf from the inside pocket of her calf-length coat and wrapped it around her neck.

It was four in the morning and freezing. She had a short walk back to her hotel and when she got there, she intended to take a scalding-hot shower, pull on her most comfortable pj's and order a cup of hot chocolate from room service. Then she planned to sleep until noon. Her flight back to Portland was in the afternoon, so she'd pass the time by sleeping until the last possible moment.

It had been a long week.

"Tinsley!"

She turned at the deep voice and saw Cody hurrying toward her, his hands buried deep in the pockets of his tan cashmere coat. A light dusting of snow covered his hair and she wondered if he had been waiting for her.

"I'll walk you to your hotel," he told her.

She started to tell him that she was perfectly able to manage the short walk herself, that she'd been navigating her way home alone for a long, long time but the words wouldn't come. Mostly because she'd run out of energy. She shrugged. If he wanted to tromp around in the snow, that was his prerogative.

Tinsley resumed walking and licked a snowflake off her top lip, thinking how beautiful the night was. Portland got its fair share of snow, probably more than most, but she loved winter. She liked moments like this when it was so quiet, when the snow softened the buildings and sidewalks. Despite Cody's presence, it was magical, picture-perfect.

Cody stopped and pulled his phone out of the inside pocket of his tuxedo jacket. Tinsley wondered whom he would be calling so late at night—correction, so early in the morning. Instead of lifting the device to his ear, he stabbed the screen with his index finger. A few moments later, a mournful voice, singing in French, pierced the quiet night.

"Edith Piaf," Cody told her with a small smile on his handsome face. "Everybody needs to dance to Edith on a cold, snowy night once in their lives."

Was he mad? It was cold, her feet were aching, she was exhausted and he wanted to dance?

He was insane; that was the only explanation.

"Cody, I don't dance," was all she could think to say. But suddenly she was no longer quite as tired, and, strangely, her feet had stopped throbbing.

Cody held out his hand, his expression daring her to join him. "I do," he told her as her hand slid into his. With his free hand, he unbuttoned her coat and slid his hand over her hip. The thin material of her dress was no barrier to the heat of his palm and she shuddered, wondering why she felt like she had been plugged into a wall socket. Or heated from the inside out.

This was Cody, not someone she was supposed to react to. He was her ex-brother-in-law.

The last person in the world who should be making her feel…hot, alive, bubbling with anticipation.

She'd been in an emotional and physical cocoon since her divorce and JT was the last man she'd kissed, made love with. Now she was wondering whether Cody's lips were as soft as they looked, how he tasted.

God, she wanted to kiss Cody.

She really, *really* wanted to kiss him. What on earth was happening to her?

Before she could find an answer to that question, Cody's big hand on her back pulled her to him, his other clasping her right hand. "Do what I do," he murmured, his breath warm against her ear.

She tried to follow along; she did, but her coordination, already bad at the best of times, was hampered by the pounding in her ears, the prickling of her skin. He was a lot taller than her and despite her heels, the top of her head only brushed his chin. If she tipped her head back, she could look into his eyes…

She was not going to tip her head back.

Tinsley stepped on his shoe and she heard his swift intake of breath. Cody released a small laugh. "Wow, you *are* bad at this," he said, sounding amused.

"Told you," Tinsley replied, releasing a long sigh.

He stopped trying to shuffle her around and looked down at her face, his eyes a deep, dangerous green in the golden glow of the streetlight. Tinsley couldn't take her eyes off him, fascinated by the intensity in his gaze, the way his fingers pushed into her lower back, his touch turning possessive. He was just holding her, but her panties turned damp and her need for pressure and friction increased.

If he didn't kiss her soon, touch her with more than a hand on her lower back, she might just scream. Not recognizing herself, Tinsley curled her hand around the back of his neck, and standing on her tiptoes, pulled his head down and slammed her lips against his. He didn't react and Tinley tensed.

She'd only ever known one other man and it had been a long time and she could be reading him wrong…

She was about to pull back when Cody's lips started to nibble hers, light, lovely kisses that fanned the raging fire in her belly, deep in her womb. But light and lovely wasn't what she needed or wanted.

She wanted to step inside the fire and burn…

Increasing the pressure on the back of his neck, she opened her mouth and her tongue darted out and slipped past his teeth. She felt him tense and thought he was about to pull back. *Please don't*, Tinsley silently begged him.

Another few seconds passed, and just when she thought this was a lost cause, Cody gently gripped her jaw and chin and tipped her face to the side and proceeded to kiss her senseless. There was no other word for it; his mouth ravaged hers, hot and hard and insistent. His other hand slid between her dress and coat and skimmed down her hip, around to her butt, pulling her closer, so close that she could feel his hard erection pushing into her stomach. Yum.

Desperate, Tinsley slid her hand between them to open the single coat button, hurriedly pushing aside his tuxedo jacket to get as close to him as she could. Through his thin dress shirt, she could feel hot skin and hard muscles and, not recognizing herself, she yanked his shirt out from his pants, pulling it up so she could lay her hands on his warm, wonderful masculine skin.

She'd missed this, missed the feel of muscles under her hands, the slightly rough texture of a man's skin. She'd missed feeling feminine and powerful and desired and sexy…

And she wanted more. She wanted them naked, him inside her, driving into her as they spun toward that fireball of intense pleasure. No, it was more than want—she *needed* him. She needed everything he could give her.

Not allowing herself to think this through, or talk herself out of this once-in-a-blue-moon madness, she pulled her mouth off Cody's and stared into his beautiful, oh-so-masculine face. "Stay with me tonight—sleep with me."

"That's the last thing I expected you to say."

She didn't blame him for saying that, acting impulsively wasn't what she did, who she was. She shrugged and tried to smile. "It's that magical hour when time and reality are suspended."

His fingers were still on her jaw and she saw the hesitation in his eyes. She shook her head and knew that if he spoke, he'd turn her down. That wasn't an option.

"One night, tonight. Let's pretend we're strangers, that we've never met before, that we saw each other in the club and started to dance. It's the New Year and we're looking to see it in with a bang," she said, hoping he didn't notice the hint of desperation in her voice, "figuratively and literally."

A small smile touched Cody's mouth but didn't reach his eyes. "Are you sure about this, Tinsley? Once we do this, we can't go back."

"When dawn breaks this will all be a dream," Tinsley told him. "And everything will be as it was before."

"You're naive if you think that," Cody told her, his voice rough.

"I want you, Cody. I want sex, a physical connection," Tinsley insisted. "One night of pleasure, no expectations, and no demands. That's what you do, isn't it?"

Annoyance flashed in his eyes, but she didn't care. All she wanted was his word that, when they reached her hotel, he'd remind her of how it felt to be held, desired... *wanted*. It had been too long...way too long.

"Are you sure about this, Tinsley?" Cody demanded.

No, not at all.

But she was going to do it anyway.

Cody knew that sleeping with Tinsley was a bad idea, that he was making a big-ass mistake, but his body wasn't listening to his brain. Tinsley Ryder-White, so lovely, wanted to get lucky and she wanted to get lucky with *him*.

He'd have to be a fool or a saint to say no. He was neither.

But, he told himself, as she opened the door to her hotel room, he wasn't allowed to complain when this came back to bite him on the ass. And it would. She thought they were going to be able to have one night of bed-banging sex and then not see each other for a few weeks, possibly a month or two. She didn't know that Callum had implied there was a lot of Ryder International work coming Cody's way...

Before he saw her naked, she should know that.

The door slammed behind him and he watched Tinsley drop her coat to the floor and step out of her heels. She lifted her hands to her hair and yanked out a series of bobby pins and her long, wavy hair tumbled down her back. She tossed the pins in the direction of the credenza and stood before him in her silver, calf-length cocktail dress, looking like a dressed-up, sexy fairy.

Sweet, sexy, a little wild...

He swallowed, looking for moisture to coat his mouth. He needed to speak, before this went any further. "Tinsley, we need to talk."

His words died as her fingers went to the zip under her left armpit and he watched, mesmerized as the fabric parted to show a slash of pale, creamy flesh and a small breast.

"I don't want to talk, Cody," Tinsley told him, her voice oh-so-serious. "I want to kiss, and touch and taste, but I most definitely *don't* want to talk."

"But—"

Jesus, he was about to swallow his tongue. Her dress fell to her hips, revealing her breasts, tipped with small, coral-colored nipples. They were already puckered—from the cold or from her being aroused—and he couldn't wait to pull them into his mouth, to taste their sweetness.

"Tonight you're not someone I've known for half of my life, you are not my ex-brother-in-law, you're just a guy I picked up in a bar, okay?"

There was so much wrong with that sentence, but Cody couldn't make sense of any of it because his head was swimming and his cock was jumping and *he wanted her more than he'd ever wanted anyone before.* He sucked in a breath of much-needed air, thinking that he owed it to her to tell her that this might be a mistake. He shook his head, trying to say the right words, to get his point across. But, before he could, Tinsley shimmied the dress over her hips and placed a hand on her hip, all long limbs, black hair and passion in her deep, dark eyes.

How was he supposed to think, and talk, when all

she wore was a tiny triangle of nude-colored lace, frothy and insubstantial?

God, he loved women's underwear.

"Are you just going to stand there?" Tinsley demanded, stepping forward to push his coat off his shoulders.

He was lost, his concerns and worries melting like early-morning mist on a hot summer's day. Cody swiped his mouth across hers, then kissed her jaw, her throat, slowly moving down to her lovely breasts. He dragged his tongue over her nipple, and it tasted sweeter than he imagined. Her sigh, followed by a breathy groan, told him she was eager for more.

He'd tried to talk to her but she only had one thing on her mind. Him.

And he was very okay with that.

So far, the morning after was living up to its reputation of being super awkward, Tinsley thought, lifting her eyes to the mirror above the sink. Her hair was a cloud of tangled curls, her mascara had left her eyelashes and had formed two dark streaks under her red-rimmed-from-no-sleep eyes and her mouth tasted like a crime scene. She wore Cody's shirt—now missing two buttons from where she'd ripped it open last night in her haste to get to his skin—and she had beard rash on her jaw. And on her breasts. And between her legs.

Tinsley gripped the basin and, unable to look at her reflection anymore, straightened her arms and dropped her head to look at the tiled floor. Last night, swept away by lust, she hadn't thought about how to deal with the morning after. Frankly, from the moment she and Cody first kissed, she hadn't thought beyond them getting naked.

But here she was, hiding out in the bathroom, wishing he'd leave.

Tinsley knew that, in theory, she was making a mountain out of a pile of rocks. He'd wanted sex, she'd wanted sex and so they'd had sex. Amazing, no-commitment sex. They'd woken up tangled in each other's arms and indulged in sleepy, best-way-to-wake-up, one-last-time-before-we-move-on sex.

It was now time to wash her face, brush her teeth and usher him out the door, hoping like hell they could avoid each other until the memory of this night faded. How long would that take? A few weeks? A couple of months? But, since it was the best sex she'd had in her life, she doubted she'd ever forget the hours she spent in Cody's arms...

Dammit.

From the moment she dropped her dress, clothes started flying, both of them desperate to be skin on skin, to discover each other's heat. They were on fire for each other, they *were* fire, both wanting to scorch and be scorched.

Surprisingly, and a little irritatingly, Cody knew how to touch her, how to make her moan and groan, to writhe and to want. He kissed and sucked her nipples, his fingers and tongue between her legs were achingly familiar, his mutters of appreciation the sweetest music she'd ever heard. Tinsley had to remind herself that this was Cody, the man with whom she'd always had a tense relationship.

And when he nudged her legs open with his knee, held her hips in his broad hands to slide into her with one smooth stroke, she felt complete, like he was the missing piece of a puzzle she didn't know was unfinished. And when he came, she relished the sounds he made—appreciative and awestruck, powerful and just a little vulnerable.

His big body collapsed on hers and she could still feel his weight pushing her into the soft mattress, his thick wavy hair between her fingers, the intoxicating smell of sex and satisfaction. After round one, they'd dozed, her head on his chest, her hand on his muscled stomach, his hand on her bare butt. And she'd felt safe, protected, a little cherished. As they drifted in and out of sleep, if she moved, he followed, tightening his hold, putting his leg across her and tangling them up tighter. And, inevitably, their sleepy caresses turned deeper and darker, more demanding.

They made love three times last night and once this morning, each time as good as the first. She hadn't wanted to stop touching him, breathing him in, touching his strong, big, powerful body.

And because the beauty of their amazing, unexpected connection threatened to overwhelm her, she'd wrenched herself out of his arms, yanked on his shirt and stumbled to the bathroom, knowing that if she didn't pull away, she'd ask him to stay.

And stay. And stay...

But this was *Cody*, she reminded herself, her ex-brother-in-law. She wasn't supposed to be feeling this way, liking him—no, loving sex—this much. She had to be reacting this way because he was her first one-night stand, her first experience of no-commitment sex, and she was making this into something so much more than what it was...

It was hot sex, nothing more, nothing less. In a few hours, the hormones careering around her body would wear off, the effects of dopamine would fade and she'd be the logical, rational person she always was. She just needed time and distance...

This was lust, and it would dwindle to nothing.

Tinsley pushed her hands into her hair, finger-combed her tangles and washed off her makeup. She brushed her teeth and, feeling a little more human, walked back into the room to see Cody pulling on his pants, his broad chest still bare. He had a light smattering of dark hair on his chest and the most gorgeous happy trail...one she'd followed with her tongue.

Stop that, Tinsley. It's over. Done. Time to move on...

"I ordered coffee," Cody told her.

Tinsley nodded her thanks and walked over to the bed and sat on the edge, looking down at the bedside cabinet, to where their identical phones lay. She wished she could find something witty and breezy to say, something that would cut through the tension. She couldn't think of anything...

"Are you okay?" Cody asked her, sitting down next to her to pull on his socks.

"Sure," Tinsley replied, knowing that even if she wasn't, she'd never admit to being anything other than okay. She was stubborn that way; the more uncomfortable or out of her depth she felt, the more confident and calm she appeared.

As Cody walked to the bathroom and pulled the door shut behind him, her phone buzzed. She picked it up, swiped her finger over the screen and saw the text message appear.

Can't wait to see you at Luca's tonight, it's been ages since we saw each other. Maybe we can have our own New Year's Eve celebration.

Wink, wink...

Norah? The only Norah she knew was a designer and decorator she and Kinga occasionally hired to stage some of their functions. She was well regarded as being one of the best in the business, but they weren't social friends and hadn't made any plans for tonight.

Tinsley pushed the home screen button and saw the higgledy-piggledy mess on the screen. This was Cody's phone, not hers. And, judging by this text message, he and Norah were more than work friends.

Cody and the gorgeous Norah made sense. Norah was loud, confident and was one of those women who oozed sexuality. Norah, Tinsley was sure, would know what she was doing in the bedroom…

Tinsley had just followed Cody's lead. Should she have been more aggressive, more demanding? Had she been too passive, too acquiescent? Was he disappointed in her? Did he think she'd wasted his time?

Suddenly what they'd shared, what had been beautiful a few hours ago, seemed tawdry, a little tasteless.

And, yeah, she didn't like feeling ick after sex.

God, this would be her first and last one-night stand. She simply wasn't cut out for them.

But she'd never let him know that. No, she'd smile, hand him his phone and find a way to ease out of this situation with as much grace as she could muster. She'd never let him see her sweat…

When he returned to stand in front of her, she nodded to his phone. "A message came through and I read it. Sorry, I thought it was mine. The phones look identical…"

An emotion she couldn't identify flashed in his eyes as he took the phone, read the message and tossed the phone on the bed without replying or giving her an explanation…

Not that she was owed one.

Tinsley slid her hands under her thighs and pulled a cool smile onto her face. "Last night, thank you." She forced herself to pick up his wrist to look at his expensive watch. "I'm going to shower and then I'm going to go back to sleep for a few hours."

Cody frowned, looking like he wanted to argue with her. She spoke again, her words rushed. "I'll see you back in the city at some point and, I'm pretty sure about this, we'll be irritating each other before long. It is, after all, what we do best."

Cody glanced at the bed, his look suggesting that they'd found something they were much better at than annoying each other. She wasn't going to acknowledge his unspoken words so instead sent him a cool smile. "Have a good trip home, Cody. Lock the door on the way out, won't you?"

She walked away from him, her head held high and her back straight. She made it to the door to the bathroom before her name on his lips halted her progress. Turning, she lifted her eyebrows.

He gestured to her torso and the corners of his mouth pulled up into a sexy-as-hell smirk. "I need my shirt and you're wearing it."

Tinsley looked down and nodded. Right. The cuffs hung over her hands and the tails almost reached her knees. It was soft and smelled of his sexy cologne. She didn't want to give it up…

"God, you are so sexy standing there in my shirt," Cody said, his voice rough with desire. Tinsley met his eyes and desire arced between them, raising the temperature in the room.

He wanted her. Again… And if she gave him the least

little bit of encouragement, he'd stay and that bed would see a lot more action.

She wanted to kiss that strong jaw again, bite the cords of his neck, run her tongue over the muscles in his arms, across his ladderlike stomach…

It would be so easy…

Her eyes bounced to his phone on his bed and she remembered Norah, and that she was expecting to see him later. The thought of Cody jumping from her bed to another woman's caused nausea to swirl in her stomach.

Yeah, she definitely wasn't any good at one-night stands…

Feeling reckless, irrationally pissed off and very off-balance, Tinsley crossed her arms over her body and gripped the hem of his shirt and slowly, oh so slowly, pulled it up, revealing her naked body inch by inch. Even though he was across the room, she heard the swift intake of his breath, and when she looked into his eyes, they were deep and dark and full of passion.

It was obvious what he wanted…and damn her for wanting it too.

But the moment was gone; it was time to move on. He had, after all, other fish to fry.

She pulled his shirt over her head, scrunched it into a ball and threw it. Without another word, she stepped into the bathroom and slammed the door shut.

And, because she didn't trust herself, she locked it.

Three

Knowing his father was out for the morning, James walked down the long corridor to Callum's corner office suite to talk to his father's longtime personal assistant. She was also the woman with whom he had an on-off affair from the time he was eighteen to twenty-three.

It wasn't something they ever acknowledged.

James rubbed the back of his neck, unable to remember how the affair started or who made the first move: the cocky, spoiled teenager, or the then thirty-year-old Emma? During the summer before he left for college, he'd fallen deeply, crazily in love with her.

Despite their age difference, their secret affair lasted all through his college career. Emma repeatedly told him they didn't have a future together— his father had other plans for him— and James countered her pessimism by violently insisting he'd defy his father to keep her in his life. Firmly believing he'd had the upper hand—

so cocky, so spoiled— he'd issued an ultimatum. They stopped sneaking around and came clean or he'd call it quits, over forever.

Emma called his bluff and shattered his heart.

In pain, and because he'd inherited his father's stupid pride, he'd immediately flung himself back into the rarefied society of the rich East Coast and met Penelope, young, pretty and eminently suitable. Within a month of meeting her, and with Callum's blessing, he'd asked her to marry him, and within three they were legally hitched and stitched.

And when he returned from his honeymoon, he realized Emma was pregnant and that her child was his.

Emma refused to confirm or deny his allegations, she simply shut down every non-work-related conversation. She also told him that if he didn't drop the subject, she'd accuse him of sexual harassment. James, not recognizing his ex-lover, and scared about the possible repercussions, backed way off.

Defeated, he set up a trust fund for her child, tried to save his rocky marriage and forget he had a son. Life became easier when Kinga and then Tinsley arrived and he could be the dad he so wanted to be.

Emma finally lifted her eyes to acknowledge his presence.

"Let's imagine I, unknowingly, fathered a child..." James said, standing behind her visitor's chair.

Emma, as he expected, started to stand. James narrowed his eyes and shook his head. "This is important, Emma, I suggest you listen. Sit down."

Emma sank back into her chair, her eyes apprehensive. But she did lift her chin and James took that as a sign to continue.

"Let's also imagine that child was raised by his single mom and was never told who his father is…"

Emma leaned forward and rested her forearms on her desk, her worried eyes not leaving his face.

"That hypothetical child might be interested in his ancestry, whether he had any relations on his father's side that he's never met, or heard of," James said, pacing the area in front of her desk. "He might have registered on the very popular WhoAreYou dot com, hoping to explore those connections."

James pushed his hand into his hair. "Once my DNA is entered into the ancestry website's database, connections will be made. The website will flag a genetic relationship between me and that child, between him and Callum."

Emma's eyes widened as she processed the implications of his pronouncement. James waited for her to speak, hoping she'd, finally, give him a confirmation of his suspicions. But she didn't speak and a pale face and worried eyes did not a confession make.

"Why are you telling me this?" Emma demanded after a tense silence.

"Because the tests results might set off a chain of events for which there will be consequences," James explained.

"Consequences for who? For you and your wife?" Emma demanded.

"For all of us," James replied, shrugging. "I just want all of us to be prepared."

And maybe he also thought she'd finally come clean and admit he was Garrett's father. But no, Emma was still an unbreakable vault.

Emma stared off into space for a few minutes before

standing up and crossing her arms over her chest. "All very interesting, James, but I have work to do."

Her expression turned cooler, if that was at all possible, and James sighed. It was Emma speak for "I'm done with discussing this."

Yep, situation normal.

She could ignore him but if Garrett was registered on the DNA site and connections were made, the status quo would seriously upend his life, his marriage and his position within Ryder International. Life, as he knew it, would be over.

Don't-rock-the-boat-James found that scenario appalling, I-want-to-acknowledge-my-son James hoped everything would come out into the open. Either way this dysfunctional cookie crumbled, he'd be disappointed.

Situation normal.

Neither of them could spare the time to meet with their grandfather, but Callum was the owner of the company and their boss and when he said jump, they jumped. They knew not to rock the boat.

Tinsley parked her butt on the edge of the conference table next to Kinga and stretched out her legs. The conference room had floor-to-ceiling windows looking out onto the harbor downtown and it was, yet again, snowing.

Tinsley remembered tasting snowflakes on her lips just before Cody kissed her, the way he heated her from the inside out. Frankly, she was surprised that during their lovemaking the bed hadn't burst into flames.

It had been the best sex of her life—hot, raunchy and oh so uninhibited. Maybe she had allowed herself to let go because she knew there would be no consequences. After all, Cody wasn't part of her day-to-day life.

She hadn't heard from him, nor seen him, since that night and that worked for her. She could pretend he was a stranger. In her head, she'd had fun sex—numerous times!—with a stranger and not with her ex-brother-in-law.

Kinga nudged her legs with her knee. "Earth to Tinsley."

Tinsley blinked before her eyes focused on her sister's lovely face. Kinga wore her blond hair cut super-short, and a pair of black-framed glasses covered her whiskey-colored eyes.

"Sorry, I was miles away," Tinsley told her.

"You've been very distracted lately," Kinga commented, leaning back in a chair and crossing her legs. "Is everything okay?"

She and Kinga were exceptionally close, something they hadn't been while she'd been with JT. During their courtship and marriage, JT came first and juggling him and her professional life had taken all the time and energy Tinsley had. After their divorce, Kinga was there for her and their friendship was now deep and strong.

But as much as she trusted Kinga, Tinsley wasn't ready to tell her, or anyone, that she and Cody had bumped boots on New Year's Eve. Since they were barely able to conduct a reasonable conversation without sniping at each other, explaining they'd had earth-shattering sex would raise questions she didn't know how to answer.

If Kinga pushed and Tinsley told her sister how she'd spent her last night in Toronto, she'd justify it by saying that it was a little end-of-year madness. She'd remind her that Cody wasn't her type, that he was too alpha, too domineering, blunt and direct. And that they'd kill each other if they spent too much time together…

"Why does Callum want this meeting?" Tinsley asked, changing the subject.

Kinga shrugged. "Why does Callum do anything?"

Kinga's question reminded Tinsley of something else she was curious about. Callum had given them—their parents, and her and Kinga—DNA tests for Christmas, hoping to find out more about their Ryder-White ancestry.

Tinsley didn't particularly care where in the world their genes originated but it was vitally important to Callum. Callum was besotted with keeping the Ryder-White bloodline untainted.

"Have those DNA tests come back yet?" she asked.

Kinga wrinkled her nose. "No, and it's driving Callum nuts. The parental unit is also acting a bit squirrelly."

She'd noticed that as well. Her normally easygoing father, who worked as Callum's right-hand person, was irritable. Their mom was distracted and twitchy. "Should we ask them what's going on?"

Kinga raised her eyebrows. "Uh-uh, I'm not that brave," she answered. "Maybe they're just going through another rough patch."

Their parents didn't have what Tinsley would call a warm marriage. They hadn't raised their voices or their hands, there had been no ugliness, but Tinsley never saw much affection between them either. She knew that theirs was, to an extent, an arranged marriage. Her mom's family had business connections with Callum, and around the time Callum decreed it was time for James to marry, Penelope had been there and waiting.

Tinsley loved her dad, but she wished he was a little more assertive in standing up to Callum. She knew there was a reason for him being obsequious, had heard an explanation, but couldn't remember the details.

They said that a woman either marries a man a lot like her dad, or the exact opposite of him. JT was a lot like James, easygoing, not one to rock the boat, happy to be managed and directed...

Until the day he wasn't.

When she married again, she wouldn't choose someone like her dad...

What the hell was she thinking? She wasn't ever marrying again! She'd placed her love and faith and trust in a man who'd promised to love her until death, yet he hadn't managed to keep that promise beyond her twenty-seventh birthday.

Tinsley knew that after all her work keeping their relationship alive and on track, if she couldn't make it work with JT, there was no chance of her having a successful relationship with anyone else.

There was simply no point in risking her heart again. Being single, she didn't have to worry about anyone else, didn't need to consult or consider anyone else. After twelve years of shepherding JT through life, she felt free.

Kinga's finger drilled into her thigh and pulled Tinsley back into the conversation. "Ow!"

"Expect more of those if you keep drifting off," Kinga told her. "You're not normally so distracted, Tins. What's going on?"

Tinsley sent Kinga an apologetic look. "Sorry. It's been a long year."

"It's the seventh, Tins, of *January*," Kinga retorted. "We're only one week in."

"God," Tinsley groaned.

Not wanting to answer any questions, or even think

about Cody Gallant, she changed the subject. "Haven't you just come back from Manhattan?"

"I flew in last night."

"And how did your meeting go with Griff O'Hare?"

Kinga released a small growl. "The man is arrogant, stubborn and far too good looking for his own good!"

Tinsley's eyebrows shot up in surprise. *Wow.* That was quite a reaction from her normally even keeled sister.

Tinsley wanted to know more, but heard footsteps coming down the hallway and she quickly stood up.

As Callum took his place at the head of the table, Tinsley turned her back to the door to walk around the table to take her seat, rolling her eyes at Kinga at Callum's irritable demand for an update on the Valentine's Day ball. Her father took his seat and sent her a wan smile. He looked tired and pale, Tinsley decided, and not at all like her normally happy and hearty father.

Kinga gave Callum her report, making it obvious that she was not happy that Callum had signed Griff O'Hare, the bad boy performer, to sing at the ball, without consulting her. Unlike James, Tinsley and Kinga both argued with their grandfather—not often and only about things that mattered—and the fact that they still had jobs made them think he tolerated their impertinence. Tinsley made notes on her iPad and when she looked up, her eyes widened at the sight of Cody Gallant sliding into a chair opposite her.

Two thoughts jostled for prominence in her brain: he looked scrumptious, dressed in gray suit pants, and a cranberry-colored sweater worn under a smart black jacket. And, secondly, what the hell was he doing here? Dark stubble covered his cheeks and she remembered how that scruff felt between her legs, the gorgeous, sexy itchiness against her sensitive skin. And then he moved his mouth up…

Heat climbed her neck and into her cheeks and she wished the world would open and swallow her whole. She wasn't ready, in any way, shape or form to deal with Cody Gallant. She'd thought she might have some time to perfect her reaction to him but here he was, just a scant week later, sitting opposite her. And all she could do was…blush.

Kinga interrupted her conversation with Callum to lean across the table, her expression concerned. "Are you feeling okay, Tins? You're looking a little flushed."

Cody smirked and Tinsley narrowed her eyes at him. She waved her sister's words away. "I think I'm getting a cold. I'll dose myself with vitamin C and zinc. They say zinc is great for upping one's immunity."

Oh, God. Now she was babbling. Tinsley wanted to bang her forehead on the conference table. She was such an idiot! Luckily her phone pinged with a message and while Callum hated being interrupted by cell phones, she picked it up and waved it. "Sorry, I need to get this."

Because if she ducked her head to stare at the screen, her hair would hide her flaming cheeks. She swiped her thumb across the screen and saw Cody's name.

Need help getting out of that hole you're digging?

You are such a jerk! was the best reply she could think of.

Tossing her head and placing her phone on the table, Tinsley looked at her grandfather, feeling irritated and off-balance.

"Callum, I have another meeting in ten minutes—" she didn't but she had no problem with lying if it would get her out of this room and away from Cody "—so can we move this one along?"

Callum frowned at her impertinence and Tinsley knew he was debating whether to remind her that he was the boss and paid her salary. He didn't need to; Callum frequently repeated those words. Tinsley had, over the years, considered jumping ship and working somewhere else, but working for her grandfather did have its perks: they were paid well above the industry norm and they enjoyed a lot of overseas travel on Callum's private jet.

And let's be honest here, they were allowed to run some kick-ass PR and publicity projects.

And if she left, there was the chance that Callum would punish James for her defection. Callum was not what one could call reasonable.

Callum tapped his index finger on the surface of the sleek black conference table. "Cody, to get you caught up, Ryder International, as part of the centennial celebrations, is sponsoring a horse race in Dubai, a yacht race in Monaco and the Valentine's Day ball is next month."

Tinsley felt compelled to look at Cody and her eyes widened when she noticed he was looking at her. His eyes dropped from her mouth to her chest and when they reconnected with her eyes, she knew where his thoughts were...

They were hanging out with hers in that hotel bedroom, remembering how they almost set the place on fire. Her skin prickled and felt too tight for her body and she couldn't take her eyes off him. She wanted another one-night stand. Hell, she wanted another three or four, ten or twenty.

She simply wanted him.

Their eyes remained connected as Callum's voice

faded to a monotonous drawl, and she forgot her father and sister were seated at the table and that she should be paying attention. All she could think of was how Cody's body felt when he settled his hips above hers, that feeling of completeness when he slid inside her, the way the muscle in his jaw contracted, how his breathing grew ragged as he waited for her to come before he did. And how, sometimes, he made her come a few times before following her over the edge...

Kinga, snapping her fingers, pulled Tinsley back to the present moment.

"Sorry, sorry...what did I miss?" Tinsley demanded, wincing when she noticed Callum's furious face. Knowing she needed to do damage control, she rubbed her throat. "Sorry, Callum, I'm not feeling too great. I think I might be getting sick. Would you mind repeating that?"

Callum narrowed his icy blue eyes but before he could speak, Cody jumped in. "Callum wants to add another function to your celebration year," he explained.

What? Was he nuts?

Did Callum have any idea what they were currently dealing with? Kinga—having found out that Callum had already sent the performer, without their knowledge, a contract for him to be the headline act at the ball—had just spent ten minutes trying to persuade Callum to break the contract.

Callum, being Callum, refused.

Kinga needed to organize the ball as well as keep O'Hare on the straight and narrow—his ability to get into trouble was legendary—so that he didn't taint the ball's reputation with his headline catching, bad boy antics. She had her hands full.

As did Tinsley. She had two more bars to open this year as well as overseeing the horse and yacht races.

They were already working long hours and the year had barely begun. Kinga bit the corner of her bottom lip, her eyes reflecting Tinsley's anxiety.

"Before I even ask what you want us to do, you need to know that if you add more functions, Callum, we'll need more staff and a bigger budget," Tinsley told him, keeping her voice firm. "Kinga and I are already stretched thin."

Callum nodded and gestured to Cody. "That's why Cody is here. I'm putting Gallant Events on retainer for the next six months and Cody's company will stage the summer promotions."

Promotions, as in plural. "What are you envisioning, Callum?" Tinsley asked, frowning.

"James, explain."

Tinsley turned sideways to look at her dad, her eyebrows raised. Her dad was a creative guy, and she was interested in what he had to say. Before she and Kinga took over and expanded the Ryder International PR division, their department used to fall under her father's control, one of the few responsibilities Callum allowed him.

"Over dinner a few nights ago, I suggested to Callum that we hold a specialty cocktail competition. By my count, we employ over five hundred mixologists and if we add our independent contractors like Jules—" Tinsley smiled at him mentioning her best friend, Jules, who was one of the best mixologists in the world and did pop-up bars, promotions and events for Ryder International "—then that figure swells to over seven hundred. The bartenders can either enter as a team or on their own, but they have to create four new cocktails inspired by four special moments over the last one hundred years. For instance, the end of the Second World War, landing on the moon, women getting the vote, the fall of the Berlin Wall… You get the idea."

Damn, but that was a spectacular plan. Tinsley felt her mind spinning with additional ideas and when she caught Kinga's eyes, she saw the excitement on her sister's face. *Go, Dad.*

"I'm envisioning a regional contest, then national, then international, with an expert panel of judges," James continued.

"That's a great idea, Dad," Kinga said, sending him a huge smile. "A hell of a lot of work, but a stunning idea. We could get chefs and food critics to judge, and we could get some of our suppliers to sponsor the prize. We could…"

Callum cleared his throat and pointed his index finger at Kinga. "You, young lady, must concentrate on the ball and keeping Griff O'Hare focused." He turned to Tinsley. "This is your project, yours and Cody's. Take the idea, flesh it out, see if it's viable and what budget we'd need. Bring me a detailed proposal in two weeks."

Tinsley scrunched up her nose. She did not want to work with Cody, not now and not in the future. "I can do a feasibility study, Callum, there's no need to involve Cody at this point."

"Cody's company is already on a monthly retainer. He needs to do something to earn the money we pay him," Callum told her, sounding impatient.

Before she could defend Cody—and why did she want to?—Callum signaled the end of the meeting by pushing back his chair. He placed his age-spotted hands on the conference table and told James and Kinga to leave the room. When the door closed behind them, Callum divided his hot glance between Tinsley and Cody.

"You two have always had a contentious relationship," Callum stated, his voice ice-cold, "and I am aware that you try not to work directly with each other."

Okay, where was her crabby grandfather going with this?

"Let me be clear. I do not care that you were once related, nor do I care whether you like each other or not."

Tinsley wanted to look at Cody but pride kept her eyes on Callum's face; she refused to cower under his hard stare. "The two of you working together on this project is nonnegotiable. And if either of you finds that untenable, you will both be fired. I will not play favorites for family."

"Callum—" Tinsley protested.

Callum's expression, if that was at all possible, hardened further. "Work together or don't work here at all."

"You are being unreasonable," Tinsley protested, standing up so he wasn't looming over them. Cody also climbed to his feet, his face unreadable.

"My company, my rules," Callum stated, straightening. "You have ten days to draw up a feasibility plan and a working budget."

It had been two weeks five minutes ago. "Callum, we need more time."

"We need, at the very least, two months, Callum," Cody told her grandfather. He sent Callum a mocking look. "And if that doesn't suit, feel free to accept my resignation. I think you've forgotten that, while Ryder International was my first client, it most certainly isn't my *only* client. In fact, you're not even in my top ten. Fire me—I promise you I'll be fine."

Damn, seeing Cody stand up to her powerful grandfather, utterly calm, was a huge turn-on. Then again, the man just had to breathe to make her feel turned on and off-balance. She really had to have sex more often if this was the way she was going to react.

Callum and Cody stared each other down while Tinsley held her breath. Her grandfather was the first to cave. "Two months and it had better be a brilliant plan, Gallant," Callum muttered.

Cody one, Callum, zero, Tinsley thought. Cody and Callum shook hands and Callum moved toward the door. He yanked it open before turning back to look at them. He shook his head and winced. "This is either going to be a stroke of genius or you two will kill each other."

He wasn't wrong.

Four

On leaving the conference room, Cody told Tinsley that he'd see her in her office in fifteen minutes, that he had a couple of calls to make before he could give her his full attention.

He didn't bother asking whether she could meet with him, whether her schedule was flexible enough to accommodate him. No, he'd just assumed…

Irritating man.

Tinsley dropped into her chair behind her desk and pulled her oversize notepad toward her, flipping past the pages filled with colorful notations, reminders and shopping and to-do lists. Her notebook was part diary, part journal, and without it, she would be lost. Opening a blank page, she did what she always did when she was feeling overwhelmed and out of sorts: she made a list. But instead of making a list of everything she needed to do to give Callum a decent proposal, she found herself writing a list of why she shouldn't sleep with Cody again.

She didn't get further than "we don't like each other" and "we are now working together" when her computer beeped, the tone signaling an incoming personal message. She turned her attention to her screen and saw that the message was from JT. Tinsley frowned, wondering why her ex was contacting her. They hadn't spoken for almost as long as the divorce had been final…

Curious, her heart beating a little fast, she opened up the email and when she saw his first sentence—"Dear friends and family"—she knew she was part of a group message. She looked at the message recipients and saw that her parents, Kinga and Cody would also receive this missive. JT wasn't one for sending newsletters, so what prompted this?

One way to find out was to read on…

Hey everyone, just a quick note to tell you that Heather is pregnant. She's twenty weeks along and we're expecting a boy. We are ecstatic and can't wait to meet our little man.

Tinsley blinked, read the message again and shook her head. What the hell was he talking about? She read the message yet again. Right, it definitely said they were having a baby, but that made no sense to her. JT didn't want kids; he never had. Whenever she'd brought up the subject, he'd told her that he wasn't ready, that he didn't think he'd ever be ready. Kids weren't part of his plan…

They'd very much been a part of hers. She'd craved a child and, to be honest, she still did. She'd begged JT to give her a baby, for them to start their family but he'd continuously refused. Unusually, he couldn't be budged on the topic and he promised her that he'd never change his mind.

But he had. With someone else.

Tinsley wrapped her arms around her stomach and rocked in her chair, the news punching her over and over again. JT was going to be a dad, but she wasn't going to be a mom.

It was fundamentally wrong…

Tinsley stood up and walked over to her window, placing her hands on the glass and resting her forehead against the cold pane. She felt hot and cold, angry and soul-deep sad. JT and Heather were living her life, the picture-perfect life she'd planned. It wasn't fair…

She wasn't supposed to be alone, divorced, childless. According to her timeline, they should've had a house in the country by now and she'd be pregnant with child number two, possibly even child number three.

Tinsley heard the rap on her closed door, heard it open and, without looking up, lifted her finger telling whoever wanted a piece of her to wait. Before she faced anyone, she needed to get her raging emotions—fury and jealousy—under control.

Don't let them see you sweat…

She refused to let anyone see that she was upset, to see even a hint of tears. Whirling around and keeping her head down, she grabbed her phone and pretended to make a call, knowing she needed time to calm down, to get her emotions under control.

Masculine fingers removed her phone from her fingers and Tinsley reluctantly lifted her eyes, up and up some more, to look into Cody's harsh expression. Emotion, deep and sad, flashed in his eyes. "Ah, I take it you got the broadcast?"

She didn't need him to explain. "You got it too? You didn't know?" Tinsley demanded, resting her flat palms on the desk.

"JT and I don't talk anymore," Cody said. "That email came as much as a surprise to me as it did to you. I thought that, like me, JT never wanted kids."

Tinsley lifted her head to frown at him. "Why don't you want kids? How can you not want kids?"

His eyebrows rose at her demand and he shrugged. "My dad was a useless father, as was my grandfather. And, remember, I did raise JT from the time he was eight. I was a surrogate father far too early."

True. JT and Cody's dad had been so inactive in their lives that Tinsley could barely remember the man. He didn't attend any of JT's graduations, nor did he grace their wedding with his presence. He was more their bank manager than their father.

Cody gestured to her laptop screen and they both looked at the picture of Heather that JT had annoyingly included. Heather wore a tiny bikini and proudly showed off her baby bump, grinning into the camera. Tinsley narrowed her eyes before standing up and crossing her hands across her chest. She lifted her chin and her eyes slammed into Cody's.

"I want a baby," she abruptly stated.

Shock flashed across his face. "Uh… I'm not sure what I'm supposed to say to that."

Tinsley knew that her next words would be irrational but she could no more stop them than she could the sun rising in the east. "JT wouldn't give me a child—he refused to. He's now having a baby with someone else and *I want my own*."

"What?"

"I want my own child," Tinsley repeated. "Maybe I should get myself artificially inseminated using donor sperm."

Color leached from Cody's face. "What? You can't make decisions like that just because my idiot brother is expecting a child!"

"I wanted a child long before he did, since when we were first married. He refused to give me one!" Tinsley shouted. Why was she so quick to lose control of her words and emotions around Cody when keeping control was her thing? It was like she morphed into someone completely different around him...

Or someone more like herself. Tinsley pushed that thought away. "So, is this some weird competition between you and Heather?" Cody demanded.

Of course she wasn't competing...or maybe she was, just a little. She'd planned on having a little boy with JT's blond hair and sparkling green eyes. Or a little girl with her blue eyes and JT's nose. Tinsley cocked her head to the side, thinking that the brothers didn't look that different, except that Cody had darker hair and was bigger and taller. JT was smarter but Cody wasn't an academic slouch. Their DNA was pretty close...

Maybe she could still have a small piece of that original plan. Knowing that she was way off base, and possibly losing her damn mind, Tinsley allowed the words to come.

"Sleep with me again—give me a child."

Cody looked at her like she'd grown three heads and a tail. "No," Cody stated, taking two steps back.

She wasn't about to back down now. "Whether I get sperm from you or a donor, what's the difference? I'm not asking for anything but your DNA. That's *it*. I wouldn't expect you to be part of the kid's life, to pay for anything. This will be as anonymous as you want it to be."

He dragged his hand through his hair, his expression grim. "Tinsley, this is madness. The only reason you're suggesting this is that you're upset that JT and Heather are having a baby, the baby you planned to have with him."

"He didn't want a child with me!" Tinsley shouted, mortified to feel tears on her cheeks. "He didn't want me!"

He moved fast and before she could react, his arms were around her and she was snuggled against his chest, her tears creating mascara streaks on his sweater. She put her fist to her mouth, and bit her knuckles, hoping to push her sobs away but they kept rising until they escaped.

She cried. For the first time ever, someone other than Kinga was witness to her distress and pain. And she didn't like it, not one bit.

She didn't like feeling this exposed, this vulnerable. Weak. Exposing her pressure points gave others the chance to hurt her. Tinsley was pretty sure she'd done enough hurting…

But JT's news stung. She felt like she'd never be whole again.

"My brother doesn't think," Cody murmured in her ear, his big hands drawing circles over her back. "He's got a massive brain but doesn't have the common sense God gave a gnat. He's not worth your tears."

"Oh, I know that! I'm not crying about him as much as about the life I lost, the one I planned. We were supposed to have a perfect life."

"There's no such thing, Tinsley!" Cody put his thumb

under her chin and lifted her face so she had to look at him. "I understand this news rocked you, but you're upset and not thinking straight."

Truer words had never been spoken.

"And let me make this very clear, you are never getting my sperm."

She sniffed and wrinkled her nose. "If you change your mind, I'll take them. I'd much rather have your DNA than a random stranger's."

Cody's lips lifted a fraction. "Good to know but...*no*. You're not getting my boys, Tinsley. Not today, not ever."

"Damn," Tinsley muttered, dropping her head to rest her temple against his chest. She was so comfortable in his arms. She shouldn't be, but she was.

"Though I wouldn't be averse to sleeping with you again," Cody said from somewhere above her head.

Tinsley tensed and, leaving her hands on his chest, put a foot of space between them. She frowned, confused. "What?"

"You heard me," Cody told her, his thumb swiping away a tear on her left cheekbone. "I'd very much like to sleep with you again."

Tinsley felt her head spinning. This was all a bit much to take in. Her ex was having a baby, she'd asked his brother for his sperm, she'd cried and now Cody was hitting on her?

What. The. Hell?

"But...you are sleeping with Norah," Tinsley said, hoping to sound matter-of-fact. Since she sounded a little squeaky, she figured she'd overshot.

"I had a fling with Norah a few months ago and we made plans to meet up the night after you and I..." Cody hesitated. "I canceled our plans."

"Why?" Tinsley demanded.

"I didn't want her. I wanted you. I still do." Cody brushed her mouth with his and Tinsley found herself sinking into him, her arms going around his waist. He felt so solid, like a giant redwood that would never shift, no matter how strong the wind or the rain. He made her feel sexy, lovely and, best of all, alive.

Made her feel safe, secure, protected.

But she was making rainbows from rope again, confusing attraction with comfort or, even worse, she was looking for a distraction. She'd told herself that sleeping with Cody was a one-night deal.

She wasn't a have-some-fun-and-walk-away type of girl. Under her calm surface, she was too intense, too emotional. There were enough things in her life she wanted but couldn't have—a husband, a happy marriage, a baby or three—and she did not need to add Cody to that big, messy pile.

But it was hard to step back, nearly impossible to move out of the security of his big arms. It was so nice to feel protected. With JT, she was always the strong one, the one he leaned on, not the other way around.

But she needed to compose herself, to pull herself together. JT was having a kid. She had the right to feel regret, but she couldn't wallow in it. Using the heels of her hands, Tinsley rubbed her eyes, hoping she wasn't spreading her mascara everywhere, and pulled up a smile.

"I never have meltdowns and I'm sorry you had to witness me losing it."

Cody lifted his hands. "I think that was a very normal reaction to hearing unexpected news," he said.

She shrugged, embarrassed. "I reacted like that because she's getting to have what I wanted, the one thing

I still want." She nodded decisively. "At some point, I'm going to have a baby. Hopefully sooner rather than later."

She placed her hands on her stomach and pulled in a deep breath. "Can you give me ten minutes to wash my face? And then I think we should get to work. We've got a lot to do."

"Are you sure you're okay?" Cody asked her, sliding his hands into the pockets of his pants, "Maybe you should take the rest of the day off and we can come back to Ryder International business tomorrow?"

He'd never suggest that if she were a man. No, he'd expect his male colleague to dust off his emotions and carry on. And because Tinsley couldn't, *wouldn't*, give herself any slack, that was exactly what she did.

But only after she spent the next ten minutes repairing her makeup in her private bathroom.

Cody paced the long, thin balcony dotted with chairs and tables outside the Ryder International break room and told himself to control his temper. He reminded himself, for the tenth time, that tossing his phone from seventeen floors was not an option.

He was relatively easygoing, but his younger brother had the knack of cranking the heat under his temper. While waiting for Tinsley to compose herself earlier, he'd video-called JT in Hong Kong.

JT answered on the first ring. "I thought my news would warrant a call from you," he said, smirking.

They hadn't exchanged more than brief Christmas and birthday phone calls for more than two years. On hearing that JT abandoned Tinsley, Cody had flown to Hong Kong to have it out with his brother, who didn't seem to care that he'd left a heartbroken wife behind.

He had a new life; the old one was behind him. Then, like today, it was all about JT and how he felt.

"You didn't think that maybe you should've called Tinsley and told her privately before you told everyone else that you're having a baby?" Cody asked him, trying to keep a lid on his temper.

"Why?" JT asked, sounding genuinely confused.

"It's a respect thing, JT," Cody replied, gripping the bridge of his nose. "I gather that she desperately wanted a child, but you refused."

"I didn't want a baby with her, but I do want one with Heather," JT replied. When Cody just stared at him, he shrugged. "This isn't rocket science, Cody. Tinsley is my past. Heather is my future. She's my everything."

"You cheated on Tinsley, abandoned her, destroyed her dreams of having a family and then you drop the news that you are having a kid in a generic email. She deserves more than that, JT!"

"We're divorced, it's over and I don't care how she feels. I have a new life. Why can't you understand that?" JT demanded.

JT was more like their father than Cody had imagined. As long as he was happy, as long as he was doing what he wanted to do, life was fine. Taking responsibility and considering feelings other than his own were not traits he possessed.

It was all about him, all the time.

Arguing with JT was a waste of time. His brother was a selfish prick and probably always would be. He'd caused Tinsley a lot of pain and maybe if he had expressed some contrition, Cody might have been able to forgive him. But he hadn't and Cody was over making excuses for him.

"Aren't you going to congratulate me, big brother?"

"Yeah, congrats," Cody replied, keeping his voice flat and uninterested.

JT was so wrapped up in himself he didn't hear Cody's lack of enthusiasm. When JT started to talk about birth plans—they were thinking about flying in a famous doula from Greece for her to assist Heather because she was determined to have a home birth— Cody decided he'd heard enough. He ended the call.

He heard footsteps behind him and turned to see Kinga approaching him. Tinsley's older sister looked a little frazzled and he presumed she'd also heard the news.

"What's a doula?" he demanded.

Kinga wrinkled her nose. "A doula is a midwife." She rested her arms on the balcony railing and shivered as a cold wind blew across the harbor and up the side of the building. "I was on my way to Tinsley, but saw you standing out here. Is she okay?"

Cody rocked his right hand from side to side. "She's mad, hurt, upset. She keeps saying she wants a baby."

Kinga didn't look surprised. "She's always wanted kids, from the time she was little. She pretended all her dolls were babies. She wanted to go off the pill when she left high school but promised JT she'd wait until they graduated college. When she raised the subject again, he told her he didn't want kids, and, not trusting her to take care of contraception, started using condoms when they made love."

Cody winced at Kinga's words. "My brother is a douche."

"Yep, he is. I think Tins wanted a baby more than she wanted a husband, so this news will hit her hard."

"She cried a little," Cody admitted.

"Tinsley cried?" Kinga grabbed his arm and dug her nails into the fabric above his skin. "She never cries! In fact, I'm surprised she even let on she was upset. Tinsley keeps her emotions hidden."

Yeah, he knew that and he hated it. "She was pretty upset."

So upset that she'd asked him for his sperm. The thought made him feel squirrelly and weird, jumpy.

"I'll go and talk to her," Kinga said, her eyes worried.

Cody shook his head. "She's calm now and she's expecting me any minute. Leave her and let her get back to work."

Kinga didn't look convinced. "I think she needs me, Cody."

The sisters had a rock-steady bond. "She always needs you, Kinga, but maybe you can chat with her later? She wants to work now, and God knows, we have a lot of it to do."

Kinga eventually nodded. "That's not a lie. What the hell was Callum thinking demanding a proposal in such little time? I swear, that old man..." she muttered.

Cody placed his hand on Kinga's back and ushered her to the door. They stepped into warmth and Cody headed for the state-of-the-art coffee machine, asking Kinga if she wanted some. She said yes and told Cody Tinsley would prefer a hot chocolate and how to make it for her.

"Is Callum okay?" Cody asked, remembering Callum's pale face and earlier ornery attitude. "He was pretty abrupt earlier."

"Have you met my grandfather?" Kinga demanded, placing her elbows on a high table next to the coffee station. "He's always abrupt, some would say blatantly rude."

That was true. "He just seemed worse than usual, and he doesn't look that well," Cody commented. "His hand was shaking."

"I didn't notice," Kinga admitted. "I know he's mad because there's been some sort of delay on the DNA tests he requested at Christmas."

Kinga went on to explain how their DNA would be entered into a genealogy website, that the family could find out where they came from originally and whether they had any distant relatives scattered throughout the world.

"He's obsessed with his bloodline and wants the results. But DNA testing has become quite popular, the lab is backed up and Callum doesn't like waiting." Kinga took the coffee he held out and blew across the liquid before taking a sip. "My parents are also acting weird, by the way."

Callum fixed Tinsley's hot chocolate. "How?"

"They're both grumpy, both snappy, both tense. Tins and I are presently avoiding them as much as possible."

"Your dad was his normal charming self this morning," Cody commented.

"Where do you think Tins inherited her acting ability from, Cody? She and Dad can both be dying inside but nobody would suspect it." She frowned. "That's why I'm so very surprised she cried in front of you. You're not one of her favorite people."

Her words punched him in the gut. "I know. But I'm hoping that will change…" He saw the speculation on Kinga's face and thought he'd better nip any ideas jumping into her head. "We need to work together, Kinga, and it would be easier if we managed to be friends."

Kinga narrowed her eyes at him. "Are you sure that's it?"

Cody picked up his and Tinsley's mugs and sent her a bland smile. "What else could it be, Kinga?"

Before she could answer, he strode away and headed back toward Tinsley's office, thinking that he never experienced this much drama at his place. Life around the Ryder-Whites was never boring.

Five

Five weeks later, in the bathroom of her hotel room in Manhattan, Tinsley stared at the pregnancy test lying facedown on the vanity, her heart beating as fast as a hummingbird's wings.

The words *be careful what you wish for* flashed across her brain and she thought she heard a witch's cackle coming from a long distance away. Her period was three weeks late and, since she was ridiculously regular, the most obvious conclusion was that she was pregnant. Courtesy of her ex-husband's brother.

Dear Lord.

The test, two pink lines, would confirm her suspicions but she couldn't bring herself to flip it over. She'd given the idea of being a single mom some thought since receiving JT's blasé email, but she never once thought she might be pregnant herself.

Cody used condoms and condoms were ninety-nine

percent effective, weren't they? She couldn't be pregnant; there was no way. She was just late because she'd been working so hard and was so stressed. Tinsley placed a hand on her stomach, pushed the tips of her fingers into her skin and shook her head. No, her carrying a child didn't make sense, didn't feel right.

Her being pregnant didn't resonate.

She glanced at the test again and shook her head. She'd just ignore the test for now, Tinsley decided, looking at her reflection in the mirror above the vanity. If she flipped it over and saw only one stripe, she'd be disappointed. If she saw two, she'd be terrified, and she didn't think she could hide either emotion. She didn't want to attend the Ryder International Valentine's Ball looking shell-shocked.

Tinsley turned and looked at herself in the long, vertical mirror behind the door. She wore a white sheath, designed by Prada. The entire outfit, and her decency, depended on a thin cord running from her right shoulder down her back to her left hip, leaving most of her back bare. A high slit left her left thigh exposed and showed off her sparkly Jimmy Choos. The dress was stark and sleek and her stylist recommended a halo braid and low bun, long curtain bangs framing her face and soft, natural makeup to contrast the severity of the dress. It worked, Tinsley decided; she looked...reasonable.

While she couldn't do anything about the worry in her eyes, at least her expertly applied makeup gave her some color. She placed her hands over her flat stomach and closed her eyes, feeling overwhelmed. How was she supposed to go to a ball, smile and flirt and laugh, while she still didn't know what was on that stick?

Maybe she should just check it...

If it says yes, you'll be thrown into a tailspin. If it says no, you'll be gutted. No, it was better to stay in limbo until the ball was over. She could cry, scream or panic after the ball when she was alone.

Her phone beeped with a message and Tinsley picked it up. It was Kinga, telling her that her family was waiting outside the Forrester-Grantham Ballroom and their guests were arriving. Where the hell was she?

Wincing, Tinsley picked up the pregnancy test and shoved it into her small clutch bag, forcing it in so that it lay from corner to corner. Lipstick went down one side, and her hotel key card on the other side. She didn't have room for her phone, but that didn't matter, since she would be with her family tonight. Not bothering to check her reflection again, she left the room and hurried down the hallway to the bank of elevators.

She just had to get through the evening, and she could fall apart later. She breathed deeply as the elevator descended and opened onto the floor housing the ornate ballroom. She pulled a practiced smile onto her face and walked toward her family, holding her dress so the hem didn't catch on her spiky heels or skim the floor.

Her eyes went to her sister, who looked stunning in a deep red ball gown, her smile as bright as the diamond glittering on the ring finger of her left hand. Kinga had spent a lot of time with Griff O'Hare over the past six weeks and had fallen in love with the reformed bad boy of rock and roll, who was also the ball's headline act. Tinsley kissed her parents and greeted Callum before placing her cheek against Kinga's and inhaling her sister's gorgeous scent.

"You look great, King," Tinsley told her, her lips close to Kinga's ear. "You're glowing."

Kinga squeezed her hands and Tinsley stepped back. "*You* look amazing, Tins. I love your dress," Kinga told her, placing her arm in hers and leading her away from the family, who'd turned to greet a Bahraini princess. "Callum and the parents can hold down the fort and greet the guests. We are going to take a minute for ourselves."

They approached a waiter holding a tray of champagne and Kinga picked up two glasses and handed one to Tinsley. They clinked, Tinsley took a small sip—surely a half glass wouldn't hurt her baby, if there even *was* a baby—and wrinkled her nose.

"What's wrong?" Kinga asked her, her eyes narrowing.

"Nothing, the champagne just tastes a little weird." It shouldn't; it was Krug Clos du Mesnil Blanc de Blancs, the '95 vintage, and it cost over a grand a bottle.

"No, it doesn't," Kinga replied, taking another sip. "It's utterly delicious."

Tinsley shrugged. "I've just brushed my teeth, so that's probably why. Where's Griff?"

Kinga's eyes softened. "With his band doing bandy things. I watched his dress rehearsal today and he's going to be brilliant."

"Of course he is," Tinsley told her, smiling. She liked Kinga's man partly because he was a nice guy, but mostly because he made her sister so damn happy.

Kinga nudged her and fanned her face. "Wow. If I was single…"

Tinsley turned to look at the trio of men stepping out of the elevator. She couldn't help her little sigh. Garrett Kaye—über-wealthy venture capitalist and the son of Callum's assistant, Emma—was the tallest of the three, topping out at six-five. He wore his light brown hair short and his beard was new and tinged with red. She recognized Sutton Marchant, previously an international stockbroker, now an author. He and Garrett seemed to be on friendly terms, Tinsley presumed they knew each other from the world of finance. Sutton shared the same coloring as Tinsley, dark hair and blue eyes, except that Sutton's eyes were a lot lighter and more arresting.

Tinsley looked at Cody, her lungs immediately forgetting how to suck air. As she could now attest, Cody Gallant looked his best wearing only his birthday suit, but he also, damn him, rocked a tuxedo. She took in the details. His suit was designer with narrow, grosgrain notch lapels matching his flat-front pants and his vest. His shirt was a crisp and classic white, with a plain front style and a perfectly knotted bow tie.

He looked fantastic.

Cody noticed her, lifted a hand in acknowledgment, turning his head to look past Garrett's shoulder. His sexy face broke out into a grin. Tinsley looked to see who'd grabbed his attention and sighed. She couldn't blame Cody; she always smiled whenever she saw her best friend too. Not only was Jules beautiful—her looks courtesy of her Swedish and Mauritian ancestry—she was also funny, supersmart and outgoing. And, as one of the world's best mixologists, she would be one of the main judges for their cocktail competition.

Tinsley watched as Cody enveloped her gorgeous friend in a huge hug and then introduced her to Garrett and Sutton. Cody kept a loose arm around Jules, and Tinsley felt a burning sensation in her stomach move up to her chest.

Kinga jammed her elbow into Tinsley's side. "Did you just growl?" she demanded.

She had, but there was no way on earth she'd admit that. Or that she was jealous of the attention Jules was receiving from Cody. Jules was her best friend, *dammit,* and as far as she knew, there was nothing but friendship between her and Cody. And even if there was, it shouldn't be a problem.

Unless she was pregnant... Then things might become complicated.

You are such a liar, Tinsley Tamlyn Ryder-White. You'd hate it if he and Jules hooked up.

God. Her grip tightened on her glass and she was sure enamel was flying off her teeth from grinding them together so hard. This evening was going to last six hundred hours, and she wasn't even twenty minutes in.

She wanted to go upstairs, climb under the covers and hide out for a while. From Cody, from life and most definitely from reality.

And from that damn test.

Standing at the bar, watching Garrett Kaye arguing with Jules Carlson, James noticed Garrett's eyes were so like Callum's—a deep, dark blue—and they flashed with irritation. But under the annoyance was a healthy dose of amusement and enjoyment.

Like Callum, Garrett wasn't used to people arguing with him. James thought that having a spirited discussion with a fiery woman would do Garrett some good. He needed a challenge and Jules was just the person to give him a run for his money.

James's son—unacknowledged but still his—was ruthless and arrogant and needed to be brought down a peg or two. Few people, so he'd heard, were allowed inside Garrett's inner world. Even Emma, his mom, was encouraged to keep her emotional distance.

James sighed. If anyone, particularly Callum, found out Garrett was his son and Callum's grandson, everything that was to come to James—stocks, shares, art, cash and properties—would go to Garrett. James didn't want that to happen. He'd done what he could for Garrett, he'd anonymously bequeathed him a trust fund when he turned twenty-one, but Tinsley and Kinga were his legitimate children. They carried the Ryder-White name and had put up with Callum all their lives.

Besides, Garrett was as wealthy as Callum and Callum's inheritance would be an excess of riches.

Garrett's head whipped up and their eyes connected. He lifted a sardonic eyebrow, said something to Jules, hopefully excusing himself, and turned to walk in James's direction, his expression mocking. He slid into the empty spot next to James, rested his elbows on the bar and ordered a fifteen-year-old whiskey.

"Care to tell me why you're watching me?" Garrett demanded.

Straight to the point, James thought. He scrambled for an answer. "I've known Jules for a long time, she's Tinsley's best friend and I'm protective of her."

"And you think she needs protection from me?"

James nodded. "Something like that."

"Bullshit," Garrett retorted. "Firstly, Jules needs no help. Her tongue is more effective than industrial-strength paint stripper. And you weren't looking at her—you were looking at me."

It took all of James's willpower to keep his expression impassive. "If you say so," he said, allowing a trace of derision to touch his voice. It was a trick he'd learned from Callum and one that was normally effective.

Garrett wasn't even a little chastised. He simply sipped his whiskey and looked over his glass at James. "Why have I caught your attention, James? Why am I in your crosshairs?"

James swallowed. It wasn't easy to see your son look at you with such a derisive expression.

"Whenever I'm around you, I get the feeling that you can affect me, or my life, in some way," Garrett continued.

James fought to keep his face impassive, unable to speak past the lump in his throat. Then Garrett's voice dropped again and turned menacing. "Why do I sense that you, the son of my mother's boss, has the ability to upend my life?"

"Maybe your Spidey sense is wrong," James suggested, his words weak.

"It's never wrong," Garrett retorted, banging his glass on the bar. He looked down at James, his eyes dark and dangerous. "What's going on, James? What are you thinking, planning? Want to save me the hassle and tell me now?"

James kept his tongue behind his teeth as sweat ran down his back. His son, this man, was tough and took no prisoners. He doubted that he would welcome being told of his parentage during one of the world's most exclusive balls.

And James had promised Emma he'd never reveal his true identity. And he knew that if he did, he and his legitimate family would lose everything. "I think you've either had too much to drink or have an overactive imagination, Garrett."

Garrett shook his head. "Nah, that's not it." Garrett clamped his hand around James's shoulder and squeezed. "You don't have to tell me. I'm good at ferreting out secrets and I'll discover yours."

That's what I'm afraid of, James thought as Garrett strode away.

Griff O'Hare was three songs in and Tinsley, sitting across the overly decorated table from Cody, looked as green as the pistachio ice cream on her plate. Not that she'd eaten any. Neither had she taken one bite from the previous five courses; she'd simply pushed her food around.

If he ignored the pallor in her cheeks, she looked sensational. And her dress, held up by nothing more than a thin cord, was the sexiest in the room. She looked, with her messy up-do and smoky eyes, fantastic but he could see beyond the styling to know that something was wrong with his once off lover and current colleague.

She looked like the weight of the world was sitting on her shoulders. And the fact that he didn't know who or what was causing her such distress pissed him off. He'd known her since she was a kid and he could read her better than he could read most. Something was eating her from the inside out and he wanted to know what it was so he could fix it for her.

She's not yours to fix, Gallant, and you don't do that shit anymore, remember?

Cody sighed and tapped his finger against the crystal tumbler holding his shot of excellent whiskey. Griff was singing an old, popular standard and all eyes, including Tinsley's, were on the superstar. Except for Cody's. He couldn't pull his eyes off Tinsley.

What was wrong with her?

She'd been tired lately, but that wasn't unexpected. They'd both been working crazy long days trying to keep up with their current work schedules while also compiling the proposal for the cocktail competition.

If Callum approved their project, plans and budget— and his fee—he and Tinsley would spend the next few months putting their plans into action before she handed over the nitty-gritty day-to-day operation to the team he'd yet to select.

But until then, their workdays would become longer. If Tinsley wasn't coping now, she wouldn't cope in a couple of weeks.

It didn't help that she was so into control and couldn't ask for help. She made life ten times harder for herself than it needed to be. But she never complained, was ludicrously efficient and he never saw her lose her cool. He wished she would. Seeing the very uptight Tinsley Ryder-White losing it would be quite fun.

Since her mini-meltdown in her office after hearing JT's baby news, tonight was the first time he'd seen her looking less than picture-perfect. Was she sick? Stressed? Feeling overwhelmed?

But, because she was as even-keeled as ever, how the hell would he ever know?

Judging by the professional way Tinsley treated him, nobody would suspect that they'd had intense, amazing, jaw-dropping sex six weeks ago. She was polite, direct and completely focused on the task at hand. When he'd tried to talk about anything other than work, whether it was politics or the ball or her family, she always cut him off and turned the subject back to business.

Tinsley was determined to pretend they hadn't spent the first hours of the New Year naked and yet he couldn't forget it. The entire night had been burned on his memory and he hadn't been able to accept any invitations for bed-based fun from Norah or anyone else.

One night with his ex-sister-in-law had totally screwed up his sex life. And, strangely, he was okay with that. He didn't want a relationship but casual sex had lost its appeal. Which left him dating himself...

But if Tinsley crooked her little finger, he'd be out of this chair so damn fast...

Cody picked up his glass and tossed his whiskey

back, enjoying the burn. He tuned back in to Sutton and Garrett's conversation. They were talking about a new cryptocurrency taking the world by storm. Cody remembered that Sutton had been an investment banker before he'd hit the nonfiction bestseller list with an easy-to-digest guide to stocks and shares. He'd then switched to writing fiction and his blood-soaked books regularly hit the bestseller lists.

During a lull in the conversation, Jules, who was sitting between him and Garrett, looked across to Tinsley. "I'm looking forward to being involved in the cocktail competition as a judge, Tins. It's such a great idea."

"It was my dad's idea," Tinsley told her, pushing away her untouched dessert plate.

Jules took a sip of champagne, her eyebrows pulled into a thin line. "I saw that Crazy Kate's Gin is listed as one of the companies you're going to ask to sponsor the competition."

Tinsley nodded. "Yeah, they've been one of our most important suppliers for decades."

Jules winced. "I don't know if they're going to come on board, Tins. They're laying off their employees and scaling down their operations."

"What?" Tinsley demanded, shocked. "But why?"

Jules looked a little green. "So many factors, including the effect of the COVID pandemic."

Cody noticed that both Garrett and Sutton were tuned in to their conversation. "Crazy Kate's is the one based in North Carolina, right?" Cody asked, racking his brain.

"No, it's a Colorado company," Jules corrected him. "I feel sick about it. Crazy Kate's was the first company I did promotions for. Kate herself suggested that I do pop-up bars. She was instrumental in getting my business off the ground. Ryder's and Crazy Kate's did a joint promotion and that's how I met Tinsley and Kinga."

Garrett spoke, his deep voice cutting through the buzz of the room. "They recently upgraded their bottling plant, right? And built a brand-new distribution depot?"

Cody shook his head, astounded by Garrett's encyclopedic knowledge of the world of business. He was famous as being one of the country's best venture capitalists, investing in companies exhibiting high growth potential.

But nothing about Garrett was simple. The guy also ran a lucrative vulture capital fund, doing the exact opposite. If he saw the opportunity to buy a business debt from a bank or a lending institution, and sell that debt or take over company assets to repay that debt, he'd do that too. Garrett was a corporate shark.

Jules pointed her spoon in Garrett's direction. "Do not go anywhere near them, Kaye," she told him, her expression fierce. Right, so Jules also knew of Garrett's darker dealings. Nothing he did was illegal, Cody admitted, but some of his decisions were morally questionable.

Garrett lifted his hands in mock surrender. "What? I just asked an innocent question!"

Jules told him that even as a baby, he'd never been innocent and Cody leaned back in his seat, entertained by their argument. Jules wasn't a fool and she wasn't intimidated by the very powerful, very taciturn Garrett Kaye. Good for her.

Cody looked at Tinsley to see how she was reacting to the heated argument entertaining him and Sutton but she'd stood up, her face as pale as her white dress. Her eyes connected with his and she briefly shook her head. Within seconds she was flying across the ballroom… Hell, he didn't think a woman could walk so fast in high heels.

Something was wrong…

He looked at Jules but she was still arguing with Garrett and hadn't noticed Tinsley leaving. He looked around for Kinga but she was standing next to the stage. Griff was on his haunches with his hand cupping her face as he sang to her.

They were together? Okay, surprising but not important right now.

Tinsley's mom… Where was Penelope? Cody saw that Penelope and Callum were talking to the Senate majority leader, one of the most powerful people in Washington. They were out…

That left him. Brilliant.

Cody pushed his chair back, excused himself from the table—only Sutton acknowledged his leaving—and followed Tinsley's path. He left the busy ballroom, stepped into the lobby and looked around. She would've headed for the elevators or the ladies' room and, judging by her speed, he bet on the latter.

Sighing, Cody headed for the room, walked down the L-shaped hallway and stepped into a beautifully decorated room, complete with a two-seater sofa covered in pink-and-black stripes and gilded mirrors. He quickly noted that only one stall, the nearest one, was occupied. The door was half-open and through the opening, he saw a sliver of white silk.

And then he heard the sound of retching…

Shit! Thinking quickly, Cody closed the main door leading into the room and flipped the lock. Whoever needed to use the facilities could hold it or find another bathroom.

Returning to the stall, he gently pushed open the

door to see Tinsley on her bare knees in front of the bowl, swaying as she tried to hold her hair back and keep her balance.

Unfazed, Cody gathered her hair in his big hand and dropped beside her, slinging his free arm behind her waist to keep her steady. "I've got you, babe."

Tinsley whipped her head around to scowl at him. "Do. Not. Call. Me. Babe. And go away," she told him before her body reacted with another spasm.

No chance in hell. Especially since she was leaning against him, relying on him to keep her upright. Under his hand, he felt the heat of her skin and the ripples of her still-contracting stomach.

He hoped she didn't have a stomach bug. He wasn't worried about catching it himself—he had the constitution of an ox—but Tinsley was too thin already. She couldn't afford to lose any more weight. Tinsley rested her head against his shoulder and he placed his hand against her forehead. She was cool, thank God, she didn't seem to be running a fever.

"Better?" he asked, tucking a strand of sweet-smelling hair behind her ear.

Tinsley nodded.

"Then can I lift you off this disgusting floor?" To be fair, it was sparkling clean but she had to want to get up off her knees. Tinsley held onto him as he lifted her onto her feet, her dress falling to the floor. He held her hips, not prepared to let her go until he was very certain she was okay on those ice-pick heels.

Her balance steadied, but she still looked like death warmed up. Cody ushered her out of the stall and led her over to the striped couch. "Sit down and I'll go and find you a bottle of water so you can rinse out your mouth."

Tinsley sank to the couch and shook her head. "I didn't actually throw up. I just went through the motions."

"Okay. But sick or not, you still look like crap," Cody told her, pushing back his jacket to put his hands on his hips. "Did you eat something strange for lunch?"

"No, it's nothing I ate." Tinsley looked up at him, her blue eyes holding a hint of purple. In them, he saw a swirl of emotions, with fear and trepidation leading the charge.

"Then what the hell is wrong with you?"

"I think it's this." Tinsley opened her clutch bag and tugged out a plastic stick, which she handed to him. He flipped it over and saw two pink stripes in a tiny window. He was old enough to know what a pregnancy test looked like and what two stripes meant. "Shit! You're pregnant?"

Tinsley reached for the stick, took it and stared down at the lines. "Seems so."

"You didn't know?" Cody demanded, feeling like he'd stepped into a complicated film with dizzying plot changes.

"I took the test earlier, but I didn't look at it. I couldn't," she explained, pushing her fingers into her hair and dislodging more strands. "But throwing up was a big clue."

"How far along are you?" Cody demanded, his eyes going to her still-flat stomach.

"Six weeks or so," Tinsley replied. Her words were accompanied by her lifted eyebrows and a searching look and Cody frowned, thinking that there was a subtext here that he was missing.

"What?" he demanded. "Just...*what*?"

"Six weeks ago was New Year's Eve, Cody, and what were we doing that night?"

He didn't...what...huh?

Tinsley rolled her eyes, obviously exasperated by his lack of understanding. "Do you need me to draw you a picture, Gallant? You and I slept together, which means that you are my baby's daddy."

Cody placed a hand on his stomach, looked back toward the stall and thought there was a good chance his dinner might make a comeback too.

Six

After she dropped her bombshell, neither of them had any interest in returning to the ball. They headed to the elevator and Cody jabbed the button to take them up to his private suite, the one the hotel owners kept for visiting friends and family. Not only was he a college friend of Fox Forrester, heir to the Forrester-Grantham fortune and the group's current CEO, but he'd also staged some of the hotel's most exclusive events.

Cody was a fixture in this hotel and had permanent access to the suite. The elevator ride up was quick and silent and the hallway leading to his suite was empty, thank God. Cody punched in the code on the door and gestured for Tinsley to step inside. A foot in and the motion sensor lights flickered on and bathed the hallway in soft, calming light.

Good, they needed calm. More than that, he needed a drink. A big one.

Cody walked into the exquisite penthouse, located on the east corner of the hotel. It had one of the best views in the city, with panoramic views of the Hudson River, the city and Central Park. The suite was over two floors, and the second floor sported two huge bedrooms with oversize windows, wonderful views of downtown Manhattan and en-suite bathrooms with Italian-marble surfaces, huge showers and large soaking tubs.

But as exquisitely decorated as the rooms were, with amazing artwork, handblown glass sculptures and designer furniture, Tinsley's words from earlier kept bouncing around his brain.

You are my baby's daddy...

Holy, holy hell. Cody ran his hands over his face and headed for the drinks trolley in the corner, automatically reaching for a crystal decanter. He sloshed some whiskey into a short tumbler and tossed it back, immediately refilling his glass and tossing back another shot.

It couldn't be possible. He didn't understand. This had to be a joke.

Holding onto the glass, he turned to see Tinsley standing in the middle of the lounge, still looking like a wraith in her white dress and tumbled-down hair. "For God's sake sit down before you fall down," he ordered.

He saw the flash of defiance in her eyes but then she sighed, sat down and pulled off her heels, curling her feet under her butt and leaning her head back. She'd just imparted rock-his-world news, but his fingers still ached with the need to touch. He desperately wanted his mouth on hers, to be skin on skin, heart to heart.

God, maybe there was something wrong with him.

"Can I get you something to drink?" he asked. "Whiskey? Wine? A liqueur?"

Tinsley wrinkled her nose. "Since I'm officially with child, I shouldn't drink."

Right. Hell.

"A lemonade would be great," Tinsley replied, her eyes drifting closed. She inched down and turned on her side and Cody suspected she was a couple of deep breaths away from falling asleep.

"Don't go to sleep," he told her. "We have to talk."

"I'm still going to be pregnant in the morning," Tinsley protested. "I'm exhausted, Cody, let me sleep. Just for fifteen minutes and then you can wake me up."

"We're going to talk, *now,*" Cody stated, his voice hard as stone. He walked over to the hidden fridge, opened it and pulled out a bottled lemonade. Grabbing a glass from the cupboard, he twisted off the cap, poured the liquid over some ice and walked back to her, pushing the glass into her hand. "Sit up and drink this. The sugar should pick you up."

Tinsley scowled at his bossy order. But she did sit up and take a few sips. Cody sat down on the coffee table in front of her, placed his arms on his knees and linked his hands together.

"Start from the beginning," he told her.

Tinsley sipped and shrugged. "There's not much to say. We slept together, one of your boys met one of my girls and here we are."

Cody pinched the bridge of this nose. "We used condoms, Tinsley. Every single time."

"And condoms are only ninety-eight percent effective," Tinsley snapped back. She banged her glass down on the table. Cody, feeling hot, shrugged out of his jacket. He ripped off his bow tie, undid the top buttons on his shirt and opened the buttons on his vest. He also picked up the remote for the air conditioner and dropped the temperature of the room.

He was in danger of overheating. Possibly exploding.

"The condom could've been damaged, had a microtear or you could've put it on wrong!" she added.

Cody glared at her. "I've been using condoms for a damn long time, Tinsley. I know how to put one on." His heart in his throat, he remembered their conversation about JT and his baby, just a week after they slept together. She told him she desperately wanted a baby, that she'd wanted one for a long, long time. She had asked him for his sperm. Maybe she'd set him up on New Year's Eve; maybe this had all been planned.

Or maybe, because she was pissed that Heather was having a kid and she wasn't, she'd hooked up with someone else without using protection, got lucky and decided to pin fatherhood on him.

"Is there a possibility that I'm not the father, Tinsley?" he asked, his voice freezer cold.

Tinsley took a moment to make sense of his question and Cody watched, fascinated as fire flared in her eyes. "What?"

"I know how much you want a baby, so I'm not taking this at face value." He looked down at the test. "These things are pretty sensitive these days. You could've hooked up with someone else and be two weeks pregnant for all I know."

God, that sounded so harsh, but he was looking for an escape hatch.

Tinsley lifted her finger, opened her mouth and closed it again. Then she jabbed a long nail into his thigh. "Are you accusing me of lying, of trying to pin this on you, Gallant?"

He didn't answer her, but neither did he look away.

"I don't need to lie! I am financially independent and completely able to raise a child on my own. I don't need you and I would *never* say you were the father if you weren't! How dare you suggest such a thing?"

Oh, he dared. "So, you're telling me that I'm the only one you've been with in the last couple of months?"

Tinsley tossed her hands up in the air. "You're the only person I've been with since JT!"

Oh…but…wow. Until he came along, this vibrant, passionate, sensual woman hadn't had sex for nearly three years? Possibly longer than that? Holy crap.

Cody rubbed his hands over his face, trying to scrub away his confusion. She was gorgeous and sexy and she had to have had offers. He told her as much.

"Offers I refused," Tinsley retorted. "Why are we discussing my sex life when we should be talking about that?"

He followed her gaze to the pregnancy test he still held in his hand. He swallowed, mentally hearing the jail doors clanging closed. He was trapped, and panic started to build in his throat. "I can't be the father, Tinsley. There's no way. I'm sorry, but you have to be wrong."

After raising JT, Cody had designed his life to avoid being personally responsible for anyone other than himself. Now she was telling him he had a baby on the way, a helpless infant for whom he'd be responsible for…the rest of his life? Tinsley swung her feet off the couch and reached for her shoes, sliding one, then the other onto her elegant feet.

"I didn't think anything could top you telling me not to marry JT on the night before our wedding, Cody, but your asinine reaction has just proved me wrong." She pulled the pregnancy wand from his closed fist and lifted her nose, eyeing him as she would gum stuck to her shoe.

"I am going to speak in short sentences and use small words so that this penetrates…

"I am six weeks pregnant, and this baby was conceived the night we slept together." She stood up and bent down to pick up her clutch bag. When she straightened, her cheeks were red with temper. "Forget this night, forget this conversation, forget that your sperm met my egg. As far as I'm concerned, you're a sperm donor and I want nothing more to do with you."

"We're going to be working together for the next few months, at least," Cody told her, knowing that was an indisputable fact.

"I would rather resign than work with you, Gallant. Stay away from me. Far, far away."

Cody watched as she stormed out of the lounge, into the hallway and out the door. He heard the door slam behind her and winced.

That didn't go well.

And that was the understatement of the year.

Heads up, Cody Gallant is on his way to see you.

Tinsley was working from home today. In her sitting room on Congress Street, she scowled at the message from her assistant before dropping the phone onto her coffee table. Moose, her massive Maine coon cat, lay over her feet and she'd lost feeling in her right foot ten minutes ago. But Moose tended to nip when disturbed so she'd left him alone.

Steeling herself, she whipped her legs out from under his solid body and narrowly missed having teeth marks on her toe.

"You're a fiend," Tinsley muttered, standing up. Her foot buckled and she yelped as tingles shot through her appendage and she spent the next minute dancing around, waiting for blood to return to her foot.

It gave her something else to think about other than Cody Gallant, who would, any minute, arrive at her doorstep. Nearly a week had passed since she'd dropped her life-changing news on the guy, and she'd been ducking his calls ever since.

On Monday, she went to London to talk to a British ad agency about a new TV advertisement and stayed a couple days longer than necessary. She could've held the meeting over Skype but since she was trying to avoid Cody, getting out of the country seemed a reasonable, albeit expensive, option.

She'd returned yesterday to another barrage of emails and a dozen missed calls from him. Cody was running out of patience, and Tinsley realized that she couldn't avoid him forever. At some point, they'd have to discuss her pregnancy and what she expected from him—nothing—and how involved he intended to be in her, and her child's life—not at all.

Her child's life…

Why didn't that phrase make her want to dance on the spot, bubble with anticipation? She'd always wanted to be a mother and couldn't wait to be pregnant, to meet and raise her child. She'd spent many hours dreaming about being pregnant, growing bigger, giving life but instead of feeling excited, all she felt was…blah. Even indifferent.

What was wrong with her?

Sure, she was upset about Cody's reaction, but she should still be thrilled to be pregnant. But she wasn't.

And she didn't know why not.

She was equally unexcited about seeing Cody but reluctantly admitted that they needed to have a, hopefully, rational conversation to figure out a way to work together going forward. Because that was today's other big news: yesterday Callum approved their plans for the cocktail competition and had given them the final budget, more generous than she'd expected. Now they had to work together to take it from paper to reality.

Tinsley glanced down at her clothes and winced. She was dressed in yoga pants and a slouchy moss green sweater. Her hair was piled up on her head and anchored by a big crocodile clip. After conversing with the porcelain god in her bathroom earlier, she'd showered, brushed her teeth and slapped some moisturizer on her face. Then she'd gone back to bed and slept for an hour.

Surely being this tired and this sick—she had morning sickness all day and all night—wasn't normal. But all the literature she'd read assured her that some women had awful first trimesters. Maybe she was feeling so disconnected from her pregnancy because her body was being utterly uncooperative. Her insane work schedule and her inconvenient, can't-stop-thinking-about-him attraction to the baby's father added to her stress and didn't they say that the body was a reflection of the mind?

And, let's be honest, her mind was a mess.

Walking over to her window, she looked out on the snow-dusted lawn and saw Cody's luxury Mercedes SUV swing into her driveway. She'd hoped to have time to change into something a little more businesslike, but she'd tarried and here he was. She watched as he walked up the drive to her front door, his stride loose, his long legs eating up the distance. He was hatless and the wind tousled his black hair. He had a laptop bag tucked under his arm and his face reflected his tension.

She couldn't see his eyes but somehow knew they were full of frustration and irritation.

Yeah, she annoyed him as much as he did her.

She heard the intercom buzz on the lobby door and took her time letting him in, thinking that standing in the cold might drop his temper a degree or two. Ten seconds later, she heard the sharp rap on her apartment door.

Tinsley opened her door and looked up, and up, into Cody's frustrated face. "Why the hell have you been ducking my calls?" he demanded, as he brushed past her to step inside. He dumped his bag on the bench and flipped open the buttons to his navy cashmere coat.

"Good morning, Cody," Tinsley replied, thinking that one of them needed to be the adult in the room. Then she remembered that she *had* been avoiding him, and admitted she didn't have a leg to stand on when it came to claiming maturity.

She took his coat, hung it up on the freestanding coat hook and led him into her sitting room. Like Kinga's place right next door, her bottom floor consisted of an open-plan living, dining and kitchen area. Unlike Kinga, Tinsley had kept all the redbrick walls and left the beams exposed. Her staircase to the second floor was steel rather than wood and she'd aimed for a more industrial look, replacing the wooden floors with stained concrete. The bones of the building were masculine and stark so she'd softened the room with feminine furniture, including couches covered in a fabric featuring blowsy pink, cream and red roses and bright, plain carpets.

And plants, lots and lots of indoor plants.

"Want something to drink?" Tinsley asked, hoping he wouldn't ask for coffee.

Because he was Cody and uncooperative, he did. Tinsley wrinkled her nose and waved at the coffee machine on the concrete counter. "Can you make it yourself? The smell of coffee makes me nauseous."

Cody's eyebrows shot up but he didn't say anything. He just walked into her kitchen and made himself at home. "Can I get you anything?" he asked.

She had to admit, he had good manners, Tinsley thought as she resumed her seat next to Moose. "I'm good, thanks."

A few minutes later Cody returned, carrying her favorite oversize mug. She caught the smell of coffee and her stomach lurched. She breathed deeply and, this time, nausea passed. Thank God.

Cody sat down on the chair opposite her and looked at her cat, who'd twisted himself into a furry pretzel and was taking up most of the couch. "Is that cat on steroids?" he asked.

Tinsley looked at Moose and frowned. "You'd think so but no, he's just robust."

Tinsley reached out to stroke Moose's ears and got a nip for her efforts. "You are revolting," she told him.

Looking at Cody, she shrugged. "Moose is a Maine Coon, and bigger than most."

Cody wrapped his hands around her cup, his gaze steady and cool. "Are we going to talk about cats or are we going to discuss the bombshell you dropped?"

"Cats are easy conversation," Tinsley admitted. She rubbed her fingertips across her forehead. She had a headache brewing. Along with throwing up, she had fairly constant headaches. The first trimester had been more intense than she'd imagined. She felt the familiar bubble of worry in her gut and pushed it aside. She'd visited the pregnancy sites and everyone's experience was different.

Cody put the mug on the steel-and-glass coffee table that separated them and placed his forearms on his knees. "I've been trying to reach you for days now, Tinsley."

"I didn't feel like talking to you. Or talking to anyone," she added.

Cody's eyes locked onto hers, dark and direct. "Who else knows about your pregnancy?" he demanded.

Kinga had left town the morning after the ball for a two-week trip down to Griff's Florida Keys island home, and their parents extended their stay in New York. Jules was in Palm Beach doing a pop-up bar at a new yacht club and Callum…? Well, Callum wasn't someone she'd confide in.

Besides, she wasn't ready to tell anyone. She was still trying to come to terms with this life-changing event. "No one knows but you."

Cody's glance didn't waver. "Okay. And I know you are intending to keep this baby… You haven't changed your mind?"

Tinsley rolled her eyes. "After acting like a lunatic when I heard that Heather was pregnant, I'd be a total flake if I said no now."

Cody's expression didn't change. "People are allowed to change their minds, Tinsley."

Tinsley lifted her chin. "I haven't. I won't. So, if you've come to talk me out of having this baby, then you can leave, right now."

Cody closed his eyes in frustration. "Did you always jump to conclusions or is this something new?"

She felt embarrassment heat her cheeks. "Sorry," she

muttered, burying her hand in Moose's coat. She didn't like being called out—who did?—and Cody, blunt as hell, had a way of slicing through all the nonsense and homing in on the heart of the matter. Of her.

She didn't like it. At all.

Because she still wasn't ready to discuss her pregnancy, and his lack of interest in being involved, she racked her brain for a change of subject. Work was unemotional, something they could talk about without shedding each other's blood.

"Did you see the email from Callum giving us the go-ahead?" she asked.

"I did," Cody replied. "Did you notice that the figure for my remuneration was substantially reduced?"

Tinsley winced. "Sorry."

"Don't be. I inflated my original price because Callum always knocks it down. My remuneration came in fractionally over where I wanted it to be."

While Cody didn't have JT's sky-high IQ, he was damn smart. And very sneaky. "I'm sorry you have to play mind games with my grandfather," Tinsley told him.

Cody shrugged. "I'm used to it and I nearly always get what I want out of the deal."

She did not doubt that. In ten years, Cody had established an international business worth a few hundred million. He had offices and staff all over the country and internationally, he owned a stunning apartment in downtown Portland, had property in LA. He owned and occasionally flew a private jet.

He was regarded as being one of the most eligible bachelors in the country. But Tinsley wasn't interested in Cody on a long-term basis. She'd taken the Gallant name once, and was perfectly happy being a Ryder-White. It was so much less complicated.

Tinsley pulled her feet up onto her couch and sat cross-legged. "I'll be back in the office tomorrow and we can draw up a schedule, decide who's doing what."

Cody leaned back and placed his ankle on his knee. "I've issued some instructions to my staff. They are getting the ball rolling."

Uh…*no*. They couldn't do anything without her. Tinsley sat up straight and held up her hand, tasting panic at the back of her throat. How did she know what they were doing was right? Good enough? Dare she say it… perfect? "That doesn't work for me. What exactly are they doing? Why didn't you talk to me about this? I need to know what's going on!"

"Since you didn't return my calls, I got the process started. Don't call me out for doing my job when you have been unavailable!"

"I was in London," Tinsley replied, knowing it was a weak argument.

"And they don't have phones or email there?" Cody sent a contemplative look toward the ceiling. "Weird, they had those the last time I visited."

"Okay, smarty-pants, I was avoiding you," Tinsley admitted.

"I know. Don't do it again," Cody told her, his voice serious. "Apart from the fact that I needed answers from you, I was also worried about you, worried about the baby."

Nice of him to say that, but she didn't believe him for a second. Cody had made it clear that he wasn't interested in being a dad.

"Talking of…"

Oh, God, here it came. The lecture, the demands, the

questions. She still wasn't ready to deal with any of it, mostly because she still somehow didn't feel pregnant— despite having done two other tests and puking every morning. Her brain was still catching up with her body.

"How are you?" Cody asked.

Tinsley looked at him, puzzled by his question. "Sorry?"

"I'm not speaking Farsi, Tinsley. I want to know how you are."

Oh. Um…right. She didn't have the energy to lie. "Constantly tired, and best friends with the toilet bowl."

Cody winced. "Still?"

"According to the literature, it should stop sometime between twelve and sixteen weeks but, in extreme cases, it can last the entire pregnancy." God, she hoped that didn't happen to her.

"Have you seen a doctor yet?" Cody asked her. He sounded so calm, she thought, unfazed.

"I called my ob-gyn, and she said that, because I'm young and healthy, I just need to carry on as normal, though she did give me some vitamins. She wants to see me when I'm twelve weeks along, for an ultrasound."

"And that will tell us what?"

He'd said us, not you and Tinsley wondered why that caused excitement to race along her nerve endings. *He's just your sperm donor, Ryder-White, not your baby's daddy or your happy-ever-after. You don't believe in those, remember?*

"That scan, the twelve-week one, accurately de- termines my due date, whether I'm having twins, or more—"

Cody scraped a hand over his face. "Jesus."

She smiled as color leached from his face. Though why he was looking gray, she had no idea; she would be the one doing everything. "The scan also checks whether everything is okay with the baby, and they also do some sort of screening test—I can't remember its name—for conditions like Down syndrome."

Cody's piercing look pinned her to the chair. "And if there is something wrong with the baby, what will you do?"

Tinsley laid a hand on her heart and jerked her shoulders up. "I don't know, Cody. I'm not thinking about that! I'm not going into what-ifs, not now, I *can't*."

Cody picked up his coffee mug and downed the contents. Tinsley winced, thinking it must be ice-cold by now. He put the cup down and sent her a brooding look, but didn't speak again. Deciding to address the elephant in the room, she dropped her feet to the floor and echoed his pose, her arms on her thighs. "Cody, this isn't your problem. I told you that I am happy to have this baby on my own, without any input from you. But—"

One dark eyebrow raised.

"But I do need you to believe that I didn't plan on this happening. I would never trick a man into being a dad. That's too big a decision to force on someone else." Because he was so very direct, she thought she could be too. After all, if he was going to dish it, he should be able to take it.

"Part of the reason I was ignoring you is that I'm still hugely pissed off that you thought I would do that."

Shame and regret flashed in his eyes as he pushed a hand through his hair. "Yeah, I should apologize for that. I was upset, a little freaked out."

Tinsley waited. And then waited some more. But no apology came. "You suck at apologies, Gallant," she muttered.

A small smile touched his lips. "I do." He glanced

down at his hands before looking up at her again. He hauled in some air. "I am sorry, Tinsley. I was out of line."

"Accepted." Tinsley rested her elbows on her knees and speared her hands through her hair.

"We need to talk about my involvement in this process, Tinsley."

Tinsley handed him a sharp look. "How involved do you want to be?"

Cody winced, then took a moment to think. "A part of me wants to let you do this on your own, then I think that I'm a goddamn coward. Another part of me knows I have to, at the very least, pay you for child support, which won't be a problem, *ever*. Another part of me, admittedly still an exceedingly small slice, could be excited. I don't know what to think or how to feel!"

And for someone like Cody, who was so decisive, that uncertainty had to be upsetting. "I don't need an answer today, Cody. Or even tomorrow."

"Thank God. Because I don't have one today and won't have one tomorrow," Cody muttered.

He was trying to wrap his head around this, just as she was. Having a kid was a damn big deal and it was a lot to think about. But they still had time, over seven months to be more precise; nothing needed to be decided now.

So much could happen between now and then, and she didn't wear rose-colored glasses. "Cody, as much as I want this kid, I am trying to be realistic. According to Dr. Internet, between fifteen and twenty percent of pregnancies end in miscarriage, but they think that figure could be higher. Those miscarriages usually happen in the first trimester."

Cody gestured for her to carry on talking.

"It's still so early in the process so I would suggest

that we take this step by step, day by day," Tinsley said. "We should try and get along, not only because of this—" she pointed to her stomach "—but also because we're going to be working together."

Cody's nod came slowly but it was there. "Okay, we can try that. What else?"

"I'd like to keep this between us, for now. Nobody needs to know yet."

"You don't want to rub it in JT's face?"

She had; she couldn't deny it. A part of her wanted to send a generic email, telling him that she was also having a baby, *with his brother.* Then she realized that was just her inner mean girl talking. "No, JT doesn't matter."

"Your breath hitched when you said his name," Cody stated, his tone harsher than before. "Are you still in love with him, Tinsley?"

Tinsley stood up and walked over to the window and stood next to a two-drawer credenza. In the left-hand drawer was a photograph in a silver frame, facedown. It was her favorite picture of her and JT, taken in Hawaii, while they were on their honeymoon.

JT sat on a lounger reading a book, and she was curled up in his lap. She was looking up at him, love in her eyes, adoration on her face. His full attention was on his book. From that moment on, for the rest of their marriage, Tinsley had to fight for his attention.

Yet she'd been so convinced that they'd had a happy marriage and his request for a divorce devastated her. In hindsight, she knew that she had looked at her marriage and seen what she wanted to see, not what it was…

She'd never do that again.

She looked out the window and watched the fat flakes of snow drifting to the ground. "No, I don't love him—I did but I don't. Not anymore."

From across the room, she heard Cody's sigh, heard the slap of his hands against his knees. In the reflection of the window, she saw him move toward her, his hands coming to rest on her shoulders. He bent his head to speak in her ear, his breath warm on her cheek. "Good," he murmured. "That makes life a lot easier and I won't feel weird for wanting to kiss you."

Tinsley tipped her head back to look at him. "And are you planning on kissing me?" she asked, her voice a little breathless.

"That would be a hell-to-the-yes," Cody murmured, covering her mouth with his.

Cody slowly turned her and placed his hands on her hips, his mouth, surprisingly tender, moving over hers. He kissed her like he was unwrapping a much-anticipated present on Christmas Day, drawing out the moment, making it last. A nibble here, a gentle suck there, a brush of his tongue against hers.

Tinsley lifted her hand to his jaw, felt the scratch of his three-day-old beard, rough against her hand. She skimmed her hand down his neck and slid her fingers under the open collar of his shirt, looking for the heat of his skin. He was so big, so masculine, and he made her feel precious and petite. She was an alpha boss girl, content to walk her own path, independent as hell, but there was something amazing about standing in a powerful man's arms.

And the fact that Cody Gallant desired her—which was fairly obvious—made her feel intensely feminine and imbued with a power of her own. Feeling his arms pulling her closer, she sighed when he deepened the kiss, his hand on the back of her head changing the angle. Tender turned to tempestuous as he cupped her ass with his big hand, the other dropping to slide under the back of her jersey, tracing the knobs of her spine.

Reality disappeared and there was only the two of them, exchanging deep kisses as fat snowflakes drifted down beyond the windowpane. Needing to get closer, she pulled his shirt out of his pants and slid her hand over his skin, her fingers dancing across the ridges of his stomach. He was so warm, so solid, so incredibly skilled at raising her core temperature to sweltering. The urge to strip him was strong.

She couldn't help the words that slipped off her tongue. "Come upstairs with me."

Cody tensed, pulled his mouth off hers and released a low groan. Moving his hands to her hips, he pulled in a couple of ragged breaths before stepping back. He raked his fingers through his already tousled hair and tipped his head back to look at the ceiling.

So, that would be a *no* then.

Embarrassed at her lack of control—what was it about this man that caused her brain to shut down?— Tinsley whipped around, conscious of her bloodred cheeks and knowing her neck would also be blotchy. She wasn't used to propositioning men; she'd probably done it wrong. Too blunt, too in your face…

But she thought that men—Cody especially because he was so damn direct—liked up-front and honest. But what the hell did she know?

She forced herself to turn around, to look at him, and when she did, she frowned, surprised. Cody stared out the window, his hands in his pockets, thoughtful surprise on his face and in his eyes. And a healthy dose of confusion…

He sighed before his eyes met hers. "I didn't come here to take you to bed, Tins. Don't get me wrong, I want to because taking you to bed is all I've thought about lately. But I think sex is a complication neither of us needs right now."

She stared at him, trying to parse his words, to find the hidden meaning. Then she remembered that he wasn't like his brother, who liked playing mind games. Cody said what he meant. And when she thought about it, sleeping together was a complication neither of them needed. They were work colleagues and they both still needed to wrap their heads around her pregnancy. She was still processing the news, working through her emotions.

It was so easy to daydream but reality had dumped a cold bucket of water on those rosy fantasies.

Really, what did she know about being a mommy? It was all very well to say that she was financially and emotionally ready, but was she? She was going to be doing it alone...

That wasn't what she'd planned. Though, honestly, if she'd had a baby with JT, that was probably what would've happened. He'd barely participated in their marriage, so she doubted that he'd have shown any interest in their child.

And people wondered why she was a control freak; it was because she had to be. In her quest for a perfect marriage and to be a perfect wife, she'd paid their bills and booked their holidays, arranged for car services and annual checkups. She balanced checkbooks and planned meals. Sometimes, most times toward the end, she'd felt like JT's nanny, not his wife.

Cody came to stand next to her and briefly, gently squeezed her shoulder. "We need to work together and you're pregnant. I think we have enough on our plate, don't you?"

He was right, so Tinsley nodded. Folding her arms across her chest, she tipped her head to the side. "I agree. So, work. Where are we and what do we need to do?"

"Everything," Cody stated. He glanced at his watch before sitting down on the sofa and picking up his laptop bag to pull out a state-of-the-art, streamlined laptop. "I have a few hours before I need to take a meeting back at the office, so let's strategize."

She could strategize, Tinsley thought, walking over to her desk and picking up her trusty iPad. She sat down opposite him, tucked her feet under her butt and rested her tablet on her knee. She'd far prefer to go back to sleep—or for her and Cody to go upstairs for some naked fun—but she could work.

She had to; in seven or so months she'd have an additional mouth to feed.

Babies, she'd heard, weren't cheap.

Seven

A few hours later, Cody looked at Tinsley, tucked into her chair, black-framed glasses on her pretty nose. Her fingers raced across her tablet's small keyboard, and noticing that she was in the zone, he decided he needed more coffee. She didn't notice when he stood up and headed for her kitchen.

It was snowing hard outside, and the wind had picked up. Wonderful. He couldn't wait for winter to be over. He wanted the heat of summer, to feel the sun on his skin. If he wasn't so swamped, he'd head down to the Caribbean and dive in those warm waters, doze in the sun and sleep with his windows and doors wide open, cooled by island breezes.

But he had too much to do here, too many responsibilities. And he'd gathered one more: Tinsley and her baby. His baby. *Theirs.*

Cody glared at the coffee machine. He'd spent the

past week digesting the news, trying to make sense of the turn his life had taken. Initially, he'd wanted to be angry, but spending New Year's Eve together had been a choice they'd *both* made. While he'd used a condom, he knew that abstinence was the only foolproof means of contraception. Abstinence had never been an option— he liked sex, dammit—so he'd taken his chances, rolled the dice and for twenty years or so he'd won against the house. This one time, with his ex-sister-in-law, he'd lost.

She'd all but given him permission to walk away, to be an anonymous sperm donor. She'd told him she was happy to be a single mom and yeah, he'd be lying if he said he wasn't initially, briefly tempted to walk away. After raising JT, being responsible for his brother's welfare at such a young age, he'd vowed never to put himself in the position of looking after anyone but himself again.

He looked at Tinsley again, taking in her thin face and tired eyes. The pregnancy was hard on her, anyone could see that, but he admired her just-push-through-it attitude.

She was a strong woman and he admired strength, tenacity, the ability to keep on carrying on.

In some ways, they were very alike. Driven, determined, stoic. They both demanded too much, liked getting their way.

And, despite the big complication of the pregnancy and having to work together, he was still insanely attracted to her, to this woman who made him feel scratchy, off-balance and out of sorts. Since New Year's Eve, he just had to think of her and his heart sped up and his lungs forgot how to do their job. He recalled, in Technicolor detail, every kiss, the silkiness of her skin, her breathy voice in his ear telling him how good he made her feel.

And when he was with her, he couldn't keep himself from touching her, partly from desire, but also because in his arms was where he needed her to be. In his arms, she could relax, and she could rest. Tinsley raised his protective instincts and he couldn't work out why.

Because of all the professional women he knew, she was the one who seemed to have all her shit together, all the time. She was smart, organized, incredibly efficient. She did the work of five men and juggled a hundred balls in the air. He knew that if there was anyone who could rock being a single mom, Tinsley would be that woman.

But sometimes Cody sensed that buried beneath her self-sufficient attitude was someone not as tough as she portrayed herself to be. He knew his brother, knew that JT expected everything done for him all the time. Cody had no doubt Tinsley had done all the heavy lifting in their marriage. Taking charge was probably a habit for her but suspected she wouldn't mind someone to occasionally relieve her of the responsibilities she carried around with deceptive ease. When she thought he wasn't looking, she sometimes looked a little lost, like she was desperate for someone to throw her a lifeline.

But Cody was always honest with himself, and he knew that could be his ego talking, his need to protect rising like a tide.

After his mom died and his father checked out, he'd taken on the responsibility of raising JT. At twelve he was planning their meals, juggling their schedules, and getting JT to school on time. His father employed a housekeeper to oversee the two boys but Cody had taken control and by the time he was fifteen, Mrs. K answered to him and not the other way around.

Until the day JT met Tinsley. Only months into their

relationship, Tinsley had JT firmly in hand. She reminded him to eat, to get a haircut, took him clothes shopping. Within a year, she had the codes to his bank cards and swiftly became best friends with their housekeeper.

JT and Tinsley left for college in Boston and moved into an off-campus apartment together and Cody took advantage of his freedom. He partied hard, slept around and vowed that he'd never again take on the responsibility of another person.

But now Tinsley was having his baby, which made him rethink everything. And, for some absurd reason, he wanted to make life easier for her. She hadn't had an easy life with his brother—JT was a difficult guy.

Cody was still pissed at JT for treating Tinsley like trash. Cody wasn't a forever type of guy, but he figured that when and if a man did jump into a relationship, he should stick to his guns, keep his word and do everything he could to make it work. JT had promised to love, honor and cherish Tinsley, but when he was sick of her and sick of their marriage , he swiftly moved on.

"So, a couple of days ago I sent an email to a TV show producer I know, someone who regularly produces shows for the Food Network," Tinsley said, lifting her voice so that it carried over to him. "I pitched the idea of a documentary about the cocktail competition, and he's interested. He wants to know if we can fly out for a meeting this weekend."

Coffee forgotten, Cody walked back into the living room, sincerely surprised. "Seriously?"

Tinsley lifted one shoulder, her eyes sparkling with excitement. "I thought it was a long shot, but he sounded excited." She placed a hand on her heart. "Frankly, I'm stunned."

He was too. "Where is he based?"

"In LA, but he's at his house in Avalon. That's on—"

"Catalina Island," Cody finished her sentence. He knew the town, had dived its waters and had taken summer vacations there. "I know it."

"He can spare us a few hours on Sunday afternoon to do a pitch," Tinsley told him. "I've emailed him to tell him we'll be there."

Cody stared at her, taking a moment to digest her words and to push down his rising frustration. "Tinsley, I have a brunch meeting in New York on Sunday morning, one that I can't blow off."

Tinsley dared to wink. "Blow her off, Cody. This is important."

Look, he knew he had a rep for bouncing from woman to woman—and it was exaggerated, mostly predicated on his behavior in his midtwenties—but he hadn't slept with anyone since her. And hadn't wanted to...

Beside the point.

"You're jumping to conclusions, Tinsley," Cody told her, his voice rock-hard. "One of the reasons I've been looking for you is to tell you that I secured a meeting with Geraint du Pont, and he's interested in judging the competition."

Tinsley's eyes widened. "Holy crap, that's amazing. As well as being one of the best chefs in the country, he's young, gorgeous and charismatic."

"He just sold his restaurant in New York and is looking for a new venture, so he has the time. But he's flying to London on Sunday afternoon, so Sunday morning is the only time he can see us," Cody told her, gripping the back of the sofa.

"Why didn't you tell me?" Tinsley demanded, temper flaring in her eyes.

"I did say, in one of the many emails you didn't answer, that I have a line on an exciting judge and to please call me urgently. But because you were ignoring me, or punishing me or something, here we are, double-booked," Cody snapped. "Why didn't you check with me before you agreed to the Catalina Island meeting?"

"Because I knew this was an opportunity we couldn't pass on!" Tinsley retorted.

"Neither is getting Geraint du Pont for a judge!"

They stared at each other; their gazes hot, equally annoyed. Cody broke their standoff. "You can't make decisions for me, Tinsley. That's unacceptable."

"Hey, you also made an arrangement I didn't agree to!"

"At least I tried to talk to you about it, and you know it!"

Embarrassment flashed in her eyes as she stood up. But her posture and expression turned defiant. "I'll go to Catalina Island. You talk to Geraint du Pont. Sorted," Tinsley said, her tone flippant.

Not by a long shot. He needed her to realize that they were a team, that she wasn't doing this alone. "You need to work on your communication skills, Tinsley. Also, this might be a Ryder project and you might be my client, but I don't work for you."

"Look, if you aren't happy with the way I work, then pull out. I'll get this project done. I always do."

She'd like that because then she would have complete control. But she'd also be working under maximum stress. "Even if I agreed to that, and I never would, have you forgotten that you're pregnant, that you spend a lot of time throwing up and that working fourteen- or sixteen-hour days right now might not be good for the baby?"

She opened her mouth to argue, backed down and pursed her lips. Taking advantage of the break in the conversation, he plowed on. "We're a goddamn team, Tinsley," he stated, glancing at her stomach, "in more ways than at work. That means we have to talk, and neither of us gets to make unilateral decisions anymore. Can you do that?"

"Can you?" Tinsley countered.

"Yeah, I can."

Tinsley pushed her hands into her hair, dislodging several strands. Her mouth moved and he was fairly sure she muttered an under-her-breath curse word. She looked up at the ceiling, out the window, at her cat—anywhere but at him.

"I'm not good at delegating, Cody," she finally admitted. He admired her honesty.

He fought his urge to run his hand over her hair, to comfort and soothe. Reassuring her now would lead to greater problems down the line. "Well, learn. And learn quickly," he said, deliberately abrupt.

She glared at the command in his voice, not at all happy with his authoritarian tone. That was fine; he wasn't particularly happy with her either.

He glanced at his watch, and thanks to the decreasing visibility due to the snow, realized that he was probably going to be late for his next meeting. "I don't have time to argue with you. I need to get back to the office."

"So you can give your staff more instructions about our event? That's pretty hypocritical, Gallant."

Cody counted to ten, to twenty. "Again, if you bothered to read all my emails, you'd know that I gave my art department leeway to work on a logo for the competition, subject to discussion. I also asked my PR person to draw up a couple of press releases, also subject to discussion." He narrowed his eyes at her, wondering how he could still want to kiss her, take her to bed, when irritation rocked inside him. "Did you hear those words, Ryder? 'Subject to discussion' means you and I will *talk* about it. About everything."

"I get it," Tinsley muttered, unable to hold his eyes.

He picked up his laptop, shoved it into its bag and walked over to the hallway and yanked his jacket off the hook, pulling it on with practiced ease. "You go to Catalina Island. I'll meet with du Pont," he snapped the words out. "But let's make this the last time we act independently, Tinsley."

Tinsley lifted her hand to her forehead in a sharp salute and clicked her feet together. "Sir, yes sir!"

"Smart-ass," Cody grumbled, yanking open her front door and wincing at the cold. This woman was going to cause him countless hours of lost sleep.

And if they had a daughter, he had no doubt she'd do the same. God help him.

The following Sunday, Cody braced himself as he stepped from his lounge onto the balcony of his apartment and cursed as a breeze blew off the water and plastered his Henley and comfortable track pants to his body. Gripping the railing, he took in his awesome view of the waterfront and cityscape, the roads and rooftops covered with snow. The sun would drop soon and, with it, the temperature. But at least the roads were clear, for now.

Another massive storm was due to hit the city in the next few hours. He hoped Tinsley made it home before she had to drive in the blizzard. Cody rubbed his arms and told himself to stop worrying, Tinsley had been driving in bad weather since she was a kid, so she was no more likely to have an accident than he was. Unless she was tired, still feeling nauseous and unable to concentrate…

He kept asking her how she was, and she kept duck-ing the question. Along with dinner tonight, they were also going to have a conversation about her going to the doctor to get checked out. They'd met several times this week and, through her expertly applied makeup, he noticed the green pallor to her skin, the dark rings under her eyes and the perpetual squint that suggested a constant headache.

Weren't pregnant women supposed to glow?

They'd agreed to meet at his apartment tonight after they both flew in to debrief and he'd told her that he'd bring pizza from his favorite place in Queens. The two massive pies were sitting on the island in his kitchen, along with a bottle of red for him and her imported gin-ger beer. It helped with the nausea, or so she'd informed him, and she drank the stuff by the gallon. He'd read the nutrition labels and saw that it was filled with sugar, but Tinsley hadn't picked up any weight. If anything she'd dropped a pound or two.

There had to be something the doctors could do for her…

Cody took in a couple of breaths, the air cactus-spiky as it slid down his throat. Clouds were moving in, and the storm was fast approaching. He glanced at his watch; Tinsley was cutting it close.

She'd be fine…

Cody glared at the sky and walked back inside. He loved his luxurious, five thousand square feet of bril-liantly designed space. His apartment had high ceil-ings, loads of natural light and amazing architectural accents. The modern kitchen opened to the dining area and a fabulous living room, dominated by a large fire-place. The floor-to-ceiling doors could be opened onto the expansive balcony, a place where he could entertain effortlessly and frequently. He had a huge master suite, three other bedrooms and a home study.

Best of all, it was just a few minutes' walk from his downtown Portland offices and, even in the dead of winter, he often walked the short distance to work. If he needed a car during the day, he could either pick up one of his company vehicles or jog back to his place to pick up his Mercedes SUV or, if he was feeling brave, the exceptionally rare and valuable 1963 Ferrari 250 GTO he'd picked up in a rare car auction five years ago.

Picking up his phone, he dialed Tinsley's number. She answered after a couple of heart-stopping rings. "How far are you?" he demanded.

"Pulling into your place right now," she replied. "The roads were empty, surprisingly, with no accidents."

Brilliant news, Cody thought. He rubbed his chest above his heart as he told her where to park. As the owner of the penthouse, and the building, he had an additional two undercover parking spaces close to his personal elevator. Jabbing a button on his tablet, he sent the lift down to the parking garage. He tossed the tablet onto a soft cushion on the couch and pushed his fingers into his hair. She was here, and she was safe.

And his baby was safe.

That was all that mattered.

His baby?

Cody gripped the back of his couch and dropped his head between his outstretched arms. Yeah, that sounded right. His baby. The one he'd never thought he wanted. Somehow, over the past week, the idea of having a child had stopped scaring him and started to excite him. He wanted to know more, know *everything*. He wanted to be involved. He'd never half assed anything in his life and he didn't intend to start now. Cody straightened. He and Tinsley were going to have some exceedingly long conversations over the next few months…

He heard a rap on his front door and then the door pushed open, and he saw her white face. He strode over to her and opened the door wider, gesturing for her to enter. When she did, she swayed on her feet and the little color she had drained from her face.

He grabbed her, lowered her to the ground and helped her put her head between her knees. "I hope you only felt light-headed once you parked, Ryder-White, because if you drove like this, I'm going to lose my shit," he told her.

She lifted her head and looked at him with purple-blue eyes. "No, I was fine, I promise. I only started feeling dizzy when I got out of the car."

"Follow-up question…so why didn't you call me and ask me to come down and help you?"

Tinsley rested her head against the wall as a smidgen of color reentered her face. Her mouth tightened and that all-too-familiar light of battle appeared in her eyes. Then she sighed and a hint of amusement touched her lips. "Because I'm ridiculously stubborn and chronically independent?"

Cody clicked his fingers and pointed his index finger at her. Standing up, he held out his hand. "Are you feeling better? Can you stand up?"

Tinsley slid her much smaller hand into his and he pulled her up, thinking that she was as light as a feather. When she pulled her hands from his, he watched with narrowed eyes to see whether she'd wobble and when she didn't, he bent down to pick up her heavy tote bag as she slid out of her cashmere coat.

He led her across the room and gestured for her to sit down on the corner sofa seat, the one closest to his wood-burning fireplace. The room was darker than before, the clouds blocking out the last of the light, and he flipped on a lamp. "Need anything?" he asked. "I have tea, various types—all of which taste disgusting by the way—soft drinks, that ginger beer you like."

"I'd really like tea, chamomile if you have it," she looked around his place, obviously impressed. "And I'd love a tour of your place. It looks fabulous."

"Sure, but later."

Tinsley bent down and removed her brown leather flat-soled knee-high boots, placing them to the side of the couch. She wore a thigh-length fisherman's sweater over tight jeans and under a blue, puffy vest. A voluminous scarf, in shades of green and blue, was wrapped around her neck. She pulled off the scarf, then the vest and placed them in a neat pile next to her boots. She gestured to her feet. "Do you mind if I pull my feet up on your furniture?"

"Go for it," he told her. " I'll go and make you that tea."

When he returned, just five minutes later, her head was on a pillow resting on the arm of his couch, she was stretched out and was deeply asleep. Smiling, Cody went to the hallway closet, pulled a soft, light blanket off the shelf and draped it over her slim frame.

And outside, the storm gathered in intensity. The wind shook the windows and fat, huge snowballs smacked his overlarge windows. She'd made it, with no time to spare, and he was profoundly grateful that she was safe with him and not out there trying to drive through the raging, wicked storm.

Eight

Tinsley shot up, disoriented. She was in a strange, but lovely sitting room. Across from her were tall, wide windows. The darkness beyond them was broken by white dots of falling snow. Pushing back her hair, she sat up slowly, and looked around, her eyes landing on Cody, sitting across from her, working on a laptop.

"Hi," she murmured, sounding like she was half-asleep.

Cody lifted his head and smiled. "Hey."

"How long did I sleep?" Tinsley asked as she sat up, pushing her hair off her face.

Cody consulted his expensive watch. "Three and a half hours."

Tinsley pulled a face. "Why didn't you wake me up?" she demanded. "I need to get home, feed Moose."

Cody closed his laptop and moved it to the occasional table next to him. "I called Kinga. She said she would feed Moose. And she doesn't want you driving home tonight. I agree."

It really annoyed her when people tried to tell her what to do. She was a responsible adult, dammit, and she'd been making her own decisions for a while now. She stood up, walked over to the window and scowled at the whirling snow.

"They're predicting whiteout conditions for the rest of the night and possibly tomorrow."

Cody's words sank in and her stomach dropped. "I'm stuck here for the foreseeable future?"

Cody nodded as he stood up. "Looks like it."

Tinsley cursed softly, partly at the idea of not being home, with her cat, partly because she was more excited than she should be at the thought of staying with Cody. Proximity wasn't a good idea. She was far too aware of Cody. She spent too much time thinking about making love with him again, remembering what he felt like, his gorgeous smell, his drugging kisses.

She wanted that again. She wanted to lose herself in his touch, slide away on pleasure, pretend that nothing existed outside his soul-stealing touch.

But she'd had him once, or he'd had her; all that remained were the memories of an awesome night. They had complicated family ties, business pressures and a baby on the way. Losing themselves in each other again was an impossibility.

"Are you hungry?" Cody asked from somewhere behind her.

She pulled her eyes off the snow and onto his reflection in the glass. He stood next to his chair, arms folded, his expression unreadable. In his supercasual clothes and with messy hair and thick stubble, he looked a little rough and a lot hot.

Then her stomach rumbled, pulling her thoughts out of the bedroom and into the kitchen. "Starving, actually. What's on the menu?" she asked as she turned around.

"Pepperoni pizza, or, if your stomach can't handle that, plain cheese."

"Frozen?" Tinsley asked, unable to stop her nose from wrinkling. She wasn't a fan—she was a pizza snob and if she couldn't get it from her favorite places, she'd make her own, from scratch—but if frozen was all that was on offer, she'd take it.

Cody walked into the open-plan kitchen and lifted two boxes with their distinctive red, white and green geometric pattern. Now they were talking!

"You have pizza from Lombardi's?"

Cody raised his eyebrows. "You know it?"

"I love it! Griff brought pizza back from New York for Kinga and when I heard about it, I was so annoyed that I didn't get a late-night invitation to join them."

"Judging by the way those two carry on, I think you would've been a very obvious third wheel," Cody said, as he pulled out plates from a cabinet. "And let's be honest here—you don't share your pizza with just anyone."

"But you'll share yours with me?" Tinsley asked, resting her forearms on the white granite counter of the island.

"Thinking about it," Cody teased. "But if you prefer girl food, there might be some yogurt in the fridge and granola in the cupboard."

Tinsley slapped her hand on the closest pizza box and mock growled. "Do not make me hurt you, Gallant."

Cody laughed. "You're about as intimidating as a pink, fluffy unicorn, Tinsley." He popped the pizza boxes in the eye-level oven to warm them. Turning to the fridge, he pulled out a bottle of her preferred brand

of ginger beer—sweet of him to stock some for her—
and lifted it in a silent question. When she nodded, he
poured the liquid into a glass before pouring himself a
glass of red wine.

Cody took a sip of his wine before lowering his
glass. "I'm presuming that you're still abstaining from
alcohol?"

"You presume right. It's not good for the baby and
the smell makes me want to gag."

Cody rubbed his lower jaw. "When are you seeing
your doctor, Tins?"

She'd been slammed at work and forgotten to make
the appointment. "I'm eight weeks now, so sometime
in the next month."

"Look, I don't know a lot about kids but I've never
heard of anyone being so sick from being pregnant.
Maybe you should see her this week."

Ah, her doctor was one of the best on the East Coast
and the chance of getting a quick appointment wasn't
in the cards. If she said it was an emergency, Dr. Higgs
would make a plan for her, but otherwise, she just had
to grin and bear it, as she told Cody.

"Then just see a family practitioner," Cody suggested.

"I want to wait for Dr. Higgs. She's a great doctor
and I can do the ultrasound and everything else while
I'm there," Tinsley told him. She wasn't a doctor snob,
she had the utmost respect for general practitioners, but
she felt—strangely and strongly—that she needed to
see a specialist.

"I wonder how Heather is feeling," Tinsley mused and
when Cody's head shot up and his eyes slammed into
hers, she wished she'd kept the words behind her teeth.

"Is this a competition?" he demanded.

"No, of course not," she told him. "But I can't deny

that a part of me, the part I name Ms. Complete Bitch, is hoping she's puking her guts out."

"You're still angry...at him, at them," he commented.

Tinsley opened her mouth to issue a denial but snapped her jaw closed at the last minute. Was she still angry? Yes. And no.

"I'm angry that I wasted so much time on him, that I did so much and he did so little. JT was so passive-aggressive, Cody, I never knew whether I was in his good books or bad." She looked down at her ring finger, bare now. "I would've done anything for him, and pretty much did. The only thing I asked for was a baby."

She scrunched up her face. "Heather moved in six months after we separated, married him a week after our divorce came through and now's she pregnant. I moved heaven and earth to make him happy, to create an amazing life for us and I'm pissed about that."

Cody's only response was a lift of his eyebrows and a quick nod. He turned to open the oven door and removed the pizza boxes from the oven. Picking them up he nodded to the plates. "If you could grab those, that would be good."

Tinsley did as he asked and followed him back into the living room, sinking to the floor on one side of his coffee table. Cody placed the boxes on the table and returned to the kitchen to fetch his glass of wine. When he returned, he sat down opposite Tinsley and nudged a box toward her.

After munching through one slice, Cody picked up another and held it in his hand, looking contemplative. "Talking about the past, I think we need to dig into why you and I have always had a contentious relationship."

Damn, just when she was feeling reasonably relaxed. Tinsley carefully laid her half-eaten slice on a plate and wiped her mouth with a napkin. "Why? My marriage is over, so rehashing the fact that you never supported us is a moot point."

Hearing her sharp tone, she winced. She picked up her slice, took a small bite and stared at the melty, gooey cheese.

Cody took a long time to speak again. "You're right I didn't support you. I always believed your marriage was a mistake. And it turned out I was right."

Tinsley tossed her slice down and placed her arms on the table. "I suppose you cracked open a bottle of champagne and celebrated me being out of JT's life," she muttered.

"No, don't stop eating," Cody commanded her. "And of course I didn't. I could never celebrate something I knew caused you pain, Tins."

To his credit, he sounded frustrated. "Do I believe that you are both better off? Yes. Did I ever want to see you hurt? No, I didn't. Believe it or not, I've always liked you..."

"But I was never good enough for your brother..." Tinsley replied, bitter. Why were they even discussing this? Her marriage was over and JT had moved on. She had too.

"Is that what you think?" Cody demanded, looking surprised. "That's such a load of crap. I never, not once, thought you weren't good enough for JT."

"Then what was the problem?" Tinsley demanded, leaning forward. She wanted to eat her pizza in peace and enjoy the crackle of the fire and Cody's company. She didn't want to discuss her marriage anymore.

"You sorta hinted at it earlier. JT never loved you half as much as you loved him. If he ever loved you at all."

Tinsley wanted to bat his words away, to shove them

back into their box and slam the lid closed. His words stung. It was said that, in any relationship, one person loved the other more, but she knew that JT hadn't loved her a fraction of the amount she'd loved him. It was her love, attention, commitment and effort that carried and sustained their relationship for so long.

She felt like a complete fool for giving so much and taking so little.

Cody wolfed down another slice, leaned back and turned his legs away from the table. He crossed his ankles and rested his linked hands on his stomach. "Let me get this out and, hopefully, we can put this behind us and move on."

Tinsley held her breath, not sure if she was ready to hear his opinion on her defunct marriage. No, she definitely didn't want to hear it, but she knew that the air between them needed to be cleared.

"JT has a very big brain, he's an intellectual giant but he knows nothing when it comes to interpersonal relationships…" Cody said, his eyes not leaving hers. "He was a huge nerd and when the prettiest girl in school, smart and popular too, started paying attention to him, he enjoyed the prestige that came with being your boyfriend. But, because he's lazy, he gave as little of himself as he could get away with."

All true, Tinsley conceded.

"He neglected you, Tinsley—it's what he does." Cody rubbed the back of his neck. "This might come as a surprise to you, but I've always been more worried about you than him."

"But…he's your *brother*! You've been looking after him since your mom died!"

Cody nodded. "And I know him better than anybody, including—dare I say it?—you." He shrugged.

"Jonathan Thomas is a cerebral guy, and, unlike you, isn't someone who needs love. He's a leech. He takes and takes."

Tinsley silently agreed. JT defined emotional unavailability. "Intimacy and responsibility scare him," Cody added.

"Maybe he's changed. He sounded so happy about being a father, about having a baby," Tinsley pointed out.

"Because he knows that is what is expected of him. Give him a couple of months, and a few hundred sleepless nights, and the novelty will wear off."

God, he was so right.

"I remember the night before your wedding so clearly. You were wearing your dress and the designer was in a flap because you'd lost weight, the dress didn't fit you properly and she needed to make some last-minute alterations."

Tinsley's mouth fell open. She'd forgotten about that. "She was so mad."

"You always lose weight when you're stressed," Cody told her. "And in the months leading up to your wedding you were as stressed as I've ever seen you." He frowned at her. "Well, up until now."

"I was determined to be the perfect bride," Tinsley told him. "And to start our married life with a perfect wedding."

"And I bet JT was less than interested." Cody scratched his forehead when she nodded. "By the way, you are far too obsessed with perfection."

Yeah, they definitely weren't going there. "Why did you ask me not to marry him?" Tinsley asked.

"Well, I was trying to protect you more than I was him," Cody admitted. "I spoke to you because, of the two of you, you were the only person strong enough, brave enough to stop the last-minute wedding."

Tinsley stared at him, not sure what to say. He'd been trying to look after her? What the hell? She recalled his exact words and winced. "You told me that marriage was a mistake and that we'd be divorced within a few years. That I wanted to be a bride and not a wife. That I was too young and too immature to marry. You never said anything about JT!"

Cody's eyes remained steady. "I might think he has no common sense, but he's my brother, Tinsley." He lifted an arrogant eyebrow. "Besides, was I wrong?" he asked.

Tinsley opened her mouth to blast him, but quickly realized that her impulse to defend JT was a conditioned response. "No, I guess not," she reluctantly admitted.

"You were all those things, but I was wrong to focus on your faults when I was most concerned about JT's selfishness and inability to communicate. We come from a long line of men who don't talk," Cody admitted.

Tinsley watched, fascinated, as Cody's green eyes heated with desire. "The fact that I managed to say anything with you in that dress was a minor miracle in itself. You took my breath away."

Tinsley blushed, remembering her wedding dress. Her skirt had been layers of cream-colored chiffon but her top had minimal fabric, just a series of perfectly placed appliqués covering just enough of her upper torso to avoid sending her grandfather to the hospital.

"JT was so uninterested in anything to do with the wedding, and I wanted to shock him into paying attention," Tinsley admitted.

"Did it work?" Cody asked her, looking interested.

"Not really," she again reluctantly admitted.

"Well, if it helps, I spent the duration of that sober ceremony thinking very unchurch-like thoughts about how I would strip you out of that dress," Cody told her, his voice rough with desire.

What? Really? "You were attracted to me back then?" she asked, her mouth slack with shock.

"Jesus, Tinsley…" Cody roughly responded. "I've always been attracted to you."

No…*really?* What? Tinsley stared at him, completely flummoxed. She'd never suspected, not once, that Cody thought of her as anything other than a pesky sister-in-law and pain in his butt.

"I don't know what to say to that."

Cody shrugged. "Nothing to say. It was what it was." He dropped his leg and leaned forward. "New Year's Eve was, for me, a long time coming." His lips quirked at the double entendre, but he didn't voice the obvious. "It was better than I ever imagined."

Tinsley sighed. It had been the best sexual experience of her life—one perfect, sensuous night she would remember until the day she died. But one that would never be repeated. Cody could pull strong feelings to the surface and, whether they were anger or frustration or heat or desire, she wasn't interested in dealing with wild emotions. She'd experienced too much turmoil with JT; she simply wanted calm. She'd had her one night of passion, and the memories of that would sustain her for a long, long time.

She'd spent twelve years floundering in a relationship, and she knew that getting emotionally or sexually involved with another Gallant was a terrible idea. If JT was a tropical storm, then Cody would be a category-five hurricane, and she wasn't prepared to allow another Gallant—or another man—to cause her to spin out again.

Tinsley forced herself to eat another slice of pizza before wiping her hands and mouth again with a fresh napkin. She sipped at her ginger beer and held the glass against her chest. "Do you think you and JT are both antikids because you had such little input from your dad?"

"To be fair, we didn't have that much from our mom either," Cody admitted. "She was a busy lady and didn't spend a lot of time with us."

Now that was a revelation since JT, the very few times she spoke about his mom, sang her praises, which she shared with Cody.

"JT and I are very different people, Tinsley, and I can only speak for myself. That's not how I remember her," Cody told her, folding his arms. His big biceps bulged, and the cotton of his Henley caressed the curves. *Yum.* "From the time I was twelve, I all but raised JT. I took on that responsibility."

"Because your father was mired in grief and couldn't function," Tinsley sympathetically stated.

"Wow, that's not true either. Your ex told you a Candyland version of our teenage years. Dad shrugged off Mom's death, took two weeks off to 'grieve,' then left every night around ten to spend the night with his long-term mistress. After a month, he returned full-time to work and resumed his insane travel schedule."

Bertram Gallant had been an international yacht salesman and the Ryder-White and Gallant families initially connected through Cody's father, Tinsley remembered. "Wasn't your dad good friends with my great-uncle Benjamin, Callum's much younger brother?"

He nodded. "Ben Ryder-White and my dad were both into yachts and my father credits Ben for launching his career selling them."

"How so?" Tinsley asked, fascinated.

"Ben asked Bertram to find him a yacht suitable for a race he wanted to enter, and Bertram did. He earned a fat commission on the deal and that led to many more."

"Really? I did not know that." There were quite a few gaps in her knowledge about her family. But that didn't surprise her, since Callum never discussed Ben, who died before she was born. Tinsley did recall her father telling her and Kinga the odd tale about their great-uncle, and she got the impression that he was a wonderful man and very different from her grandfather.

She did know that Callum and Ben once ran Ryder International together, as partners. Then Callum started pressuring Ben to marry, to produce a son. Even back then, producing the next generation of Ryder-White men had been important to Callum and he'd nagged Ben to do his part. Ben finally admitted he was gay and had met the man he wanted to marry.

And her grandfather—scared of change and scandal—instigated a campaign to force Benjamin out of the day-to-day running of the family business. It worked. Ben left Ryder International and moved in with his partner, Carlo, for a short time before passing away in a tragic car accident.

Her father's support for Ben never wavered, yet another reason Callum and James didn't get along.

"I soon realized that my father wasn't lonely on those constant business trips. His mistress joined him," Cody told her, yanking her back into the present.

"My dad was a selfish guy and so am I," Cody quietly admitted. "None of us like to take responsibility."

Oh, that was a load of hooey. Cody was one of the most responsible people she knew. When he said he was going to do something, he did it. One didn't build and grow a massive company, employ thousands of people, without being accountable.

If she pointed that out, he'd just say that was business.

"You were and you still are," Tinsley told him. "As a teenager, you were more responsible than your forebears were as adults."

He stared at her before shrugging. "Maybe. But having so much pressure on me at such a young age is also why I've avoided relationships and getting tied down."

She understood why he felt like that and couldn't blame him. "That's why I'm giving you an out, Cody," Tinsley reminded him.

"I'm not sure if that's what I want anymore." Cody raked a hand through his hair and down the back of his head. Seeing something on her face—surprise? excitement?—his eyes narrowed, and his jaw hardened. "Don't get excited. I'm not about to offer to be a full-time dad or to raise the kid with you," he muttered. No, he wasn't, at least, he wasn't *yet*. But she knew he would. Sometime between now and the birth of their baby, he'd climb on board instead of holding onto a rope and being pulled along in the ship's wake. And, if she knew him, and she thought she did, he'd soon want to captain the ship.

She'd have to work out how to deal with *that*.

"Noted," she stated.

Cody's frown deepened. "I'm serious, Tinsley. Don't expect too much from me."

She didn't need to because he expected a lot from himself and there was no way he'd shirk his responsibility, to her or her child. She knew he wouldn't offer her marriage—and she didn't want him to because a baby was a terrible reason to get married!—but neither would he walk away. "I won't, Cody."

Tinsley suspected he was trying to manage her expectations of him but she also knew, somewhere down deep where truth resided, that Cody was a much better man than he gave himself credit for. His father and brother might be a little dysfunctional, but Cody Gallant had his life together.

He stood up, looked down at her plate and then to her pizza box. "God, you've hardly eaten anything. No wonder you're on the verge of passing out every two seconds."

He'd polished off his pizza, she noticed. "I ate far more than I expected to."

Cody shook his head, closed the boxes and picked up their plates and took them through to the kitchen. Tinsley heard him putting the plates into the dishwasher, the opening and closing of the fridge. When he returned, he sat down in the chair he'd been occupying earlier.

"So, business. How did the meeting with the Food Network producer go?" he asked, placing his ankle on his opposite knee.

Tinsley pulled up her legs and wrapped her arms around her knees. "He wants some time to think about it, but he sounded keen. It's reality TV so if the contestants are dynamic and interesting, he's all-in. If the contestants are dull and boring, he's out, so he's only interested in picking up the story at the national and international level. He's not interested in the regional and state competitions."

"Neither, to be honest, are we. There's not much PR mileage in those competitions," Cody said.

"Oh, and he perked up when I told him that Jules is to be a judge. He's heard of her and would like to see her on camera." Tinsley smiled at him. "I think he has a little crush on her."

"Who doesn't?" Cody quipped.

Tinsley laughed. Unlike her reaction at the ball, she was unoffended this time around. Jules was charismatic and stunningly beautiful, and men dropped to their knees as she walked past. Tinsley was more suspicious of men who didn't have a crush on Jules than men who did. Jules was a force of nature, but she was also sweet and sincere and a crazy good friend. And Tinsley felt enormously guilty for not telling her best friend, and her sister, that she was pregnant.

She wasn't the chattiest person around, but she did talk to her sister and Jules. They knew her inside out. So why hadn't she? She'd tried, once or twice, but every time she saw them or had a moment alone with them, she couldn't get the words to form. It was the weirdest thing: she wanted to tell them but her tongue wouldn't spit out the required sentences.

Maybe it was because she still didn't feel pregnant, that the idea was lodged in her brain but for some reason, not in her heart. Was that because she was embarrassed to tell them she got pregnant via a one-night stand? Or was it because she was worried they'd think her hypocritical? After all, her ONS was Cody, the man whom she professed to detest.

Pulling her thoughts back to business, Tinsley asked whether his meeting with Geraint du Pont was successful. "Yep, he's keen to judge. As I said, he's got time on his hands, and he's waiting for his new restaurant to be built, which is going to take at least six months.

"We spoke in his kitchen, while he whipped up a quick mushroom-and-shrimp risotto," he added. One of her all-time favorite foods. Tinsley picked up a cushion from the chair behind her and threw it at his head. "You ate his risotto? I am green with envy!"

Cody caught the silk-covered cushion and tossed it

onto the sofa behind her. When his eyes sparkled with amusement, he looked years younger and irresistible. The guy rocked a suit but seeing him dressed casually, in sweatpants, a well-fitting Henley and bare feet, rocked her world. The fire in the grate crackled but it was no match for the heat running through her system.

For weeks now she'd been ignoring, or denying, her need for him, pushing her attraction away. But tonight, all her barriers were crumbling and she wanted to be with him again, kissing his mouth, exploring his body, lost in him.

Lost with him.

She was tired of thinking, worrying, strategizing, planning. Tonight she wanted to *feel*…

Tinsley unfurled her body and stood up slowly, linking her hands behind her back and arching to stretch. Cody's eyes went to her chest and his gaze heated. His hands moved to the arms of his chair and his fingers pushed into the fabric as if he were trying to restrain himself from putting his hands on her.

This was fun, Tinsley thought. She hadn't thought she could have this sort of effect on him. That she possessed the power to make the muscle in his jaw tick, his eyes soften, his pants jump. It was heady…and wonderful.

"What are you doing, Tinsley?" Cody asked her, his voice deeper than it had been a few minutes before. His voice, already a rich baritone, dropped an octave or two when he was aroused. She glanced at his pants and, yep, he was interested.

Very interested indeed.

And all because she stood up and stretched. Amazing.

There was no point in being coy; Cody wouldn't appreciate it. "I'm trying to seduce you," she admitted, blushing.

Cody sat up and ran his hands over his face, as if he were trying to wipe her words away.

Tinsley wrinkled her nose. "I know. It's not a good idea, I'm pregnant, we're trying to figure things out, we work together…blah, blah, blah." Tinsley walked over to where he sat and placed her hands on the arms of his chair, forcing him to lean back. "I know, Cody, I'm living it! But just for tonight, while the snow falls outside and the world stops, I just want to…"

Arrgh, telling a man—Cody—she wanted to make love with him wasn't as easy as she'd thought it would be. What if he rejected her? She would look like a fool, and she hated feeling that way.

She stopped, uncertain of the way forward.

She'd experienced enough rejection in her life, thanks very much.

Before she could decide what to do, Cody's hand shot up to capture the back of her head and he pulled her down so that his mouth met hers. And the world, everything she knew, slid away. All she wanted was to be in his arms, surrounded by him. She leaned in close and caught a hint of his citrus-and-spice cologne. Teasing herself, and him, she ever so softly brushed her lips against his and pulled back to look at him, to judge his reaction. His lips lifted and his smile hit his eyes, warm, delicious and dazzling.

As she still leaned over him, his hand still cupped around the back of her head, they shared a long, delicious, sexy-as-hell kiss, one that went on and on and on. She moved closer, straddled his knees and sank into his broad body, trying to get as close as possible in the confines of the chair. His fingers played with her hair and rippled down her spine as their tongues danced and dueled. His body was so different to hers, hard and solid and panty-meltingly delicious. Cody's grip on her tightened and Tinsley felt lost in him, loving the unexpected intimacy of their embrace.

It was as if they'd put everything on hold, living in the now instead of in the future. It was exactly what she needed.

She loved kissing him, but she needed more, needed him to be the puzzle piece her body was missing.

As if he heard her silent pleas, Cody's hand snaked up and under her shirt and onto her lace-covered breast, impatiently pulling down the bra cup to find her hard nipple. His thumb brushed across it, applying the right amount of pressure for maximum pleasure, and she moaned, arching her back, silently begging for more. Annoyed with the barrier of fabric between them, Tinsley leaned back and swiftly removed her shirt, closing her eyes when both his hands covered her breasts. "Take it off, Cody, and put your lips on me."

Was that *her* voice? She hadn't realized she could sound demanding and sexy at the same time. Her scattered thoughts evaporated as Cody unsnapped the front clasp of her expensive bra and looked down at her chest, his eyes that stunning green that defied description. He kissed each of her breasts, twisting his tongue around her nipples. Tinsley moved so that her knees were on either side of his hips but there wasn't enough room for her to rest her aching core against his shaft, to assuage that need to be as close as possible to him. Scooting back, she stood up, unsteady and held her hand out to him.

"Take me to bed, Cody."

Cody shook his head. "No."

Disappointment shot through her, hard and fast. He didn't want her…

He gripped her jaw and tipped her head up to look at

her, looking into her soul. "I can't wait that long. I need you here, now. Fast."

Oh…oh, thank God.

Cody yanked her to him and her breasts pushed against his chest, his desire for her hard against her stomach. He ducked his head and she stood on her toes, their lips locked together in another, hard, take-me-now, take-everything kiss.

Impatient, Cody stripped her clothes, then his. She stood in front of him, surprisingly unselfconscious—how could she feel shy when he looked at her like she hung the moon and danced among the stars? His hands raced over her body, over her breasts, down her waist, slipping between her legs. She was dripping with need and he released a long growl when he sank his fingers into her warm channel. Tinsley released a wail and found herself being turned away from his body, Cody's large hand on her back. "Grab the arms of the chair with your hands—lift your ass," he commanded.

Ridiculously excited at this new position, wondering what it would bring, she did as he asked and then his erection slid into her and he rested his chest against her back, holding her close with one arm around her waist, his other hand delving between her legs. Tinsley held on as passion soared and swirled, feeling completely encapsulated by him.

He pushed in deeper and she felt his lips on the side of her neck, on her shoulder. They established a fast, wicked rhythm, and her hips rose to meet each deep thrust. Her hands found his arms, nails raking his skin.

Tinsley felt herself on the edge of that delicious cusp, wanting to wait for him but knowing she couldn't hold out much longer. Heat flashed over her, and her low moans became tiny screams. She felt herself losing control. He thrust deeper and his response caused her to detonate into a fireball of colors. She knew that he'd come but they still kept going, unable to end this passionate tango. She felt him harden, heard his low growl and his hand slid between them again, touching that magic knot of nerves, and she flew up, exploding as she hit that fireball again.

It took a while for them to move, to speak, to unknot themselves from their sexual tangle. Cody lifted his hand to stroke her hair and dropped a brief, dazzling kiss on her mouth. "That was amazing... You are amazing..."

Tinsley blushed. "I...that...*wow*."

Cody sent her a tender smile and pulled her closer. They held each other tight, just enjoying being together. Tinsley felt his lips in her hair, on her temple and her cheek. Then he stepped back and held out his hand to her. "I have an amazing shower I'd like to show you," he told her, the light in his eyes very wicked indeed.

"I'd very much like to see your shower," Tinsley told him, walking with him up the steel-and-wood stairs. "But I'm far more interested in the fun we can get up to in it."

Nine

Their meeting was finished, and Callum had dismissed them, but instead of leaving, Tinsley stayed in her chair on the opposite side of Callum's desk. Cody turned to look at Callum, who, as always, looked characteristically uninterested. Callum Ryder was a hard man and didn't have an affectionate bone in his body. He treated his son and two granddaughters like the employees they were.

Callum's bushy white eyebrows lifted. "Is there something else, Tinsley?" he asked, his tone dismissive, as it always was.

"I've been asked by the family to encourage you to see a doctor," Tinsley quietly stated. Cody had seen Tinsley, James and Penelope in a huddle earlier in the break room, engaged in an intense discussion and it was now obvious that she'd drawn the short straw to talk to Callum. It explained Tinsley's sudden bad mood.

Callum started to respond but Tinsley spoke before he

could. "We are all worried about you. Your complexion is gray, your breathing seems labored and, occasionally, your lips seem a little blue."

Callum hadn't been well for a while. Hadn't he said as much to Kinga ages ago?

Callum stared at Tinsley, displeasure in his eyes and on his face. "I am nearly eighty years old, and I do not need to be spoken to like a child."

Now that was unfair, Cody thought, walking to the closest wall and leaning his shoulder into it. Tinsley had been rather respectful in her request. Cody glanced at the door and considered leaving them alone, but he'd been on the fringes of this family for years, was a frequent guest in Callum's home and Ryder International was one of his best clients.

He would keep his mouth shut and his opinions to himself, unless the conversation turned ugly. He respected Tinsley and would let her handle her elderly relative but, client or not, he would not tolerate Callum verbally abusing his lover, the mother of his child.

"You are not well and we all would like you to seek medical advice," Tinsley said, her voice calm. Cody just managed to contain his snort, thinking that Tinsley was the pot calling the kettle black. Despite spending a lot of time together lately—in bed and out—no matter how much he begged, pleaded or demanded she take it easier, see a doctor right away, she refused. Tinsley was the most stubborn person he'd ever met. Possibly even more so than her ornery grandfather. And that was saying something.

"Callum, this is ridiculous." Tinsley stood up and placed her hands on her grandfather's desk. Callum looked at her hands, then the desk, silently demanding her to back away. Cody thought she was playing with fire; Callum wasn't someone who took orders well.

Like grandfather, like granddaughter.

"Just go and see a doctor," Tinsley told him, frustration coating her words.

"Leave me, please," Callum echoed her tone. They stared at each other for a minute before Tinsley threw her hands in the air. Stepping away from the desk, she shook her head and when she spoke, her tone was sad. "You're not an easy man to love, or to care for, Callum."

Callum looked at her, his expression blank. He finally nodded. "I know. Leave me now."

Tinsley spun around on her heel, stomped across Callum's big office and whipped open the door. After collecting her forgotten iPad, Cody followed her to her office to find her sitting behind her desk, scowling. Temper sparked in her extraordinary eyes.

"He's not well, Cody."

Cody placed the folders and the iPad on her desk and echoed her stance from earlier by placing his palms flat on her desk to look her in the eye. "You're right. He's not."

"He needs to seek medical attention."

This was his opening, and, hell yeah, he was taking it. "I agree. But you are being superbly hypocritical, sweetheart."

It took her some time for his words to make sense and when they did, fury turned her blue eyes purple. "*What* did you just say to me?"

Her face flushed and her mouth flattened and, together with the scalding anger in her eyes, he received her silent message to back way, way off. But he'd had too many arguments with this woman to be scared of one more. Cody stood up and jammed his hands into the pockets of his suit pants. "You heard me."

"I'm hypocritical? I'm *hypocritical*?"

"Repeating it a few times isn't going to change the meaning of the word, Tinsley," Cody said, keeping his temper leashed. He'd asked her for the last three weeks or so to see a doctor, to push up her appointment and get some help. But she told him it was just a phase. It would pass.

She was the most infuriating, most frustrating woman he'd ever met. But she was also the least demanding. She didn't nag him to come around, to bring her flowers, to take her out and about. He had to wrestle work away from her—she had the nasty habit of trying to do everything herself—and, if he didn't bully her to go home, she would live at the office.

She was driven and independent. And he wanted her more every day.

"You cannot possibly be equating my situation with Callum's!" Tinsley said, her voice rising. Looking past him, she nodded at the door. "Close that, please."

Oh, and she was also bossy. "Do it yourself," he mildly suggested.

Tinsley pushed her chair back, stood up and stomped over to the door, slamming it shut. Cody winced. Way to go, Ryder-White—she'd just informed everyone else on the floor they were fighting.

Cody shrugged, unconcerned. It wasn't the first time and it wouldn't be the last. Neither she, nor their arguments, scared him.

"You and Callum are both unwell and neither of you will haul your stubborn ass off to the doc." He shrugged. "So, yeah, in my mind, your situations are comparable.

Except that you are being hypocritical in demanding that he seek medical attention when you won't."

Tinsley slapped her hands on her hips. "I am *pregnant*. These symptoms are a normal part of the process. As far as I know," she stated, sounding superbly sarcastic, "my grandfather isn't pregnant."

"Your symptoms are extreme, and you know it," Cody stated, clenching his fists inside his pockets.

"You are like a broken record!" Tinsley told him, her face flushed with irritation. "Can you give it a rest, please? This is my body, dammit!"

"It's my baby!" Cody shot back, pointing at her stomach. "You are carrying my child, and I need to know that you are okay, that my kid is okay."

Tinsley stared at him, obviously flabbergasted. And so was he. Lately they'd avoided the topic of his involvement in the baby's life. He'd told her that he would pay child support and all schooling expenses, but that was as far as they got. He hadn't told her that he wanted to be a part of their child's life, *her* life.

He'd thought they had time on their side, that they could enjoy each other, enjoy living in the moment, until their burning need for each other faded away. Because that's what always happened. He wasn't a together-forever kind of guy. Sexual boredom was just taking a hell of a lot longer to settle in with her.

After their passion was spent, they'd morph into being friends—he wouldn't accept anything less—and he'd take an active role in raising their child.

He wasn't sure he could do it, but he wanted to try.

Cody saw she was looking at him, her expression a little odd, like she was waiting for an explanation. He had none to give her; his thoughts were a jumbled mess. "I should be a part of your lives," he said, groping for words. The instant the words left his mouth, he winced. They lacked conviction and he knew Tinsley would pick up on that.

"Should?" Tinsley spit the word out, rolling her eyes. "Dammit, Cody, how many times do I have to tell you that I don't need you, that we'll be fine on our own, that I am very prepared to do this single-handed?"

"You don't have to!" Cody shouted back. "I'm standing here, offering to help."

Tinsley released a hard, brittle laugh. "Really? Well, that's the first time I've heard you say that." She shook her head and lifted her hand, palm facing front. "Seriously, don't hurt yourself making the offer. I don't need you. I don't need anybody."

"Yeah, you're so okay on your own, so stubborn in your belief that you have this all under control that you haven't told your sister or best friend or even your parents about the baby. If you are feeling so strong and so capable, why are you keeping this a secret?"

Her mouth opened and closed. He could see she was annoyed that she couldn't find a quick, cutting answer. "My relationship with my sister, my parents and my best friend is none of your business, Gallant!"

"Of course it is!" Cody closed his eyes, frustrated. "I've been in and out of your life since you were fifteen years old, Tinsley! I have eaten at your parents' and grandfather's tables, I have worked with Jules, I know all of you. So don't you dare treat me like I am some man you picked up on a whim and intend to discard when you tire of him!"

She wrinkled her nose and dropped her eyes, a sure sign that she was embarrassed. She wanted to do that, he realized. At her core, she didn't want him to step up to the plate with the baby. Because in a month or two, or three or four, she wanted to be able to walk away from him and cut him out of her life.

Tinsley wasn't interested in help or sharing responsibility. That had to be the reason she hadn't pushed him to commit to their child, because she didn't want to share control, had no interest in being half of a whole. She wanted to do what she wanted, when she wanted, to call each and every shot.

She knew he wasn't the type to stand on the sidelines, to have someone else pull his strings. He wasn't a damn puppet. He was a guy who was superbly comfortable in a leadership role, who could and did make decisions with ease.

But Tinsley wanted to do everything herself. She showed him that every day. She wanted all the control, all the time, and she knew he would never live under her direction. That was why she hadn't made any demands on him.

"You need to see someone about your issues with control, Ryder," Cody told her, pushing an agitated hand through his hair.

"What?"

Tinsley's eyes slammed into him, but he refused to look away. Yep, they were going there; she needed to know that she couldn't carry on this way.

"Seriously, you have a problem. You struggle to delegate even the smallest tasks and when you do, you micromanage them. You double-check on me, all the time. You keep telling me that you're happy to raise our baby alone but that's not because you don't want help—you just don't want to give up control."

Tinsley straightened her spine and looked at him, a cold, hard mask falling over her face. "So, I need medical *and* mental help. That's what you're saying?"

He hadn't used those terms but, yeah.

When he didn't answer, Tinsley pointed at the door. "Get the hell out of my office, Cody. And don't you dare come back until I tell you that you can!"

Cody shook his head. "There you go again. Everything has to be on your terms, your way. That doesn't work for me, babe."

"Right now, you aren't working for me, *babe*." Tinsley walked over to the door and yanked it open, her face flushed with temper. She gestured for him to leave. When he planted his feet, her grip on the door handle tightened. "I swear to God, if you don't leave now, I *will* call security and have you escorted from the building."

Cody closed his eyes, mentally shaking his head. He'd pushed her too far. They weren't going to get anywhere today, not when she was so angry, and he was beyond frustrated too. No, it would be better to postpone this discussion to a time when they were both feeling calmer. His instinct was to stay and fight but he knew he had to be sensible. It wasn't a defeat; it was a retreat. He'd fight this battle another day, in a different way.

They would work this out—they had to. They had a baby on the way. They needed to find a way to deal with each other and to compromise. They were adults and they had time.

Cody nodded and walked to the door, stopping next to her. Her citrus-orchard scent slapped him and he felt the strong hit of desire. Her face was flushed, her lips were swollen and her eyes sparking...

And he'd never wanted her more.

Too bad, so sad.

Cody reined in his base instincts and dropped a kiss on her temple, frowning when she pulled back to avoid his touch. "We're not done with this, Tinsley. I need you to let me in, give a little, *bend*."

Tinsley, stubborn to the core, narrowed her eyes to slits and made a shooing motion. "Go."

Cody released an under-his-breath curse.

All he was doing was banging his head against a brick wall, so he went.

Later that evening, in her lovely home, Tinsley pulled a cork out of an expensive bottle of red and looked at the vol-au-vents she'd quickly assembled. Spinach and ricotta for Kinga, salmon and chives for Jules. They'd both demurred when she invited them around for an impromptu snack and wine party, saying that they had things to do, but when she told them she needed to talk, really talk, they immediately agreed to be at her place around seven.

It was ten past now.

Tinsley looked around her perfectly decorated, nothing-out-of-place house and thought, for the first time, that its perfection was cold and uninviting. But living in a messy house, with a messy person—like she had with JT, who was the biggest slob alive—made her feel anxious.

Being pregnant, her position at Ryder International, living up to her deep-seated belief that she needed to be perfect—she felt anxious, all the time.

And the more turbulent she felt inside, the more she tried to control what was happening outside. Most people shrugged off chaos or ran away from it, but she dug in. She bossed people around and became belligerent about how things should be.

Cody was the first person to call her on that.

She'd been an anxious, sensitive child, and only

felt secure when everyone around her looked or felt happy, when life was rolling along smoothly. She knew that they had to keep Callum happy, that bad things would happen if they didn't. A memory hovered, just out of reach.

If they are anything less than perfect, you will bear the consequences...

That long ago sentence, spoken by Callum when she was a child, reverberated around her skull. Was that the reason she was so anxious, the root of her need for control?

As she placed her snacks on a pretty platter, she remembered being a scared child, not wanting to put a foot wrong and disappoint her grandfather or her parents. Her hair was always tidy, her room obsessively neat, her homework always done. Order made her feel less anxious, so she strived to put everything in its box.

Her need for perfection wasn't new, or born out of JT's passive-aggression; it was something she'd lived with her whole life. She'd always liked to have everything—objects and emotions—in a box. But Cody, damn him, was unboxable. No matter how much she pushed him, he stood his ground. And her growing feelings for him were becoming bigger and bolder. They were bubbling over. Cody made her feel feminine and fabulous, protected and precious.

He made her feel like who she could be if she just undid the supertight knot holding the many strands of her life and her emotions together. But losing control petrified her, so she held fast and made herself miserable.

God, what was she going to do? How was she going to resolve this? Move forward?

Tinsley heard her front door open and the sound of melodious female voices in her hallway. Walking out of her kitchen, she greeted Kinga and Jules, kissing their cold cheeks and hugging them close.

"Thanks for coming over," Tinsley told them, as they sat down on her couches, adorned with bright pink and red roses. They immediately crossed their legs, sat up straight and looked like they were at a job interview. Tinsley remembered walking into Cody's home, unzipping her boots and putting her feet up on the cushions. Her sister and friend should be as relaxed in her house as she was in his.

It was a little thing but important.

"Take off your shoes, curl up, get comfortable."

She saw the surprised look they exchanged but ignored it, walking back into the kitchen to get the tray of wine, glasses and vol-au-vents. She placed it on the coffee table and Jules, brilliant mixologist that she was, pointed out that there was a glass missing.

Tinsley perched on the edge of a chair and placed her hands between her knees. She wrinkled her nose. "Yeah, that's why I asked you over. I need to tell you why I'm not drinking."

"Antibiotics?" Kinga asked, reaching for a vol-au-vent.

"No, I'm pregnant."

Shock flashed across their faces, as bright as the sun. Kinga placed her wineglass on the table, her mouth slack with surprise. "What? How?"

Tinsley waved her questions away. "It's a long, complicated story."

Jules sipped from her glass, calmer than her sister, and picked up a vol-au-vent. "We're listening."

"During a huge fight today, Cody told me that I should've told you guys a while back. On that he was right," Tinsley reluctantly admitted. "Actually, he was right about a whole lot of stuff," Tinsley morosely added.

Kinga waved her words away. "You're always fighting with Cody. That's nothing new. We'll come back to him, and the love-hate-love thing you've got going. Who's the fath…? Oh, crap. Is Cody the father of your baby?"

Tinsley nodded.

"I didn't think he wanted kids," Jules said, once she'd absorbed Tinsley's new reality.

"How do you know that?" Tinsley demanded, curious as to why Jules would know something so personal about Cody.

"We worked an event in Rome a few years back and there were some kids causing havoc and he told me, in no uncertain terms, that he wasn't interested in being a dad," Jules explained. "That being said, I presume that your pregnancy was a great big oops? What happened?"

"We used condoms." Tinsley hunched her shoulders. "We genuinely don't know how it happened. Just that it did."

"Wow," Kinga said. She leaned forward and placed her hand on Tinsley's knee. "I've been so busy with the ball and with Griff that I've neglected you, Tins. I thought you looked tired and wan, but I never suspected this. I'm so sorry I haven't been there for you."

"Me too," Jules added, guilt in her eyes.

"It's not your fault, guys. I could've told you at any time during these past few weeks."

"Why didn't you?" Jules asked her, looking at the snack in her hand. "God, these are delicious. Have one."

Salmon? Cheese? The smell? Uh…no, thank you.

"Because I am being completely, irrationally anxious about my pregnancy and if I told you I was pregnant then I'd have to admit something else, something I don't want to face."

At her serious tone, their attention sharpened and their bodies tensed. "What, Tins?"

Tinsley walked into the kitchen and picked up two pregnancy tests lying on the counter. She showed them to Jules and Kinga. "I did these this morning and they both say that I'm pregnant, right?"

"Uh...yeah," Jules answered for them both.

"From around six weeks I have been vomiting constantly, I am extremely tired, my breasts feel like someone has stabbed them with a curling iron."

Kinga pulled a face.

"I've never felt as crap as I have the last few weeks, but those are all symptoms of being pregnant, right?"

"If you say so," Kinga replied, her tone soothing. "I'm not sure what you are trying to tell us, sweetie."

If Tinsley said this out loud, there was no going back. There was no brushing this off as her anxiety working overtime, or just the normal worry about her baby's development. If she articulated this, she'd have to deal with how she felt. And she didn't want to.

The urge to run away and bury her head in the sand was strong.

"The tests say I'm pregnant, my body is acting like I'm pregnant but I don't think I'm pregnant."

Kinga and Jules looked equally confused. "We don't understand, Tinsley."

She didn't either, not really. All she knew was that there was something very amiss with the pregnancy... She knew this like she knew her name.

And at her appointment tomorrow, the ultrasound would confirm it. She'd leave her doctor's office without a baby—that she knew for sure. And she'd have to go back to her life that wasn't really a life, filled with pressure and stress and anxiety.

She and Cody had been tied together by the pregnancy and the cocktail competition but, in a month or two, Cody's staff would take over the day-to-day operation of the competition and her time with Cody would be curtailed. The cords binding them would snap and she would be on her own.

Without a baby.

She couldn't bear the thought. She couldn't imagine a life without Cody in it. Because he was so honest, so direct and such a protector, she felt safe with him, happy to allow him to take the wheel, hold the reins. He was the least passive-aggressive person she'd ever met and she trusted him to do what he said he would, to be an adult and to consider her opinions and observations. With him, she never felt like an afterthought.

He was stable, thoughtful and responsible and being around him made her feel calm, kept her anxiety under control. With Cody she forgot to run what-if scenarios, to plan for every potential possibility; she trusted him to handle things as they came along. With him, the urge to micromanage—he wouldn't let her anyway!—faded.

He was the yin to her yang, the calm to her storm.

She loved him, as she'd never loved anyone before.

But Cody didn't want a child or a partner and, while she knew he didn't want something to be wrong with the baby, a part of him would be relieved not to have the responsibility of a child. And he would be glad to stop working with her. She was difficult and controlling and annoying.

Hell, she frequently wanted to run far away from herself too.

"Something is wrong with the baby, with the pregnancy," Tinsley repeated the words and felt the truth on her tongue.

"Are you sure you're not just overreacting, Tins?"

Because we know that you often do.

Tinsley heard the unspoken subtext in her sister's voice. It was a valid point. Maybe she was. Maybe she was just scared and feeling overwhelmed and anxious.

Maybe.

"I really hope I am being irrational, Kingaroo," Tinsley told her, tears gathering in her throat. "I have an appointment tomorrow. I guess I'll find out then."

Kinga cursed. "Crap, Tins, I am leaving for Monaco early tomorrow to meet with the organizers of the yacht race Ryder International is sponsoring. You asked me to do that, remember?"

Yeah, she did.

"And I'm leaving for Cancun on a red-eye tonight," Jules told her. "But Cody will be with you, so you won't be on your own."

"Cody doesn't know the appointment is tomorrow and I'm not going to tell him. If something is wrong, I need time to process it on my own before I tell him."

They both looked horrified. "That's not a good idea, Tinsley. This isn't something you should do alone," Jules insisted.

But it was. At some point, she was going to have to live the rest of her life alone, without Cody, so she might as well get used to doing the hard stuff on her own right away. There was no point easing into it.

She needed to relearn how to be on her own again, to not to be part of a couple, to get on without a man in her life. She needed to face her anxiety and deal with it. Become healthier and happier.

All on her own. It was her inner work. Cody couldn't do it for her.

"I'll be fine, I promise. If the baby is fine, I'll be ecstatic. If it isn't, I'll be okay because I've mentally prepared for that possibility."

"I'm sure it's just your anxiety getting the best of you," Kinga told her, trying to reassure her. "Everything will be fine, I promise."

Tinsley made herself smile, knowing that, on this occasion, Kinga was wrong. Yeah, she was anxious, but her feelings about her baby went deeper than that. It was her soul speaking.

Her soul was also telling her to face this alone. Because if she was denied her wish for a child and stopped herself from falling apart, she knew she could deal with pretty much anything.

Even Cody leaving her life.

Ten

Since Kinga sent him a text message telling him that Tinsley had a doctor's appointment this morning, Cody realized that nothing he'd said to Tinsley had registered.

Zip. Zero. Nada.

Cody looked at his watch as he approached the waiting room. He was eight minutes late for the appointment. That would do, he thought. He hadn't wanted to ambush Tinsley in the waiting room, wanting to avoid a public argument.

I'm perfectly capable of doing this on my own.

You don't need to be here.

He frowned. At some point, she needed to understand that he *wanted* to be in her life, sharing the good and bad moments, the circumstances that made them smile, others that made them weep. They were better together and the sooner she wrapped her head around that concept, the sooner they could move the hell on.

He wanted her in his bed, his hands on her body, watching their baby grow. And if she had any ideas about them living apart, well, he'd quickly disabuse her of those notions. They could live in his place—it was bigger—or in hers, but if neither option suited, they'd buy a damn house where they'd have room for a growing family.

This was only baby number one, and he intended to have a whole bunch more with that stubborn, infuriating, annoying woman.

The woman he couldn't live without.

Cody banged his hand against the door, walked into the reception room and up to the counter. He explained who he was, was directed where to go and a few minutes later he knocked on a door. A gowned technician opened the door and he introduced himself before looking past her to Tinsley, sitting up on the hospital bed, her eyes wide with surprise.

An *I'm so busted* look crossed her face.

"What are you doing here?" she squeaked, flustered.

He nodded to the nurse before speaking.

"I wanted to be here for the first scan. That isn't unusual, is it?" He kept his voice bland. During the long conversation they'd soon have, he'd explain that this was *their* kid, that he was in for the long haul and that she couldn't shut him out, not anymore.

Not with anything.

The technician told him where to stand, on the other side of Tinsley, where he had a good view of the screen. The technician pulled down Tinsley's pants and lifted her shirt, showing them her still mostly flat stomach.

"I'm going to put jelly on your tummy—it will be cold," the tech told Tinsley, smiling. She squirted a gel onto Tinsley's stomach, picked up an instrument and fiddled with the machine's keyboard. In seconds, a black-and-white image appeared on the screen.

He had no freaking idea what he was looking at.

The technician moved the probe over Tinsley's stomach and he watched her tense, saw the way her lips pinched. He wasn't the most perceptive guy in the world, but he felt the steady increase of tension in the room, a cool blanket of dread.

Tinsley lifted her hand to touch his chest but kept her eyes on the technician's face. "I think you need to call the doctor now," Tinsley told her, in a calm voice.

"What's going on?" Cody demanded as the door shut behind the technician.

Tinsley tipped her head to the side and sent him a small smile. "I'm glad you're here, Cody. I thought I wanted to be alone, but I don't. Not right now."

They could get into all that later because, right now, he wanted to know what the hell was going on. "Why is she calling the doctor?"

Tinsley's hand moved from his chest to his hand. She linked her fingers with his and tipped her head up to look at the ceiling.

"You're pretty much the only person I could imagine being here, right now. Even though your eyes are sparking with irritation, and impatience is radiating out of every pore, you calm me. It's the weirdest thing."

Cody looked down at her. "Can we discuss this later? Where the hell is the doctor?"

The door opened and Cody turned to see a petite Asian woman walking into the room, followed by the ultrasound technician. The doctor greeted Tinsley, introduced herself to him and then stood in front of the machine, exuding calm capability.

She put more gel on Tinsley's stomach, told the tech

to hit the lights and pushed the probe into Tinsley's skin, her actions speaking of competency and practice. After a few minutes of moving the probe and tapping away at the keyboard, she ordered the lights to be switched back on. Then she looked at Tinsley, sympathy in her dark brown eyes.

"I think what you have is an anembryonic pregnancy, more commonly known as a blighted ovum, Tinsley."

Tinsley nodded. Cody released a sharp puff of air and slapped his hands on his hips. "What does that mean?"

Sympathetic eyes met his. "We expect to see certain things in a scan, but I see nothing. There's just an empty sac. There's no yolk sac, no fetal pole and no heartbeat. There's fluid in the sac, so I don't think the pregnancy ever implanted."

"I don't understand," Cody said, his hands flat on the bed. "Are you saying that there's a problem with the baby?"

"I'm saying that there never was a baby, Mr. Gallant."

Bullshit! What the hell was she talking about?

"I watched and listened to her hurl her guts out! The pregnancy tests all said she was pregnant. She's also been dead tired for the past few months."

The doctor nodded. "So, basically what happens is that the body thinks there is a pregnancy and it does everything it can to support the pregnancy it assumes has implanted. The HCG and progesterone levels rise, trying to get the baby to grow. When it doesn't, the hormones up their production, leading to ever-worsening pregnancy symptoms. At some point, probably sometime very soon, Tinsley's brain will get the message that there isn't a baby and she will, in essence, miscarry."

"I'll miscarry a baby that wasn't there," Tinsley said, sounding very far away.

"You sound very calm, Tinsley. Are you okay?"

Tinsley looked at the doctor and nodded. "I thought it was my anxiety playing tricks on me, but I've known for a while that something was wrong. I didn't want to come in sooner because I didn't want you to confirm it."

So that was why she hadn't pushed him about his role in their lives, why they hadn't had any conversations about how they were going to raise this child together. She'd believed there was a problem but, true to form, didn't let him in on her suspicions. She'd kept it to herself, just like everything else.

Jesus, he couldn't live like this. He couldn't spend his life fighting to get closer, begging her to let him in.

"You can either wait for the miscarriage or I can give you something to stimulate it. Or we can do a small surgical procedure. I'll give you guys a moment to decide. When you are ready, join me."

He barely heard the doctor's words, dimly realizing that she'd left the room and the door closed behind her. He turned back to face Tinsley and watched her clean the gunk off her stomach with a paper towel, her movements calm and methodical.

When Tinsley looked at him, her eyes were clear but he noticed the churning maelstrom of pain threatening to overwhelm her. He stepped forward to hold her because, God, he needed the emotional connection, but she held her hand up to keep him at a distance.

She pulled in a deep breath, her shoulders lifted and stayed around her ears. "Well, guess that's that."

What the hell did that mean?

Tinsley pulled down her shirt and swung her feet off the bed, her face marble white in the bright light of the clinical room.

Cody gripped the edge of the bed. Jesus Christ. His

baby was gone. He felt shocked and blindsided, since he'd never, not once, thought that anything would go wrong. Tinsley, obviously, had, but she'd never once hinted at that possibility.

"Why didn't you talk to me about your suspicions about there being something wrong with the baby?" he demanded, his voice tight and cold. He couldn't remember when last he'd felt this angry.

"What could you have done?"

"Forced you to see a doctor earlier. Maybe, if you didn't have this go-alone attitude, there might have been something the doctors could've done."

Tinsley's eyes widened in her pale face. "That's not fair, Cody."

"No, what's not fair is you treating this entire situation like I'm of no importance, that my opinion doesn't matter, that I'm not worthy of you sharing your innermost thoughts and worries! I asked you, time and again, to see someone."

God, she went through weeks of hell for nothing. If they'd known sooner, she could've been spared all the vomiting and the tiredness and the headaches.

The thought made him want to punch a wall.

"I'm not sure what to say to you right now, Cody," Tinsley said, looking like she was about to break into a million pieces. He knew she was trying to hold her breaking pieces together, but he was hurting too.

She pushed her shaking hand through her hair. "Look, I might've suspected that something was wrong, but I didn't *know*. I thought it was my anxiety, me overreacting. I should've told you—you're right about that. But I have just heard that I'm not pregnant so can we postpone this fight? And the doctor is waiting for us."

Us? There was no us. There never had been. Not really. Cody shook his head, desolate at the idea of losing the baby he hadn't thought he wanted, angry at himself for losing his cool with Tinsley, devastated because he knew they could never be together. If she couldn't share this with him, a profound event that linked them together, what hope did they have of creating anything meaningful and long-lasting in the future?

It was impossible. *They* were impossible.

He might as well call it. Whatever they had was over.

He shook his head. "You go and talk to her. As you said, it's your body, your decision."

"You're not going to come with me?"

"I wasn't supposed to be here in the first place, remember? I had to get a text message from your sister." He shrugged before picking up his jacket and slinging it over his arm. "You knew that losing the baby was a possibility and you obviously thought you could handle this on your own. So handle it, Tinsley. Because being on your own is what you do best, right?"

Without looking at her, Cody walked to the door and yanked it open. His throat felt tight and his brain felt too big for his head. His heart was threatening to jump out of his chest. He needed fresh air, a drink.

To cry.

He never bloody cried, but this time, he thought he just might.

A few days later, in her parent's living room in their private wing of Callum's house, Tinsley sat on the seat in the bay window and stared at the churning waters beyond Dead Man's Cove.

She recalled spending winter days in this exact position, her attention alternating between her book and the awesome views. Though to be honest, every room in Callum's house had an awesome view, even her child-hood bedroom.

Tinsley looked up as Kinga approached, carrying what Tinsley hoped was a cup of hot chocolate. Her sister had been there when she woke up from the anesthetic after her small procedure, telling her their parents were in the waiting room. When she was discharged, nobody asked her whether she wanted to go home. They just bundled her into a limousine and took her back to her childhood home, where, her mom told her, they could keep an eye on her.

Why, she had no idea. It was a quick, uncomplicated operation. She would be tender today and much better tomorrow. Right as rain the day after that.

Or as right as she could be without a baby or Cody in her life.

Tinsley squeezed her eyes closed, trying to push the pain away, opening them when Kinga nudged her knee. She looked up to see her sister carrying their favorite mugs from their childhood and smiled. Kinga had returned from Monaco and had taken time off work to be with her and she so appreciated her sister's presence. Jules, who was working in Cancun, had sent her a dozen text messages and they'd arranged to video call later. Her parents, she had no doubt, were in the kitchen, wanting to give the sisters some time alone.

"Scoot up," Kinga told her. Tinsley did as she was told and shifted to make space for Kinga on the window seat. Kinga handed Tinsley her cup—buttercup yellow—and with her free hand, pulled up the white cashmere blanket.

"How are you doing, sister?"

Tinsley stared down at her hot chocolate and sipped. Kinga, bless her, had laced it with whiskey and she started to push it away, thinking it was bad for the baby. Then she remembered and her eyes filled. Laying her head on Kinga's shoulder, she kept her eyes on the bay, thinking that she was like that water, churning and messy, unable to stop herself from smacking against the rocks at the bottom of the cliff.

"I'm okay, physically. I'm sore but it's nothing serious."

"And emotionally?" Kinga asked her.

"I'm gutted," Tinsley admitted.

"The next time I see Gallant I am going to dismember him with a rusty, blunt knife," Kinga said, her voice a low growl.

Tinsley shook her head. "It's not his fault, Kinga. I should've told him I was worried about the baby, should've told him I had an appointment with the doctor. I should've let him in, let him help, let him be there for me. I made this bed. I have to lie in it."

She didn't blame Cody for being angry; she really didn't. She'd done everything she could to push him away, consistently telling him that she was happy to ride this rollercoaster alone. She couldn't blame him for doing as she asked.

But God, she missed him. Missed his strong arms and reassuring voice, the way his eyes crinkled when he smiled and turned that deep, dark green when he was aroused. It had been nearly a week since he stormed out of the doctor's practice and she hadn't heard or seen him since. She missed him, intensely, overwhelmingly.

With Cody, she could be herself: messy, emotional, *imperfect*.

God, she'd so liked the person she was with him and she adored him. Simply loved him as she'd never loved anyone before. He was a functioning adult, someone she didn't need to look after or take care of. When they were together, she felt like she had a partner. Someone she could rely on, someone who would never let her down.

Kinga put her hand on Tinsley's knee and Tinsley saw the flash of light in her kick-ass engagement ring. "Where's Griff today?"

"He told me I needed to be with you and that he was going to spend the day working on his new album," Kinga told her. "I'm so sorry it didn't work out between you and Cody, Tins, since I believe he's the right Gallant brother for you."

Tinsley wrinkled her nose. "Jeez, can you imagine what the Portland gossips would say if they heard I'd moved on to another Gallant?"

"JT lives in Hong Kong and even if he did live in the States, he and Cody are not close so I don't see you spending Christmas and Thanksgiving with the man. And who the hell cares what the gossips say?" Kinga demanded. "Let them talk! It's your happiness I'm most concerned about."

Her sister would always be in her corner, prepared to wade into the ring to fight her battles. She so appreciated her unconditional love. Tinsley heard footsteps and saw her parents walking toward them, identical worried frowns on their faces.

Her mom stopped and put a hand on her heart. "I have a dozen memories of the two of you, sitting just like you are."

Kinga gestured to the view. "It's a pretty special place."

Tinsley watched as her dad pulled over a chair for her mom to sit, choosing to lean his shoulder into the wall. She sipped her hot chocolate, feeling the burn of whiskey, and rested the back of her head on the cool pane of glass. "I'm sorry I didn't tell you about the pregnancy."

"Why didn't you?" her mom asked, hurt in her eyes.

Tinsley scratched the back of her neck. "I thought I would wait until I had the scan. I wasn't sure why I felt the need to keep it a secret, but I think, subconsciously, I knew something was wrong."

"As long as you didn't think we would castigate you for an unplanned pregnancy," James said.

"I never thought you would reprimand me since I am an adult, but I did think you'd be disappointed," Tinsley admitted.

"Nothing you do can ever disappoint us, darling."

Tinsley looked at her mom and lifted her eyebrows. "Mom, come on. That's a bit rich. You know that, from the time we were little, you had very high expectations for us," Tinsley snapped, wincing at her overly emotional response.

Her parents exchanged puzzled glances. "What are you talking about?"

She thought about holding back, about standing down and then remembered that was why Cody had walked, because she refused to talk, to let people in. Maybe this was a good time to start opening up. "We had to excel academically, be neat and tidy, be organized and polite."

Kinga looked at her as if she'd grown green scales. "No, we didn't." When Tinsley frowned at her, she shrugged. "Tins, they gave us a hard time if we didn't work hard, but they never demanded we be exceptional."

A frown pulled Penelope's perfectly arched eyebrows together. "You're confusing us with your grandfather. I remember your father and I telling you to *stop* working so hard, to give yourself a break, to have some fun."

"That's true. You were pain-in-the-ass driven," Kinga

commented, taking Tinsley's cup from her shaking hand and handing it to her father.

Tinsley frowned. It was as if a curtain had been pulled on her memories and what she thought was true was an indistinct collage of thoughts, emotions and pictures that now didn't make any sense.

Tinsley pulled up her knees and wrapped her arms around her legs. She looked at her dad. "I have a memory of hiding under the desk in Callum's study and you two came in. You argued about Callum's will and Callum said we had to be perfect, or you would bear the consequences. What did he mean by that?"

James looked gutted. "Jesus, I didn't know you were there."

"Yeah, that's obvious," Kinga stated. "It's a conversation that Tins remembers clearly from a long time ago, so it impacted her. What were you talking about, Dad?"

James looked past their heads, his gaze on the open water beyond the point. Penelope stared at the floor, her hands gripping the arms of her chair. Enough of this, Tinsley thought. Moving past her sister, she dropped her feet onto the floor and stood up, feeling the twinge in her abdomen. She placed her hand on her stomach and winced. Right, no quick movements.

"Mom, Dad...this has to end! What is going on with you two?" Tinsley demanded. When neither of them looked at her, she carried on speaking. "You two have been jumpy since Christmas and we're over it."

"Leave it alone, Tinsley," Penelope begged.

She was about to agree but then she shook her head. "No, I'm not going to leave it alone. If I felt secure enough to come out from under that desk and ask you what you were talking about, I wouldn't have spent the past twenty-plus years trying to be perfect, to not rock the boat. I've been anxious all my life and I think some of that could've been avoided if we'd communicated more. There's so much family history that's been ignored. We have too many secrets. We need to talk about them..." Tinsley insisted. "I think it's time we started being up-front, direct."

Like Cody.

A person always knew where they stood with Cody and, up until this moment, Tinsley never realized how much she'd appreciated his blunt honesty.

Tinsley felt Kinga behind her and when her sister's arm came to rest around her waist, she leaned into her strength. "Tinsley's right. What is going on and what don't we know?"

There was another long exchange of looks between James and Penelope, and a silent conversation. Wow, they might not be affectionate or lovey-dovey, but they did possess the skill of speaking to each other without using words. Was that something you learned after being married for more than thirty-five years?

James walked over to Penelope and put his hand on her shoulder. He looked at Tinsley, his expression regretful. "I am so sorry you felt pressured to be perfect. That was never our intention. And yes, we have been acting strange—it's been a strange time. Your mother and I need to talk, to be honest with each other. Maybe then we'll tell you what we can."

That wasn't good enough. They needed to know everything now. "Dad, enough with the secrets. They aren't doing anybody any good. Let's get everything out in the open—"

Tinsley frowned when three phones beeped with message alerts. Hers was in her back pocket and still switched off. Her parents and Kinga all reached for their phones and she saw identical expressions of disbelief and horror on their faces. Oh, God, something had happened. Something bad.

Kinga handed Tinsley her phone and Kinga read the message. It was from Cody.

Callum collapsed in his office about a half hour ago. He's been taken by ambulance to the Maine Medical Center. They suspect a heart attack, possibly accompanied by a mild stroke. I'm heading there now, suggest you do the same.

Callum? It wasn't possible.

But, since her dad was calling for a driver, her sister was calling Griff and her mom was gathering their coats, it seemed the impossible had happened.

James, followed by Penelope, rushed into the foyer of the hospital and headed for the front desk. His heart was about to jump out of his chest and a headache threatened to blow his head apart. He reached back and took Penelope's hand in his. His wife might not be the great love of his life but for the past three decades and more, she'd been his rock, his anchor, his best friend.

He needed her now. His father was irascible and difficult, hard and uncompromising, but he was still his dad.

James heard his name. He whirled around to see Cody striding toward them, a worried expression on his face.

James rushed to meet him, feeling overwhelmed. So much had happened recently—Callum's machinations, Kinga getting engaged, Tinsley losing her and Cody's baby, Callum collapsing—and he felt close to breaking.

Something had to change, he decided. He couldn't live like this anymore.

Cody gripped his hand and gave Penelope a quick hug. Pulling back, he folded his arms across his chest. "They're prepping Callum for surgery. They want to do a triple bypass and they want to do it quickly."

"But?" Penelope asked, frowning.

"But Callum is being obstreperous. He refuses to consent to the operation until he's spoken to you, James."

James swore and shoved his hand through his hair. "Really? What can be so important that he's delaying a lifesaving operation?"

"It has to be something to do with Ryder International. Nothing else is that important to him," Penelope muttered. "Stubborn old bastard."

James agreed. His father was a piece of work. "Where is he?" he asked Cody.

Cody gave him directions to where Callum was waiting. "Callum said to send you, James, and no one else," Cody said, sounding sympathetic.

Penelope's smile was bitter. She took a half step back and gestured for him to leave. "You'd better get to it, James."

James nodded before dropping a quick kiss on her cheek. "Wait for me. I shouldn't be long." He looked at Cody and frowned. "And you and I, Gallant, need to talk."

Cody looked like James had pushed him against an electric fence. "I don't think…uh… I'm pretty busy at the moment."

James sent him a hard stare, the one he borrowed from Callum on rare occasions when he wanted to get his point across. "That wasn't a suggestion, Gallant."

James walked away from his wife and the man he hoped might eventually become his son-in-law. He'd always had his reservations about JT, but Cody was a man who could handle the strong-willed and independent Tinsley. They would, if they managed to push their pride aside, have a happy life together.

As James made his way to his father, he thought about his daughters. They were, in all ways that counted, independent. They had men in their lives who loved them. Cody wasn't going anywhere; of that, James was certain. And, thanks to the trust funds he'd set up for them, they were financially independent of both their men and Ryder International. They were educated and hardworking. If everything fell apart, they would easily find work in another company. Hell, they could set up their own PR firm.

He was still tangled up with Ryder International. His fortunes still lay with the company, under his father's control. He stopped briefly, hesitating. How true was that statement, really? Was he as dependent on his father as he believed? He'd earned a spectacular salary from Ryder International but he'd also bought and sold property all his adult life, making a tidy profit along the way.

If he separated himself from Callum, he might lose the use of the private jets, the apartments in New York and Paris. They'd have to move into one of their many properties or buy another house, but they had more than enough money to do that without even feeling even the hint of a pinch.

Penelope had money from her parents, tens of millions that had not, as far as he knew, been touched. If they stayed together—and he thought they should—they'd be fine. In fact, they'd be free.

There's so much family history that's been ignored. We need to talk about it...

Tinsley was right.

He needed to get his integrity back, to find his spine,

to stand up for what was right. His actions might infuriate Callum and might lead to James being excommunicated and disinherited—and his daughters not being acknowledged as the Ryder-White heirs. But, really, was that the worst thing?

He knew what their answer to that question would be: *Hell, no.* Neither of them wanted to run the empire; they'd told him that on more than one occasion, and if Callum disinherited them, he didn't think they'd much care.

His lovely daughters respected truth and openness and honesty, and he knew their respect for him would rise exponentially if he confronted the truth.

Callum wouldn't appreciate it, but he remembered how good he'd felt standing up to his father as a young adult. He'd known that defending his uncle Ben would result in blowback, but he'd done it anyway because it had been the *right* thing to do.

He'd had more courage in his twenties than he'd had in the last thirty years combined. And he was done with being scared of his father, of his power and of what punishment he could inflict.

It was time to do what was right…

James walked onto the patient floor and was immediately accosted by a stern-looking nurse, who grabbed his elbow and marched him down a corridor. "Your father is the most stubborn, ornery man I've ever met."

Welcome to my world. "He is."

The nurse nodded to a room and told him he had five minutes. James thanked her and slipped into the dark space, his eyes immediately going to the frail figure in the bed. James approached, thinking Callum looked smaller and older. He stood next to the bed and looked down and cleared his throat.

"You wanted to see me, Callum?"

Callum didn't turn his head to look at him. "You took your sweet time getting here. They are waiting to save my life, you know."

If he could've sprouted wings and flown, he wouldn't have been able to get here quicker, and Callum knew it. "We don't have much time and they need to start working on you," James said, keeping his voice even.

Callum sighed, coughed and winced, obviously in a great deal of pain. Maybe he'd called James here to apologize for his past actions, for treating him like a servant, for being such a bastard. Maybe this attack was a wake-up call and in the last few years of Callum's life, he could have a relationship with his father...

Callum turned his head and James stepped back at the intensity that blazed within his eyes. "I'm going to be out of commission for a few months. The doctors have already told me that I won't be back for at least six weeks, probably more."

James nodded. "That's okay. I'll look after the business for you."

Callum released a half laugh, half growl. "The hell you will. You don't have the balls to run Ryder International. No, I need you to find an experienced CEO, someone who takes no crap, someone who can make the hard decisions." He lifted his hand and pointed a bony finger somewhere in the direction of James's face. "That's not you, boyo."

Of course it wasn't. What had he been thinking?

"And keep working on finding out who owns my useless brother's shares, I will not tolerate any more excuses in that regard." Callum muttered, his energy and voice fading. "And get on to that DNA ancestry company and find out why we still don't have the results of those tests."

Shares and DNA tests? That was what he was worried about right now? Seriously, his father's priorities were screwed.

"Yeah, Callum, whatever," he told him.

"Promise you'll appoint a good CEO, James," Callum said, his voice a harsh whisper.

James met his father's eyes and nodded. Oh yeah, he'd appoint a kick-ass CEO. And, in the process, he'd kick over a hornet's nest.

He couldn't wait.

Eleven

The last time Penelope met with her private investigator had been in a trucker's diner in a less salubrious part of town. To hell with that now. If anyone she knew wanted to ask why she was meeting with a PI, they could damn well ask her to her face.

And she'd tell them to mind their own business.

She was over giving people explanations on subjects that didn't concern them.

In her favorite coffee shop, Penelope leaned back in the elegant chair, crossed her legs and wished she could light up a cigarette. Ben had taught her to smoke thirty-five years ago, and how to hand-roll her cigarettes. She wondered if she could still do it.

Back when she first met him, she thought him to be a really sweet guy, oh-so-charming and considerate. The exact opposite of his hard-as-nails, ambitious brother and so very much like her husband.

But she'd been young and people were rarely so one dimensional.

A waiter deposited her espresso in front of her and she nodded her thanks. Callum had come through his triple bypass but, a week on, there were complications and he was still in the intensive care unit. He was, according to James, conscious but weak and didn't have the energy to talk.

Penelope sighed. Callum was a difficult man and not easy to love. And he'd always made their lives more complicated than they needed to be…

But had he? Years before she married James, she'd chosen to sleep with her baby's father. She'd thought that she couldn't possibly fall pregnant, that bad things didn't happen to nice girls like her.

After she left the country for six months and gave birth in London, she returned to the East Coast and met James. Both Callum and her parents pushed them to marry and when James proposed, she agreed, despite knowing there was a close connection between him and the father of the baby she'd just given up for adoption. She'd kept secrets and she'd made choices and not everything could be blamed on Callum.

James had made his move, and Penelope still wasn't sure whether he'd chosen the right person to run Ryder International. But it was James's decision and she respected him for taking action. In fact, she'd never respected her husband more. And with respect came renewed attraction, something else that surprised her.

Her decisive, clear-eyed, determined husband turned her on…

"Good morning, ma'am."

Penelope's head shot up and encountered the lovely face of the PI she'd hired. Instead of the battered jeans and hoodie she'd worn previously, KJ Holden looked like a young professional dressed in a gray-and-white houndstooth suit and with her long hair pulled back into a soft roll.

"You clean up well," Penelope commented, gesturing for her to take a seat.

KJ flashed a wide smile and sat down. "Different situations call for different clothing. I'm going to pull on my homeless-lady outfit later for a stakeout," KJ cheerfully told her.

Penelope shuddered. "Isn't that dangerous?"

"Not as dangerous as dressing up as a prostitute," KJ told her on an easy grin. "There are some weird people out there."

She could imagine.

KJ thanked the waitress for the coffee she received—she must've ordered it on her way in—and lifted the cup to take a sip. "So, I presume you want an update." KJ leaned forward and dropped her voice so she couldn't be overheard by people at the adjacent tables. "I contacted the agency you used to facilitate the adoption of your son and they stonewalled me. They refused, as I expected, to give me any information and nothing I did or said moved them."

Penelope looked at her, surprised at the intense disappointment she felt. She'd known this would happen, as she'd made a direct appeal to the adoption agency a few weeks ago and had the exact same response. Why did she think a PI making inquiries would sway them?

Penelope rubbed her smooth forehead with the tips of her fingers, feeling let down and saddened. Had she really believed KJ could perform miracles? Was she that gullible?

It had only been three weeks since she'd first met

with KJ and sent her on a mission to find her biological son. Had she conned herself into thinking that the young PI could succeed where Penelope failed?

KJ was working for a paycheck, thinking that she was trying to reunite a mother and her lost child. She had no idea that Penelope was trying to keep her reputation intact.

KJ didn't know, and Penelope would never tell her that the boy she was looking for, who was now a grown man of thirty-five, had the ability to upend her life. He held the power to expose her secrets, to make her family look at her differently for her youthful actions.

Him coming back into her life would make her husband and her daughters question her honesty and her judgement. Her daughters were independent, gutsy women with a strong moral code and she couldn't bear them looking at her with questions in their eyes, disdain on their faces.

And James! Despite thirty-plus years of marriage, James would feel gutted on hearing that she'd given birth to *someone else's* child…

That she'd kept this from him for so very long.

Her son's presence would also upend Ryder International… Of that she had no doubt.

"Have you made any progress at all? Do you have anything new you can tell me?"

KJ looked down at her notes. "I did manage to track down your case worker at the time. She's in her seventies now but she remembered you well. Apparently, you were what she called 'a complicated case.'"

That didn't surprise her in the least. "What did she have to say?"

"That you weren't the only person to contact them wanting to discover the child's real identity."

What? Really?

"Tell me more," Penelope demanded.

"There isn't that much more to tell and trust me, it took me about three hours to pry this much information from the retired case worker."

Penelope didn't bother asking her name, she didn't remember anyone from that agency and knew KJ wouldn't tell her anyway.

"Tell me everything she said," Penelope said, through gritted teeth.

KJ's calm expression didn't change. "She made it clear she would not tell me who adopted him or who he was now. She did say that she had a meeting with the boy and his parents when he was eighteen and that he was given the letter you wrote to him, informing him of his parentage. He wasn't in the least interested in opening that letter. The caseworker remembers him as a brooding, intense child.

"He has your name, Mrs. Ryder-White, and it's up to him to contact you. That's the only way you will discover his identity."

Penelope slapped her hand down on the table, making the coffee cups shake. "You implied that someone else inquired about his identity. Who?"

KJ wrinkled her nose. "Not a who, but a what. A couple of years after the adoption, an exchange of letters took place between the agency and a law firm, and they concerned the child."

"What are you talking about?" she demanded, her voice rising.

KJ gripped her right hand and squeezed. Penelope tried to pull her hand out of her grip, but the younger woman was stronger than she looked. "Ma'am, people are looking at you and I know that's not what you want. Take a breath!"

KJ's harsh words slapped her and Penelope's shoulders slumped as they penetrated. God, she was losing it, something she couldn't afford to do. This was all too complicated, too much to deal with.

"I'm sorry. Carry on."

"The case worker either had no knowledge of the contents of the letters or wouldn't tell me." KJ sighed, determination in her eyes. "I need to talk plainly, ma'am. The terms of the adoption were pretty simple, you never named the father and you gave the baby up. We can assume that the father of the child found out about the adoption, somewhere and somehow."

From her, dammit.

"But the supposed father had no legal recourse to find out the baby's identity or to overturn the adoption. Even his law firm, Gerard and Pinkler, were firmly rebutted."

Gerard and Pinkler...where had she heard that name before?

"I took the initiative to send the lawyers a letter, telling them that you'd hired me and asking whether they could provide me with any additional information."

Penelope leaned forward. "And? "

"I received a formal acknowledgement of the letter, nothing else."

Penelope slumped back in her seat. "So, we're at a dead end."

KJ nodded. "I think that's a fair statement. The ball is in your son's court, Mrs. Ryder-White. But whether he plays it or not, I cannot say."

Gerard and Pinkler...why couldn't she place that name?

She needed to do some investigating, think this

through. Something hovered at the back of her mind, misty and unsubstantial. Lifting her eyes to meet KJ's, she slowly nodded. "Let me know if the law firm contacts you again."

"Of course."

Sympathy flashed in the PI's eyes. "This must be so difficult for you, I'm so sorry."

She didn't need sympathy, she needed a resolution. To mitigate disaster or, at the very least, prepare herself for the fall out. Her world, and her family's, was going to be flipped on its head. And all because she couldn't control her emotions.

If she had simply ignored him, walked away...but she hadn't and now she was paying for her youthful temper.

Penelope released a long sigh and knew the PI was watching her, trying to read her expressions. Would KJ think her strange if she told her that her sixth sense was screaming, that there was something in the air, something brewing? That she knew her life was about to take a one-eighty turn?

She didn't want anything to change because change was terrifying. But a small part of her wanted her son to acknowledge her. An even tinier part of her wanted to tell him, and the world, who his father was, to allow the truth to spill out and move the hell on. But circumstances had recently changed and she needed to look at all the angles again.

KJ spoke again. "If there is anything else, any other way I can help you, will you let me know?"

She wished there was, but Penelope knew they'd hit a stone wall. Trouble was coming and there was nothing she could do to dissolve or divert it. She just had to deal with it when it happened. And hoped she, and her family, came out unscathed.

The chances of that happening were slim.

"I'll contact you when the lawyers contact me," KJ told her.

When... Penelope appreciated her optimism, but knew they wouldn't reach out. All the power lay with her son and it was his choice to use it or not.

All she could do was wait. And worry.

None of the Ryder-White family—except for Callum, who was still in the hospital—were happy with him, Cody decided later that day. He'd been avoiding James, refusing to talk to Kinga and Jules and ducking calls from Penelope. They'd all made it clear they wished to discuss Tinsley's broken heart. He didn't believe her heart was broken.

His, on the other hand, was close to snapping.

He'd never felt so—damn, this was difficult to admit—*lost* in his life. And he couldn't understand why. His life was mostly back to the way it had been before their encounter on New Year's Eve.

Encounter?

That was one way to put it. Another would be to call that night the six hours that rocked his world and changed his life.

Cody, still in his suit, stood by the huge bi-fold doors that separated his living room from the balcony and looked out onto the dark, clear night. He held a glass of whiskey in his hand, but he'd drunk little of it. Mostly because he thought that if he started, he might not stop.

Two weeks had passed since he'd last seen her and not having Tinsley in his life was becoming more difficult to deal with, not easier. In this case, time wasn't his friend. With every day that passed, the realization that their split might be permanent, that she genuinely didn't want to be with him, seemed to sink a little deeper into his psyche.

Cody felt himself shutting down, like he had when his mom died, remembering how desperate he felt as he came to realize his father wasn't going to step up to the plate and be the dad he needed. That he was alone and responsible for his genius brother.

God, he no longer wanted to feel alone.

He wanted to be with Tinsley, to create the family with her he'd only recently realized he wanted.

Cody heard his front door open, frowned and cocked his head to the side. He heard the sound of a bag hitting the floor and the door slamming closed. He had a baseball bat in the hallway closet, but that wouldn't help him now; he was too far away. His eyes darted around the room, looking for a weapon, and he stealthily walked across the room to pick up an exceptionally heavy glass vase.

"Are you going to brain me with that?"

He heard her voice and couldn't understand why Tinsley was standing at the entrance to his sitting room, dressed in tight jeans, those knee-high boots he loved and a short, bright berry-colored sweater worn under a leather jacket. What the hell was she doing here?

He took in her pink nose, her tousled hair and her always lovely face. She looked so much better than she had when he'd last seen her at the doctor's office, a lifetime ago. She looked vibrant, gorgeous, alive...damn near perfect.

And she was here, in his friggin' apartment!

"Can you put that vase down, Cody?"

Cody frowned and realized he was holding the vase above his head. He lowered the vase, replaced it on the mantel and, with his back to her, gathered his thoughts.

Why was she here? What did she want? And why did she have her favorite overnight bag?

"If you've come for a quick bang, you can walk right on out," he muttered, his voice sharp. He whirled around and glared at her. "And how the hell did you get in here? I never authorized my private elevator to let you up."

"I know the codes to both the elevator and the front door, Cody," Tinsley softly replied, jamming her hands in the back pockets of her jeans. "You gave them to me."

"And that just shows you how stupid I can be!"

Tinsley gestured to the sofa. "Can I come in and sit down or do you want me to leave?"

Cody hauled in a deep breath, thought of telling her to leave and then waved in the direction of the couch. "Sit. Do you want something to drink?"

"A glass of red wine would be nice."

Cody started to tell her that she couldn't have wine, and then snapped his jaw closed so hard he was sure he cracked a tooth. She wasn't pregnant, he reminded himself. She could drink wine, eat shellfish, go scuba diving if she wanted to.

He'd finally embraced the idea of being a dad, only to have it ripped away from him. It hurt...but not as much as it did to lose Tinsley.

Swallowing hard, Cody met her eyes and saw understanding there, the flash of deep sadness. She handed him a tiny shrug and released a wobbly sigh.

Needing to do something with his hands, Cody walked into his kitchen, opened his wine cabinet and pulled out the first bottle of red he saw. He found a corkscrew, pulled the cork and dashed the liquid into a wineglass. With jerky steps, and his ears up around his shoulders, he walked back to her, shoving the glass into her hand.

"Why are you here, Tinsley? It can't be for business as we've been exchanging oh-so-polite emails for the past few weeks."

Tinsley placed her wineglass on the coffee table, its contents untouched. She crossed her legs and linked her hands around her knees and Cody remembered how she'd remove her boots and tuck her feet up under her butt. But this wasn't a social call.

He had no idea what it was…

Before he could ask again, Tinsley leaned forward and clasped her hands, holding them between her knees. "As you've told me, on more than one occasion, I have control issues," Tinsley said, her eyes clashing with his. Without dropping his gaze, he sat down in the chair opposite her, arms on his bouncing knees.

"I've only just figured out why I need to be perfect, why it's so important to me," Tinsley admitted.

He cocked his head, silently asking her to explain.

"When I was very young, eight or so, I overheard a conversation between Callum and my dad. I've only just accepted what impact Callum's comment had on my life. He'd told my dad that Kinga and I needed to be perfect or else my dad would suffer. And that seeded my need for perfection. I'm controlling because I never think I am good enough, perfect enough."

He wanted to protest, to reassure her, but something in her face, deep in her eyes, had him holding back his words. She needed to get this out, he realized, and he needed to let her.

"Being controlling is like a quick hit, a fast high. At the moment, I feel reassured and strong, but it never lasts. It quickly fades and the anxiety returns. I've realized that the need for complete control, the quest for perfection, is like chasing mist. Life is uncertain and there are no guarantees,"

She was right about that. Life didn't hand out guarantees. He'd thought his sick mom would recover and be fine, that his dad would assume responsibility for them, but he'd been wrong on both counts.

"I stayed in a dead marriage because I thought that if I could make everything perfect, JT would love me. After the divorce, I micromanaged my life because I am so damn anxious about getting everything right," Tinsley continued, sounding sad. She looked at her hands, then at the floor.

"Underneath my quest for perfection is that eight-year-old me, flawed and looking for reassurance that I am enough, that I am loved. I thought that if I was a perfect little girl, Callum wouldn't punish my dad. I thought that if I made everything perfect for JT, he'd love me. I thought that if I was the perfect sister or friend or employee, I would be happy."

Oh, Tinsley, that was so much self-inflicted pressure.

Tinsley lifted her eyes and when all that deep blue met his gaze, Cody felt a fist in his solar plexus. "The thing is, around you, I never felt pressured to be anything other than the person I am, authentically me. With you, I felt—feel—like the best version of myself. Imperfect, so very imperfect, but *real*."

Her hand came out to take his and when their palms connected he felt love and warmth rush through him. He adored her, wanted her, loved her, but he also liked her. Really liked the funny, flawed person she was.

"I can be real with you. You demand it of me. I like who I am with you," Tinsley admitted. She pulled her bottom lip between her teeth and when she released it, he saw tiny tooth marks in the soft pink. He desperately wanted to kiss them away. "I was wrong not to tell you that I thought something was wrong with the baby, to try and go it alone. I should've told you about the doctor's appointment. I was so out of line and for that I apologize."

What else could he say but "Apology accepted"?

Tinsley's thumb brushed over his wrist and Cody felt heat skitter over his nerve endings. "I've missed you so much, Cody. Every day that we've been apart, I've wanted to be in your arms."

He couldn't allow himself to be swept away, to dream. Crashing back to reality hurt too damn much. "You just like the sex, Tins."

Tinsley shook her head. "No, I love the sex." She shrugged, her cheeks now a little pink. "I love the way you touch me, the way you kiss me... Being naked with you is so much fun."

"I can't have another fun-filled fling with you, Tinsley," Cody stated, his tone harsh. He reached for her wineglass and downed its contents, wondering where he was going to find the strength to let her go. But it was either everything or nothing...

"I agree," Tinsley quietly stated. "I don't want a fling either."

Cody rubbed his forehead with his fingertips. "I have no idea what point you are trying to make, Tins."

"I'm trying to tell you, very badly, that I'd like something more between us." When his head shot up and his eyes connected with hers, she quickly lifted her hands. "I'm not expecting you to agree, but I need to tell you that I think I'm in love with you, that you're the only guy who's ever got me, the one man I can see myself with for the rest of my life."

"What?"

Tinsley lurched to her feet, the color draining from her face. "Okay, obviously that thought horrifies you. Um…can you forget I said it? I really don't want to go back to sniping at you, Cody so could we, maybe, try to be friends?"

Friends? Definitely not. Not wanting to waste time by walking around the coffee table, Cody bounded across it, ignoring its protesting creak as it briefly held his weight. Reaching Tinsley, he grabbed her shoulders and bent his knees to look into her face.

"Are you proposing?" he demanded, joy flooding his system.

She wrinkled her nose. "Only if that's something you might be interested in. Not now… I mean, I know you're going to need some time to get used to the idea, to me—"

"Tins?"

"Yes?"

"Stop. Talking." To make sure she did as he asked, Cody put his finger to her lips. "Can I say something?" he asked.

She nodded, her eyes wide and purple blue.

"I love you. I am insanely, wonderfully, completely in love with you and I've been damn miserable without you. Yes, you are occasionally frustrating but then, so am I. But mostly you are wonderful and sweet and lovely and kind." He dropped a kiss on her nose, then her cheekbone. "Don't change, Tins. I love you just the way you are."

Tinsley pulled her head back to look at him, looking for something in his face or in his eyes. Holding her face in his hands, he kept his gaze steady and his voice calm. "I want to marry you, to live with you and work with you. I want to make babies with you."

"How many?" Tinsley asked, sounding bemused and a little wary. He couldn't blame her since pregnancy hadn't been a fun experience for her.

"We'll start with one and see how it goes," he said, smiling to remind her that he was teasing. "Two at least. And then we'll keep our options open."

Then he remembered that he'd have to watch her suffer. Nope, he didn't think he could do it.

"No, wait, that won't work!" he said, shaking his head.

Tinsley looked crushed. "You've changed your mind about having babies?"

"No, I just can't watch you go through hell again, Tins. Can't we use a surrogate or something?"

Tinsley's eyes turned brighter, and her bottom lip wobbled. "That's the sweetest thing—apart from you telling me that you love me—I've ever heard." She lifted her hand to touch his cheek. "But do you know what? I would walk through hell time and time again to carry your baby, our baby. There's nothing I can't do without you next to me."

Her words filled up all those empty, blank spaces in his soul, filling them with light and warmth. "Does that mean you love me a little?"

"No, Cody, it means I love you with everything I have. You are everything I want. Your love is all that I will ever need."

That was all he needed to know. With a heart brimming over with love for this amazing woman, he pulled her into him, so her breasts rested against his chest, his arms around her. He smiled down at her. "Fair warning, you are going to need more than an overnight bag, sweetheart."

Tinsley grinned up at him. "I know." She almost wiggled with excitement. "I need to call the movers, tell my parents we're engaged—we are engaged, right?—call Kinga. And Jules... There's so much to do, Cody!"

Cody smiled, dropped a quick kiss on her lips and tipped her up and over his shoulder. "You can make a mental list until we hit the bedroom. When we get there, the only thing on your mind will be me." He squeezed her butt. "That work for you?"

Her hands caressed his back and Cody shuddered in anticipation. "*You* work for me, Gallant. I can't wait to spend the rest of my life with you, Cody."

Cody, hearing the emotion in her voice, lowered her to the bed and kissed her, a hot, needy, openmouthed kiss, trying to show her how much he loved her. Tinsley moaned and returned his passion, tasting her love on his tongue, feeling it radiating from her skin.

Their one-night stand, Cody thought, was going to last the rest of the lives.

And that was the definition of perfection.

* * * * *

THE ONE FROM
THE WEDDING

KATHERINE GARBERA

To Courtney and Lucas.
I have always felt so lucky to be your mom and never
more so as I've seen the adults you've become.
Love you.

As always thanks to my girl gang, the Zombie
Belles-Eve, Nancy, Lenora, Janet and Denise. I feel so
blessed to have you in my life, and love that you always
have my back and know that I always have yours.

One

"I can't believe you told that magazine my start-up was just trying to ride your coattails."

It was a sunny Friday in June, the first big day of his maternal cousin Adler Osborn's televised Nantucket wedding weekend. Well, the first public day; Leo and his family had been on Nantucket for two days now. Two very eventful days, in which an explosive revelation involving Leo's father and the groom's mother had nearly derailed the entire wedding.

They'd all convened at today's golf scramble and were keeping up a brave front. But Leo's mom looked like she'd aged ten years overnight. His bubbly cousin, the bride-to-be, was forcing her smile and looked like she was ready to snap. He'd been hoping today's round of golf would be a relief from the pressure they'd all been under.

Seeing as how he'd been assigned to play with an upstart business competitor whom he'd dissed in an interview not more than a month ago, he guessed that wasn't going to be the case. He knew that Adler had commissioned Danni Eldridge to make the bridesmaids' jewelry instead of him because they were friends from school. But Adler had then asked Leo to supply the grooms' gifts. His line of handcrafted leather goods fit the bill perfectly.

He had no idea what Danni looked like before this moment. Her online accounts simply had her name and an old-fashioned Singer sewing machine logo for a profile picture. Seeing her now, he wouldn't say she was classically beautiful but something about her made him take notice. She was to be the fourth in their team for the scramble so he wanted to smooth things over.

Leo had never met someone he couldn't charm. He put his hand over his heart and gave the woman a humble look. "Please accept my most profound apology. Sometimes I get a little cranky when I'm bombarded with questions from journalists and just answer off the cuff. I never would have said it if we'd had the chance to meet before. Can we please start over?"

She watched him with dark brown eyes, and he had a feeling that his apology wasn't really soothing her ire. He didn't blame her at all. If someone had said that about his business, he'd never have forgiven them.

"I guess we should. Otherwise this foursome is going to be pretty awkward," she said with a genuine and sincere smile. "I'm Danni Eldridge. I'm at the wedding because I designed the bridesmaids' jewelry and Adler is a friend of mine."

"Leo Bisset. Adler's my cousin," he said, offering his hand. "Pleased to meet you."

They shook, and he couldn't help but notice how delicate her hand felt in his. Her nails were manicured but in a subtle shade. Not the latest trendy nail color that he'd seen all over his social feed from followers and influencers. Her perfume was subtle and reminded him of sunshine and days spent at the beach. She pulled her hand away and then turned to the golf cart where his brother and mom were waiting.

"So I'm going to be the only one in this group who doesn't know everyone," she said. "Tell me what I need to know."

"What do you want to know?" Leo asked. "My brother Logan is very competitive, but I'm slightly better than he is, and my mom is the nicest woman I know. She'll keep Logan in line if he acts up."

Danni smiled and shook her head. "Who's going to keep you in line?"

He winked at her. "No one can, unfortunately. But I'll try to be on my best behavior to make up for that horrible thing I said."

"You think that will work?" she asked.

"Not really, but I'm hoping you'll give me a break since you know I'm trying," he said. He'd found that honesty was always the best way to make up with anyone he'd offended. He had to admit this wasn't the first time he'd said something that had upset a woman he was attracted to. He wasn't really concerned about smaller businesses moving into the classic luxury lifestyle marketplace. He had always believed that a rising tide raised all ships, and he was captaining a big old fleet of luxury yachts, so he felt secure.

"Do you just do jewelry? I wonder why that journalist brought you up in the Q and A."

She shook her head. "I make nautical-themed bracelets and watchbands. Some people have said the quality and craftsmanship is on par with yours."

He doubted that. He had a crew of highly skilled workers who had been with him since the beginning. He'd always known he couldn't be the heir to the throne at Bisset Industries, an American multinational corporation involved in the manufacturing, refining and distribution of petroleum, chemicals, energy, minerals, fertilizers, pulp and paper, chemical technology equipment, ranching, finance, commodities trading and investing—that was going to his older brother Logan. So Leo had struck out and made his own way from the ground up. He'd taken the time to learn how to make the leather goods that he'd first sold at craft fairs and then in a thriving mail-order business that he'd grown from his online followers and now sold in a flagship store in the Hamptons. Leo had grown the company into a lifestyle brand that had gone global. He'd worked hard for everything he had, and while he appreciated that Danni thought her product was as nice as his, he doubted that she was hand-making every item. Many small crafters relied on imports and cheaply made designs.

"Are you wearing your product?" he asked, glancing down at her wrist and noticing the metal-and-grosgrain-ribbon bracelet that had a small *D* charm with an anchor wrapped around it.

"I am," she said, holding up her wrist.

He noticed how small and delicate her bones were, but then he looked more closely at the bracelet and saw how well-made it was. "May I?"

She unclasped it and handed it over to him. He had to admit that it was on par with if not better than some of the ones he carried in his store. But making one nice bracelet wasn't the same as manufacturing a large quantity of high-quality goods. He handed it back to her.

"I like it. I can only guess that I hadn't seen your product when I made my remark," he said. "Hopefully while we're playing, I can show you that I'm not the arrogant guy you must believe me to be."

"We'll see. I did hear you challenging your brother, and you sounded pretty arrogant."

"That's not fair. Logan was being...well, Logan," Leo said. "Do you have siblings?"

"Yes," she said. "An older brother and sister."

"Then you know what I mean. They can be very trying," he said.

She laughed. "I have to agree. It's just funny to think of Logan Bisset as a pesky older brother."

"Trust me, he is very...pesky," Leo said. "But I, on the other hand, am pretty charming."

"Pretty charming? I assume you're talking about me," Logan said as he rejoined them.

"Hardly," Leo said, turning to give his brother a wolfish smile before turning to Danni. "Shall we get the game started?"

"Yes," she said, walking toward the golf cart.

He watched her go, thinking, for the first time since he'd arrived on Nantucket, he was going to have an interesting time.

Danni had deliberately put her name in with Leo's for the golf scramble, but she was a bit surprised and intimidated to be playing with his mother and brother, as well. The Bisset family were pretty much American royalty, and for a small-town girl, being in their presence was a bit heady. But this was the world she aspired to and what she was aiming for in her own life. So, she tucked one of the curls that she'd tried to tame into submission in a low ponytail back behind her ear and lined up her shot.

The golf course was built near the beach, and most of the holes offered a view of the ocean. The sun was shining, and it was a perfect summer day. She knew that Adler had been worried about summer storms ruining the events she and Nick Williams had planned for their destination wedding. But Danni thought the elements were cooperating.

But apparently there were storm clouds gathering between the bride's and groom's families. Nick was the CEO of Williams, Inc. They were Bisset Industries' biggest competition, often going after the same contracts. The rivalry was pretty fierce and frequently made the headlines.

Danni had heard some rumblings at the golf clubhouse before everyone had arrived that there was some scandal brewing about the groom. Something about how August Bisset was actually Nick's father as a result of a secret affair with Cora Williams decades ago.

Had Danni even heard that right? While Adler wasn't related to her uncle by blood, the discovery that Nick was August's son had to put an incredible strain on the wedding couple. Danni hoped that whatever was going on, Nick and Adler could find their way through the crisis.

She teed up her first shot. Everything she knew about golf she'd learned from her dad at the golf course near their home. He was a big one for taking his time and using everything as a teachable moment. Danni had always been impatient, though, and now she was struggling to remember what he'd said. Swing from the hips? Keep her hips steady?

Mainly she just hoped she'd actually hit the ball and, fingers crossed, get it into the hole.

She took a deep breath and held it until she couldn't wait any longer. Then she drew back the club to swing... and missed. Ugh, she was so horrible at sports.

"Want some help?" Leo asked, coming up next to her. "I play regularly so I've gotten pretty good, but before that I was a mess."

She doubted he'd ever been a mess at anything but appreciated him pretending he had been.

"I'd love some tips. My dad said something about my hips—either swing through them or keep them steady... honestly, I can't remember, and the more I concentrate, the worse I'm getting," she admitted.

He smiled. "I know the feeling. Here's the thing— this is just for fun, so relax. I'm not a pro, but I keep my arms straight...like this," he said, moving behind her and adjusting her hands on the club. "When you swing, bring the club back straight and then turn your body in the direction you want the ball to go."

She was trying to concentrate, but honestly, he was wrapped around her like a big warm hug, and he smelled good. Like one of those luxury stores she and her mom had liked to duck into for a little pretend shopping when Danni was growing up and her parents were working for the public defender's office. She closed her eyes for a second, and it was almost like he was embracing her instead of showing her how to hit the golf ball.

"Got it?" he asked.

She smiled her thanks and then shook her head. She was here to collect intel on a competitor but also maybe pick up some advice, not start falling for his pretty blue eyes, athletic frame and grace. And he was being very generous and kind to her. He'd welcomed her as if they were old friends. Instead of reacting to her catty remark, he'd apologized…to be fair, she definitely thought he owed her one, but it had been sincere, and he'd been very nice since then.

"If I miss again, it's down to user error and nothing to do with your lesson," she said.

"You won't miss," he said. "I'm pretty sure this time you're going to connect and send that ball flying."

She wished she had his confidence.

Wait a second. She *should* have his confidence. It wouldn't hurt. She remembered her grandmother saying that if she thought she couldn't, then she wouldn't.

Danni widened her stance as she'd seen Leo do on his last putt and then set up her shot. She took a deep breath, and this time, instead of holding it, she kept breathing naturally as she swung. She hit the ball. She was so excited she turned to Leo with a squeal, not even looking where the ball went.

"I hit it!"

"You did. Good job," he said. "You'll be better than me in no time."

She tipped her head to the side. "Let's not get carried away. I think we all know that I'd have to spend most of the next few years on the course every day to get to your level. But I'll settle for at least getting the ball down the green and in the hole."

"I think you'll be able to do that," Leo said. "Are you this determined in every part of your life?"

"I am," she said. "Also, I'm ridiculously stubborn."

"I can see that. I also picked up a bit of temper. I mean, I thought you might hurt the ball if you didn't hit it."

She could see he was teasing her, and she liked it. He was funny, and that was unexpected. She wasn't sure what she'd thought Leo would be like in person. Arrogant and cocky—definitely. But beyond that, she hadn't considered that he'd be so…well, human. "I wouldn't have wanted to maim it."

He threw his head back and laughed, and for a minute Danni forgot she was trying to get business information from him and use him for his connections. She realized that she enjoyed being around him and wanted their time together to continue—something she knew would never happen. They came from two different worlds, and her brief foray into his was just that. Brief.

She needed to remember who she was and why she was here. Men like Leo didn't fall for women like her, and besides, she hadn't come here this weekend for romance. She was here for business.

Leo wasn't on his A game at all. He was a stroke off Logan at each hole and after he'd given Danni some pointers on her swing she was starting to play better. He needed to get his head in the game.

Danni was distracting him.

He finally pulled her aside while his mom and Logan were talking. He wanted to get past this awkwardness, which was totally his fault. Normally his mom would have been the diplomat who put everyone at ease but she was only half paying attention to their foursome and her own golf game.

"You're getting a lot better, but I can still sense some coldness between us. What can I do to make this right?" he asked.

Danni tipped her head to the side, studying him for a moment before narrowing her eyes. "Give me some business advice."

He was surprised by her answer. From what he'd read and heard, her business was growing quickly. "I'm not sure you need that."

"My dad always says the day you stop learning is the day you die," she quipped. "I could use a mentor."

"Uh."

"Never mind. I forgot I was talking to Leo Bisset. From Fortune Magazine's top 30 under 30."

He watched her as she turned and walked away. Was she serious? Of course she was. He'd sought out mentors and advice the same way when he'd first started out, only he'd had his father and Logan to watch and learn from.

"I see your charm isn't working, as usual," Logan said as he came over to Leo.

He elbowed his brother, intending to ignore him, but Logan dodged the elbow. "She doesn't want to be charmed."

"Oh, ho. So you're going to have to work harder to get her to like you," Logan said. "Not impossible. Even for you."

But Logan was needling him every time they were alone and rubbing in the fact that Leo couldn't get Danni interested in him. He wanted to be chill and act like it didn't matter, but there was a part of him—hell, most of him—that was always competing with Logan and, to a larger extent, their father. Both men had always been charming with everyone and had their pick of women. Even though their dad was married and should say no.

But that wasn't something Leo liked to dwell on. He wanted his father's approval, craved his praise more than he knew was healthy. But that didn't change the fact that he wanted it. He also wasn't a huge fan of the way his father had handled his relationship with Leo's mom over the years. He'd had affairs, which for the most part had been kept quiet—except for the one before Leo's sister, Marielle, was born. Until recently, he'd believed that his parents had worked out all their past troubles.

But the revelations about his father's past cheating, and how Nick Williams was really August Bisset's son, had been hard on their mom, and on the entire family. Imagine everyone's surprise when the mother of the groom turned out to be one of his father's former mistresses. Even worse, they'd had a child together who was about to marry into the Bisset family! It was surreal. The paparazzi were all over the place and gossips sites were hinting that wasn't the end of the story, but Leo hoped in his heart it was.

Logan hated Nick and vice versa, but as for Leo, he was just disappointed that his father, the man he so wanted to be like, was so flawed. It would be hard to ignore the very real possibility that he had those same flaws.

"So…what's the plan?" Logan asked, nodding toward Danni.

Leo glanced at his older brother. Logan looked more like their mom than their dad, with his blond hair and high cheekbones. They both had the same ice-blue eyes. Once Leo had left Bisset Industries to start his own business, they'd begun to get along a lot better. Leo knew it had been down to his constant need to try to beat Logan when they were both working for their father.

"I'm not sure yet," Leo said. He certainly wasn't going to discuss anything with Logan. Danni had asked for business tips and he could do that. That was one area where he didn't have to try hard.

"Sometimes you need a plan."

"I'm not you," Leo pointed out. "I do better when I go off script."

"Are you sure about that?"

Leo shot his brother the bird and then took his club to go and tee off. After they'd all taken their shots, he made sure he was next to Danni as they walked toward the hole.

"Were you serious about wanting me to mentor you?" he asked.

"Yes," she said. "But since we are each other's competition—"

"I don't think you're in my league," he said softly.

"Yet," she said, with a cheeky smile.

"Yet," he agreed. "I'll help you out this weekend. If you do me a favor."

She shrugged and turned to look out at the horizon and the ocean. He gave her the time she needed before she turned back to him, pushing her sunglasses up on her head. She looked so young and earnest, and he had the feeling that whatever she said next was really important to her. And he was scared for her. He'd never been as earnest as she appeared to be.

"What's the favor?"

"Be my 'date' for the weekend. My family is going through some stuff and I could use someone to hang out with away from all that."

"Should you do that? I mean we are talking about a business relationship," she said.

"It's just for the weekend and I've always thought that business isn't personal. It's about competing and winning and producing the best product."

"Okay," she said. But she sounded hesitant.

Which he decided he'd smooth over later.

Two

Danni went into the clubhouse and looked for her assigned table after the golf scramble. They were going to be announcing the winner, and Danni had a hunch that Logan might be it. He'd certainly been the best by one stroke in their group. He and his brother Leo had both played par on most holes and under on a couple.

He'd reluctantly agreed to mentor her in exchange for her being his date. That should assuage her conscience. She still felt a little guilty that she'd used this wedding invitation as a way to broaden her network and was planning to meet as many A-listers as she could to try to expand her business reach and discoverability.

But did she have to feel guilty with Leo? He'd said that business wasn't personal to him. She shook her head and then stopped herself from going down a rabbit hole of dithering. Her assigned table was near the middle of the room, and she started toward it just as Adler Osborn—the bride—noticed her and waved her over.

Adler was radiating a kind of glow that all brides seemed to have, but she also looked tired, and there was an edge to her smile, as if she was trying too hard to be happy. "Hello," Danni greeted her. "How are you hanging in there? According to my mother, she wanted to bolt at least three times the week before her wedding and even more so on the actual day."

Adler laughed and shook her head. "I'm doing okay. There's been a lot of unexpected stuff coming up with family, which I guess is to be expected, given that we are all in one place. How was golf? I see you were teamed up with my aunt and cousins. Were the boys good? Those two like to fight."

"They were funny, actually. They competed the entire time, but they were so sweet with their mom that it was nice to watch. I'm afraid I brought our foursome's score down—or should I say up?"

"Ha. That's okay, it's all in good fun anyway. Your business partner sent over men's and women's bracelets for the wedding guest gift bags, and I can't thank you enough for that. I wasn't expecting it, but it is a nice thing to add."

"I hope you don't mind. We wanted to give everyone something special to remember the day," Danni said. She'd asked Essie to wait until she'd talked to Adler, but apparently she hadn't. "I was going to run it by you first."

"It's fine. I love it. The one you made for my dad is cute—he's going to be over the moon." Adler's father was the rock star Toby Osborn and her mom was Leo's late aunt Musette, who had died when Adler was a baby.

"His first hit is so close to his heart, so etching the lyrics on the leather band was clever."

"Well, that song was about you, right?" she asked.

"Yes. It is. So, it's special to me, too," Adler said. "I'm so glad I asked you to do the bridesmaids' gifts. I wanted to make sure that they had a woman's touch, not that Leo isn't fabulous but...well, you have really helped make this wedding special."

"I'm glad, too," Danni said. "And I have really enjoyed working with you. You haven't been...well, like some of my more high-maintenance clients."

"I have tried to not be a bridezilla. Quinn does these high-profile weddings all the time, and she had some stories to tell. I get how easy it would be to drift into that kind of behavior. So much stress to get it all perfect and make sure all the details and events are ideally planned. But mistakes happen. Stuff happens," Adler said.

"Who's Quinn?"

"Oh, she's the producer of the Destination Weddings series, and she's filming this wedding for the show. I don't think you knew her at school but she was one of my roommates."

"No, I didn't know her. And I'm sure everyone in your family would be cool if you were to be a little divaish."

"Ha. My dad likes to be the one owning all the drama," Adler said. "But you're right. I'm so lucky to be doted on by my family. What table are you at for the lunch?"

"Twelve," Danni said. "Somewhere in the middle, I believe."

"Did you bring a plus-one?" Adler asked.

"No. I was going to bring my business partner, but she

couldn't make it," Danni said. No use mentioning that they had decided to save money and keep Essie home.

"I'll put you at one of the family tables for dinner tomorrow and for the rehearsal dinner later," Adler said. "My aunt is a good hostess, and you mentioned the boys weren't that bad."

She had to chuckle at how Adler referred to Leo and Logan. They were grown men, older than Adler, and looked nothing like adolescents. "Why do you call them the boys?"

"To keep them in line. They tend to get a little too big for their britches otherwise. They are all successful, good-looking, charming, wealthy...just a little too used to everyone being in awe of them," Adler said.

"I can imagine. Um, actually, Leo asked me to be his 'date' at the rest of these events. I hope that's okay," Danni asked.

"Of course. I'm glad you two are getting along," she said.

Danni was glad she didn't have a chance to respond as Adler motioned for her wedding planner to join them and made arrangements for Danni to be moved to the family tables for the rest of the meals. Then they both went to their tables.

She was surprised when she got to hers and found her nameplate wasn't there. There was a note addressed to her informing her to go to table nine. She looked around, holding the note, and saw Leo waving her over.

She took a deep breath. Leo certainly wasn't one to wait around. And if she were honest she'd admit there was more to the man's appeal than his business acumen. There had been a connection between them, and she couldn't help the little thrill that went through her at the chance of spending more time with him. But she had to make up her mind—either business or pleasure.

And the last thing she wanted to do was lose this opportunity to pick his brain and meet people who could help her move her business forward. She had a history of falling for bad boys who broke her heart, and she was pretty sure Leo fell into that category.

Leo had moved Danni's name card to his table after confirming his brother Logan wasn't staying for the meal. Logan was trying to reconnect with Quinn Murray, his college girlfriend, and Leo was all for his brother taking a break from the family situation. Logan was taking the news that Nick was their half sibling harder than the rest of them. Nick and Logan often went head-to-head in the boardroom, and neither really liked the other.

Logan would figure it out, though. Leo was confident of that. He watched Nick talking to his siblings and parents toward the front of the room. It wasn't too hard to see a resemblance to their family...to their father. Nick had dark hair and dark brown eyes like August. He also had the height, but then, his stepfather, Tad, was also tall. Apparently everyone in the Williams family had already known that Nick wasn't Tad's son, but none of them, including Tad, had known that August was the father until yesterday afternoon, when Nick's mom and August had seen each other for the first time in decades.

News that Nick was really August's son had thrown everyone for a loop. Poor Adler, who'd wanted a scandal-free wedding, was upset, as she had a right to be. But for once the scandal wasn't coming from her rock star father, the legendary Toby Osborn, and the drama his sexcapades with multiple younger partners had always caused.

Leo knew that Adler, with help from his mother, would sort everything out. He was more curious about this newly discovered half brother. His family dynamic with his siblings was already highly competitive and close-knit. How would Nick mix in with them? For now it seemed like he wasn't sure he wanted to. Nick ran his family business and from all reports was following in Tad Williams's footsteps. As far as any of them knew, Nick might never want to be part of the Bisset family. He was thirty-six, so finding out he had more siblings at this stage might not be something he wanted to deal with.

Leo took a moment to make sure that Danni's name card was at the place setting next to his and then walked over to Nick, where he stood with two of his brothers. One of them looked like trouble and the other had an easy smile and held his hand out to Leo as he approached.

"Noah Williams," he said. "You're Leo, right?"

"I am," Leo said, shaking his hand. "Nick, Asher, good to see you both again. How'd you do on the links?"

The conversation was easygoing as the men discussed the golf game from the morning. But it felt weird, and Leo knew he wasn't the only one who noticed it.

"Just trying to figure out this new brother thing," he said when an awkward silence built. "Figured we should at least try to be friendly."

"I agree," Noah said. "You live on Long Island, right?"

"I do," he said.

"Me, too. I'm doing the acting thing part-time, but I'll

be home all summer," he said, pausing for effect. "I'm having a killer masquerade party beginning of August. I'd love it if you'd come. Nick and Adler will be back from their honeymoon, so it will be a fun blowout."

"Sounds like my kind of party," Leo said. "Do you have my details?"

They exchanged numbers before the wedding planner came to tell them to take their seats. Leo left the exchange feeling…not sure how he felt. His father had thrown a wrench into their entire family dynamic decades earlier when he'd had an affair with Cora Williams, who'd gone by the name of Bonnie Smith back then. The affair had ended when she'd realized she was pregnant and she'd never told August. She'd kept his name a secret when she married Tad Williams because of his rivalry with Bisset Industries. Now, they were all trying to figure out how to deal with this bond that none of them really wanted but couldn't ignore.

He went back to his table and noticed that his mom's seat was empty. He hoped she was okay. As much as he admired his dad for his business acumen, he hated the way he'd hurt Leo's mom again and again. Cora… had Cora been his first affair? Was his mom wondering that now? Finding out that August had cheated on her when she'd been pregnant with his brother Logan had been a blow.

Leo shook his head as one of his uncles came over to the table. Time to put on a game face and make sure that everyone had a good time at Adler's party. He didn't want his father's mistake to hurt his cousin any more than it already had.

He noticed Adler was talking to Danni and wondered what they were talking about. Probably none of his business, he thought, chagrined. She'd sort of surprised him. The bracelet she wore was high-quality, but it would be hard to judge her and her business without seeing more of her product. He could do that later, he thought as she glanced around, looking for her table.

He waved at her and watched as she tucked the note that he'd left at her table into her pocket and walked toward him. She moved like a woman with purpose. She had an easy smile, and he saw how people readily returned it. She was the kind of person who could do well in the world of influencers. Should he help her out? Give her a hand in growing her business?

He thought about it a bit more but got distracted by the way the sunlight was making her thick, curly hair seem more alive than it had outside. He realized that she looked like one of those fairy-tale princesses from the books Mari used to ask him to read her at night. Danni had a heart-shaped face, a cute little nose and a mouth that made him think of kissing her.

Awkward.

She'd asked him to be her mentor. And he had said he'd do it for this weekend. Which meant he needed to check his libido and do the right thing. He knew in his gut that his father...well, that he didn't want to be the kind of womanizer his father had been.

All of which just added to the dilemma of whether he should have offered his help as her mentor. He had meant it when he said business wasn't personal, but if he started to be personal with her, then it would change the dynamic.

He'd been burned by that very thing. But he told himself that this time he was going into it with his eyes open. And he didn't know if he could handle another dicey relationship right now.

Leo kept the conversation at the table moving throughout the lunch, which was impressive, given that they were mixed in with his older relatives as well as his ten-year-old cousin, Jen, who wanted him to take her on his next photo shoot in Bermuda. Leo was so easygoing about his famous friends, and his jet-set lifestyle added another dimension to the man Danni was coming to know. She turned to Jen.

"Are you doing anything fun this summer?" she asked.

"Just the wedding, and then we'll be at the cottage for the rest of July and August. Then it's back to school."

"Where do you go to school? On Nantucket?" Danni asked.

Jen tucked her black hair behind her ear. "St. Francis in Boston. We live in Boston. I was supposed to go to a boarding school next year, but I didn't want to, and my mom said that it was time to make some new Bisset traditions."

"Good for her. And good for you for standing up for yourself. It's hard to tell your parents what you want to do," Danni said.

"It is," Jen agreed. "It must be nice to be a grown-up and do your own thing."

"It is," Danni said. She didn't want to tell Jen that parents still could influence your life after you were an adult. Her parents were keeping up the pressure for her to rejoin the family law firm, which they'd started when her siblings were in high school, but she didn't want to.

Everyone had expected her to practice law, and she'd

done it. Followed the family path and gone into practice with them. But to be honest it had been killing her soul.

One of the hardest conversations she'd ever had with her parents was when she told them she wanted to start her own business. They'd been supportive, and it had taken her a while to realize that they expected her to get bored with it and return to the law firm.

Her dream was to have her own business. Nothing as big and far-reaching as Bisset Industries, but her own little shop...which was why she should be picking Leo's brain at this lunch instead of talking with his cute little second cousin.

Danni knew she didn't have that killer instinct, and a part of her wanted to believe that good girls could go just as far in business. But there were times when she wondered if she was just kidding herself.

"Leo, how's your mom handling everything that's come out about—"

"We're not talking about that during Adler's wedding, Uncle Joe," Leo said.

Joe nodded and then shook his head. "Sorry to have brought it up. Your mom is a class act."

"She is. Some say that I inherited her charm. What do you think, Jen?" he asked his little cousin seated next to her.

She laughed. "You're silly."

"Hmm...not the image I want to project around Danni."

"Too late," Danni quipped, happy to help change the subject. "This key lime pie is good."

The discussion turned to the food and slowly everyone left the table until it was just the two of them.

The lunch ended before Danni had a chance to ask

Leo anything that would help her business. Though a part of her was curious about whatever was going on with his family, she had to focus on this mentorship. She'd had a few different questions in the back of her mind, but it was hard to transition from "pass the bread basket" to "how did you find a reliable production factory?"

"That was fun," Leo said. "I always forget how Uncle Luca is like a totally relaxed version of my dad. He's so much easier to just talk to."

"I don't know your dad at all. Is he intense?"

"Oh, yeah, like Logan and me dialed up to eleven," Leo said. "He always owns whatever room he walks into."

"That can't be true. I didn't even notice him today," Danni said, wondering about Leo's relationship with his father. She'd read in his bio about his family, and of course everyone—well, maybe not everyone, but most people—had heard of the Bisset family. They were like the Kennedys but without all the tragedy. They were a big, wealthy family that had connections everywhere in all branches of society. Business, politics, the arts. But she hadn't read much on August Bisset—her focus was on Leo.

"He's not here," Leo said with a dry laugh. "Trust me, when you do meet him, you'll know what I'm talking about."

"I'll take your word for it. I guess we're free this afternoon until the rehearsal dinner," Danni said. "Are you in the wedding party?"

"No," Leo said, shaking his head. "I'm taking some photos of Adler for our family, but otherwise I'm not really involved. I think Adler wanted to keep my branch as far away from Nick's family as she could."

"Yeah? I heard there was a bit of a rivalry, but surely it's not that bad," Danni said. She had heard the rumors of the rivalry, and the family businesses were often mentioned in the news for edging each other in some big deal or another. But she always thought it was media hype; she didn't think big feuds like that existed anymore. But she was the first to admit that she might be naive.

"It's bad, all right. I mean, Dad almost didn't come to the wedding, and Adler is my mom's only niece on her side of the family. Mom helped raise Adler when she was younger," Leo said.

"Wow."

"I know, crazy, right? That's the Bisset family. What are you doing this afternoon?" he asked.

She thought about it for a minute and realized this might be a good time to pick his brain. "I'm going to try to take some photos to use for my social media accounts. Got any tips?"

"What kind of tips?" he asked.

"Your pictures on Instagram are so…great. I mean, it's more than a filter, it's how you set them up and everything. I could spend hours looking at them. I've tried to analyze why, but I can't put my finger on it." She waited to see if he would be offended that she'd asked, but instead he rubbed the back of his neck and then pulled his phone from his pocket.

"I don't know if I can tell you why you like the pictures, but what I do is try to capture not the product I'm selling but more of a feeling I want to evoke. So, your bracelet isn't the focus but instead that bottle of Veuve

Clicquot in the background and the flowers, and then you reaching for the glass. Try it," he said.

She leaned over and reached for the champagne flute as he'd directed her.

"Wait. Adjust your bracelet so the charm is dangling in front of the bottle," he said, then reached over and moved the bracelet and then stepped back again and snapped the picture.

"What do you think?" he asked, inviting her closer to look at his phone. She leaned over to look down and realized that he'd captured something more than her bracelet, and for the first time when she looked at her product, she saw a hint of a different lifestyle.

"I like it," she said, looking up at him, and their eyes met.

"I do, too," he said, not looking at the phone but at her. She shivered as she felt that current go through her again, and she quickly looked away.

She took a deep breath and looked back at him. She realized how close he was, close enough to really appreciate the flecks of gold in his eyes. She hadn't let herself dwell too much on the fact that he was a very good-looking man.

She was noticing it now.

And it wasn't too long before he noticed her noticing. He lifted his hand and tucked a curly strand of hair that had fallen to lie against her cheek back behind her ear.

She shivered again and stepped away. *Focus, Danni.* Otherwise she'd be back in the law firm when the summer was over.

Three

Leo got the text summoning him to a family meeting at his gran's house and almost ditched it to stay with Danni. But given what had been happening at family meetings lately he knew he couldn't. Reluctantly he said goodbye to Danni and headed up to the cottage. Since he'd arrived on Nantucket, every family meeting had led to a new scandal. He wasn't naive enough to believe that this time would be any different.

Gran's butler, Michael, let Leo in and led him to the back of the house. His sister, Marielle, was seated alone in the sunroom when he arrived. She smiled over at him. "I bet everyone is having flashbacks to the texts we used to get to discuss the *M* problem," she said with a wink.

For the last few years, Marielle had been the most outrageous thing about the family, after her high-profile affair with a married Formula One driver, but that had all ended when the driver had been killed in a crash and Marielle had retreated from the spotlight to try to change her life. She'd managed to do that and six months earlier had fallen in love with Inigo Velasquez, another Formula One driver. One who loved her back this time.

"I kind of like that there isn't an *M* problem anymore," Leo said, going over to hug his sister and then sit next to her on the love seat.

"Me, too. How's business? Logan mentioned you had another jewelry designer–slash–social media influencer in your group at golf," Marielle said.

He could tell she was fishing for information about Danni. "Is that all he said?"

"Nah, he let slip you'd insulted her in a press interview and were trying to get back in her good graces," Marielle said with a laugh. "Who is she?"

"Danni Eldridge. She's not an influencer—well, not really. She has a small business designing bracelets and watchbands. She did the jewelry for Adler's bridesmaids, I gather. And yes, she did come up in an interview I did a while back. I said she was trying to ride my coattails."

"You really have a way with words. No wonder people think the Bissets are arrogant."

He shrugged. "To be fair, a lot of Etsy shops have copied my font and storefront images. One of them was even illegally using my photos to sell their cheap products."

"Fair enough. So what's the deal with Danni? Did she do that?" Marielle asked.

"No, she has too much pride in her own products to do that. The deal... I like her. She's cute and funny. I didn't really know who she was when I was asked about her. I just lumped her in with everyone else."

"Do you wish you hadn't said it?"

"About her? Maybe. I mean, I stand by what I said about my competitors in general, though. It's hard to do what I've done. A lot of people assume Dad or Logan gave me the money to start my business and that I'm just the face of the company. But I work hard—"

"I know you do," Marielle said.

"Hi, all. Where are Mom and Dad? Isn't this meeting supposed to be starting soon?" Leo's brother Zac asked as he came in.

"I don't know," Marielle said. "Michael told me to wait in here. Gran's coming as well, but she had a Pilates session just wrapping up, so we're waiting for her."

Leo wasn't surprised that his maternal grandmother was going to be here. Normally, she stayed away from Bisset business but she'd been playing hostess to the family this weekend. After the news that their father had had a child with another woman, their mom had been subdued and not herself. She was a strong woman, but this kind of news was hard to hear. Gran would want to show up to support her daughter.

"I'm here. What did I miss?" Logan asked as he came into the room.

"Nothing. So far it's just us," Leo said.

"Just us?" Dare asked, coming in.

"Yeah. It's been a while since we've all been together," Leo said. "This is nice. Are you thinking of staying in this part of the world, Zac?"

"I wish. I've got to get back to training for the America's Cup," Zac said. "But I hope to make more trips this way in the future."

"I'm glad to hear that," Leo's mother said, joining them.

She seemed to have aged by about ten years overnight. Normally she looked at least twenty years younger than sixty, but not today. Leo got up and went over to give her a hug and noticed his brothers and sister had the same idea. They were all in a big group hug around their mom, and she hugged them all back the way she had when they were little. But Leo heard her draw a ragged breath, and then she started to cry.

"Kiddos. This new thing…it's my fault. I don't know how to tell you—"

"Don't do it, yet," Leo's father said as he arrived. "Carlton is on his way. We can discuss it when he is here."

Carlton was his father's press relations guy and had been spinning the Bisset family scandals since before Leo was born.

As she took a deep breath, Carlton burst through the door, with Gran following close behind but at a slower pace.

"Are we all here?" the family adviser asked in the brisk, no-nonsense tone he used when handling any PR problem. "Because there are new developments."

Once the entire family, including Gran, were in the sun room, Carlton read them a newswire story about a nurse from a small rural hospital who claimed that Nick wasn't the only baby Bonnie Smith aka Cora Williams had delivered that night. In fact, she'd had twins and had given one to Juliette Bisset to raise after her pregnancy ended in a stillbirth.

Leo almost couldn't comprehend what he heard. Mari

went stock-still next to him, and he put his arm around her as he turned to his mother.

His father had stood up. "Jules, how is this possible? Nick and Logan don't look like each other. Is it true?"

One look at his mother's face confirmed it. She took a deep breath and wrapped her arms around herself as she stood there next to the floor-to-ceiling bookcases.

She recounted the story of her going into labor. Auggie had been away on a business trip.

"Skip to the part where you swap your dead baby for me," Logan said.

Leo gasped and started to lunge for his brother but Mari stopped him and he let her. Logan's face was a cold mask and Leo realized that his brother was having a difficult time hearing all of this.

"Don't be such a dick," Leo said.

"I'll be whatever I want, she's not my mom," Logan said. "Right? That's true, isn't it?"

August cursed and turned on him, but when their eyes met, Logan knew his father understood his anguish. His dad started toward him, but he just shook his head.

"Finish the story," Logan said curtly.

"My birth was quicker, and I was in the recovery room," Juliette said. "I was crying when Bonnie—I mean Cora—came back in. She was crying, too. She had anticipated having one child but two was too many for her to handle. She'd gotten a partial scholarship to go back to school and thought she could manage with one child but with two she was going to have to skip college.

"I told her that my marriage would probably be over when my husband learned about the stillborn baby. The pregnancy had brought us back together. But I knew without that baby, your father and I would struggle to stay together."

"That's not—"

"Don't say it's not the truth, Auggie. We both know that we were barely keeping ourselves together as a couple then. Bonnie said she was going to have to give up one of the babies or maybe it would be better if she gave them both up," Juliette said.

"So you offered to raise one as our son," August said.

"I did. I also gave her money to support herself and get some help for the son she kept," Juliette said. "We swapped the bracelets and Logan became my son. I nursed you, you became my baby at that moment. I never thought of you as anything other than my son."

"So how did the nurse know?" Logan asked.

"She knew my son was stillborn and had gone away to do the paperwork. Even though Bonnie and I told her that she was mistaken, she knew the truth. I offered her a bribe, which she was reluctant to take but then Bonnie—I mean Cora—said that no one would ever find out, there were only the three of us. This way the boys would both be raised by mothers who could afford them and who wanted them. The doctor had already signed the paperwork and it was simply down to us filling it in. Bonnie took it from her and signed it. I thought that was it."

"You should have brought this to me," August said. "I could have—"

"What? What would you have done?" his mom demanded.

Logan got up and stormed out of the room, Leo started to follow but Dare stopped him. "Let him alone."

Leo did, but he felt his family was falling apart. He wanted to comfort his mom, punch his dad and maybe have it out with someone.

"Did you meet him? Was he as douchey in person as we thought he'd be?" Essie Palmer asked Danni while they were video chatting. Her friend and business partner had a way of getting right to the point.

Danni was sitting on the porch of her family's cottage as she tried to figure out her next move at the wedding. "Actually, he was really nice. And Adler loves the jewelry we gifted her…"

"Did she mind if we use her name in our advertising?"

Danni hadn't had the courage to ask Adler about that yet. She nodded, but her friend must have seen the hesitation in her expression.

Essie raised both eyebrows and shook her head. "Don't even say anything. You didn't ask because you don't want to impose."

"You're right," Danni admitted.

"I know how hard it is for you to use your connections, but you want this to be your job. You have to be more ruthless."

"I know, you're right. Leo and I were talking today about how there's nothing personal about business. But it feels personal to me, especially when I'm dealing with people I like."

"No," Essie said on a laugh. "That's why you're holding yourself back. Business is business."

"I don't know what that means," she said. "But Leo did help me stage a photo. I'm sending it to you now. I want to use it on our social media. What do you think?"

She texted the photo to Essie and noticed on her camera roll that there was a photo of Leo that she hadn't meant to take. He was handsome, and there was something about him that made her think very personal thoughts. Not business at all.

"Damn. He's good. He just took this photo for you?" Essie asked.

"Yeah. I mean, I did ask for some tips, and he set this up. It looks, well, more professional than my usual shots. I want to make sure our shop links for the bracelet are updated, and then I'm going to post it."

"I'll update the links as soon as we're off the call and text you when I'm done," Essie said. "I'm proud of you asking him for help."

"I figured that it was okay. He knows that we're in the same business, and he could just say no to me. I mean, it's not like we are friends or anything."

"Anything?"

Why had she said that to Essie? Her friend was way too observant, and Danni had the hots for Leo. He had a magnetic personality that had drawn her in despite her many misgivings. And there had been that tingle that she was still trying to convince herself she had imagined.

"Just saying," she said.

"Okay. He is cute. I wouldn't blame you if there was something more," Essie said.

"I would. I want to keep my distance, you know. He's a rival. I want to be good enough that he sees me as competition, not some woman he met at a wedding."

"Why can't you be both?" Essie asked. "You are too quick to put someone in one box and leave them there."

"I don't even know what you're talking about."

"Stan. Mark. Jesse."

"They are business contacts and partners, Ess. They have never been anything else and they don't want to be anything else," Danni said, but she knew her friend was right. She'd turned down all three of them when they'd asked her out. Stan was a corporate vice president for a luxury hotel chain that she'd been trying to get to carry her jewelry in its boutiques. Mark ran the warehouse they used for their inventory, and Jesse... well, he was just a flirt.

"Leo isn't a business partner, and you could just have fun with him this weekend and then still use the connection when you get home. Not every guy has to be a serious relationship," Essie said.

"I know," she said, but in her heart, she wasn't that casual about it. She wasn't interested in hooking up with anyone just for fun at this time when she was trying to get her business off the ground and stand on her own. She didn't want Leo to have the impression that she'd used him. Or for anyone else to think that. This was her thing and she wanted to earn it.

"Okay. Enough of the lecture. I think you should try to get more photos like this one that Leo helped you with," Essie said.

They discussed staging some more photos and a media plan for the weekend. Together they created a list of images that Danni should try to capture before they hung up.

Danni stretched her legs, propping them up on the railing as she scrolled through her photos. The best were the ones that Leo had taken, but she found herself staring at the off-center photo of Leo.

His face was serious. He was staring at a point beyond the camera; she knew it was the champagne bottle, but it was almost too easy to imagine he'd been looking at her. Had he felt the same zing she had?

Honestly, he wasn't the kind of man who'd feel a zing with a woman like her. It wasn't an insult to herself; she was too low-key for a man like Leo. She knew that to boost her profile she should change her energy and her attitude and be more hard-driving. But she wasn't ready to let go of that part of herself, even to be successful. And maybe that was what Essie had been getting at. She needed to become a different woman to have the success she wanted.

But the kind of woman who would have an affair with Leo Bisset?

"Affair" was such an old-fashioned term but the truth was she did want an affair with him. She had felt a connection when he'd touched her, but this was her last chance to make a go of her small business. She couldn't—wouldn't—risk it for an affair with Leo Bisset.

He was a playboy and a flirt and she wasn't going to put herself on the line with him.

Leo was angry and hurt. He hadn't expected to react so strongly to the announcement that Logan wasn't his mother's child.

He still couldn't believe what his mother had told them. For once even Carlton had little to say. Why hadn't they discovered all this sooner? It was true that Cora had gone by a different name back then, and she'd married Tad Williams much later. The Bissets didn't realize Cora—aka Bonnie Smith—was Tad Williams's wife until they all met her the other day when they arrived for Adler's wedding. The Bissets and Williamses were enemies; they'd always avoided each other socially. It was bad enough that Juliette's niece was marrying Nick Williams.

Also, Nick and Logan weren't identical; in fact, Logan was often told he looked like Juliette Bisset, though it now turned out they weren't even related by blood.

Leo's brother had experienced a double blow. First, that his father's affair with Cora made his adversary Nick Williams his brother. And now that he, too, was the other woman's son and Nick was his twin!

Now the rest of the family sat in shocked silence. Even though Leo acknowledged that his mother had done wrong, he knew where the blame lay, and it wasn't with her. It was with his dad. August had always been so determined to take what he wanted that he never thought of the consequences.

"Dad, you never think of the consequences of your actions," Leo said. "You had an affair and then moved on and disappeared when Mom was about to give birth. I've always wanted your approval and to be just like you but now I'm glad I'm not."

There was a murmur from Leo's siblings.

"That's a little bit harsh," Dare said.

His eldest brother was used to being the voice of reason in their family and in his job as a politician. But Leo knew there was no denying it.

"Is it, Dad?" Leo asked their father.

Even Marielle was watching August, all of them waiting to hear what he had to say. Their father had lorded over them all for their entire lives, and now chinks were starting to appear in his armor. Leo admitted to himself that they had always been there but for the most part they had ignored it.

"No. It's not unfair to say. I was very determined to build an empire out of Bisset Industries. Your uncle and aunt weren't interested in running the business, and I knew if I wanted it to last for more than one generation, I was going to need kids to pass it on to. I wanted another son, because Dare wouldn't be enough."

"Thanks, Dad," Dare said, reaching into his pocket and pulling out a pack of cigarettes that was at least ten years old and looked worn from being carried around for too long. He looked at the pack and then cursed and shoved it back in his pocket. "You never do mince words. So you would have left Mom if she'd lost the baby… I mean, if you knew she'd lost it?"

August shoved both hands through his hair and then turned his back on them. He put his hands on his hips and bowed his head but didn't answer Dare. He didn't have to, Leo thought. They all knew the truth.

"Dad?" Marielle asked. "That's not true, is it? You love Mom."

August turned to Marielle, who got up and went over to him. Those two had always been close, but now Leo could tell that his sister was seeing their dad through different eyes. Probably the same way he was. His entire life Leo had wanted to be like August Bisset, and now…well, now he wasn't sure. He didn't want to be the kind of man who kept his family in line through bullying and intimidation, Leo thought. The same went for August's staff—he treated them the same way.

"I do love your mom, Mari. But it's taken a lifetime for me to realize that I didn't want to lose her. I'm not entirely sure what I would have done if I'd known about the stillbirth," he said.

Leo shook his head and walked out of the room and out of his grandmother's house. He didn't want to hear anything else his father had to say. Their relationship had always been too strained, and his mom had said it was because they were so alike. Something that Leo had used to fuel his ambition and keep himself moving toward a new goal. Never standing still, never being satisfied with the success he'd found.

But that was all confusing now. Was that the man he was destined to become? Was he going to be laying waste to everything he'd built someday because he'd never taken the time to appreciate what he had?

He didn't know. It was too much to delve into at the moment. He stepped out into the summer heat and looked at the driveway full of expensive cars. They all had to acknowledge the effect of being a Bisset and seeing the example that August and their mom had set for them. They were all overachievers who would stop at nothing to get ahead. For Marielle it had been an affair with a married man. For himself it had been ruthlessly stepping over his acquaintances and building his empire from the ground up. But was it time to step away from that model?

Hell, he knew it was. But he had no idea how else to operate. How else to build his business and his life.

He ignored his car and walked toward the town center instead. It was busy, since the summer season meant everyone was headed to the beach. But Leo just put on his sunglasses and ignored the families and tourists all seeming to enjoy this paradise of an island.

Nantucket that had been their sanctuary since they

were kids…maybe because they'd always come to visit with their mom and August had stayed in the city working all summer. Again, Leo felt like he'd been punched in the gut, and his heart was broken in a way. He wondered how Logan was handling this.

His brother had always been the best of both their mom and their dad, and now Logan was going to have to deal with the fact that he wasn't part Wallis—their mother's maiden name—as he'd always believed. But something else. Someone else.

Leo knew it was going to be a long time before his brother could forgive his parents for that.

"Leo?"

He looked over and noticed Danni was sitting on the porch of one of the smaller cottages close to the main street. She stood up as she saw him and waved.

He waved back. He didn't dwell on it but realized he'd felt so lost until he saw her. She wasn't his salvation or anything like that, but she was a distraction… and he desperately needed one.

Four

Danni's half-formed plan of asking Leo to mentor her seemed to be getting a nudge from the universe, she thought as he opened the white picket fence gate and walked up to the porch.

"Just calling?" he asked.

He seemed tense, even though he was being cordial and friendly. There was an energy around him that made her feel like he was on edge. She knew that weddings stirred up all kinds of emotions in people. In her experience it was mainly women, but she realized that was a bit sexist.

"Yeah. Want to join me?" she asked.

"Yes. But I can't sit still right now. Could I interest you in a walk or bike ride?" he asked.

"A walk is right up my alley. Let me grab my hat and I'll be right with you," she said.

She dashed into the cottage and changed her flip-flops for some Keds and put on a wide-brimmed straw hat that she'd had for years. She took a quick look in the mirror, hoping her outfit was cute, but with her curly hair responding to the humidity, she looked like...well, like Hermione Granger when she didn't use a spell to tame her hair. She tossed the hat on the bench since it wasn't sitting on her hair very well and grabbed a baseball cap that had Nantucket embroidered on it. She forced her hair into a ponytail that she anchored with the hat's Velcro strap at the back.

She stepped outside and noticed that Leo was texting, his fingers moving at a furious pace. She pulled her phone out and checked to see if there was anything in the WhatsApp wedding group. But there wasn't any news. She wondered if he was dealing with business. Or maybe it was personal, she thought, and immediately stopped herself. Because it was still dangerous to even think about mixing business and pleasure with this man.

"Have you been down to the beach yet? I have a favorite spot for looking at shells. It's a bit off the beaten path, but I think you might like it," she said. Internally she wanted to shake her head. She sounded like she was a tour guide instead of a professional businesswoman. She was struggling to find the balance between getting what she wanted from him and being friendly. She'd give anything for an ounce of Essie's boldness, but she knew she wasn't going to be able to magically gain that.

"Sounds great. I really don't want to be around crowds right now," he said.

"I get that. I bet you have fans—do you call them fans? Followers?—that recognize you everywhere you go," she said.

He smiled over at her. "I do, but that's not an issue. I love talking to them and posing for photos. Without them I'd be just another trust-fund guy who struck out on his own to try to prove there's more to him than his family's legacy. Or maybe I'm just trying to fill up my time."

She led the way down the path and onto the sidewalk. He fell into step beside her, and she wondered if he wanted to talk. She thought he had something on his mind. People often told her she was a good listener.

"Everything okay with your family? I didn't see your mom after our golf round," Danni said.

"She's oaky. Something from the past… Actually, she's not okay. Our family is having a bit of a crisis. Not exactly what you wanted to hear, right?" he asked.

Danni stopped walking and reached out to take his hand and hold it. A tingle went up her arm, but she shoved that reaction to the back of her mind. "I don't want to hear it because I like your family and want them to be okay. But if you need to talk, I'm here. Just tell me what you need."

"Why?" he asked suddenly. "Why are you being so nice?"

"You did me a solid favor earlier. It was nothing to you and everything to me," she admitted. "I owe you."

"That was business," he said with a wink. "This is…a hot mess. I mean, it's so crazy I wouldn't even know where to start."

"Then just say whatever you want to. I'll be honest, I don't know much about your family. Your dad seems a bit larger than life. Logan, obviously, is following in his footsteps, and from what I read, you are, too—"

"That's part of it. I always wanted to be bigger and bolder than Dad, but now... I'm not sure," Leo said.

"I get that," Danni said. "I mean, not on as big a scale as your family. But my entire family are lawyers. Parents and two older siblings. And I want something else. It makes every family get-together so...tense."

Leo looked over at her. "Did you ever want to be just like your mom or dad?"

She shook her head. "Not really. I mean, I wanted their approval, so I went to the schools they wanted me to and took the classes they urged me to take. I even went to law school and passed the bar and practiced for a year. But it just felt like it wasn't me."

Leo turned to face her. "Well, I have always felt like I was just like my father. That I would have been his heir apparent if I'd been born first, and I wanted nothing more than to make him see that in me."

"I think we all grow up wanting to be like our parents. They're always sort of our first heroes."

"You think so?"

She shrugged. Why else would she have gone to law school? The ultimatum they'd given her, the condescension she'd felt when she'd stood her ground and insisted she was going to make her small business work had shown her a different side of her parents. "For me. But it's hard when you realize they have feet of clay."

"Yeah, well, today... I learned some things about my dad that are making me question everything about him and about myself, and I'm not really sure where to go from here."

She had no advice to give him, and really, the pain in his voice when he talked about his father made her realize that this was more complex than she had thought.

She turned so that they were facing each other on the sidewalk. At least with her folks they still had a solid relationship.

"Well, let's start with the walk on the beach, okay?"

Leo realized there was something very sweet about Danni, which made the cynical part of him acknowledge she was probably never really going to be good in a high-stress, cutthroat business world, which the world of influencers was. He wasn't an influencer himself, though he used influencers to promote his brand and his sister was one. But he knew that it was very hard to succeed in that field. Despite the fact that Danni was trying to sell her own products, she'd need to grow her audience enough to make that crossover from Etsy shop to her own brick-and-mortar store. And looking down at her heart-shaped face after she'd just been so kind and sweet, he didn't see her making it.

He reached out to brush a stubborn curl back behind her ear under the baseball cap, and it immediately sprang back to wrap around his finger. He liked her hair. He liked her face and her mouth, which looked perfect for kissing. Normally he didn't size up mouths, but there was something about Danni and her lips that kept drawing his eyes and his thoughts to them. She had some sort of light pink gloss on her lips, and of course she had an easy smile that made him want to smile, too.

Despite all the tension, anger and hurt that he felt at this moment, she was making him want to smile. That was saying something. He saw how that was her real strength. And maybe that was what had appealed to him about her bracelet—something about the design reflected her innate kindness. He wasn't sure how a piece of jewelry could convey that, but hers had.

"You're staring at me, aren't you?" she asked. "Has my hair escaped the hat?"

"I am looking at you," he said, bringing his hand up to rub his thumb lightly along her jaw. "I'm thinking about kissing you, Danni. What do you think about that?"

The days of a guy stealing a kiss were long gone, and he had to admit there were times when he missed them, but at the same time, he sincerely hoped all the girls he'd kissed in high school and in college hadn't felt like he was pushing himself on them or taking something they hadn't wanted to give.

"I wouldn't mind," she admitted. "I've been thinking the same thing."

"You have? That's always a good sign," he replied. He slid his hands along the sides of her neck, noticing the small birthmark behind her ear, then down to her shoulders as he leaned in the slightest bit. She tipped her head more to the side and took a breath.

He leaned down and then hesitated. He wasn't in the best place to start anything right now. He was angry at his father, unsure of the man he wanted to be. Kissing Danni was a distraction, and he wasn't going to pretend it was more than that. But she was kind and sweet, and what if this meant more to her?

"It's just a kiss," she said wryly. "I mean, I can see that you probably think I'm going to be immediately starting my dream wedding wish list at retailers, but honestly, I don't know you. You're hot and everything, but that's all."

He took a step back and started laughing. "God, I'm sorry, Danni. I am just off my game today, or maybe just with you. I hope to have that kiss later. But I think you hit the nail on the head with that comment, and it's made me realize I really don't know you."

"You don't? Just kidding, of course you don't. I had an idea of what you'd be like, and let me say that it totally missed the mark. You are so not what I was expecting," she said.

He took her hand in his and started walking again. "Tell me something about you. Let's get to know each other."

She nibbled on her bottom lip, and he felt that sizzle of arousal go through him again, but he liked it. Finally, he felt something that was exciting and new.

"Okay. But I feel like I should warn you, I do want your advice for my business. So, I'm going to pick your brain for that, too."

He stopped and looked over at her. "I honestly won't be upset by anything business-related between us. I swear."

"Okay. I just don't want to use you," she said.

And those were words he'd never uttered himself or heard his father say. Every person they met was either someone who could bring them closer to achieving success or not worth their time. He realized that he'd probably missed out on a lot of friendships in his life by following in his father's footsteps. Maybe it was time to try things Danni's way.

"Gaining knowledge and using it to your advantage isn't using me. I won't let you use me if you don't let me use you," he said.

"Deal."

"Kiss on it?" he asked. His hesitation from a moment earlier had already gone up in smoke.

"Not yet. Not until you tell me something that your fan base doesn't know. Who is the real Leo Bisset?"

Before today, he would have answered that he was pretty much what the world saw on social media, but he knew that wasn't true. "Let's see…well, I hate wearing deck shoes. I mean, I know I have a brand partnership with Sperry, and we collaborated on a line. I endorse them, and I do wear the shoes all the time, but if I wasn't in a partnership, I'd wear a pair of ratty old canvas shoes that I keep at my gran's."

"That is shocking," she said with a wink. "Are they comfortable?"

"Yes. So it's not that. They make me feel like I'm working, and the ratty ones I could never photograph or wear when I was going to an event," he said.

"I like that you have them."

"Why?"

"It makes you seem more real," she said softy.

"Do I come across as fake?"

"Well…" She wrinkled her nose and then gave an awkward little laugh.

"So yes. Why?"

"Um, I asked you to tell me something real and you talked about shoes," she said.

"What more can I do to show you I'm real?" he asked, realizing that he wanted to impress her. Which was odd for him.

"Why did you strike out on your own? Not the standard answer you gave me earlier but in your gut, what made you do it?" she asked.

"Wow, that's getting very personal."

She shrugged again, that delicate little movement of

her shoulders. "You're the one who wanted a kiss and I don't kiss strangers."

Had he ever worked this hard for a kiss? No. And maybe that was why he craved one from her.

"Okay, well then." He took a deep breath. He didn't think he'd ever told another human being this. "I wanted to see if I was like my Bisset ancestors who built a dynasty out of nothing. I could have taken a senior role and proven myself to my family but I needed to prove myself to me."

He arched one eyebrow at her and cocked his head to the side. "That personal enough?"

"It'll do."

"Now what about you?"

What about her?

She wished there were some easy answer that she could give that would make her seem cute and clever, but the truth was she'd never had a filter, and she wanted to blurt out all the things that most people never noticed about her. Instead she contented herself with channeling Essie. What would Essie say?

"I think most people underestimate me," she said, speaking from the heart. "They mistake kindness for being a pushover, and then are surprised when I'm not. I'm also ridiculously competitive."

"You are? I didn't see that today on the golf course," he said.

"Not that way. More with myself. Like if I see something that I think I can achieve, like being a successful small-business owner, then I don't let anything stand in my way. I've been told that I'm competitive in the courtroom, too."

"Are you? Do you want to go back to practicing?"

"No."

He laughed at the way she said it so quickly and forcefully. "Why not?"

"I'm good at it but it's not my passion. My parents' passion is law, so they don't really get it. They've given me time off to try and make my business work and if I don't by the end of the year, I have to go back. But I won't let myself fail."

He laughed in that way of his that made her smile. "I'm the same way. It's not about the other people in my industry—it's about the next mountain that I want to climb. I'm looking ahead, not to my left or right."

She liked that. "So that's what you meant when you said you don't really see business as being personal? You're focused on your own goals, not the competition. Right?"

"Yeah, pretty much."

"I was trying to figure out how dealing with people wouldn't be personal, even in business situations. How you keep the emotions out of it. But you're not looking at them as competition. Is that how you've been so successful?"

"Perhaps. I think it was more my innate drive to build my own legacy since my father's was denied me."

"That sounds a bit…"

"Over-the-top?" he asked with a grin. "Yeah, I know. But it always felt that way. I'm the third-born son. There was no way I was going to lead the company, and I like my brothers too much to do the kind of things I would have needed to do in order to run it. So I decided to do my own thing and make my company even more successful than Bisset Industries."

There were so many nuances in what he was saying, and it spoke to the complicated family he belonged to. But also to his drive. He was a leader in an industry that was almost out of step with the price-conscious, fast-fashion world they lived in. His American-made brand had been built on old-fashioned values and an aspirational lifestyle that many emulated.

"I get it. I mean, I practice law with my family, but I'm not ever going to be as good as the rest of them, because it's not my passion. That's why I want to make my jewelry business a success, but I haven't found a mentor yet."

"I'm not going to be your mentor beyond this weekend," he said. "It's not my thing. I'll give you some pointers and answer your questions."

"Fair enough," she said. "I figured I'm going to be the one whose coattails you want to ride eventually."

"Damn. I'm never going to live that comment down, am I?" he asked.

"Not for a while," she said. "Actually, I'm glad you said it. It made me seek out more opportunities to put me in competition with you, and it's made me grow my business."

"Then I don't regret it. Competition is where I thrive. So where's this beach you were telling me about?" he asked.

She led him down to the shoreline and away from the crowds. The farther they got from the tourists, the more Leo relaxed. She learned that he liked cherry ice cream, never wore a tank top and read all the Harry Potter books once a year. She told him that she loved butter-pecan ice cream at the beach but chocolate when she was at home. That she loved wearing skirts over

shorts and had a huge stack of books that people recommended to her, but she really only read her large collection of romance novels.

They walked along the edge of the water, and she
took off her shoes. He glanced around to make sure
there wasn't anyone close by—winking at her as he
did so—before he took off the deck shoes he wore. The
sand was warm under her feet and the water cold. He
told her that his youngest brother knew more stories of
the sea than anyone else he had met and that, when he
was younger, he used to dream of being an only child.

She confessed to the same dream but added that in
her version she was a stolen princess whose family
searched endlessly for her. Which made him laugh and
that made her smile.

She was watching him laugh when something on
his face changed and he reached out and snatched the
baseball cap off her head. Her hair—always larger in
this kind of weather—caught the wind, and she felt the
tendrils and curls flying all around. She reached up to
capture it, but he caught her hands.

"Leave it," he said. "You look like the ethereal creature I'm slowly realizing you are. Some sort of sea
nymph that has soothed something savage inside me."

"I'm not that," she said. And she didn't really believe that there was anything savage about Leo. But it
was there in the husky timbre of his voice. "I'm just a
girl…well, woman."

"You are so much more," he said, taking her hand
and drawing her into his arms.

She put one hand on his chest as his arm went around
her waist and he lowered his head. His lips brushed
against hers. They were soft yet firm, and when he

opened his mouth to deepen the kiss, he tasted better than any man she'd ever kissed. She closed her eyes, felt the wind blowing her curly hair all around their bodies as he kissed her, and she forgot about everything except Leo.

Five

When they started their walk, he definitely hadn't planned on kissing her…but then things had gotten intimate—fast. She'd made him face himself for the first time in a long time. But something about the way she'd gotten past his defenses so quickly made him not trust her. She wasn't what she seemed. But then who was, right?

His mom definitely wasn't who he'd thought she was. He was having a hard time with her betrayal. If it wasn't for her duplicity, he might have been running Bisset Industries, because Logan wouldn't be in the picture. He immediately felt guilty—Logan was in a lot of pain right now and Leo shouldn't be having such jealous, petty thoughts. He guessed he understood why his mother had acted the way she did. And he loved his brother. But still.

His dad—better to not even go there.

And then there was Danni. Sweet Danni with her curly hair that seemed to beckon him to leave behind his cares and his worries. Kind Danni who made those things about himself that had at times felt cringey okay. Sexy Danni who was making this kiss into something more than he'd anticipated. Was she too good to be true? Right now, he didn't care.

There it was. That August Bisset legacy of taking what he wanted without thinking of the consequences to anyone else. Did he really want to be that man? Also how could he stop?

Her hand on his waist held him firmly to her as she went up on her tiptoes and wrapped her other hand around the back of his neck. The kiss deepened and went further than he'd intended.

Her breasts rested against his chest, and he tried to control his response. But he couldn't. He slipped his hand down her back to cup her butt and draw her more fully against him. His erection hardened, and he couldn't help rubbing it against the softness of her tummy.

She tore her mouth from his and looked up at him, though she didn't step back. He wondered what she was thinking, but her eyes were blocked by her dark sunglasses. Her lips were slightly swollen from kissing him, and her hair, that glorious mane of thick, curly hair, was dancing on the wind.

There was something in her that called to him in a way that no other woman had before. She didn't fit his image of where he wanted to go with his life. She was just…a treat, he thought. And he was smart enough to keep that thought to himself.

"I like kissing you," he said.

"I liked it, too," she said.

He felt something under his foot and looked down to see a shell buried in the sand. He stooped down to pick it up, brushing the sand off on his shirt. He handed it to her. "So you won't forget me when you are rich and famous."

She took it from him and pushed her sunglasses up on his head to look at it. "I'll never forget you after you said that crass thing about me in the press."

"I'm trying to make up for it. Give you something else to remember me for," he said. "Hey, I know tonight is the rehearsal dinner, but I am not feeling up to a big party. Would you want to skip it and go on a date with me instead?"

"What did you have in mind? Tonight is my chance to mingle with Toby Osborn and maybe do some networking," she said.

"And you are trying to grow your business," he said. "How about if I take a photo of you on the date that you can use to sell your products?"

"You still haven't said what kind of date it will be," she said, pushing her sunglasses back down and putting the shell in her pocket.

"My grandmother has a fully restored yacht from the 1930s. It's just the right size for a couple to manage under decent conditions. I'd love to take you sailing and have dinner as the sun sets."

The women Leo had dated over the last ten years had always said he wasn't romantic, but the truth was he'd never made the time to be. In his mind he'd always envisioned a romantic sail with the woman in his life, but he'd never been that far away from a cell phone signal, unable to be reached if a business emergency arose, until today.

As if a cell phone was the only thing making him hesitate. He acknowledged to himself that he wanted her because she was Danni but also she was a distraction. But was he letting himself get too distracted? She hadn't even pretended she didn't want him to mentor her. She had said they were competition and yet…none of that mattered right now.

He'd seen his father focus on building Bisset Industries during his tenure and now the entire family was paying the cost. He needed to believe he was somehow different and that he wouldn't make those mistakes. So one sail…would it be okay?

Today had changed everything, and he had no idea if this was something he'd like or not, but he was tired of not trying. Of filtering everything through what August would do—for maximum personal gain—instead of what Leo wanted to do.

Hell.

He hadn't realized how long he'd been scrambling to get and keep his father's attention. Attention that August was never going to give because Leo was his third son and not a part of Bisset Industries.

"What do you say? I can't promise it will be perfect, but it should be fun," he said at last.

"I'll take fun over perfect every time," she said.

"Good," he said as they started walking back the way they'd come. "I've had a really nice afternoon, Danni. Thank you for that."

"It's my pleasure, Leo. I enjoyed it, too," she said. "I saw an ice cream stand when we were walking here. Do you have time for a snack before you have to get back to your family?"

Leo thought about it. He had responsibilities this weekend. They were all playing a part in the wedding, no matter how big or small. He pulled his phone out of his pocket and saw he'd missed ten messages from his team, who were all back on Long Island. He skimmed them and there weren't any emergencies so he didn't reply. There was one from his mom asking if he was okay, which he also ignored. Instead he texted his cousin to see if she needed him this afternoon at the rehearsal, and her response didn't sound like Adler. It was wooden: just a smiley face and a brief message to enjoy himself. That wasn't Adler. She wrote massively long text messages. Always.

"I'm not sure I can. I want to check on Adler. This new family thing probably has her rattled, too," Leo said. "But I'll see you tonight around six?"

"Okay, see you then," Danni said as they reached town. She turned toward the ice cream stand, waving him up toward the hotel.

He stood there feeling the pull of Danni, but that was ridiculous. He'd only met her this morning. She had no sway over him…but his libido begged to differ.

Danni posted the picture that Leo had helped her stage at the luncheon on her social media accounts and then went to sketch in her art journal. She wanted to capture the day she'd spent with Leo. He stirred emotions in her that she was used to ignoring. She was on the clock if she wanted to make her dreams a reality, and sex wasn't something she normally made time for.

But Leo…the way he'd kissed her made her think of

things other than her production schedule and distribution channels. He made her want to be that ethereal
woman he'd seen her as on the beach. Someone who
lived in the moment, for passion and pleasure.

The truth was she'd never be that woman. But on the
pages of her art journal, she could be. She sketched herself the way she always did, but this time as she drew
her hair, she didn't feel the resentment she sometimes
did toward the long, curly locks. Everyone always envied her, but her hair was hard work, and it was frizzy
when she wanted it to be smooth. Though that hadn't
mattered to Leo. She sketched him, too, but she wasn't
as good with men as she was with women. He looked
odd in the picture, so she added a pair of sunglasses
over his eyes, and that fixed the problem. She took the
shell he'd found for her out of her pocket and flipped to
another page in the journal and sketched it from all different angles before she set her journal aside.

She needed to wash her hair before her date with Leo,
and it was going to take a while to dry, so if she showered now she might be able to get away without blow-
drying it. It was a mundane thing to worry about, but
her life was more easily handled when she focused on
those details instead of things like her attraction to Leo.

He had been by turns tense and then totally relaxed.
And though he'd shared things with her, she knew he
was still hiding something. Whatever was going on with
his family had shaken Leo to his core. That wasn't the
man she'd come to know through his online presence
and profile in *Forbes*. He was the kind of man who
was always certain, she thought, but this afternoon he
hadn't been.

She got out of the shower and then checked her

phone to see that it was blowing up with messages from Essie—she had seventy-five text messages waiting. Worried that her friend had been in an accident, she clicked on the thread only to see that Essie was fine. She was texting about their business.

She hit the video chat button to get the down low so she didn't have to scroll through all the messages.

"Where have you been? That photo you posted is blowing up. I mean, we've had more than one hundred orders in the first thirty minutes, and it isn't slowing down," Essie said.

"Sorry, I didn't think we'd get that kind of response. A hundred? Wow, that's great. I bet it will slow down soon. What's our stock like?" she asked. They had a warehouse with products in it, but they were a small business with mainly Danni and three helpers making everything.

"You'd know better than me, but I don't think we can handle more than five hundred orders—not that we will get that many."

"I have two other bracelets that are very similar... let me get to my laptop, and I'll tweak the shop page so that if we sell out, those will pop up as alternatives. And we should set the limit on the back end at four hundred and fifty just to be safe—okay? Once we hit that, we can automatically redirect customers to the other bracelets that I'm thinking of. We have three hundred of each of them. Also we'll set up a button for people to click so they get an email when it's back in stock," Danni said. She felt a fire coursing through her body at the thought of selling stock so quickly. This was exactly why she needed Leo's tutelage: he'd tweaked that photo and helped her sell more bracelets in thirty minutes than she had in the last month.

"Okay, I'll get on it. Dang, girl. This is exciting—stressful, but exciting," Essie said. They continued video chatting while they both worked on updating the website, both front and back end, and then she disconnected with Essie to call her helpers and ask them if they could start working on more bracelets and get them delivered by the following week.

Once she had all that done, she called Essie back and made sure her friend had everything she needed until the next day. She hung up and finished getting ready for her date with Leo, which was coming up soon.

As hot as he was and as much as she wanted him and liked kissing him, she had to focus on continuing to get tips for her business. She wanted to be partnering with luxury brands the way he did. She took out her phone and jotted down things she needed help with in the notepad app. Once she had a solid list, she decided she'd casually bring them up throughout the evening.

She could do that. And she wasn't going to feel guilty about it; he'd told her that he wasn't worried about her business. And it wasn't like she was going to ask him how he got brands to work with him. She knew that developing those relationships would take time, that she needed to get her products noticed so that brands would want her.

He knocked on her door at six, and she opened it and almost forgot her plan. He had on a pair of shorts and a casual collared shirt along with those deck shoes he endorsed. His hair was combed back, and when he smiled at her, she remembered what it had felt like to be in his arms on the beach.

Keeping her mind on business was going to be harder than she had imagined.

Adler Osborn had thought she was getting the wedding of her dreams with a nice, respectable man who came from a well-established family. Nick Williams had the upbringing she'd craved; he'd been raised by two loving parents and was tight with his siblings. Adler had grown up spending half the year on the road with her famous rock star father and the other part of the year with her grandmother and aunt Juliette after her mom had died of a drug overdose. Her father was always in the tabloid headlines and the more that the spotlight had flashed around her, the more Adler had hated it.

So, meeting CEO Nick Williams and falling in love with him was the answer to her long-awaited dream. But then yesterday when her extended family, including her beloved aunt Juliette and her arrogant uncle Auggie, had met Nick's parents, everything had fallen apart. Turns out that Nick was the bastard son of August Bisset. And the fact that the Williams and Bisset families were business rivals and sworn enemies didn't make that matter any easier to handle.

In fact, it was the kind of scandal that had hit TMZ and blown up her picture-perfect, elegant wedding scenario. Then today, when she learned that her cousin Logan was actually not her cousin at all but Nick's twin, things had gone from bad to worse. Nick and Logan hated each other. They were always trying to one-up each other in the boardroom and steal deals out from under each other's noses.

Nick was wigging out and not acting at all like the man she'd fallen in love with, and her Bisset family, her mom's relatives, who could normally be counted on to be calm in a crisis, weren't. They were in the center of a scandal that felt like a hurricane that kept getting bigger and bigger.

When her cousin Leo had offered to come and just chill with her for an hour, she'd jumped at the chance. They'd been close when they were kids, and she liked him. He was funny and sarcastic, and he had a way of cutting through the bullshit and getting straight to the heart of the matter. She had asked everyone to leave her alone for the afternoon to try to process the new family scandal that Logan was actually Nick's twin.

Leo knocked on the door to the hotel suite that she was using to get ready for the wedding, and when she let him in, she noticed his smile didn't go all the way to his eyes.

"Leo? You okay?" she asked. But she knew the situation with his father and Nick's mother had to be affecting Leo, as well. Adler took a deep breath, not sure she was ready to try to play calming influence on another male. Nick was taking all that energy!

"Yes. I'm here for you, kiddo," he said. "I could tell from your very succinct text that you aren't yourself."

She had to laugh at the way he said it. "I knew I should have put more in the message, but I'm out of words. I mean, I have words, but I thought a string of curses followed by *what am I going to do?* would be over-the-top," she said.

He laughed and then pulled her close for a hug. "Maybe for someone else, but not for you, Addie. So, what's going on? Is Nick handling this any better than Logan?"

"No," she said, leading the way farther into the suite and stopping at the bar cart. "Want a drink?"

"I'm good. I have a date later," he said.

"Ooh. With who?" she asked. "I guess that's why you wanted to skip the dinner. I thought it might be because of the other drama. But this is better." Honestly, right now, she had entered a kind of Zen calm about the wedding. She was just too numb to care if people showed up or didn't at the events. Her dream wedding was turning a bit into her worst nightmare and she had other stuff on her mind. If Leo wanted to miss the dinner that was fine with her.

"This is better," he said. "It's with Danni Eldridge."

"I like her, Leo. So, don't do your one-night thing," Adler warned.

"She's a grown woman," Leo said. "I like her, too. She's different."

"She's got a kind heart. We went to school together, and since then her dad became my dad's attorney, and he's one of the toughest lawyers I know. But Danni isn't anything like him," Adler said.

"She mentioned that she's from a family of lawyers. She wants me to give her advice on her business. What made you pick her for your bridal jewelry?" he asked.

"To be honest, I only looked at her stuff because her dad mentioned it to my dad, but then when I saw it… it's really high-quality and so unique. I told her what I wanted, and she sent me back some sketches that were better than I'd imagined," Adler said.

"It is good," Leo said. "You look like you're freaking out again."

She was. The scandal just kept intruding on her thoughts. She wished she could go back to that time before she knew that Nick was August Bisset's biological son. But she couldn't. She was just going to have to keep trying to ignore the tabloid press and paparazzi who were gathering all around the hotel and on Nantucket and pretend that her life was going to be okay.

"I just hate this. I thought I'd picked the kind of man who would give me the nice, quiet life I've always wanted," she said.

"I wish you could have that life, but it's just not in the cards for you. It never has been. You were born in the spotlight, and I can appreciate you trying to have a low-profile wedding, but you're Adler Osborn. That was never going to happen."

"I know," she said. "I'm just glad it's not Dad doing something outrageous."

"Like one of the bridesmaids?" Leo said, arching one eyebrow at her.

They both busted up laughing, because it wasn't that far-fetched that her father would have slept with one or more of the bridesmaids in years past. But he was slowing down with his wild lifestyle and seemed to finally want a life beyond the spotlight.

Leo left a short while later, and Adler felt a bit lighter for having talked to him. She was still concerned about Nick, who wasn't answering her texts and seemed to be questioning all his life choices. She loved him and wanted the wedding to go on, but she wouldn't make a mistake just to keep up appearances. In her mind, marriage was forever.

But she was starting to realize that the man she thought she knew was changing as each new secret from his past was revealed. And in her heart, she was scared that he wouldn't be that forever man she'd always believed him to be.

Six

Leo was an old hand at sailing. As soon as he and Danni were on the yacht and out of the marina, he switched his boat shoes to the old ratty pair he'd mentioned earlier that afternoon. She watched him piloting the yacht and took her sketchbook out to make a rough drawing of him and the boat.

The boat was exquisitely restored and made her feel like she was in one of the glamorous old black-and-white films her mom used to watch on Saturday mornings with her and her siblings. They'd always pile into her parents' king-size bed and drink milky, sweet coffee and watch the old films. The women in them had always been so glitzy and smart, full of sassy comebacks that kept the handsome men on their toes. Danni had loved it.

Leo would have fit very well in one of those old

movies. He had the drive and pedigree that the heroes usually had.

He dropped anchor when they were far enough out and not in a line of shipping traffic. It almost seemed as if they were the only two people in the world. The horizon stretched out all around them, and she couldn't help but feeling like he'd somehow had a glimpse inside her secret dreams from the days when she watched those movies and was now making them come true.

He couldn't have, of course, because those dreams were silly in this modern world where everyone was posting constantly. He knew all about that. In the beginning, Leo had built his brand by staging photos showcasing his products and making sure everyone in the world wanted to have his affluent lifestyle. So he was just good at conveying a fantasy, that's all.

"I had Michael pack us dinner," Leo said. "He's my grandmother's butler, and honestly he's usually spot-on when it comes to getting both meals and drinks right. He's famous for his Manhattans, so I asked him to make us a batch...do you like them?"

Not really, but she just shrugged. "I'm not sure I've ever had one. I'm more of a gin and tonic kind of girl. But I'll try it."

"I'm pretty sure the bar in the galley is fully stocked, so I should be able to whip up whatever you want. Don't feel like you have to drink something just because I suggested it," he said.

"Oh, I don't. I just don't want to start complaining on our first date," she said, realizing that was entirely true. She might have been thinking about peppering the evening with business questions, but that didn't mean she wanted the date to be all business. There was something about Leo that called to a very feminine part of her, and she wanted to explore it.

"First date... I like the sound of that, because it implies there might be more dates," he said, coming over to her and pulling her into his arms. They stood together in the middle of the deck, the ocean breeze blowing around them. His arms wrapped around her made her feel secure and safe. She wasn't a woman who had ever needed someone else to make her feel safe, so that unnerved her a little bit.

"What else did Michael pack for us to eat?" she asked, moving away from him slightly.

Leo didn't mention her move but took the picnic basket he'd brought with them over to the padded benches that lined the bow of the boat. He set it down before opening it and pulling out the items.

"Lobster rolls, homemade coleslaw, sea salt potato chips and some kind of mousse. I told him we wanted something casual."

"Sounds delicious. I swear, every summer I eat more lobster rolls than anything else," she said with a smile, trying to gain back the easy footing they'd had before she'd stepped away from him. She sat down next to the basket so they were facing each other over it.

Leo closed the basket, and it made a tabletop of sorts. "Do you want to try a Manhattan?"

"Yes," she said.

"I'll mix them up. What did you get up to this afternoon?"

Perfect opening for her to mention her business. "I spent most of it on the phone with Essie—she's my business partner. That photo you took of me generated a lot of interest and orders. So, thank you! How did you grow your supply chain? I'm struggling to find quality craftspeople who can work to a deadline."

He mixed up the drinks and then handed one to her. "Supply chain is pretty much hit or miss. I'm a member of the American Crafts Association, and that is a good place to start. There are a lot of artisans in their directory. I will say it's the one area of your business that you don't want to rush. You can look into factory machinery, but I've found that sometimes quality suffers."

"Thanks," she said, taking a sip of her drink. The whiskey was strong but smooth, and the taste wasn't as bad as she recalled. "This is a pretty decent drink."

"I try," he said, then changed the subject. "You mentioned lobster rolls—what else makes you think of summer?"

"The beach and sunburn. Friday afternoons spent sitting on my porch," she said. "What about you?"

"The beach and being here at Gran's. When we were kids, my mom would pack us all up and we'd spend a month here. Just running around on the beach and in town, sailing, eating…no curfew or rules. It was nice."

"Did you have a lot of rules growing up?" she asked.

"Yes. You?"

"It didn't feel that way, but I know there were limits," she said, realizing how much leeway her parents had always given her. And despite the fact that they'd wanted her to be a lawyer, in all fairness, she'd never really been able to believe she could be anything else until this year. That wasn't her parents' fault.

"Limits are good," he said. "Like maybe only one kiss tonight…otherwise I'm not sure what will happen."

And just like that, he made her realize that she'd backed away earlier because she was afraid that one kiss wouldn't be enough.

Leo had never been known for his tact. He knew bluntly telling Danni he wanted her wasn't the smoothest move, but he wasn't up to being someone he wasn't. He'd seen everything that had happened with his parents today, how all that sophistication they'd always wrapped themselves in had been stripped away. But with Leo, nothing was left but his most basic self. And that man wanted Danni.

He was willing to do what he needed to in order to show her that he wasn't an animal, but really at his core he felt like one. He felt like everything he'd ever believed about himself had been a big rotten husk and now it was gone. He hadn't anticipated shedding it, but nonetheless it was gone.

"Sorry if that was a bit too in-your-face," he said. "But earlier it seemed like you weren't certain you wanted me touching you, and I really don't want to dance around it all night. So, if you're not interested in that, if you just want to be friends or whatever, I'd rather you say it now."

She took a sip of her Manhattan and then crossed her legs before leaning toward him. The sun was behind her as it set, so her face was in shadow. He knew he was pushing, and part of him was doing it because he wanted to see how she was going to react.

"That's straight to the point, isn't it?"

"It is. I'm not really known for being tentative," he reminded her.

"No, you're not. Well, here's the thing. I'm not really

into much dating at the moment, because if my business isn't a success by my next birthday, I have to honor my promise to my parents and give it up and go back to practicing law...so there's that. And I like you. That kiss earlier was hot and I'd like to kiss you again, but..."

He sort of liked the sound of that. He wasn't looking for forever, and a weekend fling sounded perfect right about now.

"But?"

She nibbled her lower lip and shifted back in the seat, resting her arms against the yacht's railings. "You are very complicated. There is nothing straightforward about whatever is going on in your family, and you are the cousin of my client, so that might be odd. But also, I have the feeling that keeping things light with you is going to be hard. And I'm not sure I want to add you to the mix that is my life."

Damn.

He thought he'd dropped a truth bomb, but she had shown him that his wasn't nearly as deep or revealing as hers was. She was being honest. He owed her honesty in return. And he got it. Everything she mentioned was true. He was a mess. His family was crashing and burning in a way that would probably leave scars on them for decades to come. While a weekend fling seemed as if it might be ideal to him, for her it might not be. She would be associated with him, and he didn't want her tainted by this scandal.

"Too much for you?" she asked.

"No. It was exactly what I was fishing for when I said what I did. But I'm trying to decide if we should chuck aside our reservations and go for a weekend fling...or just finish eating dinner and sail back to the marina and walk out of each other's lives."

Danni took a moment, turning away from him to look out over the water. Whatever she came up with, he'd go along with it. He liked her. She was different from the other women he'd dated before and would probably date again after her. But he also cared about her. As Adler had mentioned, Danni had a kind heart, and the last thing he wanted to do was to crush it—even inadvertently.

"Why don't we eat dinner and see where that leads before we make any decisions?"

He nodded. "Sounds good. I wanted the chance to get to know you better."

"Me, too," she said. "Nothing about whatever is going on in your family. Just Leo stuff."

"Leo stuff?" he asked, wiggling his eyebrows at her. "What does that entail?"

"I'm not sure. Things you normally don't talk about for sure, but also what makes you tick."

"Ambition, coffee and the need to prove to my dad that I'm better than him," Leo said. He didn't need to think about that one. He'd been driven by those three things since he'd turned twenty-three and struck out on his own.

Was he still? He wanted to think that nothing had changed in the last few hours, despite the fact that he wanted it to. He wanted to be better than August, but a part of him still wanted his approval.

So stupid.

"That's what makes you tick?" she asked. "What about enjoying the journey? And good friends?"

"I mean, I can give you the politically correct version if you want, but you said to show you the real Leo."

"Fair enough."

"What makes you tick?" he asked.

"I don't know...that's sad, isn't it? I'm almost thirty and really have no idea what it is that is at my core. I know it's not law."

"That's a start," he said.

This, he thought. This was precisely why he needed to be careful of Danni. She was searching for herself, trying to carve her way in the world, and he didn't want to be the man who made her cynical and made her strive for something that Leo was slowly realizing would never be enough even for himself.

"Really?"

"Yes. Just knowing what you don't want to do is a good way to find what you do. You like making bracelets, right? What else?"

What else?

She wasn't sure. That was part of the problem with her life. She wanted not to be a lawyer and wanted to run her own business. But hand-making bracelets was taking her a lot of time to be successful. And when he'd asked if she liked making them...well, she wasn't sure. She'd seen a demo online and tried it. Then someone at the gym saw what she'd made and liked it, so she'd made a bracelet for her, and slowly her business had grown.

But it wasn't like bracelets were her passion.

"I like sketching, but I don't think I can make a living at that," she admitted.

"What kind of living?" he asked. "You have to know what you want so you'll be happy when you get it."

"Do you know?" she asked. "Because you don't seem that happy. Or maybe you haven't gotten there yet."

She knew she sounded defensive. She felt defensive and edgy, but it was only partially to do with him. It was mainly down to herself. She didn't know what she wanted. She loved her condo in the city, but it wasn't her dream home. She enjoyed the challenge of growing her business and forging her own path, but was it her higher purpose? Her mind was jumbled with images of different things she'd like to achieve in life.

He lifted both hands to her shoulders. "I do know what makes me happy, but once I get there—once I achieve it—then I want something else. So maybe... maybe I don't know what makes me happy."

She nodded. "Me neither. Sorry if I came across as aggressive. I hate that I'm not surer of my life."

"Honestly, I don't think many people are. By any definition, I'd be considered successful, yet there is still something missing in my life," he said. "Some hole that hasn't been filled."

"I can't believe that," she said. "You have everything. I can't think of a single pleasure, home, car, boat, that you don't have."

"I don't have my own plane," he admitted.

"Is that important?"

"No, or I would have bought one," he said, winking at her. "Just kidding. You're right, though. I have enough stuff, but still I'm looking for something else."

"Love?" she asked.

He started laughing. "Uh, no. That's a fairy tale."

"Is it? What about Adler and Nick?"

"I don't know. Most of the people I know who love

each other usually end up hurting each other. I'm not interested in that."

Wow. She'd never thought of love that way. Her mom and dad were still in love with each other. They fought at times, but they were definitely the kind of couple she wanted to be when she settled down. And her sister had been in love with the same woman for ten years, and they'd been married for five.

"I guess I see love differently. You're not supposed to hurt someone if you love them."

"It's not always hurting someone else. Love hurts the person who is experiencing it. It might not be something malicious, you know. Love is…it's like a storm at sea. Unpredictable, and it tends to leave nothing but flotsam behind."

"Leo, that's not love," she said. "I'm not going to pretend to be an expert. But love is supporting someone when you know they're making a mistake, and love is smiling because you see each other—"

"For you, maybe." He cleaned up the remains of their dinner and stood up. "We'll have to agree to disagree."

"Sure," she said. But a part of her realized that she wanted to show him good love. But she wasn't getting involved with him. She might hook up with him because she wanted to, but that would be it.

"What's next on the agenda?" she asked.

"You want to stay out here for a bit?" he asked. "Once the sun sets, we can swim under the stars. Night swimming is my favorite."

"I'd like that. Luckily, I have my swimsuit in my bag," she said.

"Thinking ahead. I like it. Sorry I got a little—"

"Don't be. We're just getting to know each other.

There are going to be buttons we aren't even conscious we are pushing."

He put his hands on his hips and looked over at her. "I can't decide if you're a genius or not."

"Of course I'm a genius," she said with a laugh. "I'll go and change into my bathing suit."

"Yell before you come up. I'll change up here."

She nodded and went down the gangway, carrying her bag with her. She wasn't as smart as she'd been bragging. If she were, she'd have been asking him business management questions instead of debating love.

Love. She wasn't an expert. She'd never loved anyone except maybe her family. But that was different. It bothered her that he thought love was hurtful, though.

It told her a lot about his personal relationships, and she factored that into what he'd said about business not being personal…no wonder it wasn't to him. It was more than likely his business relationships were more stable than his personal ones.

Did she want to get caught up in that? She was on the clock to get her business off the ground. Leo had so much to offer her with his knowledge, connections and business instinct. Another woman might be able to ignore her feelings and get what she needed but Danni had never been that way.

She changed into her swimsuit. It was a one-piece; she'd just never felt comfortable in a bikini. She didn't look at herself in the mirror—the temptation to see flaws was great, even though she knew the suit flattered her. Her brother had told her once that men didn't judge women the way women did, and she was her own worst critic.

She shrugged and yelled up, getting the all-clear be-

fore she went back up to find Leo standing at the edge
of the deck looking out at the ocean. He'd taken off his
shirt and wore only his swim trunks. She caught her
breath at the sight of him. He was too much to handle
in her life right now, if she was being honest, but at the
same time, she knew she wasn't going to just turn and
walk away.

Every new thing she learned about him made him
more intriguing. She might not know what she wanted
to achieve, but she knew she wanted Leo.

Seven

The water was colder than she expected. She took a quick dip and got out to lie on the deck on her towel. Leo did the same. The evening air was summery and warm. She tried to keep her eyes off his body, but he had really well-developed pecs, which were always her weak spot. His stomach was flat but not washboard lean. He looked good, like a normal man instead of some kind of perfect Hollywood specimen.

She had reviewed her notes when getting changed, and there were a lot of business questions she should be asking him. Except she kept getting distracted. He was lying on his side next to her. So close. His eyes seemed bluer than they had before. The sun was slowly setting, and there was something in his body language that made business the very last thing she wanted to concentrate on.

"So far if I had to rate this date, I'd give myself a failing grade," he said. "A cocktail you don't like, a freezing-cold swim and a rant about love...you're not getting the best version of Leo tonight."

She smiled and shook her head. "I like this version of Leo. He's not perfect. I mean, your social media feed and press image made it seem like you're someone who always has his stuff together."

Leo groaned. "I'm not sure I like where this is heading. I scrolled through your social feed earlier, and I know you didn't ask for my advice, but your feed is all over the place. You have some really good images and content, but you need a focus."

"You think so? I'm never sure if I should curate my content more carefully or be authentic," she admitted. "I don't want to come across as constantly trying to hawk my products."

"Listen, if people are following you, it's because they like your products. So, you need to give them content that builds on that. Just giving you a tip. Ultimately, you should do what you want and what makes you feel comfortable," he said.

As the sun set, the breeze felt colder against her skin, giving her goose bumps. She shivered, and Leo rubbed her arm. "Is it too cold?"

"It is chilly, but I'm not uncomfortable yet."

"Yet..."

"I mean, once the sun goes down, I might need to grab my sweatshirt," she said.

"Do you have one with you?"

"Yes. I know it's silly to carry such a big bag, but when I'm at the beach I find I need a few wardrobe essentials. I don't like to be caught unprepared."

"Me neither," he said. "I put our dessert below if you want to go down there. We can eat and chat."

Eat and chat. It sounded so innocuous and not at all what she thought Leo Bisset usually did on dates with women. But she wasn't his usual gal. She knew that. As he'd said, as far as first dates went, this one wasn't going to go down in the history books as the best one. She thought he might have decided that they were going to be quasi friends for the weekend. With no shot at being lovers.

She ignored the twinge of disappointment that went through her. That was for the best. She needed to keep her cool and focus on her real life, which was more about getting her company to make a big enough profit so she could keep doing what she wanted to do.

"What's the matter?" he asked.

"Nothing. Why?"

"Your face...you don't look as excited to be here as you were earlier."

She thought about it for a moment, weighing whether or not she should tell him what she was thinking, but she'd never really been good at hiding her thoughts. And what did she have to lose?

"I'm not sure if you've changed your mind about this date," she admitted. "I guess I was starting to enjoy Leo the man and getting to know the real you. I mean, tonight I think I'm seeing the ratty-canvas-shoe side of you instead of the polished, preppy, jet-setting man that the world knows. I liked it. I don't want you to shove me away with the rest of the crowd."

She realized after she said it that she hadn't left herself anywhere to retreat to. She was all in suddenly, and that was exciting and scary. She had no idea what his reaction was going to be, and a part of her was okay with that even though she normally liked to tread carefully.

"I don't want to push you away, either. I just figured after my many screwups that we should write this night off and maybe start over another time," he said.

"I think the screwups are what makes this feel more real."

"Me, too," he said as he reached out and ran his hand along the side of her face, then down her neck. Shivers spread down her body from his touch. It was as intense as that moment earlier on the beach when he'd kissed her.

Leo's touch seemed to be calibrated to her body. Every brush of his fingers or his gaze on her made her react as if she'd been awakened from a long sleep. She leaned slightly toward him, her lips parting. She didn't want dessert or more conversation, she wanted Leo. She wanted his arms around her and his bare chest pressed against hers. She wanted his big, strongly muscled arms wrapped around her and his mouth on hers.

She scooted slightly closer to him, and he leaned in, as well. She felt the brush of his breath over her cheek and then his lips against hers. She parted them and let him in, realizing she'd missed the taste of him over the few hours since she'd last kissed him.

He put one arm under her shoulders and the other over her waist and drew her into the curve of his body as he deepened the kiss.

Danni tasted like the sea and summer, and this kiss made him realize that he had grown complacent in his life. Maybe this entire thing with his parents was the wake-up call he needed. Because he knew without that situation, he wouldn't have taken Danni out tonight.

He just didn't take time out for himself. The question was always: How does this move my brand forward and how can I use this to take over a better position in the global marketplace?

He would have missed this. Missed the taste of her as her hungry mouth moved under his. The feel of her as her curvy body nestled in closer, her breasts pushing against his chest, her belly brushing against his stomach.

He wanted so much more from her, and he wasn't a man used to denying himself, so he didn't do so now. She wrapped one of her arms around his shoulders, drawing herself closer to him. He rolled over and realized he could have picked a better place to start this than on the deck of the yacht. He shifted her in his arms and then sat up. She adjusted her legs until she sat crossways on his lap. Her fingers pushed into his hair, and she held the back of his head as their eyes met.

He tried to remember what it was he'd been trying to do when all he really wanted to do was kiss her again. And not stop until he was buried deep inside her body. She was making him forget the chaos that had become his life.

He lowered his head, but before he could kiss her, he felt the brush of her tongue against his lips, moving over them and tracing the outline. He got hard all at once, and he groaned as she straddled him, her leg brushing against his erection.

She had both her hands on his head, holding him still as she took her time exploring his mouth. Her kiss was thorough and made him harder. It didn't allow him any time to do anything other than try to figure out the quickest way to get her naked...which made him pause.

He leaned back to break the kiss, and she arched one eyebrow at him.

"Is there a problem?"

"Yeah. I don't have a condom with me," he said. To be honest, as much as he wanted Danni, Leo hadn't been sure that sex was the right move between them. But now that didn't seem to matter. He wished he'd just brought one with him.

"It's not a problem. I'm on the pill," she said. "And I'm healthy. Are you?"

He nodded. "Had to have a physical last month for my company. Good. I'm glad."

"I'm glad, too," she said. "I would have thought you'd bring a condom."

"I didn't want to presume, and if I had one...well, let's just say I'd rather it be your choice than my pressuring you into it," he said.

She shifted slightly so she could whisper in his ear. "Do you feel pressured?"

He groaned. Whatever he'd expected of Danni when it came to sex, it was this sensual playfulness that was turning him on and making him realize that he might not have a lot of control where she was concerned.

"I feel horny."

She laughed. The sound was pure joy, and he couldn't help pulling her back and kissing her to try to capture some of her joie de vivre himself. But it quickly melted into desire. Her bathing suit and his swim trunks were thin barriers, and he knew she had to be able to feel his erection between her legs. She swiveled her hips against it, riding him through his trunks, and he couldn't help the guttural noise he made.

He put his hands on her butt to stop her from grinding against him but then found himself pushing her down on his shaft. He slipped his fingers beneath the cloth of her bathing suit, caressing her butt as she moved.

She was kissing him again, and he honestly felt like he could die in her arms and he'd be okay with it. He never wanted this feeling of anticipation to end. She rocked against him, his fingers moving over her butt, tracing her crack until he couldn't take it any longer. He wanted her naked.

He wanted to see her breasts, taste her nipples. He eased the strap of her one-piece bathing suit down her shoulder, and she moved back to stand over him, her legs on either side of his thighs.

He let his gaze move up her legs, to her body and her one breast that was now exposed. She took the other strap off, pushed her suit down over her waist and legs, and stepped out of it. She stood over him, a naked Venus risen from the sea of his dreams to distract and tempt him.

He shifted to his knees, put his hands on her thighs, kissing them as he moved higher. Using the fingers of one hand, he parted her and rubbed his tongue over her clit. Her hands were on his head, pushing him closer to her, and he made a meal of her delicate flesh. Tasting her and driving her arousal higher and higher with each flick of his tongue. Her hands tightened in his hair, and he put one of his hands on her butt cheek, drawing her even closer as he continued to taste her.

She gasped his name; it was a high, breathy sound. He could tell she was getting close to her orgasm, felt the bud beneath his tongue swelling with each brush, and he shoved his finger up inside her as he gently bit down on her clit.

She screamed his name. Her legs went weak, and he caught her as she collapsed in his arms.

Danni's entire body was buzzing as Leo lifted her in his arms and carried her to the padded bench where they'd eaten dinner. He shoved his swim trunks down his legs. She caught her breath at the sight of his fully erect manhood. She reached out and touched him, took him in her hand and caressed him.

She'd had a hunch making love to him was going to be more intense than anything she'd experienced before. He'd been raw and real with her when they talked and ate, and just now he had pushed that even further.

She'd never had filters with lovers—didn't see the point in pretending to be someone she wasn't. She hadn't ever faked an orgasm with a guy, because she felt like that just made him think he was a better lover than he really was. But with Leo there had been no time to think. No need to do the little tricks she normally had to do in order to get herself to come. He'd pushed straight past all her barriers and wrapped her in a web of sensuality, need and longing that had driven out everything except the feelings he was stirring in her.

He sat down and brought her down on his lap. His hands went to her breasts as she straddled him and felt his erection nudging at her center. She shifted so that she could feel him at her core, but he stopped her. "Not yet. I want the chance to explore every part of you in case I screw up later."

She put her hands on either side of his face and

looked into his eyes. There was an honesty there that ripped right through her. "I want that, too. You won't screw up."

"Don't. I'm not sure what I'm doing right now. I just know that I can't let you go," he said, then seemed to regret his words. He pulled her head down to his, his tongue pushing deep into her mouth. It tasted faintly salty from her. That thought made another pulse of desire go through her, and she reached down to take him into her hand and rub the tip of his cock against her center. She pushed her hips forward and down until she was impaled on him. She stayed still. This was what she'd needed. She'd felt so empty without him inside her.

"Now you can take your time," she whispered in his ear. "I needed you inside me."

He groaned and uttered a curse word as he put his hands on her backside and drove up into her. "Now I can't. I have to finish this."

He tried to bring her along with him. He teased her, bent to capture her nipple in his mouth, and she threw her head back as she rode him hard. He thrust again and again until he tore his mouth from her breast and buried his head in the side of her neck, sucking at her skin as she felt him come inside her just a moment before she came again. Her orgasm made lights dance behind her eyes, and she shivered and continued riding him until her climax passed.

She slumped forward in his arms, resting her head on his shoulder as he ran his hand up and down her back. He held her loosely to him as his breathing slowed. He didn't make any move to shift her off his lap, and she was content to stay where she was. Over his shoulder she saw the last rays of the setting sun.

He'd given her a summer memory that she knew would last forever. He started to move, and she pushed herself delicately off his lap and then stood there for a second. When their eyes met, the rawness she'd glimpsed before was gone, and the smooth billionaire was back in its place.

"You can clean up in the head downstairs first. I'll give you some privacy."

She stood there for a moment, unwilling to believe he was dismissing her, but it felt that way. Like he was tired of her and needed some distance.

"Is something wrong?" she asked. Then immediately wished she hadn't. Why couldn't she have just gone below deck and gotten changed instead of poking at him? But she knew the answer. She wasn't a woman who took lovers lightly. She knew this would more than likely be a fling, but she wasn't going to allow him to treat her as if she didn't matter. As if she could just be sent off when he was done with her.

"Everything is wrong, Danni. We're strangers, yet that sex was deeper and more...hell, I don't know what. But it was more. I'm not sure what's going on, and every time I open my mouth on this date, I make a mess of things. I figured you needed some time to yourself."

She reached over and pulled him into her arms, hugging him tightly to her. "It's the same for me. It scares me, the emotions you're stirring inside me," she admitted. "I know that no matter what we both say, this thing between us is only for one weekend, but at the same time, it feels like it could be more."

He turned his head and looked into her eyes.

"It can't be. I'm not a forever kind of man."

"And you don't believe in love," she said. "I do. And that's a nonnegotiable for me."

Eight

Being back in his grandmother's house and away from Danni made him realize how on edge he truly was. Dare was sitting on the patio in the backyard, holding an unlit cigarette in his hand, as was his oldest brother's habit. Dare was a senator and had spent his entire life being groomed for public service. There was a part of Leo that had never understood Dare's need to do that, but it was something his brother was called to do.

His father loved having what he considered an insider on Capitol Hill. But Dare seldom voted for big business's interests and often put the little guy first, something that had led to many fights between August and Dare.

"Did I miss much tonight?" he asked.

"Yeah," Dare said. "Let's see. Zac sang to Iris and won her back with some heartfelt lyrics and help from Toby."

"Glad to hear it," Leo said. Zac had entered into an

arrangement with the maid of honor to be her date for the weekend in exchange for financial backing. Over the time he got to know Iris, he'd fallen in love with her. But he'd let it slip out that she'd paid him to be her date, and it had been picked up by the gossip sites, which had caused a huge problem for Iris, who was a brand influencer who had her own show about relationships and weddings. So it had been damaging. Since then, Zac had been trying to make amends and win her back.

"Adler lost her cool and I'm not sure if Nick can fix the problems between them. Dad didn't show up. He's locked in the study with Carlton. And Mom went to talk Adler off the ledge and was instrumental in keeping her on Nantucket."

Leo dropped down next to his brother on one of the loungers that offered a view of the ocean and Gran's garden. "I guess we shouldn't be surprised that every event is highly charged. If I were Adler and Nick, I think I'd elope."

"Right? But at this point I think there are too many people here for them to even entertain that idea. Where were you, by the way?" Dare asked.

Leo rubbed the back of his neck. He wasn't sure he wanted to talk about Danni, but this was Dare. Of all the Bissets, Dare was the most levelheaded and had a way of looking at a problem that always brought clarity.

"I went on a date," he said. "After having words with Dad, the last thing I really wanted was more family drama. I visited with Adler to make sure she'd be okay with it."

"I'm not going to scold you for missing the rehearsal dinner," Dare said.

"I did sound defensive, didn't I?" He had to admit

when the family was all together, it was sometimes a little too easy to fall back into the sibling dynamic they'd had growing up. Leo, Zac, and Mari often seemed like the troublemakers while Logan and Dare had to step in and be sensible. But Logan wasn't himself right now, and that left only Dare to hold them all together.

"A tad, but I don't blame you. By the way, I am not a fan of how you talked to Dad this afternoon, but I think you were spot-on with your message. He's spent too many years selfishly pushing us all, including Mom, into the roles he wants for us and never once has acknowledged the price we've paid."

Leo looked over at Dare. "I realize I was harsh, but honestly, it was a sobering moment for me. You know I've always craved Dad's respect and kudos, and today...well, I had the first inkling that maybe I was Don Quixote, tilting at windmills instead of pursuing something real."

"I get it. I think Mari had the same realization not that long ago, and my relationship with Dad was always complex, so I keep my distance when I can. But I think he's finally starting to understand the impact of his focus on always being the best...it's not even the best. What would you say it was?"

"He thinks he's better than everyone else. That he can do whatever he wants and there won't be any consequences," Leo said. "And this weekend he's learned otherwise."

"We all have. It's made me think hard about my actions," Dare said.

"Really? What have you ever done that is questionable?" Leo asked.

Dare looked uncomfortable as he glanced away. "Never mind that. How was your date?"

How was it? Leo still wasn't sure. He'd dropped Danni off at her place, and she'd been sweet when they'd said their goodbyes. A part of him had wanted to stay the night, but after their discussion on the yacht, he knew that wasn't wise. They'd both acknowledged they weren't in a position to start a relationship, and if he'd stayed…it wouldn't have been the wise thing to do.

"That bad? Or that good?" Dare asked. "It's taking you a long time to answer."

Leo laughed and shook his head. "Both. Can it be both? She's complicated, Dare. She brings out my most real self, and that guy isn't as polished as I'm used to being. I feel like I have no game when I'm with her. And then something unexpected will happen and we connect…"

"That's good, Lion," Dare said, using Leo's child-hood nickname. "It means that you are probably with a woman who is going to change your life. Tell me more about her. What does she do?"

"She's got a small Etsy shop to sell her jewelry and leather goods. I pretty much dissed her in an interview and then of course she was in the foursome at the scramble. But…there's something about her."

"You don't sound like you. I think that's good," Dare said.

"Is she? Or is it just that everything with Mom and Dad has me in a tailspin?" Leo asked. "I'm so confused about everything. No one is who I thought they were, and for the first time ever, I don't respect Dad. I mean, he's always been tough and, as you said, arrogant. But I kind of got why up until today. Today when I heard

Mom talking about how he was when she was pregnant...he just seemed like a bully, and I don't want to
be that kind of man."

Dare tucked the unlit cigarette into his shirt pocket
and spun around to face him. Leo stared up at his older
brother and waited.

"You're never going to be that kind of man," Dare
said. "Dad would never be able to honestly look at himself the way you are. And I think the woman you went
out with is more important to you than you want to
admit."

"Maybe."

Dare didn't say anything else, just squeezed Leo's
shoulder before going into the house. Leo stayed where
he was, thinking about Danni and if there was a way
forward with her or if he should just let himself be satisfied with one night.

Danni took a shower and then climbed into her bed,
taking her sketchbook with her. There were so many
images tumbling around in her head after the date with
Leo. She'd toyed with asking him in when he'd walked
her back to her cottage, but in the end, she had decided
that she didn't need to do anything else spontaneous.
She needed to remember her focus, her goal. She didn't
know how Essie did it, but her friend never seemed to
really have any problem staying in complete boss babe
mode.

Danni vacillated between wanting to be a titan of
industry and needing to curl up with her sketchbook.
Or, in the case of this evening, curling up with Leo. She
hadn't asked him in, but she missed him. She found her
pencil moving over the page and saw the images she

was sketching were all him. He'd been so…all man. Normally he had a sophisticated polish that made everyone in the room notice him. Men wanted to be him, and women wanted to be with him. But tonight, when he'd stood on the deck of the yacht, she'd had a glimpse of a different man. Probably the reason why he was so successful in business was because he had that wildness inside him.

She realized that he had a killer instinct. Something that she'd been told to develop by many of the TED talks she'd watched and business seminars she'd attended. Actually, her father had advised it as well for when she was in the courtroom, but that wasn't her. It just never had been.

She closed the sketchbook, realizing that staring at drawings of Leo wasn't what she needed to do. She opened the notes app on her phone and looked at the list she'd made before her date with Leo. He had given her a few tips and she was glad of that; she would use them when moving forward, but she still needed to learn so much more from him.

She had one more chance tomorrow at the wedding, but honestly, how was she going to turn the topic to business advice at the reception? She doubted she'd get a chance to talk to him at the ceremony. And honestly, should she even continue on this path?

When she thought back over the night, she realized he'd just volunteered info that would help her with the business. But she wasn't very good at shutting down her emotions and just getting the information she needed. Maybe she needed to be more like that. But how?

She rubbed the back of her neck, enjoying how parts of her body were pleasantly sore from Leo's lovemaking. She felt a tingle between her legs as she remembered his mouth on her. She definitely regretted not inviting him in now.

He seemed like the kind of man who would have wanted sex again, and she realized she wanted him now.

She rolled over. Was she finally turning into a sexual creature? After all these years of just sort of liking sex, she was now obsessively reliving every moment on the yacht with Leo. He'd brought out a side of her that she hadn't really given much weight in the past, and she wanted to be more of that woman.

She got out of bed and went into the living room. Getting out her laptop, she forced herself to work. She was on Nantucket to grow her business and to keep her client happy. Not to develop an obsession with Leo Bisset.

She opened up the order page on the website and saw that they had reached capacity on the bracelets. She was both thrilled and surprised but also a little worried. She had to sort out her supply-chain issues if she was going to take her business to the next level.

She was trying to concentrate on that when her phone pinged, and she glanced over at the notification on the screen, expecting the message to be from Essie. But it was Leo. She picked up her phone and read it.

I know you're probably sleeping but I can't. I miss you.

She thought about ignoring it, but she couldn't.

Not sleeping. Trying to work to take my mind off you. This is so crazy. We're practically strangers.

She saw the dancing dots and waited for his response, closing her laptop and curling her legs underneath her. She didn't have long to wait.

It is crazy, but I like it. My family are all sleeping, and I don't know if I can.

Why not? she immediately responded.

Thinking of you and...

And?

I said some douchey things to my dad and mom earlier and I'm not sure what to expect when I see them in the morning.

Best to just apologize...do you think you should?

Yes. But I'm still mad so I'm afraid I might say something else hurtful. And tomorrow is the wedding so I should try to just be chill.

Is there anything I can do?

Run away with me. Jk. I can't do that. And I know you wouldn't.

Danni sent back the zany face emoji, but a part of her wished he'd meant it. But she was starting to suspect that it wasn't her—Danni Eldridge—that Leo was obsessed with at this moment. It almost seemed as if any woman would do. She was just holding a place, being the distraction he needed. It was the distraction that he wanted and not really her. She realized she had to be very careful not to make Leo into a man she wanted him to be but that he wasn't.

I have to go now, she typed. See you at the ceremony tomorrow.

Okay. Good night.

Good night.

She put her phone away, knowing she'd done the right thing. No matter how intense and real the feelings between herself and Leo were, she was wise enough to know that a man who didn't believe in love wasn't going to fall for her.

Juliette Bisset was sleeping in the same room as her husband, in the same queen-size bed they always shared when visiting her mother. But it felt bigger than king-size. She was careful to stay to her own side and had been pretending to sleep since Auggie had come into the room.

She hadn't been able to talk to Logan; he was refusing all conversations with her, and her heart was breaking.

The secret of his birth had always been tucked deep inside her. From the moment she'd held him and then breastfed him, Logan had been her son. As he'd grown up, he hadn't seemed any different from her other children, and she'd believed that the secret of his birth would be one she'd take to her grave. But she should have known better.

She felt tears burning her eyes and struggled to keep her breathing even so Auggie wouldn't hear her crying. But when he rolled over and put his hand on her shoulder, she let out the ragged breath that she'd been holding. She didn't know what to say to him or to her kids. She was sorry she'd kept Logan's birth a secret, but she'd been convinced the only way to keep her marriage together was to bring home a healthy son to Auggie, and a part of her had been proven right. They had gotten stronger as a couple after that. It was only after Leo's birth, when Auggie had a public affair, that she'd realized she might have been lying to herself for years. But at that point, with four sons, she'd felt like she had no choice but to stay with him.

"Jules…"

"Don't," she said. Her voice was ragged, and no matter how much she wanted to stop crying, she couldn't. "I can't talk about this."

He pulled her into his arms, curving against her back and just holding her, which made her cry that much harder. She'd always struggled with why she stayed with him for all these years, but this was the very reason why. There were times when August was the best man she'd ever known. Of course, he was also the worst man she'd ever known. It was a constant balancing act. After Mari's birth they'd found a new truce, and over the last twenty years, they'd really fallen in love and committed themselves to each other and their marriage. Or so Juliette had thought.

"I'm sorry," he said. "I know you don't want to talk about this, but I'm very sorry that you went through the loss of our son alone and that you felt as if you had no other choice than to bring another baby home in his place."

She shook her head. "Me, too."

"Where did you bury our son?" he asked her.

She had been keeping this secret for too long. She'd had the baby cremated and put his ashes in an urn that she'd kept hidden here at her mom's house until Musette had died. Her broken, lost sister, who wouldn't be there to see her daughter grow up, and Juliette's lost son were buried together in the family plot on the property.

"Here, in the family plot with Musette. I figured my lost sister and son should be together."

"That sounds about right," he said. "Honey—"

"Don't *honey* me. Not right now, Auggie. I can't…"

"Okay."

She didn't say anything else and neither did he, leaving her wondering if he'd fallen asleep. But then he squeezed her tight. "I'm sorry I was such an ass for so many years. You were always too good for me."

"Now I'm sure you don't feel that way," she said. She'd deceived him for a long time, and that had to rankle him and make him mad at her. Though the way he held her made her believe that he wasn't upset with her after all.

"I do still feel that way. It makes me realize my influence on you… I always hoped you'd make me a better man and never thought how I would affect you. My behavior changed you. Made you afraid for our family. I don't want you to think that I didn't love you and Dare and our unborn child. The affair…well, sometimes I think it was my way of proving I was still a stud. Still the biggest, baddest man in the room, never realizing that I was sacrificing what mattered."

She didn't want to hear any of that. August was looking back on that time with regret, as he should do, but Juliette remembered how it was, and the pain was still very sharp. He'd needed to be the man every woman wanted, and he'd had a string of affairs around the time of each of her pregnancies. It seemed that as much as he wanted to build a dynasty, at the same time each new child was a bond that tied him closer to her, and he'd resented that. He'd wanted to be seen as his own man.

He rolled her over to face him. His face wasn't clear in the dappled moonlight coming into the room, but decades of sleeping with the man made it easy for her to discern his strong features. Age had added lines by his eyes and mouth, and gray at his temples, but she still saw the man she'd fallen in love with all those years ago.

"Why did you stay with me?" he asked.

"Did you want me to leave you? Was that why you had the affairs?" she asked. She'd often wondered if her own stubbornness in not just leaving and letting her marriage fail had made her equally culpable in their relationship.

"No, I didn't. But I did have a lot of guilt. Thinking you were better than me," he admitted.

"But now you know I wasn't," she said. "I didn't leave you because when you turn that charm and attention on me, you make me feel like I'm the only woman in the world that matters to you. I guess we both know that was never true."

"Jules," he said.

But she was already turning her back to him, and after a moment, she heard him get up and leave the room. She didn't cry anymore, but sleep eluded her for the rest of the night.

Nine

Saturday dawned bright and sunny, almost as if to make up for the hovering storm cloud of paparazzi and scandal-sheet reporters in the lobby of the Nantucket Hotel.

Danni made her way through the lobby to the elevators, carrying a box of doughnuts and a thermos of coffee. She was headed up to meet Adler and her bridal party. To be honest, Danni wasn't sure she was needed, but she had wanted to ensure that Adler was beyond happy with not only her product but with her customer service. So, when Adler had texted to ask if she minded stopping by the bakery and bringing doughnuts and coffee to the suite, Danni had texted back an enthusiastic "of course." She didn't mind and would love to do it.

She was here for business. In fact, last night she should have been schmoozing at the rehearsal dinner instead of going on a date with Leo. She'd heard that Toby Osborn had given an unscheduled performance. The two people who were talking about it in front of her in line at the doughnut shop mentioned that some of his music industry friends had been there, too.

A part of Danni had wondered if maybe she should be going after that crowd for business. She hated to think in clichés, but most musicians did wear a lot of jewelry. But she wasn't really boho chic. She never had been. She was too preppy for that. And she knew it. Which was why she was schlepping doughnuts and hoping to cultivate some of Adler's more sophisticated brides-maids as future clients.

She rapped on the door to the suite, and someone Danni didn't know opened it. The woman motioned for her to come in while talking loudly into her phone. The woman nodded toward the other part of the room, and Danni headed over to find the bride and her maid of honor sitting together and chatting.

"Hi," she said, looking for a spot to deposit the doughnuts and coffee thermos before turning back to-ward them.

"Hey, Danni," Adler said, standing up and coming over to greet her. "You're a lifesaver. This is Iris. Have you two met?"

"Not officially," Iris said. "I love the bracelet you designed for me to wear today."

"Thanks. It's nice to meet you. I feel like I know you because I'm a huge fan of your show," Danni said. "I hope that didn't sound weird. I just meant it's great to meet you in person."

Iris laughed. "It's totally cool. I have done the same

thing a million times. Tell me more about your jewelry business."

"Well, I have a few products in stock that I made in bulk and sell from my web shop, but I prefer to do custom work. That's where my main focus is, trying to grow that side of the business. I'm hoping to have a little storefront of my own one day," Danni said.

"I can see where that would be possible. Your designs are really unique, but also the quality is top-notch. When you're ready to open your store, look me up. I'm always interested in investing in women-run businesses. Let me grab one of my business cards," Iris said.

Danni just nodded and stood there while Iris went to her purse and got a card. "Here you go. Can't wait to hear from you."

"Thanks for this," she said, pocketing the card and trying not to get too excited. For all she knew, Iris was just being nice, but Danni couldn't help wanting to squee with joy.

"So what doughnuts did you get for us?"

"They already had a dozen boxed up with Adler's name on it, so I'm not sure what's in here."

Iris opened the box, and a few of the other bridesmaids came over, including the woman who had been on the phone when Danni had arrived.

"Sorry for being so rude earlier," she said by way of introduction. "I was dealing with a catering issue. I mean, it's the wedding day, and the last thing Adler needs is for him to text her about nonsense. I'm Olivia Williams."

"Danni Eldridge."

"Bridesmaid?"

"Jewelry designer. You?"

"Soon to be sister-in-law, bridesmaid and all-around fabu person," Olivia said with a wink. "Actually, I'm also trying to keep everyone calm. Every day there's another bombshell from the parents. Gah, what a messed-up situation."

"You seem totally awesome," Danni said with a return wink. "I'm not up on all the gossip. Figured I'd just keep out of it."

"Good idea," Olivia said. "My mom had an affair with August Bisset. You knew that, right?"

"Yeah, I had heard something about that. But then I heard…it can't be true, but I heard Logan Bisset is actually Nick's twin."

Olivia nodded. "Yeah, that shit's true, too. Adler said if one more revelation comes out today, she's running away, and truth be told, I'm going with her."

"I don't blame you. Surely that's all that is going on between them, right?"

"I hope so. I have been looking forward to having a sister all my life, and I am not letting Adler slip away. So whatever I have to do, I'm going to do it," Olivia said.

Danni liked not only Olivia's attitude but also the love she could hear in the other woman's voice for Adler.

"I've always wanted a sister, too," Adler said, coming over to them. "So I'm happy to get you! Thank you again for bringing these, Danni. I was afraid to go myself because of all the paparazzi trying to snap a photo of me and make a story out of my expression or whatever."

"It really is okay. I can't imagine being in your situation," Danni said.

"Well, to be honest, this isn't the way I thought my wedding day would play out," Adler admitted.

Which made them all start laughing. Danni helped

out with hair and makeup where she could but then left the other women to go and get ready for the ceremony herself.

Leo wasn't too sure what to expect when he went down to breakfast. Dare had been chill last night, but he had no idea what he would get from the rest of the family.

Logan looked the worse for wear, as if he'd been drinking too much or not sleeping. He had a pair of Wayfarer sunglasses on and was sitting at one of the chairs in the middle of the table with a Bloody Mary in front of him.

Normally Leo felt like he was in competition with Logan. A long time ago their gran had said it was natural for younger brothers to feel that way, but Leo wondered if a part of him had sensed that Logan was different, then he immediately dismissed that thought. Logan was his big brother, someone Leo had always looked up to and wanted to be like. As much as Leo had competed to get their father's attention, it was Logan he'd emulated the most.

"Bro, you okay?" he asked, pulling out the chair next to Logan and sitting down.

"Fuck, no," he said. "I haven't talked to Mom, and Dad is mad at me. I made a deal that's going to set Nick and Williams Inc. back, and I know everyone in the family is going to think I'm a dick for doing it. And I have to go to a wedding today and put on my happy face…"

"What deal?"

Logan shoved his hands through his hair. "I bought a patent that Nick has been trying to get for eighteen months and he needs it to move forward with a deal he already had in the works. God, I'm such an asshole sometimes."

"You're not an asshole. You just have to win at all costs. If it helps, Dad is pissed at me, too," Leo said. "Mom will understand, no matter how hurt she might be. She always does. She loves you, Logan. When you are ready, I have no doubt she's going to be right there. Business is business, and Nick knows that better than anyone else. It's not personal, right?"

Logan shrugged and took a sip of his Bloody Mary before he pushed his sunglasses up on his head. "When did you get so smart?"

"I always was, you just never noticed," Leo said. "Seriously, though, no one is going to be looking too closely at you today. So be happy for Adler if you can. This is her day, and I'm pretty sure all eyes will be on her."

"All eyes should be on her," Logan said. "That's the part of all this that really rubs me the wrong way. I mean, I've never made any bones about the fact that I don't like Nick, but even I wouldn't have wanted to see Adler's wedding singed like this."

"Um, what about the patent?"

"That's business."

"Not personal like the parentage thing," Leo said. "No one deserves this kind of situation. Especially not Adler. She's always seemed so strong and able to roll with anything, I guess from bouncing between two worlds like she did. But yesterday…she seemed like she was barely holding herself together."

"Yeah, makes me feel like a douche for having my own feelings."

"She'd be the first to tell you not to beat yourself up over that," Leo said.

"Are you speaking for everyone now?" Logan asked sarcastically.

Leo shook his head. His brother took all the burdens of their family on his shoulders. He got it. They all had a sense of loyalty and guardianship when it came to being Bissets. But in this case, none of this was Logan's fault. "I spent the afternoon with her. We chatted. She doesn't blame you for this, and she even was worried about you. She understands the rivalry between you and Nick probably better than anyone else."

"She does," he said quietly. "I wish I could change things."

"I'm pretty sure you're not the only one," Leo said. "I'm not sure about Dad, though. He probably doesn't think he did anything wrong."

"Or maybe he knows that the past can't be changed, and he has to move forward," their father said from the doorway. He wore a polo shirt and a pair of khaki pants. His salt-and-pepper hair was neatly groomed and his jaw clean-shaven. Leo looked over at his father with a twinge of guilt at what he'd said. But the truth was, Dad hadn't acted as if he felt bad about any of it.

"You should still apologize," Leo said.

"To whom?" Auggie asked.

"Mom, Logan, Nick, Adler…do I need to go on? Also, what about Dare and me and Zac and Mari?" Leo felt that anger stirring in him again. "You never once made our family your priority, and I get it. I know what it's like to close big deals and watch your profits soar, but until this weekend I had never realized how little you valued us."

"Not everything is about you, Leo," Auggie said. "I'm not answerable to you."

"No, you're not," Leo said. "And to be honest, it doesn't matter anymore. There was a time when I thought you hung the moon. I wanted to follow in your footsteps and have everyone say I was just like you, but not anymore."

He pushed back from the table and stood up.

"Leo. That's enough," Logan said.

"No, it's not. Part of the problem is that no one ever told Dad that he was being an asshole, so he thought it was okay to keep on being one. But not anymore," Leo said. "Sorry if you don't like that."

He walked away from his father and brother and out of the house. He hadn't meant to say any of that, but he hadn't been able to help himself. He knew his father wasn't one to show emotions easily, but he also had never doubted that his father loved him and his siblings. And this weekend he'd realized that he wasn't as sure of that love anymore. Because what man who loved his family would have affairs and father children he didn't know about?

Worse yet was how Leo still wanted to be just like August. How could he? What was it going to take for him to finally break free of that? He just wished it would happen.

Danni arrived at the wedding ceremony a good forty minutes early. She'd had time to think about Iris's offer, and it made her realize that if she was just herself, she could probably cultivate a few more contacts while she was at the wedding. She was pretty sure Leo would be busy with his family, and after talking to Olivia she got why Leo had needed a distraction the day before. She wasn't even part of their family, and she would have needed more than a distraction if everything she'd ever believed about her siblings and her parents was revealed to be a lie.

She imagined that was going to take him some time to get over, and she knew the last place his mind could be was with her. They'd had some fun, and she was determined to keep that thought firmly in mind.

Then she caught a glimpse of him in his tux standing slightly apart from his brothers. He had on dark sunglasses, and his expression was pensive. He was hotter than she remembered. She wanted to go and try to distract him again.

Except that wasn't her job.

She wasn't his girlfriend. She'd been his Friday-night hookup. That was all.

As tempted as she was to try to make it into something more, she knew better than to lie to herself about him. He wasn't going to suddenly change from his jet-set lifestyle to being a Netflix-and-chill guy. She had to remember that. But it was harder than she wanted it to be.

She saw a few people she recognized as buyers for a large US retail chain. Adler had mentioned that they were going to be here today, and Essie had looked them up on the internet and sent Danni their photos so she could find them. She had a moment where she was torn.

She could do the business thing and go and introduce herself. She had just about convinced herself to do that when she saw Leo turn and walk away from the guests who were milling around on the lawn where the outdoor wedding would take place. She noticed that no one followed him, and she knew it made no sense for her to go after him. Sleeping with Leo wasn't part of her plan for the weekend, yet somehow, he had become that. Somehow, he'd become as important as meeting retail buyers.

She didn't analyze it; she just went right off in the direction where Leo had disappeared. She quickly found him facing the ocean with his hands in his pockets and his head tipped up toward the sun. She stood there for a moment watching him. He was solitary. A man who didn't want or need anyone else around him. She could see that he was conflicted, and to her he seemed...lost.

She knew she couldn't be the one to find him and bring him back to the wedding in this moment. He wasn't physically lost, he was spiritually lost, and she recognized that because she had been the same way for so long until she'd decided to quit practicing law and turn her Etsy shop into a profit-making business. Which was why she should be talking to those buyers so she wouldn't have to go back to the law practice. But she was here.

Because this man called to her in a way that she struggled to understand. She didn't want to be standing here watching him. Aching for him. Witnessing his pain over the fact that the father he loved and looked up to wasn't the man Leo had always believed him to be.

"Want some company?" she asked, feeling like she had to say something. If she kept staring at him, she was going to start trying to convince herself that all sorts of things about him were true.

"Not sure how good I'll be, but yes," he said, glancing over his shoulder at her. "Damn, you look good."

She smiled at the way he said it. "Thanks. Figured

I couldn't just show up with my hair blowing around me like a storm."

"I would have liked it," he said. "You try too hard to be this buttoned-up version of yourself. I like it when you are wild and free."

She'd come out here to help him, to bring him back to the fold, but he was looking at her, looking past the barriers she'd put up and dropping truth bombs she wasn't ready to deal with. She did try hard to be the woman she wanted the world to see, but she wasn't sure if that was who *she* truly wanted to be.

"I like you when you smile," she said, ignoring his remark as best she could. "But you're not today."

"Yeah. I keep saying things that I shouldn't. Keep getting angry with my family. I wasn't kidding when I said I'm bad company today."

She walked over and stood next to him. "You might be, but you were smart enough to remove yourself from them for a little while. Was it something about your brother?"

"Logan?"

"Yes. You two seemed awfully close yesterday. I hope you still are."

"We are," he said. "I'm not mad at Logan. I'm mad at my parents, and a part of me knows that I shouldn't be. I'm not the child most affected by their deceit, yet I am still hurting. I can't help it. I want them both to realize that they have shattered what our family was, and I'm not sure I can go back to being the loyal son I was before."

She had no way to help him through this. No words that would ease his conscience or make him feel okay. So she did the one thing that her gut told her to do. She put her arm around his waist. He stood there stiffly for a moment before he put his arm around her shoulder and hugged her to his side.

He didn't say anything else and neither did she until the wedding coordinator came to get him because the wedding was about to begin.

Ten

Leo wasn't surprised when his mom pulled him aside after the ceremony while the photographer was taking photos of different groups. As soon as she was done being photographed with Adler, Juliette looped her arm through his and walked him away from the rest of the family.

"Mom, this isn't the time," he said, having an idea that he was going to be getting a talk, which was how his mom had always referred to any type of discipline she had to mete out to them when they were children.

"It's the perfect time, Lion. We don't have to be at the reception for thirty minutes or so, and I think you need someone to talk to."

"Not you, Mom," he said. "I don't want to say any of the things that are in my head to you."

She stopped near some of the seats that were still set

up from the service and gestured for him to sit down. He did, and she sat next to him. Putting her arm on the back of his chair, she turned so that her knees were facing toward him, and he did the same. Looking into her pretty eyes, he couldn't help but remember all the times in his life that he'd come to her for comfort and advice. All the times he'd just turned to her knowing she'd be the solid rock of the Bisset family.

And for the first time when he looked at her, he wasn't just seeing the love that he always saw in her expression. He saw her pain, too. This was what he'd wanted to avoid. He didn't want to be his asshole self with his mom. She was already tearing herself up with guilt and recriminations. He knew she didn't need to hear it from him. God knew how she was going to deal with Logan.

"Lion, if you don't say it, then we can't move past it. I know what I did was wrong and that it has really had a profound effect on the family. I also heard what you said to your father...thank you for defending me, but the blame for my deceit is mine and mine alone. You know I believe that we are all responsible for our actions," she said.

He did know that. Many times when he was younger, he'd tried to defend doing something he knew she wouldn't approve of by using the justification that Logan or Dare had done something worse. That argument had never worked on her. "I know that. But at the same time, you're the one who always was home with us and loving us... I can't blame you for this, Mom, not that it's even my right to place blame. I guess what I'm saying is I don't want to direct the anger I feel at you. I hate that the family we had was a lie, and I'm trying to sort out where that leaves me. I've always been so proud of our family—even our arrogance. I thought that was okay because we were good people."

She didn't say anything in response, and he wondered if he'd gone too far. Then he got mad at himself and her. She'd been the one to force this conversation when he hadn't wanted it. He should have dashed out of the photo session to go find Danni. She was just the excuse he could use to get away from this.

"We are still good people. Good people aren't perfect, Leo, and I'll thank you to remember that everyone makes mistakes. I was trying to do the right thing, and once I took that action, I had no other option but to stick with my lie. You've made mistakes, as well," she said. "Your father and I have a complicated relationship, but the one thing that even you have to admit is that we have always loved you and your siblings."

She was right, but then, she knew she was. He stood up. "I know that. This is why I didn't want to talk. I'm not ready to be a grown-up about this yet. I feel like all of my life has been a lie, and I have to figure out how to get past it. There is nothing that's going to magically make this okay, which I think you know. I love you, Mom, but I need time to get over being mad at Dad and, in some small way, you."

She stood up, as well. "Fair enough."

She stood so straight, her pride lending her the illusion of being taller than she already was. He put his arms around her and hugged her close. "I love you."

She hugged him back, and for a minute it felt like everything would be okay in their world. He stepped back and moved away from her. "I'll see you later at the reception."

"See you there."

He walked away, knowing that his other siblings and the Williams family were probably watching him. A part of him knew that he needed to reel in his emotions, but for the first time in his life, his path was broken. It wasn't that he couldn't see it—it was that something impassable had grown up in front of him and the way forward was barred. He had no idea what to do next.

And it wasn't business that had him flummoxed, it was his personal life. He had Danni, who had been a breath of fresh air and comfort when he needed it, but he had no idea where that was going. If anywhere. She wasn't looking for anything with him, and he was leaving his family and racing to be by her side. Did that mean as much as it seemed to?

Or was she just an escape?

He didn't want to use her and would hate himself if he did that. But at the same time, he wasn't going to let this bring him to his knees, and he would use whatever—or whoever—he needed to in order to get his mojo back.

Danni enjoyed the wedding more than she'd expected to. After knowing all that Adler and Nick had been through in the last three days, Danni had cried when they'd looked into each other's eyes and said, "I do." It was a special moment that had made Danni realize that once she got her business off the ground, she wanted to find a man who looked at her the way Nick had looked at Adler.

She had been seated in the same row with some of Marielle's influencer friends, and they were nice and friendly but had immediately left to post videos and photos from the event. Danni stood off to one side trying to observe them, but she was distracted, watching as Leo and his family posed for their photos with Adler and Nick and then with Adler and her dad.

And one thing that Danni observed was how they all smiled. They were really good at looking happy and like everything was perfect for the photographer. Her family would have all been glaring at each other if they were having the kind of weekend the Bissets were. As soon as the photographer was done with them and they were dismissed, Leo started to walk away, but his mom caught up to him and drew him off to the side for a private conversation.

Danni watched for a moment before realizing what she was doing. It wasn't any of her business. She needed to get herself to the reception and start schmoozing like the other guests instead of watching Leo.

But again, she felt that pull toward him. It wasn't just sexual. Of course, she wasn't denying that he was hot, and she had thought about their time together at odd moments during the day—especially when the minister had said Nick could kiss the bride. She'd had this weird little vision of herself as the bride getting kissed by Leo...

But that wasn't going to happen. He wasn't the marrying kind, especially after the huge mistakes his parents had made. To be honest, it was enough to make her think twice about marriage.

"Hey, you on your own?"

She glanced over to see Olivia Williams walking toward her, swinging her bridesmaid bouquet in one hand. "Yes. I guess I should have brought a plus-one, but I figured I'd be working."

"But now you wish you had? It's so awkward when

you're doing a social event for business. Happens to me all the time. Dad tends to make one of my brothers go with me but that's even more annoying, because then they are trying to ditch me so they can find someone to—"

"Someone to what, Liv? Are you going to deny that you ditched me the last time to hook up with Beau Montrose?"

The guy who came up and put his arm over Olivia's shoulder bore a strong resemblance to her. But for the life of her, Danni couldn't remember the name of any of her brothers except Nick, and that was because he was the groom.

"Why shouldn't she do that?" Danni asked.

"Good point, Ash. You've done it often enough," Olivia said.

He put his hands up. "I was trying to say there was equal dumping going on. I'm Asher, by the way, and you are?"

"Danni Eldridge."

"Nice to meet you," he said, holding out his hand, which she shook and let drop. "Are we heading over to the reception?"

"Yes, Danni's going to join us. She's stagging it," Olivia said.

"Are you looking for a—"

"Stop now," Olivia interrupted him. "She's not interested in you."

"Liv, we don't know that for sure," Asher said. The two of them cracked Danni up. It was clear to see they had a close relationship. She envied it, having never really been that close to her siblings.

It was different than the way Logan and Leo had interacted but just as sincere and solid.

"She's right. I'm kind of seeing someone," Danni said. It felt odd to mention it. It wasn't like she and Leo had solid plans. But she wasn't going to pretend that he didn't exist.

"Of course you are. You are too lovely to be on your own," Ash said.

"Stop it before I gag. Do you ever get a girl to go home with you?" Olivia said.

"Women like a guy who treats them with kindness, Liv. Also, they don't like to be called girls."

Olivia rolled her eyes as she looked over at Danni. "He's so woke."

"I am," Ash said. "Come on, ladies, I'll escort you to the reception."

He held out each of his arms. Olivia looped her arm through his left and Danni was reaching for the right when someone slipped his arm through hers first.

"I'll escort Danni," Leo said.

She looked up at him. His expression was inscrutable and fierce. Ash just nodded. "That's cool. She was standing all alone, and that's never comfortable at a wedding."

"That's true. Thanks for being a gentleman," Leo said.

"Uh, before you two start patting yourselves on the back, Danni and I were taking care of ourselves just fine," Olivia stated.

"Of course you were. That's not what we were saying," Ash said. "Come on, Liv, let's go."

Danni watched them walk away. "I didn't know if I should wait for you or what."

"I know. I haven't been the best guy to be around today. But when I saw you with them… I want you with me, Danni. I want to enjoy the party and pretend that I don't have to deal with the messes I've made. Just for a few hours. What do you say?"

She wanted to just say yes. But he had no idea how complicated he was. How much he was pulling at her in so many different ways. She wanted to figure out a way to fix him but knew she never could. But for a few hours…

"Yes."

The reception was fun. The band was good. Toby Osborn sang a song to Adler for her first dance with Nick that made everyone cry. Then he did a set of his hits to get everyone dancing. All in all, Leo was finding Danni made it very easy for him to shove all the messy stuff with his family aside. He drank the signature cocktail, a blackberry whiskey lemonade that went down very easily, and Danni kept pace with him.

They danced and laughed a lot. She looked perplexed a time or two, as if she wasn't sure why he was dancing just with her, and he could have told her it was because she was the only woman he had eyes for. But he knew that was the alcohol talking. Yet it wasn't just the drinks that made him possessive of her and want to express feelings he knew he needed to keep to himself.

When Toby and his band played the opening chords of "Brown-Eyed Girl," Danni leaped to her feet. "This is my song. You have to dance with me."

He threw back the rest of his drink and grabbed her hand, leading her out onto the dance floor. They walked by the Williams family, and Danni saw Olivia in the group.

"Girl, this is our song," Danni yelled over to her. "Yaas!"

Leo wasn't sure how, but he found himself dancing in a group with Danni, Olivia, Asher, his brother Zac and Zac's girlfriend, Iris. Somehow it made sense to stay on the dance floor for the next few songs, and when the band slowed to "Tenerife Sea" by Ed Sheeran, he pulled Danni close.

She was supple and pliant, her body fitting into the curves of his as she wrapped her arms around him. She ran her fingers against the back of his neck as she sang the words she knew—every other one—and closed her eyes, resting her head against his shoulder. He wanted this moment to last forever.

They weren't in love, but right now he felt like they could be. That he could be a different man. He held her as the music played, and even with everyone swaying around them, it felt like it was just the two of them. He could be the man she needed him to be. But hell, he wasn't even sure she was looking for a man.

He'd never been one to put a woman first. Not like this. Not like he was feeling it in this moment. He danced her to the edge of the dance floor and then took her hand and led her outside until they were alone under the clear moonlit sky.

The music could still be heard in the distance, and she looked up at him with those wide, kind eyes, her trusting heart in them.

God, she should never look at him like that.

He was feeling so many things. He wanted to remind himself that tomorrow he might once again consider her a distraction, but tonight...tonight she was everything he needed.

He didn't want to think about anything else in the world except Danni and how she looked tonight. Her hair was curling a little more wildly around her face than it had during the wedding ceremony.

Her eyes sparkled with the passion and intelligence that he realized she brought to everything she did. When her full lips fell into an easy smile, he admitted to himself he couldn't resist wanting to kiss her.

"Why did you bring us out here?" she asked.

"I wanted to kiss you," he said. "And there are too many people in that room for the kind of kiss I want."

"Are you going to ask my permission again?" she teased.

He groaned.

"No," he said. He was a goner where she was concerned.

He lowered his mouth and kissed her. She opened her lips under his, and her tongue rubbed over his as she held on to his shoulders and went up on her tiptoes to deepen the kiss even more.

She tasted of blackberries and whiskey and Danni. Something so uniquely her that he knew he'd never forget it.

He pulled back. She was still on her tiptoes. The skirt of her organza dress swirled around them when he lifted her off her feet and kissed her again. He knew he was running from something and that kissing her was the path he'd chosen.

This kiss was going to take him away from the family complications he'd left behind at the reception. Now he was on a path that his gut wasn't sure was going to lead anywhere. But he knew he wouldn't be steered away from her.

"Want to go back to your place?" he asked. "I'm staying with my entire family at my gran's cottage and that could make the morning awkward. Also I've had enough of the party and I just want you."

His words sounded raw when he said them, and he wondered if she could feel the need in him. He hoped she didn't sense how much he was craving her and needing her in this moment. He didn't want her to see that.

"Yes. Let me get my bag from inside and we can go," she said.

She took his hand in hers, and they walked back into the reception, bumping into a couple who were leaving. He looked up into his father's eyes, then saw that August was holding his mom's hand.

"Good night, son. Hope you had a nice evening," his dad said.

"Dad." He nodded his head. "Good night."

Leo started to move by them, but his mom reached out and hugged him. "Love you, son."

He nodded. And Danni tugged her hand free. "I'll grab my purse while you say good night."

He let her go but then stood awkwardly next to his parents. The cocktails and his regret and anger all mixed together. "I'm sorry I've been so vocal about things."

"You wouldn't be our son if you weren't," his dad said.

And Leo realized that he *was* their son. No matter what else he might feel, he was always going to be the best and worst of his parents.

Eleven

Leo was a little bit drunk, and it was funny to see the normally buttoned-up, intense man so relaxed. He took her hand as they left the reception at the Nantucket Hotel and walked toward the cottage she'd rented for the week.

"Did you see my parents?" he asked.

"I did," she said. "They seemed pretty solid despite all the gossip about them. You were right about your dad. He kind of draws all the attention in the room."

"Yeah, I guess they are. I've been a jerk to both of them," Leo said. "It's so hard to stop seeing my mom and dad from a kid's perspective. From how I saw them growing up. I mean, I know they are adults who have another life entirely, but still…"

"I think that's always the way of the parent-child relationship. We see our parents' choices in terms of how they affect us. We don't really see how they're making the only decision they can for themselves and what they think was right for you."

He took her hand and tugged her into his arms, kissing her lightly. "You're really smart."

"Thanks," she said. Knowing she was just of average intelligence but hadn't downed as many cocktails as Leo, she probably seemed smarter to him at this moment.

"And pretty. And sexy. Why are you single?"

"Because I'm a modern woman who isn't defined by being in a relationship," she said. She'd had a lot of time to practice that answer, because she got asked the question a lot. She had goals and things she wanted to accomplish and, yes, at some point, she wanted to find a man to share her life with, but right now she had other things going on. Something that Leo had complicated this weekend.

He dropped her hand and put his up in surrender. "I was just asking. Seems like some guy would have snatched you up by now."

"I guess I'm not as great in the everyday," she said. "Why are you single?"

"It's my brand and my parents have had a very tumultuous and complicated relationship, so that example is always one I wanted to avoid following. I want to be successful and don't want to be absent the way my dad was."

She thought about what he said. It was funny how the older she got, the more she realized that her parents were the driving force in everything she thought she had to do and that she felt like a rebel when she did the things she wanted to.

"Good thing we're both single then," she said.

"Definitely good. We wouldn't have had last night or tonight together," he said.

And that was it, she told herself firmly. Tonight was going to be it. Tomorrow after the brunch to celebrate Nick and Adler, she was supposed to head back home, and Leo was going back to his life on Long Island. Which was how it should be.

"Where do you live?" he asked. "I don't know anything about your real life."

"I live in Boston, in one of the suburbs there," she said.

"Own your own home?"

"As a matter of fact, I do," she said. "My parents co-signed the loan. They have a thing about rent being a waste of money."

"Good point, and property is always a good investment. I own my own home, too," he said.

"Yeah, I know. I've seen the Leo Bisset Clubhouse photos on your social. Your place looks so dreamy and perfect. I always want to curl up on the chair by the fireplace."

He had used his elegant home as the setting for many of his ads and he decorated it with the items he was selling. He'd somehow managed to tap into the zeitgeist and created a home that appealed to many people and made them want to try to recreate it for themselves.

"Yeah? You'll have to come and visit some time. It's really comfy and seats two easily," he said.

She knew she wasn't going to visit him. He was drunk, offering something that wasn't going to happen. A minute before, they'd said this night would be their last together. Yet here he was mentioning something else... Which was his real desire? And which was hers?

Most of the time she was on her own through her own conscious decision to steer clear of men who wanted more. Yet with Leo she was torn. He could be so beneficial to her business with his knowledge and skills. But time after time, she found herself doing this instead of picking his brain. She preferred holding his hand and talking to him about life things.

Where was her focus?

Why couldn't she put Leo back in the box of hot hookup, instead of whatever this was?

She didn't like the answer circling around in her mind, so she shoved it away. She wasn't falling for him. He wasn't her kind of guy. He was too business-focused and not himself because of the scandal rocking his family. He'd needed her this weekend. But in the real world, he wouldn't need her at all.

Remember that.

But when they got to her cottage, he pulled her into his arms and she started to lose her resolve. "This night was about the best one I've had in a long time. Thanks to you."

He lowered his head and kissed her. Just a soft, gentle kiss as his hands fell to her waist and he held her lightly next to him. His tongue made languid strokes into her mouth, igniting a fire deep inside her.

She put her hands around his shoulders and kissed him back. She wasn't going to dwell on anything but Leo tonight. This Leo, the one who was with her, not the one he was going to be on Monday when they were back in the real world.

He was her perfect wedding date, and she was going to enjoy every second she had with him. Every brush of his mouth over hers. Every caress of his hands on her skin. Every single passionate moment that she could wring from this night.

She wanted it and wasn't going to hesitate to take it. She needed him, and it seemed he needed her. She realized that being with him had awakened something inside her that she'd ignored for too long.

He made her want to be more than the boss babe she was always aiming to be. She wanted to be a complete woman. Not that he completed her, but he made her realize that by ignoring this passionate side of herself, she wasn't being true to the woman she was.

Leo found the night air refreshing, and being with Danni brought out his Zen side…well, maybe not really, but right now he didn't feel that anger that had been his constant companion throughout the day as his family had been forced to smile and act as if everything was okay.

With Danni he'd just let all that fall to the wayside. He thought it was probably because she tasted so damn good when he kissed her. Or maybe it was because she dressed with such elegance and grace, but her body was pure temptation. Or maybe it was… Ah, hell, he thought, who really cared?

He had Danni in his arms, and he was going to take complete advantage of the fact that she was letting him back into her bed. One last night. It was just what he needed so that when he looked back on Adler's wedding it would be with fondness instead of that murky bitterness that everything else had stirred.

"Want to come inside?" she asked. "Or were you planning on kissing me on the lawn all night long?"

He leaned back from her, looking down at her heart-shaped face with a tendril of hair curling over her cheek. "You are the sassiest woman."

She lifted both eyebrows, and her eyes seemed to sparkle. "Thanks. So, are you coming in?"

"Oh, I definitely am. I don't think anything could make me leave you alone tonight," he said, lifting her off her feet and swinging her up in his arms as he carried her to the front door.

She put one arm around his shoulders to brace herself. When he got to the front door, he set her on her feet, and she pulled her key from her purse. She opened the door, and he followed her into the hallway of the cottage. She tossed her purse on the table as she turned to face him, her face illuminated by a light left on in the main living area.

He reached up and took off his tie, putting it on the table next to her bag. She kicked off her heels, and he toed off his shoes and then his socks. She glanced down at his bare feet, then back up at his face. "Only you could look sophisticated with no shoes on."

"Oh, I think you could give me a run for my money," he said. She looked to him, as she always did. Somehow too good for the jaded world he lived in.

He knew from the moment they met that she was different, and each minute he'd spent with her just reinforced it. She held her hand out.

He took it, and she led him down the hall to the bedroom. He saw her open, partially packed suitcase on the end of the bed as she flicked on the light. The reminder was stark. She was leaving tomorrow. She'd be back to her old life, and he'd be back to his.

Back to creating products that promised a dream that millions aspired to have in their own life while knowing how hollow and fake those picturesque images really were.

"Sorry about the mess. I didn't expect..."

"To bring me back here?"

"Yeah," she said, moving around him to close her suitcase and take it off the bed. She put it in the corner and then turned back to him, and he smiled at her.

"I wasn't expecting it, either, but I'm very glad I'm here," he said. He sometimes felt that he didn't say the right thing when he should, and with Danni he wanted to give her all the words he usually kept tucked away.

"Me, too," she said.

But she was standing there awkwardly, looking like she didn't know what to do next. He realized that there had been too much time since that fiery kiss in her front yard, and she was slowly coming back down from the wedding reception haze.

"Do you still want me here?" he asked.

"More than anything," she admitted.

"Me, too," he said. "But I think we need a dance or something to get us back to where we were. Suggestions?"

"You could strip for me," she said, blushing only the tiniest bit as she said it.

"Strip for you?" he asked. No one had ever asked him to do that. He'd had a few women do a striptease for him before, but he'd never been the one... "Okay. But only if you are naked on the bed watching me."

"Fair enough," she said. She reached for the side of her dress, drew the zipper down and then lifted the dress up over her head. Now she was standing there in just a tiny pair of lacy panties and some kind of strapless bra.

She walked over to the bed, piled up the pillows,

and as she leaned over, he couldn't help but groan at the shape of her ass. She had curvy hips and shapely legs. He remembered how good they had felt when she'd straddled him on the yacht.

She glanced over her shoulder at him. Then she straightened and removed the bra and slowly worked her panties down her legs, stepping out of them before climbing up on the bed. She rested her back against the pile of pillows. Her legs were slightly parted, and she draped her arms out to her sides.

"I'm ready."

"So am I," he said. But he wasn't sure he was ready for Danni. Not for anything more than a night of sexual fun—and that's all this was. Why, then, did something in his soul crave more?

Leo's expression was inscrutable, and as she'd never been to a strip club, she wasn't sure what she was expecting. But he took his time, slowly unbuttoning his dress shirt to reveal his tanned, lithe body. He had an innate sensuality in all his moves, and as he took off his clothes for her, his gaze captured hers and she felt her temperature rising. She was already turned on from a night of dancing and laughing.

She realized that when she was with Leo, she felt like she was the woman she wanted to be. A part of her was afraid she was just pretending but another part believed that they had connected on a different level. A deeper level than either of them really wanted.

She felt her breasts getting heavier as she got moist between her thighs. He took his shirt off and tossed it toward the chair next to the window. Then he turned and put his hands on his waist, and she caught her breath as she realized how hard he was. His pants weren't hiding his erection, and she sat up and held her arm out, beckoning him to her with the crook of her finger.

"Not yet, baby. I'm not done giving you the show you asked for," he said.

"I can't wait to see everything," she said.

He undid his pants and swiveled his hips as he lowered them. They fell down his thighs to his ankles, and he stepped out of them. He wore a pair of tight-fitting boxer briefs that hugged his package, and she shifted forward again, getting on her hands and knees and crawling across the mattress to the side of the bed where he was standing.

"I'll do the last part."

She didn't wait for him to say yes or no, just took the elastic waistband in her hands and shoved his underwear down, careful to maneuver it over his erection. Once his boxer briefs were down to his thighs, she took his hard-on in her hand. He was bigger than she remembered, and harder. She stroked him up and down, leaning forward to take the tip of him into her mouth. He groaned, his hands falling to the back of her head, urging her to take more of him in her mouth, which she did. She sucked on him until he pulled away and urged her to lie back on the bed. He then eased himself up her body, letting his entire torso caress her as he did so.

His mouth was hot and heavy on hers, the kiss deep and dark with sexual promises that she would make sure he kept. She wanted everything he had to give her.

He shifted his shoulders, his chest hair abrading her sensitive nipples. Feeling the tip of his erection at the entrance to her body, she parted her thighs farther and wrapped one of her legs around his hips as he drove himself into her.

She closed her eyes, wrapping her arms around his shoulders. His mouth was on hers, sucking her tongue deeper into his mouth as he drove into her with a strong rhythm that pushed her toward her climax. She felt it just there, out of her reach, but then he rubbed her clit with his thumb, as he thrust deep in her and she tightened around him, arching her back as her climax rolled through her.

He groaned—a rough, guttural sound that rumbled through his entire body. Cupping her butt in his palm, he drove into her at an even faster pace, pushing her toward a second climax. She clung to him, threw her head back and cried out his name as she came again. She was losing all control, but she didn't care. She felt him come just after her and held him to her as he continued to thrust a couple more times, causing another tiny orgasm to ripple through her.

She fell back against the bed; his head dropped to her shoulder, and he kept his weight off her with his arms and legs. She opened her eyes a few minutes later to find him watching her, and there was an expression on his face that she couldn't define. She didn't even try to, because she didn't want to risk thinking this was anything more than these few carefree nights on Nantucket.

"I think you should know that if your business fails, you would probably be able to strip for a living," she finally said, breaking the silence.

That surprised a bark of laughter from him. It made her happy to see him laugh, but another part of her wondered why she'd done that. Why she'd deflected her fears with a joke, to make light of a deeper emotion that she was still feeling all the way inside. Because this was definitely more than sex, as much as she was afraid to admit it to herself.

"Woman, you are a constant surprise," he said as he rolled to his side and took her with him.

She cuddled against him but felt dampness on her legs and knew she should get up and clean up. But at the same time, she knew that she had only a few more opportunities to be curled in his arms. To hear his heart-beat beneath her ear and feel his hand languidly caress-ing her back. She looked up as she felt a tug on one of her curls and saw he was winding it around his finger, looking down at it like…like he was lost.

She knew he was.

That was why this was just for the weekend. Just a wedding fling, nothing more. It couldn't be, because she had stuff she needed to do, and no matter how much her soft heart wanted to add saving Leo to the agenda, there wasn't room for that. Not mentally or emotionally.

Twelve

Waking up a married woman was nothing like Adler had expected. Nick was snoring, as he'd had too much to drink the night before, and she had a champagne headache. Not sexy, not glam, not at all how she'd thought they'd start their life together. But that was par for the course.

They were scheduled to have a brunch with their friends and family later this morning, and they could both deal with everything that had come up over the last few days. It was so hard to remember how excited she'd been about becoming a bride just a few short days ago, before all the scandal hit. Life had felt...so full of promise.

"Adler?"

She glanced over at Nick. He'd rolled to his side and was watching her. He was so handsome, with his square jaw and brown eyes that always seemed so bright in his dark face. He had a bit of stubble on his jaw, but to be honest, he didn't really look the worse for wear after all his drinking the night before.

"Husband?" she said back. A lot of stuff had gone on between the two of them this weekend, and she wanted their first day as husband and wife to set a new tone. All that crap from the Bissets wasn't going to have a negative impact on her life. She wasn't going to let it.

"Wife," he said, pulling her into his arms and hugging her tightly to him. "That sounds good. I'm sorry for how crazy my behavior has been over the last few days. It's just been a lot and if I didn't have you by my side I think I might have lost it."

She hugged him back. "It's okay. How are you feeling today?"

"Surprisingly good. I know there's still crap to deal with in terms of August and my mom, but last night was nice. And ultimately, though I think that our two families aren't ever going to be friends, they can at least be cordial."

"Good," she said. "I don't even know what you're going to do with August. But my cousins are all decent—it's still hard to believe they're your half siblings."

"I know. I still hate Logan, and now I come to find out he's my twin. How is that even possible?" Nick said.

"Yeah, it's a mess. But we are leaving for Fiji tonight, and we can have two weeks away from the world. Will you be okay with that?"

"Yes. I need it. I want to get back to us instead of focusing on this stuff. It never really bothered me that I didn't know who my biological father was, you know? I have my dad and he's always been one hundred percent that man for me. I wasn't missing anything, and my family felt complete. So, learning that someone like August was my biological father was hard to handle."

"I bet. He's been my auntie's husband all my life, but I've never really had a close bond with him. He's sort of all about business and making sure that the world knows that the Bissets are on top."

"Yeah, Dad hates that about him."

She nodded. She didn't want to be talking about her uncle the morning after her wedding, but he was Nick's biological father and he'd been so quiet about it up until this point. She knew he'd been shaken and he'd been dealing with it by drinking too much, but otherwise he'd kept it all locked in until she'd pushed him to show her what he was feeling. That's what being married was about.

"You do, too," she said. "I guess you aren't going to suddenly have a father-son relationship with him, are you?"

"You know, he hasn't even tried to talk to me," Nick said. "So I guess not. I'm more concerned about Logan. I think… I'd like to get to know him better. He seemed open to that, as well. He offered to give me the patent he stole as a wedding present. Maybe I can find a way to make that work."

"I'm pretty good friends with Quinn, and she and Logan seem to be an item again now. We can all do a dinner party after we're back from our honeymoon," she said. "I can help you navigate that if you want."

"Yeah, that might be the way to do it," Nick said. "I don't want it to affect our business. I mean, I'm not proposing a merger or going softer on Bisset Industries now that we are related. I still don't really feel that we're family, you know?"

She nodded and realized that this was the conversation she wished they could have been having all along instead of dodging the paparazzi and trying to deal with the scandal through the media instead of with each other. Part of her nerves, she knew, came from the fact that everyone who wanted to could know her business. She'd always hated that part of growing up in the spotlight.

"I get it. And besides all of that, we are family now. We are starting our own little Williams clan, and I don't want any of that scandal to touch us."

"I can't promise it won't, but I'll do my best to keep it away from us," he said. "I don't want to spend my life living a lie with you. That was one thing I thought about a lot. How Auggie and my mom's affair had led to all of this…and then your aunt Juliette…"

"I know. I was shocked to hear she'd do something like that. But she always has been the kind of woman to do whatever was needed to do. She's been a surrogate mom to me, so I know how much she loves all of her kids. She never treated Logan any different."

"I thought so. She was welcoming to me from the first, even though she knew my family and the Bissets had this business rivalry. She's a gracious lady. This has to have been hard on her."

"I think so, too," Adler said, knowing that her aunt had done her best to make this wedding perfect for her but at the same time had struggled with her own guilt over her part in the scandal. "Your mom, too. Who would have thought those two would be at the heart of this?"

"Not me," Nick said. "I'll be glad to get the brunch over and have you to myself."

"Can't wait," Adler said.

Danni woke to the smell of coffee and Leo sitting on the edge of the bed, dressed in a polo shirt and khakis. She wasn't sure when he'd had time to go get a change of clothes. She pulled the bedsheets with her as she sat up.

"Good morning, gorgeous," he said as he handed her the steaming mug.

She took it from him, pushing her hair off her face, and then panicked as she realized her curls were probably doing their normal Medusa-morning thing. She reached up to try to pat them into place with one hand, but Leo caught her wrist and drew her hand down.

"Don't touch it. I love your hair all wild and free," he said. "You seem to spend most of your waking hours taming it, and I wonder if you aren't taming yourself, too."

She wasn't sure she was ready for this much honesty on a Sunday morning. She took a sip of coffee and then leaned back to study him. "Feeling philosophical?"

"Yeah. That, and I don't want to leave you with the impression that I was just a big ball of anger and rage."

"And sexy stripteases," she said, trying to keep it light. But her throat was tight. He was saying goodbye. He was right to do it now, before they saw each other again in public. She knew that, but she wasn't ready. She had just woken up. She hadn't had time to tame her crazy hair or reel in the emotions she wasn't going to acknowledge she had. She still needed to lock them away before she could deal with this conversation.

"Yeah, that…no one would believe you if you told them," he said.

"Seriously, you were fun. A bit of a complication that I wasn't anticipating, but given the impression I had of you, you were much better than I thought you'd be," she admitted. He had been human, which sounded silly when she said it in her head, but the truth was, he had seemed like a cardboard man until they'd first met and played golf together at the scramble.

"I like that. I wasn't sure why you were with me," he said. "The novelty of being with a Bisset or something else?"

She was taken aback by that. "I don't care that you are a Bisset. I think your family puts too much stock in your name."

She knew her words were harsh but didn't really care. What he'd just said wasn't very nice, either.

"You're right about that. I didn't mean it the way you took it. I was just trying to figure us out."

"You're hot. Apparently, you thought I was, too, and we hooked up, Leo," she said, feeling a little mad that he'd taken the conversation in this direction. "That's all it was."

He nodded, but his jaw was tighter. "I guess that is all. You seemed like a woman who would need more than heat to sleep with a guy," he said at last.

"Maybe I thought you were a different sort of guy, or maybe you're not as smart about me as you think you are," she said. "But that doesn't matter. Thanks for the coffee."

She wasn't sure how to ask him to leave. She was lying naked in the bed where he'd made love to her the night before. She'd thought she was storing memories for the future, but he was plotting how to make his escape.

"You're welcome. I phoned up to my grandmother's house and asked Michael to bring breakfast with my change of clothes. How about if I leave you to your coffee and wait in the other room? We can have breakfast together, if that works for you."

"Sure," she said.

"I think I upset you," he said. "I'm sorry. I'm still not in my right mind after everything that's happened with my family this weekend."

She softened toward him but then realized what she was doing and just forced a smile instead. He was projecting his wounded feelings onto her, and she was allowing it. But she needed to stop, because that kind of bond didn't really exist between them.

He'd been upset and needed a distraction during the wedding, and she'd been there waiting for something from him that he couldn't give her.

"You're fine. Will breakfast keep if I take a quick shower?" she asked.

"Yes. Michael brought the ingredients and instructions. Your fridge was empty," he said.

"I know. Okay, give me fifteen minutes," she said.

He got up and stood there as if he had something more to say, but then he just turned and walked out of the bedroom. She braced herself for the rest of the morning and everything he'd set in motion. He was walking out of her life—he'd made that clear. If there was any lingering hope from the night before, it was time to kill it.

Leo had been trying to be a good guy, not like his usual self—or like his father—but he knew it had backfired. He wasn't super in touch with his feelings and would never think of himself as having a good read on women, but he could tell he'd pissed Danni off. He was a second away from texting Dare and asking him for advice. But this wasn't a relationship. He'd been trying to give them some closure before they both had to get on the ferry and go home. Though first, he was taking a helicopter to Martha's Vineyard for a photo shoot with Tommy Hilfiger for a partnership he'd worked on.

And he realized after watching his dad's past affair bite him in the ass that Leo didn't want any surprises years from now. He should have used a condom, even though Danni had said she was on the pill. But this weekend he'd been shaken, and it had made him stupid.

Danni seemed like this wild, ethereal woman, but he remembered when they first met she'd definitely had an agenda. Somewhere along the way, as he'd been rocked by the revelation of his parents' secrets, he'd forgotten all that and let himself fall for Danni. He needed to get them back on track. Fix this, make sure she knew if anything resulted from their nights together, he wanted to know now, not thirty years from now.

He heard the shower shut off and looked at the instructions that Michael had written for him. The breakfast casserole he'd brought for Leo to fix was already partially baked and needed to be reheated for fifteen minutes, so Leo put it in the oven. Michael had set the table on the back porch for them, complete with a bottle of champagne in an ice bucket and a chilled pitcher of fresh-squeezed orange juice.

Everything was perfect, the way his grandmother's butler always did things. Leo knew that the only thing messing up the morning was him. He wasn't sure why. It wasn't as if this was a first for him; he'd done this before. He'd slept with plenty of women then said goodbye. But this was Danni, and she'd seen him in a more vulnerable state than anyone else. And now he regretted that.

He should never have revealed so much of himself to her. He should have kept his guard up. But he hadn't been able to. He'd been reeling and falling, and he'd landed in her soft arms.

He looked around the tiny kitchen while he waited for her to finish getting ready and saw some notes she'd jotted down. They were all about partnering with brands and meeting buyers.

He remembered how she'd asked him about keeping their relationship business-focused. She'd wanted something from him, and he was pretty sure he hadn't delivered anything other than some hot nights.

Her list was small, and he knew she'd have to broaden her goals if she was going to make it big. She was taking tiny risks, and so her results would be smaller. He jotted a few things on the paper underneath each of her topics. Just advice that would help her.

At the bottom he wrote, *You have to stop being timid and asking politely for what you want. Take it, Danni, and you will get more than you realized was out there.*

He put the pen down as he heard the bedroom door open. Danni walked out, dressed in a pair of white slacks and a floral blouse with a bow at the neck. She had her hair pulled back in a low bun, and her makeup was flawless. He knew he was seeing Danni Eldridge, businesswoman, not the Danni he'd been with all weekend.

And somehow, as much as her appearance signaled that she'd gotten his message, a small part of him was disappointed. Did he want her to beg him to stay? To keep seeing each other after they went home?

No, he scoffed. He wasn't in the market for a serious girlfriend, and if he was, Danni didn't fit his image. She was too real and solid. And that worried him. He wasn't what she needed. She had that earnest authenticity that he could never achieve.

"You look lovely. Breakfast has about five more minutes," he said. "I hope you don't mind, but I had the table on the patio set up."

"That sounds perfect. It's such a nice morning. Do you need my help with anything?"

"No. Let's go outside. Can I get you a mimosa or just orange juice?"

"A mimosa would be great," she said. She was so calm and collected. Honestly, he'd never seen this side of her. Even the day they'd met she'd been fiery, ready to confront him for his rude remark about her to the press.

He walked ahead of her to the French doors and held them open for her. She gave him a tight smile as she walked by, and in that moment, he had a flash of what felt like déjà vu. But he knew it was a childhood memory of his mother treating his father the same way.

Leo felt something inside him die. He'd spent all his life trying to emulate his father, trying to be the business titan that August Bisset was. He'd craved that more than anything, but he'd always thought he was better than his father. Better at treating the people—the women—in his life with kindness and respect. And until this morning, he might have been.

But he'd used Danni as a distraction from the pain and confusion that had plagued him since his parents' secrets were announced, and now he was realizing the cost. He'd done damage that there wasn't an easy way to undo.

And since he was walking out of her life today, he knew that he couldn't really undo it. He was going to have to live with the fact that he'd caused that tight smile. That she'd put up a barrier with those extra-fine manners and the polite small talk that he had no doubt was waiting for him at her breakfast table.

Fuck him.

He wasn't just the son who should have been the heir to Bisset Industries, he was also the same lover who left behind more collateral damage than he'd realized. And that hurt more than Leo would have guessed.

He reached for the champagne, but honestly, did she even want to have breakfast with him? He was tempted to leave, but he hadn't yet decided that he was going to be this much of his father's mini-me. Was there a way to fix this?

He was going to try. He couldn't offer her anything else as a man, but maybe as a business mentor, he could help out. It wasn't much, but it might be enough to make him feel better about the morning.

But he doubted anything was going to fix the hurt he'd caused.

Thirteen

Danni kept her back stiff and her dignity around her, but at this point she had to wonder what had happened to her pride. He'd asked her if she was with him because of who he was when they'd been in bed together as if he didn't know her at all. As if her business meant nothing.

"I can't stop thinking about what you said to me."

"Which part?"

Which part? Oh, this was harder than she'd expected. This was veering away from taking what she needed for her business and into personal territory that would leave her scarred.

"Was I with you because you were a Bisset?"

"Oh, that."

She raised both eyebrows at him, waiting for him to continue.

"I can be an asshole. But you knew that when we

met. You wanted me to mentor you. And I don't know what more I can do."

Clearly, he thought that he was better than her. Did she really want business advice from a man who had that kind of mind-set?

"You know, I can't do this," she said. "I think you should just leave."

He stared at her for a long moment and then nodded and pushed himself back from the table. "The food will be done in five minutes. I set the timer on the microwave. I'm sorry. I was trying to make this easier. If you ever need me for anything…or if you are pregnant, please let me know."

If she was pregnant?

"I'm not going to be pregnant. I'm on the pill," she said.

"It's not one hundred percent infallible, and I don't want to follow in my father's footsteps and show up at a wedding thirty years from now and learn we had a kid," he said.

"That won't happen. I'll let you know if there's a kid," she said.

She was reeling, her emotions so out of control in this moment. First he was worried she'd been with him because of his family connections, and now this. She wasn't sure what she'd expected from Leo, but once again, he'd surprised her. And not in a good way. But still, she couldn't necessarily blame him for making sure that the pregnancy issue was out in the open.

"Thanks," he said.

She stood up and followed him through her rented cottage. The smell of food cooking filled the air, as well as the faintest scent of his cologne. He paused on the threshold with the door open and turned to her, the empty street behind him.

"I really did enjoy this weekend with you, Danni. I'm sorry that I'm not better at easing out of your life," he said. "It was never my intention to hurt you."

She nodded. Hurt her? Had he? Of course he had. She'd known all along that realistically this wasn't going to last, but there had been a part of her that had hung on to hope. Probably the same part of her that wanted to keep her business small but make a huge profit. "Of course. I'm not hurt. We said this was for the weekend. I had a good time, too. Take care."

She sort of shoved him lightly out the door and shut it before her throat closed over the lies she'd told. She thought she'd kept her lawyer's face on the entire time until she caught a glimpse of herself in the mirror in the hallway and realized from her pale complexion she hadn't. She'd never been good at hiding her emotions, and that was especially true with Leo. She hated that.

The timer on the microwave started chirping, and she went to turn off the oven and take out the casserole his grandmother's butler had prepared for them.

God.

If she needed further proof that they weren't meant to be together, there it was. Her grandmother lived in a trailer park in central Florida and drove a golf cart to play bingo and swim with her friends. She didn't have a butler who took food to her grandkids. Her family were lawyers and they made a good living but it wasn't this kind of wealthy. And her family...well, they didn't keep secrets like the Bissets. Her family talked things out, all things, even when they were uncomfortable. Danni had been dabbling with someone whose life was so different from hers that it was no wonder he'd made that comment about her being with him for his name.

The funny thing was, she *had* sort of been with him because of his business. Which might be the same thing? She didn't want to think too much about that, because her heart knew the truth. She'd been with Leo because she liked him. She was starting to more than like him when he'd woken her up with a goodbye on his lips.

She looked down at the counter and saw the note she'd made of questions to ask him and shook her head. He'd written answers to them all and then left her a piece of advice. To dream bigger.

Would she ever really know him?

No. She wouldn't. He'd been pretty plain about that as he'd walked out the door. She would just have to take his advice and make that work for her. Forget about Leo and all the thoughts and feelings he'd stirred in her.

He'd made her almost believe that she was some otherworldly creature who could be comfortable with her wild, curly hair and independent entrepreneurial spirit… just for a moment before he'd walked away.

She wasn't changing her life based on a man who'd done that.

She needed to change her life based on her own opinions. What did she want? Where did she see herself going? She had to make a profit this year—a big one. She decided she'd go to the wedding brunch today and make those connections she'd ignored yesterday because she'd been giving in to the need to be with Leo.

Today, she was a different woman.

He had changed her, she realized. He'd shown her that business and pleasure didn't mix, but pleasure could certainly distract her.

She made a plan for the people she needed to talk to before they left Nantucket and then followed some advice her father had given her long ago—she pictured the meetings in her head, imagined her prospective partners inviting her to collaborate with them and submit her products for a pop-up in their retail chains.

An hour later, when she walked into the banquet room at the Nantucket Hotel, she had that vision firmly in her head, and though her steps faltered when she heard Leo's laugh across the room, she completely ignored him as she sought out the people who could make a real impact on her life.

Not a man whom she'd allowed to distract her from her goals. She wasn't interested in Leo Bisset or anything he had to say. Not anymore. Maybe if she said that enough times in her head, it would actually become the truth and her heart would stop aching at the thought of never seeing him again.

Leo was aware of the moment that Danni entered the banquet hall. He had meant for their break to be clean, and given all his experience with women in the past, he'd sincerely thought that he would be able to ignore her once he walked out her door. But his body hadn't gotten the memo and wasn't interested in ignoring her. His skin felt too tight and his blood felt like it was rushing heavier in his veins as he watched her move through the sparse crowd. He saw her turn to speak to Martha Dillion, a buyer for a large retail chain and Tad Williams's first cousin, but all he could focus on was how with her hair pulled back, her neck seemed so long. He remembered how it had tasted when he'd kissed her there.

Which made him harden, and he had to adjust his stance to avoid anyone else noticing. With perfect timing, Dare walked over to him just then. His oldest brother usually had an air of almost uptight dignity about him, but today he seemed…well, more relaxed, and almost as if he didn't have any worries. Not like Dare at all.

"Had a good night sleep?" Leo asked his brother.

"Something like that," Dare said, snagging a drink from the passing waiter. "You?"

"Great night, sucky morning," Leo said. But he had no one but himself to blame for that. He could have just left things as they were with Danni and been standing next to her as she worked the room. Which she was doing now. Really working it, as far as he could tell.

She must have found his note. That was a tiny sop for his conscience. He knew no matter what she said that he'd hurt her. And that hadn't been his intention at all. True, he wasn't himself, and he'd been acting out all weekend but with her—with Danni—he'd felt like he'd found some solace. And repaying that with hurt wasn't what he'd wanted.

"How was your morning sucky?"

"It's been the worst," he said. "I had to wrap things up with Danni. Didn't want to put it off until she had to leave. Thought it would be better and more dignified."

"Ha."

"Ha?"

"Dignified? When have you ever given a crap about that? You must have had another reason," Dare said.

"Whatever," Leo said, but his older brother had him thinking. What had he hoped for? Maybe that she'd say she wanted them to try to figure out how to keep seeing each other? Something he knew wasn't possible because he had a very demanding work schedule and lived in the Hamptons and she lived in Boston.

"Look, are you sure you're not being too impulsive here? The truth about Nick, and how he and Logan are actually twins, has rattled all of us. We're dealing with the kind of family drama that normally we don't have to. We leave that to everyone else," Dare said.

"Do we?" Leo asked. "You don't sound like you."

"Good. I've been spending time with someone who suggested I shake things up."

"A woman?"

"Yes," Dare admitted. "And it was nice not to have to watch my back constantly for a change. She's...well, different. She doesn't care about Dad's scandal, Bisset Industries or how I might vote on any issues."

"She sounds...interesting."

"She is. And I didn't cut things off with her. Life doesn't have to always be cut-and-dried."

"Not in my experience," Leo said. "Dad's, either. I mean, Cora Williams was a loose end he should have tied up a long time ago."

"You think Danni is like Cora? I didn't get that read on her, but I really just exchanged small talk with her."

Danni wasn't anything like Nick's mom. For one thing, Danni would never have had an affair with him if he'd been married. Also she wasn't the kind of woman to let Leo off the hook. He knew if she was pregnant, she'd want him to do his part with their child. And he would do it.

He watched her moving around the room, talking to the legendary American designer Peter Drummond, and he realized that he wouldn't mind if she was pregnant. It would give him an excuse to keep seeing her.

Did he need an excuse?

That felt cowardly to him, and he'd always prided himself on facing his problems like a Bisset. Like a man. Not dodging them. If he wanted to see her again, he should just ask.

"You are staring so hard at her right now," Dare said. "It's a wonder she hasn't turned around."

"I am, aren't I?" Had he screwed up this morning? He knew he hadn't. There was no scenario where the two of them actually could be a couple. He had made the right choice. She had her own business to run and a life of her own back in Boston.

But listing all that didn't lessen the fact that he wished he had the right to go up to her. Put his hand on the small of her back and kiss that spot at the base of her neck that he knew turned her on. He wanted that more than he wanted his next breath.

And if he needed more proof that he'd made the smart choice when he'd ended things with her, there it was. He wasn't going to give up his life to build one with her, and he knew from watching everything that had happened with his parents this weekend that he couldn't ask her to do that, either.

They'd had fun together.

That had to be enough. Because as he watched her throughout the brunch, it was clear to him that she had moved on and was determined to let him know it.

Danni collected a lot of names and information throughout the morning. She maneuvered herself through the crowd the way she should have been doing all weekend. Essie was going to be very happy with the results she'd gotten today.

She knew that part of the reason she'd been so successful was that she'd tried to put as many people between herself and Leo as she could. Still, she was putting her connection to him to good use. Something her sister had always told her to do but that Danni had struggled in the past to actually do.

Adler and Nick seemed to have a rosy glow about them. Danni smiled and waved to her client and friend. Adler waved her over to them. Quinn Murray, who had been producing the televised wedding stuff, was now here as a guest and friend to the bride.

"Congratulations again," Danni said after she hugged them both. "Your wedding was fabulously gorgeous. I can't wait to watch when it airs on television."

"Thank you," Nick said. "Your jewelry added the perfect touch to the day. It looked great on the bridesmaids."

"That's sweet of you to say," she responded.

Nick just nodded and then turned away when his brother Asher tapped him on the shoulder.

"He's not wrong," Adler said. "Your jewelry really was a nice touch, and you were, too. Thank you again for everything you did yesterday. Just coming to the prewedding session… I needed you and you were there. I appreciated it so much."

"That's okay. I'd do it again."

"I'm glad. I hope you and Leo—"

She cut Adler off. "There isn't a me and Leo."

"What did he do?" Adler asked.

"Nothing. We weren't planning to be together forever. It was just a fun weekend fling," Danni said. And if she never had to explain it to anyone again, she'd be eternally grateful.

"Oh. I thought it was…something different after all. I hope you had a good time despite the paparazzi and the reporters here. You really helped to make my wedding special."

"I had a great time," she said. "Thanks again for inviting me and for giving your guests my gift bags."

"I didn't mind. Dad loves the bracelet that was in his. I think he wants you to make some for his next tour," Adler said. "I gave him all your details."

Wow, that would be great, Danni thought.

This wedding had netted more than she'd expected. As she drove her car onto the ferry later that afternoon, she realized she was leaving Nantucket a different woman. She'd learned so much, not only from being with Leo, but from watching how he interacted with everyone. The way he'd shown her how to take pictures and, to some extent, how to take risks.

She wasn't sure she was ready to look back at the sketches she'd made when they'd been together, but she knew she would soon. She wanted to just keep this nice numb insulation around her until she got back home and she could let her guard down.

She sat there on the ferry trying not to remember the last time she'd been on the water…it was on the yacht with Leo, and she knew that was when she'd stopped seeing him as a business rival and started to view him as a man.

A man she'd never thought she'd fall for. But she had. She'd definitely fallen for him over the long weekend.

Essie texted to ask if she wanted to have dinner when she got back to the city, and Danni knew that fooling her friend would be hard. Essie would know that things had gone too far with Leo, but at the same time, she couldn't hide that. She felt the pain of it inside, and it was going to take some time and a lot of work to move past it.

Plus, she had a lot of new information to share with Essie, and they needed to get moving on reaching out to the contacts Danni had made.

It was time to stretch her dreams bigger, just as Leo had recommended, and start making her life her own.

She was going to have to thank him for this someday.

But right now, she still felt too raw. She did take comfort in the fact that if she had her way, he was going to see her name a lot in the future. And she hoped it made him remember what they'd almost had.

She hadn't had the courage to call him a coward, but in her heart, she felt like he had been. That he'd walked away from her without even considering ways to make a relationship work. He hadn't even tried.

God.

Oh, but what if he hadn't cared at all? What if the reason he'd been able to walk away so easily was because she'd been the only one who'd felt anything? He had been pretty plain when he'd said his life was a mess and he was trying to get over it by having a fling with her. He'd said he was rudderless, and she'd made herself the wind in his sails.

That was what she did. Dream small and put herself into someone else's vision instead of creating her own. But as Nantucket faded into the background, she vowed she'd never do that again. If anyone was going to be riding someone's coattails in the future, it would be Leo chasing after her. She wasn't going to let this be the last time he saw her, and when they did see each other again, he'd regret that he ever had her and let her go.

Because the new Danni wasn't someone who led with her heart. She was only going to lead with her head... and business smarts that would leave Leo Bisset in the dust.

Fourteen

After two months of strategy sessions with Essie, growing their supply chain and hiring and firing artisans to satisfy the growing demand, Danni had reached a new milestone: the fashion designer Peter Drummond was interested in her work. He'd contacted her to ask if she'd be interested in submitting some designs for a collaboration to be released next summer.

She hardly ever thought about Leo or the last time she saw him on Nantucket. Of course that was a lie; she saw his ads on billboards and on television all the time. Leo Bisset wasn't just a person, he was a brand, and he was everywhere.

Not that she was going to let that matter. Peter Drummond was interested in her work, so she'd focus on that.

It was the kind of opportunity that would take her business to the next level. She now had a good stable

of artists working with her to create high-quality jewelry that would meet the standard for collaborating with
America's living design legend. And after speaking to
her parents, Danni had decided to sell the expensive
townhome she was living in and scale down her lifestyle
so that she could pump money into her business and ultimately live on the profits alone. It had been a difficult
conversation to have, but she had told them frankly she
was going to invest in herself. She believed in her jewelry business and wasn't willing to take a back seat on it.

They were encouraging and suggested she rent out
her townhome instead of selling it—that way she'd have
it when she was back earning what she'd made practicing law. She liked the idea, and once they knew she
was serious and wasn't looking to them to support her
as she dabbled in her art, it changed the dynamic between them. Danni admitted that even though she was
just months away from thirty, it had been the first time
she'd actually felt like an adult with her parents. She
knew taking responsibility for her own life and decisions had played a huge part in it.

She also admitted to herself that it was Leo who had
given her the drive to make the change. A big part of
her wanted to be so successful that he was constantly
reminded of her. She'd taken her vision bigger, which
had made her focus smaller in so many ways. She knew
what she wanted, and that had made her stop chasing
trends and fast fashion. As a result, she'd gained the
clientele she'd always wanted.

In finding herself as a businesswoman, she realized
that she missed Leo, too. It had just been a weekend, and
she was trying to remind herself of that, but she knew
that she really cared for him. It had taken her about two

weeks to admit that she was a bit heartbroken. She'd spent another two weeks obsessively stalking him on social media before she'd mentally slapped herself and stopped that masochistic behavior.

He'd sent her a few texts, which she had longed to read and respond to, but had refused to let herself. A clean break was the last gift he'd given her, and that had to be enough. Still, she'd fashioned the shell he'd found on the beach into a charm for a bracelet. As a base, she used one of the leather bands from his signature line. She'd cut the leather to add in a ribbon that suited her personality and then threaded the ribbon through the shell.

She only wore the bracelet on her days off at first, afraid to let Essie see it because for Danni it was so bittersweet. It combined her and Leo's work, reminding her of when they were at their best, walking together on the beach on Nantucket. But that wasn't reality, she thought as she boarded the flight to New York the day of her big meeting with Peter Drummond's team. While she was in town, she also planned to have lunch with Adler, who wasn't finding married life to be as easy as she'd hoped.

Nick and Logan were at war again thanks to some of Logan's actions before he'd known that Nick was his twin. And scandal still seemed to dog the Bissets, as the board of Bisset Industries required all the Bisset children to have a DNA test to prove they were August's children. Danni had almost texted Leo then. She knew how much he prided himself on being a Bisset, and that had to have stung.

But in the end, he'd made the break with her, and she hadn't reached out. She was trying to be okay with what he'd left her with—after all, Leo had made her stronger in so many ways. She had new business skills that had impressed even her family. She had new connections that she'd been using to the best of her ability. She had learned that business was better when it *was* personal. Those handwritten notes she'd sent after the wedding to tell each of those buyers and designers how nice it was to meet them had paid off.

But that had been her. She'd realized that she couldn't be coldhearted when it came to business. Her products were a reflection of her, and once she and Essie had figured that out, everything else had fallen into place.

In a way, even the sadness she felt when she thought about Leo had made her stronger. She was determined to succeed if for no other reason than to make him have to remember her and their time together.

But in the end, she had to admit that it all added up to one stark truth: as hard as she'd tried to forget him, she hadn't been able to.

She still woke in the night reaching for him, but the bed next to her was empty and cold. She still felt the brush of his lips against hers, which left her mouth tingling and craving a kiss she knew she'd never experience again.

And her hair brought back the worst memories. She'd come close to chopping it all off because she remembered him touching it, twirling it around his finger and claiming that he liked that wildness to her.

In the end she'd taken to wearing it in a tight, low bun at the back of her neck. She didn't want to risk her heart being that vulnerable again, and somehow, the more he'd seemed to accept her secret hidden self, the easier it had been to fall for him.

She wanted to believe she was stronger and would never do that again. And she'd almost convinced herself—until she walked into the Drummond Designs reception area and saw Leo standing there in a suit and tie. In that moment, she knew that all the tight buns and hard talk had just been a facade.

She still cared about Leo; in fact, it was getting harder to deny that she loved him. No matter how badly he'd hurt her when he'd ended things with her.

The last two months had been hectic and life-changing for Leo and his entire family. His business had been his safe haven. More and more, he'd found himself questioning what he wanted out of life as he watched his parents navigate through the mistakes they'd both made.

One thing that had struck him when he'd had dinner with them last weekend was that they were both committed to each other. The scandals they'd endured had left them stronger together, and he wanted that. As much as he'd at one time believed he was a chip off the August Bisset block and then had hated that he was anything like his father, he now realized that his father had accidentally done the one thing that truly mattered when he'd married Leo's mom.

He wondered if he only believed that because he missed Danni. It was funny to think of how close he'd grown to her over the long weekend, but he knew he'd been more himself with her than with any other person, including his family.

He'd texted her once and she hadn't responded, which was fine. It had stung, but that was her prerogative. He knew he'd been the one to make a clean break, but forgetting her was harder than he'd imagined, and after a night out drinking with his brothers before Zac had to head to Australia to start training for the America's Cup, he'd drunk texted her again.

But that also had gotten no reply, and he'd decided he needed to man up and move on. He knew he'd hurt her, and he guessed that it was the kind of wound she wasn't interested in letting him try to heal. He didn't blame her at all...well, maybe a little, but only because he wanted her back.

So when Peter Drummond had mentioned a collaboration for the coming summer campaign, Leo had done something that wasn't like him at all. Or rather, wasn't like the old Leo. He'd suggested that Drummond take a look at Danni's online portfolio and perhaps invite her to contribute some ideas. He knew he'd be presenting designs as well, and he'd hoped that Drummond would be impressed by Danni. Impressed enough that he'd call them both in about the collab.

And the designer was impressed. *Very* impressed. He'd let Leo know that he thought in a few years she'd be serious competition for Leo. He couldn't help but feel a small sense of pride at all that Danni had accomplished since they'd met. But he also wasn't about to make it easy for her. He was still a businessman who liked to win.

So, when he got to Drummond Designs' offices early for the meeting where the project parameters would be rolled out for the competing designers, he was ready to see Danni and make an impression. To make their business personal. He'd worn his best suit, had his hair trimmed the day before, and he knew he looked good. This was his last chance to try to make amends for how he'd ended things and ask her for a second chance.

He was sober and ready to face her as Leo Bisset. Not the arrogant man he'd been on Nantucket, but a more realistic version of himself. He was no longer just driving himself and his business higher, he was taking steps to make sure that he was going after goals that actually resonated with him.

He'd stopped working seven days a week and had found he liked the downtime. Of course, it had sharpened the ache left by the absence of Danni in his life. And it made him realize that Boston and the Hamptons weren't that far apart.

In his head he had a few ideas of how he wanted this meeting to go. She'd see him, their eyes would meet and she'd run into his arms, confessing that she never should have let him end things.

It was a nice daydream, and a part of him knew that was never going to happen.

But until he turned and saw her standing in the Drummond Designs reception area, he hadn't truly realized how deeply he'd fallen for her. And he was never going to settle for anything other than getting her back into his life.

She had her glorious hair pulled back in a bun, like she had their last morning together. She wore a pencil skirt that hugged the curve of her hips, a flowy blouse with a tie at the neck and heels that made her almost his height. She gave him a smile that he could see was forced. She clearly hadn't expected to see him here today.

He had the advantage, because of course, he'd known she would be. He walked over to her and held his hand out for a handshake.

"Danni, hello, it's good to see you again," he said.

"Leo. I didn't realize you would be here," she said. "But Mr. Drummond did mention there would be other designers submitting work."

"I'm glad he selected you to be one of them," Leo said. "I've been impressed with your new designs."

"Thanks," she said.

"You're welcome," he replied.

She was businesslike and almost a little cold toward him. He knew that he'd hurt her by the way he'd ended things, but had he done too much damage? He didn't have a lifetime bond to fall back on the way his parents had. Was there a chance that he wouldn't win Danni back?

He knew there was that possibility, but he refused to even give it credence. He'd overcome a lot of stuff, and winning Danni back wouldn't be easy, but it was one fight he was going to win.

She knew it would be rude to refuse to shake his hand, but as soon as their fingers brushed, she realized it was a mistake to think she could touch him even in this business setting and not feel that tingle all through her body.

She'd had too much time away from him, and the anger that had kept her back stiff on that Sunday morning at the brunch was no longer driving her. She was sad that he looked so good and she still wanted him as much as she did, even knowing he didn't want her. She was excited to see him again, too. Ready to show she could compete with him and maybe best him, but she also wanted to talk to him. Tell him all the things she'd been doing with her business and catch up on what he'd been doing.

She heard more people entering behind them and tried to step back, but Leo kept hold of her hand.

"Have a drink with me after this meeting," he said.

He wasn't asking, not really, but she knew if she said no he'd let her go. A part of her wanted to make this a second chance. She knew what she wanted in her life now, and she wondered if Leo could fit into that plan. She hadn't been consciously thinking of him but now that he was here, she knew it was going to be so much harder to pretend that she was over him.

"Okay. But I'm not sure when this will end," she admitted.

"Normally Drum is a big fan of a showy presentation, and then he'll ask everyone to go away and come back with some designs," Leo said.

"Good to know," she said.

"Want to sit with me?" he asked.

She frowned. Did he think they were just going to go back to how they'd been before he told her it was over? Did he think that she had been waiting for him to come back into her life? She needed to know where his head was. She didn't want to spend the entire meeting just sitting there thinking about damned Leo Bisset instead of this important collaboration that she wanted. She turned and gestured for him to follow her into the hallway so they'd be alone.

"What are you doing?" she asked. "Why are you acting all chummy?"

He reached up to rub the back of his neck, and his expression tightened. "I was trying to gauge how things were between us."

"Dude, you broke up with me and then offered me business advice. How do you think things are?"

"Well, I don't know, do I? I screwed up, Danni. I was afraid of dragging you into my family mess that I needed to sort out myself. I was also afraid that I was just using you as an escape to forget the mess that was going on."

Those words hurt, but it wasn't as if she hadn't had those same thoughts. "Exactly, that's why I want to know what you are doing. I need to pay attention in the meeting and not be thinking about you and how good you look today and how I'm not sure what 'having a drink' later means to you. Is it something more, or do you just want to get laid again? I don't want to be on that hamster wheel, Leo."

He cursed under his breath and turned away from her for a moment before turning back. His eyes were so blue and bright in his dark face, his expression a mix of emotions that she couldn't read but looked like anger or maybe something else.

"I don't want that for you," he said. "Seeing you today reminded me that in trying to avoid making the same mistakes as my father, I may have made an even bigger one. I don't want to distract you during the meeting, so if you'd like we can skip drinks and wait until after Drummond has made a decision to talk. But know this, Danni—I regret what I did on Nantucket. I'm sorry I hurt you, and I want a chance to start again."

Start again?

The words were still lingering in her mind when Mr. Drummond's assistant came to call them into the meeting. Leo gestured for Danni to go in front of him, and when she got into the meeting room, she saw that there were at least ten other people there. She took a seat, and Leo took one on the other side of the table away from her.

She tried to pay attention to the presentation, but she couldn't. She didn't want to be that kind of woman, but Leo had said things she couldn't just ignore. He had regrets—which part? Ending things with her or sleeping with her?

The lights dimmed, and a film started. She pulled her notebook out, flipped to a blank page and forced herself to try to make notes. And ignore Leo, though it was hard. Why was he doing this? Was he toying with her?

Her gut said no, but the last time she'd trusted it, she'd woken up to a fully dressed Leo, who was trying to make a quick exit from her life, all while telling her he'd do right by her if she had a kid. So she was confused. And angry. And not about to take this quietly, as she suspected that Leo might want her to.

When the film ended, Peter Drummond walked to the center of the room. He was over six feet tall and had a leonine mane of white hair. He also had one of those long handlebar mustaches but it was jet black. His eyebrows were sleek and his face showed signs of his age but not too much. He had an easy smile, which he flashed to the room.

"Thank you all for coming in today. Sorry I was so vague in my invitation but I wanted you to come to this fresh. Now that you've seen the film I hope it's clearer what I'm after."

Danni glanced down at her notebook, which was empty. The film had consisted of images of couples running through fields of high grass and riding horses down a beach. There had been footage of a man diving into an infinity pool that overlooked the Adriatic. So no, it wasn't clear what he was looking for.

Leo nudged her arm and showed her his notepad, which had a big question mark drawn on it. She smiled, glad to see she wasn't the only one not sure what Peter was looking for.

She raised her hand.

"No need for hands here, Ms. Eldridge."

"Um, okay. I'm not entirely sure what you're looking for. I have an idea of the feelings you want the campaign to evoke but that's about it."

"Yes. That's it precisely. I want you to tap into the next big thing. I'm afraid if I tell you what I think it is, you'll be limited. I want every part of this project to feel fresh and new."

"What about price point?" Leo asked. "Are you going for the luxury market as you have in the past or are you going to try for the mass market again like your last campaign?"

"A great question," Peter said. "Don't put limits on your designs. Bring me what you want to create."

Again not very direct but Danni wouldn't say it was completely useless. Peter had a chaotic energy and joy that she liked. There was something about him that seemed to want to be surprised.

"Any other questions?"

She shook her head as an idea started to take shape in the back of her mind.

"No. This has been very interesting, Peter. I can't wait to get to my studio," Leo said.

There were similar comments made by the other designers and Danni looked over at Leo, who smiled at her. Something entered her mind, a trigger of a memory from when they'd been together on his yacht, and she knew that would be her inspiration. As unsure as she was of why Leo was back in her life, she had really learned more from him than she realized. He'd showed her a glimpse into a world that she'd never been a part of before.

By the time the meeting finished, she had no idea what she would submit, but she was determined that her design would stand out. Leo was one of the last to leave the meeting room, which she knew, because she'd waited for him in the hallway. It was time for Leo Bisset and her to have a talk. One where she wasn't just forcing a smile and doing the "nice girl" thing.

Fifteen

Leo hadn't meant to unload on Danni before the meeting, and as soon as he saw her waiting for him in the hallway, he knew he'd screwed up again. Why was it with this one woman he never got it right? He wanted to be his best self around her, and instead it seemed as if he was always his worst.

She didn't look that happy to see him, and he realized that he might have blown his last shot to win her back.

"I'm sorry."

"About?"

"Everything," he said. "Come on. There's a coffee shop in the lobby. We can talk there, or I have a car waiting. We can sit in there and talk if you want more privacy."

"The coffee shop sounds good," she said.

So she didn't want to be alone with him, and he

couldn't truly say he blamed her. She'd been asking him to just set her mind at ease so she wouldn't be distracted in the meeting, and he'd been unable to do that.

He wanted to tell her that it wasn't his fault. She went to his head and everything got jumbled inside him, and truly it seemed like the harder he tried to make things right, the more they went wrong. Was there ever another person in his life that he'd been this way with?

He knew the answer was no.

Why? he wondered as she stood silently next to him waiting for the elevator to arrive.

When it did, she stepped on and punched the lobby button angrily. And right then, he knew that this wasn't a conversation they could have in public. He wanted to lay his cards on the table, tell her how he really felt and let her tell him everything on her mind. He got on, took her arm and led her back out toward the emergency stairs. He opened the door and pulled her into the stairwell.

"Leo. What the hell are you doing?" she demanded.

"We can't do this in the lobby coffee shop. Paparazzi are still following me around, and I don't think you want pictures of us talking about this splashed on gossip sites," he said.

"Okay, but you could have said something," she said.

"Good. I'm glad," he said, feeling a sense of relief that she was still there with him and hadn't fled the stairwell.

"So what is it you want, Leo? We can't just stand here staring at each other," she said after a moment.

"Who knows when it comes to me and you? I didn't mean to say everything I did earlier. You just go to my head, Danni. I always start out with a plan that seems to go out the window as soon as I'm close enough to smell your perfume or see that small birthmark on the side of your neck just under your ear.

"Then I stop thinking and my most primal self takes over and I have to get you back. Why did I ever let you go? And that's not rational, is it? We only spent a weekend together, and my life was complete chaos during it, but I truly feel like being with you was the realest thing about that time. That our time together saved me. I can't figure it out, but being away from you has only made me want and need you more. And that's not normally how I am. I think…hell, I don't think, I know that I love you, and I can't figure out if we can ever make a life together work because we've never tried it, but at the same time I know—like, down in my soul—that I can't live without you."

She just stood there looking up at him, blinking, and then she shook her head. "You love me?"

"I do," he said. "I was afraid that what I felt on Nantucket was just a reaction to you being the only bright spot in that weekend for me. But I've known for weeks now that I love you, and I'm going to do everything I can to prove it to you and win you back."

"You love me."

She just spoke the words back to him as if she wasn't sure if he was playing a game or not.

"Yes."

"Now you tell me, when I'm trying to get over you and prove that I'm not running after you and following your lead? Now you tell me, when I have the chance to get a big brand deal and finally get my business off the ground?"

"Yes."

"Leo Bisset, you suck," she said. "I hate that you said you love me now when I'm still mad at you. I'm not ready to hear those words when I'm busy thinking about how I'm going to kick your ass in the presentation and win this client. But now I can't do that, can I? Because I love you, too. I hate that I haven't been able to write you off as a wedding weekend hookup. I thought you didn't care about me at all."

"I care too much," he said. "I didn't want to be like my father and drag you into a lifetime of ups and downs. Over the past few months, I finally figured out what I want in my life, and it's you. If I have to give up this collab, I will. If you say move to Boston and we can try dating, I will. If you say you never want to see me again..."

She just stood there watching him, her brown eyes full of emotions that he wished he could read but couldn't. He knew that he had to be able to let her go if he had any chance of making this work. He had realized while they were apart that love wasn't a one-sided, get-your-own-way-every-time thing, it was a selfless emotion that meant putting her first.

He loved her so much that her happiness mattered to him in ways he was only beginning to comprehend.

"You won't see me again?" she asked. This was it, she thought. The moment when she'd know for sure how he really felt. She felt like she was seeing ratty-canvas-shoes Leo. The real Leo and not the smooth, sophisticated man she'd spent the afternoon watching during the presentation.

This was the man she'd fallen in love with, she realized. The man who'd answered her business questions on that note in the cottage kitchen without show or fanfare because, at his heart, Leo Bisset was a good guy. He worried too much about following in his father's footsteps and leaving behind messes that would have to be dealt with thirty years in the future, when in reality he'd never do that.

He was too caring.

"It will kill me, but if that's what you truly want, I'll do it," he said. "I can't imagine that even if you never saw me again, I will ever stop loving you."

She nodded.

The gesture was more for herself than him, but when he sighed, she knew he'd taken it to mean she never wanted to see him again. He turned away, but she put her hand over his, turning him back to face her.

"Thank you for being willing to give me the space I need, but what I really want is a life with you. A way to figure out if this can work. I love you, too. I've spent the last two months trying to forget you and realizing that I never will. Like you said, I'm not sure that we can merge our lives together, but I truly want to try. I've been living with the ghost of you for these last months and that's not enough.

"I looked at that note you left me and tried to dream bigger because of you. I've made huge changes in my life, but the truth is without you in the picture, my dream was only half-real. And it could never actually come true. I don't want you to think I need you to complete me or anything like that, but having you by my side rounds out the life I'm making. I'd rather come to this realization now than spend the rest of my life regretting that I didn't take a chance on love when I could."

He pulled her into his arms and lowered his head to kiss her. He tasted better than she remembered, and she wrapped her arms around his shoulders and clung to him. Happiness overwhelmed her; she'd never dared to think she'd be able to have him back in her life. And on her terms...well, their terms.

He stepped back. "We need to get out of here. I have an apartment in the city. Would you come with me? I want to make love to you and then figure out our future."

"There's nothing I'd rather do," she said, reaching out and taking his hand in hers. As she did so, the sleeve of her blouse fell back, revealing the bracelet she'd made from his leather band and the shell he'd found on the beach.

He lifted her wrist and looked at it. "I didn't know you had made this. This is us, isn't it? A mixture of my business and yours, but also the start of our life together."

"It is, though I didn't realize it when I made it. I thought this would be a reminder not to let my heart get involved in business decisions, but it has turned out to be my good-luck talisman when I make deals."

"It has?"

"Yes," she admitted. Though she hadn't wanted it to be true, looking back, the bracelet had given her the confidence to pursue her dreams. And it had represented their love when Leo wasn't with her.

"I have an idea for the collaboration. How do you feel about working with me instead of competing?"

"I'm listening," she said.

"First things first," he said as he led her back into the hallway to the elevators. He didn't say a word as they rode down to the ground floor. When the elevator doors opened, he quickly ushered her through the lobby to his waiting car.

When they got back to his apartment, Leo carried her to his bedroom and made love to her. He took his time making sure she realized how much she meant to him. He had missed her more than he realized and though he wanted to go slowly, he found he couldn't. But she was just as hungry for him.

Afterward, as she lay in his arms, he outlined his idea to take her bracelet and use it as the jumping-off point for his-and-hers bracelets for the Drummond collection. They both knew it would be a winner.

But it wasn't the business idea that was keeping them together.

It was their love for each other.

Adler was a bit surprised when Danni brought Leo to their lunch meeting. But as soon as she saw her friend and her cousin together, she saw why. No matter how much heartache she'd had at her wedding, and from the ongoing issues involving the rivalry between the Williams and Bisset families, at least Zac and Leo had found love. Logan had, too, and despite the chaos he'd caused for Nick and his business, she was happy for him and Quinn. But Adler's new husband was putting in a lot of extra hours, thanks to Logan's sneaky buying of that patent company.

"Well, hello, you two," she said, forcing a smile, determined to keep up the facade of happy new wife, even though her existence now revolved around dodging the paparazzi and trying to keep her husband from ruining the new life she wanted for them.

"Hello, Adler," Leo said, coming over and giving her

a warm hug. "I hope it's okay that I came. I know there's a lot of tension between Nick and our family these days. But I miss you, so I decided to try to tag along. If you want me to go, I will."

She hugged him back, realizing how much she'd missed her cousins since she'd gotten back from her honeymoon and everything had blown up between Nick and Logan. "I'm happy to see you, too. Are the two of you together? When did that happen?"

"At your wedding," Danni said. "But you knew that. We just got back together a few days ago."

"And it's good?"

"Yes," Leo said. "It's really good. Like you and Nick."

She hoped it wasn't like her and Nick. Things had really deteriorated between them. She wanted better for her cousin and Danni. But Adler realized that she was going to take steps to get her marriage back on track. If that meant telling Nick how she really felt about his feud with her cousins, then so be it. She was tired of trying to keep the peace when no one else seemed interested in that.

Danni's and Leo's phones both pinged, and they turned to look at their screens. Then they glanced at each other with secret smiles and love in their eyes.

"Good news?"

"Yes. We've both been chosen to do a big-time collaboration with Drummond Designs," Danni said.

"This calls for champagne," Leo said. He got up to go find their waiter.

When he was gone, Danni leaned in closer. "I would never have guessed that I'd be this in love with Leo Bisset."

"I'm glad to hear it. He's a good man. And you two

met because of me. I'm taking all the credit," Adler said, winking at Danni. She forced herself out of her funk because she was so happy to see the two of them in love.

She suspected it wouldn't be long until they were collaborating on more than just designs.

* * * * *

COMING SOON!

We really hope you enjoyed reading this book.
If you're looking for more romance, be sure to
head to the shops when new books are
available on

Thursday 14th April

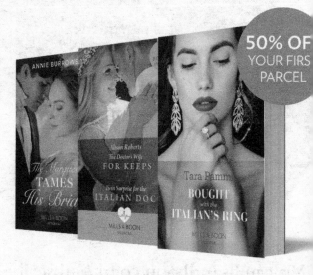

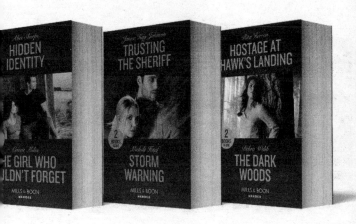

MILLS & BOON
MEDICAL
Pulse-Racing Passion

Set your pulse racing with dedicated, delectable doctors in the high-pressure world of medicine, where emotions run high and passion, comfort and love are the best medicine.